Time is Relative
for Wavering Loyalties

Written by

Brett Matthew Williams

ISBN: 0692807187

ISBN 13: 9780692807187

Library of Congress Control Number: 2016918937

Brett Matthew Williams, Round Rock, TX

For my sisters:

Hannah, Betsy, & Meridith.

...Oh, the places you'll go...

Edited by J. Morrison

Time is Relative
for Wavering Loyalties

Table of Contents

Act I:

Act II:

Act III:

Warning

Ignorance is bliss – should you decide to read further you might learn something truly shocking.

All dates and events are true. The participants... maybe not.

Historian's Warning

Keeper of Records

Welcome back dear readers to the second part in humanity's history, also known as the *Time is Relative* series. While I am ecstatic that you have chosen to journey back to Eden, I would be remiss not to warn you of the heartbreak to come. For with the introduction of Rolland Wright, and his discovery of Eden, begins the final act in the brutal war between the mythical paradise, and Vilthe's domain of Tartarus, also known as the Underworld.

As with all wars, losses are inevitable.

We begin at the eleventh hour; where it is still early for a few to appear, yet far too late for a great many more. Shrouded by thinly held beliefs of immortality, the bravest amongst them walk with their heads held high, never knowing if their next breath will be their last. This is their story.

Six weeks have passed in Eden since our heroes, the Knights of Time, escaped the swamps of Florida with their mission (somewhat) accomplished. Since then Rolland Wright, the young Father Time, has been imprisoned under charges of illegal tampering and manipulation of the Time Stream. Indeed, Rolland had utilized the Dream Phoenix to transport himself and the Knights back to 1817 Pensacola to save his grandmother, Princess Blaisey of the Nabawoo, in order to somehow prevent his own mother's (Taylor Wright)'s death. Unfortunately, the entire ordeal ended up being little more than a lesson in the harsh truths of how time travel works.

Rolland's new mentor, Marcus Turtledove, leader of the Knights of Time and Protector of Eden, also faces similar charges. With Eden's bureaucracy against them, can either Rolland or Marcus escape with their lives intact?

Patience.

Patience is a virtue that all creatures must learn to comprehend in their own due time. For too often it is out-waiting one's enemy that can sometimes make all the difference between victory, and defeat.

... Or so the ancient ones say...

It is with great pleasure that I present to you part two in the Time is Relative series:

Time is Relative for Wavering Loyalties

Chapter 1:
Grief

Tartarus (Underworld)

Six weeks following the events in 'Knight of Time'

"Woe is the grieving left after a loved one sheds their mortal coil. Where comfort once filled a part of existence, so too does the empty void left by their passing. It is a tale told by many, with fond memories, stories, and anecdotes of days gone by. Yet unlike other experiences that connect us in a primal fashion, death only alienates us further from one another."

The words from J.S. Alexander were as timeless as they were haunting. Each syllable echoed in her conscious mind as Sephanie Kelly read them again and again. It was always the same on nights like this when she was locked away in her tower. Time had become nearly immeasurable to her while in Tartarus. Though she knew that time moved here as it did in Eden, she was unsure as to the conversion rate compared to Earth.

The days dragged on longer than Sephanie could have imagined possible. Though it was not her first stay in the desolate kingdom known as Tartarus, it had by far been the bleakest. She had been his child bride here for eleven years, this season making it a dozen. In all of that time the closest thing the two had ever come to being intimate were the long, soul crushing moments when Vilthe would let his hand, or arm, linger on her when they spoke.

Skillful from a young age, Sephanie had been assigned many missions over the years. All of them at Vilthe's demand. Images of the man, Vilthe, whom she had released from the cave imprisonment following the 1817 Pensacola Florida encounter filled Sephanie's mind. That man was human looking, albeit an older and frail, but human looking nonetheless. But her husband, the man who she had been forced to marry, did not resemble a human in anything but body shape. As to the reason behind this Sephanie could only speculate. She knew Vilthe had lived in Eden once upon a time, as had been taught in her history class at the Academy of Light, and was later exiled based on his high crimes and prejudicial treatment of Elemenos and other races. Some even spoke of an epic fight with Marcus Turtledove before his banishment, but she never had summoned the courage to ask either one of them about it.

The land of Tartarus, also known as Hell, the Underworld, and the land of the Damned was as large as Eden if not larger. There were multiple cities stretching over thousands of miles, where both indigenous and non-native creatures lived side by side. Also like Eden, citizens of Earth would often wander into one of the two-way fountains that were scattered across the globe, finding themselves in the dark, desolate, foreign land of sorrow. That was where the similarities ended. The continent of Tartarus was shaped like a large horseshoe surrounded on all sides by oceans as black as ink. Despite having never travelled to the coasts before Sephanie had read stories of sailors disappearing in the Sea of Woe to the East, the Undead Ocean to the West, and most famous of all, the dark waters of the ominous River Styx that ran though the continent like a large, throbbing vein. The river itself was treacherous with its choppy waters, but it paled in comparison to the lakes that split into four separate directions that beckoned for the new entrants to Tartarus to choose one.

While Eden existed as a never ending paradise of lush, forested areas surrounding the flowing Time Stream, Tartarus was a dark, desolate landscape that seemed just as vast, with suffering filling nearly every space. Her place, as Vilthe saw to it, was caged, complacent, and under her Lord husband's thumb at all times. Sephanie sat upon a simple perch, one reminiscent to that of the fabled princess Rapunzel; a figure with which Sephanie felt she shared a great deal in common. Yet where Rapunzel awaited for her prince to rescue her from a prison on high, Sephanie was a powerful, independent woman whose dreams awaited not a knight in shining armor to save her, but an opportunity to use her wits and cunning to advance her position in life. Goals were her driving force behind her actions, the cause of the blood that flowed within her veins. The effects of which she knew would be ill tempered and painful, always painful. But that was future Sephanie's problem. For now she needed to feed her soul, consequences be damned.

The usually somber atmosphere surrounding Tartarus, and Vilthe's palace in general was especially dark for the past six weeks. As the minutes turned into hours, and hours turned into days Sephanie's thoughts were focused on the past, both the immediate and the distant. Memories of the Marcus Turtledove, the overly lecherous Andrew Jackson, the deep regret over Scott Wright's murder, and the mountain of lies that stood between herself and her best friend Joan filled her with both comfort for the outcomes, and remorse for the paths not taken. Yet one person stood above the rest in haunting her dreams; Rolland Wright.

In the dark sky above a crescent moon rose slowly as the ever barely visible sun countered, fading into the night. With it went the notion that Sephanie could ever find any peace of mind regarding the youngest and only surviving member of the Wright family. Though she could admit to herself that she cared for the boy in a romantic way, anything beyond that was but a pipe dream. A sharp pain ripped through Sephanie at the thought, causing her to place a hand above her left breast. It was gone as quick as it came, just like her time with Rolland nearly two months past. It was illogical to obsess over something so brief, she told herself brusquely.

Still... when she closed her eyes at night Rolland would make appearances in her mind's eye, often smiling at her and offering a fresh chance at adventure. A fresh chance at life. Sometimes they lived where they were not citizens of Eden, or Knights of Time, but people, simple people. People who knew nothing of extraordinary powers, who swore no allegiances, and acted not as bartering chips between the yin and yang of good and evil. People who could be together forever, or walk away any time they pleased. But every time she would open her eyes, Sephanie remembered that these were nothing but wishes wrapped in fantasies. They were not those people. They would never be. Her current surroundings proved that much.

Sephanie shook herself out of her reverie and began to dress. She, along with the rest of Vilthe's closest confidantes, had been summoned to a meeting in the hall at the base of her small tower. Its close proximity to Sephanie's room struck her as no accident, nor did the fact that sentries walked the hall outside her door every ten minutes. After she was finished primping, Sephanie cautiously opened her door. Looking out she spied a box shaped man marching slightly down the hallway away from her, obviously making his rounds. After he disappeared from sight, Sephanie slunk out into the dimly lit hallway before jogging in the opposite direction from the guard.

'There is something very wrong with this place,' Sephanie thought to herself as she crept down the stairs from her tower cell. The

narrow, ancient, stone laden passage curved sharply in a counter-clockwise motion as it descended from the fourth story of
her jail. Though she'd never had the opportunity to explore the
rest of Tartarus, Sephanie had heard rumors of the squalor
and misery that plagued the citizens of Vilthe's kingdom. *Her
kingdom.*

This thought consumed Sephanie, filling her with an overwhelming sense of anxiety and dreadful responsibility for the
peoples' suffering. It was more than just apathy, however, as
Sephanie proved to the people of Tartarus yearly. As sure as the
sun sets in the east, so had Tartarus with its queen's bi-yearly
arrival. Because their king forbade public displays of celebration
and joy, the local peasantry had instead begun leaving tokens of
appreciation for her at the base of the high tower in which she
was normally kept. Piles of molded fruit, homemade crafts, and
scattered coins lined every nook and cranny of the scorched
black brick structure that stood an impressive thirty-three stories
high. Though the tribute to their queen took up nearly the entire
first floor, not a soul dared make off with a single cent. For if
they did, there was nowhere in all of Tartarus they could hide
from her husband's wrath.

Each stay with Vilthe brought with it a fresh hell for her to
maneuver through until Spring came again, and she could go back
to Eden, the light at the end of the tunnel. As the years crept
onward, Sephanie found herself longing for the vast open spaces,
fresh air, and freedom that awaited once her six-month obligation in Tartarus was complete. Sephanie's current surroundings
were a world away from that. Her head spinning, feet wobbling
slightly, and mouth dry as a bone, Sephanie was more than happy
to reach the end of the staircase. She leaned against the wall, her
weight pressing into the cool stone. Across from her was an oak
door and behind it lay the main hallway, a long, narrow corridor
with walls made of stone that connected to every other room in
the castle.

While catching her breath, Sephanie raised her head and looked through a small, tinted window near the top of the door. She spotted a cloaked figure striding along the hall. The person, though not recognizable from its outline alone, did display a few distinguishable characteristics. Despite the cloak, the silhouette revealed broad shoulders and a slim waist. It was a man. A tall man who had just began what appeared to be a prayer of some sort, though Sephanie did not understand the words from his mouth, she recognized the language.

Imhotep, or Otep as he preferred to be called, was tall and muscular with a black beard that covered his mocha colored skin. Sephanie recognized the meticulous look that sat on his peevish face. She had grown to know, and loathe Otep's vigilant behavior quite well over the years. As her mind wandered Sephanie neglected to remain within the shadows at the end of the staircase, calling attention to her location.

"Get back inside your room, Persephone," Otep ordered. "Good wives do not go gallivanting about the corridors until they are called for."

"Not that it is any of your concern," Sephanie spoke with a false sense of confidence. "I was summoned."

"I'm sure you think that," Otep said in a manner not dissimilar to the way one would a dog, or extremely slow witted child. "Go now. Go back to bed sweet child."

Yet before she could spit out another angry retort, her eyes caught sight of a figure slumped over further down the hall. Rudolph Hess placed a cigarette between his lips as he lit a match to begin smoking it, capturing both Sephanie's and Otep's attention at once. The weeks that passed since his sister Alora's death had blended together for the once proud Hess, who now appeared despondent, malnourished, and little more than a shell of his former self. Much to Sephanie's surprise, even the swastika arm band that had so prominently adorned Hess' left bicep sagged downward in a depressed state, symbolic of its owner's overall demeanor toward the waking world.

"Perhaps, you should listen to him," Hess spoke, his voice deep and raspy from a lack of use. Ash fell from the end of his cigarette fell on to the dirt floor between his feet as he inhaled another drag, filling his lungs to the brim. "This time."

"Hello Rudolph," Otep offered casually in his odd accent. It was proper, but old, rustic in its simplicity, just as Otep himself was.

"Save it, *arschloch*," Hess said from behind his cigarette. The dimly lit butt glowed orange and red as he inhaled, pacing the conversation with every breath. His usually polished black boots were scuffed, revealing to both Otep and Sephanie more than the man would ever let escape through his lips. "She isn't your woman to order around. You know how *ze* master hates to share his property."

Breathing deeply, Otep took stock of the obviously disheveled German filling the hallway with smoke. Although his adversary was mostly cloaked in shadow, the rich stink of nicotine marked his presence. Since that was the case, Otep need not even keep his eyes open while fighting the Nazi, for his nose would surely do the job. With this in mind, Otep threw a quick glance in Sephanie's direction. She returned it with an uneasy stare of her own, wanting nothing more than to run away from them both. She considered it, considered turning around and walking back to her room to wait for their liege, but as soon as she turned around Sephanie ran into another one of her husband's closest henchmen.

The emergence of the new man brought a smile to Otep's bearded face. He was a tall, large, and bulbous fellow with a noticeable overbite and broad forehead. He wore a boiled leather breastplate over a mustard yellow tunic and noticeably wrinkled khaki pants. The two men spoke quietly to one another, both growing bolder with the advantage of numbers as they slung threatening stares across the hallway to the German smoker. More laughs followed, accompanied by impressions of rigid marching, and even a dirty wiggly finger over the lip in a bad attempt to fake a mustache from the ugly man. Hess watched all of this with a quiet, if not contemptuous indignation, all the while smoking his cigarette slowly, each drag creating a cadence by which he judged how best to kill the other two men.

"Hey Rudy, you over that slut sister of yours, yet?" Ivan asked, sitting on Hess's left side as Otep did the same on Rudolph's right. "You two weren't, you know...where you?"

As Ivan's insinuation sunk into Hess's mind, all forethought of consequences beyond satisfying the growing sense of rage within his gut flew away faster than it took for Ivan to realize that the fight was on.

The first blow came in the form of a head butt, which hurt both men equally, and causing them to temporarily lose their bearings. Fortunately for Hess the adrenaline rush he was enjoying allowed him to bounce back first, righting his feet before balling his left hand into a fist and swinging a wild haymaker in Ivan's direction, connecting squarely on the other man's chin.

The resulting blow knocked the bulbous man off his feet and onto the hard ground. His leather breastplate split open, enveloping his elbows and legs while he attempted to prop himself upward, only to be met with a small rock as it hit him square in the temple.

Sephanie looked over at Otep for signs of his impending entrance into the fray but he simply looked on with an almost bored expression on his face. She then looked at Hess who smiled, boyishly, for the first time since his sister's death. Although she held no affinity for Hess, she did appreciate his need to retaliate for Ivan's comments. Usually this displaced display of masculinity would have entertained her, there was little time before Vilthe would summon them, and she had other things to worry about. Her wish that this would be the end of the altercation was dashed as quickly as it was thought of soon after Hess' smile reseeded.

"You will respect my sister's memory," Hess proclaimed loudly while sauntering closer to the cowering Otep, the limp in his walk more noticeable in the firelight. "Or join her in death."

"STOP THIS!" Sephanie suddenly screamed, emphasizing the two words as she sent two large gusts of wind in both of their directions, forcing Ivan and Hess apart.

"Silence!" commanded a shrill voice from beyond the cavernous hallway in which they stood. The cool, moist air suddenly went bone dry. An elongated, brooding shadow crept down the hallway toward them at a slow, methodical pace. Every head, including the two involved in fisticuffs, turned toward their leader before falling to one knee. All except for Sephanie.

A tall, thin man with his hands held together behind his back glided effortlessly into the dimly lit hallway. He wore only one article of clothing, a long gray robe tied at the waist and that was tattered at the end and eerily, the garment appeared fixed, almost independent of its wearer's movements. A common reaction to the sight of Tartarus's overlord was the sense of impending doom, a sense Otep, Hess, and Ivan were all feeling now. The number of dead since Vilthe had taken power was upwards of twelve million in Tartarus alone, a boast both Ivan and Otep proclaimed during every tavern outing to attract wenches. Sephanie had to control a shiver as her husband stopped directly in front of her.

"There is a special task that I've set aside just for you," Vilthe said to her softly, his right hand lingering on top of hers for what seemed like an eternity. His touch was cold. The bones that peeked through his nearly translucent skin did nothing to comfort his bride as she forced herself to look him in his sullen, sunken in eyes. Where normal humans held a black pupil, Vilthe had not but a bright, golden white void staring back in the middle of both of his eyes. It was a souvenir picked up upon his exile from Eden.

"Thank you, my Lord," Sephanie said, squeezing Vilthe's frigid hand tightly as Vilthe released her hand and turned his attention toward Hess.

Taking a wide, calculated step toward his most loyal lieutenant, Vilthe extended his right hand, closing the gap between himself and Hess, before resting it there on the grieving Nazi's shoulder. Taken by complete surprise, Hess suppressed a sudden urge to lash out at his master, Ivan, Otep, and everyone else in his immediate vicinity.

"As for you, Rudolph..." Vilthe said, gripping Hess's left shoulder. Though his cloak hid Hess's skin beneath it, the purplish hue that set in began to turn a shade of blue as the skin bruised further. "I have other plans for you."

"Where are we going, my liege?" Hess asked, despite the known repercussions for speaking out of turn in Vilthe's presence.

"To obtain what human beings would call, an ace in the hole," said Vilthe, leading Hess to a rock cut out into an oval-shaped archway which they both passed through, entering a small chamber no bigger than five by five feet squared. Here, the two would wait until summoned by another of Vilthe's agents before walking, hopefully effortlessly, through a fountain at the place of Vilthe's discretion. When nothing happened immediately, Hess' heavy breathing became noticeable in the quiet. A strangle, cracking sound filled the air as the master tilted his head toward his lieutenant. "Does this put your mind at ease, or shall I accommodate you further?"

"No my Lord, actually my mind is not at ease," Hess said nervously, the wine he had been drinking earlier in the evening reinforcing his boldness. If there was one cardinal rule in which Vilthe's inner circle lived and often died by was that the word 'no' was said uttered within Lord Edward Vilthe's presence. Finding himself, Hess lifted his lower jaw, which he had allowed to slack greatly, before pressing the issue a bit further in an attempt to lay it to rest. "What is our mission objective?"

"We are going to find something that has been dangerously misplaced," said Vilthe clasping his hands together behind him in a militant stance. This rigid stance provided a glimpse of the man, if you could even call him that, who had rallied the lords of the underworld thousands of years ago, only to lure them into a trap before their mass execution. *'Chaos reigns supreme,'* he had thought at the time; a maxim the Lord of the Underworld reminded himself of on daily basis. He did this, and many other things, without hesitation or any sign weakness to any of his loyal subjects; not until the day his son brought her home. Not until Sephanie, his one weakness. As he re-entered the hallway the militant stance slacked, breaking as the black robe cascading across Vilthe's bony shoulders upon seeing the mournful look on Sephanie's face.

"My sweet..." Vilthe hissed at her, the hollow sinus cavities of his nose whistling as he spoke. "Whatever is the matter?"

"N-nothing," Sephanie said in a barely audible tone. "Do you want her brought in dead or alive?"

"Alive," Vilthe said, the slightest hint of regret saturated his voice as he spoke the word. "Take Otep with you to break her spirit before bringing her to me. I do not have a lot of time for her not to cooperate."

With an intense sense of longing inside of her that raged like wildfire, Sephanie wanted nothing more than to bash her husband's head in, and kill as many of his lieutenants as possible before her inevitable death. Instead of giving into those urges, Sephanie bit her bottom lip softly, smiled sweetly, long enough for Vilthe to return with a hideous smile of his own.

Knowing that his queen would not ask a follow up question, Vilthe returned to Hess, drawing the sullen man into his gaze before facing the doorway from whence he came and asking a curt, "Shall we?"

Exhaling audibly Sephanie looked down at her hand. Clenched within her white, cramping fingers was a simple piece of sheep-skin with a name written on it, one she recognized almost immediately:

AMELIA EARHART - LAE ISLAND, 1937

Chapter 2:
Strangers in the Night

Nestled inside of the Holmes family dining room was Tina Leigh Holmes, returning the hostile glare of her twin brother Timothy from across the table's hardwood surface. Timothy's left hand was tapping aggressively to a rhythm that purposefully skipped beats which he knew would further annoy his sibling while the family watched the television and waited for the verdict in the Council of Light's case against Marcus Turtledove.

Next to Timothy sat their mother, a sallow faced woman whose dreams had never seem to come to as much fruition as her waistline. But that was before Eden's latest craze, her self-proclaimed 'life-changing surgery' known as the gastric bypass. It was but the latest in the blonde woman's many phases, fads, and trends that she subscribed to in order to fill an inner void she could not quite put her finger on. Tiffany Holmes had lost nearly eighty pounds via the surgery following Tina's initial acceptance into the Knights of Time Internship Program. Therefore, Tina found the hypocrisy of her mother preaching virtues like temperance and good judgment following her 1817 Florida encounter with Rolland nothing short of ridiculous.

An evil grin crept across Timothy's face as a special news bulletin began flashing on the television. Tina cringed, remembering that grin from the days of cruelty on the playground throughout their younger years. Though she assumed herself to be the smarter twin, she had never thought of her brother as stupid. On the contrary, Tina had learned to both respect and fear Timothy's wrath over the years. His cruel pranks and destructive tendencies left little doubt in her mind that there was no line that Timothy would not cross. Tina looked away from her brother as the news bulletin flashed across the screen again and a man's voice came through the speakers.

"Good evening Eden, it is seven o'clock and this is your news. I'm Brad Burkhart with tonight's top story involving the Protector of Eden Marcus L. Turtledove. We now go live to our field reporter Jennifer Morrison on site at Eden Courthouse. Jennifer?"

A split screen introduced a moderately attractive woman in her late twenties holding a microphone. Dressed in a tasteful, deep purple business skirt and blouse, the industrious Ms. Morrison had worked hard on her journalistic career and credibility in Eden for years. She now somehow managed to keep a calm visage despite the idiots that currently surrounded her in full blown protest. Few citizens of Eden supported the interventionist policies that the Knights of Time espoused, believing that the Time Stream did not need protecting, and never would. This ideology was based on the preposterous notion that Eden truly was a good embodiment of a modern paradise; completely ignoring the socio-economic policies that marginalized and disenfranchised the lower classes. Jennifer explained all of this, again, for what felt like the one hundredth night in a row, into the camera. The protesters, nearly all of which held more of a personal vendetta against Turtledove and the Knights of Time rather than the accusations at hand, held signs and screamed crude, belligerent, and often sexually explicit slurs at Jennifer.

Tina watched from the comfort of her dining room table as Ms. Morrison attempted to overcome the adversity that presented her. Onlookers, some of which came to gawk at the Ms. Morrison more than follow Turtledove's sentence, took immediate notice - bellowing out catcalls and inappropriate sexual innuendo at the young reporter. Though their eyes saw a pleasing sight, not a one of them understood the power that lay underneath the able bodied Edenite.

"Just moments ago the Council of Light, in a near unanimous decision, voted for the acquittal of Marcus L. Turtledove," Jennifer Morrison said, staring directly into the camera as a gust of wind blew past, tousling her perfectly placed curls of blonde hair. The momentary gust of wind also had effect of slightly elevating her skirt, showing off another inch of skin above her knee. This flash of skin prompted more lewd catcalling from a group of men to her left.

With a sudden snap of her fingers Jennifer immediately exhausted every decibel of human made sound within a twenty-foot radius. Though the rude onlookers still shouted, each vulgar insult harsher than the last, their despicable words fell upon deaf ears as all that could be heard to both Jennifer, and the viewers at home, was the reporter's voice.

"With a vote of eight to one Mr. Turtledove was found innocent on all charges stemming from the incident that took place several weeks ago which involved using Dr. Judah Raines's Dream Phoenix machine to travel back in time without legal consent. This is the same incident in which Rolland Wright, a minor, and recent arrival to Eden, will face judgment for tomorrow. Wright is accused of sending himself, Turtledove, and fellow Knights of Time, including Councilman Holmes' underage daughter, nearly 200 years into the past. While Turtledove was charged as an accessory to the crime, Wright is charged with the actual illegal use of the Dream Phoenix, a far more serious charge. And while the Council of Light showed favorability to Turtledove due to his long history of service to Eden, Wright shares no such good will. Frankly Brad most people I've spoken to are surprised that more accomplices, including Tina Holmes, and Doctor Raines were not brought under indictment. This leads many to believe that the swift hammer of justice will fall hardest on Wright."

Tina snapped to full attention at the mention of her name. The screen changed from Jennifer Morrison back to a split screen between her and Mr. Burkhart in the studio. Perhaps it was the near imprisonment her father had forced upon her since her return from Florida, but in that moment she felt connected to both reporters than she did any member of her immediate family. Without realizing it, Tina found that she was hanging on both reporters' every word. As was her father, Councilman Thaddeus Holmes - the caster of the single vote in favor of Turtledove's conviction earlier that day.

"Now Jennifer," Burkhart began, a silver ear bud protruding from his right ear. "Can you tell us what nature of the relationship between Councilman Holmes' daughter and Wright?"

"Well right now preliminary reports confirm that there is *some* type of relationship between them and while she was not on the official list of accomplices, eye witnesses have her square at the middle of this incident alongside Wright, and several others who form the fringe group the Knights of Time."

"Do you know if they have had any contact since his incarceration?" Brad Burkhart asked.

"Well, since Wright's incarceration," but the young reporter was cut off by an especially vocal protestor, a man with a shaggy beard and potbelly.

"Hey baby, I got something here you can replace that microphone with," the man yelled as three or four of his group joined in with a chorus of laughter and approval.

Without batting an eye Jennifer Morrison lifted her right hand to face level, snapped her fingers twice, and again expelled all audible traces of sound within an immediate area of herself, including the potbellied man and his group.

"That's difficult to say Brad, as Ms. Holmes has not been seen in public for weeks. Our sources do confirm that she DID return to Eden following the incident," Jennifer continued, her posture returning to normal as she regained her composure.

Brad Burkhart nodded his head in apparent agreement of his co-worker's actions before continuing with the broadcast. "And what are your thoughts on Wright's trial?"

"With only hours left in his appeals process, the situation looks much more grim for Wright than previously thought. We will know more tomorrow when the trial takes place. For Eden News 1 this is Jennifer Morrison signing off," she said, before snapping her fingers again, returning the noise to the surrounding area.

"Thanks Jennifer," Brad Burkhart said, grinning broadly to flash his teeth, highlighted by two razor sharp canines resting on either side of his mouth. "What a cool trick, eh folks?"

"So how did Turtledove get out of it, Pop?" Timothy asked his father before jamming a piece of pork chop into his smug mouth, chewing furiously.

"Fucking politics," Thaddeus murmured under his breath, while sopping up stray juices on his plate with a flour biscuit. He repeated this process until the roll in his hand was sopping wet, only stopping once it had fallen apart and onto the plate below. "I'll tell you one thing though - that Wright kid will not be getting off so easily."

As if by cue the three members of the Holmes family not named Tina looked at the youngest female in the Holmes clan to gauge her immediate reaction upon mention of Rolland Wright's name. Noticing this, and knowing the negative response she would receive upon voicing her real thoughts Tina chose instead to ignore their desperate attempts to goad her into an argument. Instead, she bit her bottom lip with an increasing severity as the conversation progressed along.

"So Pop," Timothy continued on. "What's your strategy going into tomorrow? You think those rumors of Wright stealing pirate treasure are true?"

Raising his right eyebrow while simultaneously tilting his head ever so slightly in his daughter's direction, Thaddeus Holmes thought for a long moment before replying to his son's question with a snort, and a very pronounced, "Probably."

"Probably?!" Tina incredulously, throwing her efforts to ignore her family out the window. She grabbed the end of the dining room table with both hands and stood up in indignation. "You've got to be kidding me!"

Prepared for this reaction, Thaddeus Holmes raised his left hand above his head, index finger lifted in a manner by which to indicate that he was calling for order amongst the chaos. But it was his wife, Tiffany Holmes, who spoke first.

"That is enough, young lady," Tiffany said, her eyes burning a hole into her daughter's wide blue ones. Though they looked alike in build, and hair color, there was little in the way of personality traits were shared between mother and daughter. Where Tina was capable and inquisitive Tiffany was complacent with the way of the world. "Sit down."

"No," Tina said between gritted teeth, looking from one parent to another. However, the moment she locked eyes with her father she immediately regretted it.

"So you want to defend the rebel, then?" Thaddeus roared, standing up from the dinner table, causing the plates and silverware to clash.

"He's not a rebel Daddy," Tina said meekly, her eyes widening while her bottom lip protruded further outward in a desperate attempt for leniency.

"Oh, not a rebel?" Thaddeus said, wiping his mouth with the off white cloth napkin. "Care to try out deviant, degenerate, hoodlum, or punk?"

"Try trailblazing, misunderstood genius!" Tina fairly screamed as she flushed with agitation.

"Not another word," Tiffany said sternly, her voice completely devoid of compassion for her daughter.

"But Mom, I love-" Tina began before being cut off by an irate Thaddeus.

"Don't you dare mention that word in the same sentence as that wretched boy's name!" Thaddeus screamed, his face turning to a new shade of purple.

"The word is love Daddy!" Tina shouted, throwing both of her arms down to her side and making fists. "I love Rolland Wright!"

"YOU DO NOT!" Thaddeus said in a furious whisper as his wife stood behind him, gently massaging his tense upper back.

"Go to your room young lady!" Tiffany Holmes shouted, pointing toward the staircase at the end of the hall.

Nearly an hour following the confrontational conclusion to the Holmes family dinner, two feminine hands emerged from a second story window in which a room sat. For Tina, who had mastered the skill of sneaking out of her window when she was twelve years old, the task was not so much difficult as it was time consuming. Though she had followed the same steps in almost exact succession every night for the past six weeks, she reminded herself that it was the confident fool who was always caught. With that thought in mind, she took her time, moving silently, slowly, stepping out onto the steep, three-foot wide rooftop of the cottage. From there, Tina crawled, as stealthy as a cat, to the edge before extending her left hand, groping blindly in the dark.

From his bedroom Timothy Holmes watched as his twin sister shimmied down the drainage pipe outside her window, jumped to a nearby tree limb, slid down, and land mid-run toward Eden Town Proper. Within minutes he was following her exact path, and was sprinting after her over the grassy hill. Although he had kept far enough away to not be noticed, it was still close enough to keep an eye on his sister. He had to. It was his job.

A bit chunky for his age, Timothy was never known for his athletic prowess, relying heavily on his technical abilities instead. The roundness of his belly and sweat on his brow weighed him down as he kept on after his skinny sister and her annoyingly persistent nature. One in which he was growing tired of accommodating as he followed her closer and closer to the exact spot he hoped she was not going, Eden Prison.

It was not until they entered Eden Town Proper, specifically the wall farthest to the east, that he knew for sure where his sister was going. At the far side of the wall a large boulder stood directly in front of a gaping hole large enough to accommodate a single average sized teenager. With a practiced ease, Tina wiggled and squeezed her way through the slim fitting gap. After slipping through the wall and into Eden Town Proper Tina made a beeline for the north side of the city, keeping mainly away from the central road. Keeping her head down, Tina felt the tension in her stomach increase as she etched along the farthest side of the prison before locating the window to Rolland's cell. Arriving at it, Tina crouched down low before allowing her eyes to adjust to the darkness that surrounded her.

"Big bear," Tina whispered repeatedly as she climbed the ledge of the fortress that normally housed Eden's criminals. Built during a strange trend of utilizing levels in architecture, the fortress holding Rolland was pushed back behind two twin towers with spiral ceilings that blocked the sun ninety percent of the time and concentrated it first thing in the morning onto the cell's occupant. Planting her feet carefully Tina was able to hop across, clasping the edge of the stone spiral tower as she made her way to the cell where her beloved was being held.

"Little bear," came a deep voice from beyond the shadows above her. There, in between the two towers, with slight stubble gracing his otherwise boyish face stood the world's only living natural born time traveler, Rolland Alan Wright.

"Sorry I'm so late tonight," Tina began to say, moving the short distance between her perch on the spiral tower and over to the ledge where the cell was built into the stone enclosure, removing the grapple from her pocket and tossing it through the window. "Got into a fight with my parents."

"Again?" Rolland asked, catching the hybrid fruit and immediately taking a large bite. Its sweet juices flowed freely from both sides of his mouth. In that moment he was grateful Tina could not fully see him, or his poor eating habits.

"Yeah, but this time I have news," Tina whispered, a slight jump in the enthusiasm to her voice. "They found Turtledove not guilty - eight to one."

Not guilty - two words that Rolland Alan Wright had longed to hear for the better part of a week's time, yet they applied to a man that he was conflicted about. Alone with his thoughts Rolland had begun to resent Turtledove and felt that he had not done nearly enough to protect him from his arrest at the Halls of Time upon their return from Florida. Add to this the fact that he was now taking what Rolland guessed to be the one and only not guilty verdict the mysterious council would hand out, the resentment grew.

"Did you hear me?" Tina shout-whispered. The dank interior of the cell told every sense in her body to stay away, yet her heart pulled her closer to the soul she knew to be inside.

From behind a thick patch of bushes, Timothy Holmes watched his twin sister silently. Seeing her as a traitor to his family, and his father's position on the council, the young man could think of little else but the building fury inside of him. Sharp stabs of betrayal made him clutch at his belly without realizing it, all the while glaring at his twin sister. Though he could not hear every word, the two he spied upon were good enunciators, making their lips easily readable. So far anyway. He hoped Rolland's silence meant that the guards had come in and beaten his blonde ass senseless.

"I did," Rolland finally answered back, walking back to the window to meet Tina's eyes, prompting the girl to smile brightly.

"Your trial is tomorrow," Tina said, her mouth working before her brain could command it to stop. She reached out and wrapped her hand around his.

"That it is," Rolland answered, refusing to betray the sense of impending dread that consumed his insides. "I like my chances."

"Me too," said Tina, with a single tear falling down her left cheek, catching the moonlight as it traveled back to Earth. "It sounds horrible but I, well I've just really, really enjoyed the time we've spent together over the past couple of weeks."

"Yeah, me too. I don't think I would have been able to make it without your nightly visits," Rolland said, squeezing her hand a little tighter. "Thank you."

For Timothy, this spectacle was sickening to the point of nausea.

"It is the east and Tina is the sun," Rolland spoke softly, his soot covered left hand lightly brushing Tina's face as he pressed the top of his forehead up against the rot iron bars that separated the pair. "Arise fair sun and kill the envious moon, who is already sick and pale with grief."

"Do you recite Shakespeare to all the girls, Rolland Wright?" Tina asked, leaning ever so slightly closer to the cold concrete that surrounded the iron bars. Her steady footing fought her rapid heartbeat as the pair drew closer to one another, neither seeing the bars that kept them a world apart.

"You would be the first, Miss Holmes," Rolland said with genuine affection building within his heart as Tina's free hand found his on the cell window's ledge. His head had reached the edge of its zone of freedom, cut off by the restrictive nature of the bars covering the windows. There were seven altogether, each an inch and a half thick, spaced two inches apart from one another, making the window only big enough for someone with shoulders smaller than his own to crawl through. While he had hoped for a more PG-13 rated encounter tonight, the night before his trial, the bars once again acted as an agent of cold water on their shared passion.

"I should get going," Tina reluctantly admitted.

"Thank you for coming out tonight," Rolland said to her, finding her eyes once again in the dark and looking directly into them. "I know how much you hate sneaking around."

"It's...." Tina could barely hear herself answer; she was so transfixed within Rolland's touch.. Rolland's stare...

From his perspective nearly fifty feet away from the couple, Timothy Holmes saw all that he needed to in order to leverage his sister, blackmailing her for the foreseeable future. Opening his cell phone, Timothy touched the camera application, springing the video to life, and with a touch of the red button marked 'record' forever captured the balcony moment between the prisoner Rolland Wright and the rebel Tina Holmes.

Chapter 3:
Uncharted Territory

Morning came sooner than Rolland expected based on the conversation he heard amongst the guards following Tina's departure from his cell window, he was unsure as to if the speedy trial guaranteed by Eden law would result in his favor. Guilt, much like historical accuracy, is subject to mass consumption, and rarely confined to one person. The dank smell of the cell reminded him of the distinctive, corrupt streets of downtown Los Angeles in all of their putrefied glory. The parallels of the two places flooded Rolland's mind as he mindlessly fingered the magnetic collar around his neck.

The blasted device that incased Rolland's neck left a red mark from sleeping on his side the night before, making his skin tender to the touch. So instead he watched as it circled, again and again, around the precious few centimeters of open space between skin and steel. Though he was never much for jewelry before his recent vacation at Eden Prison, the shackle about his neck was by far the cleanest, and most hygienic part of his wardrobe. Perhaps it was a good thing that Tina could not get too close during their nightly rendezvous, as he had been without a shower in nearly two weeks, and without a change of clothing in twice that length of time.

The days had been long and tedious for the native Californian who had for nearly two years before this spent the majority of his time outside. Yet this place was a far cry from the sandy beaches and shady palm trees of southern California. Besides Tina the only friend Rolland had made was a white mouse that often appeared before dawn most mornings. Unsure if the creature was there seeking discarded scraps of food, or something else entirely, Rolland was happy to have the company. This was what his life had become in the past few weeks.

All around Rolland the walls were a dark green, mixed with the brownish red hues that came from iron oxidizing and becoming rust. If not for all of the time he had to take notice of every small detail of his surroundings, the loneliness might have driven Rolland to the point of insanity. Though he had learned to survive well enough on the streets of Los Angeles, the survival skills he had learned in prison were coming in far handier. It was if he had been using his senses all wrong, like the volume in his ears had been turned on low his whole life. Never had lights been so angelically illuminated as those outside the dank cell window where Tina came to visit almost nightly. Food, though it came in small portions less often than he cared for, tasted like a culinary experience each time a morsel passed his lips. Rolland thought about this, and wondered if he was developing new abilities, or just appreciated the gifts bestowed upon him before the inevitable hands of death closed in.

It was this grim thought that distracted Rolland from the sound of the wrought iron door that swung open forcefully behind him, slamming against the cell wall and leaving yet another small indention in the rusted green siding. Rolland felt a bit stupid for noticing this small indiscretion, but the truth is that after a few weeks the cell had begun to feel like home and part of him did not want to see it marred.

"Get the hell up, boy!" said a guard, as he charged into the cell. Blinded and confused, Rolland winced as the light poured into the room. Before his eyes could adjust to his surroundings, however, he found himself back up on shaky feet, which only barely caught the rest of him as he swayed back and forth, much to the amusement of the guards. A few forceful pushes later and Rolland was through the narrow doorway of the cell, walking between the two rude guards, each of which took great pleasure in his suffering. Both of the guards were male, middle aged, unkempt in appearance, and wielded crudely made long spears seven inches wide by fifty inches tall, not counting the black, razor sharp points that rounded out the lethal skewers.

"They say this one can travel through time," the taller of the two guards said to the other, completely disregarding Rolland. "But I don't believe it."

"Why not?" the second guard asked his companion, staring at Rolland for a long moment before the three turned a corner past numerous oak doors with various nameplates positioned to the top right, many of which also had small windows. "He looks like Scott Wright well enough."

"Maybe," the taller guard said, his long spear keeping a close watch on Rolland's slow, steady shuffling through the hallway between his owner and his partner. "But if could travel back in time, why wouldn't he just blink 'imself outta here?"

A long moment passed between the two guards, forcing a smile to Rolland's lips for the first time since he had seen Tina. Rolland too had thought about the exact same paradox for hours while lying motionless inside of his cell, yet came to no finite conclusions. The shorter guard scratched an exposed patch of forehead skin peeking out from under his brass helm before finally answering, "I don't get it.."

While he was being manhandled, thoughts of the future rushed into Rolland's mind like fleeing survivors of a catastrophe. He wondered if Eden believed in the death penalty, and if his supposed 'crimes' even warranted such an extreme punishment. As the trio made their way out of the prison and into the winding corridors of Eden Courthouse, darker and more ominous thoughts clouded the mind of Rolland Alan Wright, draining him of what little confidence he had left.

Their caravan grew as three more guards joined them in their journey through long hallways, curvy staircases, and past vast windows with skylines larger than Rolland had ever seen. The sight was a spectacle to be sure, though not one that the teenager could enjoy. They passed even more offices with more nameplates, all of which were identical to the previous. After a while Rolland began to wonder if there were actually people inside of those offices; people toiling away at some assignment or task given to them from another office dweller - all of them like ants working collectively for a nameless, faceless figure of bureaucracy. Allowing his mind to wander, Rolland barely realized that they had come to slow their steady pace as the hallway hit a T shape before opening up to a large, vaulted ceiling above two double doors that led to where he guessed he would be judged. Outside of the chamber stood two more men, both carrying long, ornately carved wooden spears with glistening metal tips that begged for trouble. One of the men Rolland had never seen before, but the other he had once shared a brief conversation with.

"Morning! Rolland, isn't it?" the town guard named Michael, whom Rolland had met shortly after coming to Eden, said to him before lowering his spear before nudging the guard next to him in the ribs to do the same. Michael, who was an imposing man of his own accord, looked a good thirty pounds lighter than his counterpart, who appeared downright intimidating. His partner, an unshaven, glassy eyed looking man with a long face and hard jaw snapped out of his stupor and complied.

Oh hey Michael," Rolland said, glad to see a familiar face. "I thought you guarded the town gate, what are you doing here?"

"Put in a special request to work here the second I saw you were arrested. Thought you might need someone for support," Michael said, looking around nervously. "Or to execute plan B."

"Thanks," Rolland said, a little too loudly for his surroundings. "But what's plan B?"

"We'll worry about that later," Michael said, guiding the conversation. "Listen, as soon as you walk into that room, the council is going to lay into you hard. They're trying to force a confession, it's General Falocco's favorite tactic. Don't let them talk you into anything Rolland."

"General...?" Rolland asked, suddenly concerned with the repercussions that come from being found guilty by someone with a military designation.

"Yeah, but don't let his direct demeanor rattle you," Michael said, slapping Rolland's back before re-gripping his staff tightly. "Here we go, boy'o."

"The defendant may now enter the Chamber of Light!" proclaimed a nearby sentry, who then proceeded to bang his long, ornate staff against the marble courthouse floor.

The action seemed to prompt a great many things, the most important of which for Rolland was the literal shepherding of him from the cramped hallway to the largest room he had ever seen. In a sequenced, much rehearsed procession, the group made their way past Michael and his brother at arms through the now open chamber door.

The chamber's nearly one hundred foot high vaulted ceiling, a long, curved desk with nine chairs on the far side that ran the length of the room, and too many stained glass windows to count caused Rolland to think that he had accidently stepped into a cathedral, not a courtroom. The blinding Eden sunlight scattered across the room as he was walked the length of it toward a single, isolated chair that sat before the long desk. With his eyes squinted, Rolland barely had time to register his new surroundings before a large, deep voice spoke loudly enough to send an echo throughout the chamber.

"Did you do it?" the deep male voice asked, coming from somewhere dark and high above his head. Though he could not make out who posed the question to him, Rolland decided that the answer mattered a hell of a lot more than who was giving it.

Suddenly, as if a curtain was drawn from over the sun itself, a harsh yellow light poured into the council chamber from above, illuminating the high oak table that ran across the entire room. Propped up at least ten feet off of the ground the perched long-table was spacious, featuring nine black leather chairs, each with a golden embossed nameplate sitting neatly at the edge. Though eight of the chairs were empty, standing in front of one, the ninth one, directly in the middle was the silhouette of a broad shouldered man.

"No," Rolland said, raising his still shackled hands above his head in a vain attempt to block the blinding golden light seeping in from the windows as the silhouette of the man in front of him became much clearer. As he grew accustomed to the light Rolland began to see more features present themselves, the first of which was the nameplate that gave away the man's name, rank, and affiliation. In response to Rolland's denial the man offered a curt, "We shall see."

General Falocco was bald save for a rim of dark brown, verging on gray, hair that lay upon his head like a horseshoe. He was diligent, strict, and efficient beyond a doubt - or at least Rolland inferred as much based on the royal blue military uniform he wore. Even in silence the General retained a sense of unquestioned authority and purpose to his actions. With Falocco seated, glasses on, the case briefing in his hand, Rolland was forced to take in his surroundings once again.

The chamber, though illuminated via the now open skylight above them, was drab and seemed to resemble more of a medieval style courtroom than a modern place to practice law. Perhaps it was by design, or perhaps it was truly so old that it actually was from medieval times. Whichever the case Rolland did not know, but he made a mental note to ask Tina about it later. The thought of her fill Rolland with many emotions, the least of which was hope. He knew little about the council except for what she had told him. Over the last few weeks she had gone over its various members, always focusing on their positive attributes, their respective careers and their many life achievements. Though Rolland knew she was leaving things out, he decided early on never to call her on it.

With less fanfare than Rolland expected, the oak double doors that he had been staring at opened down the middle, revealing a brightly lit chamber beyond their narrow split. Quicker than he anticipated, individuals of various walks of life filtered out before going their separate ways to their respective seats.

A fresh faced woman with short hair and a cheery demeanor entered the chamber in a quick fashion. Her walk seemed to Rolland almost prance like in its over exuberance; that is until he realized that she was not walking, but gliding a full two feet off the ground. This fast paced means of transport led her past the other chairs to the far end of the council table before taking a seat in the second to last chair. Her nameplate bore the title **Councilwoman J. Oskam**.

"Had a rough morning, eh?" Oskam asked Rolland, her left hand clutched around a warm mug of steaming coffee, her black leather swivel chair bobbing slightly as she smiled down at him. The acknowledgement made Rolland smile, slightly. But if Councilwoman Oskam was hospitable member of the council, then the woman who entered the chamber immediately following her was surely her polar opposite.

Her attire was drab, yet complex in its intricacy. Little knick-knacks such as pins, and buttons adorned her blouse, skirt, and shoes as she waddled to the overly spacious chair prepared for her generously large posterior. Her spectacles, black frames with a thin gold chain tied to both ends, sat sturdily upon her short, squat nose that sniffled slightly as she squinted at Rolland.

"Eleanor," Councilwoman Oskam said before turning away from Rolland.

Rolland watched as the two seemingly conspired against him, each shooting quick unreadable glances downward towards his lone, isolated seat. Deciding to rid his mind of such paranoid thoughts, Rolland veered his glance away toward the other members of the council, hoping for a friendlier face.

Instead Rolland, unfortunately, caught the eye of who he was sure was Tina's father, and the only man in the room that he knew he would never win over. Rolland watched as Thaddeus Holmes sat down in his large, leather chair before meeting Rolland's gaze, and smiling coyly; like a spider playing with its prey.

A kindly looking man entered next proceeded to take a seat behind the desk with the nameplate **Councilman J. Yick, Ph.D.** The man's thin horn-rimmed spectacles rested on the middle of his nose, steadily slipping downward as he composed himself in his chair. Rolland guessed he was Chinese based on his name and outward appearance. His demeanor was calm and his eyes, black and deep, revealed an inner sense of wisdom and duty.

A well-dressed, dark skinned woman followed Dr. Yick into the chamber before taking a seat at the far right end of the shared desk. The golden embossed nameplate sitting in front of her read **Councilwoman L. Fluker** and Rolland found himself wondering if she were a friend or foe. Not a moment later a large, white, toothy smile flashed across her elegant face, and for second all was right with the world. A slightly older man entered the council chamber behind Dr. Fluker. Rolland immediately noticed multiple distinctive features about this man, who found the seat behind the name plate **Councilman Pierre Cagniart, PhD**; the first of which was the random disbursement of chalk stains that lined the man's tweed blazer, slacks, and upper lip. If he were a betting man Rolland would have placed money that Dr. Cagniart was a professor of some sort, though mad scientist would be a good guess as well.

A frazzled looking woman wearing a white lab coat toddled along with her head down, and her eyes lost in some sort of electronic device clutched within her left hand. Removing her rectangular bejeweled eye glasses from atop her nose, she simultaneously sat down and pocketed them within her coat pocket; all the while betraying nothing in the way of body language that might reveal the severity of her ethical leanings toward Rolland's guilt or innocence. Though the plaque on the desk in front of the woman's desk read **Councilwoman Shannon Duffy, PhD, M.D. J.D.**, Rolland was doubtful that any one person could hold that many advanced degrees. He did not have much time to ponder the thought however, as soon the lights in the council chamber dimmed.

Rolland's attention then reverted back to General Gary Falocco. In front of his desk were two plaques, one that read his name, and another that stated **MAGISTRATE OF EDEN**. It was in that moment that Rolland put two and two together, remembering everything that Tina had told him regarding the Magistrate, whom he now knew to be the man before him. Apparently this man, known was the council's 'lion' was also the commander of all of Eden's Armed Forces and the defacto leader of the Academy of Light. Above all else he had learned about her in the past few weeks, it was the passion and love for the Academy of Light that stood out the most about Tina Holmes. Knowing that should the best case scenario transpire, he would be then attending the Academy of Light alongside Tina; directly in the backyard of General Gary Falocco.

"Rolland Alan Wright," General Falocco barked while simultaneously sliding his chair toward the crescent shaped oak desk. "Did you manipulate the Time Stream and intentionally travel back in time without permission?"

"No sir," Rolland replied without missing a beat, his voice steady. He watched as another council member, followed by harried two clerks, entered through the doors. It was Anthony Varejao, the man who had arrested him in the Halls of Time and who was now shooting him a very dirty look.

General Falocco eyed Rolland suspiciously, his bushy unibrow furrowing slightly as he squinted a bit.

"My apologies for my tardiness Gary," Councilman Anthony Varejao interrupted in a smooth voice. Like Falocco, he was dressed in full military uniform, complete with small medals, sigils, and a crisp, tight fit. "But I-"

"That's General Falocco," Falocco stated curtly, his eyes unblinking as he stared daggers into his subordinate. "Though we are equals within this room, I kindly ask that you extend me the courtesy of remembering my rank when addressing me, Councilman. Now that you are finally here, let us commence with opening statements."

"Apologies General," Anthony Varejao said sheepishly before continuing. "Today we convene to determine the fate of this..boy. A one Mr. Rolland Alan Wright, son of Taylor and Scott Wright, registered members of the Knights of Time and citizens of Eden."

"Opposing counsel?" Councilwoman Fluker asked.

"I'll be taking the lead today," Councilman Holmes stated, in a tone Rolland believed to be a little too gleeful.

"Big surprise there," Dr. Cagniart retorted sharply, a slight lisp evident as he spoke. It was not easy to understand the councilman, due to the lisp as well as his heavy French accent. What he did hear, however, filled Rolland with a sense of hope. "I surmise that you would like to drag every boy who made eyes at your daughter in front of this council, *non?*"

A ripple of stifled laughter shot through the courtroom like lightening, much to the chagrin of the rising tide of anti-Wright supporters. From both sides of the long council desk Councilmen Varejao and Holmes dealt with this first blow by fidgeting in their seats in agitation.

"And counsel for the defendant?" Doctor Yick questioned, but before anyone could answer the chamber doors swung open, filling the entire room with the same radiant beams of early morning sun that cascaded across the hallway outside, setting the stage for the emergence of the man acquitted in the same very courtroom the day before, Marcus Turtledove.

"Are you taking that position because you truly believe in his guilt, Thaddeus? Or because of the favor your daughter has shown toward the defendant?" Turtledove asked, never breaking eye contact as Holmes fumed and shifted uncomfortably in his seat. Stifled giggles from Doctors Yick and Duffy burned against Holmes' ears like a fires back draft, turning them red with embarrassment.

"Order!" Councilwoman Oskam shouted, banging her gavel numerous times to emphasize her point. "There will be order here!"

"Bailiff, please have Mr. Turtledove removed from the courtroom," Councilman Holmes requested, lurching forward in his chair a bit as he spoke.

"That will not be necessary, bailiff," Councilwoman Duffy said in a firm, yet gentle voice.

"What the bloody hell do you mean that won't be necessary?" Councilman Varejao inquired. "Remove this man at once!"

"Marcus Turtledove was an invited guest of the court yesterday accused of the same crimes as the boy here," Councilwoman Duffy proclaimed, staring Varejao directly in his cool, humorless gray eyes. "Who better to serve as a character witness?"

"I'll be serving as defense for the young Mr. Wright if it so pleases the council," Turtledove said in a nonchalant manner while walking to the desk where Rolland sat, hands shackled. His pace was practiced, slow, and deliberate. It dawned on Rolland that it was a tactic, possibly meant to upset the opposition to throw them off their game. A quick glance at Councilman Holmes and his suspensions were confirmed.

"As you please, Marcus," said Councilwoman Oskam. "Shall we begin?

As the color returned to his face, Councilman Varejao sorted through a stack of papers before selecting one, standing up, and walking it to General Falocco, who read the following:

"To reiterate, we are convened here today to determine the guilt or innocence of Rolland Alan Wright on the charges of Time Stream manipulation and traveling back in time without permission," General Falocco said, reading from the paper. "The defendant has pleaded not guilty by means of necessary action, is that correct?"

"That is correct, councilman," Turtledove said, nodding his head twice before looking over at Rolland. "I would like to put the boy on the stand, if it pleases the council of course."

"It does not please the council!" Councilwoman Menninger said between pursed lips and a burrowed brow. "He is not from Eden and does not have the right to speak in this room."

"True," Councilman Falocco said, casting more doubt onto which side he might choose. "That is a privilege to those who serve Eden with citizenship. This boy is not a citizen. This boy is unregistered. This boy is.."

"An abomination!" Councilman Holmes blurted out, his face a mild shade of purple. "He is a weapon born in secret that corrupts everything he touches. He is dangerous! Today it's the Time Stream, but tomorrow it could be our homes, our children, even our lives!"

"I'm not after your children!" Rolland insisted, speaking out of turn for the first time since entering the chamber. "I never meant to break any laws, I swear. All I meant to do was help the Knights of Time and my parents."

The council was nonplussed by Rolland's admission, each member appearing ambivalent to his passionate decrees of innocence. But he did not care, for Rolland had come too far and given up too much to be convicted of something he did not feel guilty of.

"Mr. Turtledove," Councilman Falocco said in a manner befitting his rank of general. "Please control your client as he is not permitted to speak while council is in session."

"Understood sir," Turtledove said, throwing a quick glance of disapproval to Rolland before addressing the council once again.

"What we have here, ladies and gentleman, is both an opportunity, and a risk. In short, this boy, this lump of unkempt and untrained clay is our element of fire, our gunpowder, our nuclear weapon," Turtledove said, lowering his voice for dramatic effect. "For within him lies the key to traveling through time freely, harnessing that power toward our own goals, and, perhaps, even unraveling Vilthe's long-term invasion plans."

The longwinded statement by Turtledove shocked many of the council members, sending them into a series of whispered fits amongst themselves. The ruckus went on for several long moments before Councilman Falocco exercised his authority as Magistrate with a liberal use of his mahogany gavel on the desk. The sound that followed was only drowned out by the councilman's own voice calling for order.

Rolland thought that perhaps the post of Magistrate might be based on whoever could speak the loudest, or call a room to order. He then noticed how Falocco's gavel was slightly larger than the other councilmen's gavels, and wondered what other perks came with the job of being Eden Magistrate. He would think of anything except the terrible situation he had found himself in.

"This is a jarring revelation," Councilman Falocco exclaimed, his face turning various shades of pink at what he perceived to be such an outlandish statement. "This is what you bring to us? Empty promises and fancy jargon? I might forgive you for insulting my intelligence, but I cannot forgive your sense of stupidity."

This verbal volley stung Rolland in a way that felt physical, gripping his heart, and squeezing it for its stupidity. Suddenly he regretted everything - every decision he had made since the bookstore and deciding to trust Turtledove. Florida was bad enough, but now he was being martyred to a group of super-powered bureaucrats in the name of... what, exactly? Rolland stopped listening after Turtledove promised them his life on a silver platter in exchange for his freedom. He looked over at Turtledove, the snake, expecting him to look devastated by Falocco's response. But strangely, Marcus was not fazed at all. On the contrary, he looked poised as he delivered his counter argument.

"Do not blame the tool for your inability to utilize it properly. Instead inspect yourself for defects," Turtledove said without batting an eye, citing the Academy of Light Code of Conduct verbatim.

A series of rumbles and guffaws shot through the chamber. From all sides Rolland heard an explosion of murmurs, stifled laughter, and small gasps as all nine councilmen gossiped more than he expected grown adults, much less elected politicians, to do. The distinguishable sounds of shoes squeaking against the chamber's marble floor furthered the interruption and any momentum that Turtledove had been picking up with his controversial argument. While he had never thought of himself as anything other than what he was, whatever that was, the idea that he could be a 'key' of any sounded like a poor defense, even if he could travel through time.

"Order!" Councilman Yick demanded, his glasses slipping off of his nose slightly as he raised his left hand in a stopping motion. Much to Rolland's surprise the entire room, spectators, council and all complied. Obviously Yick carried a great deal of respect for reasons Rolland did not yet know. "Go on, sir."

"We are venturing into uncharted territory," Turtledove said, walking the length of the council table. "Rolland Wright could one day be the key toward a final peace."

"Preposterous!" exclaimed an outraged, red-faced Thaddeus Holmes before rising to his feet. Both of his hands were extended, bracing his near obese frame as he rose, face scrunched into an indistinguishable flame of fury turning his round face pink with indignation. "The boy is a degenerate and nothing more - just look at him!"

"You say that which you perceive to understand with your eyes," Turtledove spoke softly. "Might I recommend a different organ by which to make your decisions?"

"Not smart," Varejao stated, sporting a smirk over what all around him knew to be a clenched jaw and grinding teeth. "Not very smart of you to come in here all half-cocked and aggravate the council before we render a verdict on your little protégé here."

"Councilmen, please!" Councilwoman Fluker insisted, her short, raven colored hair dancing over her right shoulder as her fever grew. "Can we all please act like adults?"

Yet in place of reason stood nothing but more banter and high winded speeches regarding the 1817 Florida incident by both sides for nearly three hours. Everything about Rolland was called into question; from his own conception, to his actions as a child, all the way to the time spent since his mother's death, which was brought up by more than one council member. None of it noteworthy, all of it depressing, it made Rolland feel as if he were about three inches tall and guilty of every non-violent sin ever committed.

"Have you any surviving family members, Mr. Wright?" Councilwoman Duffy asked Rolland with a note of sympathy to her voice. Not knowing how to answer this quandary, Rolland again looked to Turtledove.

"No," Turtledove said to the council at large with utter certainty to his voice. "He has no remaining blood relations upon this, or any other plane of known existence. If you get rid of him then his family line goes as well. Years of dedicated service from his mother, father, not to mention others, would all be in vain. Tell me, is that the sort of impression that this council wishes to send to the citizens of Eden? That multiple lifetimes of service will be punished?"

Rolland thought, rather erroneously, that this line of logic might find an audience with those wishing to find him guilty. But alas, it only strengthened their resolve. Lead by Thaddeus Holmes, the opposing council even called his personality traits into question, with the back and forth game only hitting its climax with Turtledove's impassioned closing speech.

"There is a difference between being intelligent and being capable," Turtledove said, turning slowly on the spot in which he stood, moving from staring Rolland in the eyes to Varejao, and Councilman Holmes. "The inept will never understand this."

"That will be enough, Mr. Turtledove," General Falocco barked from the council's perch before shifting some papers in front of him, removing his glasses, and folding his hands. "I've reached a decision. What say the rest of you?"

"Guilty," bellowed Councilwoman Eleanor Menninger, her fat lips quivering gleefully as she spoke the words of condemnation as she leered at Rolland's shackles.

"Guilty," said the next council member, Dr. Oskam, though her face betrayed no sense of joy, merely civic responsibility.

"Not guilty," came the vote of Duffy, her eccentric tone of voice stressing the word 'not' while looking directly at Thaddeus Holmes.

"He's guilty," stated Holmes with a fair amount of certainty to his voice. "Guilty, guilty, guilty."

"Just because you say it three times does not make it so," Turtledove interjected, very aware that he was grating on Councilman Holmes' last nerve. Rolland felt thankful to have the old man in his corner, but wondered if he might not be pressing the opposition too much.

"I agree, obviously," Varejao said with a smug certainty. "Guilty."

"Not guilty," said Councilman Yick, nodding a few times before lowering his head in self-contemplation and repeating to himself. "Ah uh, ah uh, ah huh."

"Not guilty," Councilman Cagniart said solemnly his boyish humor gone as he crossed his arms, awaiting the end result. With only two votes left, and the tally at a respectable 4-3, all eyes fell to the last two councilmen.

"Not guilty," Laurie Fluker agreed, shifting in her black leather seat.

It came down to Falocco, as it had done so many times since the division along ideological lines blocked any real progress from coming to Eden. The final vote, subsequent decision, and Rolland's entire future rested on the shoulders of the highest ranking military officer in Eden. The first to enter, the last to leave - the one who holds all the power and balances the scales.

"Yours is an interesting case, Mr. Wright," General Falocco said, inhaling deeply, his chest pushing up against his crisp blue uniform. As their eyes met like two warriors on a battlefield, Rolland could see no hints of apprehension, no mercy. "Did you do it, son? Did you mean to tamper with the Time Stream?"

"No sir," Rolland said adamantly, and in a confident tone. He then locked eyes with every member of the council, moving from one to the other, before settling back on Falocco's and waiting for the result that would determine his entire future. The gesture landed well with everyone, save councilmen Varejao and Holmes. Even grumpy Councilwoman Menninger gave what the casual observer might call a cross between a smirk, and the face one makes right before they are about to sneeze.

"Well then… not guilty," General Falocco bellowed loudly, his gavel already in mid-motion towards his desk before anyone else in the large chamber had an opportunity to draw breath. Though a large, if not instantaneous, response of verbal objections, physical protests, and angry gesturing followed, the verdict of the day had been handed down.

Rolland was innocent.

Chapter 4:
Eden Revisited

Eden—The Same Day

In a diamond shaped house located on greenest hill in all of Eden sat a maroon brick two bedroom domicile where a great deal of love was shared. It was circled by a white picket fence, with overgrown ivy covering the awning over the front door. In the master bathroom the lady of the house, Joan Raines, was putting the final touches on her long, now curly, golden hair.

"I'm just saying that there are worse people to be on the Council of Light is all," Judah said from their bedroom. "Imagine if they put George Hart on the council, that bloody moron would yammer on for days about cutting funding to the Elemenos."

"Yes dear, I know you don't care for the extremists," Joan said, unplugging her curling iron and putting it off to the side of their shared counter.

"No one does, love," Judah said, placing one hand into a pocket of an overcoat that hung from a hook on the back of the washroom door, fishing out a pack of cigarettes. Eyeing him carefully, Joan caught his hand instead, cradling it in her own softly while simultaneously drawing her husband close. Judah loved it when she did that. It was moments like this when she was more than a saint to him, she was an angel - a mixture of beauty, grace, and sophistication perfectly wrapped up into one five foot, five-inch blonde Frenchwoman. It was moments like this when Judah knew that he was completely and utterly wrapped around Joan's finger.

Joan knew it too.

"So, where are we going?" Joan asked, batting her eyelashes at her husband, intertwining their fingers as the vanilla scented perfume she had just applied wafted over Judah, enticing him further under her spell.

"Going? What? Where?" Judah asked, placing his free hand on his wife's hip in order to pull her closer.

"On our honeymoon. The one you promised me weeks ago when we got back from Florida," Joan said, removing her hand from his before crossing it, and the rest of her arms in front of her; a visual display to the human male of his impending doom. "We've been together for how many years, and you still haven't taken me on a proper honeymoon."

There it was. The subject Judah had spent the better part of their entire marriage dancing around was sneaking out from beneath the foot rubs, breakfasts in bed, and salon weekends, only to rear its ugly head at a time when both were half naked.

Thinking quickly, and fearing for his sexual short term future, Judah stood up straight, looked his wife dead in the eye, and asked with a completely straight face, "Wait, are you really asking how long we've been together? Because, you could at least remember.."

The gamble, however folly, worked for the moment as Joan rolled her eyes before reaching up on her tiptoes to kiss Judah deeply. Breaking their embrace, Joan stepped away to pull on her blouse. As her perfectly manicured nails draped the dark green garment across her slender shoulders Judah could not help but marvel at how utterly desirable his wife was. After a few final touches to her hair, make-up, and skirt, Joan threw a quick, seductive glance at her husband before slowly walking out of the bedroom, teasing him with a look at what she knew he wanted most at that moment.

"Smartest man alive..." Judah muttered to himself before shaking his head and following his wife. Today would not be his lucky day.

"All I'm saying is that asking for a week or two off wouldn't be the end of the world, especially since we know Turtledove is in the clear," Joan said to Judah as the two exited their home in the country and began the trek to Eden Town Proper. "Plus it might be nice to get away for a while if the Wright kid is found guilty."

"You're right, I know you're right," Judah said, taking his wife's hand. "But just so we're clear, I'll never admit to that in public."

"Uh-huh," Joan biting her lip to hide her smile as they walked.

"There's a lot of things I wouldn't admit to anyone but you. All my deep, dark secrets and what not," Judah confessed playfully. "But it's not like I'm the silver shaded pervert, or anything."

Joan smiled coyly as she remembered how the infamous Judah Jacob Raines had mumbled, and fumbled through their first two dates, displaying none of the intellect he was so famed for. Then, early into their third date, just when all seemed lost, the pair happened upon an Eden street performer impersonating a statue. As they passed him, the performer held steady, ceasing to breathe until he was in Joan's blind spot before bending over, extending his hand, and pinching her bottom.

Joan had jumped in startled surprise, dropping her purse in the process. She eyed the man and while normally she would be on him in a second, her ensemble for that evening, a tight red dress and high heels, did not allow for it. No sooner had she freed her left foot from its high-heeled prison than she noticed the blur that was her eventual husband. Judah, in a mixed flurry of physical and mental jabs, took the performer to task, pummeling the man without hesitation.

"Couldn't get a real job, could you? Why else would a grown man be painted like a bloody idiot on a street corner?!" Judah hollered, alternating between his left and right fist as continued his assault on the silver shaded pervert.

"Judah," Joan had said, taking a tentative step toward her date.

"Your parents must be SO proud of you!" Judah said, picking the silver shaded pervert by his collar and standing him. By the time Judah was done the performer's silver paint had rubbed off his face, neck, and forearms and now covered his attacker.

The memory of Judah covered in silver paint while the pervert scurried away to tend his wounds, forced a smile across Joan's face as the two neared the gateway to Eden Town Proper.

"What are you smiling about there?" Judah asked.

But before Joan could answer they saw a face near the gate that they had not seen in a month. From behind a large, seven foot tall male bodyguard walked a thin, bony blonde woman and her two twin children. The boy was unfamiliar to them, but the girl they knew quite well as a friend and comrade.

"Joan?! Judah?!" Tina Holmes screamed in a tone that was half question and half exclamation. Once the two had locked eyes it was impossible to keep the teenage girl from sprinting over and embracing them both in a running hug.

"Hey there," Joan said, awkwardly, patting Tina on the back. While Joan and Tina knew that theirs was not great friendship, their relationship was far from hostile, more like a tepid comradery. Regardless, there was a general sense of kinship for all three of them since the incident in Florida. After a quick introduction between the groups, both parties remained outside of the gate to talk.

"Have a good summer?" Judah asked, turning his face away before Tina could answer, his focus shifting to something in the distance. Used to the quirks of the eccentric genius, Tina instead shifted her focus to Joan, smiling as she went. "The local news sure thinks you did."

"So.." Joan said, placing her hands upon her hips, "Academy starts in a few days, huh?"

"Yeah," Tina replied, her smile faltering and a bit of color draining from her face at the mention of her impending studies.

"I'm going too," Timothy Holmes said suddenly. "I hope to be in the Class of the Coyote."

"How about you, kiddo? What class do you want to be in?" Joan asked Tina, punching her playfully on the right shoulder. The hit was slow, but firm as it grazed Tina.

"Ocelot," Tina said nervously. "Class of the Ocelot."

"What's an ass-el-lot?" Timothy asked with his toothy smile gone, replaced instead with an expression of utter confusion. Luckily for all, their conversation was interrupted by a shout from the direction Judah had been looking.

"Oyi!" came a far-off, deep, bellowing voice from across the valley to the west. Tina and Joan both turned to look, instant smiles donning their faces as Victor and Geoffrey hiked up over a field of dead grass the size of a football field, just within eyesight. Although they could only guess as to it being Geoffrey with him, Victor was rather distinguishable, even from a difference.

It had also been a month since Joan had seen either of them, for Tina two weeks. Invoking his right as Protector of Eden to issue an executive order, Turtledove directed his Knights to keep a low profile, keep contact at a minimum, and enjoy some much needed time off during their period of limbo. In the media frenzy of condemnation toward both Turtledove and Rolland it was good to see familiar faces. Tina allowed herself to get lost in the warm, comfortable feeling of friendship before snapping back out, remembering that her eerie little brother and snobby mother were still at her side. Setting her brain to task, Tina thought desperately of a reason why they might need to excuse themselves.

"Tina, honey," Tiffany Holmes said in a hoity tone of voice. "We really need to be going. So, say goodbye to your little friends."

"Little friends?" Judah said, turning around sharply to reveal a cigarette hanging limply between his lips.

Perhaps it was the tension that filled the air like a magnetic wave, or the heart palpitations she felt within her chest that drove Tina to the anxiety ridden response that she blurted out indirectly toward Joan, "We have to leave!"

Sensing trouble, Joan acted first, hugging Tina close before turning the girl around, and pushing her back toward her mother with a curt, but friendly, "So good to see you, I'll give you a call sometime soon."

Then, without missing a beat, or waiting for anyone else to respond, Joan of Arc turned toward her husband, took his arm. "There's our party, we're off to the court to support Rolland you know. Sure you've heard all about it. Great meeting you, hope you have a nice day!"

"What was all that about?" Judah asked as they walked closer to Victor and Geoffrey the cigarette that was there before conspicuously missing.

Joan shrugged without answering and turned her attention to the two Knights that had caught up to them. "Hey you two," she said, extending her arms outward to hug Victor. "So good to see you. How have you been?"

"Oh, you know," Victor offered. "hanging in there."

"Yeah, it's been a rough few weeks. But no convictions for anyone equals tequila for everyone!" Geoffrey said, changing his face from Andrew Jackson, to Councilman Anthony Varejao, and back to his own, chuckling slightly in all of their respective voices.

"Easy there," Judah said to Geoffrey. "The brat hasn't been acquitted, and most likely won't. You think Turtledove is going to want to celebrate then? Fat chance."

But try as he might Judah's condemnations and doubts could not dampen the spirits of Victor or Geoffrey who both insisted as the four knights made their way the rest of the journey into Eden Town Proper together that good things were on the horizon for the Knights of Time.

After his acquittal Rolland was taken, still rather forcefully, and still in shackles, to the communal showers before being stripped down to his underwear and cut loose from his chains. Removing the last vestiges of his dress, he was then given exactly five minutes to wash before the lukewarm water was cut off, leaving behind a shivering, naked teenager who then had mostly damp, yet somewhat cleaner, versions of his own clothes from before his shower thrown back at him. Another quick change later and Rolland once again had guards on both sides of him as he was led away from the showers and back toward the main court hallway.

To Rolland Wright, the warm Eden sunshine that greeted him as he walked out of Eden's Courthouse was sweet beyond words. So much so in fact that he completely disregarded the swarm of people awaiting their party as they exited the courthouse, and entered what was known as Eden's Downtown District. Like a plague of locusts the reporters, camerapersons, producers, and writers filled the steps outside, all waiting to throw a microphone or other electronic device in Rolland's and Turtledove's faces. Though for some reason, none of them were paying attention, or even facing the courthouse when they exited, leaving a rare window of opportunity to get away unnoticed.

Rolland walked directly behind Turtledove, who was surrounded on both sides by the guard Michael and his partner, Gabriel. The two guards met them outside of the council chamber and walked them through the entire length of the building before marching with them down the imposing, steep granite steps that led down to the street in front of Eden's courthouse.

"Thank you guys, really," Rolland said, meaning every word, catching the eyes of both men as they smiled politely and headed back inside the courthouse. *'Their lives are in there, not out here,'* he thought to himself, finding it difficult to let go of the one place he wished to get away from for the past month.

Suddenly a street vender appeared in Rolland's view. The middle aged man walked behind a self-driving cart with a picture of large pretzels on it. He screamed, "Pretzels! Pretzels!" as he passed a group of technical workers doing sound checks on their boom microphones. For a moment Rolland thought of buying one, but then he remembered that he had no money. The thought was only superseded by the pretzel vendor's presence as he passed by the courthouse steps, still crying out his wares as he went. But the only thing the pretzel vendor accomplished was attracting attention toward both he and Rolland.

"They're here!" screamed a cameraman, creating a mob, a series of flashbulbs, and chorus of name calling that filled the sensitive eyes and ears of Rolland Wright. The howling of both spectators and inquirers swarmed Rolland and Turtledove like ravenous dogs, scarcely giving the pair but an inch to breathe. All around him there were cameras, lights, and a sea of unrecognizable faces calling out his name. The odd familiarity of people that came with his re-entrance into Eden was as strange to him as his initial arrival if not for one key difference. Just when the sweat on his brow built, and the panic within his chest and stomach mounted, Rolland heard a soft voice call out his name from above the chorus of others doing the same.

"Rolland?" Tina inquired, making her way through a group of reporters before stopping directly in front of her love. The task of becoming separated from her family, getting 'lost' long enough in the crowd of people in front of the courthouse, giving her mother the impression that she had already gone inside and up to her father's office was her odyssey to get to him, but that was over now. They were together at last. Their eyes and arms magnets toward their positive ionic finds.

As the two embraced, arms wrapped tightly around one another, opportunists surrounded them with a vicious tenacity that threatened to swallow them both whole. Flashes of lights from cameras popped into existence from all around them as reporters, gawkers, and onlookers hoped to catch a glimpse of Eden's newest pseudo celebrities. Yet neither Rolland, nor Tina cared; for they were together at last, and no tabloid journalist, parental figure, or government bureaucrat was going to ruin that, try as they might. Each thought that the other's lips tasted like honey.

Eventually the crowd of reporters parted, annoyed with the lack of a juicier story. So too did both Tiffany and Timothy Holmes, who retreated inside the administration building next door to find the patriarch of their family, no doubt to once again sooth his nerves with their kind words of support they would never grant Tina. For his part, Timothy knew both what his sister was doing, and the ignorance of his mother she pushed hard against the crowd she was so accustomed to whenever she visited her husband at his place of employment. Deciding not to create a conflict at that moment, Timothy made a mental note to fight another day.

It was not long before the Knights of Time who travelled to Florida, all save Sephanie Kelly, were reunited upon the steps of Eden's courthouse. It was not much, but for Tina Holmes, Rolland Wright, Marcus Turtledove, Victor Aquasi III, Geoffrey Miller, Judah, and Joan Raines it was a sweet moment that none would ever forget.

Behind them, walking down the large granite steps by himself was the surprisingly chirpy looking Councilman Anthony Varejao. Though he lacked the same calculated confidence to his walk that he had when entering the courtroom earlier, he still had a very specific, and determined look about him. Approaching the Knights, all lost in jovial conversation, the councilman cleared his throat before speaking directly to Judah. "Mr. Raines."

"That's Doctor Raines, Polish," said Judah, removing his left hand from his wife's interlaced fingers before searching his pocket for his pack of cigarettes. "What do you want?"

"What I want, Doctor Raines is to be rid of the problem I have," Varejao said, looking from Judah to Joan, addressing her directly as the commanding officer in the group. "Which happens to be official council business."

Choosing to take the high road instead of rubbing their victories over Varejao's agenda in his face, Turtledove ushered the knights a few steps away from the trio in their conversation. They milled a bit, unsure how long the interruption might take, or if they had an obligation to stick around. Joan looked from Varejao to Judah, watching as her husband mouthed the words 'HE'S GOT CRABS' before smiling for a moment and turning back to Varejao.

"What problem is that, councilman?" Joan asked, her face revealing no sense of the disdain for bureaucrats, or the good humor her husband exuded. Though there was no love lost, she still felt honor bound to at the very least listen to the council's request.

"I need something, and someone, extracted from a remote island in the Pacific circa 1937," Varejao said removing a folded piece of paper from his pocket and handing it to Joan. "The council has voted unanimously to use the Dream Phoenix to accomplish those ends."

"The hell you will!" Judah exclaimed, interjecting into the conversation and getting Varejao to turn around to face him. "You bean counters forgot to ask the one man you'd need for such a little ride through the lilies. Me."

While not expecting full cooperation from Judah in handing over access to the Dream Phoenix, Anthony Varejao did not, and would not accept such rudeness from anyone. But before he could protest, he was greeted by Joan's soft but commanding hand as it found his wrist. He looked at it, and at her before hearing the words that told him it was time to leave.

"We would be happy to cooperate, Councilman," Joan said with a smile before letting go of Varejao. "On one small condition."

"And that would be?" Varejao asked, straightening himself.

"You send us, Dr. Raines and I, in lieu of a council appointed extraction team," Joan said with a fierce stare and a motivated agenda. "And give us a week, I mean month, off from active duty afterward. About time I had a proper honeymoon."

"Mrs. Raines, I-" Varejao began before being cut off by the blonde Maid of Orleans.

"That's Mrs. Doctor Raines, councilman," Joan said before crossing her arms, and raising one eyebrow.

"Ha!" Judah shouted somewhat uncontrollably as Varejao sputtered for a valid excuse as to deny Joan's request. When none came, the aging councilman composed himself before continuing to delegate.

Though he was probably not supposed to be listening, Rolland heard nearly every word spoken between the three adults, and for the first time, found himself genuinely liking Judah. Then Turtledove clapped him on the shoulder before murmuring his goodbyes and promises to speak to him later on. Geoffrey morphed into a cupid like figure with Victor in tow before the three made their way through the crowd, leaving the teens alone to continue their eavesdropping.

"So, what now?" Rolland asked Tina, attempting to change his mood into that of a more jovial and less skeptical pessimist.

"Well, since you're a free man, we can attend the Academy of Light together," Tina said, a smile creeping across her blushing face. Her eyes were large, round, and sparkling with various shades of Rolland's favorite colors. She could have offered him ocean front property in Arizona and he would have bought it. He was hers.

"Oh, yeah, right," Rolland responded, forgetting all about the fact that these people expected him to go back to school for some sort of training. The very notion had seemed preposterous an hour before, much less a day. Yet now this girl, his girlfriend, wanted him to go back to school, back to a normal, well, normal for Eden, lifestyle. He pondered this as he looked over at Varejao, the enemy and very man who arrested him, speaking with Joan and Judah, his teammates. It was all so strange how quickly his world had once again changed. But looking at Tina it didn't all seem so bad. On the contrary, the future was looking up.

"Care to grab a bite to eat?" Tina asked Rolland, her face positively beaming with the idea of an impromptu first date. Thoughts buzzed through her mind of her favorite cafes, shops, and secluded spots around town to take her new beau. Simultaneously cupping her hands together behind her back and praying that Rolland could not hear how fast her heart was beating Tina did her best to hide her excitement as such a prospect.

Thinking of the moldy food he was offered in Eden's prison, Rolland too showed signs of interest in a day on the town, complete with a smile and raised eyebrows, before offering his hand, and in a higher than usual tone of voice proclaiming, "Yeah, shall we?"

Together Rolland and Tina walked through the ocean of cameras, reporters, and would-be journalists eager to capture a story of the two together. Hand in hand they went past a sign that read **Winifred Street** before passing several shops Rolland could not see the names of due to people crowding around in front of them. With a very exaggerated push of her arm Tina cast a great divide between patrons as they passed, causing a great deal of people to anticipate her will, and move out of the way. One star struck straggler lingered in the couples' wake, an older woman whose green dress and burnt orange CROCS shoes struck right at the middle of Rolland's pity quota. After wishing her a good day they marched on, each lost in their own world. A short while later the couple entered a small bistro Rolland guessed to be French based on the simple wooden sign out front that read: **La Petite Peche**.

The low key atmosphere of the bistro was obvious from the onset, which put Rolland's anxiety addled mind at peace for the first time that day. After being shown their seats from a waiter with muttonchops the couple held hands, and made small talk. Although both enjoyed each other's company immensely they knew that the desire to find somewhere more private was a pipedream for the time being. In the background behind Tina stood a small stage where a man wearing a cowboy hat was playing guitar behind a microphone.

Being from present day Earth Rolland was used to people not making eye contact, it was just a byproduct of how busy people are in modern society. Yet the second he looked in his general direction the musician in the cowboy hat found Rolland's eyes before nodding in acknowledgment. Bemused by this act, Rolland nodded back, a bit surprised by both the friendliness, and the proceeding musical exit that indicated he was done with the song. It was familiar and from his childhood. He loved that song.

"She'll leave you with a smile," the Musician sang before tipping the brim of his hat to the audience and waving before removing the guitar from around his neck and walking away off stage. Despite repeated requests he did not reappear for an encore.

"Rolland?" Tina asked, gaining Rolland's attention once again.

"Yes," Rolland said, snapping back to reality.

"Whatcha thinking about?" Tina asked nonchalantly.

"Just dumb music. So, French food, huh?" Rolland said, looking around at the eclectic atmosphere. It was not that Rolland was surprised to find that Eden had restaurants, as obviously everyone has to eat. But a French restaurant seemed so...particular.

"I know what you're thinking," Tina began to say before Rolland could explain himself. "But people come to Eden from all over the place, and all across time. My grandfather actually came here via a portal he found in the Swiss Alps. I'm the second generation to-"

"What's going on over there?" Rolland asked, motioning his head across the restaurant. At a nearby table two women were also holding hands, though their eyes were glazed over. On both of their right hands was a black glove attached to an electric chord that split and ran up every finger, encasing them all in some sort of cybernetic mesh webbing. These clashed dramatically against their otherwise normal sundresses, neither of which featured any sort of outlandish pattern or material such as their gloves. He guessed they were communicating in some private way that was beyond his immediate comprehension, but his Earth manners got the better of him. "What is it they're doing together?"

"Rolland.." Tina said under her breath. "Don't say stuff like that so loud, it's rude." Knowing that she was right, but not liking being chastised for such a small offense, Rolland grimaced, which in kind elicited a mingled look of regret, shock, and pitiful sorrow from Tina. "I am so sorry. I just sounded like such a bitch didn't I?"

"Don't worry about it," Rolland said with a slight laugh. He did not like the look Tina got when she was on the brink of tears so instead he decided to change the subject to lighten her mood. "So, what's the deal with the school we're going to? The academy of something, right?

Noticing Rolland nudge to another subject, one that he surely knew Tina must be well versed in as an Eden native, the youngest of the Holmes family gave a small, playful smile before giving him her reply. "The Academy of Light, yes. And it's more than just a school, dear. It's where you're going to learn how to do, well, everything really."

Furrowing his brow at this, Rolland gave her a quizzical look before shifting slightly in his seat and fingers still intertwined with hers. "What do you mean? I thought we just had to go spend a semester there before.."

But in that moment Rolland realized that he did not know what came after the academy any more than he knew what being at the actual Academy of Light would be like. He was, as he had been for so very long, completely clueless. Nor did he know what exactly a traveler of light was. He decided to press the issue, but only after reading the menu for the first time. The dishes were as eclectic as they were plentiful in their selection.

After ordering the drinks, and food, Rolland decided to bring the academy training up once again. Deciding this meal was as good of a time as any to learn, Rolland pressed the issue with his new, and first, girlfriend.

"It isn't difficult really," Tina said, though she did not sound completely convinced of herself. "There is a seven month basic training program for cadets where each is taught everything they'd need to know to survive and contribute as a citizen of Eden. The hard part is mastering B.E.T.S.I."

"Who's Betsy?" Rolland asked, feeling quite stupid as he did so.

"Not who, what," Tina said, her eyes wandering again. "It's an obstacle course that simulates virtual reality in an attempt to get you to fail your objective. I've read that they use plasma from every former Eden citizen to maximize the difficulty levels. Can you imagine? Anyway, you get two tries to complete the course and if you still can't you're kicked out. Is something wrong?"

"No, I'm fine," Rolland lied as he shifted again in his chair. The prospect of joining only to be kicked out after two consecutive failures was as deflating as one could be, but Rolland still had a thirst for more knowledge of his short term future, and without any sensitivity at all, encouraged his new girlfriend to keep talking. Luckily for him Tina loved to do so.

"Everyone in Eden, no matter where or when you're from, is considered a traveler of light. It's kind of a blanket term for meaning you've been through time, but now call Eden home. But you can be more if you want. I mean, you don't HAVE to attend the academy, but you do if you want to be a citizen. That's the legal difference between humans and Elemenos anyway, citizenship.

Those who complete their training at the Academy of Light and serve two years in the protection of Eden are considered citizens and can do all sorts of things. Unless you're an Elemeno."

"Like what?" Rolland asked her, seriously contemplating whether or not all the hassle of going back to school, no matter what kind, was worth it at all.

"Hold office, own lands, firearms, vote, almost everything really," Tina said as if this simple bit of segregation were another fact of life for a native Edenite like herself. "And anyone can do it, so there is really no excuse. Plus, it's responsible to know how to use your abilities."

"Hang on," Rolland said, pulling his hand away from Tina's. She noticed this, and before she could ask yet again if something was wrong, he put his back on hers. "Why can't Elemenos be citizens?"

"Because Elemenos aren't allowed to attend the Academy of Light. Only humans, MerPeople, and Nocturns," Tina said, her free hand playing absent mindedly at the small white menu lying on the table before her. "It's all in accordance with the Sapien Act of 1914."

"Why aren't Elemenos allowed to attend the academy?" Rolland inquired, feeling this "justifiable" explanation of this brand of injustice of the Eden bureaucracy as bullshit, even if they were Elemenos.

"I just told you, the Sapien Act prevents them from registering for anything that the rest of us can do. For Elemenos everything is segregated. Eden Town Proper, the place with the prison, courthouse, really everything inside the gate, well all of that is divided into two segregated groups, the humans and the Elemenos," Tina said her voice steady and full of confidence.

Growing up as the child of a councilman prepared her for many things needed in a political career. Knowing her history was but one of the many virtues gleaned from her parents' otherwise lackluster careers as guardians to her and her twin brother. "It's been like that since around World War I. Humans aren't native to Eden, you see. Not originally. The elves are though."

"Elves?" Rolland said a bit too loud for their setting. Looking around the bistro he saw no eyes find his with indignation and decided he was safe. "For real?"

"Well, I mean they aren't exactly elves," Tina began, her eyes rolling a bit as she went. "But they have pointy ears, are light on their feet, and are very private with their culture. They're called Nocturns and they live in an enclosed city called Elysia. But it's here on Eden too!"

Although Rolland recognized what Tina said as valid English words, they seemed strange in their placement, and he found himself repeating them over and over in his mind as he stared blankly at her. Several beats passed between them before she broke the silence.

"Sorry sweetie, I know that's a lot of information to take in at once. The elf like people who are native to Eden are called Nocturns," Tina said, the index finger of her left hand unconsciously drawing a small heart on Rolland's palm as she delved deeper into her knowledge. "About one hundred miles from Eden Town Proper is a large fortress called Elysia. That's where the Nocturns primarily live. A long time ago they used to live all over the place, but following the Thousand Year War with the humans..."

Another awkward pause blanketed the conversation as Tina's mind wandered to a darker, more sinister part of Eden's history that neither were sure if they wanted to cover at that particular moment. Sensing this, Rolland again pulled the same trick out of his bag of charismatic tricks, and steered the subject back to its starting point. "So, why exactly do we have to do that?"

"Do what?" Tina asked, her straw turning over on her pink bottom lip.

Her sparkling eyes looked at him with adoration, not question, leaving him comfortable with the idea of pressing the issue. It wasn't as though Rolland had an alternative plan. Far from it, the surprising revelation that he would not be banished from Eden, or worse, was setting in, and allowing his mind to hear what she said. But despite the elation he felt from a clean verdict, he could not get past how pink Tina's lips were, and how the air around her seem to smell faintly of cinnamon and honey.

"Why must we, you and I, go to the academy, become citizens, and all of that? Why do we have to do any of it?" Rolland asked, scooting his creaky wooden chair closer to Tina's.

"Well, what else are we going to do?" Tina asked, her mind racing with the possibilities. Her heartbeat grew faster as the inches between them grew smaller. It was the perfect moment for a first kiss, or a twentieth, as it were.

"I've got a few ideas..."

The two leaned inward toward one another, steam percolating within their hormone laden teenage brains as they intersected. When flesh met flesh a ripple of pleasure cascaded through him like the Santa Anna winds that used to remind Rolland of safe things. Familiar, comfortable, homey things. All of which Tina reminded him of. Lingering thoughts peaked out from behind a veil of doubt masquerading as momentary joy when they broke apart, eyes opening to reveal a spark that could not be manufactured. For Tina it was puppy love bliss wrapped in serene

Chapter 4: Eden Revisited

chocolate, ooey gooey goodness. Yet for Rolland there was no chocolate, or bliss, or anything short of a frustrating, and somewhat painful longing in his nether regions the longer they exhibited public displays of affection. Rolland was about to bring this exact subject up, even going so far as to clasp Tina's hand with his own before opening his mouth when he was interrupted by the strangest, gruffest voice he had ever heard.

"My date and I would like to eat," said the rough voice from across the cafe, followed by several indignant noises coming from other patrons. It sounded angry, yet reserved, almost as if it were gearing up for a more offensive attack. "I don't mean to be rude but I have a right to.."

"*Monsieur*, please..." said the overly French accented host with mutton chops who had seated Tina and Rolland. He had made a somewhat distinctive impression, eyeing the teenage Wright's wardrobe with a judgmental eye as he had led them to their table.

Looking beyond the mutton chopped host Rolland saw the last thing he could ever expect. There, standing nearly six and a half feet tall, covered in fur so green it could rival Astroturf, was an Elemeno. Yet this one did not look anything like the Elemenos working for Vilthe that Rolland had seen in Pensacola. This one was wearing a dark gray suit, complete with vest, slacks, and black tie and despite his gruff voice, he was articulate and reserved.

Before another moment passed a portly man with a thin mustache, one whom Rolland had never seen before, rushed as fast as his little legs could waddle under his massive frame from the back of the cafe toward the well-dressed Elemeno, his human date, and the host. Manners cast aside, Rolland recognized the gestures of rudeness the portly man immediately began showing toward the Elemeno and his human companion. Without thinking Rolland was up and in mid-motion before his mind even began forming a plan as to what to do once he did intervene. No. What drove

65

that moment that instinct was the rotten smell of oppression, the decaying stench of bigotry, and the foul taste of discrimination that made his skin boil, temper rise, and brow to sweat.

"Excuse me," Rolland spoke in a commanding, yet overly friendly way to get their collective attentions. Beneath his cool exterior Rolland was all a fluster of nerves and apprehension, still, the overriding feelings of oppression were stronger, forcing him onward to speak his mind.

"*Monsieur* I..." the mutton chopped waiter attempted to interject as Rolland looked passed him toward the restaurateur, who obviously held more authority.

"Do you know who I am?" Rolland asked, eyeing the restaurateur with as much threatening presence as he could muster in his still dirty garb. The man did not respond in words, but instead with a slow nod of his head up and down, his jowls bobbing slightly on either side of his fat face as he did. "So you know what I'm capable of, who I have influence with..."

"I will not be threatened," the portly restaurateur said, inhaling sharply while puffing out his chest, harrumphing away as he did so with the pride of a fat peacock in bloom.

"Oh no, no of course not. Nor would I ever suggest as much. You misunderstand me, good sir," Rolland said, lifting his hand to divert the portly man's attention to Tina, who was sitting at the table equally as engrossed in the action, yet divested of hearing any of the dialogue. A thought, one so bordering on the line of evil that he questioned to himself for a split second if it was a wise decision, popped into Rolland's mind before he sprung it into action. Taking another step toward the portly restaurateur so that they were less than a foot away from each other face to face, the teenage Wright motioned toward the watching Tina, who gave a nervous, half-hearted wave in recognition of their attention. "You know my date as well. You know who her father is, I trust?"

"*Oui*," the portly restaurateur said, looking Tina up and down in a way that he had to know made her uncomfortable.

"Then you'll know not only who her parents are, but also that she's their golden child. She also graduated early at the top of her class and is headed to the Academy of Light soon. So maybe you shouldn't be so concerned with what's considered normal, or who might be in charge right now. Because Tina Holmes will be on the council someday, if not the head. Now, ask yourself, do you really want her as an enemy?"

The portly restaurateur shook his head from side to side, this time the color drained from his face as he turned back to Rolland, leaving behind chubby, white cheeks. Without another word he turned toward the desk before mumbling something in French to the mutton chopped host. After a few short exchanges between them, the restaurateur again turned to Rolland, this time with a little more color in his face from exercising his authority over a subordinate.

"We have a table available for you and your date, *Monsieur*. If you'll just follow me," the portly restaurateur said to the well-dressed Elemeno in the politest tone possible. Gone was any sense of disdain.

"Thank you, but no. We shall dine somewhere else tonight," the Wlemeno said, his beady black eyes landing on Rolland, encompassing him in a net of warm gratitude one only gets from assisting others when they most need it. "I fear your efforts were a waste. Mr. Wright, I presume? I saw your photograph in the newspaper."

"Never a waste," Rolland responded, speaking directly to an Elemeno for the first time in his life. Realizing this, and the ignorance behind it, Rolland desperately wished that he could say or think of literally anything else. He had fought these creatures, perhaps even killed a few while in Florida. Yet now, after weeks of time to reflect on his actions, Rolland regretted the damage that he inflicted on these beasts, not the hurt he put on Andrew Jackson. No. That was justified. As was what he did to Puck. What was left in the six long weeks of solitude, what he had found, was remorse for being so brash, and accepting truths on face value. A mistake he refused to make again. "Though you do have me at a disadvantage, knowing my name but not sharing your own."

"Darius," the Elemeno said, extending his fur covered muscular right arm to Rolland, offering his right hand to shake. Rolland took it, immediately noticing the lack of a thumb in favor of a prolonged dugong. The shake was firm, not too hard, not too soft, and above all else sincere. It was a good shake that spoke highly of Darius and his people. "It's nice to meet you, Rolland Wright."

"It's nice to meet you," Rolland said with a smile of his own. "Darius."

Chapter 5:
Orientation

Eden - Present

The first morning that Rolland awoke outside of a prison cell was like a sweet dream, one so fine that he thought himself unworthy of experiencing it. Then he heard the unmistakable sound of Victor's snoring in the room next door and knew it was real. With the sun peeking through the paper shades that covered the windows it became increasingly difficult to ignore the dawning of a new day, forcing Rolland to get out of the bed. The air outside of the blankets was cool, raising the hairs on the exposed skin of his arms, and chest. He was in the middle of pulling on his pants when the unmistakable aroma of something familiar found its way into his room. Zipping up, Rolland sniffed the air, tilting his head as he did. The smell was tempting, indulgent, and fatty. It wafted through the walls, seeking out the quickest way to his nostrils. It wasn't..it couldn't be.. but it was.

Bacon.

Suddenly Rolland was a man on a mission sent from the gurgling of his stomach, reminding him that he had not eaten since the cafe with Tina the evening before. Rolland raced out of the room, through the hallways, and down the stairs to the dining alcove. Turtledove and Geoffrey were already there waiting, their smiles greeting him as he arrived. Breakfast was a veritable buffet of every type of morning food imaginable. Rows of cereal in various types sat in their cardboard boxes lining the long countertop. On the next countertop sat heated trays containing an abundance of scrambled eggs, bacon, steamed spring vegetables, potatoes, and waffles in their respective bins. Jams, syrups, jellies, and other condiments of various sorts sat nearby, waiting to be plucked and added to the many dishes.

"You guys really know how to do breakfast," Rolland said, not able to take his eyes from the food. His mouthed watered, though he did not notice it due to the growling coming from his stomach. "Thank you so much."

Wolfing down the pile of food on his plate, Rolland scarcely made eye contact with Victor, Geoffrey, or Turtledove. The bacon that he had smelled from his dorm room was nothing short of spectacular. Cut to a generous diameter, the hickory smoked pepper bacon was crisped up nicely while still maintaining an even reddish-brown hue. It was sweet, and plumped up just the way Rolland liked it.

It was it was like being home again. Home, a feeling Rolland had not known since before him mother passed away.

And so it passed for three whole days. Rolland spent most of his alone time sleeping or otherwise just lying in his feather bed, happy to never see the inside of a prison cell for as long as he lived. Victor and Geoffrey were only too happy to provide companionship as the three explored the confines of nearly every room at the Halls of Time, including a particularly revealing trip to Turtledove's office, ate themselves silly on the finest foods Eden had to offer, and played numerous games of a game called 'Blissball' which Victor described as a hybrid of baseball, American football, and fireworks. The concept took days to explain properly. Tina was actually quite good at it, the best amongst their group by far.

Tina did not visit on the final day, which Rolland found somewhat strange, but dismissed it as her over-prepared nature for their first day of classes at the Academy of Light. Instead he spent the day mostly speaking with Turtledove, whom he had found sipping coffee in the Halls of Time kitchens early that morning. What began as a simple question about his mother turned into a day long conversation regarding everything from his parents to Eden, to the way time is perceived when one is on a mission. The two went to lunch in Eden Town Proper and talked. Went window shopping and talked. Hell, they even followed the same path that they took when Rolland had first arrived in Eden and talked; it somehow feeling much shorter the second time.

What struck Rolland most about this time was how adamant Turtledove was for his forgiveness surrounding the trial. The reassurance that he, Rolland, would not be turned into an instrument of warfare, or any sort of weapon was calming, if only because someone with real power actually said it out loud. This came toward the end of the day when the two were joined, and later left by Victor, who had a date that evening and wanted Turtledove to tie his tie for him. Needing a space big enough to accommodate all three, they choose the downstairs entry parlor where the Knightly Creed hung proudly on the wall. The talks between Rolland and Turtledove only became awkward late into the evening when the topic of conversation somehow led to Turtledove's past, and the revelation that he was somehow responsible for the unicorns' existence in Eden as well.

"Hang on, you're telling me that it was you that brought them here?" Rolland asked, forgetting his manners for a moment as the hour grew nearer to midnight Eden time.

"Aye, yes," Turtledove reaffirmed with a sketchy eye before fidgeting in his seat. "It was a long time ago. Many decades. I'd hope to have accomplished more since coming to Eden, but, alas. We cannot always get what we want. And with that grim thought, I bid you goodnight."

Turtledove left Rolland there, alone, to once again ponder not only his own situation, but that of Eden itself. Such a strange place, yet so inviting to outsiders. Almost as if the land itself wanted him there. He thought on this perplexing conundrum as he dressed for bed, and fell asleep in the same dormitory that he had months before, though this time he did not sneak out of bed. This time, with no mysteries to solve, no one to rescue, no attractive females to bump into, Rolland instead let himself fall victim to the hypnotic, steady rhythm of Victor's snores, and drifted off into a listless sleep.

When the morning of his orientation arrived Rolland prepared for the day just as he had the previous three. Another good meal and then it was off to either meet his destiny or become the laughing stock of a group of supernatural meta-humans. Rolland pondered this over his bacon and cereal before being interrupted by Victor.

"Good luck, brother," Victor said to Rolland, slapping him so hard across the back that it knocked the spoon out of hand. "I remember my time at the academy. Good times man. And when it comes to your female classmates... how do the kids say..no glove, no love."

A bit uncomfortable, Rolland gave a tense laugh in response before offering his final goodbyes to Geoffrey, and moving toward the massive front door of the Halls of Time. There Turtledove beamed at him as if he were a proud grandfather before stepping aside and likewise wishing him well. As the doors shut behind him, Rolland realized that he was alone in Eden, truly alone, for the very first time. Rolland lingered there for a moment. His eyes were fixed on the rot iron letters of 'KoT' that labeled the doors, and subsequently, the entire Halls of Time as well. It was a weird place yet it was his place. He couldn't explain it, but in his heart, he knew he had a connection to the building, and was sad to leave it. Taking a deep breath he turned, facing the vast green Eden hillside before him, and took a step forward.

The trek to the Academy of Light from the Halls of Time was not a long one, but it was one that did not ease the tense muscles in Rolland's stomach. Chalking it up to first day jitters, he decided to dismiss the uneasy feelings. The worst was behind him after all... right? Nothing could be worse than a stint in Eden county lock-up, right?

As he passed the Blackard Family Orchard, Rolland spotted Sherman, the blind groundskeeper, picking low hanging fruit outside the parameter wall. He thought about waving, but quickly realized how foolish it would be. Instead he pressed on along the steepest hill he had yet encountered, putting him at a one-hundred-twenty-degree incline. Sweat appeared, pooled, and beaded down around Rolland's collar as he leaned in, forward, onward. His breath quickened as he went on, up, up, up. It was strenuous, but once he reached the top the entire landscape of his understanding of Eden changed and he forgot his exhaustion entirely.

The view was nothing short of breathtaking.

Before Rolland lay the round-shaped enclosure that comprised the Academy of Light. It was huge, stretching out the entirety of the flatland that lay in the valley before him. A strange, soft golden hue reflected off of the white, twenty-foot tall limestone walls that surrounded the place. It wasn't until Rolland was half way down the hill separating him from the Academy that he realized he was moving toward it without choosing to, as if it were a magnet he was drawn to. It was another heartbeat before he realized the golden hue was coming from a thin, contorting river of shimmering golden water acting as a large moat. The Time Stream. It was continuous, stretching from the hillside to the east around the Academy, forming a protective, albeit small, barrier before naturally moving towards the Blackard Family Orchard. Rolland was suddenly filled with a powerful reverence for the Time Stream, though he could not fully explain why.

Upon approaching the gate, Rolland noticed that it was not like the large, wooden gate that led the way to Eden Town Proper, nor the doors to the Halls of Time. Instead these gates seemed to be made of the same, semi-swirling golden material that he had seen on only one other item - Turtledove's sword as he slew the beast known as Ballua in 1817 Florida. As Rolland walked, his pace slowing with each step in anxious trepidation, visions of the past few months filtered into the forefront of his mind. The heat of the glass windows at Books Half Price, where he first encountered Victor….and the Nazi, Hess. The look on the librarian June Lin's face as he ran shirtless from the library bathroom followed by a 4-inch tidal wave of toilet water. The night he kissed both Sephanie and Tina. It was with that last pleasantly confusing thought that he pushed the gate open, revealing a large courtyard nearly full with people.

They were students everywhere, all of various age, races, and nationality. Their only shared trait, aside from being mortal, was that each was green and inexperienced. This was their proving ground. This was their training. This was not voluntary. In that they all knew, if only deep down within the bowels of their individual minds, and accepted this rite of passage that was the academy of light. And yet most, if not all, of them were happy.

The many cadets chatted away in small groups scattered throughout the courtyard as he slipped in unnoticed to join them. Rolland walked further into the courtyard but took no more than ten steps before hearing the only voice he was searching for.

"Hey sweetie! We're both cadets now!" Tina shouted, giving a small squeal before rushing to his side. Their embrace was longer than it probably should have been for public setting, but neither cared about the looks it attracted from other cadets around them. When they broke their kiss, Rolland noticed Tina's twin brother standing beside them.

"Hey Timothy," Rolland said, extending his hand out only to have it rejected in turn.

A curt scowl and nod were the only responses Timothy Holmes offered, choosing instead to act like Rolland was not there, speaking only to his sister. "Do you think we'll get to pick our Class? I hear it's determined by whoever has the most psychic link to the animal. If that's true, then I'm sure to be a Raptor, I know it."

Stifling a laugh, Rolland coughed instead, turning his head to face away from Timothy as he let out a chuckle in response to Timothy's ridiculous expectations. The gesture did not go unnoticed.

"You laugh at me now, convict, but my father will see to it that I get what I want," Timothy offered, tilting his head upward while simultaneously twitching the left side of his lip, raising it slightly. "You'll see."

"That's stupid Timmy," Tina chided her brother as she wrapped Rolland's right arm around her. "Daddy doesn't do favors like that."

"Does so," Timothy defended, his face contorting in anger. "He got you into the Time Nights, didn't he?"

Tina bit the inside of her cheeks, irritated beyond words at her brother's blatant disrespect. She wanted so much to scream, to hit Timmy like she did when they were young children. "You know I got the communications internship on my own accord. I aced it by translating a lost Native American language therefore averting certain death, but you wouldn't know anything about that, would you, Timmy?" The verbal smack down of fact laid upon her brother complete, Tina turned her attention toward her boyfriend. "Which class do you want to be in, honey?"

But Rolland's attention was diverted elsewhere, across the yard, to a slender African American young woman who was staring at him intently. Although he did not know her, he recognized the look on her face - it was almost as if she had seen a ghost. He brushed off the thought and looked away but he could still feel her eyes on his face. He shivered involuntarily.

"Rolland?" Tina repeated herself while simultaneously grabbing her boyfriend's upper arm. Rolland turned to face her, smiling despite the troubled look in his eyes.

Suddenly the sound of a whistle filled the courtyard, eliciting a hive-mind reaction from all of the cadets, Rolland and Tina included. Without realizing how it had happened, each found themselves lined up in loosely created rows, none of which were straight or uniform in any way. At the front of Rolland's line was a tall, broad shouldered young man with tan skin who Rolland guessed to be near his own age. He wore no shirt, only a light vest that seemed to be made of seaweed. Tina, after telling Rolland to stand at attention, turned away before straightening her back, hands at her sides, and eyes wide open. Although he knew he should keep his eyes straight forward, Rolland could not help but stare at her backside.

A tall, fit woman approached through two of the columns of cadets, the cause of the commotion pressed firmly between her chapped lips. She wore olive pants that ended just above a pair of perfectly polished, brown boots. Her beige tank top clung tightly to her torso, attracting the attention of many of the male cadets. Above her left breast a small, pewter nametag said **Sergeant Tillman** in black, engraved letters. Tucked away in the small of her back was a clipboard, the metal top sticking out from above her bottom. She was a very attractive woman, yet her immediate presence was both imposing and authoritative as she eyed every cadet she passed over the top of her golden aviator sunglasses.

"You all will be broken, and rebuilt by yours truly, turned into highly effective soldiers to protect Eden from those who wish to do her harm. Is that understood?!" Sgt. Tillman asked the group at large.

"Ma'am, yes ma'am!" came the loud, automated response from all forty of the cadets, though not all at once. They were a group of individuals, but soon they would learn to work in cohesive groups together.

"Good, good. Not a clown among you, it seems. But you know what that means, right?" Sgt. Tillman asked as she walked in front of the column of cadets, eyeing each one as she went along. While most of their eyes dared not move from their fixed positions. "Means I'll have to root one out."

"This year the five classes will be trained, tested, and miracle upon miracles, pass through this Academy prepared for not only anything thrown at them in battle, but also every day civilian life. I believe in balance. There will be eight to a class and the names for each have already been chosen, so do NOT ask!" Sgt. Tillman declared, her methodical pacing continuing through the ranks of cadets reinforcing her command. "The classes are as follows - Ape, Caribou, Parrot, Raptor, and Tiger!"

A small ripple of excited murmurs shot through the lines of cadets. For Rolland it meant almost nothing. For Tina it meant the world. She had heard rumors of the Class of the Tiger returning after nearly eight hundred years, and had hoped against hope that they were true. It was tradition at the academy to name classes after animals that represented values important to them as a group. The Class of the Tiger was once considered one of the five main classes, often reappearing every year as a tradition, creating former members who greeted one another in fraternal bonds of friendship. That is, until the last Class of the Tiger. No one talked about that Class of the Tiger.

Sweat formed on nearly every brow as Sgt. Elle Tillman eyed the cadets with disdain. Her extensive battle training and field combat experience made her the perfect individual to train these new recruits. The fact that her mere presence struck an intimidating chord in the heart of nearly everyone she met did not hurt matters either. In raising the clipboard that was tucked away in her olive pants, she caught the eye of the young, wide hipped, redheaded girl who might as well been screaming 'fresh meat.' Elle Tillman smiled at the girl menacingly before asking, "What is your name, cadet?"

The redheaded girl stepped forward, tripping over her pink Converse sneakers. Her voice was small, meek, and without the slightest bit of confidence as she offered a soft, "Amara. Amara Hart."

Looking over the clipboard, Sgt. Tillman saw the name under the third column, listing the young girl as a liability, part of the curve for training purposes. It was a common tactic, a measure that Councilman Holmes insisted on nearly a half a dozen years prior. Girls like this Amara Hart helped bolster the overall numbers, made the other cadets look better by comparison, and help inspire underdogs teetering on the edge of passing their training. With this in mind Elle Tillman lowered her aviator sunglasses before shouting in a loud, shrill voice that carried and reverberated throughout the entire courtyard, "Class of the Ape."

Sgt. Tillman wasted no time in moving on to the next individual, bucktoothed boy with freckles on his face who went by the name of Derrick Noldb. He was assigned to the Class of the Parrot, as was the man after him, and the woman after.

"Wright!" Tillman hollered before tilting her head and reading the name again. She let the clipboard slack a bit before turning to Rolland. Although he immediately wished he had not, Rolland's eyes went to Sgt. Tillman's. "What the hell are you looking at, cadet?"

"Nothing, sir... I mean ma'am," Rolland said shakily. He wondered if they were being divided into class by talent, or size, or what the criteria was for him to pass.

No sooner had Rolland formed this thought than Sgt. Tillman shoved her face into Rolland's and began to breathe heavily, leaving no personal space between them. "Says here that you can travel through time? Is that so?"

For a brief moment Rolland felt blocked in, and considered fighting his way out. Yet he knew, deep down, underneath his childish ego and entitled sense of pride, that he was being hazed. Tested. "Yes, ma'am."

"That's good. Real good," Sgt. Tillman began, her attitude completely changing, as she remembered a dream. She fumbled a bit before reading the clipboard once again and announcing, "Class of the Tiger!"

And there it was. Rolland was going to be in the Class of the Tiger.

So lost in reflection was Rolland that he did not hear the designated classes of the next six or seven candidates. When he did zone back in, it was the leader of the line's turn, the boy with the seaweed vest. He too was assigned to the Class of the Tiger, a fact that Rolland immediately had mixed feelings about. Then came a series of able bodied, dark skinned young men with broad shoulders. They each sported a similar short haircut and their behaviors were staunch, rigid, and unyielding. It was as if they had already been attending the academy, judging by their attention to detail and strict code of behavior when at attention. Whereas Rolland's eyes met Sgt. Tillman's as she called his name these men did not. Each looked, dead eyed, directly in front of them. All were accepted as members of the Class of the Raptor. Rolland wondered if they came from Eden, or some other world in another dimension. Surely there were more people in Eden than those who lived in the city, right? Judging by the diverse cast of cadets in the courtyard he guessed his assumptions were correct.

Soon it was Tina's turn, and although he strongly considered using his abilities to slow down time to check Sgt. Tillman's clipboard (and if need be change it) so that he and Tina were in the same class, it turned out to be unnecessary. Tina was also placed in the Class of the Tiger. A smile, a look, and a hastily wiped happy tear were the only reactions she could offer her significant other but they meant the world to Rolland. Their moment was short lived however, as Timothy Holmes was also assigned, rather unceremoniously, to the Class of the Tiger. A shocked look of disappointment fell upon both of the Holmes twins' faces, both for very different reasons.

"Wait, what?" Timothy asked, his shock getting the better of his senses. "I'm not a Tiger, I'm meant to be a Raptor. My father said!"

Wasting no time, Sgt. Tillman stopped dead in her tracks as Timothy's insolence reached her ears. Turning her heels, she marched intently toward the Holmes boy. Bracing for an impact as she closed in on him, Timothy sucked in his gut, and prepared for the blow. Instead, Sgt. Tillman, not one to suffer for fools, simply stopped in front of the boy, crooked one eyebrow and proceeded to take off her aviator sunglasses. Her face was slender and purposeful, as if she was descended from the ancient military captains of folklore. Hell, in a place like Eden she might have been.

As Sgt. Tillman stared into his eyes, every bit of happiness and hope drained from Timothy's body like water from a sponge. His brain, his very psyche, which had been spoiled rotten, crashed around him as every bit of his soul cried out for an ounce of compassion. His breath escaped him, as did control of his legs, eyes, and ears. The periphery of his vision darkened, became cloudy, disjointed, and erratic. In his mind Timothy held out for a long time, perhaps hours in his estimation, before giving in to the urge to cry, tears pouring down his cheeks before he fell to his knees, ending in the fetal position. In reality it took six, maybe seven seconds. With a nod to the psychologically broken Holmes boy his nightmare ended, and the Sgt. moved on, never needing to utter a word of resistance to his objections. He stood, looked around a bit, humiliated, before standing back at attention, never once stopping to wipe the tears from his eyes, or the wet patch from the front of his pants.

Next came the woman with mocha-toned skin in her late teen years who had been staring so intently at Rolland earlier.

She wore a tasteful maroon dress with rose shaped earrings, and matching sandals. Much to Rolland's amazement the staring girl, whose name turned out to be Hannah, was also placed in the Class of the Tiger. Not sure how he felt about this, he tried not to think about it and instead watched the rest of the placement process. Two more boys, one Hispanic, and one he guessed to be Chinese were also added to his class. Both had a strong sense of outward ambivalence to the entire process. When the last cadet was assigned to the Class of the Ape the process was done.

"We will now begin with our first exercise," Sgt. Tillman shouted whilst taking her place at the front of the rigid lines of cadets before her. "Lieutenant! Bring me the Judificator!"

Rolland could only guess that he knew the inventor of the item in question. Leave it to Judah Raines to invest something brilliant only to insist on naming it after himself, regardless of how stupid it might sound. He mused on the arrogance of Dr. Judah Jacob Raines as the lieutenant rolled out enormous stacks of dried straw, bringing one stack directly in front of the line of cadets. A small blonde woman with slender limbs and extremely pointed ears literally fluttered out of the way of the straw pile nearest to Rolland. She bumped into his chest briefly before turning around with a lightening quick speed; all without ever touching the ground. With an even quicker smile she was gone, back into the crowd.

Then a noise drew all of their attention. A low, hollow screeching sound followed by the loud ticking of a clock. When the ticking ceased the straw burst open at its points, streams of crimson, gossamer, magenta, teal, and gold began pouring out in focused jetties of energy toward the sky. It rumbled, slightly at first, before picking up momentum. Once it had enough propulsion to move, it turned on itself, creating a rotation, and coincidently, a stream of brilliantly beautiful light that followed it. Then without notice it burst, creating a flashing bulb effect, blinding everyone in the courtyard for a split second before reforming itself into a small, slightly glowing yellow boomerang.

"The straw represents the current state of each of you," Sgt. Tillman announced, still moving through the columns of cadets, circling them like a sheep dog would its herd. "You are all the same, each a straight, malleable, fragile piece of straw; held by the constraints of your lives before. But here, this boomerang is bent, forged and forced to change course in the name of teamwork. Each team will try to find their boomerang in a pile of straw."

"Sounds too easy," said an Asian teenage boy who was standing close by Rolland and Tina. It was unclear to either if he was speaking to them, or to himself. Either way he spoke their minds clearer than they were able in that moment.

"Break into your teams and solve the problem," Sgt. Tillman screamed, her already loud voice increased somehow to echo in every square inch of the courtyard, accompanied by the loud whistling sound that had heralded her arrival previously. "You have five minute probies, go!"

As if on cue all five towering piles of straw, each large enough to crush a grown man, lifted five feet off of the ground, spun on themselves in a counter-clockwise motion, and landed with an unceremonious thud in front of each group.

"First things first," the broad shouldered teenage boy in the seaweed vest said, leaning in to the others. "The name is Kniff and I'm in charge."

"Like hell you are," said one young man, the Hispanic gentleman with intense eyes.

"You can't even dress yourself properly. Unless you're going to lead us into the nearest fish pond, I think you're out of luck," said another, the skinny Asian teenager in tan corduroy pants.

Rolland laughed, prompting others to do the same. Though it did not matter. The broad shouldered boy in the seaweed vest heard Rolland laugh first and took offense to his indiscretion alone. "Something funny, convict?"

A hush fell over their group as cries of jubilant teamwork from other groups became of no concern to anyone amongst them but Tina, though her loyalty and need for approval from Rolland superseded her concerns.

"Just admiring your choice in fashion accessories," Rolland said, his eyes darting to the bracelet on the boy's wrist. It was a rectangular outline charm on a silver chain, each side featuring a clasp surrounding a large, red ruby, cut into the shape of a human heart. Although it was flat on one side, the inner workings were as clear as a bright Eden afternoon. Rolland recognized the shape immediately, and chose to resist complimenting the literal nature of a symbol. Instead he took the low road, offering up a rude, "Did you steal that from your Momma's jewelry box?"

"Alright, convict," Kniff said, the second word hissed through gritted teeth. An evil smile splashed across his face as he glanced toward the girl named Hannah. "We'll vote for it, aye? Now who wants to follow me? How about you, girl? You'll do as I tell you, right?"

"I am no one's slave," Hannah said, a small pink bubble jettisoning out of her right hand. As it exited her mocha colored flesh it formed a hard shell, rotated on its axis, and shot across the short distance before impaling itself upon Timothy's forehead.

"I'm on your team!" Timothy Holmes screamed at Hannah. As fighting broke out between all but one of the classes, a clear picture of the task at hand began to form in the most astute of minds. Surviving the Academy of Light was not only an exercise in self-preservation, but also one of sacrifice in teamwork. A lesson that their class had failed to learn.

"Winner - Class of the Ape!"

"Thus concludes orientation!" Sgt. Tillman bellowed, her voice seeming to come from everywhere and nowhere at once. "Report at 0:500 in the am for your next assignment."

When the exercise was over, and the authority figures had left the cadets alone, the rules of the playground took effect.

"Maybe we should start off by introducing ourselves," Tina said, in an obvious attempt to defuse the situation. "I'll go first. Hi, my name is Tina Leigh Holmes and I.."

"We know who you are," the Hispanic teenager said. "You're a council brat, just like your brother, and the Asian one. We're sooo lucky to have the favor of your presence in our class."

"Hey now!" Rolland protested.

"It's fine," Tina assured him, placing her right hand gently on Rolland's arm. "I'm all right. And you are?"

"My name is Jaime," the Hispanic teenager said, his eyes intent on the conversation despite his distant demeanor. "And it's *Jaime*. Pronounced 'HI as in hello' and ME as in call ME Jaime."

"Nice to meet you Jaime," Tina began but was interrupted by a cold gust of wind followed by a blur to the groups' right, then left, and back again to the area where Jaime had been two seconds before.

"Well I think that's pretty neat, your running, I mean," Tina offered politely.

Another awkward silence filled the courtyard as each of the other seven cadets held their tongues. This was getting them nowhere. Deciding to keep the ball rolling, Tina asked the Asian teenager his name.

"Stew - Stewart, Stewart Yick," the boy said bashfully. "But everyone I know has always called me Dodger."

"Why is that?" Rolland asked, before watching Dodger literally disappear before his eyes. It was not sudden, but happened gradually, over the course of about three seconds. Then, a few heartbeats later, a gentle poke on Rolland's left shoulder told him that Dodger had re-phased back into reality behind him. "You...what?"

"I teleported," Dodger said with a great deal of proud enthusiasm. "It's what I do. I dodge things, teleport; generally an overall badass."

"Wait, Yick - I've heard that name before," Rolland said, the thought mulling over in his mind.

"My granddad is on the Council of Light," Dodger said, somewhat embarrassed. "I'm here because I want to make him proud of me. He's done a lot, and I have some big shoes to fill. So you're a mermaid right?" Dodger suddenly asked Kniff, his overzealousness getting the best of him.

"Merman," Kniff said through gritted teeth. "And it's Kniff."

"Oh?" Dodger asked in bored voice.

"I am not to be trifled with, dodge boy," Kniff barked. Without so much as a warning, Kniff punched Dodger, hard, and squarely in the stomach, sending the poor boy flying backward a few feet onto the cold, dirt floor of the courtyard.

"What about you, Nocturn?" Kniff asked the much smaller blonde girl, eyeing her up and down while smirking and nodding his head. "Got any accessories you'd like to show off while we're all here?"

Knowing that Kniff was begging for trouble, Rolland immediately thought of going to the blonde woman's aid, and even took a few steps toward the pair before the demure blonde with pointed ears spoke for herself. He was more than surprised by what he heard.

"You talk tough, Merman," the blonde woman said, speaking for the first time. She, like Kniff had done to her moments before, eyed him up and down, her head tilting sideways in with a look of disappointment, her head level with his stomach and crotch. "But my people have known your kind for millennia. We know of your boastful ways, your plentiful promises, and your... shortcomings."

"Burn!" Dodger shouted, throwing both of his hands over his mouth and laughing obnoxiously. "I like this gal."

"Gal?" the blonde woman asked, cocking one eyebrow at Dodger. "I am no gal. I am Gwendolyn of Clan Murrow."

For his part Dodger might as well as have cartoon hearts bulging out from his eyes. "I'll call you whatever you'd like..."

"Dodger!" Tina chided, smacking his chest lightly with the back of her open right hand. Her teeth were grinding against a tense jaw, as she hated confrontation, and only recently discovered, in no small part thanks to another situation that Rolland had put her in, that she was even capable of being level headed under pressure, much less of any use. The sound of muddled war hammers beat deep within her head as the energy surrounding Kniff began to glow a very faint shade of lilac purple. "You're not helping the situation. We have to all get along if we want to do well so can't be fighting all the time."

"Thanks for your help baby, I appreciate it. I mean, I'm no weather man," Kniff began, looking Tina up and down before licking his lips in an overly animated way, "But tonight - you'll be getting a few inches."

"Fucker," Rolland said without missing a beat, the short distance between them becoming but a few inches as he descended on his would-be enemy. With a lightning quick grasp of his vest, Rolland had Kniff up, and in the air before the momentum that he used to perform the move could wear off, or Kniff could retaliate properly. "Take it back!"

"Wa-oh now,'" Dodger began, holding both of his hands up even toward his chest. "Tina is right, none of this hostility is necessary. Hey I've got a question for you - why did Sgt. Badass call us all probies, what's up with that?"

The attempts at changing the conversation fell on deaf ears as the lines of battle had already been drawn.

"I challenge you to *Davhor*," Kniff said boastfully, his statement nothing short of a declaration.

The blank expression on Rolland's face told the entire Class of the Tiger that he was completely clueless as to the implications of Kniff's challenge. One by one they waited with bated breath as the blonde teenager weighed his options.

"Rolland," Tina began to say, inching closer to her boyfriend. "He just challenged you to a duel for leadership of the group."

"Oh," Rolland began, tilting his head slightly askew in a pitiful, half quizzical statement of fact. Within a heartbeat the broad shouldered teen had breached the gap between them, getting uncomfortably close to Rolland before landing a sucker-punch that connected Kniff's knuckle to his own chin, a reaction that left him tripping over his own feet on the way to a barrel roll of sorts to the ground. All Rolland knew was that one moment he was debating the merits of averting a fight with his new teammate, and the next he was struggling to find his footing.

"I knew you were all hype!" Kniff exclaimed, bending over Rolland as he scrambled like a jungle cat that had been startled awake. "I am the strongest!"

A knot formed in the pit of Tina's stomach as her boyfriend tumbled, fumbled, and then remained still on all fours, choking and catching his breath. With both hands covering her pursed lips and nose she initially thought of rushing to his aid. But then she caught Rolland's eye, and the mischievous brown eyes signaling her to step back. With a quick snapping of his fingers, Rolland brought his left palm down hard onto his fisted right hand, causing time to slow to a stop. Slow to his will.

From the perspective of anyone else the scene must have appeared to be some sort of magic. One moment Kniff was smiling broadly, his cocky hands resting comfortably on his hips, chest stuck out. The next Kniff was flung like a rag doll across the courtyard, his face being contorted as if being hit by an invisible wall. When Kniff landed hard on the concrete with little more than a thud, he wasted no time in rolling forward, scrambling to his feet despite an intense embarrassment bordering on true shame.

"We're done here," Rolland said, his chest heaving up and down, breath quickening as fast as the heartbeat that raced from deep within. Drips of sweat fell freely from both sides of his brow. Behind him the classmates assigned to join Rolland in their collective training watched with eager eyes at what exactly he was capable of.

"Damn," Jaime said. The sentiment was shared by all of the others, including Tina. None had heard Rolland strike, or knew that he was playing possum, luring Kniff into his trap before striking hard and fast. That made Rolland dangerous in Jaime's eyes.

Inside the humiliated merman Kniff simmered fury and embarrassment. Logic abandoned him like a boat made of paper upon a river of self-doubt. Never before had he ever been so humiliated and belittled by a commoner, much less one of such ill repute. Searching for an ambassador to deliver his declaration of war, Kniff found one in a nearby rock that had taken up residence surrounding the still untouched pile of straw that was their task the previous hour.

The rock flew past the blonde locks of Gwendolyn, the small, lavender scented brown fuzz of atop Hannah's head, and the tresses of gold silk that Rolland loved to run his fingers through while kissing Tina before making final contact with the small of the time traveler's back. Although a shirt, cotton fabric, lay between rock and skin, the edge split the difference, drawing blood, pain, and a great deal more annoyance back to the situation than Tina was hoping for. When she saw Rolland's nostrils flare as he exhaled sharply, Tina knew the fight was far from over.

"What the hell!" Rolland shouted before closing in and shoving the Merman backward as hard as he could. But Kniff was a large boy, beefy, and broad shouldered with an excellent grip that latched onto to Rolland, and used the already shifting momentum between them to break his inevitable fall. Though both went down, only one landed flat on his back.

For Rolland the free fall was interrupted by a dull, purple flash out of the corner of his eye. Before he knew what was happening to him, Rolland's legs were manipulated, as if someone was pushing on them, straightening them. It felt as if each of his toes were being pulled independently from his body.

"DODGE!" came the overzealous voice of someone Rolland knew to be close by, even if they sounded very far away. His head was woozy, though returned quickly to normal. The voice came from Dodger, who was prancing about it a small circle with genuine glee, though Rolland was unsure as to why. Then he saw Kniff flat on his back and tentatively extended his hand to the merman.

"Get away from me," said Kniff, refusing Rolland's hand. Instead he flipped himself over, assuming a push-up like position before slowly making his way back to his feet, all the while refusing to make eye contact with his fellow teammates. "You know nothing about nothing."

'He *isn't so really tough*,' Rolland thought to himself, his eyes locking on to Kniff's as the two would-be gladiators circled each other for supremacy. Then and there he swore to himself that he would change. Maybe. If he lost. Then, the fight began again. With a low arc the palm of Kniff's right hand came down, inches away from the middle of Rolland's face.

Blocking Kniff's left hand with his own, Rolland next focused his attack on his opponent's midsection, pummeling away with four alternating jabs focused upward into the chest cavity. It was a careless move, Rolland knew, but he did not care.

"Rolland!" Tina shouted amidst the noise, "Stop it right now before someone gets hurt. I mean it, stop it! You guys...!"

Ignoring Tina, Rolland dodged another jab as the pair continued their dance. Suddenly, Kniff lunged and before Rolland could react the merman had a hold of Rolland's legs. Kicking as if his life depended upon it, he paddled his assailant as if he were a kangaroo. Then, when he could kick no longer, a sharp pull caused him to lose balance, causing both Rolland and Kniff to fall clumsily in a heap on the ground.

For the other members of the Class of the Tiger the anti-climactic ending of the duel was underscored by the distinct lack of a winner, as both combatants were momentarily down for the count. Though it did not matter, as even the dimmest among them realized that whoever held the role of leader would also find themselves accountable for the collective failures they experienced that day.

As his classmates dispersed around Rolland, no closer to an answer for leader than when they had started, he noticed that none of them seemed to be in any sort of hurry. Like wandering protons they searched for a charge, a spark, anything to ignite them into believing their survival at the academy was assured. Yet in his heart, Rolland knew nothing he said could assure them. Add to it his need for more physical training after the display with Kniff, and it was no wonder they found him wanting. He stood up, straightened his shirt that had become off kilter during the fight and walked toward the exit where the other cadets had left after their first task. He was the only one to do so..at first.

But no sooner had Rolland began to walk, his head held insufferably high for someone who just suffered such a public humiliation amongst new acquaintances, then he was joined by Tina, and oddly enough, Hannah. Then Dodger and Gwendolyn. Cliques had formed between the class and Rolland had just become the leader of the biggest one.

While Kniff had bested Rolland in hand to hand combat, his victory came at the cost of earning no other friend but Timothy.

Jaime left outright, lending his support to no one following the bout. Rolland on the other hand, had not only acquired a new friend in the aspiring class clown Dodger, but also that of the pixie looking blonde woman Gwendolyn and the quiet Hannah. It was then he noticed the single door on the far side of the stadium-sized courtyard, one that had but a single word written on a small plaque that hung on the upper center.

GLORY

"Hey, check it out Wright, there's a chick in here named Glory," Dodger said, teleporting away from the group before re-appearing directly in front of the mysterious door, his hand already on the handle.

"Dodger, ok, you know that's not what's in there, right?" Tina said in a flat tone that everyone, including herself, realized was drenched in the spirit of a buzz kill. She looked up at Rolland with pleading eyes and a scrunched mouth before saying, "Sorry!"

A toothy smile and the wrapping of his arm around Tina's waist was all that it took for Rolland to put her at ease, neither of them noticing as Dodger opened the marked door some ten feet in front of them before stepping inside, his eyes growing large as he advanced. Immediately the lights to the first four sections of what Tina guessed to be a nearly mile long hallway turned themselves on overhead, illuminating the multicolored marble floor and glass display cases on both sides. Florescent lights made the golden trophies glisten through the glass as far as the eye could see. The vaulted ceiling was nothing short of spectacular, as the class banners, each with a different animal from throughout the millennia sown on to it below its iron setting, hung with an aura of importance.

"That. Is. Impressive," Dodger said, creeping inside on foot before noticing a large, solid gold award in the shape of a cup to his right. It was easily as tall as he was, not including the base, and stood behind a solid inch of glass display case. Running to it, not teleporting, he stopped short of complete awe as his eyes were drawn to the diamonds adorning the rim, handle, and base. Crouching down low to read the names of the **981 Bliss Ball Champions**, Dodger raised his left hand to his eyes before pressing them against the glass to get a better view. "This place is crazy old."

"Is that Turtledove?" Tina asked, eyeing the large black and white portrait carefully.

It was, although there was no plague to display his name. The facial features of the smiling young man standing amongst other students were indistinguishable. As were the ones of another man that looked an awful lot like Rolland. Upon inspection his suspicions were confirmed; Scott Wright had been the star athlete of the Class of the Manatee.

"You think your picture will wind up in here one day?" Dodger asked Rolland, his eyes still darting from one display case to the next, ribbons, banners, and trophies glorifying cadets who had long since passed on over the centuries. Their tales of valor in sport, combat, and competition lived on here, in this little hallway just off of the courtyard where the cadets first met. A short distance down the hall four words were written in large golden letters that shined against the florescent lights hanging from a lamp above them.

FAME.

PRESTIGE. NOTORIETY. GLORY

'*Aspirations of someone made of tougher stuff than I am*,' Rolland thought to himself as he turned to leave the hall his other new friends.

"I'm not that guy."

Chapter 6:
As Knight Falls

Eden - Halls of Time

The Following Day

Victor never saw himself as a hero. Or a leader. Or anything else really besides a guy just trying to get by. Yet since coming to Eden, he had been called upon to fill each of these roles time and time again. Another role he never saw himself in was that of brother – a role he felt himself more and more filling when around Rolland. It was not because he felt sorry for him, which he did, but that wasn't just that. He genuinely liked Rolland. Even so, he couldn't tell him, or anyone else the truth regarding what the Knights were monitoring the Time Stream for, not in the current political climate. No, Victor would remain like he always had been; stoic, dependable, and dedicated to the task at hand.

All was quiet the day that until the sirens rang out all over the Halls of Time, startling Victor upright. He immediately began scanning the computer screen in front of him for the cause of alarms. All over the Time Stream censors were going off due to disruptions within a particular quadrant just beyond the inhabited land around Eden Town Proper. The sirens continued to sound, prompting Turtledove and Geoffrey to join Victor in the lab after a few more moments of wailing.

"Anything serious?" Geoffrey asked Victor. "This Ranger Vaughn character keeps pinging us with requests."

"Nah, seems like all we got is a tripped sensor and a spooked forest ranger," Victor replied, zooming in on bend in the Time Stream in question. The flow overlapped at a certain point, causing a tide of the Stream to splash against one of the large rocks that cut the water in half.

"Better check it out anyway," Turtledove commanded kindly, placing both hands behind his back and walking the length of the room. "The both of you. Take Aurora."

Aurora was the name lovingly bestowed upon the daily business vehicle for the Knights of Time, the Rip-Rora 3000. A Rip-Rora appeared very much like a standard early 21st century automobile. However, the major difference lay in how it moved, as it hovered a good three feet off of the ground. Needless to say, driving the Rip-Rora (for business or pleasure) was a popular past time among all of the Knights of Time.

"I get to drive!" Geoffrey shouted, before grabbing the keys out of Turtledove's hand and racing out of the room.

After giving his mentor a look of feigned anguish, Victor was summarily dismissed with a smile. Turtledove smiled to himself as he watched the doorway, and listened for the familiar sound of car doors shutting. A few moments went by before the unmistakable sound of the Rip-Rora's engine sprang to life, grew louder, and then out of earshot.

Minutes after Victor and Geoffrey had left the compound, the Protector of Eden walked briskly to his office. Locking the door from the inside, he removed a file from behind a painting above the marble fireplace. Placing the file on his tabletop desk, Turtledove read the words "PROJECT DREAMCOAT" that were written prominently in green, splotchy ink.

Turtledove eyed it longingly, as if it were a bottle of ice cold water and he were trudging through an endless desert. It was then that he had done something he had only done once before; Marcus L. Turtledove opened the file, flipped through its contents and gazed warily onto the last page.

On the page was a photograph of a man walking down a busy city street. His left eye was covered with an eye patch, and it appeared as if he was missing a few fingers on his left hand, but otherwise the man's face was identical to Turtledove's own. In the crook of his arm the strange Turtledove carried a folder, the exact folder with the exact writing on its cover that Marcus Turtledove how held. With a long sigh he flipped back to the beginning, eager to crack the mystery within.

All of the pieces of the puzzle were there.

The Rip-Rora flew through the Eden twilight air. Beneath its small, jet propelled engines sat a variable labyrinth of machinery developed by Eden's leading scientists before the Raines era began. Despite an ignition sequence similar to that of a helicopter, the vehicle acted more like an airplane, or hang glider, as it hovered along the heavily wooded landscape that composed Solomon Forrest. Though the road was both paved, and well lit the ominous feelings of estrangement grew deeper and deeper the further away they travelled from the Halls of Time. The GPS tracking device on the dashboard spouted off instructions in a soft, soothing English accent that always brought a smile to their faces. As the GPS spoke visions of the 21st century British actress Emma Watson filled Geoffrey's head, spinning off into a world where the two of them were alone and clothing was optional.

"Those Brits," Victor said with a toothy smile as his saw Geoffrey's hand slipping a little on the steering wheel. He knew what, or rather WHO his best friend was imagining, but always resisted teasing Geoffrey about his choice of women despite their shared affection for the gorgeous celebrity's 'assets'. On this day, however, he decided to press his luck. "They're just so sexy."

The only reply Victor received was the sound of the wind buzzing by their ears as he spotted a clearing coming up ahead. As the vehicle slowed, he turned to his left to see not Geoffrey sitting next to him, but Judah. Except it wasn't really Judah, as he also wore a pair of obviously female lips that looked overly comical perched atop the British man's chin. "I am quite sexy, aren't I?"

"Turn right at the next fork in the Time Stream," the Emma Watson GPS said loudly, startling Geoffrey a bit, causing the plump lips and Judah's strong European features to melt away as easily as candle wax. "Location will be on your right in approximately 200 yards."

Upon arriving at their destination, the Knights noticed a small, mousy man sitting on the front porch of a log cabin. He was bald, very skinny, and wore clothes that even Victor knew to be stereotypical of an American forest ranger from Earth. Green denim shorts that cut off nearly six inches above the knees, and off white socks pulled up to just below the kneecap seemed to comprise most of the man. The other half was cloaked in a puffy brown vest covering a long sleeve white shirt, and a beige hat that read 'Ranger' in big black letters across the top. He stood up as their vehicle approached and it appeared that Ranger Vaughn was eager for their arrival.

"Hello there boy-os!" Ranger Vaughn shouted enthusiastically, setting an immediately off putting tone to their collective interaction. "You two Turtledove's men, the Knights?"

"We're Knights of Time, yes," Victor said a little irritably. "How can we help you?"

Ranger Vaughn gave an uneasy smile as he looked from the large Victor down to the average sized Geoffrey. He hesitated several times before breaking into a sweat, and timidly saying, "Sensor's been tripped."

Suddenly realizing how intimidating he was, Victor's mind raced with regret about how rude he must have been. "Ranger Vaughn?" he asked breaking into a smile and extending his baseball glove sized right hand to the demure man.

"Yeppir, that's me alright," Ranger Vaughn said cheerily. "I don't think there is any reason to worry about this," he continued, leading them through thick, jungle like vegetation to the bank of the Time Stream.

"Why's that?" Geoffrey asked, tip-toeing between the two men on his way to the bank. The Time Stream was lapping lazily against the side of the bend, right before it narrowed, picked up pace, and met with the fork, splitting into two. It was then that Victor noticed the larger, golden scepter in Geoffrey's hand. Seeing Victor's puzzled look, Geoffrey tipped the weapon in Victor's direction before stating, "You can never be too careful!"

The three men split up and investigated the surrounding area, but came up with nothing the slightest bit suspicious. So much so that Victor began to wonder if they really were there on a fool's errand. It wasn't until they reported back to each other that a strange odor wafted into the clearing by the Time Stream where they stood.

"Do you guys smell that?" Victor yelled at the other two, his nose working overtime to isolate and decipher the aroma surrounding them. "Like old chicken eggs left in the sun."

The other two men did smell the strong odor that Victor spoke of, but neither would quite describe the repugnant stench exactly in those terms. Each continued on their separate way in search of the smell's origin, though Victor was more concerned that it was coming from Aurora than anything else. Geoffrey guessed that an animal had died, or an Elemeno hunting party had made their way through, tripped the sensor, and fled before their arrival. That theory, of course, would mean the complete incompetence of Ranger Vaughn, a reality that he was bracing himself for more and more.

Rising silently from the Time Stream like a submarine in the open sea was a man in a short tunic named Nero whose intentions as sneaky as they were sinister. Pressed tightly in his left palm was a long, gray steel knife with an ivory handle. He held it behind his back, choosing instead to don a malicious grin as he announced his presence to only man facing the bank.

"Ghost in the Time Stream..." Ranger Vaughn sputtered in a quavering voice, horror overcoming him, as he took several steps backward before falling down on his posterior. His glasses, the taped up feats of engineering that he claimed they were, did not live up to their reputation, and instead fell off of his face, landing in the grass below. Flipping over, his hands groping desperately as he went, the Ranger was able to get back to one knee before he heard a *crunch* that told him all was lost. Then he felt his hair jerked back sharply, exposing his all-too vulnerable neck and suddenly he felt very wet, very wet. And cold.

The blade of Nero's knife made quick work of the flesh protecting Ranger Vaughn's throat. It swept across the jugular rather haphazardly before coming to a rest, bathed in the sticky, life giving blood that glistened against the Eden sunlight. The assassin smiled boyishly as the last jolts of life escaped through the Ranger's gasp. The old man clawed in a vain attempt to delay his inevitable fate, tugging at the bottom of Nero's tunic, annoying his would-be killer and preventing him from a seamless sneak attack on the other two Eden dwellers. When the fight left him, Nero pulled the blade out from its flesh casing, raised it to an attack position, poised himself accordingly, and set upon his next target - Victor.

"Wait, what?" said a confused Geoffrey as he turned around, just in time to see both Ranger Vaughn's lifeless, blood spurting body fall to the ground while Nero simultaneously launched himself nearly eight feet into the air above them, his ivory handled knife, held it high above his head in a threatening position.

The initial attack was quick, meant only to gauge his opponent's weakness before moving in for the kill. Landing between the Knights with a roundhouse kick to the larger, dark skinned target's chest, Nero was able to isolate the smaller of the two, of whose supernatural abilities he was not aware. The skinny man whom he faced was not on his liege lord's list of expendables; yet there he was. And there he would die. Although he was armed with a long, golden scepter it seemed nearly useless with the bearer's hands. A gamble, but one that Nero would gladly take if it meant leaving Eden's smothering presence of morality but one second sooner.

All it took was a false attack, a bluff, from the assassin to lure Geoffrey into a full on offensive. Flashes of gold swept through the air as Geoffrey wielded the scepter, each swing missing Nero by more inches each time. On the fourth swing the scepter was caught on the downswing, jerked, and turned against Geoffrey before he knew how to react. Pain filled every inch of Geoffrey's skull as something hit him under the chin very, very hard. Stars, colors, and shades of black circled in around him as he lost consciousness. In and out he went before silence engulfed him.

Geoffrey might have been knocked out, and Vaughn dead, but Victor still fought on against the capable attacker. The term fighting might be a bit too generous given Victor's strategy of avoiding attacks by leaping out of the way whenever the assassin went on the offensive. Thinking quickly, Victor decided that the numbers game would be his best bet, and with trembling fingers, removed his satellite phone from his pocket.

"This is Victor Aquasi III. I am approximately ten leagues east of Eden Town Proper and request immediate back-up. Repeat: send immediate back-up," Victor whisper-shouted into his phone. Huddled behind the Rip Rora, knees bent to his shoulders, Victor repeated the message again and again as he listened to Geoffrey bide him time. When the noises stopped he knew it was time to re-enter the fray. Standing upright, he peered over the edge of the vehicle, immediately spotting the assassin standing upright, staring at his position, just waiting for the next altercation to begin. Panicking, Victor ducked down, turned, and closed his eyes shut tight before softly saying a prayer to himself, and slowly standing up again. Only this time the killer was not standing at a distance, but above him in mid-air, barreling downward on top of him.

Acting quickly, Victor sidestepped Nero's attack, using the man's own momentum against him, and propelling the strange attacker headlong into the neatly stacked pile of firewood beside the cabin. Bits of flaming wood flew everywhere as Victor got to his feet and spun around, fists glowing with fire, only to be greeted with a thick, hard blow squarely to his chest. The stinging by Nero's hand was reminiscent of the time he accidentally punched a concrete wall after imbibing too many spirits with Geoffrey one night. The hit had the dual effect of both knocking the breath out of Victor's lungs, and temporarily causing the flames lighting his hands to sputter out. The latter of which caused Victor to bend over, back toward Nero, in hopes that he would catch a moment for air. This would prove folly.

Propelling himself into the air nearly a foot, Nero raised his right knee while at the same time forcing Victor's face downward into it; the result of which knocked the larger of the two men clean off of his feet and into the sea of fallen orange leaves nearby. Before he could take a breath, or right himself, Victor was again under attack - this time from a pair of very wet, blood covered hands that grasped tightly to both sides of his thick, brown neck and pushed down violently. As the leaves began to catch fire, their would-be instinct to act as kindling propelled the flames to spark all around the pair, creating a small inferno as they fought. The two men struggled for a moment, neither willing to give the advantage to their opponent. Then, with a sudden second wind of energy coursing through his veins, Victor's right leg freed itself, bent, and delivered a crippling blow to Nero's groin that sent a shockwave of indescribable pain from brain to toenails. Nero released his hold, coiled, and fell to the ground.

Alternating between choking and fighting for sweet, life giving oxygen Victor made the decision to fight back. Grazing his left arm across his chest in anticipation, and to re-ignite the flame within him, Victor brought it down on Nero with a thunderous roar that sent the smaller man to the ground again, writhing in pain.

"You aren't so tough now, are you?" Victor asked his attacker while stepping back and beginning to circle the assassin. He thought of creating a ring of fire to trap the man, much like Hess had been kept in back in Pensacola months before. This was a common tactic, and one he had learned in his first week at the academy, Victor knew to always be moving around when facing an enemy, never to plant his feet or stop. It was good to know that he could hurt the man, though he had yet to expose any solid weaknesses that might have been hiding. Thoughts of the darkest nature entered the young Knight's mind as he watched his opponent rise to his feet, stumble a bit, and join the circling dance Victor had set in motion.

"I will not be tricked, young one," the assassin Nero said, attempting to hold onto the blade in his left hand despite the wet, slippery blood that covered both hands almost entirely. "Soon you will perish, just like the ranger. Soon you shall feel the fire of Tartarus."

"I was born in fire," Victor said before striking his free hand on the ground in a quick, igniting motion, and raising Geoffrey's scepter above his head. Victor was ready for the coming onslaught. "Bitch."

Poised, Nero again advanced on his intended prey, his weapon tucked tightly against his forearm, the blade facing downward. He leaped, weapon at the ready as he tucked, rolled, and landed on the opposite side of Victor, turning him around and throwing him off balance a bit. Flames and the glint of steel danced around them in a ballet of carnage and close calls. The moment was all that the assassin needed as he latched on to Victor's left wrist, twisted, and brought it down hard against the ground - popping it right out of its socket.

The pain angered Victor, who used his legs to kick his assailant away as he fumbled to his knees. It slowed Nero, but only for a few seconds as he righted himself and again pursued his target. A blocked shot with his left hand landed upon Victor's upper wrist, gliding off with little effort. Another attack, followed by another block, and another, and another with little in the way of progress for either individual. The destruction they caused, however, was on a scale not seen in that part of Solomon Forest for nearly seven thousand years. It wasn't until fatigue began to set into Victor's lower back, a long standing injury he had been nursing for some time, that the tides began to shift in Nero's favor.

After another few minutes the two circled around, back to the shore of the time stream where Geoffrey lay, still unconscious. Nero ran his weapon upon the ground, creating more flames than Victor was comfortable with, given their proximity to his unconscious teammate. With his naked eye, Victor watched as a single spark willed its way against the wind toward the spot where Geoffrey was, landing softly on his cheek, and drawing a pathetic whimper of frailty.

"Geoffrey!" Victor screamed desperately, knowing full well that Nero was sauntering back toward him. A wicked smile twisted its way into their fight as the invader of Eden planned his next move. With a determination on par with a fully-grown rhinoceros Nero bull-rushed Victor as hard as he could using his right shoulder, knocking the Knight of Time backward, directly into Geoffrey's feet. A semi-conscious Geoffrey stirred as his best friend fought off their soon to be murderer with one good arm.

Knocking Victor backward toward the Time Stream a few feet, Nero picked up the discarded golden scepter and began poking Victor in the chest, herding him further backward a few feet at a time. When he was backed up against the bank on the Time Stream, with the golden white mists of existence lapping at his shoulders, Victor suddenly realized what Nero's endgame was.

Victor had heard stories of people who had fallen into the Time Stream over the centuries, although often times they were just that - stories. Actual accounts of Edenites who disappeared were undocumented due to the fact that they disappeared, lost in time and space. The prospect of joining them was as unappealing as ending up like Ranger Vaughn, yet Victor knew that he had but one choice. Go out fighting.

Upon the next poke with the scepter, Victor grabbed the shaft, pulled it with all of the strength of his good arm, successfully jerking Nero off of his feet and onto the ground next to him. Victor then latched on to the man, wrapping Nero in a headlock, and taking a position on his back, hoping his size advantage would make up for his lack of arm. It didn't.

Biting Victor's finger nearly to the bone, Nero threw the large man off of him before kicking him numerous times in the stomach, chest, and head. He was then rolled the remaining five or so feet toward the edge of the Time Stream, kicked again for good measure, and unceremoniously scooted into the misty waters feet first. The way it cupped and clung to every pore of Victor's skin as fought to pull his feet back. It wasn't until Victor was clear from the swirling mist that he noticed he was no longer under attack from the mysterious stranger. Looking around for the madman he found the figure skulking on the edge of the forest, seemingly laying a trap for the stirring Geoffrey. The shape shifter was slowly getting back to his knees, but was still in no shape to assist in the struggle.

With seven large paces he reached for and caught the smaller man by his lilac colored collar that stuck out from beneath his tunic. Despite the lunatic's slashing at him the larger of the two held on, keeping the edge between them by utilizing a mixture of sudden movements and shifting his weight from foot to foot. The technique was clumsy, poorly trained, and not poorly suited for the stamina heavy fight Victor often found himself in with people brave enough to face him in battle. Eventually the would-be assassin got the best of Victor, backing him up against the edge of the Time Stream once again, this time Victor's heels feeling the icy cool bleakness of a lost eternity amongst a mysterious populace. The thought was enough for Nero to gain the advantage, a moment of weakness capitalized on by the cunning Roman as he swept Victor's weak left leg out from under him during a shift of weight.

"Ahhhhh!" Victor hollered, turning his head sideways as he fell backward into the oblivion. Unyielding, the Time Stream took him in with an embrace that slowly but surely consumed whatever it wanted; which was now Victor Aquasi III.

"No!" Geoffrey screamed, scrambling to his feet and reaching for Victor as his friend and fellow knight fell further into the Time Stream. Geoffrey was just able to touch the tips of Victor's fingers as they journeyed into the great golden abyss that was time infinite. And then he was gone.

Gone from Eden. Gone from the Knights of Time. Just gone.

Falling to his knees, Geoffrey was at a complete loss for what to do next. He was no leader of men, no decision maker under times of duress. He was the jokester, the class clown, always good for a laugh. Then, as if matters could get no worse for, the pale, tunic wearing assassin looked back at him with a mixture of distain and pride in his work. The man eyed Ranger Vaughn's corpse before snickering, a sick perversion that words could do no justice as his yellow teeth displayed themselves like badges of rotten past accomplishments.

Geoffrey could feel the anger welling upside of him as he sat, knees folded under him, helpless to do anything as the assailant brandished his weapon nearby. He prepared himself for one final attack to avenge Victor, summoning every ounce of courage conceivable before he heard the man speak for the first time; the words quelling any sense of retribution he might have planned.

"Remember who nominates you for the noose," Nero said, looking down at the crying Geoffrey before running full force toward the Time Stream, jumping in feet first.

Once the assassin was gone all fell silent in the clearing by the woods where Ranger Vaughn had called home so many years. Still in shock from Nero's assault, Geoffrey's refusal to move did nothing to prove his innocence once the authorities arrived. Blood still covered his hands as men in police uniforms took his statement, again and again, but he felt numb to the entire encounter. In a blur Turtledove arrived, wrapped Geoffrey in a blanket, and led him away, back to the Halls of Time. But it wasn't the same. It would never be the same again.

Chapter 7:
Down Under, To the Left

Lae Island - 1937

Despite an uncharacteristically sunny morning, the afternoon promised nothing but showers and precipitation on Lae Island. A peaceful incubus cloud, seemingly benign as it instantaneously became a twisted, gnarled portal to another world as purple, golden, and forest green swirls of time and space opened in the void where the cloud hovered moments before. Yet it was not the weather that created this phenomenon, but rather the portable Dream Phoenix, created by Dr. Judah Raines, was responsible. This was a prototype device that served as a miniature version of the Dream Phoenix and could only transport no more than four people.

Shooting out feet first, Joan Raines caught a bit of air as she fell freely, only opening her eyes as she passed through the threshold and saw the Lae Island landscape form through a plethora of colors. As the blurry scenes of nature came into focus she realized that the green blobs were actually large trees that seem to be filling the majority of the land around her. The scent of salt air filled her nostrils, along with a strong wind that drew her attention to her right, where she caught a quick glimpse of the ocean before it fell out of view as she continued downward. Then she landed in a neat upside down barrel roll on a tiny patch of short green grass situated among the trees. A quick look around revealed her husband had done the same; only it appeared that he was fortunate enough to have landed on his feet.

"You're like a cat, dear," Joan told her husband a bit irritably, brushing her legs and bottom off before standing up. Looking upward she realized that wherever they were it was in the middle of two nine foot tall lush green hedges with small, prickly thorns protruding out from almost every square inch.

"Don't you just love that you married an inventor?" Judah said in more of a statement than a question.

"Mad scientist, you mean," Joan said, kicking a bit of mud off of her right heel. She could feel the ocean breeze creating goose bumps up her neck, and had little patience for her husband's hubris. "Did you pack your revolver? And your back-up pistol?"

"Yes dear," Judah said dryly before pressing a small red button near the inside heel of his right boot. It activated a device of his own invention that he had built in to both his and Joan's shoes; the aptly named Rocket Tight Boots contained two small engines that burned cold fusion to propel the wearer short distances forward, up, and backward depending on the direction their toes were pointing. Activating her own, Joan too waited for the familiar feeling of weightlessness as she rose nearly seven feet off of the ground, just above the top of the maze. Reaching outward,

Judah moved closer to his beloved, grasping her hand in his as he straightened his toes, putting the Rocket Tights in neutral.

It took but four minutes for Joan and Judah to float to freedom from the hedge maze, the small light blue engines glowing at the bottom of their shoes as they moved through the air. Flying was still a strange feeling for Joan, who came from a time where the thought of man flying was impossible. Nevertheless, she had taken the lead once the pair became airborne. The entrance to the maze, or perhaps it was the exit, was spotted by Joan first, but Judah decided to take advantage of the moment, flying close before swooping in on top of his wife in an attempt to pin her as the two landed. They rolled a bit, but alas, the tactic was no match for Joan, who was already on her guard. However, the gesture did not go unappreciated.

The two kissed, a sweet moment uninterrupted by anyone or anything. Their limbs were as intertwined as only two lovers could ever be, joined in the bonds of genuine affection and years of familiarity. A small THUNK sound nearby revealed that the portable Dream Phoenix had landed alongside them. The two kissed again, tongues caressing in a carnal symphony of delight. Then another THUNK sound. And another. And another. Finally, after the fifth THUNK Joan broke her husband's embrace and checked to see what was making so much noise.

"The landing was much smoother this time," Joan said coyly. "A lot better than your last prototype."

"Yeah," Judah concurred, pressing a small red button that caused the boots to stop humming, their engines coming to a complete stop and returning to their original state as simple tan standard issue boots. "The landing probably busted the synchronizing mechanism. I'll have to fix it if we ever plan to leave. But hey gets the job done. Speaking of which..."

Their lips met again, only to be interrupted by a very rude, very determined third party shouting something incoherent in the distance. Breaking the embrace, the pair of Knights ducked behind a large boulder. They cautiously looked eastward to see a small man, dressed in a dark blue military uniform complete with button down jacket, high top boots, and sporting an old turn of the century rifle complete with bayonet at the end was making his way toward their position in a slow but methodical pace.

"Who is he?" Judah asked, his left hand exploring his wife's chest. He knew her attention would be drawn away, and that this, like many of his other attempts at outdoor intercourse, would probably fail. Never the less, he felt entitled to a little bit of tit-for tat after freeing them both from the maze in a fraction of the time. "You know what, I don't care. Just snog me some more."

Casting him an exasperated look, Joan Raines sighed heavily for emphasis before peering over their hiding spot at the oncoming stranger. He was of Asian descent, and judging by his uniform, a solider of the early Japanese Imperialist army. No sooner had Joan come to this conclusion than she felt a sharp, yet still playful nibble upon her earlobe. Choosing to pick her battles, Joan swallowed her desire in lieu of pushing onward toward their intended extraction target. Toward Amelia Earhart. Unfortunately for Judah, this also meant having to push him away, literally. But before she could Judah dropped the charming act of seduction in favor of a more cautious, vigilant demeanor. Confused by this, Joan looked at him, and followed his eyes back to the small Asian soldier, who was now joined by what appeared to be a dozen more soldiers fifty or so yards behind him, moving at a similar pace in their direction.

"Our numbers game just went the other way, love," Judah said in a flat tone of voice. Scrambling to their feet the pair looked around for something, anything that might work to their advantage. Off in the distance Judah saw what appeared to be a small, wooden shack propped up by four tall stilts so that it stood a clear ten feet off of the ground. "Over there, higher ground."

As the two activated their Rocket Tights and made their way across the field inland, they began to hear the sound of gunshots as the now thirty Imperialist Japanese soldiers entered the fray yet the shots were not coming in their direction. When Joan and Judah landed on the porch of the shack, both were dismayed to find a locked door waiting for them. Jiggling the handle with as much force as he could muster, Judah shook the door before kicking it and swearing loudly.

"Just stop, ok?" Joan said. They couldn't afford for Judah to panic, a habit he developed whenever on mission with his wife but never with anyone else. More gunshots rang out, this time all around them as the Imperialist troops moved closer on their position.

"You're right. Bollocks! What I wouldn't give for a good pair of.." Judah began, but was interrupted by the sound of twin propellers sputtering from above. The couple looked up to see a small airplane set ablaze by what appeared to be a red and green supernatural flame. It was a small, faded black, twin engine plane with a half missing left wing, and a poor painting of a scantily clad woman on the left side. The distinctly human screams coming from within sounded both male, and female. Without thinking both Knights took off running after the plane as it careened through the sky, back toward the hedge maze, the coastline, and the gathering crowd of Imperialist troops.

The plane's tail, engine, and right wing were ablaze with the odd green and red flames, whipping against the wind as it nose-dived to Earth. The aircraft zigged, zagged, and maneuvered six different times before finding a holding pattern, turning its nose upward, and spinning on itself, all the while knocking down Imperialist troops like little blue bowling pins. The force of the landing, mixed with the various people, and objects it hit, caused the plane to lift several times before finding a groove in-which to settle and skid across the ground.

The makeshift runway, a field of dead grass next to the old, wooden shack served well enough a place to park as any. It was just too bad that the pilots parked nowhere near it. Spying two large boulders a few yards away one of the pilots of the small plane steered the smoking aircraft back on the spot as if it were a land vehicle. The craft slowed to a halt, turning at the last minute so it wasn't quite facing forward before a fresh spray of bullets from the remaining Imperialist troops rained down. Although there were only eight or so left, the remaining soldiers were quite determined to carry out their mission despite the casualties. Within seconds two people jumped out of the plane, seemingly unhurt and both wearing pilot uniforms, complete with brown bomber jackets, tan colored pants, and goggles that covered the majority of their faces. The taller of the two pilots spied the Imperialist Japanese troops running toward them and, tapped the other one on the shoulder before starting off in a sprint without waiting on the other. Despite this, the smaller one quickly caught up, both making their way directly toward where Judah and Joan stood watching.

"Look dear, party crashers," Judah said before breaking out into a full run toward the pair of pilots, removing from his pants what looked like a nightstick, not unlike a policeman would carry.

Unsure if he was a friend or foe, but with an armed Imperialist at her heels, the shorter of the two pilots chose to duck as the strange blonde man came hurtling toward her. Much to her relief, he was a friend, or as close to one as she would get considering the circumstance. Pulling off her flight helmet, the leather straps tugging at her dirty blonde hair as it went, Amelia Earhart breathed fresh air for the first time since landing. She looked up, and with as much appreciation as she could offer, gave a polite, "Thanks stranger."

Amongst the chaos, Joan began to experience an odd sensation. What started as a foreign tickle in her nose quickly spread toward her eyes, forcing them shut, and then suddenly her feet felt as if she were glued to the ground. Rubbing her eyes furiously with her palms, she opened them slowly with a gasp as she did so.

Before her, distorted though they were, stood dozens, perhaps hundreds of English soldiers poised for battle. The men, dressed in various alternations of chainmail and peasant garb, were armed with 15th century armory, which she knew to be completely out of place with her 20th century location. Standing in a loose formation, each with their weapons at the ready, the Englishmen lined up in columns as they watched her and calculated their next move. Knowing it to be an impossible sight, Joan again closed her eyes before once more rubbing them furiously, this time with a sense of foreboding to her action.

Luckily for her sanity's sake, when Joan opened her eyes again the only thing that greeted her was the sweet sight of her husband Judah as he screamed her name, hands gesturing wildly for her to join him at the stilt of the wooden shack. Shaking her head, Joan instead pointed behind Judah and the two pilots to the new additions to their party as they approached from the South. This time she knew she was not imagining things, as the fifty Elemenos currently storming the beach were very real. As was the tall man with curly black hair, black beard, and mocha colored skin leading them. Unlike the Japanese soldiers, however, these invaders did not move at a methodical pace, but a brisk one that was as menacing as it was determined. The war cry of an Elemeno rang out, causing Joan and Judah running out to meet them. A quick WHACK of Judah's weapon to the cranium of an oncoming Elemeno was followed by a quick spin to his right to directly engage the next Elemeno before doing the same, only this time in a stabbing motion. He continued his maneuver as Elemeno after Elemeno closed in on them.

Joan, still reeling from her vision, decided to focus on the task at hand; taking down every Elemeno and Imperial Japanese warrior charging at her and Judah. Within milliseconds the neurons inside Joan's brain sprang to life, analyzing the situation, its variables, probable outcomes, contingencies, and finally a battle strategy. Using a nearby tree no taller than she was, Joan put on an acrobatic display of combat pageantry that only comes with years of field experience. She began by raising her pointer fingers behind her head like ears, taunting the Elemenos into accumulating around her in a dense crowd. With every punch, every kick to the head, every duck, she knew, deep down, that the result would always be the same; Joan would be left standing tall as the victor.

Laser fire rained down on the Knights as the armed Elemenos stormed their way toward their enemies. It was at this time that Judah suspected something was amiss, as most of the Elemenos were aiming for his feet. Yet before he could warn his wife of this, a fresh barrage of laser fire hit them both squarely in the heels, frying one of Judah's favorite bits of tech that he had ever created. "Now I'm angry!"

Joan merely shook her head at this, knowing full well that her husband would have zero problem creating more. Hoping for a challenge equal to her skill set, Joan looked across the field to see the man she now recognized as Otep standing stock still, his eyes watching her for any signs of weakness. When it became clear that more of his troops were dying than were getting anywhere close to the two pilots, Otep dropped to one knee. Eyeing him suspiciously, Joan barely saw between attacks from two large Elemenos, being forced at the last second to refocus her attention. With Joan occupied, Otep bowed his head, mumbled a few unintelligible words, and then arose almost as quickly as he had taken a knee. The ground beneath them all shook for a moment before settling; a small thing, but symbolic of the shifting nature of life and death. After that, it did not take Joan long to deduce what the mocha skinned man had done.

Suddenly the battle was raging again, with the numbers quickly growing out of Joan's control. What appeared to be dead Elemenos and half burned Imperialist Japanese troops began to launch fresh attacks on both Knights, most rising from the spot in which they been recently been killed. In a few instances, the bodies even lacked heads, not to mention the coordination needed to launch an attack. This challenge, though cumbersome, proved no match for either Judah, or Joan, both of which spent less time with the second wave than they did the first.

Momentarily distracted by the attractiveness of his wife kicking so much ass, Judah was brought back to reality by the high pitched screams of the co-pilot, the taller one he now knew from the mission log to be Fred Noonan. Surrounded by what appeared to be newly resurrected Elemenos, Noonan fought of flailing, severed limbs, torsos, and bushy green tails. As if by instinct Judah stood, rushed to Noonan' side, and shoved off the five crooked arms as they groped for the pair to join the ranks of the undead.

The two men fled back across the landing strip, away from where Joan was holding her own against an ebbing flow of freshly reanimated Imperialist Japanese troops, their weapons held high above their half missing heads. With bodies piling up, Joan again took in her surroundings, this time finding a more desirable location to conduct her business the form of a small drop-off cliff that overlooked a rocky section of beach below. Backing closer to it, she repelled a fresh wave of attacks from two armless Imperialist troops, both of which appeared to have gotten mixed up with Earhart's propeller as she landed.

The cliff behind Joan had what she guessed to be twenty-foot drop. The fall would not be fatal, but would render anyone unlucky enough to befall such a fate unfit for battle for at least a few minutes. Long enough for Joan to gather the others and make an escape. With a strategy in place, Joan set about the task of dodging offensive attacks from Imperialist and Elemeno alike. Her first step was a left pivot, faking a movement to garner an opposite reaction from her opponent, and throw them off balance. Once off balance, their attention would be drawn to correcting themselves and then the free fall over the cliff would be Joan's parting gift. One by one they went over the hillside cliff that overlooked the beach below.

From her point of view Amelia Earhart saw what appeared to be an Amazonian like display of raw, feminine power as Joan bested man and beast alike. Though she still had no clue what the green furry beasts were that attacked them, the fact that they carried firearms, strange, futuristic looking things at that, was enough to tell her that they were not her friends. What, or who they were was still a question mark in her mind; but one that would have to wait as she was suddenly beset by a one armed Elemeno. Without thinking, Amelia grabbed a loose piece of metal debris from the plane, roughly the size of a stop sign, and swung it across the Elemeno's face with as much force as she could muster. The foreign creature cried out one final time before it fell limp across her feet.

"I guess the little squirrel has got some fight in her after all," Judah said, believing no one heard him. But Amelia did hear him, and smiled broadly because of it.

After it became clear he would not be winning the day Otep retreated quietly away from the scene, his black hair wafting in the salty ocean air as he went. He felt no shame, for he did not feel defeated. Following his exit, the re animated Elemenos and soldiers fell where they stood, the remaining live ones following Otep and the soldiers fleeing through the forest. The two Knights and two pilots then reconvened in a less cluttered part of the field. It wasn't until then that Fred Noonan, the taller of the two pilots, finally took his helmet off to reveal a head of very messy looking short black hair. He cringed with disgust as he noticed the blood spots on the front of his bomber jacket.

"A messy thing, death," Judah said to Noonan, wiping off his hands on a piece of woolen cloth he picked up from the discarded pile of personal affects building up around Joan's position.

"That was Otep, wasn't it?" Joan asked Judah over the dying sounds of the battle.

Craning his neck, Judah was clearly able to make out the retreating form of the man he recognized as Imhotep, master of the undead, and one of Vilthe's favorite agents. Judah knew that Imhotep, former scribe to an infamously mad Pharaoh of what Earth mortals living in the natural time stream called ancient Egypt, was a bad guy by reputation. While his original notoriety came from being the father of anatomy mapping, and early autopsy development, he was known now more so for his experiments with resurrection and other horrendous acts on Vilthe's behalf.

"Guess we know what kind of situation we're dealing with," Judah said, reaching around for his wife's hand without looking.

Finding this particular habit to be sweet, Joan smiled at Judah before asking the inevitable set up question she knew he was waiting for. "What kind is that, my love?"

"The kind that ends with me getting me teeth kicked in," Judah said, sniffling a little as he noticed how wet the tip of his nose was. He touched the back of his left hand to it, before bringing it back to his line of vision, and gazing upon it with little surprise. Blood. "Let's take this party somewhere more private, yeah?"

Once their party of four was cleared from the chaos of battle and it became clear that the immediate danger had passed, the task of getting the pleasantries out of the way became the first order of business.

"You're Judah," said Amelia with a smile.

"How'd you know that?" Judah asked, stopping his momentary search for his cigarettes to look Earhart directly in the eyes.

"Oh come on now, Judes," Amelia said, her tone thick with mockery as the new nickname hit him hard, eliciting a facial twitch. The couple stared at her, a bit bewildered. Amelia however simply smiled adoringly. Although she could not explain it, something in the back of her mind told Amelia that these folks were alright. "Every squirrel has their secrets."

Joan laughed at that, and strangely immediately knew that Amelia Earhart could be trusted. It wasn't a feeling that she had often felt toward other women. Hell, she had only had it for Sephanie Kelly and Taylor Wright before, but something about Amelia caused Joan to like her immediately. Perhaps it was her moxy. Joan loved moxy.

"I'm Amelia Earhart," the perky woman with the dirty blonde hair said, her flight goggles bobbing on her chest as she moved in, extending her hand to Joan. "This is my co-pilot, Fred Noonan."

"We know," Joan said, shaking both of their hands in turn, completely dismissing the bewildered looks upon their faces. "We were sent to find you."

"Sent?" Fred asked, his look of relief morphing into one of trepidation. "Not by the same people who shot down our plane or tried to kill us just now, I hope."

"Fear not mate," Judah said, smacking Noonan in the chest with the back of his hand. "We did just kill a whole bunch of them, after all."

"He does have a good point," Amelia said, looking from Noonan to Joan. "So who sent you then?"

"That's a bit more complicated to answer, squirrel girl," Judah said, removing a cigarette from his pack before producing a lighter.

Judah's comments did nothing to soothe Amelia and Noonan's natural inclination toward paranoia on their current espionage mission. Realizing this, Joan decided to step in, offering the rarest of all commodities regardless of what age one might find them-selves in - the truth.

"I'm Joan, Joan of Arc," Joan said, deciding not to mince words. This attempt at complete transparency drew more than just the quizzical looks from Amelia and Noonan that she expected, but also a severely animated objection from her husband.

"Well why don't you go and tell the whole bloody world our secrets, woman?!" Judah exclaimed, throwing both of his arms up in the air and pacing madly around, a lit cigarette still bobbing between his lips.

"They need to know, my love," Joan offered, a look of the utmost compassion in her eyes. "For their own safety. It is why we're here after all. To extract them, to make sure that they have a better future."

"Oh, we're all about the future," said Amelia proudly, a small smile creeping across her face. "I'm going to be the first woman to ever fly across the..."

"About that," Judah said flatly "I just wouldn't get your hopes too if you know what I mean. Can't be a part of the future if you aren't in it."

"I don't understand," said Amelia nervously, afraid to ask the follow up question they all knew was to come. "What did you mean, we're not in it?"

"You're dead," Judah said bluntly, lighting another cigarette in flagrant disregard for his wife's preference on the matter. "Or you will be soon if we fail in our mission."

"Wait, what?" Amelia asked, becoming more apprehensive of the two strangers as their story unraveled.

"Are you two really married?" Noonan asked Judah. "Because you couldn't be more different. She seems nice but you're acting like a bit of an asshole."

"Yes," said Judah and Joan in unison, eliciting shared laughter between them.

Nearby, a pair of eyes watched the group of four from behind the entrance to the hedge maze. As silent as a cat, and twice as patient, Sephanie Kelly sat, crouched with her legs under her at the base of the tree limb. Though she had expected Joan and Judah's presence, it was not the end for her like it would be for other agents of Vilthe; nor would it be the first time she had sabotaged a Knight's mission in order to accomplish her own ends. Where her concern did lie was with Joan spilling too many secrets to Amelia in case Otep resurrected the flying bitch after she murdered her. She couldn't have that.

No one could know what Sephanie was really doing.

Chapter 8:
Sweet Sorrow

Eden - Victor's funeral

The news of what had transpired in Solomon Forrest spread quickly throughout Eden. Inevitably, people were most interested in who was responsible for the incident. After numerous hours of questioning by Eden's authorities Geoffrey still adamantly claimed that it was a mysterious man who rose from the Time Stream to murder Ranger Vaughn and Victor before taunting him and leaving the same way he came. Needless to say that few believed Geoffrey's story, fewer still thought he was innocent of committing the crime himself. Yet without solid evidence of his guilt, Geoffrey had been released under house arrest to the guardianship of Marcus Turtledove. Therefore, he had found himself unable to attend his best friend's funeral. A fact that Rolland Wright sadly noted as he and Tina made their way to say their own goodbyes.

Rolland also surprisingly noted that there were but a few mourners at Victor's funeral. It was a simple service that took place upon a high hill near the Halls of Time. There sat the small cemetery where distinguished members of the Knights of Time were laid to rest. For Victor, Turtledove had chosen a simple headstone made out of dark pink marble.

Raised as a Catholic by his Kenyan parents, Victor was openly proud of his faith, often carrying his rosary on missions as a Knight of Time. Despite the freedom of everyone in Eden to practice whichever religion they chose to, Turtledove found it incredibly difficult to find a Catholic priest on such short notice. It was not until the name 'Joan of Arc' was mentioned that a Father Thompson suddenly became available to preside over Victor's funeral. A small victory, but a hollow one at that.

"Yea, though I walk through the valley of the shadow of death, I am not afraid," Father Thompson intoned to the sparse few in attendance for the fallen Knight. He was an old priest, one who had not only found the light of his savior but also the one that lead to Eden. In keeping his faith, he also kept the garb of his era, a long brown cloak that covered his simple olive covered tunic and pantaloons. It was simple, but so was he. Even his quarters at the Eden monastery, located a few blocks away from the Eden Synagogue, was a simple room with only a few books and a spare change of clothing to distinguish it as his dwelling.

Simple too was the ceremony. With Joan, Judah, and Sephanie away the front row of white chairs was left empty out of respect, along with one for Victor himself. In the fifth row on the left side of the aisle, sat Rolland and Tina in plain white chairs. Both were sitting silently, deep in thought.

"There are only like ten people here," Rolland said stiffly, teetering on the edge of unleashing a stream of tears as each word spilled from his lips. "Why aren't there more people here? Where are all of the people?"

As Rolland nearly hit his breaking point, Tina grabbed his hand and squeezed comfortingly. There are not many in the world that would, or even could, go through the things that this pair had already experienced in such a short time and a special connection had been forged between them. Each was in the other's heart now; a place neither would leave for the rest of their lives. This episode of grief was but one is a series of events they would share together. There was some comfort in that. The pair was soon joined by none other than Turtledove, who was seeking anything but company.

For Marcus Turtledove, the occasion was marked with nothing but a quiet sense of responsibility for Victor's death and Geoffrey's arrest. He had spent nearly all night pouring through numerous casebooks at the Eden Hall of Records chronicling hundreds of years of legal cases regarding secondary manslaughter charges but had yielded no satisfying results. Worse yet, horrible news that Geoffrey had been removed from house arrest and taken to Eden Prison had greeted his early morning return to the Halls of Time. Moving off to the side of the line of gravestones that composed the Knightly cemetery, the leader of the Knights of Time stood solemnly, having not spoken a word to anyone the entire morning. Not since the death of Taylor Wright had a loss so fundamentally shook the Halls of Time. It was a natural process, Turtledove knew, but one that he had personally hoped never to see applied to one as young as Victor.

As Rolland looked around he saw a few faces he knew. There were two council members from the Council of Light that he recognized, Dr. Yick and Dr. Fluker. The town guards, Michael and Gabriel, were also there, as was the blind gardener from the Blackard Family Orchard, Sherman. There was one man who Rolland did not know, however, who stood up almost immediately following the priest's words to address the small crowd with words of his own.

The tall stranger was muscular, handsome, with distinct air of ruggedness about him. A tugging on his skinny necktie and starched shirt gave Rolland the distinct impression that he was not used to dressing so formally. Yet it was none of these things that drew Rolland's attention as the man approached the podium to honor their mutually fallen friend. It was the gun belt, and dual six shooters that sat on either side of the black leather strap straddling both hips that sent a jolt through Rolland.

"Victor was my student," the handsome man said, his brown hair staying perfectly in place as he spoke. "He was a good man, and too young to go."

"Who is that guy?" Rolland asked Tina, nodding to the man speaking.

"That's Lieutenant Jesse James," Tina said, a shaky reverence to her voice. "He teaches at the academy."

"What subject?" Rolland asked with some amount of incredulity to his voice.

Tina merely took this in stride, like she had done so many times before. "All subjects really. He acts as a personal mentor. You'll be assigned one, as will everybody else in our class."

"Huh," Rolland said, distractedly, listening to the rest of the eulogy. He wondered if Lt. James was the American outlaw Jesse James; the thought was a welcome, if not momentary, distraction from the suffocating grief that stabbed at his heart. It also brought a neglected thought to Rolland's mind regarding who his mentor would be. Deciding that he would ask Tina more about it after the funeral, he focused his attention back to the man talking at length about the great person Victor was. While flattering, he knew that if Victor happened to overhear it he would most certainly roll his eyes at such flowery descriptions.

After Lt. James was done speaking Turtledove gave his own short, abrupt eulogy before nodding curtly and walking back to the spot where he had been standing. Rolland was irrationally angry at this, as he felt that the eulogy spoke nothing of the magnitude of Victor's character, his large goofy grins, or the good natured heart that was as big as the man himself. Moreover, it neglected the mentor/mentee relationship between the two that Rolland himself had witnessed on numerous occasions as nothing more than a casual observer while at the Halls of Time. A rather taken aback Father Thompson stood up hastily before thanking the small crowd for their attendance, and bidding them to leave in peace. Each mourner stood in a timely manner and walked away, all appeared ready to move on. All but one; Rolland Allen Wright.

It was over. Victor was gone.

Shock set into Rolland's mind when he realized that the funeral was over; that Victor's death was final. Perhaps it was the extraordinary circumstances in which Rolland had come to Eden, or the adventure in Florida against Jackson and Vilthe, but for some reason he expected Victor to return triumphantly, revealing that he was alright after all, and ready to lead a charge against the assassin who killed Ranger Vaughn and sent him hurdling through the Time Stream Lost deep in this fantasy of thought, Rolland offered no resistance as Tina pulled him to his feet, walked him up the aisle, and stood next to the tombstone that marked Victor's eternal presence.

It was a small plot, much smaller than Victor himself had been by far. Though without a body there was no need for a casket, and without a casket there was no restriction on the size. Choosing a plot near Scott and Taylor Wright, Turtledove had maintenance workers construct the standard black, rot-iron gate around the five by five plot that housed nothing but grass, and the pink, marble headstone.

"Goodbye, Victor," Tina said softly, kissing the tips of her fingers before placing them softly upon the cool marble. She then hugged Rolland tightly, kissed him on the cheek, and turned to leave before stating quietly, "I'll give you a minute."

Rolland stood there dumbstruck. It was all happening so fast. What happened to the days, the weeks that dragged on while he was rotting away in the dungeon of Eden's courthouse? Memories of meeting Victor outside of the used bookstore in California flooded his mind again, and with them a new wave of soul crushing grief and suppressed tears.

Tina brushed away her own tears from her baby blue eyes as she walked away from Victor's tombstone, spying Turtledove standing at the end of the row. But before she could call out to her mentor strange sounds filled her ears. Faint at first, but louder with each step she took toward Turtledove. It was if someone were playing both a maraca and a xylophone at the same time. The sound was very unpleasant, causing Tina to stop dead in her tracks. She looked at Turtledove, who did not return her gaze, or even acknowledge her existence in the slightest except for a quick hand motioning her to the direction of a large tomb. Tina tilted her head in confusion but hurried to a spot behind the tomb nonetheless as she watched Councilman Anthony Varejao approach Turtledove.

"I understand that Geoffrey was arrested last night, without my consent," Turtledove said flatly, his voice heavy with burden. "Your cronies said that he was being charged with the murder of Ranger Vaughn, and of Victor."

"He's guilty Marcus," Varejao said unapologetically. "Or don't you think so?"

"Do you?" Turtledove asked Varejao, scanning the councilman's eyes for any sign of mercy. It was a gamble, he knew, but one Marcus Turtledove felt necessary given the circumstances. For his options were limited, at least until Judah and Joan came back.

Rolland approached Tina, who had been listening to the conversation with rapt attention. When he attempted to speak she hushed him, pointed at the pair of men talking, and he immediately understood.

"What I think is irrelevant, Turtledove," said Varejao, his back straightening as a Cheshire cat-like smile crept over his slender lips. "But what the rest of the Council thinks, well, their opinions carry more weight. And following this little stunt in the woods Falocco will swing in favor of.."

"When was the last time you spoke to the General?" Turtledove asked Varejao, turning away from the gloating councilman and toward the rod iron railing that surrounded fallen Knights' headstones.

"Yesterday," Varejao stated indignantly, his smile disappearing in an instant before his face turned red from being interrupted. "He's the one that insisted that your shape shifter be brought up on the charges."

"What is to happen to him, Anthony?" Turtledove asked, a pleading in his voice that gave Councilman Varejao a jolt. Perhaps to emphasize this point Turtledove, for the first time, displayed a sign of weakness in slackening his posture, and leaning on a nearby railing. This act, simple as it was, displayed much more than a momentary lack of comfort, but seemed to exemplify his age, and underscore that despite the title of Protector of Eden Marcus Turtledove was an old man.

"He is to be put on trial Marcus. Much like you were recently," Varejao said, stretching both arms behind his back before cupping his hands together. "Or don't you remember?"

The news, while not monumental or unexpected given the circumstances, was still surprising to anyone who had ever met Victor and Geoffrey. Never in his wildest dreams would Rolland ever have thought of one man killing the other, much less the larger Victor being the victim. He had seen them go at it a few times, all in the name of fun. But in those rough housing sessions Victor had always, without fail, come out on top due to his massive size and equally keen intellect.

"So," Turtledove began, likewise removing himself from a position of comfort to one of direct defiance. "Why don't you tell me what you're really doing here?"

Like a patient hunter stalking his prey, Varejao took a few, calculated steps toward Turtledove, before saying softly, "I think you already know, Marcus."

Deciding that something she did not want to hear was about to transpire, Tina turned to Rolland, grabbed his wrist, and marched him the opposite direction of the two men, back to the line of seats that now stood vacant.

"What did you do that for?" Rolland asked in earnest.

"I just thought," Tina began, but immediately stopped when she looked back, and saw Councilman Varejao walk triumphantly away from Turtledove, who hung his head where he stood. A beat passed before the leader of the Knights of Time righted himself, turned toward them, and began walking, his eyes finding hers as Rolland stood on, completely unaware. "Umm, well. I just, I just thought that when he talks to us it should be on his terms."

More confused than ever, Rolland was greatly relieved when Turtledove approached, albeit in a strangely sloppy fashion that seemed to be taken more out of obligation than actual desire.

"Mr. Wright," Turtledove said, his eyes a bit puffy. "How are you?"

Honestly not knowing how to answer such a question, Rolland opened his mouth in anticipation for his response, yet none came. Instead he simply stared into Turtledove's blue, wisdom filled eyes held by a leathered, grief stricken face.

"I've been relieved of my duties, Mr. Wright," Turtledove said, his voice resolute. "The Knights of Time are to be disbanded, or at the very least, stripped of their responsibilities and titles."

"You cannot be serious," Rolland stammered through a slightly dropped lower jaw. "But you had nothing to do with-."

"Mine is not the place for such decisions," Turtledove said meekly, placing one hand on Rolland's back and giving his shoulder a squeeze.

Rolland watched as the wandering eyes of the old man looked off toward the mid-morning sun. "I will keep you up to date."

Agitated by what he perceived to be his mentor's blind devotion to authority, Rolland did not feel like meeting Turtledove's gaze, turning instead away from the hillside. He looked into blue Eden sky as he let the so-called 'Protector of Eden' make yet another promise to keep, which he strongly doubted would be kept.

"Thanks, but I'll," Rolland began to say, turning around to find no one there.

Turtledove was gone.

The strange mix of emotions that filled Rolland's heart and mind were as complex as they were contradictory. He wanted to fight, he wanted to cower, he wanted to run, and wage war at the same time. It was all too much. Memories of his mother's death, the emptiness that followed, and the hopelessness that was Victor being lost in time were too much for his teenage emotions to take. With a thumping head and a beating heart Rolland clenched his fists, closed his eyes, and breathed deep in an attempt to stem the tide of fury raging inside of him. Then, like a gentle breeze in the middle of a desert, a hand landed softly on the small of his back, its light fingernails grazing his skin through his shirt in a circular, soothing motion.

"I'll wait for you by the cemetery gate," Tina said softly, gently taking Rolland's hand in her free one and squeezing before walking away.

Looking around Rolland found himself alone save for the graves of his mother, and father to the right of Victor's. For the moment he decided to ignore his parent's graves, for it was not their day to be mourned, he had years of that ahead of and behind him. Instead he focused on the pink headstone that bore Victor's name. Rolland read it again and again, somehow still unable to process its meaning. Perhaps it was because he never had time to mourn his mother and father, but the loss of Victor hit him somewhere hard. Somewhere realistic.

Visions of the flames from the bookstore back in California filled Rolland's mind. Flames that he knew would probably never be extinguished. Not now, not after this. Praying to himself silently, Rolland asked for the power to better himself over time, fully develop his abilities, and the capacity to travel through time at will to find lost souls like Victor, despite the real-world ramifications that might ensure. With a last, meaningful glance at the tombstone, Rolland read it once again before deciding it was time to leave.

VICTOR AQUASI III

FRIEND. BROTHER. KNIGHT.

"I will do right by you," Rolland said, grazing his fingers into the black etching on Victor's marble tombstone. The tears that he had fought so hard to suppress finally left his eyes as his mind wandered again back to the bookstore and where Victor had saved his life.

"Somehow."

Chapter 9:
Witness

Lae Island - 1937

The night sky was bursting with stars. They sparkled brilliantly set against the backdrop of the cosmos in a casual, easy illusion to the human eye. The problem with stars is that when you get close to them half are already burnt out, and the other half are full of hot air. It is rare that such a flower, a diamond in the rough, lives up to its perceived shine from afar.

"It's called moonshine and it's bloody brilliant," Judah said, taking another long swig from the glass bottle, allowing a bit of the liquid to dribble down the front of his chin as he drank. Normally he was not one for drinking on missions, having hated the inevitable early morning hangover that followed as well as dulling his senses. And yet tonight he did drink, happily imbibing on a newfound spirit of friendship with Amelia and her buffoon of a co-pilot. "Really put some hair on your chest!"

"You could use some of that," Amelia said, coyly, to her co-pilot Noonan. With a flirty demeanor and toothy smile, the world renowned pilot made quite the impression with her male companions; a fact that Joan did not miss. "Maybe it'll help you fly straight."

"I satry flate," Fred Noonan said before taking a long swig when the bottle came to him. As the other three struggled to mentally piece together what he had said, Fred gave a little wink to indicate that he did indeed mean to misspeak. This attempt at charm fell flat with the females, but did warrant a single, half-hearted laugh from Judah.

"Honestly, you forget a knife but not a bottle of booze and cigarettes. Good to you know you have your priorities in order," Joan said to her husband a little irritably.

The four of them had taken refuge in an old, abandoned barn with an open roof to ventilate the smoke from their small fire. Joan objected to this risk, as it gave away their position, but the spirit of the moment carried the day, much to her continued dismay. The accommodations, while far from ideal, worked well enough for the four as the early evening hours turned into night. The song of the night played all around them as howls, hoots, chirps, and rustling from the nearby wooded area and tall grassy fields behind the barn worked in perfect sync with the wind to drown out the nearby crashing of ocean waves against the beach. Joan listened to all of this, and thought of Tina Holmes, whose insistence that everything had its own theme song, or something to that effect. She looked at Amelia, who was eagerly waiting a turn for a pull from the bottle of moonshine.

"So Amelia," Joan said, steering the conversation. While Joan found Amelia easy to speak with, there was something about her that stuck her as... off. The entire mission was top secret, so neither she, nor her husband were privy to exactly WHY they were there, except to extract Earhart. "How long have you been flying?"

"All of my life, really," Amelia said with a laugh, her cheeks flushed due to the alcohol.

But before Joan could press the matter the bottle of moonshine came to her, as well as all six of the eyes accompanying her party. With a sigh, Joan held the bottle high above her head and took a long, slow swig that quickly turned in to multiple gulps. The liquor burned her throat, chest, and stomach from the inside but in a pleasant way that also warmed her blood. Forgetting what it was she was thinking about, Joan passed the bottle to Judah on her left, completing the circle and looked around for a new topic of conversation.

"I would kill a dozen Elemenos for some chocolate right about now," Joan said, kicking a small rock as far as it would go.

"Oh, so you like chocolate, then?" Amelia asked nonchalantly. "Me too. Belgian is the best. Do you like Belgian chocolate?"

"Yeah, but I'm partial to French chocolates. You know, the strong stuff from San-Luc..." Joan began.

"Sebastian," Amelia said happily.

"The little ones?" Joan asked, her fingers making a measurement of something small.

"Yes!" Amelia concurred, nodding furiously.

"I love those!" both Joan and Amelia exclaimed at the same time, followed by a fit of giggles from both parties. Their regression to fast speaking school girls was more than obvious to Judah and Noonan, both of which looked on with blank stares of their own.

"What I love is when you roast some sausages before we all starve," said Judah crossly.

"I've gotta sawsage," Noonan asked, drunkenly attempting to place his sausage on the end of his stick evenly, and failing miserably to do so.

"I'll bet you do mate," said Judah as he reached for a sausage in the crate they had found in the plane's wreckage.

"Oh you poor mistreated thing," Joan crooned mockingly, taking the meat from Judah and skewering it before thrusting it over the fire. "I'll take better care of your sausage from now on darling."

Amelia giggled and blushed at this comment while Judah laughed loudly and took another swig from the bottle and tipping it in the direction of his wife.

"I just can't, can't wait for this to be over, ya know?" Noonan said swaying. "But that won't matter once those Yankee bastards pay us."

"What are you talking about? What about the Yankees?" Judah asked, causing the mood of the barn to shift dramatically.

"Oh no I was just.." Noonan said, remembering himself before he said another word. He looked at them suspiciously for a moment, his eyes darting back and forth. He then took a deep breath before continuing on. "Shucks, you folks rub me as being trustworthy enough."

"Freddie," Amelia said warningly, eyes darting to Joan and Judah.

"No, no," Noonan began, holding up his right hand in a 'stop' motion to Amelia.

"So there was this Yankee peddler who bet me I couldn't fly across the ocean..." Noonan began, a broad smile plastering itself to his face as a long, drunken story about some old man from Nantucket came spilling out of him.

Silently exhaling, Amelia laid her head against a large wooden log as Noonan slurred, closing her eyes against the firelight. When Noonan asked her a question, the curly haired pilot pretended to be asleep, softly offering an easy agreement before rolling over to face away from him. Though her eyes only opened slightly, it was enough for Joan to notice, and appreciate.

As the night grew longer and the fire died down the trio joined Amelia in various sleeping positions, Judah the last to do so. For a long time he watched his sleeping wife with a silent appreciation for her ability to read people, interacting with them in a way he felt impossible to do. Thinking back on her history, he knew how she had inspired millions of people over the centuries, and counted himself among them.

It was some time later when Joan awoke to the sound of faint screams. The noise was strange, deep and resonant, almost like a hymnal. Lifting her head from her makeshift pillow of straw she looked around into the darkness of the barn, finding only her sleeping husband to her right, and Amelia a short distance away, close to the door. Then, through the corner of her eye she saw it - the familiar stranger that she had not laid eyes upon in a very long time. It was soft, yet indistinguishable with its white light contrasting against the country night sky. Where some might see a star, Joan knew what it was that came to greet her; and greet her it did, making its way through the open barn window it hovered at eye level, glowing and vibrating with a pulse that urged her to follow.

The white orb whirled through the air wildly as it made its way east through the tree line, illuminating the night and guiding Joan's path toward an unknown destination. For almost three miles she jogged in an attempt to keep pace, following behind the white orb, over the hills and long grassy plains where they had fought the Imperialist Japanese troops that afternoon. When the white orb finally slowed in a little patch off the marked trail it did not linger in one spot. Instead the little ball of energy bobbed merrily in the direction of two green tents and the crackling logs that composed a fire. With a final, counter-clockwise whirl the orb ended by throwing itself into the campfire, disappearing completely.

"What?" Joan asked aloud before hearing a strange, choking sound coming from one of the two tents. Passing the last few trees in the clearing she came to a thick patch with multiple thick, dense branches that she could hide behind while still seeing the encampment surrounding the fire. She wanted to move closer, but something inside held her back. Rightly so, as within seconds three people emerged from the tent farthest from her before moving closer to the fire. What Joan saw next made her heart skip a beat.

There, amidst a screaming Fred Noonan and Vilthe's henchmen Otep stood Sephanie Kelly dressed in all black, pushing the captive pilot along with a knife in her free hand. With her hair pulled back in a tight ponytail Sephanie looked almost unrecognizable as she sauntered along closer to the firelight, setting the pace with Noonan from behind. The pilot's nose was bleeding from what looked like multiple blows to the face.

Joan could scarcely believe her own eyes. Suppressing her instinct to approach Sephanie, Joan watched her longtime friend engage in what could only be described as treason against Eden. Someone once told Joan when she was a little girl that there was a large difference in knowing something, and believing something. Seeing Sephanie there with Otep Joan knew no matter what Sephanie's explanation might be, in her heart it would not matter.

"I told you," Noonan said through a bloody lip and a chipped front tooth. "We're just trying to set a record. We're not spies. I don't know-"

"Silence!" Otep screamed, grabbing Noonan's collar before wrapping his other hand around the pilot's neck. Never in his life had Fred Noonan felt such pain. But just when his surroundings grew dark, and he was on the brink of passing out, the hand around Noonan' neck slackened, and oxygen once again moved through his lungs.

"Otep!" Sephanie chided her colleague as Noonan fell to his knees while gasping for large swaths of air. Shooting a quick look of disapproval to Otep she turned to Noonan before bending down and helping him back up to a kneeling stance. "Admit the truth or I will kill you myself."

"I, I uh-" Noonan began, looking up at her with a confused look. He was not sure if she could be trusted. She seemed the more reasonable of the two, but something about her demeanor was peculiar. "I don't know what you're talking about. Honest."

"Lies!" Otep screamed, raising his hand again before striking Noonan, this time across the pilot's forehead. When the prisoner popped back up a fresh welt adorned the right side of his fore-head where fist made contact with cranium.

"HELP!" Noonan hollered, his voice high and loud, cutting the night air like a knife slicing into hot bread. The noise had the dual effect of both attracting attention, and acting as a deterrent to Otep, who for some reason moved several steps away from Noonan while he shouted. Fearing that the cry for distress might indeed bring Judah or Joan to their campgrounds was enough incentive for Sephanie to take control of the situation.

"Enough of this," Sephanie said, already in motion and mov-ing faster than any of the others anticipated. Removing the slen-der knife from her back pocket Sephanie flipped it open, exposing the blade.

Sephanie's knife made quick work on the flesh of Noonan's throat. The cut was so sudden that it took all but Sephanie by surprise, but none more so than Noonan, whose eyes bulged for several long moments before clutching the large gash across his throat. As his fingers clutched frantically, Noonan's mind raced with thoughts of his mother, little sister Abigail, and Amelia.

"My apologies," Sephanie said, removing a plain black cloth from her back pocket and wiping Noonan's blood from the blade. But as she looked at it glistening in the moonlight, fixating on the bits of blood that did not come off, it was taken from her by brute force by Otep.

As Noonan sat on his knees, his left hand holding his throat together in a vain attempt at a last few precious moments of life, he knew the end was near. While he lay on the ground, his brain telling him that this would slow the bleeding until rescue could arrive, the pilot's eyes watered as his world, literally, went upside down. The voices of his attackers were of secondary concern once he saw the blonde locks of Joan Raines through the tree line. Remembering her as an ally he reached for her with his freehand before attempting to scoot himself in her direction. His lack of traction was due to the pool of his own blood that saturated his entire neither regions, but the progress he made toward assumed safety was made a moot point as Otep walked up, grabbed Noonan roughly by the back of his jacket, pulled him to a kneeling position, and plunged the knife into the middle of his chest in a decisive mortal blow that knocked the wind and hope out of the victim. With a last fleeting thought of Amelia's safety Fred Noonan closed his eyes for the final time, shedding his mortal coil as he passed on.

"Clean this up," Otep asked coldly. "Now."

Sephanie had watched the whole scene like a cat viewing a dying bug. Though she held no personal hatred for the pilot or his comrade Earhart, their superior officers were early 20th century warmongers in her mind - regardless of their nationality. Along with an unhealthy prejudice for the people of Earth who always seemed intent on wasting her time more than anything else, came an equally unhealthy desensitization to the violence they constantly waged against one another. Still, the wide-eyed dead corpse of Fred Noonan once had a mother, father, and friends who all probably cared for the man. With this in mind she crossed the small distance between them before closing the dead pilot's eyes with the side of her left hand.

Sephanie went to move Noonan's body, even going so far as laying him down, and folding his cold hands over his chest in a restful manner. The knife that did him in was still sticking out from the center of his chest. So engrossed in her task was she that she did not notice the reemergence of Otep.

"The head," Otep barked in a low, resonate voice. "Cut off the head."

"What.." Sephanie began to say before she was interrupted.

"Those were our orders, bitch," Otep barked, removing the knife from Noonan's chest. The tip of the blade became lodged beneath a particularly tough tendon that made a snapping noise as it dislodged itself. A spurt of crimson blood followed, making its way down the lifeless pilot's chest, settling on the brown leaves below. "Now then, you're going to behave like Master told you to, aren't you, sweet Sephanie?"

Joan watched as Sephanie nodded before hanging her head. The expression on the teenage girl's face was not one of shame, or regret. Instead the girl that Joan had taken under her wing along-side Taylor Wright wore a cold, hardened face that fit in alongside the likes of the nefarious Otep. It was something directly out of Joan's worst nightmare; yet it wasn't. It was real.

Sephanie's betrayal was real.

Chapter 10:
One Small Addition

Eden

The Academy of Light

Life at the Academy of Light went on without incident following Victor's funeral. The week following the gathering was marked with classes, tutorials, and other obligatory gatherings that Rolland and company were forced to participate in together. Worse yet, the dormitory situation, while working out for Rolland in the form of his roommate, Dodger, was not working out so well for Tina, or any of the other females in the class of the tiger, none of which were matched with one another. One by one he and the other males were forced to listen to the nightly exploits of the conceited women of the Classes of the Ape, Raptor, or whomever comprised the owner of the small bit of hair that lives at the bottom of their shower drains. And so it went, day by day, little by little, as Rolland grew more and more into his abilities and skill set.

When the morning of the first B.E.T.S.I. test arrived Rolland awoke with a strange mixture of excitement and trepidation that he had not felt since the morning of his trial a few months earlier. The churning butterflies in his stomach were a welcome break from the lingering sorrow that had followed him since Victor's funeral. Indeed, even Tina seemed to have found a strange solace in the pressure surrounding a solid performance within the B.E.T.S.I. obstacle course. Whereas the two lovebirds normally took comfort in one another, the morning tension allowed for not even the slightest of relief from their collective nervousness; a trait that they shared not just with Tina's twin brother Timothy, but also Jaime, Gwendolyn, Hannah, Kniff, and Dodger - who had taken to teleporting around the breakfast hall nervously whenever he heard a noise that sounded like footsteps.

The events of the morning went by too quickly for all eight of the cadets in the Class of the Tiger, each wishing they had studied and prepared more effectively for their first true test. Despite the fact that Tina had explained to all of them at various times the purpose of the commanding officers allowing what is usually a middle, and end of training exam at near the beginning of the process, none of them seem to comprehend the idea behind assessing a standard of individual strengths. Instead each chewed slowly on their respective morning meals, made forced conversation, and tried to act as if it were a normal morning. Following a half hour of breakfast their worst fears were realized as Sgt. Tillman arrived to greet and escort them to the undisclosed location of the B.E.T.S.I.

The long march from the main courtyard where they followed Sgt. Tillman took them across nearly three miles of Eden landscape before arriving at a dark, obviously neglected part of the path. Here the road thinned to little more than a poorly carved series of wooden planks hammered into the ground to show the way. The sky overhead was blocked out by the thickness of the trees, each as the path narrowed, and the outline of a tunnel emerged. As the group approached the tunnel they were suddenly joined by a solider running up behind them.

"Sgt. Tillman!" the soldier said between long, elongated breathes. "We've, we've got a problem with the Class of the, the Ape. They're..."

But no explanation was necessary. Holding her left hand up, index finger standing straight up in a clear sign of both understanding and a request to cease his pitiful attempt to relay a message, Sgt. Tillman gave a small nod before barking, "Understood, return to your post solider. All right listen up Class of the Tiger we have a change of plans. I'm needed onsite ASAP so you will continue the rest of the way on your own. I am now handing out your assignment folders. These are personally tailored to your traits, abilities, strengths, and weaknesses. Show them to no one, and know them like no one. These principles will get you through your obstacle course today. Good luck."

The words did not seem to form properly in Rolland's mind. The next thing he knew Sgt. Tillman had turned and walked away along with the still panting solider, leaving the eight of them to wander to their destination on their own. He did not see the sergeant hand the folders to Tina, but next thing he knew half of those around him held one their assignments.

"Here ya go sweetie," Tina said in high voice, handing Rolland his folder, her eyes shining. Finding this display slightly embarrassing, Rolland reluctantly took the folder and turned from his girlfriend without a word. Opening it, he saw the short, to the point blurb written in the middle of the page.

Name: Wright, Rolland Alan

Ability: Time travel - extent unknown

Assignment: Strengthen leadership skills

Leadership skills? Rolland asked himself.

When Tina decided no one else was going to do it, she began to walk toward the B.E.T.S.I. facility before being followed by all seven of her classmates. Purposefully hanging back to speak with Dodger, Rolland decided to pose a question that had been bothering him in order to attempt to distract them from their collective nervousness.

"So, I've been wondering about something. The other day someone, and I'm not saying it was Kniff, because well, you and I both know it was him," Rolland said, hearing Gwendolyn stifle a giggle further up the line. "But this "someone" called me a, a 'Meno'. Do you know what that means?"

Dodger, a bit taken aback by Rolland's casual tone, looked at him for a long moment as if he were a strange animal that had flown in through his kitchen window before nodding and offering a wary, "Yeah, I do."

Sensing Dodger's reluctance, Rolland pressed the issue a little firmer. "Well, what does it mean then?"

"It's short," Dodger began, averting his eyes from his friend. "For Elemeno. Kind of a racial slur, basically like calling you an idiot or worthless."

"Oh," Rolland said, quite surprised at the revelation. While he knew there was an understood acceptance of racism and segregation between humans and Elemenos, he had no idea it went this deep. From experience he knew that any feud that had sunk to the level of name calling the other side in order to offend was beyond the point of a peaceful resolution without bloodshed. Thoughts of the French cafe with Tina floated to the surface of his mind, thoughts of the Elemeno man named Darius and his pursuit to enjoy a simple cup of coffee in peace. Rolland wanted to say something, something moral and righteous to express his outrage but when he tried to form the words in his mind; all Rolland could think about was the sound of sixteen feet marching down the path toward their collective unknown fate. In the end he simply stated, "That's pretty messed up."

When the path split the eight came to a halt in front of a small, very old looking wooden sign that indicated they were but a quarter of a mile away from their destination. Not knowing why they had stopped, Rolland looked to Tina for instruction. Instead he was met by the predictably cocky Kniff.

"I'll take lead now," Kniff said brashly, drawing the irate stairs of no less than four of his teammates.

"Oh, will you?" asked Gwendolyn, crossing her arms in a clear sign of displeasure. "Are you sure you don't want to march in behind me? I know how you love the view."

A crunched, yet patronizing expression was exchanged by the blonde headed Gwendolyn, and the Merman Kniff. This uncomfortable butting of heads between the two was becoming as repetitive as it was predictable for the other six of their class. Almost all of their disputes would result in the division of sides with the other cadets choosing who to support. The conflict always ended with the winner being decided upon by the swing votes of Jaime and Hannah, who held equal amounts of inexplicable annoyance for both the pointed eared young woman and the Merman.

"Step aside, woman," Kniff said brashly, hurling himself in front of Tina, to the front of their group. While Timothy and Jaime admired this and followed Kniff, Tina and Gwendolyn clearly did not, choosing instead to stop dead in their tracks, creating a large space between them and the three males.

"I'm just trying to do what is best for this team," Kniff said, a proud pretense to his voice that Rolland recognized as the same ego laced narcissism of used car salesman from his own time.

"No," Rolland said, stepping forward to face Kniff head on. "You won't be leading us again. Not today, not any day."

Raising his left eyebrow, Kniff in turn stepped toward Rolland, his chest puffed up slightly before saying, in a cold, challenging voice, raising what sounded at once like both a statement and a question, "Suppose you're going to do it then?"

Looking from the Merman's left, to his right eye, each a different, ever changing color between brown, grey, green, and teal Rolland watched as Kniff struggled with the questioning of his authority. Rolland knew very little about Kniff, except that he was indeed a Merperson, and Merpeople controlled something valuable to Eden, resulting in a sense of entitlement throughout most of their kind. In a way he pitied Kniff, as Rolland knew from experience that expectations were the first step on a path to eventual disappointment. Taking a deep, study breath, Rolland spoke in a low voice, yet loud enough for the entire class to hear before pointing at Tina with as much conviction as he could muster. "No, actually. But she will."

A strange hush fell over the eight souls standing between the edge of the forest and the B.E.T.S.I. training course. It was followed, predictably, by a series of eyebrow raises and head tilts that did little in the way of inspiring confidence in Tina's leadership ability. No one among them expected Rolland to step to the side, revealing Tina as his pick for Tiger team leader.

"Her?" Kniff asked rudely, his head jerking in Tina's direction, his eyes never meeting hers. "A woman?"

"Me?" Tina asked simultaneously, her hand resting on her chest in surprise.

"Fuck that!" Timothy Holmes proclaimed to the group at large. He wasn't in the mood for another one of the idiot's speeches about how great his twin sister was.

"Hey now, "Dodger said, teleporting from his perch on a tree limb down to within a foot of Timothy. "Might be your sister, but she's still a lady."

"She's more than that," Rolland began. "Tina is smart, capable, but more important - she has experience in the field."

"She does?" Tina asked, her sparkling blue eyes bulged at the thought of added responsibility. "I mean, I do?"

Wishing that Tina had said something else, anything else really, Rolland knew that he would have to turn on the charm if he was to convince the others not to follow Kniff.

"During our time in Florida," Rolland began, catching each of his classmates' eyes as he walked between them. "Tina not only gained the trust of the local indigenous natives, but they actually elected her as their new leader. Unprovoked."

This revelation came as news to the six Tiger classmates and noticeably impressed all but Timothy. Even Kniff, seemed to really look at Tina for the first time since the conversation began. His lips parted slowly as if a question were begging to escape the

inner workings of his mind, yet the plateau of a lifetime of prejudice against both humans and females held it at bay.

"But most importantly, she won," Rolland said, walking
behind Tina and putting his hand on the small of her back before
gently nudging her forward toward them. "Tina rallied strangers
behind her in battle and won. Actually won! Isn't that the mark
of a true leader?"

Straitening her back, and donning her stern face, Tina Leigh
Holmes did her best to look the part of leader that Rolland
made her out to be. As she walked between the other six cadets,
catching each of their eyes as she went along, Tina could tell
that for the first time they each saw her as more than just an
entitled child of privilege. Looking back at Rolland with tears
in her eyes, Tina appreciated every syllable that he had spoken
on her behalf.

The rest of the walk to the B.E.T.S.I. facility was not nearly
as difficult as any of them would have anticipated. Indeed, the
forested terrain that greeted the beginning of their journey,
thinned out to reveal a relatively flat, grass filled landscape that
clearly showed the path to their destination. Taking it as a positive omen, Tina led the way with as much confidence as she had
ever possessed in her life. While the realist in her knew that it was
extremely unlikely for any class to master the B.E.T.S.I. course
on their first try it was not unheard of. She recalled reading in
one of her textbooks, *The History of the Academy of Light,* that the
1033 Class of the Squid beat their initial training course on their
first attempt. Tina thought about sharing this fact with her team,
but then recalled Dodger's propensity for asking follow-up questions, and subsequently remembered how out of seven members

of the 1033 Class of the Squid five were killed before graduation from the Academy. Tina held her tongue.

To Rolland, the B.E.T.S.I. course, whatever it was, looked a lot like a fat water tower. This image was not deterred the slightest by the fact that immediately surrounding B.E.T.S.I. was a field of what appeared to be very thin wheat plants, each as high as three and a half feet tall. As the Class of the Tiger drew closer to the five story tall building that their commanding officers had made such a fuss about, a few things began to become perfectly clear. The first, judging by the two unconscious cadets in the wheat patch closest to the back of the building, was that the level of difficulty was far greater than any one of them expected. The second, according to the small, crying girl who stood out front with her face hidden in her hands was that the place was probably pure evil. Rolland remembered the girl from orientation and thought her name was something strange sounding like Shamara, or Pamara, but he could not remember. They all watched as one of her teammates, a large dark skinned girl with black braided hair running down the middle of her back comforted her before waking their unconscious classmates. The sight was nothing short of intimidating. All eight of the cadets were so enthralled by this scene in fact that none of them noticed Sgt. Tillman's emergence from behind B.E.T.S.I.

"Time for the test then," Sgt. Tillman proclaimed before bringing a whistle to her thin lips and blowing four times in a row. The sound blistered eardrums, reverberating menacingly in all sixteen ears that suffered through it. Through the ringing each watched as the whistle free fell like a bungee around Tillman's neck before she spoke loudly. "To demonstrate team unity and proficiency in your skill set all of you will compete, individually and as a group, within the confines of B.E.T.S.I."

Kniff looked bemused by this; as if nothing could penetrate the shell of unconditional resolve and fortitude he had built up.

Both Timothy and Hannah noticed his expression, and both drew very different conclusions from it. For Timothy the sense of confidence exuded by the Merman Kniff was to be admired, perhaps even fawned over. Yet for Hannah, the brash, entitled attitude reminded her of many guests to the Madison White House back home who would attempt to give her orders. She promised herself then and there that she would not follow Kniff that day or any day. Though, as Hannah was about to find out, the universe does not deal in absolutes.

"Be advised cadets!" Sgt. Tillman hollered while pacing in front of them. "Completion of this course is required for graduation from the Academy. You will be tested again in exactly one month. Should you fail then, you will not be asked to come back for the remainder of your training."

The bluntness of Sgt. Tillman's statement sent shivers down the spine of everyone in attendance, including the four soldiers who stood idly by, waiting to follow the class inside and test their individual mettle. With nothing more to say, Sgt. Tillman turned, clicked her heels, and marched straight toward the blue, heavy iron door that contrasted sharply against the dark brown building known as B.E.T.S.I. It opened automatically as she approached, revealing a dark chasm in which she walked to fearlessly.

"Here we go," Dodger said under his breath, though only Gwendolyn and Rolland heard him. Tina went in first, followed by Kniff, Timothy, Dodger, Jaime, Hannah, Gwendolyn, and finally Rolland, each of which walked with more than a mild trepidation.

Once inside the building everything was pitch black. With the bit of sunlight left from the doors behind them, Hannah could see little in front of her but the back of Jaime and a strange orange glow in the far off distance. Once all eight of them had passed the threshold the doors snapped shut as if they were loaded on a spring. The sudden sound of iron on metal echoed and reverberated in the unyielding dark before puttering off into nothingness, followed by an eerie, quiet that dulled the senses.

"I can hear my heart beating," Tina observed, tilting her head slightly. Hearing the all too familiar thump sound that was her pulse, Tina looked to Rolland. Although she could not see him, she knew he was searching for her too.

"Me too!" came many voices all at once, the loudest of which belonged, oddly enough, to Jaime.

"What are we going to do?" asked Gwendolyn, her voice drenched in panic. A dull thud of a headache was creeping in to her mind as her disoriented brain struggled to adjust to the lack of stimulation. If B.E.T.S.I. could read minds and pull nightmares from its victims, then this room was surely Gwendolyn's version of hell. "I, I can't..."

"We move," said Tina sternly. The resolve in her voice was evident, empowering, and all together appropriate. Despite this, it did little to comfort her classmates against the seemingly black hole they had found themselves in. With the anxiety of their surroundings simmering into their respective brains it was little wonder that none of them saw the torches appearing in the distance. Small at first, and growing larger with each passing second Timothy and Hannah were first to notice then, each screaming, "Look over there!" as the little blobs of gossamer light pranced toward them.

There were a dozen of them, followed by a few dozen more, each bobbing merrily toward them like welcome strangers in the darkness. The trick was so effective that several of the cadets forgot altogether that they were in an obstacle course, therefore they let their protective guard down and began calling out to the flame-wielding strangers for assistance. It was not until they drew close, what Rolland guessed to be ten feet away, that he noticed the pointed, furry ears sitting on top of a green fuzzy faces half hidden in the firelight.

"Shit," Rolland said flatly before instinctively throwing his left arm behind him until it found Tina. "They're Elemenos."

Yet before any of the other cadets could react to this revelation, the ground beneath them began to tremble. Everyone - cadets and Elemeno alike shook along with the ground they stood upon as it fought the tectonic plate beneath it into a violent battle of submission. Without warning a large crack, broke through between Rolland and Tina's feet. Looking down they both saw it widen against the dim light, looked at one another, hands intertwined, before being ripped apart by forces stronger than either one of them.

Hurtling through the air at breakneck speed, Tina felt a sharp pain in the pit of her stomach. She felt a rush of wind through her hair before opening her eyes to see a large crater filled with debris and a pair of purple sneakers that she recognized as belonging to Dodger. All around her the high-pitched screams of Elemenos filled her ears. The dim firelight brought by the invading Elemenos was gone, replaced with a lone, strange glow that seemed to be coming from high above her head, yet still very far away. Casting these distractions aside, Tina struggled to her feet before walking to the smoking crater, squatting down, picking up the purple sneakers, and tossing them aside while checking for the body that matched them. Unfortunately for Tina, her abilities never worked their best when she was unable to concentrate, and in that moment of frustration filled anxiety she was every bit the definition of flustered.

"I'm not in there," came a boyish voice from behind Tina. Turning around she saw Dodger standing there, a wide grin upon his face, soot staining the right side of his cheek, and shoeless feet rocking him back and forth on the spot in which he stood. "But if you're looking for buried treasure..well, in that case I'm right here."

"Dodger?" Tina asked, rubbing bits of dirt from her eyes. "Where is everyone else? Where is Rolland?"

"That's him over there, I suspect," Dodger said solemnly. He was looking out across the vast abyss that separated him and Tina from two people who were lying down, obviously unconscious on a small platform that barely had room for the two of them to sprawl out.

"Where?" Tina asked, her mind still reeling from the earthquake.

"Just a minute," Dodger said before turning on his heels and disappearing, leaving but a faint trail of purple smoke in his wake.

Out of the corner of Tina's eye she saw a third person suddenly appear next to the two unconscious people. She watched as Dodger rolled one over, the larger one, put a finger on his neck, and then give the thumbs up to indicate that Rolland was indeed alright. After he flipped over the second person, who turned out to be Hannah, Dodger again gave the thumbs up before attempting to wake the pair up. It did not take long.

Startled by the fact that he had never fainted before, Rolland Wright awoke to a new setting. He remembered entering B.E.T.S.I. and even recalled the small army of Elemenos that ran toward them, but could not for the life of him recall how he ended on the ground. How much time had passed? After they were reunited via Dodger teleporting Tina to their little island in the dark, the four did little but look at one another, silently wondering about Timothy, Jaime, Gwendolyn, and Kniff. After a moment Dodger disappeared again, this time for what seemed like ten minutes.

Upon his return the intrepid traveler informed the others that not only had he found the way forward, but that he'd be taking them one at a time.

"Great. But when we get there I think we should split up," Tina suggested, looking out into the darkness. "Teams of two."

"Sounds good to me," Rolland said in a tone that was perhaps a little too overly enthusiastic. "So it'll be you and me, and-"

"Actually," Tina began, placing a hand on Rolland's shoulder. "I'll be going with Dodger, you take Hannah."

"Oh," Rolland said, attempting to find Tina's eyes in the shadows. When she did not meet his, Rolland mumbled a short, "Right."

The first time Rolland teleported alongside of Dodger he felt a subtle lightheadedness followed by an immense feeling of drowsiness, concluded by a shocking feeling similar to having a bucket of cold water poured on top of his head. The process felt like it had taken hours, but Rolland was surprised to learn it had taken mere seconds. This hard to believe fact, coupled with the perceived insult of Tina choosing to accompany Dodger instead of him, put Rolland into something of a distant, displeasing mood. So much so that when the four of them reached the door Dodger had found, a yellow painted old oak door with a rusted knocker and doorknob, Rolland completely refused to make eye contact with Tina, choosing instead to hang back with Hannah.

Beyond the door there was a hallway, also dimly lit, with a cream colored carpeted floor that wound to the left some thirty yards inward. With a final look back at Rolland and Hannah, Tina gave a halfhearted smile before stepping over the threshold.

"Madame Holmes," Dodger said, gesturing for Tina to walk in front of him into the long, narrow hallway. As she went he stole a quick peek of her backside, admiring what he saw. Fearing he might be caught doing this, Dodger checked on Rolland, who was attempting to make awkward plans with Hannah. Dodger had never seen the two speak to each other alone before, and wondered if this was their first time. With his mind lost in thought, Dodger momentarily lost track of Tina, who had wandered past his line of vision. Panicking, he ran to catch up with her.

"Oh my.." came Tina's voice, loud and clear through the hallway toward the pair of remaining cadets. Fearing the worst, both Rolland and Hannah ran through the door toward her, their plans of splitting up becoming an afterthought in the wake of their leader's disappearance.

Teleporting around the corner Dodger saw what looked like a completely different world than the one he had just been in. Gone was the ominous debris and dim firelight; replaced by a many windowed room surrounding the most extravagant golden throne he had ever seen. White and black checkered marble tiles adorned the floor, fine crown molding on the top of the walls, and a suit of armor stood nearby standing guard, a large silver sword with a slender handle pointed upward several feet toward what looked like a small wooden perch situated in the top corner of the room.

"Pretty chair," Hannah offered, running her hand against the purple satin that covered the throne's seat. She had beaten Rolland into the room, walked past a still awestruck Tina, and made her way to the throne, its glittering golden hues shimmering against the sunlight windows.

The scene made little sense to Rolland, which made it much like the rest of Eden in his opinion. Deciding to just go with the flow Rolland put both hands in his pockets in a bad attempt to act casual. The truth was that the anxiety of not being in control of the situation was killing him, and despite a little voice that kept saying he should trust Tina's judgment, he did not. He knew, however, that there was little he could do about it. It was him who had recommended her for the post, and despite wanting to speak out against what he perceived to be her failings as a leader, Rolland knew that as her boyfriend he needed to keep his mouth shut. So, instead of voicing his objections, he instead studied the armor intently, as if it were about to attack him and he were checking for signs of weakness.

"This is awesome!" Dodger exclaimed, teleporting twice around the room before reappearing again nearly ten feet away, a cautious look of half trepidation, and half pleasure plastered across his face. Perhaps it was because of this sparse attention to detail that he missed the trip wire, placed upon the perch before where he finally landed. Stepping on it as he repositioned himself, the barely visible line gave off a distinctive noise that resembled a very out of tune guitar chord.

"Hey Rolland, did you hear that?" Dodger asked nervously, crouching on his haunches and gripping the perch.

Before he could answer, Rolland strengthened his grip on the suit of armor's sword as the room around him began to shake violently.

Within seconds the white and black checkered floor opened down the middle, pulling both Hannah and Tina in with it. All of the room's contents, including the ornate throne and suit of armor, seemed to be stuck to the floor, and did not move along with its occupants. Neither girl let out so much as a scream as they fell freely away from Rolland and Dodger, who were spared from this pitfall due to their respective grips on the sword and perch.

After what Rolland guessed to be ten seconds the floor righted itself again, and both he and Dodger found themselves alone in a very different, very foreboding room. The windows, which had previously displayed a bright spring day outside were now open, revealing a backdrop of utter desolation and despair.

"You alright, Dodge?" Rolland asked shakily, finally letting go of the sword's handle. His hands were red, swore, and imprinted with the hilt's lines that ran across both palms.

"I think so," Dodger offered, jumping down from the perch instead of teleporting. "What now? What about Tina and Hannah."

"They're ok," Rolland said with more conviction than he felt. "Remember, Tillman said we would be tested individually too, so that's probably what they're doing. Feel like going outside?" Rolland asked, desperate to shake the thoughts of his girlfriend and tilting his head toward the windows.

"What the hell else are we going to do?" Dodger retorted, while shaking his head slightly.

Together the two climbed through the windows and walked out into the Eden night. Although Rolland knew this was all a simulation, he could not for the life of him tell much of a difference. The barren ground beneath their feet felt real as they walked across it. The air was sweet with the mingled smells of smoke and something foul that he did not recognize. In short the effect was as realistic as it could get, despite being nothing more than one of Judah Raines creations; a virtual hologram. It was not until they had walked for nearly fifteen minutes in silence that either one realized where they were going. Perhaps he had led them there on instinct, but whatever the reason both Rolland and Dodger soon found themselves standing at the edge of the Time Stream. Another five minutes of silence passed between them, neither sure as to what to do or where to go next.

"Hey Fearless Leader," Dodger said, shaking his head slightly, a noticeable buildup of sweat having accumulated around his neckline. "Did it suddenly just get blazing hot or is it just me?"

"What?" Rolland asked, before looking down at his own shirt. Sure enough sweat stains around his neck, chest, and armpits had appeared. "When...?"

But before Rolland could inquire further someone jumped out of the Time Stream and lunged at him, his hands immediately wrapping around his neck. Gasping for air as he fell to the ground, Rolland tried in vain to thrash about as the life was being choked out of him, but was unable to break free until he opened his eyes to see two more hands, small, and attached to Dodger, prying the stranger off from behind.

Breaking free of his would-be murderer, Rolland scrambled to his feet just in time to see a dazed Dodger lifted up by the man high above his head before dropping him down in a swinging position, and kneeing Dodger to the forehead. Having seen this maneuver performed before as a child, Rolland knew how effective it could be. A flood of memories from watching Saturday morning wrestling burst into his mind. Yet they were gone almost as quickly as they appeared, extinguished by the icy stare and daunting body language of the stranger.

The man was thin, morose, and held a hungry look in his eyes that instantly reminded Rolland of an old wolf. His nose was slanted to one side at the end, and he wore a strange tunic that half resembled something ancient Greek or Romans might wear. Beneath it was a makeshift belt that held multiple compartments, from which a practiced hand removed a long, thin blade that for a split second shimmered against the golden hues of the Time Stream.

"What the hell is going on?!" Rolland exclaimed, jumping backward as the man lunged for him again, the edge of his knife grazing the center of Rolland's chest. The cut drew a little blood, but not enough to be noticed in the moment, allowing Rolland to press onward in his fight to survive. In his mind the priorities of the situation became clear. #1- Survive. #2 - Keep Dodger safe. Looking for an excuse to get past the man and his knife, Rolland searched for a momentary distraction, finding it in a patch of loose soil that he scooped up in his cupped hand. Pivoting to his left, Rolland led the attacker in that direction before quickly snapping his fingers, bringing the palm of his left hand to the cupped fist of his right, and slowing down time.

The effect was immediate. No sooner had Rolland done this, however, then he threw the soil into the air before the now charging stranger, doubled back, and ran toward the Time Stream; which Rolland noticed was moving quite normally despite everything else being in slow motion. This thought seemed to break his focus, as time righted itself, and he heard a bellow of pain from the temporarily blinded attacker. Zigzagging left, Rolland headed for the spot where an unconscious Dodger lay.

But Dodger was gone. In the spot where Rolland's teammate had been a mere minute before lay nothing but the barren, desolate Eden soil where he landed. Confused, and distracted by this, Rolland did not see the quick kick to his chest coming, which sent him hurdling across the distance and into a small pile of rocks that did little to break his fall.

"Ok," Rolland said, rolling over to see multiple cuts along his exposed arms. He looked up at the ceiling, at whatever was watching and shouted, "I wasn't ready for this. I concede."

But the pleas fell on deaf ears as the man again wrapped his hands around Rolland's throat.

It was then, and only then, that Rolland finally realized what he should have known all along; that this man, whoever he was,

was one hundred percent real and hell bent on killing him. With a face that was turning more purple by the second, and eyes that watered around a line of vision that was only getting smaller, Rolland began to resign himself to the idea that he was nearing the end. His mind flooded with thoughts of Tina, of Sephanie, Turtledove, and his parents, Scott and Taylor Wright. He had missed them more than he thought, and in that moment he knew that if he let go perhaps he would see them soon. The feelings of comfort suddenly gave way for another thought, one of unfinished business, and a promise he swore to someone else special to him. Victor. With his promise of vengeance in mind, Rolland's eyes bugged open to the surprise of his attacker, throwing both off guard as they renewed their respective resolves.

Suddenly long, jagged yellow teeth stared back at him as they covered both his and his attacker's arm before squeezing shut. The pain was incredibly strong, but did not linger. Immediately the pressure around his neck weakened, and he was able to breathe again. A dull throbbing pain pulsated in his head, clouding every judgment over the line between reality and fantasy.

"Holy hell!" Rolland wheezed. Falling backward he struggled to sit up and looked, wordlessly in wonderment at the sight before him. There, locked in what seemed to be an epic struggle was his assailant and what looked like a fully grown female white tiger. With its back claws dug firmly into the attacker's thighs it clawed ferociously, taking out chunks of his neck as the two danced around the Time Stream. Shielding himself with his forearms, which were becoming little more than bone, the stranger jerked in every way imaginable to shake the beast off - yet it would not yield.

Using its own weight, the tiger finally removed its claws from the man before circling back around, and charging one last time, hitting him square in the chest. Falling off balance immediately, the attacker stumbled backward into the Time Stream from which he came, his knife doing nothing to stop either he, or the tiger that intervened in the fight from slipping into the golden hues of time indefinite. With a final howl of pain, the assassin named Nero cried out as a black and white colored tail was the last bit to leave Eden, taking all sense of immediate danger with it.

Silence filled Rolland's world. He was alone, bleeding, still out of breath, and confused beyond his wildest imagination. Was that all part of the trial? Was that man even real? Where the hell did Dodger go? Turning these questions over in his mind, Rolland almost missed the soft mewing sound that broke his train of thought like a penny on railroad tracks.

Standing up shakily, his legs still wobbly from a lack of oxygen, Rolland walked toward where he though he heard the noise coming from. Amongst a lose assortment of burnt logs, rocks, and built up soil seemed to be a small nest of sorts where a bundle lay hidden away from the utter destruction of their environment. Leaning in, Rolland could see the outline of a small, very young white tiger cub. Shocked by this discovery, Rolland thought for a split second of leaving it alone until it opened its crystal blue eyes, and met his for the first time. He crouched down, extending his hand hesitantly to the young beast, who took it gladly, nuzzling the side of her face against his fingers before mewing again.

So engrossed by his discovery, that Rolland did not notice when the world around him changed yet again, this time into a seemingly normal, if not round warehouse with boxes and large piping overhead. With an interest in the noises beyond her new human friend, the tiny tiger cub stood up, stretched a bit, and sat down looking at Rolland before mewing again in an obvious request to pick her up. Rolland obliged.

"Bang, I killed you," said a voice from behind Rolland. He stood up, the blood rushing to his head only adding to his confusion as he saw a small, squat looking man standing there aiming what appeared to be a cheaply made toy pistol at Rolland's chest. The man was a solider the same one who had asked for Sgt. Tillman's assistance earlier that day.

"Wait, what?" Rolland asked, completely confused by this turn of events.

"You're dead sir, please move along so the next class can come in here," said the intern, holstering his plastic weapon and feeling around the wall for the trap door that would soon become his exit.

"You cannot be serious!" Rolland exclaimed, standing up. "What about the guy who tried to kill me? And the tiger?!"

"Tiger?" the solider asked in surprise. "What tiger?"

"A white tiger," Rolland began, his breathe and wit catching up to his objectionable mouth. "Big one, huge fangs. It saved me from the man with the knife trying to kill me."

"Look kid, I don't know what you're talking about, but-" the solider began to say before his eyes moved to the pool of blood at Rolland's feet as well as noticing the purple bruises on his neck. "The hell..?"

Then the solider saw the tiger cub nestled in the crook of Rolland's arm. The creature began to fuss, causing the man's eyes to widen before he took several steps backward. Staring at the solider as he backed away in fear, Rolland could tell that the man had no knowledge of the events that had just transpired at the Time Stream. While he found this frustrating, Rolland could not blame him for his reaction given that the simulation was over yet the tiger and the blood still remained.

"Where did you get that?!" the wary solider asked, taking a large side step to his right, further away from Rolland and the staircase that led to the exit beyond the trap door.

Seeing his opening, Rolland shook his head before descending the L shaped staircase, exiting through the steel door at the bottom of the stairs, and back out into the Eden sunlight where the rest of his class was already there waiting for him, including a now wide awake Dodger whose eyes widened with relief at the sight of Rolland. The initial reaction of disappointment at their failure was quickly replaced by shock at Rolland's blood covered clothes and bruises, and after an affirmation that he was mostly unharmed, an onslaught of gushing love for the tiger cub. None of them said a word as he recounted the tale best as he could, but instead alternated their gazes from him to the tiger with a mixture of horror and fascination. Well, all except for Timothy, who showed no interest in either.

"She's adorable!" Tina exclaimed while holding the white tiger cub up for Hannah and Gwendolyn to pet. The cub seemed to enjoy their touch, and did just as she had done inside, nuzzled their fingers with both sides of her face.

"Aye, she is quite cute. And will perish out here without a larger animal to hunt for her," Gwendolyn said, interjecting logic into the now generally held belief that the group should adopt the creature. "But we can help her with that."

"It's settled then," Tina said, holding the cub up to the light while scratching her under the chin. "Now this little lady just needs a name."

A long moment of silent contemplation between the cadets was followed by rapid exclamations of loud suggestions, each one growing more ridiculous than the last. Believing that half of the team objecting to any one suggestion was enough of a veto to disregard it, Rolland voiced no objections to any name, instead choosing to smile at Hannah as she looked up from the grass where she sat, seemingly choosing not to participate in the proceedings. Hugging the little white tiger cub tightly Tina kissed its head multiple times in a display of emotion that had both her twin brother, and Kniff laughing while casting mocking looks at Rolland.

"We'll decide on a name later, for now I'm just glad everyone is alright," Rolland said, looking from Hannah, skipping over Timothy, and resting his eyes upon the gathering females who circled in on the cub.

"Looks like we've got ourselves a mascot," said Dodger, envying the affection being heaped upon the cub by the three females. The little cub cooed, and nuzzled the long fingernails offered to it as another chorus of awes were elicited when it began to purr.

Rolland watched, though with much different emotions than that of Dodger. For him the attempted attack that brought the little white tiger into their company was nothing short of an unexpected, and unwelcome, surprise that cost the team an early victory. Coupled with his already uneasy feelings about Tina, and even Kniff's leadership skills, he knew that the paper he received earlier in the day was correct; it was time to take some responsibility for himself. For his classmates. For the tiger cub. Deciding that these negative thoughts, and the subsequent feelings that it brought to the forefront of his mind, were best suited for another time, Rolland decided instead to smile, pat Dodger on the back, and nod his head in agreement.

"Looks like it."

Chapter 11:
A Tale of Two Women

Lae Island - 1937

The orb was pulsating with a violent glow that shone brightly over Joan's tears of frustration. It nudged her left arm gently, leading her away from the scene of carnage down the path from whence she came. With no eyes, ears, mouth, or language to communicate its wants to her the little orb merely led the way through the dead of night. Joan walked listlessly, a ship lost in a sea of betrayal. Questions buzzed about her head like a swarm of locusts, each swarming with a hiss that clouded and muddled her psyche. Timelines of events led Joan down paths laden with conclusions of even more potential backstabbing and deceit. White hot fury swelled inside her, ebbing and flowing around in her stomach, creating intermittent minutes of both extreme rage, and severe heartbreak, verging on self-pity. It wasn't enough to be deceived by the best friend she had ever had. What made it worse was knowing how blind she herself was to the entire situation.

In joining Vilthe Sephanie had done what only one other person in her life had managed to accomplish, cut to the very core of what made Joan a warrior and question the fundamentals therein. As she trudged Joan attempted, albeit in vain, to take rational stock of her situation, deciding what course of action to take next. In the way of council she had Amelia, whom she did not really know all that well yet, and of course, her husband Judah. She knew that Judah would advise an immediate, direct, and perhaps less than logical retaliation in response to Sephanie's unspeakable action. It would surely be violent. Swallowing the last bit of moisture in her mouth, Joan readied her vocal chords to articulate what her mind couldn't fully grasp to be the truth.

"Sephanie.." Joan said, under her breath in a half whisper. She quickened her walk, making every step more brisk than the one before it until she was jogging along the rocky countryside. She reached the sandy beach with no fanfare or notice, the orb of light following her like the tail of a comet. There, passing as she went along, the moonlight bounced off of the water's edge, reflecting back a scene of what anyone else would call majestic beauty. Likewise, the trickle of giving a damn about the world at large slipped past Joan's consciousness into the universe, beckoning energy to conglomerate around her position. The electricity within her rose as she closed her eyes and her feet continued doing the work of both navigation and mode of transportation.

It was then that the orb acted, sensing Joan's distraction that bordered on narcissism. It flew, fast as it could toward the jogging blonde warrior, meeting with Joan in a high paced crash that temporarily blinded her eyes, but did nothing to deter her still sentiment feet. As her world filled with a white light in an explosion of dizzying deafness, Joan tried desperately to adjust her eyes best as she could. The main problem with this did not become apparent until the white faded from her eyes like a film, revealing a world of sunny blue skies, green pastures, and run down 15th century dwellings. She was still moving, but it was not of her own accord. Far from it, as all of a sudden a horse's hooves became clear every time she looked down. Joan was riding a horse!

What had been moments ago night had become the middle of the afternoon in what felt like the blink of an eye. The effect was disorienting at first, but it wore off after a few long moments of confusion. Joan instantly recognized her surroundings, but once again her mind and eyes could not concur on what it was they were both witnessing. It wasn't until the smell hit her nostrils. It was the smell of boot leather, lilac, horse dung, and embers of campfires freshly put out. The skin around her eyes tightened as the world around her formed solid shapes again. Joan's heart spoke loud and clear as to where she was; Joan was home.

Compiegne, France 1430

Gone was the glittering ocean that Joan had been walking along aimlessly as it had replaced by endless muddy fields. Her left hand, which Joan raised to her eyes, was gloved in gray wool. Then, as suddenly as if the knowledge was a cool rain falling on her head, it all made sense. Her hand flew to her boot, which if her theory were correct would contain a small shard of looking glass that belonged to her mother. Finding it there, wrapped in the same wool that comprised her gloves, she looked astonished at it

The reflection in the mirror was herself, albeit some years younger. Gone were the slight wrinkles she had noticed appearing in the past few years. Gone were the fully developed breasts and womanly figure that her husband Judah spoke so highly of.

All replaced by a heavy silver breastplate, black woolen britches, and an overly anxious horse beneath her. Remembering herself despite the layer of fog that clouded her brain, the middle aged Joan, the woman so full of experience and good judgment, tried to make sense of the situation she found herself in.

In Joan's previously empty hands were a crudely made steel sword, and an equally hastily constructed wooden crossbow, respectively. Tools of a trade she had given up on long ago; and had not picked up since. A promise to herself that she had not only failed to keep over the years, but. Still, she could not deny how happy she was to cast aside the real world worries regarding Sephanie and just be a young warrior again. Taking a deep, satisfying breath as her chest swelled with pride, Joan smiled for the first time in what felt like days. Looking around her, Joan's eyes revealed a plethora of wonders from a time only whispered about in romanticized literature, glazing over the brutal savagery that was her 15th century homeland set against the Hundred Years War between France and England. Little cottages, simple in design, stood in a row along the mud road, each with a little yard equally full of mud. The owners of the homes were deep within, hidden from the coming onslaught of what they predicted to be a slaughter brought on by the Almighty in retribution for putting their trust in a woman. Joan remembered the offense well, for it was the greatest she had ever felt. What she had hoped never to feel again was suddenly back, back in at her lowest moment; a waking nightmare.

But before Joan could process this information another one of her senses was bombarded with an undeniable truth that terrified her even more. Filling both of Joan's ears the sounds of footsteps marching in an awkward succession behind her, clomping through the mud and earth. They wore the makeshift armor of her recollection, tarnished antiques in their own day, into battle with their heads held high. A quick count revealed that nearly fifty men trailed her, all armed to the teeth and attentive to the task at hand. It wasn't a large army by any means, but each man was as capable a soldier as she could hope to find. A strange sensation filled her as she gazed at them, sloshing and mumbling along. Joan had thought on them often, in both dreams and nightmares, yet never wishing to return back to this moment. This moment, the one she found herself, regressed back to the age of a teenager to once again face her greatest challenge. Her greatest defeat. The group's pace continued steadily for minutes, or hours - Joan wasn't sure, before a geographic obstacle slowed their collective momentum to a crawl.

When the tree line narrowed, Joan's chest once again filled with the same anxiety that grasped as her heart when she had first arrived on horseback. Unnerving to the point of madness she decided to ignore the thoughts of running away into the brush of the woods around her, believing it might convey the opposite of the strength she has worked so hard to cultivate within the souls of her soldiers. No, Joan had to think other thoughts, strategic thoughts, full of sound and fury. No sooner was her plan moving past the initial forming stages when the woods gave way around a bend before opening wide up to reveal a large, open field of green grass some half a mile from the gates of a large village beyond a hillside. Compiegne. She knew it well, well enough to remember that inside was the key to crippling the English king's economic rule over the gentry of his lands, thereby rendering him moot and handing the French a long awaited victory. Well enough to recall that the town gate, which currently stood in a half open, half closed tilt, blocking access to the village entirely, was the key to entering the city with as little bloodshed as possible.

Inside Joan's teenage hormones blazed at the thought of basking in riches and glory. The emotions were so powerful, in fact, that it was not long, perhaps one hundred yards, before her adult mind, still fighting for control, began losing the battle over her teenage body and its own wants. Thinking on this very fact Joan was broken from her reverie by a familiar whistle coming from her first Lieutenant, a swarthy man named Renoir. Expecting the banner men on her left to lift their flags, Joan was surprised one final time as the banner men on her right rose theirs instead. Dark and ominous, the red and black flags of war swayed once, twice, three times in the chilly morning air, followed by the sounds of the war horns of the isles. Their meaning was clear; it was time to fight the English.

The soldiers lined up in columns behind Joan, all wearing a steely reserve within their posture. These were war-hardened countrymen of hers. Hers. Her countrymen. Joan saw this and thought about how far they had come together. It wasn't so much about the distance as it was the gradual acceptance, though respect earned via shared combat experiences, that each and every one of her men knew and trusted her to lead them into the mouth of hell itself. Each stared dead eyed straight ahead as Joan rounded on them, pacing from the far side of each column to the next. Although the memories of what she was supposed to say wafted over her senses like a fresh mist filled morning, a sneaky, nagging suspicion clouded her judgment as she took center stage on the hill outside of the fortress at Compiegne.

"Men of France!" Joan screamed, turning on her horse to face them. Their faces gaunt, haggard, yet eager for any measure of approval, be it plunder, destruction, or simply a warm meal. Another rush of adrenaline hit her, this time harder, giving her the endorphins that drove so many of her actions. Joan smiled, a bit of madness behind her eyes. Raising her weapon high above her head she screamed, "Today we liberate a fortress!"

Cheers of, "The Maid! The Maid!" were bellowed in different tones and timbres throughout the ranks of men. From the diaphragms in their collective bellies they shouted, rallying one another into a frenzy soon to be quenched in battle. They were the sons of peasants, not noblemen, aiming to fight as such. As individuals they knew only loyalty to their own kin, cottage, and

Lord; yet as Frenchmen, as soldiers in *Jeanne d'Arc's* army, each found a greater purpose in their shared experiences that equaled a greater sum of themselves. Another round of isle horns wafted over the symphony of battle cries, heralding the arrival of the first band of English in their midst. Seven in total the ornately dressed riders, each on horseback, were either the bravest, or most foolish men on the field that day. Regardless, their goal became as clear as the clouds on a sunny day - reach the gates of Compiegne before Joan's men to fortify and protect.

Instantly it became a race with Joan versus the seven. Two of the English noblemen made the gate just as it lowered. Joan, a good twenty yards behind them, was forced to pull up hard on her horse's reigns as the gate rose to the height of the beast's eyes. Coming up short Joan rounded her horse before the fortress' main gate, looking upward at the castle's defenses. With a quick glance she spotted several guards eyeing her, weapons at the ready. Knowing she was standing in such a vulnerable position, Joan somewhat welcomed the challenge. Out of her periphery vision Joan saw three of the English soliders chasing after her, their swords drawn at the ready as they charged.

'*Funny*', Joan thought to herself, her smile confusing her opponents further as their momentary pause allowed more than ample time for the superior teenage warrior to best their efforts. With minimal effort Joan released her feet from her makeshift saddle's holsters before curling her legs into a crouched position. Using her leg muscles for all that they were worth Joan thrust herself off of her horse and onto her first startled opponent, his jaw literally dropping along with his sidearm as the comet that was Joan of Arc landed with all the force of a merciless, celestial object hell-bent on finding a permanent resting place.

Dispatching them quickly with lightening fast swordsmanship Joan hopped from one horse to another before moving onward, the line of her French lieutenants shaking their heads in exasperation as she adjusted herself with finesse. A mewling English solider whose yellow femur protruded through the top of his breeches called out for support, all of which fell on deaf ears. Joan watched as one of her men walked the short distance to the noblemen before removing his sword and ending the mewling through a soft bit of flesh through the neck. This mission was going much the same way previous ones against other English outposts and defenses had. But they did not care. Not as long as there was plunder to be had and a profit to be made. For their loyalties, unlike their 'chosen leader' were not based on religious beliefs or national identities.

"*Mademoiselle* Jeanne," said a soldier from Joan's first column. Joan eyed him for a moment, trying to remember his name. The words Jean-Luc leaped out at her despite herself so she decided to run with the feeling. "The advancing column is not far behind them, my lady. Perhaps we should flank them with the bulk of our remaining forces?"

The suggestion, a good one, meant leaving whoever stayed behind to act as bait extremely vulnerable. Knowing full well that she would lead said force, Joan accepted the fate with a continued grace that astonished even her most reluctant soldier. It was, after all, the fourteenth century and Joan was but a teenage girl of fourteen. Remembering this, Joan squared her shoulders, hardened her reserve, and readied herself to give the hardest order she would ever be forced to utter.

"Jean-Luc, take the auxiliary force and head back around to flank them," Joan said, her eyes purposefully avoiding both of her lieutenants as she tip-toed around the fact that she would be staying behind. "Cut them off, kill as many of them as possible, and for goodness sakes don't let yourselves be captured. Retreat if necessary. I want to see all of you again."

"But *Mademoiselle* Jeanne.." Jean-Luc began, eyeing his commanding officer suspiciously. She seemed... off somehow. The embodiment of French courage and steadfastness, the Maid of Orleans had come to represent so much while also meaning so very much to a great deal of people, noblemen and peasant alike. "I do not think it wise to be.."

"You are to take the auxiliary back around and fortify there," Joan reiterated, her resolve strengthened by making eye contact thins time. "Is that understood?"

Though his pride would not let him physically say the words in front of the other males, Lieutenant Jean-Luc did as he was told, divvying precisely half of the groups forces, their weapons, and horses before taking one last look at the woman he had come to know. Never one to believe her own hype, Joan was able to shield herself from much of the gossip that made its way around the French court and the streets that she fought to protect. Questions regarding her chasteness, her character, and even her dieting choices were hot topics of conversation - depending on the audience. Knowing this, and knowing that Joan's bullheadedness would carry the day regardless, Lieutenant Jean-Luc did as he was ordered and before long took the bulk of the French army serving under Joan of Arc back to around to control their own fates instead of falling victim to the trap that was becoming Compiegne.

The numbers did not lie.

15th century warfare was a dirty business, one started with a gruff word and ended with a wave of death from the sky; also known as the most sophisticated use of weaponry for the age. The line of English arrow men stood at the ready, each eager to simultaneously do their duty for King and country, and to stay as far away from any actual fighting as possible. Their current allocation provided a means to said end, so they did their duty happily indeed.

"Back! Fall back!" Joan shouted, turning around just in time to avoid a pointed arrow that would have struck an individual two inches taller. She, along with five of her company, were able to move backward enough to retreat and mount an offense on the opposite side of the ridge. The rest of her troops were cut off in a sea of crimson colored cloaks as the English advance moved faster onto the French side of the clearing. Joan fought hard, to cross the divide that separated her forces, and for the briefest of moments the battle seemed to turn; raising the hopes of the doomed French soldiers and the Compiegne witnesses that would live on long past them. Rounding about until she found her core, her inner circle of remaining officers, Joan raged with a screaming charge before leading her small brigade back toward the English line in a pointless, yet all important rally to the pride of their nation.

The first clash rang out, claiming the lives of all six opponents, each French sword and spear landing beneath English chainmail, breastplates, and overcoats; meeting fresh flesh against the morning sun. Clamoring aside from the second onslaught, Joan subdued another two men, then three English cavalry before something sleek caught her attention from the corner of her eye above. Looking upward, she watched as the first line of slender, and ominous bolts, each tipped with a deadly piece of flint, made their way across the heavens above them before arching downward onto their position. Without thinking Joan released herself from her horse, leaned as far and as fast as she could to her right, and allowed gravity to take her to the Earth below.

"Duck! Fucking, duck!" Joan screamed in English, narrowly dodging an English broadsword aimed by a portly fellow as she hit the ground with a thud. Rolling under a nearby splintered, wooden wagon she avoided the spray of arrows that thudded and landed all around her protected position. Beneath her the grass grew heavier with blood as she looked out to see one of her brave fellow Frenchmen fall, skewered by the rain of wood, claiming his body back to the Earth in which it came. Angered by this, Joan rolled to her left, popping up into a standing position just as a new wave of English crossed her path. Acting on instinct Joan twirled around, unsheathing the dagger she kept on her hip, before thrusting forward into the belly of the soldier. The remaining four that stood behind the falling corpse had little time before they too fell into Joan's web of revenge. When more English regulars appeared, all intent on intimidating Joan to make a name for themselves, the Maiden of Orleans spotted the heaviest, targeted him, and then roundhouse kicked the fat fellow into his peers.

"Judah!" Joan said aloud, momentarily distracted by the remembrance of her most cherished one. The momentary distraction crashed whatever momentum Joan had amassed as another squad of English cavalry officers on foot marched up behind her. This group, consisting mainly of scouts and retired knights of the land, saw the advantage in killing the 'French whore' before she could be taken. Lost in thought she did not see the danger approaching until it was on her. With a very loud and boisterous battle cry one of the knights raised his weapon high above his head, revealing two rows of rotted teeth all aimed at the still distracted Joan.

Suddenly the sounds of choking rang through Joan's ears, drawing her attention back behind her. An axe fell from a previously unseen English soldiers grasp, severing the young scout's wrist clean off before lodging itself within his upper thigh. Bloody lips screamed a call of the damned before the Earth claimed him for itself.

"*Merci*," Joan said to Renior before whipping the accumulated sweat off of her brow. A momentary smile flashed between the two, the last two, Frenchmen to hold their ground that day. Another noise, this time the sound of cannon fire, drew Joan back in the direction in which they came. Joan's eyes bulged at the sight of the hundreds of hostile English, all making their way, in loose ranks, up the hill toward her. They were armed, and each had a hungry look upon his face; the kind of look a starved dog or newly freed prisoner dons when out on the prowl for the first time in a while. A look that still haunted Joan's dreams.

Joan turned around, jogged the short distance to the city doors, and balled her fists before pounding hard against the wood gates that had been shut for the dual protection of the village's citizens and Joan's now wiped out force. She banged until her hands bled and the war drums beat like thunder in her ears, yet the doors would not budge. As the seconds ticked by and the English circled inward to surround them the pair clutched their swords and looked at one another, silently considering their options. For Joan the thought of surrender seemed worse than death for several reasons, rape being the least of her problems. Renoir too saw little honor in such an end, conveying as much with a simple shake of his head.

And so it was, standing armed on the outer gates of the city of Compiegne, that the girl known as the Maid of Orleans took her stand. The man at her side did very little to comfort to her as the English line advanced in their direction, nearly seventy strong; every one of the dressed in the age's finest armors, and wielding the most advanced weaponry. Joan's mind did cartwheels of logic trying to remember the gadgetry and technology that Eden has brought. Although she could not remember how, solace came from the dull memory and knowledge that in order to get to wherever Judah was, Joan had to survive this onslaught. No sooner did this thought bring a modicum of comfort to her than the last bit of friendship she held left her physical side.

Renoir, on Joan's far left, fell as the fifth and final arrow to penetrate his torso rained down from above, grounding him forever. A similar fate befell the two local soldiers on her right, neither of whose names she had learned. With another sweep of her sword against another English neck before flipping around, and gliding it into the chest cavity of another. Remembering the next several actions, and determined to avoid the mistakes of the past, she kept her guard up, while simultaneously summoning every bit of courage she could.

This was Joan's least favorite memory.

Between the pushing and pulling of sweaty male bodies, multiple hands groping at her every inch, her armor was undone and chest plate released. It fell dispassionately to the Earth before her tunic joined it, ripped apart like tissue paper by the hoard of hands grappling for a go at her bare breasts. It was horrific. Joan fought, elbowing, scratching, and biting whomever she could before they could go after her pants like they did her top. Somehow, she'd never remember since, Joan managed to get a hold of another sword, fighting off two more before having it knocked out of her hands by a pair of rather ambitious Yorkshire privates utilizing the age old game of bend over behind the victim and push to induce them falling on their ass.

Betrayal, anxiety, and never-ending pains of abandonment gripped at Joan's heart as her arms tightened up, making them heavy from overuse. The numbers were getting to her as the rough hands of the dozen or so English soldiers who grabbed at her chest, waist, and midsection were too much under the force of will from the second dozen behind them. Within a matter of seconds, she was surrounded, covered in a sea of flesh as fingers pinched and squeezed at every bit of her. The violation was too much, and Joan closed her eyes, pushing the trauma as far away as she could before...

"Joan," Amelia asked, extending her arm outward before placing it on the shoulder of the stock-still women who claimed to be there to save her. The reaction she got was anything but warm. "Joan wake up!"

Joan sprang upward suddenly, her hands quick enough to find her knife.

"Jeepers," Amelia said, standing up quickly before taking a giant step backward to give Joan some room to breathe. "Relax, would ya? So you going to tell me what's going on with that orb you've been following?"

"Wait a second," Joan began, stopping short as the breath in her lungs turned to ice. "You can see it too?"

Never in all of her years alive had she spoken to anyone about the orb, or its many frequent visits. But then, as the white orb buzzed around Joan's left and up above between the two, Amelia turning her head to look first, it became clear to Joan that someone else could see the orb. So, Joan wasn't crazy. At least not when it came to seeing small balls of light that appeared in her darkest, most challenging moments. Now if she could only explain the recent hallucinations.

Returning to her own tent Sephanie wiped off her knife, the instrument of murder, on the canvas of the tent. The red liquid was only gone following the third complete rub down of the blade, yet the teenage girl continued to clean it regardless, her eyes veering off to nothing in particular as her mind wandered far away from Lae Island. Sephanie had never thought of her life as anything but a series of sequential, miserable events. It never once dawned on her that a purpose, a destiny might befall her, a meager daughter of a pig farmer. He had offered her something different. Something exciting.

Greece - 3403 BCE

Nights are the toughest time to remember that you're gone, Daddy. I love Momma, and there isn't a lot I wouldn't do for her, but if you were still around I know that I wouldn't have made the same mistakes. You died in October, just as the massive storms flooded the fields, so you never got to see Mama's flower garden come Spring. They were beautiful flowers, made even more beautiful by the fact that it took that long before she smiled after your passing.

Oh Daddy the dandelions were so delicate that they fell apart in my hand. I remember when I was a little girl you used to fill your hands with them, surprising me by covering them up with your fingers before blowing them in to the wind. There, on that day, I was happy. But never again. Not after you went away and left us, Momma and me. Not after I had no one left to share my secret with. I know that both you and Mama know what I can do, I know that you've both kept it a secret from me for a while. Still, Daddy, you were the only one who would talk to me about it. The only one who made me feel.. just like everybody else. After you left, Mama wouldn't even admit to what I could do... even when the bad storms came after the news of your death.

I got so, so mad Daddy. So mad.

Since I could not speak to Mama about missing you, and since my kitty couldn't understand me, I would often sneak out just after supper to scream and kick about the old back acreage where you taught me to ride. It was there that I met him, the little boy who would change my life forever. He was tall and skinny like a bean pole, though his shoulders look like they could have filled out someday if he made it to manhood. He wore a dirty gray tunic the first time I saw him spying on me through the tall grass on the western part of our land. The first few times I spotted him I didn't say anything, just let loose with my emotions, or 'tinkering with nature' as you used to say. Suppose I thought I'd scare him off, but he didn't go.

One night in the late summer we were getting a late rain when Momma was having one of her grief fits. After calling me every bad name I could think of she threw one of her brass cooking tools at me, driving me from the cottage. Without thinking I ran out to the field where I kept seeing the boy, the field where I could be myself. So I did...

...I gave it everything I had.

It wasn't what I expected, the first time I flew. The feeling of weightlessness gripped my hips first, forcing the weight of my legs under me to disappear. If it wasn't for that feeling of shallow gravity, giving me a pain in the middle of my stomach, I might not have even looked over at the boy again. But I did look, and I saw how far away he was; how far I was from the ground. I know you taught me to always be brave but I just couldn't, Daddy. I just couldn't. After I fell back into the grass a warm, wet hand clasped my shoulder in a firm, yet tinder way. I knew before I looked up at him that it was the boy who had been watching. He was lankier than I thought, but held himself with a kindness that reminded me of you. Our clothes were soaking wet, heavy, and weighing us down. Yet somehow, Daddy, somehow I felt free after he touched me. All of a sudden I had someone back in my life that I could maybe talk to. I just wanted a friend.

"My name is Souza," the boy said to me, offering his hand. It was wet and slimy, but felt comfortable as it rested within my own. He squeezed it once, and I instantly trusted him. I shouldn't have done that Daddy. I know now I shouldn't have, but I did. I never dreamed that going with him would be the biggest mistake of my life. Oh Daddy, I'm so, so sorry.

He took me home with him, somewhere dark. I remember a large tree that was bigger than any cottage I had ever seen. At first I thought it was a castle of sorts because I had never seen one up until then. But there were branches, tall and long, that seemed to stretch so high they blocked out the sun from above. It was a place I had never been before. It was scary, exciting, and all together different than the sheltered life that you and Momma had provided for me. Souza took me down into the bellows of the tree, far beneath the Earth. There was nothing but darkness down there, darkness and cold. If I could see anything it would have been my breath. I remember that it was when I felt like my skin was on fire from the cold when a light appeared. It was purple and horrible with its temptation. Still, I was afraid, so I reached out to it, grasping it within my palm. That's when he made himself known.

"Hello there," a man that emerged from the shadows said, his voice a thin, sleek baritone. Like yours. I remember that I couldn't see his eyes beyond his cloak, which was black and shadowy like the rest of him. But his eyes.. they were different somehow. Not human. Not like an animal.. but something else. Something foreign. "I am Souza's father. What's your name?"

"Persephone," I remember telling him, although I'm not sure why I was so honest. Maybe because he scared me. It doesn't matter now, I suppose. Not once I said my name. Once I said my name it was too late. I was his. Now, every September, I return back there, back to that horrible place I was once tricked into going. Momma cries whenever I come back, just like she cries whenever I go. No matter what I do, I'm always making someone unhappy. But still, I do it because I know that sometimes we do things for those we love, even if we don't particularly enjoy those things.

Following these words Sephanie stopped her writing, ceasing to continue her train of thought.

Chapter 12:
Pinchers, Prowler, Puddles, & Ponies

Eden

Pinchers

It was the first day of individual basic training, a previously foreign concept to someone like Rolland Wright. The fact that his parents had kept their lives in Eden a secret from him and he from it, suddenly filled Rolland with annoyance that he could have been more prepared for this day. It was with this thought at the forefront of his mind that Rolland began most of his mornings in Eden. But this morning was different; this morning would not be like the others. This was the day the cadets schedules arrived.

Two white sheets of paper were thumb-tacked to wall outside of Rolland's dorm room door, their black letters glaring down at him. Rolland eyed the papers passively as he skulked by in his night attire, boxer shorts and plain a white t-shirt. The paper would become a constant companion during his first few days at the academy, as it told Rolland then when, where, and why he needed to be in certain various places around Eden. But that was only the first week. According to Tina, their third week, and every other week afterward, were to be a completely different change of pace from the first two. As his mind wandered to thoughts of Victor's funeral and the attempt on his life during the first B.E.T.S.I. trial, Rolland could not help but welcome this news of change.

Rolland went into an autopilot mode of showering, and dressing in an order that left his dorm mate Dodger shielding his eyes on more than one occasion as he too prepared for the day. The friendship that had blossomed between the two was like a shining beacon in the sea of uncertainty that was Rolland's life in Eden. Stewart 'Dodger' Yick was clean, polite, and genuinely funny. All in all he was the best roommate that Rolland could have ever hoped for at the academy. A pleasant thought, but not enough to overcome his anxiety for the day, or the uncertainty of the tasks ahead. In that moment Rolland strongly regretted coming to Eden. But then he thought about it again.

It was a strange thing, regret. For within his heart Rolland knew he held much regret over many things. The way he acted after his mother died. Never really getting to know his father, Scott. Killing Puck. Not killing Jackson. Not bringing Blaisey back to Eden with him. And not kissing Sephanie the way she had kissed him when they last saw one another. His feelings for Tina were strong, sure, but never had he been kissed the way Sephanie had kissed him in the woods back in Pensacola. With a tinge of guilt Rolland shoved those thoughts aside, dressed, and went back to re-open the door to retrieve the sheets of paper containing his and Dodger's new schedules. Rolland then read through it through a few times silently to himself.

<u>Monday/ Wednesday</u>

Zero Hour

None (1st Term) Not eligible

First Period

Hand to Hand Combat - Professor Danielson - DERR 245 - 9:00AM to 10:00AM

Second Period

Basic Survival techniques - Professor Grylls - Old Main 103- 10:00AM to 11:00AM

Third Period

Agility Training - Professor Garcia - Arena #4 - 11:00AM to 12:00PM

Lunch

Fourth Period

Communications Techniques - Professor Vianello - TMH 201 - 1:15PM to 2:15PM

Fifth Period:

One on one mentor study - M-F - 2:30PM to 6PM

Nareau- 17015 Copperhead Drive, Eden Town Proper

Wishing he could skip right to dinner, Rolland took a deep breath and set out on his way to Derrick Hall where hand-to-hand combat was taught. Putting on his light gray jacket, he closed the door to his small room and entered the dorm common area. Looking to his right he saw his roommate leaning against the front door of the building like an Asian version of James Dean. Dodger looked up as Rolland approached, smiling his big, toothy smile. Just like that the illusion of cool was gone.

"Who you got for one on one study?" Rolland asked Dodger as they sat down in a pair of beige chairs.

"None of your business, Probie," Dodger said with a smirk. But before Rolland could reply a familiar looking piece of white paper was in unfolding in Dodger's hands. He read it quickly, a sense of nervousness about him. "Well hot damn. Looks like I've got your old boss."

"What?" Rolland asked, suddenly very ready to leave.

"Marcus Turtledove," Dodger said, turning his paper around and offering it to Rolland. Sure enough there under the category that read 'One on one mentor study' were the words 'Turtledove' and 'Halls of Time' under location. "What do you think?"

"That's... uh," Rolland tried to say something, anything, but could not. Words and sense escaped him as his mind tried in vain to make sense of why Dodger, not he, not Rolland was chosen to be mentored by Turtledove. The man himself had issued yet another executive order following Victor's funeral to maintain no contact, but Rolland had assumed that meant for everyone, not just himself. This action, however, seemed to imply that Turtledove merely wished not to see Rolland specifically. Odd feelings of rejection ran through Rolland like hot liquid swallowed too fast. The jealousy that washed over him in that moment was so powerful that he felt a physical pain in his chest. Realizing that he had been silent for more than a few minutes, and that his heart was beating incredibly fast to where surely Dodger heard it in the interim silence, Rolland forced a smile of his own before continuing on. "That's great, Dodge. You'll really like Turtledove."

"But do you think he'll like me?" Dodger asked without missing a beat. "I've seen him around enough, always being around my granddad and all. But I've never spoken to him. He's, well... he's too intimidating. Don't you think?"

The tension in Rolland's jaw, shoulders, and torso slackened, allowing him an opportunity to breathe deeply, think for a moment, and answer honestly. "I think he'll like you just fine, Dodge."

And with that the two walked together to their first shared class of the day with Professor Danielson. There they joined Tina, Gwendolyn, Hannah, and Jaime in a row of seats to watch their fellow classmates who were assisting for the day as sparing models. The demonstration was entertaining, as Timothy's brash temperament was only matched by Kniff's boastful pride during their sparing matches. The spectacle went on for nearly half an hour with Professor Danielson barking instructions, technique, and things of that nature at the two. Dodger's commentary was the highlight of the entire lesson, however, as his teleporting ability was not confined to his physical body, but also included his voice, which he used to disrupt and distort both Timothy and Kniff while they boxed. As the minutes passed frustrations mounted as the small noises and name-calling doubled, causing their punches to become hard enough to leave bruises. Sensing the budding hostility Professor Danielson called it a day nearly ten minutes early, dismissing the Class of the Tiger completely.

The rest of the morning turned out to be completely uneventful to the point of boring. While both Basic Survival and Agility Training were fine courses by themselves, they hardly offered the sort of adrenaline pumping good time that Hand to Hand did. Rolland was pleasantly surprised to find that the Agility

Training instructor, Professor Martin Garcia, a stocky man who could move like a leaf in the wind, was but a substitute for the academy's real teacher, Joan Rothouse Raines. Unclear as to how this could be with her dual responsibilities as Lieutenant of the Knights of Time, Rolland made a mental note to ask Tina about it later. Lunch provided more of the same bland food as the weeks before but it was always nice to hold Tina's hand and get a quick kiss before the next class.

After the overly long communications class that included tips on how to signal for help in smoke, Morse code, and locate the nearest public library, Rolland was more bored than he had ever been in his life. The only distraction from the dull subjects that Tina seemed to eat up like they were candy were Dodger's performing antics. Harmless enough to some these practical jokes usually involved teleporting an object, but in one case an entire person, to a new location without their knowledge or consent. They began amusingly enough with Professor Vianello's laser pointer being misaimed to follow him around wherever he went, but quickly escalated as the simplistic, yet mind numbing lessons in various forms of communication dragged on. Because it was a joint class, the eight members of the Class of the Tiger shared the instructor and lecture hall with the much quieter Class of the Raptor, and louder Class of the Ape.

While Rolland had little taste for the history of communication, Tina had found it illuminating to the point of annoyance. She had a knack for not only recognizing words in various languages, but also finding ways in which they could be universally connected. If not for Tina's amazing ability to multi-task in asking the instructor engaging questions while writing cute notes to Rolland, he feared no one in the class would like her. Gwen especially found her brand of know it all-ism to be especially annoying, though she never spoke of it. But after the debacle of Tina's leadership in the first B.E.T.S.I. trial almost all of his classmates had sought a private audience with Rolland to discuss it. All save Kniff and Timothy.

"That will be all for today," Professor Vianello said under his bushy, gray and brown mustache. The tall, slightly hump-backed instructor slumped a little as he turned from the class and sauntered back to his desk. "Say thank you Professor Vianello.."

"Thank you Professor Vianello," the entire class said in a slow, practiced unison before gathering their belongings and leaving.

Zoning out during Tina's excited babbling about unicorns, Rolland did not even notice the quick kiss on the cheek and squeeze of his hand before Tina left to go meet with her new mentor, her purple backpack but a blur out of the corner of his eye. Looking down at his schedule Rolland read the instructions there, again and again, re-affirming his next course of action for the afternoon. He had no idea where Copperhead Drive was. Looking up he thought to ask someone, but they were all gone. Everyone, every student, even old Professor Vianello and his mustache.

"Well, shit," Rolland said under his breath.

After asking around the academy, Rolland was guided eastward back toward Eden Town Proper by Sgt. Tillman. Thinking this pity was due to his confusion, his gratitude quickly fell away as he realized where exactly it was he would be going. Back to East Eden, where he had become lost shortly after arriving to Eden for the first time and almost killed. With great hesitancy he marched out of the academy, walked the distance over the hills and fields to the gate of Eden Town Proper, and knocked three times on small oak door next to the tall ominous gate. The small window no bigger than the size of a shoebox opened and there staring back at Rolland was the face of Michael, one of Eden's town guards.

"Hey there Rolland," the guard Michael said with a genuinely friendly smile. The two had not seen one another since the day of Rolland's trial, and the younger of the two had a question or two regarding the back up plan that was to transpire if Rolland was found guilty. "Here for your basic individual I suspect. The Captain was expecting you nearly an hour ago. Best not keep him waiting any more, eh?"

Michael disappeared before Rolland could answer, the scrape of his sword hilt scraping against the wooden door as he moved along the other side toward the gate.

"The Captain?" Rolland asked, his voice drowned out by the clanking of the gate opening slightly for his passing through. Following a now silent Michael, Rolland realized they were taking the same path as he and Joan had taken on his first day in Eden. He swallowed with trepidation as they walked deeper into the poorer side of Eden Town Proper, where Michael left him with a salute and a smile. Much to his surprise, he located Copperhead Drive easily enough. 17015 Copperhead Drive was a one story, gray painted, run down shack with no windows surrounded by broken down Rip-Roras. A blue and red painted door with what looked like a new brass knob stood out as the buildings best, and most redeemable features.

Reading the address over and over Rolland's mind confirmed what his eyes would not tell him to be true. This was indeed the place he was supposed to be, and through that door was the answer to the mystery that had plagued him all day. He thought briefly of slowing time, entering, and then coming back out before fixing time again. But the more he thought about it the more he decided it was not behavior befitting someone dating Tina, or the son of his mother, Taylor. With as much nerve as he could muster Rolland approached, grabbed the knob, and turned it before stepping through the threshold and entering the dark building.

"Hello?" Rolland asked aloud to no one in particular. Given the state of the yard out front, he assumed to find nothing but cobwebs and dust. To his immediate horror, however, much more would be waiting that day for him. As he walked in the door shut behind him in a clichéd way that made him chuckle a little before he noticed that his surroundings were completely different; no longer was Rolland in a room, but a white void, with absolutely nothing appearing within his line of vision. With an anxious feeling in his stomach, he was suddenly floating wildly through the air. Tumbling with his eyes closed, Rolland did numerous front flips as he tripped, heels over head, the uneasy feeling in his stomach growing bigger and bigger with each jarring movement before he finally fell roughly to the ground.

"Do you know what you are, Rolland Wright?" a voice asked from beyond the infinite brightness surrounding.

"Terrified?" Rolland answered sarcastically before thinking about the consequences of revealing such levity. Lights appeared from all around him revealing an octagon shaped room surrounded by a steel cage on all sides. "This can't be good."

From a small slit in the ceiling of the cage dropped an eight foot tall beast with foot long ivory tusks, a pig nose, crooked fanged teeth, and beady, yellow eyes that sat on both sides of his tan prune shaped face. In the great beasts hands was the longest battle axe that Rolland had ever seen, it's two sides curved in a sickeningly sharp prophecy of bloodshed and mayhem. Small spikes dotted the hilt of the axe, each glistening with a black substance that reeked of poison. Raising the weapon high above its head the beast swung wildly at Rolland, forcing him backward into one of the corners within seconds of its arrival into the octagon.

"This is neither here, nor there, nor anywhere," the baritone voice said, booming with tones that were both inside and outside of Rolland's head. "The Minotaur knows wait ails you, Rolland Wright."

They fought, man and beast, back and forth until Rolland was sweating as profusely as he ever had in his entire life. The monster before Rolland was neither man, nor bull, but an odd combination of both. What stood out the most, and gave Rolland the most cause for concern, were the large crooked horns that jettisoned up and outward above the creature's head, their pointed ends nearly clipping him on numerous occasions. There was little doubt in Rolland's mind that the strange booming voice was telling the truth, strange as it was he was facing a minotaur in hand to hand combat.

The Minotaur charged at him, missing by a mile as Rolland again dodged out of the way in a manner that would make Dodger proud. Then again, and again, and again, and again, and again. When the plan of wearing the beast out failed the teenage Wright thought quickly about the arsenal at his disposal. It was then, and only then, that he remembered that he could slow down time. He snapped his left thumb and forefinger together, which seemed to draw the Minotaur's attention.

Swing

The axe swung toward Rolland, missing his left hand by inches. Again the beast charged, forcing Rolland into a defensive position instead of an offensive one. His mind raced with times he lay awake at night, wishing for adventure, battle, and a life that included any combination of the two. But the reality was much,

much different than any fantasy. Thinking quickly he remembered his basic training from day one of the academy.

Step #1: Take stock of your situation. Find your strengths and rely on them.

"There's nothing," Rolland said under his breath, immediately wishing he had not for fear of being heard by the mocking voice from above. After a few beats of silence he realized that his luck would hold, at least when it came to his momentary pride, and decided to focus on taming the beast. But how, there was nothing but a cage that surrounded them with barely twenty feet of space to maneuver around to defend himself. Then, with a quick gamble he decided was worth the risk, Rolland decided not to run not away from the beast, but toward it, aiming for the monster's chest. Surprised by the offensive attack the Minotaur swung madly, and randomly in both all directions as he waited for the hit. Knowing in that moment that he had the beast outwitted, Rolland brought his hands together, snapped, and slowed time down around him.

Acting instinctively, Rolland took the long axe from the Minotaur's firm grasp, a task that forced him to literally climb up the beast's leg to gain enough strength to accomplish the task. It fell, along with him, to the ground, with a loud thud that left a bruise on his tailbone. Yet before he could stand, or even right himself, time corrected itself without his assistance, and the now unarmed Minotaur was aware of the different circumstances. Letting out a mighty roar the Minotaur lifted its muscle arms high, giving Rolland a clear shot at its chest. Rolland lunged the pointed end of the axe into the Minotaur's stomach, causing it to bend over in pain. The distraction allowed Rolland to spin around onto his feet, lift the axe and swing it directly into the Minotaur's back. With another bellow of pain the Minotaur fell to its knees before crumpling into a quivering heap of fur and flesh.

Backing away as far and as quick as his aching muscles would let him, Rolland leaned back on his elbows until his head met the floor and he closed his eyes. Still breathing hard, Rolland only saw the faintest blur of brown as something else dropped into the cage alongside of him. Startled, he looked up to see not another monster of ancient lore, but a man. Simply a man.

The stranger was tall, African American, and in his mid to late sixties based on the graying of his short hair. He had a thin, black mustache that spilt over his lips and pooled in a patchy, somewhat gray area around his chin.

"What, what was that?" Rolland asked, his sweat drenched shirt clinging to his chest like glue to paper. "Why was it in here? What - what is all of this?

"You ask a lot of questions. I am Captain Nareau," the booming voice stated bluntly as the man's lips moved. The stranger offered Rolland a hand to assist him to his feet, which Rolland accepted, bending his sore knees as he did.

"Why are you-?" Rolland asked before having the wind knocked out of him by the strangers fist.

"Hesitation," Captain Nareau quipped. "Hesitation is what almost just got you killed."

Annoyed beyond words at both his failure to control the situation, and be lectured about it by his supposed 'mentor' Rolland focused all of his energy on his breathing - not on the building rage bubbling inside of him, as he struggled to his feet.

"You're upset. Good," Nareau offered with a crooked, wily smile. "As well you should be. Failure can make us either angry or stupid. Your father was.."

"I am NOT my fucking father!" Rolland shouted, his ears burning with a fireball of frustration and rage.

Unfazed by his protégé's outburst, Captain Nareau wheeled around the room behind Rolland, letting the pot simmer a bit before elevating the steam of emotions. "You're right about that, young pup."

The pet name, which Rolland found as insulting as the constant comparisons to his father Scott, was in the middle of working on a personal insult to sling back at the Captain when he was interrupted yet again.

"Your father was not half the man you are," Captain Nareau stated flatly, much to Rolland's surprise. Not only was it the first and only compliment that the man had paid to him since their time together began, but it was also the first time that anyone besides Rolland himself had spoken ill of Scott Wright. The warm fuzzy feelings did not last long, however. "Or ever could be even with the proper training. You're an amateur at the moment. Unmolded clay."

Swaying a bit where he stood, Rolland wondered to himself where all of this was going. So lost in thought was he that he completely missed the room change again from a octagonal steel cage back to the dimly lit warehouse it resembled from the outside. A large chair stood off to the side next to what looked like a very old computer the size of an old telephone booth.

"But you've got one thing going for you - you're the most powerful time traveler ever born. It would take a complete fool to miss that," Nareau said in a voice that sounded more like an accusation than a compliment.

"Huh?" Rolland asked ungraciously. He had heard this before, as Turtledove had said something very similar to the Council of

Light during his trial weeks ago. "How could you or anyone know that?"

Captain Nareau stared at Rolland Wright with the same look in his eyes a cat would a strange bug that crossed its path. In studying the boy the grizzled old sailor saw many qualities that stood out; some good, some bad, some indifferent. Yet the one that stuck out the most, the one that he made him and all other empathically linked humanoids was the golden hue that seemed to surround the teenage Wright, clinging to his skin. There was no denying that the Time Stream itself ran through his veins, giving him access to great power.

"My what?" Rolland asked skeptically after Nareau explained.

"The glow that surrounds you, the hum of your soul. Surely you know what I'm talking about.." Nareau said again in a tone that mixed two expectations.

"You're messing with me again, right?" Rolland asked, his nerves almost settled.

"See your Pop, well, he used to be able to follow the Time Stream and manipulate it a little bit. Think he capped out at two hundred years into Earth's past," Captain Nareau said as he fiddled rather clumsily with what looked like an old barber's chair attached to numerous cables, hoses, and chords that ran the length of the room back to the door in which Rolland came. "You though, you appear to have more control over time. Which is good because this is a fight between you and it - never forget that."

"I don't.. understand," Rolland admitted, slumping his shoulders as he did so. Perhaps it was this sign of exasperated submission that caused Nareau to soften his stance, or perhaps it was something that reminded the old man of Scott Wright, either way the iron fist of discipline that he had displayed since Rolland walked in slacked, never to be tightened again. For this was not just another pupil, this was Scott and Taylor Wright's son.

"It's the difference between fighting with one hand, and fighting with two," Captain Nareau stated.. "Scottie was good, but in the end he was only able to fight with one hand. You kid, you're not only using both hands, you've got fuckin' lobster claws."

"Lobster claws? What the fuck?" Rolland said, more than a bit dumbfounded. Being compared to fish was one of the last things he expected to happen this evening, but perhaps only secondary to fighting a Minotaur hand to hand.

"Don't like lobster claws?" Captain Nareau asked, brushing the seat of the chair off before straitening the cushion that adorned the center. "How about pinchers?"

"Here, watch this for a minute," the Captain said before pressing the play button on a nearby VCR, prompting the large screen beside it to spring to life. Rolland watched as a young man his own age appeared on the screen. He immediately recognized the teenager as his father, Scott.

"This was his first day, the cheeky bastard." Captain Nareau said, crossing his arms.

Images sprang to life on the screen before them, filling their senses with sight and sound. The young Scott took a defensive position, just like Rolland did. Scott had just taken a large swing, followed by a large miss. In a manner very similar to the one that had just befallen him, Scott went through the motions of losing his balance, being caught by the giant hand, and beaten mercilessly by the beast. Much to his delight, however, Scott did not handle the entire ordeal nearly as well as he had. Quite the contrary, the young Scott Wright on the videotape was clumsy, stubborn, and stormed off in a huff after a much younger Captain Nareau revealed himself.

"Any questions so far?" Captain Nareau asked, no part of his face moving a millimeter as he spoke.

"Yeah," Rolland said, knowing right away that he shouldn't, but could not resist himself. "Who owns a VCR anymore?"

Expecting another beat down for his insolence, or at the very least a 'firm reminder' as Sgt. Tillman put it, Rolland was pleasantly surprised when he heard Captain Nareau chuckle instead. "Just watch it, smart ass."

Yet when the tape was over Rolland felt no sense of comfort or happiness from knowing he was not the first in his family to suffer an indignation at the hands of Captain Nareau.

"Why did you show me that?" Rolland asked, deciding to level with the larger than life man standing before him.

"To show you what he was," Captain Nareau began, walking behind Rolland, his arms crossed behind him in a military taught fold.

"The Academy told you that you would be broken, well with me you will be split further," Captain Nareau said, elbowing Rolland directly in his left pectoral, which left a stinging sensation reverberating throughout his whole body. "And before you ask, yes, I will be training you harder than I did your father."

The words were straight and to the point, meant to hit a nerve and force a reaction out of the boy, but they did not. Much to the surprise of the good Captain Nareau, the boy seemed to care little for his father's memory, or any comparison to him. He took a mental note of this, remembering to use a different motivational facet in the future. For now tough, a simple shift in priority would suffice.

"Say goodbye to your free time, goodbye to your life outside of training," Nareau stated, pressing a button before walking off and out of a previously unseen door. "I'll be seeing you, Pinchers."

"Well hoo-ray," Rolland said sarcastically and under his breath. A small victory, if you could even call it that. But one of many that he knew would be his in the weeks, and months to come. With a heavy heart he wandered through the dark warehouse back to the door that led to the street.

Once outside the night air hit Rolland's face with its crisp autumn chill, causing him to shiver with a deep sense of cold that shook him to the soul. Gone was the humidity of the day, replaced with something else. So too had something changed inside of Rolland. Eden was turning out to be a bigger web of intrigue than he had originally thought, and that was with a full on Eden media blackout that was mandatory at the Academy of Light. But as long as no one else found out about his new nickname of 'Pinchers' he figured he would be all right.

Prowler

Eden - Night

Gwendolyn had started the day envious of her other classmates, most of which already knew who their mentors would be, and what location they would be reporting for duty. As the day lingered, and she was still not given her assignment, she began to worry that she may have been forgotten. This sense of doom only grew when the Eden Detectives arrived, each dressed in their casual, yet still very professional looking suit and ties. It wasn't long before she was called to accompany them, the feeling in the pit of her stomach growing from bad to worse. When one abruptly left she was left alone with the sterner looking of the two, not knowing what was in store for her next; a stranger in a strange land.

Night in Eden was a time of great movement amongst the roving beasts of the field that called the forest home. Although the open area that encompassed roughly twenty miles around Eden Town Proper, the Academy of Light, Halls of Time, and the Blackard Family Orchard contained a paved, lit street made of cobblestones and cement, it was far from civilized or safe. Travelers were as conspicuous as could be due to the rare animal or dark creature that would venture out into the open. Though, more often than not it was an Elemeno on its way to or from the Solomon Forest. On this night, however, the creatures coming from the forest were an older, silver haired human man named Samuel Bigott and his twenty four year old Nocturn protégé, Gwendolyn Murrow.

As they approached their target site, the Holmes Estate, the two figures emerged from their place in the darkness, onto the overly manicured lawn, just next to the patch of Tiffany Holmes prized azaleas. It made Samuel sick to his stomach to think that these people were running the world, and held sway over literally millions of people, Nocturns, Merpeople, and Elemenos. A good thing Bigott thought, for those comfortable with such oppression rarely make it to life's final act. He looked over to Gwendolyn, so young and so fair, before nodding twice.

"You know your assignment," Detective Samuel Bigott said while raising an eyebrow. "Don't muck it up or we'll both have trouble."

Gwendolyn nodded before she rose silently into the air and curved, gliding in to the open window that belonged to Thaddeus and Tiffany Holmes. Inside the point of view was a world away from the savagery that was the wild Eden night. The walls were bare except for a few framed pictures and knick knacks that the lady of the house no doubt put up to fill a void she could not describe. The walls were painted puce, and the floor was carpeted in a plush, fine velvet material that Gwendolyn yearned to touch as she hovered nearly three feet above it. Yet none of it compared to the treasure near the back of the room. There, nearest the closet, measuring at least seven feet long was a pristine mahogany and glass display case. It was not very high, which forced Gwendolyn to lower her hovering distance from the floor. Regardless, based on the treasures in front of Gwendolyn she was beginning to see the reason for their high social standing. There before her, nestled snugly on a royal purple velvet blanket that covered the entire bottom of the glass display case, were coins, paper dollars, and assorted currency from over one hundred different countries, time periods, and cultures throughout Earth and Eden's histories.

The gold coins glinted in the light of the stray moonbeams as Gwendolyn lifted her jaw back to her mouth. Next to the various monies were solid gold bars, each the size of a child's shoebox. The bars were stacked and lined the entire back of the display case as a sort of anchor for the collection. Silver pieces featuring the imprinted silhouettes of political leaders not taught in Nocturn schools caught her eye as the various sizes and conditions seemed random at best. The paper money, divided by color and country of origin, featured no bill smaller than one hundred, and there seemed to be more of these than anything besides the piles of gold. Copper, the least precious of the metals featured, played a prominent role in the older coins, each of which had a faded infinity symbol, strange, non-human eye, and a chipped edge in three places.

Breaking from her trance, Gwendolyn was brought back to her task by the sound of an owl hooting outside the open window accompanied with the rolling over of Thaddeus in his bed. Keeping as silent as she could, the floating Nocturn woman lowered herself to the point of being directly above the display, breathed heavily upon it until a fine steam revealed the single laser that represented the haphazard alarm system Thaddeus installed, and with cat-like precision she proceeded to open the latch and slide open the glass door above the treasures. Lowering her hand into it, she selected a single gold coin and a piece of the purplish green paper that had a man's face she didn't recognize on it.

In fact, Gwendolyn barely recognized any of the money in the display case. So vast was the collection, spanning thousands upon thousands of years, that it defied even the written record of her own people. Her mind wandered back to the blind school-teachers back home, and how the historians among them would find this treasure trove of history quite fascinating. Another turn of the restless Thaddeus in his bed gave Gwendolyn a start, causing her to lift her arm out of the display case awkwardly, and for the lid to fall shut, letting out a small but very distinctive *snap*.

"Hmmm?" Thaddeus Holmes said while simultaneously sitting up in bed. He looked around, thinking he had heard something impossible but saw no one and nothing to give him pause. The window was still open from earlier when his wife's new hair product had caused their master bedroom to fill with the vomit-inducing stench of cinnamon and barley. Throwing off the blanket that warmed him, he bent his naked knees before rolling a bit into a sitting position on the edge of the bed. Standing up, he rubbed his eyes lazily before sauntering over to the far side of his room closest to the closet. There, lying as peacefully as it had ever been, were his families treasures, the pride and joy of the Holmes estate. Feeling pleased by their security, Thaddeus turned around, headed back to bed, and was asleep again within a matter of moments - never bothering to look directly above him at the prowler Gwendolyn Murrow as she hugged the ceiling and wished for the best.

After waiting for what felt like an eternity Gwendolyn lowered herself and made a straight shot for the window in which she had come, eyeing Detective Bigott still standing where he had been since they arrived.

"Is this is?" Gwendolyn asked, tossing the coin wrapped in purple paper down to Detective Bigott who caught it, turned it over, and shook his head.

"No," he whisper shouted, his left hand cupped over his mouth to slightly amplify it over the slight, random winds that separated the two. As Gwendolyn watched him she lowered herself closer, until she too was standing instead of hovering. "I told you, grab the ones with Andrew Jackson on them. It has the number twenty on it."

"I don't know who Andrew Jacks is," Gwendolyn said through shallow breaths. Although she was back on the ground she was still more than a little jumpy and paranoid about the slightest noise or movement, two things for which the Eden night had no shortage of.

"It's Jackson, Andrew Jackson," Detective Bigott grumbled through a clenched jaw. From what little he knew of his assigned protégé there was a good, direct connection between herself and the rebel known as Rolland Wright; whose name was now as synonymous with Jackson as Kennedy was with Castro. While Bigott wasn't 100% sure what Rolland was up to, he knew enough about the measure of a man's family to wager that with enough surveillance he could discover something illicit, if not illegal, to report to the Council of Light. Still, that might alienate Samuel from Gwendolyn, and his first responsibility was to see to her education. No, he wouldn't risk that. "Just forget about it."

"I'm sorry," Gwendolyn said solemnly, her big, round eyes slightly watering due to the stronger winds, adding to the effect of a warrior princess set against the backdrop of the double moonlight.

"There's nothing to be sorry for," Detective Bigott said, holding up his right hand in a stopping motion. A second later it held the coin, again wrapped in the now crinkled paper note, which he threw upward back to the spot where Gwendolyn had begun to hover above him. "It was my own fault. Now run this back up to where you found it and let's get us out of here before first sunlight."

"Yes sir," Gwendolyn said before levitating higher, rising the thirteen feet to the Holmes' second story master bedroom window before disappearing inside. After placing the money back where she had found it, the young Nocturn turned back around toward the window and moved onward before turning to look at the sleeping master & mistress of the house one last time. Tiffany's nose was narrow, like Tina's, and Timothy shared his father's widow's peak hairline. Gwendolyn wondered silently to herself if she could abstain from mentioning such hereditary abnormalities the following day when she saw the snoring couple's offspring. Another shift from Thaddeus startled her into action, and with a click of her heels Gwendolyn shot out of the room with a completely silent, yet lightening quick speed that put her classmate Jaime to shame.

Watching his pupil complete her nightly mission Detective Bigott nodded in proud approval. He thought Gwendolyn was a fine young woman, courageous, astute, and wise beyond her years. What he feared, however, was not the talents she possessed, but the company she kept. It was no secret that her class had the lowest expectations among the academy's faculty, with all but a few expecting them to fail or quit outright before the first term was over. Not Samuel though. After only spending a little bit of time with Gwendolyn he had decided that she was the future of this world. With the wind whispering sweet nothings of revolution and unrest among Eden's populace Bigott knew that everyone would soon have a part to play. Gwendolyn would be his to mold into the soldier she had to become in order to survive, a process he had gone through with many students over the years to great success. He thought of one in particular, his favorite trainee who ever came through the Academy, as he watched Gwendolyn leave the window of the Holmes estate once again, and wondered, silently, where Persephone Kelly found herself on this starless evening.

Puddles

Eden

Kniff hated humidity. Humans never understood how too much of a good thing simply ruined whatever it was one began with; to them, he presented the foul beast known as humidity. Land seemed always full of the thick, noxious, sticky mist that filled the air yet was invisible to the inferior human eye. Yet Kniff could see the humidity that clung to his skin in a thin film as the late afternoon was a particularly rough time walking on dry land for MerPeople. Even the brass knocker at the gate of Eden Town Proper was hot to the touch. With a knock he made his presence known, prompting the guard on duty to allow him passage inside. He felt the air around him raise what felt like another five degrees as he crossed the threshold into the city. Perhaps he was being a bit dramatic, but Kniff really hated humidity.

As the ramparts that held up the guard station gave way to a city sidewalk below his feet, Kniff walked along the now familiar path to Eden's courthouse. Having grown up as a child of a diplomat of the MerPeople, he had taken many trips to and from Eden's capital city, with most of the time during those trips being spent in the courthouse, and exploring the basements for untold treasures, though the most valuable thing he had ever found was an old pair of maintenance work boots. After he entered the courtyard and walked up the courthouse steps Kniff took the elevator to the third floor where he knew his appointment was to take place. Exiting the elevator he stepped over the patch of floor where old shag carpet gave way to plush, velvety soft flooring as the inner domain of Councilman Thaddeus Holmes beckoned Kniff to come closer.

To Kniff's surprise the usual secretary was absent from her place outside of Councilman Holmes's office, replaced instead with an unwelcoming brown leather chair and empty wooden desk. Before he could contemplate this, however, the door behind the desk opened, and the invitee of the meeting emerged.

"Ah Mr. Youngblood," Thaddeus Holmes said with an air of noxious superiority. "Come in then, won't you."

Obeying, Kniff walked past the secretary's desk through the door and into an office that was smaller than he imagined. Books lined the shelves to his left, all of which were in meticulous alphabetical order. To Kniff's right was a dark brown painted wall adorned with various plaques and a couple university degrees. The largest of which had the words **'University of Eden'** stamped across the top in bright red letters.

"I'd offer you some refreshment but my secretary is out today," Councilman Holmes said as he shuffled past the sitting Kniff to a very fine looking black leather office chair with small silver buttons adorning the inside of its armrests. His desk, unlike his former assistants, was full of clutter. Pictures of his wife, Timothy, and Tina Holmes sat on the far side closest to the guest chairs across from the desk.

"What can I do for you, councilman?" Kniff asked, his weariness clouding his judgment as the words spilled from his mouth.

"Right to the point then, I like that," Councilman Holmes said smiling wolfishly. "It's come to my attention that you have certain ties to the Mer royal family."

"One could say that, considering the Queen is my sister by blood," Kniff said automatically, stating a fact that both men knew the other was aware of before it was mentioned out loud. It wasn't enough that his family was a spectacle under the sea; he had grown accustomed to the media frenzy down there. But on land.. well, Kniff thought it would be different up on land as most dwellers had never taken interest in the political hierarchy of the MerPeople. Oddly, most folks above the surface were obsessed with questions pertaining to a debate over fins vs. legs and which were more practical in water. "What interest have you in my sister?"

"A great interest," Councilman Holmes said. "The Council has big plan for Eden's improvement and a big part of that is interspecies relations between humans and Merpeople. Don't you agree that would be beneficial?"

"I do, but if you'll excuse me I need to get to a meeting with my ment-" said Kniff before being cut off as he stood.

"Your mentor looks otherwise preoccupied," Thaddeus said, motioning toward the window.

The courtyard below was green with plants and flowers that were pleasing to the eye, and in the center stood what looked like a tall man wearing a gray cowboy hat, holding a pistol, and shooting tin cans that were lined up in a row roughly one hundred yards away at the end. One by one Kniff watched them fall, each in a different direction and performing a different 'trick' as they were shot. One flew straight up in the air so high that the next two were already at a complete stop by the time it did.

"Might I propose that you start thinking about your future in Eden?" asked Councilman Holmes from behind Kniff.

"I have," Kniff said, turning back to face his classmate's father. "That's why I am attending the Academy of Light this term."

"I mean after the academy," Councilman Holmes stated patiently. "You don't have to return to the sea, you know. You could come work for Councilman Varejao, or myself, if you wish."

There it was. While Kniff knew that most land dwellers did not take interest in his royal connections, he suspected that someone in the Eden government might try to use them to their advantage. At least this proposal was merely one of employment, a contractual partnership that he could void at any time. This case was much simpler than the ties that come along with a marriage proposal - which is by far the MerPeople's favorite means to solidify a contractual obligation or bloodline.

"There are benefits to working for me, " Thaddeus said, motioning to a picture of his daughter, Tina, that sat on the far corner of his desk. "Some more personal than others."

"My people are a proud race," Kniff said, straightening his back and puffing his chest a bit as he spoke. "We do not accept bribes, carnal or otherwise."

"You've mistaken my kindness for flattery, Youngblood," Thaddeus stated bluntly, all kindness forgotten. A fire had ignited in his eyes that eclipsed all that surrounded them. "You are here at my pleasure and I will not hesitate to end your land visa if you prove unworthy of my invitation. Do I make myself clear, cadet?"

Kniff was furious. He mentally added Councilman Holmes to list of things he hated. Why hadn't Tina told him what a jackass her father was? The rage inside of Kniff was so powerful he feared that a bit of steam might escape from his ears or the gills located behind them. When a few minutes passed without another word the Councilman broke the stare between the two, picked up a nearby pen, and began signing his signature to a series of documents sitting near the picture of Tina.

"You may go," Thaddeus Holmes said curtly while waving his hand in dismissal, his eyes not moving from the papers.

Without another word Kniff stood, turned, and walked out of the office, through reception area, to the path that led to the courtyard behind the building. With his mind still on the infuriating confrontation with the councilman, Kniff didn't even notice the first couple of bullets whiz by his head.

Sting

The strange noise made Kniff turn his head to see the man in the cowboy hat still holding the pistol, only this time it was pointed directly at him.

Sting

Acting instinctively Kniff ducked down, scraping his knee on the concrete walkway as he did. He then crawled behind the nearest bush, dropping his daily schedule as he did. Doubling back he grasped it before rolling over behind the bush for safety. The man who was listed on his schedule was a legend amongst the Eden bar scene, but those folks were mainlanders who didn't know a gill from a hole in the ground. Word around town was that Lt. Jessie James was a bit of a ladies' man, gambler, and the poster child for the fringe wing of Eden's bureaucracy. Another whistle in the wind rang out overhead and Kniff decided to act.

Sting

The bullet sang through the afternoon air like lightening as Kniff rose to his feet. He immediately wished he hadn't as the bullet found its target - the top of his right shoulder. Blood poured from the wound quicker than he anticipated, causing him to fall into a large puddle and to scrape his other knee in the process. Between nursing his wound, and concentrating on breathing, Kniff barely noticed that his assailant had approached him.

"You could have killed me," Kniff complained, his indignation knowing no bounds as the man in the gray felt cowboy hat came within five feet. The man laughed, shook his head, and again stared off into the distance before answering in a curt, yet polite "If I wanted you killed, then you'd be dead. This was more of an initiation of sorts."

When the armed stranger looked down again, the Merman's eyes were already set upon his, biding their time. An intimidating tactic to other humans, Kniff found the strategy quite useful on dry land despite the fact that his eyes would not moisturize themselves like they did under the sea. This stare down did nothing to the man holding the revolver, however, as outlaws of the American Old West rarely backed down from a good, old-fashioned duel.

"Professor..?" Kniff asked, his throat dry as a bone. It had been so long, years even since he was rendered speechless that he was stymied as to what to say. "You are Professor James.. right?"

The armed stranger smiled, his toothy grin on display as he holstered his weapon on his right hip. He wore a casual uniform similar to the one Kniff had seen on General Falocco years ago, but could not place the rank from his point of view on the ground, and the stranger did not offer to help him to his feet. So, Kniff continued to sit, childlike, and wait for an answer.

"I am, I suppose," he said sheepishly. "But I prefer my military rank if it pleases you."

"Which would be..?" Kniff asked.

"Lieutenant Jesse James," the man said, smiling at the sound of his own name. "And you, sea boy, you think you're kinda special, huh? Don't look like much to me, cowering in a puddle of your own sorrow."

"I beg your pardon?" Kniff asked, his day not going at all like he had hoped.

"I'm going to call you Puddles," Lt. James said with a toothy, uninhibited smile that unnerved his potential protégé to no end.

"What the hell does that," Kniff began but stopped himself before he could continue his sentence. "Will that - be all, sir?"

No stranger to encounters with Merpeople, Lieutenant James also knew better than to mince words with the likes of Kniff. Still, he felt like he had driven the point of tough love home for the day. With a small nod of his head Lt. James ended their introductions with a breezy, "Dismissed."

And then, lying there in the courtyard, his shoulder bleeding from a grazed bullet, Kniff decided that he now hated three things: humidity, Councilman Holmes, and Lt. Jesse James.

Ponies

The elegance of a unicorn is almost indescribable for those who have never seen the wonder for themselves. With its graceful nature and near unending capacity for majesty the unicorn had come to symbolize everything that was right with the world in the mind of a young Tina Holmes. As a child, she would sneak out of her window every evening to watch as the four-legged wonders made their nightly sojourn back to their stables on the grounds of the Halls of Time. Her fascination with the unicorns was more than a small part of why she decided to join the Knights of Time and now with the sudden addition of the Rolland Wright seemed to further strengthen her conviction to join the group.

On this day, however, Tina did not feel such conviction, as it was the first day of her meeting with her mentor. Despite her excitement at discovering that the meeting place were the unicorn stables, the thick, black, **"TBA"** letters on the piece of paper in her hand seemed ominous and forbidding to the teenage girl. In that moment she regretted the tantrum she threw to her father the day he knocked on her bedroom door asking about her education. After insisting that she wanted to be treated like any other cadet at the academy Tina recalled how she stood straight up, looked her father dead in the eye, and the proceeded to reveal the worst kept, though long suspected secret of her young life; she wished to join the Knights of Time. Feeling obligated to pull at least some strings for his little girl Thaddeus obliged with the secret hope that her familial ties would alienate her enough for her to quit outright herself. Yet the summation of his efforts, the internship as the Jr. Communications officer that opened when Taylor Wright was killed, brought with it an unexpected result. As fate would have it, another young would-be member joined the Knights, and with him came any hopes that Tina would ever be anything but a Knight of Time. It was only while Rolland was away, those many nights spent half scheming a way to go visit him in jail, that she allowed herself to remember the feelings of isolation she had before they met.

Deciding to cast thoughts those thoughts aside Tina made her way deeper into the valley outside of the Halls of Time where the unicorn stables stood uninterrupted and empty. The pleasant sunshine bathed the teenage beauty in a warmness that seemed to fill every pore of her skin, and every crevice of her heart. Shaking aside her concerns, Tina had a sudden idealistic burst of enthusiasm for what her training would be like, as well a boy-friend whom she perceived every other girl her age was jealous of. In that moment, Tina Leigh Holmes was happy, truly happy. Another gust of wind blew up her khaki shorts, hitting her upper thigh playfully as she leaned against a wooden fence. Nearby a unicorn whinnied, followed by another in a long, drawn out call of friendship. She smiled, and as she adjusted her light blue blouse the unmistakable sounds of footsteps greeted her ears.

"Excuse me," a voice belonging to a curly haired brunette woman in a lab coat said as she made her way up the far side of the hill to the stables. In her right hand was a clipboard, coat breast pocket a series of pens in various colors, and maroon scrubs poking out from underneath it all.

"Doctor Duffy!" Tina exclaimed, taken aback by the presence of not only one of her father's co-workers, but also one of her personal heroes. "I uh..."

"Are you the new intern?" Doctor Duffy asked, not bothering to look up from her clipboard to acknowledge Tina's exact presence. Yet another added benefit of wanting to be treated like just another cadet.

"Yes, Doctor," Tina said with the utmost respect to her voice. This gamble paid off immediately as Duffy raised her head, cocked her left eyebrow, and thought for a long moment before realizing just exactly whom it was she was speaking to.

"I know you from somewhere," Doctor Duffy said more to herself than to Tina. The look they exchanged made Tina feel as if she were a particularly interesting specimen that had crossed the good doctors path before being fitted for her microscope. "You used to hang out by the court house. Back when you were smaller.

Played with a boy your age, as I recall. Were good with the animals back then too, the birds and such. Not the boy though. He was cruel and uncaring. You, though, girl, you exude a kind spirit."

"Yes, councilwoman, my name is," Tina began but was interrupted.

"No, I don't want to know your name," Doctor Duffy said curtly. "Too often we are judged not by the content of our character, but by the associations that come from our birth. No. I have my suspicions on who you are already, but I'll reserve final judgments until after I learn more about you. For now I shall call you.. Ponies."

"That's, uh, generous of you," Tina said nervously. Without looking Tina stepped in a large patch of unicorn dung, which squished and spread itself onto the bottom of her shoe like paste. Despite Tina hating her new nickname she felt that in time it could become a term of endearment, despite her unicorn feces fueled humiliation.

Slightly amused by this, Doctor Duffy smiled to herself as the young intern struggled wit her footwear. In examining her surroundings more closely the scientist in her saw ample opportunity to learn something new about unicorns, and the teacher in her saw a means by which to test her new charge. A fresh chorus of unicorn whinnies gave rise to her first question. With that in mind she asked "Tell me about these unicorns."

"That's Comet," Tina said, catching her breathe as she knocked still more mud off of her left boot. "He's got a really bad attitude, so I had to put him in the same pen as the only other corn he gets along with, Blitzen."

"Oh?" Doctor Duffy inquired with a smile. Although she had known the factoid for nearly seven months the conclusion took her twice as long to deduce. A clever little intern indeed. "I have a question, Ponies."

"Yes Doctor?" Tina asked, her razor sharp mind kicking into action at the prospect of flexing her strongest muscle.

"Your hypothesis about the patterns displayed in the outer coat of Elemenos in relation to their geographic location of origin were quite fascinating." Shannon Duffy said, walking at a moderately brisk pace in relation to her much younger potential pupil toward the aforementioned pair of unicorns. "Tell me, how did you come to that conclusion?"

"Oh, uh, well..." Tina began, feeling positively redundant in her hero's presence and full extent of her intellect. "It was your theories that led me to it, Doctor Duffy."

"My theories?" Dr. Duffy asked Tina, petting Blitzen on the top of the head above her nose. She had expected a dense girl of privilege, not a smart young woman who wasn't afraid to challenge authority. "Elaborate, immediately."

Not knowing whether this was a request or a demand the nervous Tina elaborated on her findings, much to the good doctors delight. "The expedition you did when you followed Eden's spotted timber owls. In your field journal you wrote that as you followed the tagged birds south the newer ones that you encountered had more spots than the ones you had followed since the beginning. I thought that if that pattern held with all animals indigenous to the region."

"I remember that expedition well," Doctor Duffy said in a voice that was rich with nostalgia. "But you'd do well to remember that a pattern is three or more. But what you've found here, my dear, is not a pattern. Though I do not doubt that you your assumptions were done in the best spirit of tenacity. I admire that.

That's why I take my expeditions. I like to go out and study a new breed native to Eden one every eighteen months or so. Perhaps you'd like to accompany me on one of these studies some day."

Again the councilwoman's voice did not indicate if her statement was a question or an offer. This not only excited Tina, but drove her absolutely crazy as well.

"Please," Tina said, feeling as if she had no choice following her rant. "I apologize if-"

"No!" Doctor Duffy shouted, switching gears faster than Tina had expected. "Never apologize for your theories. In all truth I am but a bit embarrassed is all. Bad enough that you proved my theory on geographic Elemeno genealogy incorrect, and with who I suspect your father to be; well, you didn't have to prove to be SO much like me."

"I, uh, well..." Tina began before being stopped again mid-sentence.

"I didn't want to like you, Ponies, but I find that I have no choice. You're smart, assertive, and damn it, you're prettier than I was at your age. So fine, Ponies, you got me. I was wrong. " Dr. Duffy went on, only turning to face Tina once she was done speaking.

Tina's lower jaw dropped for the briefest of moments as she heard the words of praise tumble from her idol's lips. Never in her wildest dreams would she have expected this level of praise from THE head of the Academy of Light's Science Department, much less a councilwoman, or, on a much less professional level, a role model who she had been a long running feature as poster on her bedroom wall growing up.

"Thank you, Doctor Duffy." Tina said, almost by instinct. "I am honored by your kind words."

"Tomorrow, following your regular training with Sgt. Tillman you will report to my office for private tutorials for the rest of your term at the academy." Doctor Duffy stated, her tone changed back to its usual commanding presence, leaving behind no trace of the down to Earth individual who offered such unbridled honesty a mere minute before. "You might be my boss someday, but that doesn't mean I can't train you to be a good one."

Chapter 13:
Beware the Sheep

Marshall Island - 1937

At first Joan could not distinguish what was happening, the weight and emotional toil that was being forcibly taken by so many men at once leaving a scar that forever reverberated through her psyche. Flashes of a burning pyre blanketed her mind, filling her with fear. When finally, after what could have been either several minutes or merely a few seconds, Joan realized that she had fallen over on the trail back to the old barn where they had slept. She sat, her legs stretched out before her in a very juvenile fashion, looking up at a somewhat familiar face. Once again mixed emotions of wanting to trust the woman, yet also harboring an uneasy suspicion about her diced her insides, causing a stomach cramp to bellow ominously via her small intestine. A cough overhead, mixed with the sound of birds chirping snapped Joan back to a right, grounded, state of mind. Add to it the fact that this woman, this somewhat famous woman, Amelia Earhart, was there, standing before her, eager to be a supportive friend, and it was all simply too much for her to process. Exhaling disparagingly, feeling very French doing so, Joan stood, straightened her back until her chest stuck outward, and then turned to face the American pilot, sans white orb.

"I'm not," Joan began, distracted by the looseness of the skin on her arm due to the ravages of age. She thought, if ever so briefly, about telling her newfound companion about what she had just gone through, just in case it was a dream, but thought the better of it. Her mission, as Councilman Varejao had assigned it, was to retrieve Amelia Earhart, not to entrust her with any state, or personal, secrets. While she might be friendly and easy to talk to, there was something about the entire situation that still gave her pause. "I don't know what you're talking about."

"Oh," Amelia said, a bit taken aback, but only for about ten seconds before her hands raised to her hips, her weight shifted to her dominant, right foot, and her left eyebrow crooked upward. A slight, intent expression, complete with a closed, smirking mouth and casually accepting eyes flashed across Amelia's face, offering an olive branch of trust and new friendship. Unfortunately for both of them, Joan was not in the same headspace. "So it's going to be like that then?"

Feeling the tension, Joan decided the best thing to do was to change the subject. She looked around them at the little trail that she had been wandering down back to the barn when her... flashback... had happened. With the disjoined from reality feeling dissipating, and her brain becoming less foggy as the seconds went by, Joan said the first thing that popped into her time travel addled mind. "The sun came up."

"Yes it did, some time ago, actually," Amelia said, grasping Joan by the left shoulder in a poorly chosen, and poorly timed sense of wanting to connect. "What are you doing all the way out here, anyway?"

"I was..." Joan began, completely unsure as to how to finish her sentence. Should she lie, and tell Amelia, who she had just met, a complete fabrication of the truth? If she did, wouldn't that make her just like Sephanie? Would Amelia somehow feel betrayed by Joan's lie? Or, would her betrayal somehow be less serious because they had not been friends beforehand? These silly, seemingly random thoughts zigzagged like checker patterns through Joan's depression addled mind. Finally, Joan decided that a variation on the truth would suit her needs just fine, at least for the time being. "I saw something I didn't want to. What about you? What were you doing all the way out there?"

No sooner had the question been posed than both women were back on the trail that led to the barn where they camped the night before. Small clouds of dust from the dirt path kicked up around their four feet as they went along, passing deeper into the woods. As they double backed, passing within fifty yards of where Joan witnessed the aforementioned Fred Noonan's murder hours before, feelings of guilt and responsibility crashed with the secrecy of her knowledge. Pushing these thoughts aside as they went, Joan, averting her eyes from Amelia's searching ones, convinced herself her silence was for the best. Much to Joan's dismay, the female pilot noticed this unusual behavior and countered it with her own, slightly downtrodden, limp shouldered, morose way.

"Just looking for Fred," Amelia finally said, while stepping over a small, dried out creek bed. With the woods ending in an inclined clearing that slanted up a grassy hill, both women met it, stepping gingerly onto the evenly spaced cobble stoned steps that guided the path upward. Amelia, who had more experience with the land, was quicker for a change, her feet finding the right position on each stone as she effortlessly moved up the hill. Joan, whose mind was elsewhere, slipped several times, leaving a bruise on her right knee that would cause her a bit of pain in the days to follow. To Amelia's pleasant surprise the time traveler wasn't upset at this turn of events, but rather began to giggle softly to herself. Smiling, Amelia too joined in with Joan's laugh before extending her hand and offering her new friend up off of her feet. The two walked for a bit longer, perhaps five more minutes, before reaching another, steeper hill. This time they went up together and without incident. Upon reaching even footing, the pair found themselves within yards of their starting point, the old, abandoned, turn of the 20th century constructed wooden barn.

"Judah isn't here," Joan said as she made a quick assessment of both the inside and outside of the barn. The perimeter seemed clear, but with Judah nowhere to be seen it was just as likely they were about to step into a trap set by Otep or worse, by Sephanie. No sooner had those thoughts crossed Joan's mind that Amelia, oblivious to the larger, more political world around her, entered the barn without the slightest fear of possible danger. Sprinting after her charge, Joan raced into the old barn, skidding to a halt as she turned to see the reality of her perceived danger.

Nothing. There was nothing there besides a slightly confused, and a bit winded in the lungs looking Amelia Earhart.

"You sure you're alright?" Amelia asked, her doe eyes falling softly upon the windows of Joan's fractured soul.

In that moment again Joan was presented with an opportunity to come clean with her newfound friend. And, for a second time in no less than ten minutes, she chose not to take advantage of Amelia's kindness. Biting her bottom lip fiercely, Joan's cheeks turned a light shade of pink before she let out a small but firm response of, "I'm fine."

Abashed, and wanting to change the subject, Amelia nodded furiously before looking around the scarce barn for a distraction. It was minimalist, made out of old cheap wood that probably came from the hull of a retired naval ship from the 19th century. Amelia was just beginning to wonder what the name of said ship could be as she traced the wooden beams and planks that comprised the interior with her eyes, when Amelia noticed the pattern of two by three that the designer had used to interlock the wood to maximize efficiency. A good barn was like a plane engine, and for both symmetry was the key. It was with symmetry in mind that caused the pilot to approach the dust covered sign that hung roughly four and a half feet off of the wall on a rusted old nail and piece of string. There, in big, bold letters that were carved into the mahogany nearly a centimeter thick were the words:

BEWARE THE SHEEP

"That's hilarious," Joan said, nudging Amelia in the ribs and pointing to the old rustic sign. The Frenchwoman thought it a nice touch, and one desperately needed in such a morose environment. Although she had spent the night there something was rather unsettling about the place - almost as if it were haunted. It was exactly the kind of place Judah would have loved to spend an afternoon in trying to deduce its history, his morbid curiosity always getting the better of him.

"Yeah," Amelia agreed, looking around the far to the rest of the walls, and not seeing anything out of the norm. While grateful for this continuation of the norm, it yielded zero clues as to the ware bouts of the two gentlemen of their party. Displaying her worst habit for her newest friend Amelia began speaking on the topic mid-thought, leaving zero context for Joan to comprehend the topic at hand. "I'm pretty worried. I mean, they're... out there."

"Ohh no, not the sheep!" Joan said, rolling her eyes as her hand absentmindedly ran along the rotting wood that comprised the old structure. "Or, were you talking about the boys?"

The downtrodden look on Amelia's face struck Joan like a physical blow, straight to the heart. Hiding the truth was tantamount to a lie in her code of belief, a sin by which there was no penance, or forgiveness, given their still new friendship. A forced smile, a skewing of perspective, and Joan was back to her own set of half truths, her own impression of Sephanie. "I can only imagine what you're thinking. I've been thinking a lot about Judah, myself. Where do you think he went? I, I just... don't know. "

"You too are really crazy about each other huh?" Amelia asked, curious as to what true love might be like. Once upon a time she had thought that true love was something that presented itself in due course, but that was before her own love life turned out to be nothing more than a series of uninspired suitors. Even Fred Noonan had taken a shot at vying for Amelia's hand, yet she cared not for him, or anyone else she had ever met, in a romantic sense. She had thought she loved her husband, George, for a while but realized quickly that they did not share the kind of love people had like Joan and Judah. Knowing full well that her own happiness was not, nor should it be dependent on any other person, Amelia's attentions turned further toward the sky; further toward achieving new goals. Such things left little time for a love life.

"Yes," Joan answered, looking out the window at the clouds in the sky. "He promised to take me on a honeymoon after we complete this mission. All we've got to do is find some trigger. Merde, I'm only even telling you now because I feel a million leagues away from it. And Judah. Bloody hell!"

"I'm sure he and Fred are alright," Amelia offered, more than a few questions racing through her own mind. The mention of the word 'trigger' in particular peaked her interest, as she too was assigned a similar chore before departing across the deep blue sea to chase history. Like Joan she too held worry within her heart for her co-pilot, Fred Noonan, but it was not a romantic, or familiar concern. She let it fade from her mind as she opened her mouth to speak again, but was cut off by the taller blonde woman.

"Sure," Joan said to her new friend with a meek smile that they both knew to be but a kind social gesture. While Joan wasn't sure of why exactly Amelia had to be extracted from time, she knew enough about Varejao then to ask too many questions. Because of this, she did not know the extent of Amelia's abilities, or even what they were. Yet in this moment both seemed to be of one thought, the two kindred spirits met somewhere between women's intuition, and a hive mindset to find strength against a looming threat, still unseen. "But as soon as we find them we need to begin looking for the trigger. We're already behind, and I really want to know where it's located."

"I too would like to know that information," said the deep, rich voice of the former Egyptian priest as he made his way into the old Winston barn. His black hair was loose, falling upon his broad shoulders. His beard, which was neatly trimmed with pinpoint precession, had been shaved into the form of dual flames on each side of the bottom of his cheeks. Odd enough, the flames had been enchanted somehow to move independently, creating the illusion that his facial hair was indeed harboring within it some ancient fire to be feared. The robes he wore were long, fine silk, black, and as ornamental as either woman had ever seen.

"Otep," Joan said flatly. Her feet took a fighting stance, planting themselves firmly with the tips of her toes facing her opponent. "What are you doing here?"

"I was sent to serve at my master's behest," Otep retorted, his long fingers flexing sporadically within the palms of both of his hands. He watched the pair of women with a mixture of curiosity, and contempt. His pity of them, their mortal coil and imperfect genetic make-up, was tantamount to the pity he might hold for an orangutan, or domestic housecat. In such he wished them no ill will, but would not go out of his way to ensure their safety. "But you appear comely enough. I am always in the market for new concubines; should you wish you submit an application."

"Joan," Amelia said, "Who the heck is this guy?"

Cocking his head slightly to the right, Otep examined Amelia for a long moment, taking her in fully with his tar colored eyes. Thinking that Otep was most likely given a similar assignment to herself in retrieving the American pilot, Joan did not like the way he was staring at her at all. To her great surprise, however, the man with the dark complexion did not linger his attention on either woman, but instead took in his complete surroundings in silence. Which, as it would turn out for the women, would be a critical mistake.

With a peaceful, yet ominous concentration the dark pupils in the center of both of Otep's eyes began to rotate slightly counter-clockwise, creating a small, but steady buzzing within his head. In a low voice, he began to speak in a harsh language that neither Joan nor Amelia understood.

"*Vah rooma moonchique ceroque!*"

Standing roughly eight feet away from the Egyptian priest Joan recognized the early signs of an attack only too late. As it was, the running spin kick that connected with the center of Otep's chest was enough to stop what she guessed to be the second wave of the beasts that were responsible for the ground rumbling. Landing on her feet Joan spun around in time to see that all around Otep the ground shook violently, cracking and breaking at the seams while scattering bits of dirt into the chasms created between them. Though Otep's clothes grew dirty due to the dirt in the air, his mind was clean and his concentration true. The task at hand was clear to Otep, and one he had performed thousands of times in his life; to raise the dead.

"Let us see how meager you seem when dealing with the full force that is the undead," the necromancer proclaimed, his arms sprawled outward as the wind caught his long, straight black hair from falling on his shoulders and face as his silent spells rang out through the heavens, lying waste to all in their path. In his own mind he was all powerful, regardless of what reality told him. Soon the two women would be dead, and he could curry more favor with his master. A smug, satisfied smile appeared on the ancient Egyptian's face, sparking a fresh bout of unease in Joan Raines' stomach. All of this he did, without even standing up.

From the bowels of the Earth came the cries and scratching of the souls once laid to rest lifetimes before. Jagged claws flew this way and that in a flurry of undead fury between two women and a small army of giant crustaceans, formerly of the crab variety. As tree roots and stones caught onto lifeless limbs the creative method by which Otep built his madness became apparent, as the massive crabs' legs, each measuring at least three feet long, unhinged before latching onto the Earth beside them, and forcefully pulling what remained of their physical bodies up from the ground like common carrots. The process worked for some, but not all, as several of the unnatural creatures disintegrated themselves doing this, with a few ripping their legs clean off before lying upside-down, legs kicking furiously.

Amelia was confused, but that was becoming a trend since she met Joan and her husband. What was disconcerting though, was the fact that not only was the ground shaking beneath her, but that something, or rather multiple something's, were frantically clawing their way out from several evenly spaced holes breaking through the impacted Earth by her feet. Bits of old bone, tattered flaps of rotted flesh, and darkened shells appeared in clumps of viciousness complete with claws that seemed to sharpen in death. "What in the blue hell?"

But no sooner was Joan prepared to answer than their problem doubled in the form of a small army of very much alive coconut crabs, each fully grown to their four by three foot size with large, jagged claws clasping away at the air between them. Upon locking eyes with the two women the first group of twenty of the beasts let out a blood-curdling, unified screech of unbridled terror.

"Stop this now Otep!" Joan screamed, turning around expecting the dark skinned man to be gloating. But the necromancer was gone, replaced by nearly a two dozen undead, re-animated zombie coconut crabs, all of which wanted nothing more than to feed off of the two women until they joined their ranks. *"Merde."*

Although the coconut crabs started their attack off slowly their gathered, unified momentum launched each forward in a coordinated effort to knock either Amelia, or Joan to the ground before pinching as much exposed skin as possible. Focusing on the women's necks, the skeletal remains of what was the island's main export gnarled and clawed their way with dead eyed determination to inflict as much damage as possible per the direction of their hypnotically controlling master, Otep. The attack was sloppy but was not long, and within ten minutes the pair of unlikely allies subdued the plethora of creatures, ending their second lives before they could even begin. The living coconut crabs, each more ferocious than the next, retreated shortly after the third grouping fell to Joan's expert cracking abilities.

For Joan, the knowledge that her new ally could not only handle herself in combat, no matter what sort, was of great relief, as her thinking mainly centered around locating Judah and going immediately back to Eden. Once there (and not a moment sooner) she would tell her husband about her little 'flashback' episode and together they would talk to Turtledove to try to make sense of it all. Using the back of her shirt sleeve Joan wiped the sweat and blood from her forehead, closing her eyes for a long moment of contemplation before being interrupted by a somewhat recently recurring visitor. The white orb hovered with a coy aura that walked the line between fate, and fatality. Instantly all eyes fell upon it, causing a diverse array of reactions. The most animated of these was Otep, whose verbal curses were only punctuated by his abrupt exit from the scene; a cloud of kicked up dust in his wake.

This left the two women alone with the orb, the opportunist, determined to impose its will on the scene, regardless of the outcome. Without a moment's notice the white orb re-appeared from behind Amelia, swirling wildly through the open barn window, and diving right toward her, hell-bent on impact. Thinking fast, Joan thought to run away, but there was no time to hide, or detract Amelia's attention away from what was coming.

"What?" Amelia asked, preparing herself for a fresh wave of undead crustaceans. When none came out of the ground she eyed Joan suspiciously.

"No!" Joan tried to holler out in protest, but it was too late. Another blinding flash of white light engulfed her completely, and she was back the body of a teenager again.

Orleans. France -1429

The first thing Joan noticed was the sound of the horses' hoofs she was riding on as they walked across the crudely made road beneath them. Her horse was gray like ash and clashed oddly with the tan colored reigns that were grasped tightly within her fair, youthful looking hands. The initial shock of being, once again, in France, much less her own time, threw Joan for a moment as she got her bearings. Gone was Amelia, gone were the crab corpses, and gone was the impending sense of doom that came the last time the orb brought her back in time. No, this time Joan felt something else, something different. Feeling of elation and nervousness filled her breast as she thought for a long moment. Behind her was a caravan of other French soldiers on horseback, none of them looking particularly battle ready. Suddenly forlorn, Joan decided to reach for the skin for drink of wine. Bending to swing her arm down to the horses' side Joan felt around blindly for a few moments before furrowing her brow and trying again, this time using her eyes as a guide.

'If I'm reliving past glories,' Joan thought to herself, her horse galloping steadily beneath her as she made her way through the undisciplined French columns of soldiers, *'than nothing I do now can change the past. So, I might as well enjoy it.'*

With this thought in mind Joan pulled on her horse's reigns and took off toward the end of the row of troops. Once there the beast doubled around, before riding to the center front where it's rider cupped her hand to her mouth, just as she had done dozens, or was it hundreds, of years ago in both recorded history, and a young girl's memory. Each man watched her as she passed, many of them seeing a woman for the first time in recent memory. On both sides of the conflict men watched her move until she held enough of their attentions to consider it a captive audience. "My countrymen!"

The soldiers, each there for different reasons, be it by choice, or by force, were interested in many things, chief among them gold, food, plunder, and women. Truth be told many of the ones in attendance would have followed Joan into bed, rather than to battle that day. Though, none would get the opportunity. "Today is a day in which the fortunes of our country change! I have but one thing to say to our English oppressors."

Turning around, Joan attempted to make eye contact with as many of the English as she could before declaring her proclamation.

"I have a bigger cock than every one of you!" Joan screamed at the top of her lungs, forcing every head within earshot to turn directly to her, many of which had not yet noticed her. Joan smirked as she felt the cool rush of countryside air brush by her young face. It stung her eyes, but only briefly, and only in a way that drew tears of happiness, tears of remembrance in a time of victory and great confidence.

"The Maid!" screamed a Frenchmen from behind Joan, who rushed past his new commander headlong into the crowd of armed English soldiers. His overzealous nature, which cost him his life rather quickly, became contagious as fifty more Frenchmen did the same before Joan followed them, her sword drawn into a defensive position as she advanced.

The sounds of swords clashing together in a melody of triumphant combat greeted Joan's ears as she whirled around, her cape flying valiantly as her steel met the sword of an opponent, easily overcoming it and knocking it out of his hand. The solider was a boy, no older than fourteen, but no wiser in defeat than he was whence armed. Refusing to accept defeat at the hands of a female, the boy foolishly grabbed the blade of Joan's sword with both hands, causing both appendages to bleed instantly. In that terrible instant Joan had her first battle decision to make; one that she would carry with her into every conflict that followed in a long, storied career in protecting Eden and its people. There, with her sword in prime position to cripple her opponent, Joan had to decide if mercy was the best policy, or if peace would only be attained through resolution to a conflict in progress.

The boy screamed as his fingers fell, one by one, into the mud below. The last digit, a pinky, sprayed some blood in Joan's direction, landing sparsely across her face. The young English soldier cried out in anguished misery, grasping his fingerless hand with his useful one, doubling over, and falling into a fetal position at Joan's feet. She smiled at that, taking it all in again as if it were the first time. The smell of battle was strong around her, as for the first time in decades her countrymen stood side by side with a sense of patriotism and purpose toward their oppressors. Gunpowder, blood, and the scents of burning wood caused her get lost in the moment all over again.

Taking his position on the rampart of the castle wall, in the designated space his commander had told him to, the young English solider named Jonas, who had never met Joan, nor would he live long enough to see the sunset again, prepared his bow in the same manner he had done hundreds of times over the years in training exercises. Removing a finely stringed arrow from his lambskin quiver, Jonas placed it delicately in place before cocking it back on the string and resting his eye on a sight. To his surprise, a woman stood in the middle of the battlefield, her eyes closed, and blood splattered upon her face. Feeling pity within his breast for the defenseless creature, he decided the quick action on his part would spare the little damsel in the long term. With a quick release of his finger he sent the arrow flying through the air on a direct course where it hit Joan of Arc's left shoulder, sinking deep enough to simultaneously knock her off of her feet, and break through the skin to the other side.

Two French squires rushed to Joan's side, each grabbing a free body part before carting her off a few hundred yards. The pain was a strange mixture of intensely tangible, and extremely gratifying in its sweet duality of causation. Between gritted teeth, Joan smiled to herself, relishing every millisecond of her first taste of pain in battle.

Joan laughed as the medic, an older man with long, gray hair snapped the arrow lodged in her shoulder before pulling it out and patching her up with a poultice of leaves, mud, and vinegar. Without saying a word the medic gathered his materials and moved on to the next fallen Frenchman, murmuring something about women and battle under his wine drenched breath.

"I must go back in!" Joan screamed at the medic, inching the armor off of her chest with the few remaining muscles that functioned properly.

"Not like this you won't," the old medic said, tying a bit of fabric around Joan's shoulder would, exposing her budding breast slightly under the sling. Fortunately for Joan, this man, unlike many of her other fellow countrymen, was more interested in the teenager's battlefield prowess than what lie beneath her trappings. "But you won't lose the arm if you go back. Guess you'll be dead long before it falls off."

"*Merci*, Doctor," Joan said, grabbing her sword with her free hand before leaving the bewildered old man to tend to the other fallen soldiers.

The first two waves of the French attack were in full retreat, leaving the third wave, which was majorly comprised of peasants, to die or be captured into slavery by the English dogs. Sensing this, and getting lost in the rush of the moment, Joan unsheathed her sword with her non-dominant hand, catching the afternoon sun on the blade, causing a reflection to bounce off of the castle wall and blinding one of the English defenders.

"Send them all to hell!" Joan cried out, raising her sword high over her head before running headfirst back into the battle.

Clashing and crashing through the stunned males surrounding her on all sides, she was able to get through the previously insurmountable line of English soldiers that had spilled over the castle walls and engaging French troops in hand to hand combat. With a slice to an English throat, a stab to a full belly, and a thrust of her sword to the midsection of another, meaner looking man in full armor Joan no longer felt any residual pain from the wound she had sustained minutes before. With the adrenaline pumping through her veins Joan never noticed the return of the quirky, unpredictable white orb. Swirling, the orb freefell the length of the castle wall before rolling through the chaos of combat before bouncing upward and surprising Joan, engulfing her in the same white light as before.

Marshall Island - 1937

The room was pitch black, save for the fire, which crackled almost angrily in the far right corner near the door. Two occupants, one tied down, one walking freely, filled the room with a tepid sense of foreboding. Judah awoke with a start as he felt his shoes being roughly removed. The last thing he remembered was relieving himself on the far side of the old barn whilst waiting for his wife to return from doing (what he assumed) was the same. After a strange sound from the bushes caused him to stop midstream, he felt a sharp pain in the back of his head, followed by his entire world going dark. It was a few moments before his eyes adjusted, and Judah was able to recognize his captor's dark skin and black robes. Otep.

"Morning sunshine," Judah said, leaning back in the chair. He could smell the smelting of iron as something manmade heated inside the fire nearby. "This thing is pretty comfortable. Odd since the whole point is to make me feel like utter shit. Go on then, get to the torture, I haven't got all day."

A door opened across from Judah opened with a creaking noise of metal on metal that moved slowly, revealing a middle aged Elemeno male who held three long, iron rods that he handed to Otep before disappearing just as quickly. Once gone the room was once again cloaked in the pitch black of despair that Otep was so good at cultivating. Finally, footsteps made their way across the length of the room before another sound of metal on metal, followed by more footsteps. Then silence reverberated through the room like a symphony of empty spaces falling gently upon cracks of the same nature. The only break from this was the fire, wild, and with a seeming mind of its own as it cracked, and crackled merrily while the dashing, if not somewhat bull-headed Doctor Raines awaited his horrific short term fate. The iron poker, which Judah remembered had entered the room a rusted shade of metallic gray, was now glowing orange. Rolling the poker back and forth with an even, zen-like procession Otep as his mind resided miles away, deep in solemn prayer.

Crossing the room in the blink of an eye, Otep's quick movements spared his victims the run-up of a preamble before the main act. The red-hot poker in Otep's right hand found its way to Judah's unprotected flesh with little resistance. Murmuring old English obscenities through sobs of stifled tears the scientist donned a steely resolve that rested within his nose, eyes, and mouth - culminating in a determined set jaw and gritted teeth. Again Otep rolled the scolding hot poker, just as he had done over the flames, only this time it was what remained of Judah's skin that received the sadistic treatment from the ancient Egyptian's practiced precession.

Otep, who had once been a surgeon, found that it was only in moments like this, moments where he had someone at his complete mercy, that any semblance of peace was felt within his breast. The dark thoughts, not to mention the actions they preached, were unrelenting, and he knew that no matter what they would never stop. But in his heart, where his faith and trust for his master lied, there was nothing but peace in doing the bidding of such a great and ancient man. It wasn't until the smell of searing flesh caught his nostrils that Otep realized that even though he had taken the hot poker off of his captive's direct skin, it had been hovering slightly above

"Just bloody say something already!" Judah hollered, the pain searing into every nook and orifice of his body. "Tell me what you want!"

"What I want..." Otep finally said, never missing a beat in his now practiced rhythm of heating the iron poker over the fire before bringing it to Judah's flesh. "Is to watch the fire take you..."

Another wave of fresh pain jettisoned through Judah as the burning sensation filled his senses, blocking out all other stimuli and hogging all of his focus. While blinding in its fury, part of him understood why his kidnapper was being so thorough in his brutality. Breaking one's spirit is no easy task, especially someone of his caliber of celebrity. Or so he imagined.

"How's about this then," Judah began, spitting a large glop of blood out onto the wooden floorboards of the room by Otep's feet. "You untie me and we settle this like gentlemen, eh?"

Chapter 14:
The Great Elemeno Mystery

Eden - Dusk

"Jackson called him a fool, which made Rolland let go of the bow string, releasing the arrow toward his neck!" Dodger exclaimed, raising his arms high, and casting a shadow on the rocks opposite against the firelight as the sun disappeared behind him. The tale, told to him by both Rolland in the dorms several nights before, was bringing him as much attention from Hannah, Jaime, Timothy, and Gwendolyn as he had hoped for. "But then, just as it was about to pierce Jackson's throat, forever changing the history of Earth as we know it..."

"That's when Puck teleported in front of it, knife in hand, blah blah blah," Timothy Holmes said in an exasperated tone of voice while simultaneously rolling his eyes. He was tired of hearing the praises of Rolland Wright. "So Wright shot and KILLED Puck. Which is shit, total shit. He's a murderer!"

Nearly five weeks had passed since the Class of the Tiger had begun their mentor training, yet their relationships with each other were still tenuous. While some real friendships had developed, no group dynamic had yet to take hold. This trip, a tradition from Earth that Rolland had called 'camping' was meant to change that. Therefore they found themselves on the outskirts of Solomon Forest, surrounding a campfire and all watching Dodger recount the latest bit of gossip to cross his path.

"Well, yeah," Dodger stated, his expression changing from one of excitement to one of extreme disappointment. While he had never fully shared Rolland's distaste for Timothy himself, Dodger was beginning to see the appeal of hating Councilman Holmes' son, despite their many shared commonalities. Fortunately for both Dodger, and his pride, none of the other cadets seem to care that Timothy had spoiled the ending of his tale; as all but he was still gazing intently at Dodger for the next bit of his story. "But that doesn't mean he did it on purpose. I don't think he meant to do it. The way Rolland talks about it... he might have killed Puck, but he's no murderer."

"He told you about it? Personally?" Jaime asked with squinted eyes.

"Uh, well, yeah," Dodger said, suddenly realizing that he was the only one amongst them standing. "A couple days ago. Completely out of the blue."

"No shit?" Jamie asked, the kettle-corn he had been so adamant about making for their group falling by the wayside as only one of every four pieces made its way successfully into his waiting mouth. So engrossed was he in what Dodger had dubbed *The Battle for Pensacola* that neither he, nor any of the others had done anything but listen since Dodger began to speak. All except Timothy, whose sour face and grumpy disposition were punctuated by his constant sighs of annoyance.

"So what happened next?" Hannah asked softly. The quietest cadet in their class, Hannah had yet to open up to anyone since arriving in Eden. This air of mystery was a mixed bag, however, as despite having made no enemies with her cold reception, she had yet to make any friends either. Perhaps it was her age difference to half the class, though in truth, she was but a year away in chronological time from Gwendolyn. Silently, she wandered to herself for what felt like the hundredth time if she should have just stayed in her dorm.

"Well.." Dodger began, the smile returning to his face. "The arrow was already in mid-air by the time Puck teleported in front of Rolland so Puck didn't see the arrow coming toward him until it was too late."

"So," began Gwendolyn, who was leaning toward the campfire. "So the arrow got him in the neck and then Rolland killed him. Correct?"

"Right," Dodger said proudly, almost as if he was the one who had directed the order.

"Wait," Jaime asked, his renewed interest pressing Dodger for an answer to the question that plagued all of Eden, the Council of Light, Marcus Turtledove, and Rolland himself for months. "So did Rolland mean to kill Puck, or was he really just trying to kill Jackson?"

Thinking on the situation for a long moment, Stuart 'Dodger' Yick thought back on the past couple of months he had spent with Rolland as his roommate, ruminating on Jaime's question. In that time he had picked up on no hostility, no signs of madness displayed by the teenager that Eden papers had labeled a 'menace', 'weirdo', and 'outsider'. Moreover, Rolland had never been anything but a good, encouraging friend to Dodger since their first meeting. Despite these facts, the wide, even tempered voice of his more educated grandfather Dr. Joseph Yick rang clearly in his ears, reminding him to separate intention from opinion. This, above all else, forced Dodger to be honest.

"No idea," Dodger offered, taking a sip of grapple wine from his cup. His lips became a little purple, and cheeks flushed as the alcohol hit his system with a purpose.

"I think he meant to kill them both," Timothy nearly screamed, standing up from the mossy, fallen tree he had been sitting on, alone. His heart was beating so fast he didn't notice how loud his voice was until the end of his sentence. Feeling the need to defend his actions, Timothy decided to soldier onward in lieu of retreating away from his minority opinion. "He's not such a great guy, you know. And he has NO people here. Like, nobody knew him before a few months ago. Nobody loves him. Nobody except you all and my damn sister, apparently."

The mood around the campfire darkened as the last vestiges of Eden's setting sun melted away behind Timothy. Timothy had worked himself into a fury, his chest heaving up and down in an odd, yet perfectly timed rhythm with an owl that hooted softly somewhere nearby. His head was swimming with a buzz as his exclamation filled him with a newfound confidence he had never felt before. Strangely, Timothy found it nice, comforting.. powerful.

"I believe that you're just jealous," Gwendolyn said softly as she walked over to him as she stood to look her barely taller class-mate dead in the eyes. "Perhaps you wish she looked at you like the way she looks at him?"

Timothy Holmes stood shocked, his face turning two shades of red while his somewhat plump fists balled into themselves to form tight, angry melons of rage resting on either side of his outer thighs. Nearby Dodger's face formed into a joy filled 'O' with his mouth, eyebrows raised as high as they could go. Though Hannah did not understand what Gwendolyn meant, she knew by his response that it was of a negative connotation. The deafening silence that followed further cemented this suspicion. For Timothy, whose thoughts could not stop from pining for his cell phone, and the video he had captured on it, this bit of public humiliation was not but a roadblock toward that goal. With a deep breath he began to prepare for his verbal comeback when he was interrupted by the breaking of twigs from a dark spot in the wood behind their tents.

"It wasn't on purpose," came a deep, baritone voice from the darkened trees behind where Hannah sat. After a few moments two silhouettes joined the other six that formed a circle around the campfire, which now that the sun had finally finished setting, was their only source of light. The shadows, one broad shouldered, the other slender and short belonged to Rolland Wright and Tina Holmes, who had been listening to the end of Dodger's story in the safety of the woods before making themselves known. As they approached, all twelve eyes, Timothy's included, darted in their direction as they emerged, their arms filled with freshly cut wood for the fire. "I just felt like.. like it was what I was supposed to do in the moment, you know? It wasn't malicious, and I didn't wish Jackson dead. Well, I might have, the guy was a total dick. But not like that. It was instinct more than anything else."

Silence filled the campsite. More hooting from their neighbor, the owl, followed, as both Timothy and Gwendolyn still stood next to each other, their conflict forgotten.

"I know what you mean," said Kniff, who had not spoken until this point. Since their initial meeting the power struggle between Kniff and Rolland had been one of cheap shots, physical violence, and snarky insults flung by their respective seconds, Dodger and Timothy. Now the two teens saw each other, eye to eye, over the light of the campfire, for perhaps the first time. "I too had to kill a man once. An assassin who attempted to take my sister's life shortly before her marriage into the Mer Royal family. He had a blade of some sort hidden in his robe. No one else saw him go for it but me. When I launched myself against him, he had yet to turn the blade around, and it plunged deep into his torso."

'*A night for revelations*,' Gwendolyn thought to herself, taking mental notes on the two men in the group she suspected posed the best networking advantages after the academy. This was a practice encouraged by her mentor, Detective Samuel Bigott, whose number one rule of survival was getting to know one's enemies and friends equally as well. Examining Kniff, and then Rolland - who had somehow managed to wrap his hand around Tina's in a fashion befitting the teenagers that they were, Gwendolyn doubted she would be sharing with her classmates on this particular evening.

"Sometimes you cannot help but trust your instincts. Other times, your instincts betray you, leaving you nothing but your better judgment," Kniff concluded before taking a long sip of his wine. The kick of the alcohol hit Kniff's brain much in the same manner as it would a human beings, the only difference being the color variations between green and blue swapping within his line of vision. The now emerald, red, and orange fire that emitted such warmth and comfort added a new characteristic, which only got more pronounced as he continued to drink. "You did what you had to do."

Without pause all six of the other cadets nodded their heads and said supportive things, like 'yeah' and 'right', much to Rolland's amazement. For the first time there was support, REAL support for his actions that morning in dealing with Jackson, and it meant the world to him.

"Well, thanks guys," Rolland said, fighting back both tears and the inflation of his own ego. "Anybody bring any marshmallows for the 'smores I told you about?"

"I did!" Jaime said, jumping up to his feet lightly from his sitting position before rummaging through a green bag sitting between Hannah and Tina.

"How about a ghost story?" Dodger asked, looking around hopefully from Kniff, to Rolland, to Jaime. "These woods are ancient as hell. I bet they're at least a little bit haunted."

"But Dodger," Tina began, donning a face that was of the utmost seriousness. "The forest IS haunted. Don't you know about Fred Solomon?"

"What?" Dodger asked, his joyful expression at the prospect of 'smores and ghost stories fading at the serious look on Tina's. "Who's he?"

"Fred Solomon is the witch whose spirit haunts the forest," Tina said, taking a seat on the fallen limb next to her brother. "Roughly one hundred years ago the witch died here, and in the moment of death the witch's spirit gave new life to the trees, turning them from brown and dead to green and leafy."

"Shut the fuck up, really?!" Dodger asked in total disbelief of what he was hearing. "I thought there was no such thing as magic, or witches, or, umm.."

"Oh yes," Tina said in a flat voice, surprised that of all the people in their party Dodger was the one to fall for her ghost story. Putting a little bit of a scare into one of her more liked classmates would be a nice change of pace. "But the truly scary part, the part that will really get under your skin, is just HOW Solomon died."

"How did he die?" Dodger asked, completely entranced in Tina's tale.

The eerie calm of Eden surrounded them all with its enticing promise of tranquility. This lie, like many falsehoods, was based on a shred of truth; for once upon a time the land of Eden did use to be a paradise. Long ago, long before the time of humanoids or mankind of any sort. Before elemenos, or even before the first Mer-person breathed a lung full of Eden oxygen. But that was then, that was before the haphazard, disposable, and disrespectful treatment of Eden at the hands of its inhabitants. Since then the land has taken its due just as much as the those who call her home, a fact that Tina Holmes attempted to bring home as she revealed the name of the most despicable offender to grace Eden with his repugnant presence.

"Edward Vilthe killed him," Tina revealed, her face now so close to the fire that the heat was becoming uncomfortable. "Boo!"

Dodger jumped as the laughter around him landed like a punch to the gut. Deciding to play it off, he acted like he was in on the joke instead of the butt of it. Like his grandfather had taught him, Stewart Yick laughed right along with his classmates.

But one person wasn't laughing. The plethora of information that came out of Tina's soft, luscious lips regarding Vilthe had captured Rolland Wright's attention, despite its farcical nature as a lame attempt at a campfire story. He didn't know who Fred Solomon was, or if he was even real, but the story reminded him that he needed to find a way to kill Vilthe once and for all. A way to avenge his mother's murder. A way to bring closure to her. Filing a mental note to research Fred Solomon, Rolland mind went back to his most recent loss, Victor. With his abilities increasing and focusing every day he looked forward to the day in the not too distant future when he could sneak away, slip into the Time Stream, and rescue Victor from... wherever the hell he ended up. Although he did not know the when, where, or why of how to find his friend, Rolland figured those problems were for future him to worry about. This thought brought a smile to his lips, simultaneously as he looked back up in time to catch Tina's eyes watching him suspiciously. A casual wink and a smile righted her again.

"How menacing," Jaime said to Timothy, who laughed for the first time since Gwendolyn's confrontation. "I bet her next story will make me wet myself."

"Do you," Tina asked before fidgeting a bit in place. Nervously, she flattened her skirt, a poor choice in hindsight, especially when camping. "Is there something you'd like to say, Jaime?"

"Oh come on *chica*," Jaime said squinting his eyes and smiling an empty smile. "I didn't mean nothing by it, really."

"Yeah?" Rolland interrupted, forcing himself into the conversation. Not having ever had a real girlfriend before he was confused as to where to draw the line between standing up for your lady love, and allowing her enough space to be her own person. Actual rudeness seemed to be the line on this night.

"Yeah man," Jaime said with the utmost sincerity. "Despite what you think of me I actually respect what you've been doing here. I think you're really good, really impressive during our training. And Kniff - hey Kniff, don't get me wrong buddy, I like you more as a person but Wright here is a born leader. I'm going to fall in line behind him."

"Plus this," Jaime stated, motioning loudly and spilling the remaining little bit of grapple wine he had in his cup. "This is fucking fantastic."

"Your wine?" Tina asked, a little disgust in her voice barely masked by the crackling of the fire between them.

"No, camping! It's fantastic! And we might as well enjoy ourselves, right?" Jaime said, pouring a large amount of wine into his plastic cup before placing it somewhere in the shadows behind Timothy. "We'll all be out of here soon enough, one way or another."

"What do you mean?" Gwendolyn asked cautiously.

"Just look at us," Jaime laughed, choking a bit as he spoke. "We're a damned mess if I've ever seen one."

"Hey now," Rolland objected. "Speak for yourself."

"Ok boy scout," Jaime said sarcastically, the wine giving him courage to speak his mind for the first time since coming to the Academy of Light. "Let's do the math on our little gang of amigos here. There's you - the orphan convict who pulled the last strings his parents had to beat the rap on altering the timeline. Good job by the way, I was real impressed."

"Jaime," Tina said. "Stop it."

"Nah, let me finish, let me finish," Jaime said, spilling a bit of his wine as he turned from Tina back to Rolland. After eyeing him for a moment, Jaime decided that he had said enough on the matter, and turned to point at Timothy and Tina. "We've also got the council brats: number one and number two."

Timothy's cheeks turned a shade of red with indignation. He liked Jaime, but felt their game had grown out of hand, and swore never to drink with the Hispanic young man again.

"Sorry, but it's true. Oh! And the other council brat - that would make you number three, Stewie." Jaime knew Dodger found this particular pet name particularly distasteful, and continued to call him by it regardless. He then pointed at Hannah with the hand not holding his near empty cup of wine and spoke in a loud tone. "Then there's the other outcasts. The Merman, and the Nocturn aren't even human, and no one know who or what the hell she is!"

"I was a lady in the service of Mrs. Madison, first lady of the States United," Hannah said with a smile and a far off expression on her face. "Please do not pity me, I never worked in a field, and I was not a slave. I mean, I started my life as a slave, but gained my freedom at a young age. Only 17. Ms. Dolley, err, Mrs. Madison saved up and bought me from her husband's estate. Then she moved me into the big house to tend to the family. Lady Madison was very good to me, fed me well, and loved me..."

The burning itch of release just below Hannah's eyes urged her to continue, despite their demanding presence of infuriation the tears came in their own time, cascading down her cheeks. Still she persisted. "It wasn't until the night the one you all call Vilthe attacked my home, the big, white house where the swamps used to be, that I had to show my power to the world," Hannah continued, her eyes filling with tears as she looked directly at Rolland. She, more than Dodger, Tina, Rolland, or Kniff before her, had his complete attention as she spoke. "A man named Scott Wright saved me that night. He gave his life so that Lady Madison and I could escape. Then Dodger's mentor, Mr. Turtledove, brought me to Eden."

Rolland's eyes bulged at the mention of his father's name, much less the new knowledge surrounding Scott Wright's death. He looked at the African American girl with new perspective, taking her in against the shadowed firelight. Her coarse, black hair was tied back in an intricate weave that complimented her already beautiful face, despite a complete lack of any beauty enhancement products. Hannah's was an inner beauty that stemmed from a lifetime of hardship, perseverance, and determination to rise above whatever adversity she encountered.

"Great, so she's a former American slave. Anybody else here a former slave? Anybody? No? So, she's an outcast, just like I said. Add her to the other two, plus the three council brats, the convict and myself," Jaime said, his voice a mixture of sadness and scorn. "You think any of the other classes are like that? You think the Class of the Raptor is this messed up? Hell no!"

"Face it *cabrons*, we've been set up to fail,"

The mood amongst the Class of the Tiger was unsettling, despite the peaceful presence of the two moons and sparkling stars. Deflated by Jaime's statement, none said a word as the conversation took another, sharp right turn."But I meant what I said about your leadership skills Wright. And this camping, this is wonderful! Hey, can we do this again next Saturday?"

"Sure," Rolland said without thinking, drawing several stares, perhaps none of which filled with as much venom as the one from Tina. And with that, each of the cadets found a little spot of their own private sleeping area, shook out their standard issue sleeping bag, and pillow before crawling inside, hoping to put Jaime's haunting words aside and fall into a listless sleep under the stars.

The week between the camping trips was relatively uneventful, but on the day of their second outing, Rolland decided, rather spontaneously, that he needed to have a chat with Hannah following her revelation the previous Saturday. The brief recap of the night she was taken to Eden stuck out in his mind for several reasons, the least of which was the mention of Scott Wright. Of his father dying for her. Leaving the dormitory earlier than usual he noticed Dodger's bedroom door was still shut, and a soft resonating of music made the wall vibrate a bit as he walked out. Dismissing it, Rolland made his way across the main courtyard toward the entrance, left through the guarded gate, maneuvered around the columns of special OPS groups training in the field out front, and made his way up the steep, grassy hill away from the academy. With his shoulders slumped, weight distributed downward to balance as he climbed, Rolland never saw the gunman as he opened fire.

Sting

The bullet whizzed by Rolland's ear as he found even footing. Then another, and another before he even realized what was happening. In an instant, Rolland was frozen in place, panicked to the point of confusion as the thunderous noise of the handgun, followed by the whizzing noise of each bullet as it missed him forced him to act impulsively. Spotting a nearby boulder big enough to shelter him from immediate harm, Rolland jumped behind it just as he felt the sharp, painful contact of one of the bullets connecting with his right shoulder.

Sting

The pain was intense, forcing Rolland to cry out with a swear word he would never use in front of Tina. Rolling over into the fetal position he used his non-dominant hand to roll up the sleeve of his shirt and prepared himself to find the worst. But there was no blood. No blood! As if in disbelief, Rolland looked again, and again to reveal the same solution to the problem every time. He had not been shot, only bruised by the bullet that came so close, too close, for comfort.

Sting

Sitting up at the waist, Rolland was immediately visible to the gunman, who continued to shoot madly all around Rolland's position. Bending his knees, he stood up, turned around slowly, and began to walk toward the man at an even pace. It took seven steps before Rolland recognized the man as familiar, though he could not place his face. Thinking on this, Rolland completely missed the hole in the ground before him that was partially covered by leaves and twigs. Stepping in it inadvertently, he tripped, falling to the ground and scrapping the palms of both hands as well as his left knee.

"You do well under pressure, grace under fire is what keeps one alive," said the male voice as he holstered his revolver. "Lt. James, Jesse James."

"Rolland Wright," said Rolland, checking himself over for any more bullet holes. Finding none, he decided that there was no harm done. This fact, although simple enough did not escape Rolland, but instead imprinted within his mind a deep respect for James' skill set and unique way of expressing it. "You could have killed me if you wanted."

"Could have," Lt. James said with a boyish grin. "If I wanted to."

"Help me up?" Rolland asked, extending his right hand toward the stranger. "Please?"

"The first thing mankind looses in times of crisis is his manners," Lt. James said, outstretching his arm, offering Rolland his hand. "Yet you keep yours under duress."

"Well," Rolland began, dusting the dirt off of his shirt and jeans after he stood. "I lived in Texas for a while and there you are surrounded by racism and manners. One of them is bound to stick."

Tilting his head to one side Lt. Jesse James started at Rolland for a long moment, his piercing blue eyes engrossed with the spunky young cadet's defiance in the face of authority. It was refreshing in a landscape of fawning students, each more enamored with the wisdom their famous mentors had to offer. If he had any 'wisdom' it wasn't on matters pertaining to life, or being a human being, or even being a good soldier. Jesse James knew he was good at one thing, and one thing only, handling a gun. Still, he wasn't absolutely terrible at recruiting talent when he recognized it.

"So where are you heading?" Lt. James asked the plucky cadet.

"In life," Rolland asked, raising his eyebrows for a moment before lowering them. "Or at the moment?"

Smiling at the coy response, Lt. James was pleased as punch at the response. He nodded his head and rested his hands on his hips. "Dare you to answer both."

Puffing his cheeks out with concentration, it was Rolland's turn to shake his head, thinking at lightning speed before answering. "Right now I'm going to look for Doctor Joseph Yick. His nephew, Dodger, er, Stewart, is a friend of mine and I need to speak with his protégé this semester, Hannah. She apparently knew my dad."

"A lot of people knew Scott Wright. I did," Lt. James said without a second thought. His honesty was refreshing to most people, especially the non-native Edenites who recognized him from American history. When he first arrived in Eden his celebrity status was merely a jest, a joke that brought him free alcohol from men and added attention from women. Then it morphed into something else, something unwanted. Years of ass kissing later, Jesse preferred seclusion to people. "And the other?"

"Honestly?" Rolland said in more of a statement than a question. "I have no idea."

"Perhaps you'll come work for the Academy after graduation," Lt. James said, taking aim with a different kind of pistol.

Rolland laughed for a second before realizing the man with the gun was serious, and quickly donned a face to match. After a few more pleasantries Rolland left the folk legend to continue his target practice. Although the encounter left Rolland with more questions regarding both Lt. James and Eden's bureaucratic structure in general, his brain was tired, and he wanted nothing more than to relax, spend some alone time with Tina, and generally unwind with his classmates. The bonfire that night had provided the perfect opportunity to do this. Unfortunately, neither Hannah nor Councilman Yick were where he thought they would be, and he was forced to go back a different way to avoid becoming shooting practice again for the Lt. Jesse James.

"I think we should name her Aphrodite," Gwendolyn suggested that night shortly after they got the campfire going.

In the time period since the young tiger pup's arrival into their lives she had been something of a blessed curse. On one hand the logistics behind feeding, keeping, and hiding an actual baby tiger had tested the cadets to the very limits of their problem solving skills. The best temporary solution they had found, thanks to Tina, was to enlist the help of the local man Sherman, who lived at the Blackard Family Orchard, to supervise the somewhat structured releases of the tiger cub every day when he let the unicorns out of their stables. This newfound relationship between the two animal subgroups led to some mildly fascinating behavior whenever the tiger was taken away from her 'pack' for too long. This included increased snuggling, listlessness, and the occasional thumping of her tail, much like a domesticated house cat.

"Aphrodite is cute, but it's a bit too long," Tina said with an easy hand. "Plus the guys would end up calling her Afro or something stupid."

"That's a good point," Jaime said, agreeing with Tina for perhaps the first time since they met.

"Thing #1!" Dodger offered, laughing at his own joke before anyone else had the chance to. "That way when we holler for it people will think we have another one too. And really, what's better than one tiger besides two tigers?"

"Oh Dodger, stop" Tina said, stroking the tiger cub's stripped head, the fur flattening down before springing up with each pet of her hand. "But I like the way you're thinking."

"Oh yeah?" Dodger asked, his eyebrows rising comically, before taking a quick peek at Rolland before a moment of silent contemplation. After deciding that the inevitable punch that was sure to follow was worth it, Dodger looked Tina dead in the eyes before saying, "Here's another one for you. Bet you didn't know that there's a wocket in my pocket"

Jaime and Timothy guffawed boyishly as predicted while Rolland playfully punched Dodge in on the shoulder. Neither Kniff, Hannah, nor Gwendolyn seemed to understand Dodger's joke, as all looked confused. Their confusion was doubled when Tina's eyes lit up, and she unexpectedly let out a large squeal of delight.

"Oh, Dodger!" Tina proclaimed, her toothy smile shining brightly against the fading Eden sunlight. "Wocket! Wocket is a perfect name!"

"Nah, doesn't seem to *fit* right," Rolland said, eliciting a snort of laughter from Dodger. He actually liked the name Wocket, but could feel the popular opinion against it amongst the group.

"Blaisey," Hannah offered. Rolland looked at her aghast, not knowing if she was reading his mind or not. She was so mysterious, and he knew so little about her, despite her knowing quite a bit about him, his father, and what constituted the events that led to him being forcibly brought to Eden by Turtledove. The uncomfortable silence that filled the campsite was not totally unfounded, the persistent rumors of Hannah being telepathic in addition her constant silence in social situations, plagued the girl everywhere she went. Since she had yet to share her special gift with the group at large, every one of them, including Rolland, suspected them to be true.

"Tiikeri," Kniff offered with little fanfare, breaking the silence. Without prompt the tiger cub sat up from her kneeling position at Tina's feet and walked the short distance to Kniff. The cub sat at his feet, tilting her head until her eyes met the Merman's. It was a simple thing, but something about the way the tiger looked at Kniff, its crystal blue eyes conveying so much emotion and expression, told all eight of the cadets that it was attempting to express itself in their conversation. A soft, but firm meow from the animal confirmed the suspicion they all privately held; she had picked her own name.

"What does it mean?" Rolland asked with some interest.

"It's Mermish," Tina offered to no one's surprise.

Kniff nodded, his eyes still locked with the tiger cubs own bright, sparkling, blue eyes. "It means 'cat.'

"I like it," Rolland said in a low, but resolute tone.

"Yeah, yeah me too," Dodger seconded, clasping his hands together.

"Aye," Gwendolyn offered, nodding her head.

"It fits," Hannah agreed, her pearly white teeth shining as brightly as her eyes.

"Then it's settled," Kniff said.

Following the naming of Tiikeri, who loped about the eight cadets intermediately, alternating between getting her head petted and cuddled by all of them, the grapple wine came out of the bags brought by Jaime and Kniff. Somehow the naming had created eased some of the remaining uneasiness and this outing was going markedly smoother than the last. The increased social interactions allowed two particular cadets to wonder off to participate in some.. more private social activities.

"Tell me about yourself," Rolland said, in a tone of voice that Tina wasn't sure what to make of. They had laid down together in a clearing twenty yards away from the others, which was far enough away that Rolland thought he could successfully make a move.

"What do you mean?" Tina asked, reaching up and kissing Rolland's neck softly.

"Listen to you," Rolland began with a smile. "Asking me what I mean when you know perfectly well, Ms. Holmes. I want to do is know you, inside and out."

Playing coy, the usually timid Tina knew at once that the opportunity she had long sought was presenting itself. Here was the chance for the two of them to cross the line, both emotionally and physically. Biting her lip in what she thought was a seductive fashion, Tina suddenly moved herself on top of Rolland. Her big, sparkling blue eyes caught the light of the fire, making them even more spectacular contrasted against the dark of the night.

"Ok, Rolland Wright," Tina said softly, feelings of warm joy bubbling in her blood. "I was born here. In Eden, I mean," she said, a little embarrassed about her lack of exciting or foreign cultural heritage. This fear was unfounded, much to her pleasure, as within seconds she was caressing her tongue against Rolland, and his hand was resting gently on her left buttock.

"Boring!" came Dodger's always charming, blunt summation of the situation.

Looking up Rolland knew that he definitely would not have any alone time with Tina; his goal of bringing the Class of the Tiger closer together had been accomplished. All six of his team-mates were standing looking down at the pair, unified in their curiosity to see where their friends had gone. This far cry from the week before, at what Rolland had guessed would be their last meeting after Jaime's drunken declaration. Indeed, the Class of the Tiger, and their collective REAL tiger, Tiikeri, seemed insep-arable as they watched Tina straddling Rolland on the ground amongst the fallen leaves.

"Now there you go," Dodger said to Rolland, nodding his head as Tina awkwardly rolled off. "That's what I call getting close to nature!"

"Shut up!" Timothy barked suddenly, his arms crossed and his face as pinched as if he had just been forced to eat a lemon whole.

"Well since everyone here seems know everything about me as well as seem to agree that I won't be getting any alone time with Tina tonight," Rolland said, eyeing them all individually, "I thought I might talk about the man who tried to kill us during the B.E.T.S.I."

"Kill us?" Hannah asked.

"Yeah, during the end of the B.E.T.S.I. simulation. Remember the guy who 'you know what-ed' Tiikeri's mother?" Tina said, covering the tiger cub's ears. In retaliation for this, the cub nipped at Tina with its small, but extremely sharp teeth while wrapping its paws around he left hand for leverage. Pulling it away easily, Tina knew it wouldn't be long before the animal was stronger than her, and such games would be out of the question.

"Oh, the one you and Dodger said came out of the Time Stream," Hannah asked, her eyes gazing upward toward some previously believed inconsequential memory.

"That's the one!" Dodger shouted, teleporting the short, seven foot distance between them.

"He is Nero - Roman emperor, arsonist, assassin for hire, and all around terrible guy. To top it all off it says that he hates cats. I ask you, what kind of madman could hate a cat?" Rolland asked the group at large to a series of eye rolls, minor snickering, and shaking of heads.

"Rolland," Tina said in a concerned, yet understanding tone of voice Her piercing baby blue eyes glistened inside her tilted head. This confused Rolland until he looked past Tina to a similarly skeptical looking Kniff, Gwendolyn, Hannah, and Jaime.

"How do you know all of that?" Kniff asked, his posture subtly changing from one of moderate relaxation to one of a defensive nature.

For his part, Rolland felt a pang of embarrassment in revealing that his source of information was the Time Stream itself. This thought passed, however, as Dodger joined the conversation with his usual sense of timing and ease.

"The better question is, why was he targeting us?" Dodger asked, playing mindlessly with a long blade of grass he snapped off of its base.

"Targeting your boyfriend, you mean. He didn't come after the rest of us so why should we be worried?" Timothy interjected, his arms crossed in front of him as he leisurely leaned against a tall tree.

"I disagree," Gwendolyn said, stepping forward "He went after both Rolland and Dodger but how do we know he was targeting them? It could have been any of us."

"Would you listen to this girl talk?" Dodger asked, pointing to Gwen and getting no response whatsoever by any of his teammates. "Ridiculously sexy. Go on girl, talk logic to me!"

"She's right," Tina pointed out, staring icy daggers of repressed childhood animosity into her twin brother's eyes. "He would have settled for a kill, regardless of who it was."

"Guess we should just chalk it up to another unsolvable mystery then," Jaime said, shaking his cup a bit to check the amount of its contents. "Right up there the Great Elemeno Mystery."

"Wait, the what?" Rolland asked.

"You've never heard of the Great Elemeno Mystery?" Kniff asked Rolland, looking at him a bit as if he had been bathing all of his life without using soap.

"Non-native Edenites," Tina said with a smile. "You explain, please?"

"It is said that the Elemenos were the first to settle in Eden, but that they are not from Eden. Humans think they are, but the MerPeople know things humans do not. The Elemenos came or were brought here from a world that died, a place like Earth that had gateways to Eden."

"Do the MerPeople know what world it was?" Tina asked. This information was not what her parents, or the Eden public education system had taught her.

"No one knows," Kniff said solemnly, drawing an overly skeptical look from Tina, and a genuine lack of interest from the hormone driven Rolland. "But that doesn't matter. Legend has it that there was a group of Elemenos, an educated elite class and assimilated with human culture who were banished by the Edenites. They're known as The Shunned."

Both Rolland and Tina thought back to the elemeno they had met in the French cafe weeks beforehand. He had gone by the named Darius, seemed very polite, and spoke so eloquently that Rolland had not a single disparaging remark to say about him. He thought of brining Darius up to the others, but decided against it when Tina's eyes met his and gave a small, but definitely noticeable shake to her head. Prejudice it seemed, was commonplace in Eden.

"Anyway, they know the secret of where the Elemenos truly came from, and what's more, they know the ENTIRE history of Earth, including when and where this Edward Vilthe was born, his family, even all the kids he's had over the millennia," Kniff concluded.

"Vilthe had kids?!" Rolland asked, standing up suddenly, forcing the chair he was sitting in to fall backward to the marble floor.

Every one of them looked at him, some with the expression as if they had heard this story a thousand times. For some reason the revelation shocked him a great deal than it logically should have. Vilthe was a man after all, and all men have biological needs. It only made sense that he would have created an offspring or two. Still... the prospect seemed like a can of worms he was not eager to open for the time being.

"Of course he did," Tina said to Rolland, squeezing his hand. "But they're all dead. The first Council of Light saw to that after the Great War."

With a quizzical look Rolland eyed Tina, one brow raised above the other. He asked, "You mean World War I?"

"Yeah," Tina said, a bit indignantly. "Of course after the first World War. But like I said, they're all dead."

"All but one..." Kniff said, his voice lowering for effect as the meaning behind his words sunk in for each of them. In their group, only three, Rolland, Tina, and Hannah, had actually met Vilthe. "Who he is, and what he is, is all a part of the Great Elemeno Mystery."

Chapter 15:
Simple Things

Lae Island - 1937

The water made its way down the steely pipe until it found its destination in a circular bowl, hovering above Eden's smartest son, Judah Jacob Raines. There was a small hole in the center, where gravity took hold of each molecule as one by one they fell onto the forehead of the waiting scientist, who had been suffering this torture for hours on end. His resolve was shooting to the breaking point, as Judah knew that his time was running out. It wasn't that he feared death. Death was a finite event that was going to happen regardless of his actions. It was the variables in life that scared Judah, not the definite things. Not death. It was losing his mind, his most prized possession and asset that terrified the world's smartest man the most. With his sense of anxiety rising, Judah opened his eyes wide with the resolve of a man hell bent on surviving. All he could see was darkness. The room was black all around him, meaning his eyes were useless in his escape plans.

Regardless, Judah did not want to wait for his host to come back before finding out. It was not that he feared Otep, or even the torture he had been inflicting on him. No, the need to escape was intertwined with the need to right himself, and think of the next step in the process to complete his mission. Getting himself untied was easier than he anticipated, but his arms and legs ached with sharp, pulsating jolts of pain that added yet another obstacle to overcome. His heart and mind were beyond this place, beyond this darkness. They were with Joan, and he knew he had to get to her. Had to make sure she was safe. Groping around in the darkness, Judah finally found what he believed to be a door, and, tracing the outline with his fingers, pushed and jiggled it open to reveal the great wide world beyond the confines of small, smelly cabin.

The sweet smell of the cool Pacific breeze hit Judah's nostrils like a wave as he came bounding out the door of Otep's torture cabin. The sunlight, after hours in total darkness, was almost painful to his eyes, forcing him to his knees and to cup his hand over his face for a bit of comfort. His feet were bare, as was his chest, both of which felt cool and wet when he fell against the green grass that surrounded him on all sides. The wounds on his feet ached, causing him to fall over, yet the physical pain was nothing compared to the inner turmoil he felt in not knowing if Joan was safe. Determined, Judah got back on his feet. His right ankle rolled slightly on the grassy incline that awaited his escape path away from the place he was forced to spend the night, but the pain was nothing compared to the burning desire he had to get away; to get to Joan. After a few minutes of moving at the pace of someone thirty years his senior, the smell of the ocean grew stronger, and the sound of waves crashing against the beach led to his first geographic marker.

Making his way back to the site where Amelia's plane crash landed the day before, Judah trudged along the seashore, just beyond the point where the sand met the dirt, kicking small rocks into the water as he went. Dirt kicked up all around as he made his way to the shore, collecting more and more in midair behind him without his notice. After slogging through the water, Judah moved inland toward the green valley that Amelia had been using as a runway when she first arrived.

What began as a dust storm quickly turned into broken bits ·of Earth, separated only by what appeared to Judah as long, stiff limbs clawing their way out from below the ground. One of these, a long broken thing that still held patches of flesh covered with hair, and a loose scalp upon its head, spotted him with empty eye sockets and began to draw closer to the scientist at a slow, but steady crawl. The pace was stopped briefly as one of the corpse's legs became entangled in something beneath the ground, still buried out of sight. Crying out in a blood-curdling scream of anguish long passed, the lifeless form snapped it's obtrusive leg off at the hip before continuing on its journey toward living flesh.

Judah watched with rapt attention as the re-animated arm of a corpse that was too decomposed to deduce anything aside from its height, popped off of its body, before being picked up by one of the more whole, and fresher dead things that was newly resurrected. This time, however, the lifeless brown eyes belonging to the dead man looked directly at Judah and saw its prize. While he could scarcely believe the physics behind a near skeleton, Judah guessed this was anything but normal behavior for the recently departed.

"What in the bloody hell am I going to do now?" Judah asked himself under his breath.

Low murmurs of inaudible words escaped the bits of fleshy lips that clung to the jaw lines of the walking dead that meandered slowly toward Judah. Taking a few quick steps backward in the shin high grass behind him, Doctor Raines assessed his current predicament with an uneasy trepidation. The creatures were obviously enchanted by necromancy- an art that made Judah sick to his stomach.

Picking up a long, curved stick lying in the nearby grass, Judah held it high above his head in a stance like a baseball player before swinging violently at the closest corpse walking toward him. The stick connected with the monster's skull, knocking it cleanly off of it's still moving shoulders, which continued to meander toward Judah.

With one down, he turned his attention toward the eleven other undead creatures making their way in his direction, all in various stages of the same journey from the ground to his position. The brown-eyed corpse was the closest, and the thought of a pre-emptive strike against it yielded positive results in his mind. On the other hand..

"To hell with this," Judah said, dropping the curved stick and quickening his pace away from the grassy hillside where the undead meant to drag him back to hell with them. A grim fate to befall the self proclaimed smartest man alive. As fast as his injuries would allow him, Judah moved as quickly as his body would allow back to something familiar, back to the barn where he slept the night before. Back to Joan.

No sooner had Joan gone with the orb after the battle before suddenly she was on Lae Island again. The nearly four minutes of Joan's catatonic state meant four very awkward and uncomfortable minutes for the clueless Amelia. To the American pilot the white orb was a serious threat, one in which could only be kept at bay with a long, pointy stick that she found conveniently placed on the ground some fifteen feet away from the rigid, sheet white skin of Joan Raines. Then, after a few minutes of poking at it, the orb sprang back into life from its stalled position above Joan's head, made a diving motion for Amelia, and whizzed upward before disappearing into the forest. When the Knight of Time awoke from her stupor she felt more than a bit hung over. Deciding not to directly answer the quizzical looks her traveling companion was giving her, Joan instead pressed onward in the direction they had set fourth nearly fifteen minutes, and one trip through time, ago.

The two women walked in moderate silence with Amelia making a casual, albeit interesting observation of their surroundings every few minutes. After a while Joan found herself wanting to speak more in depth with her charge, but remembered her own strict code of not fraternizing too much with the mission objectives, and kept her mouth shut.

The intentional silence did not go unnoticed by the sharp tongued Amelia, who finally asked, in the most ladylike way possible, "What the hell was that back there?"

"Nothing. Well, not nothing, it was something but it's not something I want to talk about, ok? It's just that I.." Joan said, trailing off as something in the tree line caught her eye.

"Ok, so I'm really going to need you to tell me what that thing is," Amelia asked, slowing her pace a bit as she lifted her head toward the orb. Eyeing the ball of white light suspiciously, the pilot knew something paranormal was going on, a theme that seemed to follow her new friend around as much as anyone she had ever met. She pointed directly at the orb as it floated casually above their heads. "Spill."

"Wait, you can see that thing?" Joan asked in shock. "Like, really see it? You weren't just saying that earlier?"

"Of course I can see it," Amelia revealed. Her eyes betrayed no sense or shock or fear, which was reassuring to Joan in a way words could not describe. "Not my first rodeo."

"First what?" Joan asked, failing to understand Amelia's turn of phrase. Regardless, the revelation that she was not alone in seeing the orb was the one of the happiest moments she had experienced in what felt like a long time. Yet before she could begin to explain the orb, her history with it, or what she suspected it might really be, the ball of white light zagged sideways again, before buzzing away westward with a small, whirling noise.

"Ugh, never mind," Amelia said in annoyance, before pulling on Joan's wrist toward the orb's zig-zagging direction. "Come on."

Much to Joan's surprise, she did not automatically flinch, or attack the woman who pulled her along after her. She did not move against the direction at all, almost as if she was more comfortable with the near stranger Amelia than she ought to have been. So engrossed by these thoughts, all of which were completely new to the somewhat aloof Joan that she failed to notice the change in behavior emanating from the orb itself.

"Hey Joan," Amelia asked warily. "What's it doing now?"

Looking up just in time to notice the transformation that was taking place, Joan's mind was thrown off track by the bombardment of her senses by the foreign object. With another blinding white light the orb expanded, intensified, and enveloped Joan as she shielded her eyes with her forearm. Trying in vain to call out to Amelia, Joan felt her mouth open, but the words would not come out against the radiant heat that saturated them both. Then, a cool breeze against her arms told Joan the process was over, and she was, once again, a different woman.

France 1430

Without even the slightest hint of warning Joan was once again transported away from the scenic shores of Lae Island. Looking up she saw the long, winding dirt road that she rode along, she smelled the fresh air of a place that had been untouched by pollution.

Her entire world had shifted yet again, Joan attempted to take it all into her mind and process the information as fast as possible. Although this was the third time that she had experienced the phenomenon, Joan was not fond of the uneasy feeling in her stomach that accompanied the change, or the throbbing ache it left in her head. Lost in thoughts of physical hurt, Joan did not notice the small details of her surroundings, such as the one hundred and forty pounds of extra weight that rode behind her, with her hands on Joan's hips.

"Well, I don't think they have airplanes in this place," said a voice Joan knew to be more out of place than her own. Looking over to its point of origin she saw Amelia Earhart, hands wrapped around Joan's hips as tightly as they could be, and with a dizzyingly optimistic disposition as she rocked along with the ebbs and flow of the horse they rode.

"How did you?" Joan asked, completely taken aback at this unexpected turn of events. Up until this point Joan had assumed that she was suffering from delusions of her past life but now she wondered if she really had been traveling back in time.

"How did I?" Amelia asked, looking Joan over from head to toe. "How did YOU turn back the clock on what was already quite a few favors from the Lord?"

Thinking this over, it took Joan more time than she'd admit to deduce that Amelia was paying her a compliment. With a half-hearted smile Joan attempted, in vain, to hide this fact from her new friend.

"I really don't think Judah or Freddie are going to be here," Amelia said, the wind muffling every other word as they rode faster and faster. But Joan heard her just fine.

"We aren't here to look for them," said Joan in a voice that seemed to travel on the wind with the grace of a Nocturn.

"So then what are we doing here?" Amelia asked her head and chest lurching forward as their horse came to a sudden stop. Before them was a small, quant looking church that would look right at home in a Norman Rockwell painting. It's small, unassuming windows were not stain glass, or held much regular glass at all. Instead the majority of the church was comprised by very old, very brittle looking wood, the kind that ramshackle buildings defined themselves by. After breathing it in for a long moment, Amelia drew breathe to, again, ask Joan about their reasoning for traveling through time when she was interrupted by the opening of a small door at the front center of the church.

Seven men, six of whom were dressed in identical robes poured out of the little church's narrow doorway into the court-yard to greet the two women. The leader of the men, who Amelia guessed to be a priest, had a quizzical look on his face as he eyed the pair suspiciously. The looks they gave Amelia were so familiar in their sexiest, and chauvinistic cognitive reasoning, that the blonde pilot took an immediate dislike to the lot of them, but she still decided to don her fakest, brightest smile.

"The Lord has sent me here to retrieve a weapon," Joan began in French, passing her horse's reigns from her right hand to her left before swinging her leg over the side, and hopping onto the hard ground below. It will aid me in defeating our English oppressors. Will you help me find it?"

While Amelia had taken French in school, the French Joan was speaking was flavored with different inflictions and phrases that she found hard to translate. However, she understood the gist of it and quickly went over her options in her head. She knew there were but two, and striking out on her own in what was obviously a completely different geographic climate than the one she was in minutes before would get her in nothing but trouble.

"Greetings *Mademoiselles*," the priest offered, bowing deeply before gesturing toward his parish. "If you will step inside we can discuss what you are looking for and how we may be of service. We have lodgings for the night if you require. Food as well, despite our meager harvests this year."

"Thank you, *Pere*," Joan said, holding up one of her gloved hands to silence the priest before looking past him at the church. "But that will not be necessary. We will not be staying long."

"Oh?" The priest questioned, as low rumble of disapproving murmurs coming from the monks behind him. "So then, if may ask, what exactly are you doing here?"

"I was sent," Joan stated bluntly before she was on the move. Dodging the monks, she walked behind the church to the small graveyard that rested peacefully between a pair of sycamore trees. "By the Lord, as I said - to retrieve a weapon."

"Father," one of the monks said. He was the shortest by far, and was balding beyond the point of dignity. "These, these WOMEN come here alone and clad in the most improper clothes! They must be removed at once!"

Sensing danger brewing, Amelia found herself playing referee between Joan, who had fallen to her knees and begun clawing at the ground like a dog, and the group of clergymen. Deciding to be as proactive as she could before matters got out of hand, the pilot leapt across the distance that separated her from her friend, landing on her knees in front of the men.

The gamble worked, as all of the men stopped dead in their tracks.

"Father, forgive me for I have sinned! We know we should not be here!" Amelia shouted in her schoolgirl French, waving her arms around to distract the men from what Joan was doing behind them. Out of the corner of her eye Amelia saw Joan locate a nearby rock, examine it, decide it was no good, select another one, and then begin to bang it against the ground in a digging motion next to her claw marks. After a few more moments of this a few of the monks, those who had not yet made any vocal noise, began to also stare at Joan's digging, so Amelia waved her hands again - making her breasts jiggle beneath her beige tank top. " Please, please forgive our intrusion on your," her French failed her so she offered a lame, "shindig?"

The 20th century vernacular, being more than the priest could understand, turned out to be the breaking point for the amount of perceived disrespect he could tolerate before acting. Wasting no more time with Amelia the priest turned on his heels before marching straight over to where Joan sat crouched, a series of monks following him like a line of ducklings. Silent looks of shock were exchanged among the seven monks, all of whom were dressed in identical dark brown robes interlaced with maroon crosses and roughly woven belts.

"But that is our garden! What are we to eat if you destroy it?" The balding monk asked indignantly, obviously not impressed by Joan's claims.

"I was sent from the Lord," Joan screamed, still digging as fast as her youthful limbs would allow. "To find weapon! Busy!"

"*Excusez moi,* Amelia repeated again and again waving her hands at the priest. "Have any of you heard of *Jeanne d'Arc?* The maid of Orleans? *Oui? Non?*"

Handful after handful of dirt went flying through the air, separating Joan from the prize she knew was awaiting her. *'This is a truly interesting experience'* Joan thought to herself as she dug, alternating between using a rock and her fingers. She recalled the first time she had done this, the first time, when she did not have Amelia to distract, and had to rely on physical violence. The decision had haunted her for years, which in and of itself she knew was silly, as she only caused the monk minor discomfort at best. This was nothing compared the hundreds of lives that had been ended at the point of her sword over the centuries.

With an intently focused ferocity to her actions Joan scratched and dug her way into the cold, hard Earth beneath her. Clawing away at the cold soot she remembered performing the task the first time, and how it was not until she had searched in a counter clockwise, circular pattern that she found what she was looking for.

Then, just as she was about to give up, Joan's thumb pressed down on to something sharp that caused her to jump back from her crouched position over the hole in the monks' garden. With an intense ferocity reserved for this occasion and her wedding

night, Joan clawed away at the ground that housed the lost treasure, eager to liberate it from its Earthy prison. For a few minutes
Amelia too helped dig, unearthing one half of a bejeweled handle that reflected a deeper desire within Joan to take control of
the situation. Finally, after a bit more grit and determination than
Amelia thought possible given the extraordinary circumstances,
Joan pulled the long sword out from the ground, the first human
to wield it in nearly five hundred years.

The others in attendance stood in awe.

"*Mon Dieu.* How, how did you know that was...?" the priest
asked Joan in French, backing away from the teenage girl who
brandished the large, ornate, and recently unearthed blade. The
weapon was as sharp as it was intricately designed, clashing like a
jewel in the sunlight.

Joan had forgotten how beautiful the sword was. It had been
years, centuries really, since she had last seen the weapon, and
holding it now she felt its power and majesty once again wash
over her. So entranced in the moment was Joan, so full of life and
hope for the first time since coming to Lae Island, that she didn't
notice the hair standing up on the back of her neck that signaled
the white orb was near.

"Incoming!" Amelia hollered, her hands cupped around her
mouth as Joan fell backward, the sword slipping away from her
as she went. With a buzzing whirl that disorientated everything
around them the snow white colored orb zoomed over Joan's
head, around the monk, and hit Amelia square in the back, causing her to disappear before Joan's eyes.

Joan's jaw dropped, the physics and fiction of her predicament rattling around in her brain like bingo balls waiting to spit
out which matter to tackle first. The surprise 'attack' of the white
orb that spun around the small church like a tornado of blinding

white energy gave way to the pain in her stomach as another cramp hit her. Overhead, the orb barreled downward and instinctively, Joan raised the sword to meet it, causing the two objects to collide in an explosion of radiant heat that caused everyone in attendance to shield their eyes from the result. Joan's last thought before her scheduled blackout was of Amelia, and the hope that she too would travel back to Lae Island. The clasping of feminine fingers intertwining within Joan's was reassuring on a number of levels.

The cold, grooved hilt of the sword as they landed together beside the salty seaside on Whiting Beach on Lae Island was even more reassuring.

Chapter 16:
B.E.T.S.I.

Eden - Dawn

Rolland awoke early that morning. The memory of bacon haunted him as he suffered through yet another morning of dry cereal and orange juice with pulp. He hated pulp. Hated it almost as much the anxious knot lodged in his stomach at the thought of another meeting with Captain Nareau. A small part of Rolland felt like quitting his mentor relationship but it was overridden by the strange question that all warriors experience during basic training: can I survive combat? The prospect, while intriguing, was one he feared that would be put to the test that morning as he was summoned for what would be one of the final training sessions he'd have with the Captain. Rolland thought it to be a necessary evil, especially if he ever hoped to become proficient enough at using his time travel abilities to travel to.. wherever to save Victor. Rolland's stream of thought was cut short as his roommate came gliding into the room on his socks, his loose strands of black hair falling in his forehead in a leisurely fashion.

"Can't be late today, finally getting the boss out of the house," Dodger said in a mockingly chirpy voice.

"Nice," Rolland said automatically without really registering what his friend had said.

Dodger finished putting his light jacket on before eyeing Rolland quizzically. He could not decide if his roommate was being serious or not, but thought better to air on the side of caution and just tell him the truth. " When's the last time you've seen Turtledove dude?"

Jolted by the name, Rolland's mind fought to keep up with the sudden and rapid beating of his heart within his chest. "Turtledove?"

"Former leader of the Knights of Time? Arrested for the same crimes as you? My mentor? Ring any bells?" Dodger asked as Rolland nodded his head woodenly. "I'm assuming it's been awhile since you've seen him. Well trust me, that guy is in no condition to be doing much of, well, anything these days."

"What do you mean?" Rolland asked, immediately regretting his decision to do so. As guilty as he felt for not looking in on the man who brought him to Eden, ignorance was bliss, and the pain behind losing Victor was still relatively fresh in his heart.

"Just everything... everything. That guy is a mess," Dodger stated bluntly, his mind awash in where to begin to describe the sharp decline that was Marcus Turtledove's life. What at first seemed like a easy gig had turned out to be an endless cycle of essentially caring for an eccentric, aged former leader of the

Knights of Time who had provided zero to nothing in terms of mentoring. Dodger's head hurt the longer he thought of it, and suddenly realized that neither he nor Rolland had spoken for several long seconds. "You want me to tell him you said hi?"

Rolland might have obliged if they were discussing nearly anyone else. The Turtledove he had known was as a strong, capable leader who he never would have thought capable of an emotional breakdown. As sad as he felt at the man's state, every time he thought of Turtledove he thought of Victor and that pain still seared like a white-hot knife to his heart. The blinking red clock on their communal oven from the kitchen read 7:21, which told Rolland that he was running late. He thought to relay this information to Dodger, but when he looked up his friend was gone. As he stepped out into the bright sunlight thoughts of Turtledove's depression, Victor's death, and the dissolution of the Knights of Time weighed heavily on Rolland's conscience. Making his way down the now familiar path through the impoverished East Eden, Rolland found the Captain's warehouse and made his way inside the dark, unassuming space with relative ease. Given past experiences in the same part of town Rolland was thankful for the small miracle of an uneventful day. Less than an hour later, he would learn that it was only the beginning.

The lesson today would be the final building block in what Nareau had called Rolland's training wheels before giving his abilities a real try. Prior lessons had focused on learning the fundamentals of the astrophysics characteristics, behavioral patterns, and temperaments, behind the Time Stream. The revelation that the Time Stream, the physical embodiment of time incarnate, was not only alive, but self-aware and cognizant of its' importance to humanity had confused and intrigued the teenage boy.

Nareau had explained to a stunned Rolland that it was only by making direct contact with the Time Stream that he, or any other beings [1]with time travel capabilities were able to somewhat direct the flow of themselves into the fabric of the stream itself. What separated Rolland from other natural travelers weren't his capabilities to travel through time, it was the ability to travel through time with a precision that was tantamount to the difference between a person arriving at the correct month as a party and a person arriving the precise moment the party starts. This major difference also meant that Rolland could physically transport both farther into the past and with more energy, which equated to more people, equipment, and things he could transfer between the two destinations safely. While Nareau had explained all of this the best he could, Rolland did not fully understand the magnitude until he began to speak to Ananke.

It had happened during one his routine meetings with the Captain. Instead of their usual meeting place at the warehouse, pupil and mentor had met outside of Eden Town Proper at the banks of the Time Stream. He had stood there as Nareau stared silently into the waters, unsure of what to do when suddenly he heard a voice. Because Rolland was unsure of what to do he ignored the voice at first, dismissing it as merely his own self-doubts. But the longer he listened, really listened whilst in proximity to the time stream the more he heard the same message over and over again, *'Greetings traveler.'*

The words were so odd, and so obviously carefully chosen that Rolland knew they had to be coming from somewhere. After staring at the never helpful good Captain, he decided to mentally answer the voice back, feeling ever foolish in the process. *'Hello - my name is Rolland.'*

'Rolland, yes,' the voice said, accentuating each letter of his name with a pronounced diction that rang out in his mind like

---

1   Including human beings, Nocturns, MerPeople, or Elemenos

a wise voice that sounded very much like his mother's favorite poet, Maya Angelou.

'Who are you?' Rolland asked without speaking.

'I am yesterday, today, tomorrow, and forever. I am everything and nothing. I give, I take, I yield to no mortal. I am Ananke."

'Tell no one of this Rolland,' Ananke said before retreating back in to silence, ending their first meeting. In the many weeks since that first time, Ananke had proven to be more than just an otherworldly voice; she had become a friend to Rolland, a trusted companion who gave advice, and guidance regarding his abilities. Despite the burning urge he felt to tell someone of this phenomenon, he stayed true to his word and told no one of her existence, including Captain Nareau, whom he suspected already knew of Ananke somehow but never brought it up. In exchange, the phenomenal entity that called itself Ananke told Rolland the answer to what his heart truly desired to know.

'Nero,' Ananke had whispered at the end of their first meeting when questioned about the man who attacked Rolland and Dodger during the first B.E.T.S.I. *'Nero'.*

This prompted Rolland to venture to the Eden public library, a general search on their computer system, and the connecting of the dots. The man in question, Nero, was a hired assassin wanted by Eden Police Department on the charges of first degree murder, regicide, and multiple counts of burglary. In addition to this, Rolland learned that Nero's last know job, confirmed by an unidentified eye witness, was working for Edward Vilthe nearly one hundred years prior. Though intriguing, this still did not answer the one question Rolland felt was most important about Nero; what his superhuman ability was. In this Rolland could find no detail, received no help from Ananke, or Captain Nareau, and kept up empty handed during every spare minute doing research at Eden's library. Rolland thought on this, and debated if Nero was a time traveler, like him, or an immortal being like Vilthe as he walked to training.

Casting these thoughts aside as he arrived, Rolland opened the door to warehouse with a false determination and got right to work. With a snap of his fingers, and clasp of his hands, Rolland did what he had been preparing to do for weeks, despite the uneasy feeling in the pit of his stomach. The effect was immediate and undeniable, as the entire warehouse was filled with a sound like an eagle screeching. Rolland was surprised by this, but did not allow his eyes, or concentration to falter. The reward was instantaneous for both men, as within seconds a small hole, no bigger than that of an American baseball, filled with the familiar hot white light, appeared before them, hovering nearly four feet off of the ground. It emitted power, personality, and for Rolland Wright - a newfound feeling of accomplishment.

"Yes!" Rolland hollered, a feeling of deep accomplishment filling every part of his mind and heart. After weeks of frustrating training, many of which produced nothing but a deep longing to return to the 'carefree' days of being a homeless teenager, the result of his hard work was staring him in the face like a small, burning sun in his own orbit of accomplishment.

"Easy there Oppenheimer," Captain Nareau said with what Rolland thought to be a small smile peeking out from the corners of his mouth. "It's a good start, but it's only that. You hear me?"

Rolland heard his mentor but did not care, for the joy of seeing the first physical proof of an extraordinary ability that came from him, and only him, was too much of a high point to downplay. Smiling broadly, Rolland turned around to face Captain Nareau, and without warning or permission, gave the older man's bare, outstretched palm an enthusiastic high five. When he saw the look on his mentor's face, he immediately regretted his decision to do so and decided to change the subject.

"So, how long do you think before Varejao learns about this and invites me back for a luxurious stay in Eden Prison?" Rolland asked, only half joking but hoping that he would get a real, direct answer in return.

"Hmmmpppff," Captain Nareau said without looking at Rolland. He found a strange comfort in double checking the knobs and switches that comprised his older looking super computer to verify that they were all turned off that was indescribable to anyone who doesn't obsess over the details. In doing so he was satisfied that indeed the Wright boy had managed to create a wormhole into the Time Stream. Yet he was afraid of that, and the implications that such power might incur. The boy was too young, too raw and unprepared for the world around him and for the dangers that would surely follow.

"I was only joking, you know," Rolland retorted after several long seconds of silence filled the room in a blanket of discomfort.

"That's horse shit, kid," Nareau said bluntly, walking over to the bar in the corner of the warehouse to pour himself a drink. His footsteps echoed throughout the chamber, filling it with the sound of the Captain's military issue boots, circa thirty years prior. He arrived at the bar and found his glass, the bottle, and unscrewed the cap. It was always whiskey, always from Tennessee, and always had the same black and white label. It was a good metaphor, good enough, so he decided in the moment to go with it. "You can't think of ideas as black and white, there are various shades of gray."

"What?" Rolland asked, taken aback by the philosophical turn of the conversation.

"Ideas are gray. They're never evil, never bad. There's always a nugget of good in every one, no matter how sinister or fool hardy," Nareau said, extending his right arm, bottle in hand, toward the door and Eden at large. "But they're never pure either, never 100% good or perfect. Remember that."

"But ideas are everything. They're the fabric of our society. They're morality. Are you saying morality is relative as well as time?" Rolland asked.

"Not morality, no," Nareau said, taking a long sip from the glass but only drinking half of the portion. He savored the way the liquid burned his tongue and slid down with a warmth that rivaled no other. "Morality involves the variable of people and people are different, Rolland. People cannot be treated like ideas. The day will come when you'll have to be clear cut, black or white, with those you come across. Both in love, and war cause when you get right down to it, they're the same damn thing."

The last comment threw Rolland, who suddenly realized how deep their conversation had gotten. "But I thought that you just said it was a grey area?"

"It doesn't matter what I said," Nareau snapped at him, ending the chat in its tracks. Rolland merely nodded before turning toward the front door to leave, the small rip he had created vanishing in the blink of an eye as he passed his mentor toward the warehouse exit.

"Courage doesn't mean you aren't afraid," said Captain Nareau, pouring himself another two fingers of whiskey at the bar before raising his hand slightly to his mouth, pressing his lips against the glass. "Just means you're paying attention enough to know better. Good luck tomorrow."

The tomorrow that Captain Nareau spoke of came entirely too soon for Rolland Wright.

The walk toward the dreaded B.E.T.S.I. obstacle course was filled with anxiety, remorse, and for one of the cadets - the idea that redemption could be attained via a little bit of hard work. For Tina, whose leadership during the last attempt led to not only the groups failure, but also left a window open for possible assassinations, the time was imminent to prove her worth; both to the Class of the Tiger, and to herself.

Before long the eight cadets stood in a line in front of Sgt. Elle Tillman and her small squadron of interns. Two of the Class of the Tiger cadets, Tina and Gwendolyn wore small tan backpacks, one of which contained Tiikeri the tiger cub that mysteriously appeared during the groups' last trip to the B.E.T.S.I. compound. Despite the fact that none of them wanted to part from the cub, the group decided unanimously that they would at least attempt to return the little girl to her home. This was the first of two serious subjects the group had discussed, with the other being the elephant in the room that Jaime had brought up during their first camping trip; that they were all placed together to fail. Also concerning was the question was whether or not the Academy of Light was actively trying to sabotage their training, or if the setbacks, the odd mentor pairings, and what a few of them perceived as under preparedness wasn't part of a grander, more sinister scheme to undermine each and every one of them.

"While each of you will be tested individually, only one of your team must retrieve the red flag in order for your class to pass the course and move on in your training," Sgt. Tillman said with a smile while holding the side door open for the cadets. "Good luck, Class of the Tiger."

As all eight cadets walked into the B.E.T.S.I. compound an otherworldly hush fell over the group, enveloping them in a new world of possibilities and danger. A cold breeze blew around their ankles, causing the cadets to abruptly stop in their tracks.

"This isn't a good sign," Dodger said as the sounds of his teleporting filled the otherwise quiet air around them. The teleporter could not see especially well in the dark, but knew that his 'trail' of teleportation left a small flash of light behind each time that illuminated the section of empty space it was created in. After seven blinks in and out of reality Dodger came to a land directly next to the small Nocturn woman.

"Stop that this instant!" Gwendolyn chided, grabbing Dodger by the wrist in the seemingly pitch black confines of the room. "We must collect ourselves and be steadfast against the many threats we are bound to cross as we progress."

Intentionally allowing a few seconds of awkward silence pass between them, Dodger smiled at the realization that a real life female had been touching him for what was going on over thirty seconds. Once Gwendolyn too realized what she was doing she let go of the somewhat taller young man, causing him to stumble a bit backward before falling over onto the suddenly dusty, dry ground.

"Ahhhhhhh the Nocturn's trying to eliminate me already!" Dodger said, checking his hands and elbows for injuries. "I like aggressive women, but not like this!"

"Are you hurt," Gwendolyn asked, holding out an arm to help her teammate up. She ignored the overtly sexual comment, chalking it up to his adolescent nature and little else.

But before Dodger could answer, a strange whistling noise filled the room along with a blinding yellow light. The cadets looked at each other in confusion as the noise grew louder and the light came closer and closer to them. Only once the sound of wheels screeching across a steel track did Rolland finally realize what was happening.

"Move" Rolland screamed before throwing himself out of the train's path. The Class of Tiger scattered, with Tiikeri rolling out of Tina's backpack in the chaos. The19th century steam engine cut a path between the separated teammates, casting off bits of light that formed the shape of lassos in the darkness. The particles of light, eight in total, wafted lazily to their intended targets before falling around each of their feet in a line of gold, not unlike that of a thin rope.

"It's trying to separate us," Tina hollered over the howling of the train. "We have to stick together!"

"What are those things? They look like-" Kniff said before being cut off by the lasso of light that circled around him. Once the two ends of the bright yellow rope had Kniff trapped not only did all noise cease to escape its confines, but it grew upward like a bean stock before forming a cylindrical prism of light around him. A few moments later and a bright *FLASH* of the same shade of gold color of the lasso, Kniff was pulled into the light of the train.

"Where did he go?" Gwendolyn asked. Within seconds Gwendolyn too had her own prism, and so too did she disappear following a flash of light that revealed nothing of its' intention, or her elimination.

With two of their team down within seconds the remaining six members of the Class of the Tiger could do little as each of their golden lassos picked up speed in enveloping each within its soundproof confines. Because there was no pronouncement, none were sure if the two had been eliminated, or simply taken elsewhere. Thinking quickly, Rolland knew it was up to him to at least keep things moving forward. Taking a deep breath

before he began, Rolland focused all of his energy and concentration on the energy surrounding the lasso's circumference
as it bonded with itself, forming the seal around his immediate
vicinity. Clap snapping his hands together, the muted sounds of
a roaring eagle overtook the cone of silence, snapping the lasso
into no less than ten pieces, and freeing Rolland of his prism
prison.

"Woah," Jaime and Dodger both said, watching the scene
transpire. They saw each cylindrical prism being ripped open by
Rolland on both sides with ease. For the first time their predicament felt like a battle, awakening a hunger within each to fight,
to survive.

Doing it again as he moved straight toward Dodger's impending golden lasso as it was on the edge of creating a bean stock
prism, Rolland was able to focus enough energy to open another
rip in time, his hands clasping together post snap, this time focusing the wormhole straight onto the lasso. The result was a very
girlish scream from Dodger, and the literal imploding of the
golden lasso that held him in place moments before. Out of the
corner of his eye, Rolland saw both Timothy and Tina disappear
along with their lasso prisons.

"Damn it," Rolland screamed, scaring Hannah as both he and
Dodger made their way into her lasso, both of them grabbing
one of her wrists before dragging her out, the lasso imploding as
they fled. No sooner had they taken another step before Jaime,
who was visibly anxious at not being rescued sooner, vanished
to wherever his teammates had gone to. He was just about to
say something to Dodger when the very far off, but very distinct
sound of a mighty ROAR filled the air. Staring out at the great
darkness that had surrounded them since they entered the warehouse, the backdrop of black melted away into a primitive jungle
setting, complete with overgrown palm trees, long extinct fauna,
and again, another loud ROAR.

Tilting his head sideways Dodger too watched the change in their environment wondering if perhaps he should be concerned when he felt the vibrations. Small at first, then steadily larger as each second passed, Hannah using him to prop herself up to her own feet numerous times, the ground beneath them shook harder, and more often with each passing moment. Dodger Yick thought he knew what might be coming, but couldn't admit to himself what it might be. Couldn't yet admit that it was his deepest fear coming to fruition within the confines of the all knowing, all seeing B.E.T.S.I. simulator. Childhood memories of monster movies, where large pre-historic beasts would attack humans just for recreation flooded his mind, re-enforcing the budding fear that had already set up camp in his psyche. Snapping himself out of this dark spiral of fear, he saw that likewise Hannah and Rolland were also entranced on whatever was causing the ground to vibrate.

"Dodge to Rollie, come in Rollie," Dodger said, snapping a finger directly in front of Rolland's face. The time traveler blinked before facing his friend, any time they might have had to formulate a solid plan gone due to distraction. Although neither of them needed to say it, Dodger felt obliged anyway, taking it upon himself once again to point out the severity of their situation. "We're pretty fucked, huh?"

It was in that moment that a forty foot tall, spotted dark tan and crimson colored Tyrannosaurus Rex with two rows of foot and a half long jagged, pointed teeth made its presence known to the trio by emerging through the brush of squished palm trees. Letting out another bellowing roar that sent Hannah running in the opposite direction, the king of lizards raised his head toward the heavens, stomped its meaty feet, and paced slightly in a menacing show of its dominance. With the poorest eye sight among all dinosaurs, the tyrannosaurus possessed a keen sense of hearing, and knew it merely had to wait until its prey made itself known before moving into an attack position.. Scared beyond anything she had ever been up until that point, Hannah tripped while running, which resulted in a tumble where she hit her head. Again Rolland and Dodger helped her up before all three stared at the beast, the hundred feet or so of extra distance doing little to comfort anyone.

"Go," Rolland said in a voice that was surprisingly calm. "Dodger get Hannah out of here. I'll do... something."

"Where do I go? I- should I take you too? Let's go together." Dodger said, having the opposite reaction of Rolland. His speech was fast, tense, and alerting suspicion to the dinosaur that lowered its head a bit toward them.

"No, no take Hannah," Rolland said, squinting his eyes against the howling wind that resulted whenever the beast moved. "She stands a better chance of finishing than if she gets out of here."

"I will," Dodger said, a hint of confidence under pinning his status as Rolland's trusted number two. "Should I come back for you?"

"Come back, but only if there's time," Rolland said, making his wishes known over the roar of the tyrannosaurus, which had yet to move from its position at the base of the tree line. It was almost as if it were waiting for something, or someone. Thinking to ask Dodger, he turned to open his mouth to ask, but they were gone, leaving Rolland alone with the T-Rex.

Tina

The soft feeling of a familiar pillow, the scent of a comfortable room, and the glow of her night-light filled Tina with a sense of comfort that she had not felt since leaving home for the Academy of Light. Opening her sleep heavy eyes, she found herself staring at the pink and purple comforter that had been on her bed as a child. As flashes of the B.E.T.S.I warehouse poured into Tina's mind, she snapped up at the waist as she kicked the blanket off violently and before taking a closer look at her surroundings.

She was definitely her room in her parents' house, or at least it looked like it. Yet the longer she sat there, the more Tina realized that something was wrong, very wrong. The walls were painted the strange shade of pastel pink that had been painted over when she was ten. That fact stuck in her mind for some reason, reminded her of something important that she couldn't quite access yet. She walked over to the white vanity and peered cautiously into the small, oval shaped mirror and was confused as to what she saw.

Her blonde hair was short, and separated into two long braids that sat just out of reach on the back of her head. She wore a frilly pink dress that grossly matched the walls of her bedroom. As she fingered a piece of her lace dress, a sense of realization hit her. Her research had told her that the B.E.T.S.I. simulator dug deep into a cadets' subconscious, and forced them to face their deepest fears before continuing on to their training. She realized that her studies had proved true, as the thought of a perpetual childhood under the thumb of her controlling parents who would never treat her as an adult, was her worst nightmare.

"Tina," came a singsong voice from outside of her bedroom.

Tiffany Holmes was the last person Tina wanted to see under the circumstances. Focusing her attention back to her surroundings, Tina noticed something that did not exist in her real room, an air vent that sat at the top right hand corner of the wall opposite her bed. It was larger than usual, large enough to fit into - which meant that it wasn't designed for home use, only industrial. While her brain urged her to be cautious, her instincts told her that the vent would be her ticket to freedom. She began planning her escape as the shape of her mother suddenly filled the doorway.

"Well hey there sleepy head," Tiffany Holmes said with an overly cheerful demeanor, startling her busy daughter as she entered the room. The woman was heavier than the woman Tina had seen a few months ago. With her hair pulled back into braids that matched her Tina's, an apron tied around her waist, and a large sundress on underneath, Tiffany was every bit the picturesque version of the perfect housewife.

"Mom? Where's..?" Tina asked, before being cut off by her mother's gratingly chirpy voice.

"Where's who, Tina darling?" Tiffany Holmes asked with a smile, her expression changing the longer she looked down at her confused daughter. "Oh of course you mean Timothy! Do you miss your brother? I bet he misses you."

Shaking her confusion aside, Tina focused on her priorities, and the fact that the 'mother' she spoke to was not real, only a holographic impression of her subconscious portraying Tiffany Holmes. With a sigh she smiled politely at her mother until she waddled away, her heavy thighs rubbing together as she went back down the stairs before Tina could answer her question. But then something odd happened, something Tina had not counted on. The room around her began to shimmer, much in the same manner heat bounces off of warm sidewalks in summer time. Disoriented but determined, Tina fell from her bed and on to her knees before hauling herself back up. The strange shimmer only lasted a few seconds, but the effects were immediately felt.

Behind Tina brass bars appeared on the foot and headboards of her previously box string bed. The bars were familiar to her from fuzzy, half faded memories of her early childhood, sometime around early grade school. Another uneasy feeling in the pit of her stomach that did nothing to quell her fears lurched over her insides, grasping tighter and tighter, and forcing her into the fetal position.

"Tina!" came the chirpy voice of her mother from downstairs. "Almost bed time!"

What? How could it almost be time for bed? Hadn't she just woken up? What was going on here? The terrifying thought of being forced to relive her childhood motivated Tina beyond perhaps what anything else could, propelling her back to the air vent. She sat for a long while studying the vent's grate, not knowing exactly what to do. Her feet were asleep to the point of being numb, as were most of both of her legs. Shifting her weight distribution off of them, still sitting on the plush carpet of her bedroom floor she noticed the oddest thing yet; her shoes were no longer the polished Mary-Jane shoes they were when she woke up, but instead pink, juvenile themed Velcro sneakers that strapped across the top to keep them on her feet. Tina swallowed nervously before taking a deep breath. Moving the vanity chair directly below the industrial air vent, Tina removed the grate with a loud clang.

"Tina Leigh! You better be in bed or your father and I are coming up there!"

As she threw the grate towards the bed, the edge caught one of the brass bars with a piercing noise. Tina heard her mother call her name again and the sound of footsteps coming up the stairs as she thrust herself in to the vent. As the darkness surrounded her, a sense of foreboding hit her but she forced herself to remain calm. In her head the same mantra repeated over and over again on a loop as she heard her parent's voices nearly screaming her name. *'Just keep going'. 'Just keep going'.*

Just keep going.

Kniff

He awoke in a room, not entirely sure that he had been asleep at all. Only slightly disoriented by the transportation to another part of the facility, Kniff Youngblood stood up straight, undeterred from putting up a good fight against B.E.T.S.I. Armed with nothing but his courage and conviction, Kniff immediately charged forward though the hurdling darkness toward a open door that spilled a warm, muted light. A pop in his ears told him seconds before his arrival that he was, somehow, back under the ocean. Torches of contained firelight lit the path around the final bend before entering the throne room of Mer where he had come to visit his sister so often in the past few years.

Despite his taste for leadership while at the academy, Kniff did not share the same desire for power in Mer. On the contrary, despite being fifth in line for the royal crown as ruler of the Oceans of Eden, Kniff Youngblood, brother to the Queen of Mer, despised politics. Besides, he was only royal through marriage, as his sister had married King Tecumseh of Clan Neptune. The line of succession went from Tecumseh, his son Troyson of Clan Neptune, then Tecumseh's brother, Etra of Clan Neptune, before Kniff would have any claim what-so-ever. Still, this positioning made him a celebrity amongst the populace of nearly a billion Mer that lived in Eden's vast oceans.

Plush, ornately decorated, and carved out of driftwood the throne of Mer stood at eight feet tall and four feet wide. Made out of a wood that his father told him had been extinct in Eden for over five thousand years, it's arms, legs, and back were carved and decorated with battle scenes from Mer history. Approaching it cautiously, Kniff noticed for the first time how inviting the wood looked, how tempting the idea of power could be. A sudden spasm of pain shot through his lower back, forcing Kniff to jerk as it spread up along his invertebrate. Breathing steadily to manage the unexpected torture, he did not notice that he had both sat down on the throne, and that he was no longer alone in the room.

"Enjoying yourself, nephew?" came the voice that Kniff knew to belong to his uncle, Etra.

"Etra," Kniff said in relief, his heart skipping a beat at the sight of another Mer. He had hoped that another presence would lift his spirits, even if it were his uncle through marriage with who he had never really been close to. Then he noticed another change in the room, more dark and sinister this time.

Blood stains, deep, dark, and sporadic made their presence known all over the room the closer his uncle got to the throne. Standing up on his feet Kniff again experienced another jolt of pain surge through his body, causing him to double over, sitting on the throne yet again. Gritting his teeth, Kniff looked up to see another change; the deceased bodies of the royal family were lying in various parts and positions of the room.

"No," Kniff screamed while simultaneously hurling himself forward toward his sister's lifeless body. Her cheeks were cold, eyes open, and a small trickle of blood had formed before hardening around her mouth, neck, and the carpet below. Close by were the bodies of Tecumseh and Troyson, both broken, both lifeless. "We must do something!"

"Why have you come back here?" Etra asked solemnly, his folded hands not moving an inch as Kniff approached.

Perplexed, Kniff tilted his head as if the answer to his uncle's riddle would come to him naturally. A few beats passed before he realized his uncle Etra was not blinking. Taking a step backward toward the throne, Kniff saw for the first time the blood that ran down his seemingly harmless, interlaced fingers.

"What have you done, Etra?!" Kniff exclaimed, extending his right hand in grabbing his uncle's shoulder. As it was, he did not see the knife that slid cleanly through his stomach. It disappeared into him before he could object, the cold feeling of nothingness coming in contact with his bare skin.

Lifting his woven vest in a panic, Kniff examined the middle of his stomach fully expecting to see the mortal wound that was momentarily to end his life. It didn't, it wasn't real. None of it was real. The deaths, the betrayal, the stabbing. It was the B.E.T.S.I. simulation and nothing more.

"You're eliminated."

Hannah

"Stay here, alright? I'll be right back for you," Dodger said to Hannah before teleporting away. The two had appeared in what looked like a peaceful field on a sunny afternoon day. Because she did not want to be alone Hannah did not object to Rolland sending her and Dodger away, but now that she was it was if her worst fears had come true.

Chapter 16: B.E.T.S.I.

Not a moment later a group of ten people, eight men with skin as dark as hers pulling an old cart, being led by two older white men, one holding a long bullwhip, who rode along top pulled into view on the road beside her. The cart they were dragging, an old wooden thing that carried pick axe, shovels, and pitchforks was untethered from the wrists and leg shackles each of the dark skinned men wore before their tools were dispersed, and they were directed to the field where Hannah stood. She knew she should run but her head was still pounding and her limbs felt sluggish and wooden. As if sensing this, the two older white men took notice of her presence, arming themselves, and giving approach before she could run away. The two men looked identical, save for the fact that one wore a long, scraggly looking gray beard and one merely whiskers.

"What're you doing out here girl?" the first white man asked, eyeing Hannah up and down.

"I, uh," Hannah began, swallowing hard and trying to think of an acceptable answer. "I just.."

"Looks like we got a runaway!" the bearded man shouted, reaching for his bullwhip once again and turning his back to Hannah. Unleashing the instrument of torture, it whirled around, hitting Hannah full in the face leaving a small gash under her left eye.

Overwhelmed by the situation, a longing began to swell deep within the confines of Hannah's soul. Suddenly all of the despair, all the anguish, all the resentment and pain of being kept as a slave and second class citizen for nearly two decades of her life accumulated in a massive pink ball of energy that flowed within her veins before coalescing into a surge of physical strength. Holding out her left hand as if by instinct a tremor of acidic pink energy flowed out like a sonic wave into the world, passing over the racist old white man completely while simultaneously melting away all of the flesh and beard on his face. Choking for life, the older man fell sideways.. right onto the waiting pitchfork, it's barbs pointing outward ready to strike. Making their way through his chest as easily as if he were comprised of butter, both Hannah and the man with the whip watched in abstract horror.

"You killed him," the man said under his breath before turning to stare at Hannah with cold, dead eyes. The hysteria in his demeanor rose to the surface like an unstoppable force of nature, completely enveloping Hannah within its web of fury. He saw that her eyes had changed color, the corneas were a dark orange that didn't look natural at all. "You killed him!"

"No!" Hannah tried to say, backing away quickly while throwing both arms upward in defense. The man too was on his feet, and ready to once again use the bullwhip on the insolent Hannah, but she was too quick. A jettison of metallic pink daggers flew from the palms of both of Hannah's hands in such a rapid succession that the force literally melted the face of her attacker as he closed in. She fell to her knees as the screams enveloped her ears, mind, body, and soul. Turning to face the small crowd of five Hannah raised her left hand, releasing a fresh spray of deadly deluge upon their unsuspecting flesh, burning it all away instantly upon contact. Within the span of fifteen seconds the small clearing in the woods where Hannah had once been taken into forced servitude now stood as a tomb, a final resting place for six out of seven souls who stood there a minute before. This was her nightmare - unleashing the violence tendencies she knew could come out of her if she let them. Losing control, losing her mind, losing everything...

"Hannah?" came the small, beleaguered voice of Gwendolyn Murrow as she crept into the dark clearing in the woods. Stepping over the bodies of the men still holding whips as he made her way toward her teammate, Gwen put both of her hands up in the air to signify that she was unarmed.

Hannah could see tears falling down the cheeks of the Nocturn women as she edged her way closer to the former slave, and she wondered what had happened to her. A small part of her even took comfort in the idea that she wasn't alone anymore, but she wouldn't admit that, despite their shared emotional turmoil. The orange glow that filled Hannah's corneas faded away with the steadiness of her breathing leveling off with each passing second. She was unsure if Gwendolyn was real, or yet another one of the simulations tests.

"I heard you," Gwendolyn said shakily. Her hands were still up in the air despite not having any fear of her teammate. "I saw them all die. My people. My home. I was all alone. I was lost and then I, I heard you, Hannah. I found you."

Timothy

Walking into the front door at the Holmes Estate Timothy went through the repetitive motions he did each and every time he came home. Taking his shoes off by the front door, left one first, then the right, he took special care to leave his jacket on the floor next to them, rather than hang it up on the coat rack a mere two feet away. Looking around for his mother, Timothy saw no one and nothing that would otherwise give him pause. It was all normal, mundane. Except for the fact that his mother would never let so much time go by without doting on him, nothing was a miss at all.

"Hello?" Timothy asked aloud, shouting up the long staircase that led to all the bedrooms. He didn't feel like going upstairs to search for anyone, and was thinking about how stupid his parents were for not getting an elevator when he got the shock of his life.

"Hey there, handsome," his sister said with an air of seductive dutifulness. Dressed in a black and white polka dot pattered dress with a white petticoat peeking out underneath and high heels, Tina L. Holmes scurried over to Timothy before throwing her arms around him and giving him a quick kiss on the lips. The bit of her bubble gum flavored lip gloss that stayed behind served as a reminder that no, this was not a dream. "How was your day?"

Stupefied Timothy could not believe what he saw. As if she had read, agreed upon, and decided to act out his deepest, more secretive fantasy his twin sister was acting very much the part of lady of the house while accommodating him and him alone. Looking every bit the picturesque stereotype of a mid twentieth century American housewife, he was willing to bet that she would also be at his beck and call. Which meant it was a dream. But it didn't feel like a dream. So, was Tina playing a cruel trick on him? Had she somehow figured out his hidden feelings? It was in that moment of self-doubt that he realized Tina, standing there biting her lower lip and widening her eyes to maximize her cuteness, that his twin sister was literally hanging on his every word. Oddly discomforted by this, he finally settled on a tentative sounding, "Good."

"Oh that's wonderful!" Tina exclaimed, bending her knees before jerking back up to give the impression that she literally jumped for joy. It was something he had seen other girls do before in placating their boyfriends, and always wanted a girl to do it for him. Now, not only had a girl shown him attention, affection, and adoration but THE girl had. His girl. His other half. His every-thing. "Would you like me to get you a drink? Oh! How about your slippers? Silly me, of course you'll want both. Ok, I'll get them if you just go sit down in the den and relax."

'This has to be a dream,' Timothy thought to himself before turning that prospect over in his mind a few times. He remembered waking up that morning in the academy dorms, remembered eating breakfast, remembered what his sister decided to wear that day, and remembered the long walk through the forest to the B.E.T.S.I. facility. 'I'm in the simulation,' he thought to himself.

Tina bit her lip again as she placed her hands behind her back and shifted slightly while staring at him with wide, wanting eyes. When Timothy nodded, Tina hurried to his side before bending down, and then giggling a bit as she pranced off back the kitchen and out of sight, taking extra special care to wiggle her bottom seductively as she went around the corner.

"No!" came a scream in distance beyond the open door. Timothy knew that it was Jaime in peril yet somehow could not bring himself to care. He stood, paralyzed at the genuine fear of losing this fantasy, and he knew that if he went back out the front door that stood open and unknown he would surely never come back. Not to this, not this perfection. For Timothy Holmes could now define bliss, for he had found it this day within the confines of B.E.T.S.I. He knew it wouldn't last, it couldn't, for eventually his team would lose and the simulation would end; which it did, though not before Timothy got his one perfect day.

Rolland

The Tyrannosaurus Rex reared its scaly, leathery head backward, baring its teeth against the backdrop of jungle setting that Rolland suspected might be his final resting place. Having met, adventured with, and learned to dislike Dr. Judah Raines he knew exactly what kind of dangerous invention the mad scientist might be capable of creating. To this end, Rolland was unsure if injury or death in the B.E.T.S.I. simulation would equate to injury or death in the real world; both of which he was surely to toe the line of when dealing with a Jurassic beast such as the one that stood before him.

Jumping out of the way Rolland was able to avert the first lunge of the massive dinosaur's attempt to consume him by landing in a pile of tree brush. Rolling over onto his back, Rolland got a good view of the tyrannosaurus rooting around the spot where his human prey had been seconds before, trying desperately to find a scent trail. With a short lift of his head that send an almost electric response down the animals spine the massive head turned directly to look to look at Rolland, and with another mighty ROAR that rivaled it's first, it came at him with no regard for mercy.

Panicking, Rolland snapped both his thumbs against his middle fingers before bringing his palms together while in mid-run. The slow motion of the tyrannosaurus' jaw as it bit and grasped at bits of debris that still held Rolland's scent was the oddest sight he had ever seen. Although time was moving slower, fifty times slower by his concentrated effort, the extinct, yet majestic king of the lizards fought like a warrior in an attempt to catch Rolland Wright. Estimating that each tooth was nearly as tall as he was, Rolland jogged backward, never taking his eyes off of the still snarling, very angry looking dinosaur, whose beady little black and yellow eyes were as fixated as could be residing on either side of its head. Picking up his pace as he fell following another ground shaking snap of the mighty beast's jaw, Rolland saw a small cave opening ahead of him that was too narrow for the monster to fit. For some reason time around him was quickening, and he knew he had the option to either once again slow it down, or proceed to the cave. Running for it full out, he made it with enough breath in his lungs to spare a good taunting before time corrected itself fully, despite how tired he was becoming.

Angered by this turn of events, the Tyrannosaurus began circling around several times and let out many consecutive roars in what Rolland could only describe as a temper tantrum. After a few minutes in which the beast settled down and both man and dinosaur were able to catch their breath, another strange happening transpired. From the narrow opening in the cave Rolland looked outward to see two very distinctive portals, each resembling very much his own wormholes that he had created with Captain Nareau opening on either side of the dinosaur.

They each came with their heads down to better see any immediate threat that might be approaching. Although their teeth were much smaller than those of the Tyrannosaurus, there were more of them and being closer to the ground, both had easier access to whatever they were hunting. Their claws were the size of fully formed icicles in the dead of winter, and twice as sharp. There were three on each of the scaly arms that gave the first, and often last, impression the velociraptor had in interacting with other animals. Often described as vicious, velociraptors garnered a reputation of their ruthless cunning during the hunt, relying on their instincts and intellect above all else. The pair of them, both hungry, saw Rolland immediately upon arrival. A sudden POOF of light and smoke appeared next to him, returning Dodger Yick back to the battle, but positioned just outside of the cave's safety from the dinosaurs.

"I'm back to help," Dodger said, smiling at Rolland before hearing the screeching sounds coming from the two velociraptors that stood on either side of the Tyrannosaurus, waiting to attack. Seeing that the situation had gotten even worse Dodger's jaw dropped ever so slightly as he eyed both smaller, yet somehow scarier looking beasts before turning back to Rolland and offering a meek, "Just in time."

Pulling his friend into the cave by the wrist, Rolland whirled around snap clapping his hands together to slow time down again. He did, but only by half as he knew it would be easier to sustain given the fact that the velociraptors were small enough to fit inside the enclave, essentially trapping them if the two stayed. They ran, picking up bits of debris that could be used as weapons if necessary. Dodger found a metal pipe that he used like a poker toward the velociraptors when they lunged at the fleeing cadets. The two velociraptors were strange in that unlike the tyrannosaurus, who was relentless in his pursuit to the point of becoming discouraged, the two velociraptors appeared casual, calculated, and beyond anything else, patient. After about ten more minutes of this pursuit, they switched, and Dodger teleported Rolland from safe location to safe location within the confines of the jungle room yet they could not find an exit. Eventually the two were too exhausted to continue and were forced back into the cave from which they started.

"I expected to see Vilthe or something," Rolland panted between labored breaths. "I thought this place would make me see him, not dinosaurs."

Looking abashed, Dodger gave a single shake of his head before shrugging his shoulders and said, "My bad."

"Dinosaurs?" Rolland asked incredulously, his fingers grasping tighter to the sharpened pipe he had taken from Dodger during their last switch. No comfort was found in this action. "Your biggest fear is DINOSAURS?!"

Dodger smiled sheepishly in response as behind them two more velociraptors popped into existence from the still opened portals, each stripped with various shades of green and brown stripes, interlaced with bellies of spotted gray and white. Oddly ornate feathers of tope, purple, and lilac grew on both sides of their heads, lightly grazing their bulbous yellow eyes that looked past the tyrannosaurus and locked onto the two cadets. "Aren't you scared though?"

Rolland turned towards the portals, but immediately wished that he hadn't. It was too much. He turned to Dodger and was about to ask what the process was for surrender when he heard familiar female voices. Bridging the gap between them and the dinosaurs, with the tyrannosaurus hot on their trail, were Gwendolyn and Hannah, both of who were in full battle mode.

"Need some help?" Gwendolyn called to Rolland with a smile as the two passed through to the safety of the cave.

"Always," Dodger said, looking over at Hannah who blushed lightly at his gaze. Just then one of the new velociraptors made its first move on their ground, launching in a full out sprint toward the narrow opening of the cave in an attempt to break away the rock and widen it. Seeing it coming, Hannah pushed Dodger aside, extended out her left hand, and blasted the dinosaur with a jetty of molten hot pink plasma that caused the beast to screech in agony before retreating.

"Good job!" Rolland offered.

"I don't think we can hold this position," Gwendolyn said, whirling around to kick a velociraptor who had stuck its head into the cave. With her natural grace, and Nocturn instincts taking over under duress, the Nocturn made a formidable opponent to any man, or beast. Running out of the cave to mount an offense before it could expect one, Gwendolyn flew at the beast, rounding around its small neck until she was in a sitting riding position on its back.

"Just a little longer," Rolland said, as he ran out of the cave holding the square piece of steel up like a shield to deflect the claws of the third beast. A flash out of the corner of his eye told him that Dodger had also left the cave and, sure enough, he appeared with Hannah in tow, to assist in distracting the velociraptor that was halfway jammed in the enclave opening. Suddenly an idea came to Rolland.

Waiting for the right moment, Rolland snap clapped his hands, filling the jungle with the eagle screech before creating a rip in time that Rolland willed bigger than any he ever had before, all while the raptor hurdled itself toward it. Once the last bit of its sinister tail was clear Rolland closed the portal with a sigh of relief before running out to see a smiling Dodger nod approvingly at him.

But suddenly another portal opened right above their collective heads. The familiar majesty and sound of a screeching eagle filled the chamber as the same velociraptor that Rolland had banished moments before returned, leaping out of the window as it closed, and landing on the stone ground before them. Drool fell freely from its yellowing teeth as it mocked the four cadets with its very presence. It took a swipe with its left claw that connected with Rolland's shoulder, leaving a shallow gash two inches long.

"Damn," Rolland said under his breath. He then ran, attracting the attention of all five of the dinosaurs as they watched him scurry away from his three companions. Then, a great many things happened at once. Just as it had shortly after Nero's attack months before the lights turned on, changing the interior of the B.E.T.S.I. obstacle course from a holographic, if not deadly, simulation back into an old, rather plain looking warehouse, complete with a black metal catwalk over head and a multi-colored lighting rig. With the lights on the menacing looking building was nothing more than a place where adolescent fears came to either die, or be invigorated by fresh exercise in power.

"SIMULATION OVER!" said a booming yet flat female voice that sounded from everywhere at once, filling all ten of their ears again and again. "SIMULATION OVER!"

Rolland, Gwendolyn, Dodger, and Hannah looked at one another with complete confusion. Moments before the quartet had been battling for their lives against ancient beasts, and now were once again mere cadets in an academy simulation that each believed they had lost somehow. The dinosaurs had not been vanquished, they had not been eliminated, and none of their other teammates had come to their assistance. Each cadet silently worried that the worst-case scenario was about to transpire, with all but Rolland believing he would be the target for any attack to come. Dodger remembered the man who had risen from the Time Stream and braced himself for a re-introduction.

"What did we do?" Gwendolyn asked, her small hands placed palm downward over her pointed ears. What none of her classmates realized was that Gwendolyn possessed heightened hearing abilities. An ace up her sleeve, the young Nocturn never felt the need to share this fact with anyone, seeing as how it served little purpose besides being boastful. The downside of sensitivity to loud, repetitive, human made noises was most evident in the situations where she was nearly crippled due to the genetic variation.

Behind Hannah Rolland spotted a vibration stemming from the catwalk overhead as it connected to the air vent. It shook again, this time with more violence, before the bottom of the vent came crashing down to the floor, followed by two familiar, female legs, a torso, and the face of Tina Holmes, a red flag of victory clutched in her left hand. "I got it!"

Dodger got to Tina first, spotting the flag but not understanding its meaning until the other three arrived on the scene to confirm that Tina had succeeded, and that they had collectively passed the test. His world turned upside down.

"What's the matter Dodge?" Tina asked, her face covered in splotches of vent grease, and one of her hair braids mostly untangled, hanging lazily over her right shoulder. "Cat got your tongue?"

"Tina!" Rolland shouted, his face turning a bit red as his tongue choked on itself in surprise. He wanted to hold her, grab her, KISS her, but stopped for some reason. The moment was too big, too grand for it to be just for the two of them. Rolland knew, deep down in his heart, that the humble surprise Tina's victory brought was nothing short of spectacular. "You did it!"

Bowing her head slightly to the four of them, it was then Tina's turn to propel herself forward, landing with her arms outstretched into a collective group hug between herself, Rolland, Gwendolyn, and Hannah. For his part Dodger, who was only left out due to space, was happy with the red victory flag being flung in his face following a quick flick of Tina's wrist. She looked at Rolland, intense affection in her baby blue eyes as she stood on her tiptoes to match his height, leveling their lips together. A sloppy, moist kiss between the two as they walked through the exit door behind Dodger and Gwendolyn left little doubt as to who underestimated whose abilities that day.

"WE did it!" Tina screamed happily, walking slightly in front of him. Her hair bounced off her shoulders, falling down her back and giving the distinct sense of accomplishment as she moved.

Humbled, Rolland walked out to find Kniff, Jaime, and silent, visibly upset looking Timothy Holmes waiting outside discussing their failure loudly. Between the chattering pair stood the tiger cub, Tiikeri, smelling the night air with an upturned nose and whiskers. She had enjoyed spending time frolicking with the unicorn pups by the pen where Tina met Doctor Duffy for lessons in the past few weeks, but the time for action was near, a sense the animal picked up from her human counterparts by the change in their respective heartbeats. It wasn't until they were all outside that they broke off to turn to the others. The comical moment of awareness as their angry expressions melted away at seeing the red flag clutched in Tina's hands was one that Rolland would cherish for a long, long time. No one spoke. All of them, the morose looking Timothy included, merely sat down on the ground in a semi-circle, and relaxed for the first time in hours. Later Tina would find out that she had spent four hours, seventeen minutes, and forty five seconds inside the simulation before she reached the flag. But for now the Class of the Tiger enjoyed tranquility, peace, and each other's company for what none realized would be the last time.

Seizing the opportunity, Rolland asked Tina for a moment of privacy. As the two stood up and walked roughly ten feet away from their classmates, they elicited a series of whoops from almost all but Timothy, whose sullen silence was becoming his trademark. Taking it in stride, Tina smiled and shook her head, though Rolland noticed the two were not walking far, and would only be out of earshot - not complete privacy. Still, the moment was as perfect as Rolland could want as he circled Tina's waist. His hand slid a little lower, resting comfortably on Tina's buttocks.

"Naughty," Tina said with a slight smile to her voice. She enjoyed Rolland's company in such close proximity, the little voice inside her head that told her to draw a line with him sexually grew smaller, and father away. The two kissed again, their tongues caressing each other on every fourth or fifth kiss.

Then it appeared. Knowing no boundaries of time, or space, or any respect for the interpersonal schedule its targets might be keeping the brilliantly white orb that had last greeted Rolland in 19th century Pensacola, Florida appeared. It was coming toward him fast and its brilliant light contrasted sharply with the deep black of Eden's Solomon forest. Its sudden appearance brought many things to Eden, the least of which was immediate dread that filled the heart of the only surviving member of the Wright family.

"No," Rolland said, staring at the white ball of energy as it hovered above him for a long moment before rising another foot into the air and beginning a zig-zag pacing dance. He recalled that it had done this before, whenever it was stationary for too long. Once upon a time the orb was a savior, a guiding light in a world of fire and uncertainty. In this moment, however, Rolland Wright was not lost, or alone. In this moment Rolland was in no need of the orb, and frankly, didn't want anything to do with it. He knew he had to follow it but resisted and yelled, "No, no, no!"

"What?" Tina asked, furrowing her brow as she watched her boyfriend's face go white.

"It's a long story, but I have to do it, I have to follow the-" Rolland began, stopping short when he felt the soft, slender fingers of Tina interlacing with his own.

"Go on, follow the what?" Tina asked, a gentle smile gracing her understanding face as she looked deep into Rolland's eyes.

This was it; this was the moment that Captain Nareau had warned Rolland about regarding the secrets he kept. The choices were two - tell Tina the truth, risking the idea that he might come across as crazy, or lie outright to her, and choose the path that he knew would end like every failed friendship and familial relation he ever had. In the end Rolland chose the path of most resistance.

"Do you remember that morning I told you about, the one at the bookstore?" Rolland asked, his heart beating a mile a minute.

"Yeah, as much as you and the field reports told me," Tina said with a straightforward smile that comforted Rolland, encouraging him to go on with his story. She had never admitted to him outright that she had read almost literally everything she could concerning Rolland, his trial, and his family heritage while he was in jail. "Sweetie, what is it? What's wrong?"

"There is a reason that I saved those people," Rolland said, stepping over a large rock as the pair made their way away from the Academy. "Someone, er, something showed me how. Gave me a path to follow."

Confused but not deterred, Tina nodded her head and asked, "What was it?"

"It was this white ball of light." Rolland said desperately. "I know this sounds crazy."

"Crazy is relative," Tina said breezily. "Go on, so you followed the white ball of light through the fire…"

"Yeah, except that wasn't the only time I've seen it," Rolland said, thinking back to his time in Florida. "Remember when you set Hess on fire, and I found my knife in that little cave? Well the orb lead me to it, and now.."

"Now, what?" Tina asked, squeezing Rolland's hand. The night air was colder than usual, creating small bumps on her bare arms and neck.

"It's back," Rolland said, looking Tina dead in the eye and hoping against hope that she wouldn't think him a mad man. "And it's buzzing around your head as we speak."

Fascinated, and not at all alarmed by this revelation Tina merely smiled the same understanding smile before nodding her head in support, urging him to continue. "So what does it want?"

"I think it wants me to go help Turtledove," Rolland said, knowing somehow that it was true. He didn't exactly know how he knew the orb was leading him to Turtledove; all he knew was that he needed to go. He watched as Tina's jaw dropped, and her eyes grow wider than he had ever seen them. "What I can do.. what ONLY I can do, is to follow this thing."

Not knowing what else to do Tina nodded her head as tears welled around the corner of her eyes. "I understand. You should go."

Surprised by Tina's acceptance of what Rolland could only describe as a useful, if not annoying otherworldly visual hallucination, he turned to face the ball of light, which floated slowly away from him and toward the hills that led to the Halls of Time. Thoughts of Turtledove flashed into his mind as well as a sense of trepidation at seeing him. He hadn't spoken to the man in months, and according to Dodger, he wasn't in the best state.

"I have to go," said Rolland again, watching the little white orb dance merrily in the distance beyond the academy's gate. He was so focused on the light's movements that Rolland did not notice that the other members of his team had gathered around them.

"Pardon?" Kniff asked, eyeing Rolland warily. A flash of his uncle Etra stabbing him within the simulation filled his mind's eye once again, and he had to shake it away.

"There is.. something that I have to do," Rolland said, unable to take his eyes off of the white orb and hoping desperately, silently, that one of his classmates would see it to. Each eyed him carefully before following his line of vision to the spot where the orb was, yet none of them said a word to the affirmation of its presence.

"Wait, right now?" Dodger asked, his voice betraying a hint of anger. He was hoping for an impromptu campfire, alcohol, and a first attempt at getting some one on one time at speaking with Hannah, who intrigued him to no end. "Seriously?"

"But we just passed the B.E.T.S.I !" Hannah exclaimed, followed by a chorus of like-minded chants from the rest of their class, and a small roar that was really more of a meow from

Tiikeri. Feeling a bit of comfort from the cat, Hannah picked her up and cradled it in her arms as she watched Rolland attempt to explain himself. She had heard the rumors of his madness too, but held the only proof she ever needed to argue otherwise.

"I know, alright? And I'm sorry, really I am," Rolland said, his eyes watching as the orb did another series of cartwheels down the nearest visible hillside in the nearby woods. It left a strangely beautiful glowing trail that evaporated after a few seconds in its wake. The scene was eerie, yet oddly comforting somehow - much like how Rolland felt about the orb itself. Suddenly he was very aware that he had seven other people staring at him, waiting for him to answer them back. Kicking his brain into overdrive, Rolland thought before he spoke. "You are all my friends, and I would do anything for you. But right now another friend needs me."

That was it. There was nothing else to do but give Tina a quick, but meaningful, kiss on the lips, pat Dodger on the back and take off running toward the orb, which upon Rolland's movement began a steady pace away from the Academy of Light eastward toward the Halls of Time.

"He doesn't really expect us to wait here, does he?" Jaime asked, looking at Timothy, Dodger, and Tina as they watched Rolland disappear out of sight.

Shaking their heads quizzically, both Hannah and Gwendolyn looked out of sorts, each still bearing the battle scars from earlier. Both young women looked to Tina who was still trying to process all that Rolland had told her. Tina frowned, raised her shoulders and simply stated, "It will be dangerous."

"My blood still boils," said Kniff thinking of his dead sister lying in a pool blood. He pushed his way past his teammates, all of whom were watching Rolland striding in the distance. "We go."

Chapter 17:
When Next We Meet

Marshal Island - 1937

Upon returning to the present, neither Amelia nor Joan spoke of the incident beyond the initial asking of each other's condition after landing. With their bits and pieces all accounted for, Amelia opened her mouth to ask one of the hundred burning questions bubbling in her brain, but thought better of it when her eyes caught the sword Joan had retrieved from the church. Suddenly the trivial questions of 'How had they done what they had just done?' were secondary to the severity of the situation. So, they walked. And walked, and walked some more until both the deafening silence between them and the greenery surrounding them broke with a dramatic revelation of a modest cabin in the center of the forest.

"We have to go inside," Amelia said suddenly, walking forward and past Joan, who was squinting to get a better view of the place. The events of the last few days suddenly faded and Amelia snapped back into the mindset of her mission. The one assigned to her by the President of the United States himself; retrieve the trigger to a top-secret covert operation titled: Project Dreamcoat. Though she had no idea what it was, Amelia didn't care. She had always longed to escape the drudgery that came with being a woman and with an aptitude as high as the planes she piloted, Amelia was quickly spotted and subsequently recruited into Uncle Sam's payroll. No matter how she justified it, called it something different, or placated her own conscience, at the end of the day Amelia knew exactly what she was, and was damn proud of it. Amelia Earhart was the first, and best, female spy of the early twentieth century.

The pair of women stopped suddenly as they came upon the bloody bodies that created a less than inviting trail leading toward the small cabin. The massacre, totaling in what Joan quickly guesstimated to the final action for some seventeen men of two starkly contrasting cultures and appearances. On one side of stony pathway that led to the small structure were the corpses of fallen Imperial Japanese soldiers, each still wearing their helmets - even in death. On the other side of the wreckage were six dark skinned, and very tall men wearing jewelry comprised of crab claws. Although neither woman knew who the men were, they each noticed that despite their ultimate fate, they had obviously taken out quite a few of the soldiers before falling victim to the superior numbers of the Imperial troops.

Amelia, whom before that day Joan would have assumed was unfamiliar with the sight of fallen soldiers in battle, was taking it all in stride, stepping over the corpses of both Imperial Japanese and who Joan now suspected were Eke warriors alike as if this were a daily occurrence. Without meeting each other's eyes, both women visually checked each and every corpse they encountered for familiar physical traits that they would recognize, silently hoping they wouldn't find Judah or Fred Noonan among the carnage. Thankfully, neither found the horrific closure they sought.

The door was wide open, giving the immediately ominous impression of danger as the two entered inside. Joan half expected the thin, poorly built door with its oddly new looking brass doorknob to swing shut behind them when they walked in, and, without realizing it, only let go of the breathe she was holding when it did not move.

"Woah," said Amelia.

The cabin consisted of a single room with a small dining nook off in the far right corner, complete with a small wooden table and two crudely made wooden chairs with hearts etched into the back supports. Across from the table was an old wood-burning stove that gave off an rich earthy scent. The walls were covered from base to ceiling with books of various sizes, colors, and bindings. Authors with names in multiple languages, among them English, French, Italian, and Latin embossed the spines of each volume of knowledge, creating a structure of their own as they amassed around what looked like a wide, cushy, light brown chair with a seat filled with cotton that peeked out from both sides.

"What is this place?" Amelia asked, her hands already grazing the shelves of the nearby bookcase. She knew that Joan was watching her warily and despite knowing more than one secret to hold over Joan's head in return, was not yet ready to reveal her true motivations or mission. Not yet.

"It looks like someone's home," Joan said, taking a moment to look for any signs of a bed, pillows, or blankets. When she found none, her sense of wariness increased. "Nothing inside looks too disturbed, so I'm guessing none of the departed outside ever made their way in here."

It was then that the item caught her eye. A book entitled *Saint Joan* was sitting neatly in the middle of a stack of books that was as high as her waist. Joan grabbed the red book, opened to the first page, and looked for a table of contents. There, her entire life before coming to Eden was chronicled, and documented by no less than at least twenty different scholars. One chapter titled **CHARACTER** struck her curiosity further, and she flipped to the prescribed page before beginning to read.

Joan displayed exemplarily character and pose under the worst of conditions. Despite the odds, monarchs, and persecution against her, the young woman inspired the hearts and minds of an entire country of displaced Frenchmen.'

It still took Joan by surprise that history would remember her so fondly considering how little she was appreciated in her own time and by her own people. The great ironies of life are ones best savored in hindsight. Pondering this, positive feelings of nostalgia, not just for her military life, but of meeting and marrying Judah, being recruited into the Knights of Time, and teaching various students at the Academy of Light gave her a comfort she had not experienced in days. Hard days. Days filled with betrayal, deep delves into her psyche, revisiting her past, and crabs. Big, big crabs. As she grew further lost in thought, the unpleasantness of what she knew was to come regarding Sephanie faded into the ether of her mind as happier memories took hold.

With Joan distracted, Amelia continued her inconspicuous search for the trigger. She did not know exactly what it looked like specifically, only that it was the size of a human adult fist, made of metal, and would be housed in some sort of containment receptacle. Hell, even if she found it, the item in question might be one of perhaps four or five trinkets that would match the description given to her by America's 'finest intelligence committee'. Just when the thought of taking a knife and hollowing out each book she encountered fleeted through her mind, her eyes spotted a mahogany and walnut box the size a large book on the top shelf to her right.

"Jackpot," Amelia whispered to herself while standing on her tiptoes to reach the item. Lifting the walnut inlayed box off of the bookcase with the same care one would an antique, the young pilot looked again to see Joan's attention still wrapped in a book before taking stock of the treasure she had found. Any doubts that she might have had regarding the validity of the item that was described as the trigger to Project Dreamcoat were dashed upon first inspection. Resting on a soft velvet cushion behind a thin pane of glass that comprised the top of the box was a metal trigger, much like the one used on a firearm, except bigger, and bend upward sharply at the end. Two golden latches on either side of the box beckoned to be opened, and as she flipped the first one a dull thud filled the room.

"Don't open it yet," Joan said suddenly, startling Amelia, who almost dropped the box. "Someone's coming."

The bloody scene that Sephanie Kelly found when approaching the otherwise unassuming looking cottage was some of the worst mutual destruction she had ever witnessed. Recognizing the darker skinned individuals as members of the island's indigenous Eke tribe, she plucked a crudely made machete out of the of the more intact tribesmen's corpses before stepping over what was left of his two nearest comrades. She then saw the cottage with its front door wide open. Visually sifting amongst the rest of the corpses, Sephanie did not see the prize she sought after and knew at once she would have to travel the path of carnage to look inside the building. 'How peculiar' she thought to herself as she tip toed around the remains of the skirmish, 'that I'm capable of taking a man's life, but my stomach still grows uneasy amongst so much death.'

Sephanie thought of the incident with Fred Noonan in such terms; she had 'taken a man's life' because she was indeed the one who had caused his final breath to be drawn. She saw it as both a necessity, and a means of survival in world where cruelty was simply another form of currency. With no sign of life, Sephanie held up her machete and slowly entered the cabin. Inside she found books scattered everyone as well as a pleasant humming noise coming from the table by the stove on the far side of the room. Sephanie ducked behind the entryway to avoid being seen, but not before spotting the mahogany and glass box that sat on the table next to the humming woman.

The occupant, whose back was turned away from the doorway, was reading a book while humming a jazzy tune that Sephanie did not recognize. Another quick look and Sephanie spotted the curly locks of the woman she recognized to be Amelia Earhart. Taking no notice of what exactly Earhart was doing, only that whatever the task it was in proximity to the location of the trigger for Project Dreamcoat, Sephanie's mind struggled with creating a more eloquent plan than to simply attack while Amelia's back was turned. Steeling herself, Sephanie clutched the Eke machete tight within her left palm, and stepped sideways beyond the entryway so that she was lined up a mere eight feet from her unsuspecting victim.

Suddenly a pale hand shot out like a cobra and gripped her wrist so tightly that she gasped aloud. Before she even looked up she knew whose hand that was. "Joan?"

"Hello Sephanie," Joan began coldly. Out of the corner of her eye she saw Amelia spin around to watch the two.

"Joan…" Sephanie gasped again. "What are you doing here? Is Judah with you? Turtledove?"

"Just stop. You have one opportunity to explain what you're doing here," Joan continued. Deep in her mind, beneath the intense feelings of betrayal and bitterness were questions and the lingering want to give Sephanie the benefit of the doubt. Yet she was not fool enough to ignore signs from a higher power, signs like giant glowing orbs that send you back in time over five hundred years to re-learn numerous lessons on the subjects of trust and betrayal. "One opportunity."

A long moment of silence passed. Part of Joan expected her friend to outright deny the accusation before it was launched. But it never came. Long breaths, in and out, came one right after the other, joining in the symphony of the island's outside noises as day turned to dusk and the wind picked up. The two friends looked at one another some more, memories of good times clouding the already murky waters of judgment between them. Both women knew what would happen next, then after that, and where their paths would eventually meet after each chose their role before it all ended in bloodshed. Joan knew it always ended in bloodshed. "Are you working for Vilthe?"

Deafening silence engulfed them.

"I can explain, I-" Sephanie began, before being cut off by the woman who had been her closest friend in the world.

"Save it," Joan said in a flat, unfeeling tone that chilled Sephanie to the bone. "I saw you with Otep last night."

Knowing that she was caught Sephanie saw no other conclusion than to come clean with her friend and mentor, and hope for the best possible outcome. Her free hand fell to her side as she took a deep breath and begin to speak. "Joan, I-"

"I said save it!" Joan shouted as she let go of Sephanie's wrist, her face turning bright red with rage and her posture straightening with the strength of a warrior in her spine. "I watched you torture Noonan, Sephanie. I watched you *kill* him."

"You what?" Amelia shouted, her attempts at being small or uninvolved cast aside at the mention of Noonan's name. "Fred is dead, and, and you knew about it?"

"We'll discuss that later," Joan snarled through gritted teeth. She didn't dare even look at Amelia, lest she appear unsympathetic while cooling down from her inner rage. "Let's go."

"Vilthe is my husband," Sephanie admitted, a fresh wave of tears cascading down her cheeks. "He tricked me into marrying him, Joanie. I was so young and I- I just couldn't help it."

"You're Persephone, aren't you?" Joan asked bluntly, her eyes wet with pitiful tears of frustration. Joan had wondered about her friend's identity for years, all the unexplained absences during the winter months made sense now. Except it didn't. Joan made a motion to leave before giving out what she anticipated to be her final thoughts on the matter. "Vilthe's wife and spy. How could I have been so stupid?"

"Wait," Sephanie shouted, looking up at her friend with the impudence and fear of a child about to be scolded. With tears in her eyes, her hair matted with dirt, and a smell surrounding her that can only be gained from camping outdoors for several days, Sephanie looked as pathetic as she ever would and under any other circumstances short of betrayal or adultery with her spouse, Joan might have forgiven her long time friend. "What happens now?"

"What happens is you are going stop looking for the trigger, or Amelia, or whatever the hell it is your *husband* sent you here for," Joan fairly spat out. Too long had she confided in the woman she now stared holes of white-hot rage into. Too long had she trusted her with matters of the utmost sensitivity. Too long had she loved her like a sister. "And then you leave this place."

"But what about.. Joan, what about," Sephanie began, desperate to gain a bit of her comfort back. "What about us, Joanie?"

"Don't ever call me that again. There is no us anymore, Persephone," Joan said, both of her hands balled into tight fists that sought a meeting with the face of her former best friend.

"We need to leave. Now." Amelia said to Joan, her anger and sadness at Fred Noonan's death overwhelming her. "We need to find Judah."

Yet as the two women made their way out of the cottage, around the corpses of Imperialist Japanese and tribal Eke alike, and down the cobblestone path that led back to the grassy hillside, a crying Sephanie suddenly came after them, tears streaming down her face.

"Joanie, Joanie please-" Sephanie began.

"No! I don't want to hear anything you have to say," Joan said, a single tear escaping her left eye, sliding its way down her cheek and landing on her pink bottom lip. It would be the only one she would shed over the loss of Sephanie from her life, regardless of their sisterly affection. "Not another word."

"Please..." Sephanie managed one last time, inadvertently nailing the final nail in their coffin of trust and friendship.

"When next we meet," Joan said, turning to Sephanie full on with the utmost sincerity to her voice. "One of us will die."

Hours later, long after Joan and Amelia had put some distance between themselves and Sephanie, they finally had the discussion about the events surrounding Noonan's death. The extent of the details to which Joan would tell Amelia, she decided, would only be as far as the pilot asked for, and much to her relief, she only wanted the big picture. After another hour of speculation regarding Judah's whereabouts, the two called it a night and drifted off to a listless sleep under a blanket of stars and regrets.

Joan awoke from a dream more tired than when she had initially fallen asleep. Feelings of forced sympathy for Sephanie flooded her mind, second only to the feelings of rage and betrayal the girl had left in her wake. It was barely dawn and the fire from the evening before was nearly dead, only a few coals left to glow against the brink of day. Joan thought of Judah and wished he were there to comfort her. Worried that the day time illusions were carrying over into her night time dreaming, making it impossible to gain any foresight into the future. Lost in her thoughts she realized with a jolt that Amelia was nowhere to be found.

And with her the trigger to Project Dreamcoat.

Chapter 18:
Unwavering Loyalty

Eden

Bracing himself against the wind, Rolland pushed the small strands of hair out of his eyes for what felt like the hundredth time. He knew instinctively where the orb was leading him, even before the Halls of Time came into view. Despite his aching calf muscles that shot spasms of pain through his legs with each step, an urgent sense of duty forced him onward. He had told Tina that he knew he had to follow the orb but he didn't tell her everything, having known he already sounded like the insane criminal half of Eden thought he was. Somehow, he knew that the orb was leading him to not only Turtledove but to Victor. Another strong gust of wind hit him, pushing his hair to the side, exposing the right side of his slight widow's peak hairline. Goose bumps rose on his exposed arms as he ascended the hill and stood before the

Halls of Time. The building's shadow loomed large over Rolland as the twin waxing moons arose to bathe the valley in their soft glow.

Opening the heavy door for the first time since he had left for the Academy of Light. Rolland continued down the wide hallway, his shoes squeaking loudly, until he entered the foyer. To his right was the library, where Tina and he shared their first kiss. There were the tables where he and Victor had spent so much of their time talking and laughing after his release from prison. They were good memories, memories worth fighting for. With that thought in mind, Rolland steeled himself for the confrontation yet to come.

To Rolland's surprise, the dining room was dark, darker than he had ever seen it. The effect left an uneasy feeling in the pit of his stomach as he flipped on the light switch. With the room illuminated Rolland saw the full extent of the situation. The long table where he had dined with the Knights of Time his first night in Eden was pushed to the far side of the room with the majority of its chairs stacked neatly against the north wall. Dirty dishes, empty bottles, and books were scattered everywhere. The soft sound of a pen scratching from the far edge of the room reached Rolland's ears, and looking his found the one man he had both yearned and dreaded to see; a disheveled, beleaguered Marcus L. Turtledove.

"Mr. Wright," Turtledove said with a ghost of a smile. "How good of you to drop by."

"Er.. No problem. How've you been?" Rolland asked awkwardly, making his way through the sea of food containers. When he reached the table, he noticed it was covered with black and white photographs, and scrolls with writing he couldn't even begin to comprehend. Stranger still were various maps with seemingly random pins but with a second glance Rolland realized the pins all formed the same pattern.

"Oh, I've been..." Turtledove began before breaking off with a hacking cough, his eyes looking up at Rolland for only the briefest of moments before drifting off again toward the room's only window. The sky outside was scattered with blinking white stars, all emerging as dusk made way into night. Deep down it was a nice metaphor, a peaceful one that described how he had been feeling for the past several months. Time was a heavy, burdensome thing to him now. One that weighed upon his shoulders in a meta-physical toll of grief.

The lines under the old man's eyes were never more prominent to Rolland as they were in that moment. Unsure as to how to proceed, Rolland thought about what he had learned in the past few months while at the academy. Training with Captain Nareau forced him to believe in himself, and mastering B.E.T.S.I. had taught him humility, and trust in others. While these were not the essential lessons he had expected to learn at the Academy, he knew why he had to learn them.

"Let's just cut the bullshit, Turtledove," said Rolland flatly. Startled, Turtledove turned to fully face Rolland and his eyes suddenly seemed more alert. Rolland wanted to ask the man who had pulled him into the life they both shared why he had chosen to find him. Why he had waited so long to do so? And most of all, why his father had tried to lead a double life. Scott, who had wanted it all, the life in Eden, and a nice, happy, 21st century suburban Californian life of the upper middle class. Instead he simply said, "Do you know why I'm here?"

"I have my guesses," Turtledove began, his eyes piercing into Rolland's. " This is in regards to Victor is it not?"

"It is," Rolland said, softly. Though he had heard the rumors and whisperings of people who fall into the Time Stream being lost forever, an inner voice told him that he needed to at least try. The orb, mysterious as it was, had never steered him wrong in the past, and being that it was thinking along the same lines as he was, fed off of his need to play the part of hero to Turtledove, Victor, and the rest of the presently absent Knights of Time. Fleeting thoughts of Sephanie and Tina blurred as he grabbed a long parchment off of a nearby table and read the strange numbers written in scribbled letters. "These coordinates, what are they leading to?"

"As far as I can deduce," Turtledove began, choking back a fresh round of coughs as his voice rose. "Victor is currently on the island of Haiti, in the year 1803."

Stunned, Rolland sucked in his breath. While he knew the orb was leading him to something to do with Victor. He hadn't actually let himself believe that his friend was alive somehow.

Noticing his reaction, Marcus Turtledove let out another long sigh before closing his eyes before saying, "Please understand Rolland, I can't be 100% of any of this."

"So what do we do?" Rolland asked, still unsure as to what exactly the cost might be.

"When you and I first met you expressed disapproval in the methods by which I employ in extracting individuals from the timeline, do you recall?" Turtledove mused.

Rolland merely nodded his head.

"Many years ago, eleven to be precise, I was tasked with extracting a boy from the late part of the twentieth century," Turtledove began, his voice taking on a ragged tone as if this were a story he had long held within his heart. "The place was a war torn country in Africa, Nigeria, in the year 1990. Unlike other extractions I had performed this boy was not in any immediate danger, as his identity only came to us via an embassy consulate who recognized that the boy in question did not feel any pain following a fall he took one day while his father led him home. Anyway, I arrived just in time to see the boy, his mother, brother, sister, and his father, ambassador Aquasi II, get into their Lincoln town car just before it exploded, sending it five feet off of the ground."

"That's.." Rolland began, but the loss for words struck deep within his mind. "Horrible, Turtledove. Just awful."

"Quite. The mother died instantly, but not the father or his children. The girl, poor thing, had her left arm, leg, and face blown off before the fire ravaged what was left. The father, Isaac, managed to exit the vehicle and assist his oldest son out, but the firing squad, my guess consisting of at least a few of those who placed the bomb in the vehicle to begin with, made short work of both of them before they suspected a thing. The last child..." Turtledove said, his voice growing distant and broken as the moments passed. The faint sound of a clocks second hand filled the otherwise quiet room as Rolland waited with baited breath to hear the end of Turtledove's tragic tale. "The last child was the boy I was sent to extract. I did not know it at the time, but once he had been shot eight, twelve, fifteen times and kept walking toward the terrified crowd I knew who he was. Unfortunately there was nothing I could do for the lad. So, I watched."

"You, you what?" Rolland asked, totally unprepared for this confession from a man he had previously respected. "You watched? You mean, you didn't help him?"

"No, I did not help. The flames were too thick, there were too many bystanders, and I do not possess the same abilities to slow time that you do, Mr. Wright. No. All I could do was watch, weep, and watch the flames as they burnt the child's flesh off of his bones as he reached out for his likewise charred parents and siblings. In short, it was the most grotesque thing I had ever seen up until that point. Finally the boy stopped fighting and allowed the mob to beat him, shoot him, and watch him burn. But I knew, deep down, deep in a place beyond using the extraordinary abilities I was blessed with, that this boy was still alive," Turtledove said, his eyes filled with a well of tears that refused to fall.

"That's awful," Rolland said softly. He had known that Victor had been somewhat invincible when consumed in fire, but he had no idea that ability went so far as to make him bulletproof. The entire ordeal sounded dreadful.

"I waited until the crowd had dispersed, never taking my eyes off of the boys vacant, milky white eyes as they stared at me, tunneled into me as he separated himself physically from his body while it was beaten and bruised from those who feared him," Turtledove said, his unapologetic tone morphing into one of contempt and anger. "He looked dead, and no doubt they all thought he was. But I knew differently. I knew that the boy was still alive. Broken body, broken soul, but ALIVE Rolland. Do you know how I knew this?"

"How?" Rolland asked automatically, so wrapped in Turtledove's story that he did not hear the opening of the main hallway door behind him.

Turtledove took a deep breath, looked down at his feet, and spoke in a very soft, but composed tone, "Because, Rolland Wright, corpses do not shed tears."

The pain within Rolland's heart was palpable to say the least. Feeling more motivated than ever to save his friend. "Let's go get Victor, Turtledove."

"Then get him we shall," Turtledove said, unaware that his audience had grown by nearly four times its size before he finished his tale. "Logic is a messy, complicated thing. One to which the heart chooses not to subscribe."

"Wooo hoooo, looks like you two are planning a va-ca-tion," came the pitchy, overzealous voice of Dodger from the hallway beyond the open-air foyer.

What came next was a series of sights and feelings that Rolland would cling to in his lowest moments for decades following. Rounding the corner, each the picture of the words haggard yet hopeful was the caravan of Tina, Dodger, Gwendolyn, Hannah, Kniff, Timothy, Jaime, and the tiger cub Tiikeri.

"I'm sorry sweetie, I couldn't stop them, I..." Tina began, her doe eyes pleading for forgiveness she knew at once she would receive.

"You're here," Rolland said, his thoughts jumbled at his teammates' sudden appearance. He was happy to see them, upset that they followed him, and relieved at no longer being alone with Turtledove. The touch of Tina's hand was comforting, even if it came with a death glare from her brother Timothy. "You're all here."

"Aye, you left in such a hurry, we thought we would miss you," Kniff said, his hands still covered in soot from the last stage of B.E.T.S.I.'s wrath. "Trying to get rid of us that quickly?"

Looking into Kniff's eyes Rolland thought of a quick lie, something simple enough to get them to go away before slipping out with Turtledove and the Dream Phoenix. Then Hannah's eyes caught his, two brown orbs of genuine affection and reverence for Rolland's leadership skills. Next came Gwendolyn's green eyes, and Jaime's brown ones. Every one giving him the same pleading look as Tina. In that moment Rolland realized that all they wanted, despite their rough night of trial, was the truth.

"Turtledove thinks that Victor, my friend, is still alive, lost in the Time Stream," said Rolland in one long breath. All of them save Gwendolyn and Kniff gasped at this, as it was tantamount to announcing the revival of the deceased. Yet none interrupted him as he spoke, propelling him to continue with his train of thought. "We're going to Haiti, 1803. We need to get in, get Victor, and get out. No telling how long he's been in there, and we want to keep unnoticed, so, just the two of us are going to go."

For a few moments the silence that hung in the night time air that filled the foyer convinced Rolland, however foolishly, that his teammates might drop the matter and return to the academy. This did not last long.

"Then we're going as well," Kniff proclaimed, garnering a series of head nods and general agreement from the rest of his class.

"Oh captain my captain!" Dodger proclaimed, accompanied by a genuine salute that prompted a fresh smile on Rolland's face.

"Yes, what the weird one said," Gwendolyn spoke, stoned faced and then confused at why the others began to laugh at her unintentional joke.

"We are all with you, Rolland," Hannah offered, her small, soft smile stretching the bounds of her face. Behind her eyes was something mysterious, hidden, and potentially dangerous to everyone but Gwendolyn, who had witnessed the 19th century girl's power inside of B.E.T.S.I.

"Word," Jaime said, raising one hand in the air. "Always wanted to see an island!"

"We will follow you anywhere, especially if it's to find Victor," Tina offered, her eyes glistening with fresh tears.

Facing the rest of his class, Rolland's apprehension began to melt, though he was still unsure. He remembered Pensacola and his run in with Jackson. "I'm not so sure guys, I mean, a few of us have experience in the field, but by and large we're a pretty green bunch."

"Life does not wait land dweller, trust me." Kniff said, clasping one hand on Rolland's shoulder.

"This is indeed unwise," Turtledove said, standing up from his chair for the first time since their arrival. Through weary eyes the leader of the now defunct Knights of Time saw a group of bright eyed, enthusiastic, promising pupils set on a specific goal; his goal - to right a wrong. "But, if you all insist on accompanying an old man into the past, you would be welcome."

"Insist? We're practically forcing you and Rolland to do it," Dodger said with a wink to Turtledove. Their rapport as mentor and mentee over the months had been strange in its familiar simplicity, which had been comforting to both as they went through turbulent and stressful times. Still, Dodger was careful never to take advantage of this, or the elevated place he held in Eden society as a 'council brat.' This felt right to him, like the end of a long road where he had found purpose to his life. Filled with a newfound confidence that can only come from self acceptance, Dodger smiled, slapped Rolland on the shoulder, and said, "Seriously though, we've all got your back."

Rolland smiled the toothiest smile Tina had ever seen him smile. Although he wasn't looking at her, she could tell how much the role was agreeing with the wild fire that burned within his soul. Tina watched as the boy she was falling in love with shifted gears quicker than she thought humanly possible, changing from instantaneously excited to strategic, and battle ready. His music never played so loudly, or sounded so sweet to her ears as in that moment. With a snap of his fingers a portal opened before them, it's shimmering plethora of various colors beckoning them with a tranquil ease that soon welcomed each at Rolland's direction. He was ready and eager to finally do right by his fallen friend.

But eagerness can be both a blessing, and a curse - a lesson never learned without a little bloodshed.

Standing on the hillside graveyard where Victor's grave lay empty, a lone man stood holding a half burnt cigarette in one hand, and a five foot long spear in the other. His name was Dom and he had been sent by Councilman Varejao to watch the Halls of Time for the past several weeks with nothing to report but that didn't stop him from doing his duty. Nothing would, as long as the checks kept clearing at Eden Savings & Loan. Dom was just about to put his cigarette out, his mind already thinking about getting a fresh one, before he saw the light.

A brilliant flash of white hot light inside the Halls of Time beamed outward, temporarily illuminating the otherwise dark Eden landscape surrounding the building, cemetery, and valley immediately surrounding it, just as his boss claimed it eventually would. Without wasting another moment, the scout named Dom removed a cellular telephone from his left breast pocket, pressed the number one on the screen, and was instantaneously connected with his superior.

"Sir" the scout named Dom said, breathing heavily into the mouthpiece of the telephone as he reached for another cigarette. "The den is empty, repeat, the den is empty."

Chapter 19:
Mission Accomplished

USSR

St. Petersburg - 1991

Red was the day the union fell.

By December of 1991, the great Soviet Union found itself on the precipice of collapse. Despite a long history filled with numerous men of acclaim, victories in war, and an indoctrination of an ideology of numerous subjugated nations the top brass of the country found themselves unable to collectively hold on to power amidst a growing call for reform among the majority of its population. Indeed, the onetime superpower of twentieth century Earth was on its knees, awaiting a death sentence that all who slept under her colors knew was inevitable. Pitiful would be the soul that might take advantage of their mother country in such a state, regardless of intention. Yet for one of the land's most infamous souls, whose very actions led to the destruction of the Romanov monarchy, the opportunity was too rich, too rare to ignore.

The day was calm on the west side of St. Petersburg despite the political chaos inside of its government buildings. Ironically, the setting sun cast the sky in a reddish hue, the heavens seemingly mocking the fallen Soviet state. Yet while the government might have been falling apart around them, the people of St. Petersburg went about their daily business. All along the streets, venders sold their wares of fruit, meats, and novelties without the slightest care or concern for the laws that governed them. Each wore the fashion of the day, if not the previous era, as trends were slow to fall over into the part of the world where Communism still held supreme. Because of this, and much more, the stranger dressed in an all black three piece suit with wild, tangled black hair did not garner much attention. As he turned the corner that led to the church, sinister thoughts brewing below the surface of his mind as he passed an older, pale woman who was hunched over her cart of turnips and his face twisted with contempt.

The church was centrally located in the main square, almost perfectly so. While officially disregarding religion, many of the government's top comrades had been finding sanctuary within the church's walls. Some had even sought the priest for confession. Therefore, the elderly priest paid little attention when the old wooden doors creaked open to reveal yet another lost soul in an expensive suit. However, once he met the stranger's eyes, something cold snaked through his gut. They were piercing, bright with an almost animal magnetism that seemed to bore into the priest's eyes. The stranger held his gaze for a minute longer before turning into the confessional. Trying to shake off the inexplicable uneasiness he was feeling, the priest hurried after him and entered his own side of the booth.

"Forgive me Father, for I have sinned," the man in the black suit stated in tone that seemed to care little for forgiveness..

An hour ago the priest, Father Alexei Belsky had little else on his mind besides what might be served for supper that evening. Now, he felt like something evil had come to find him, his church, and would not be leaving without enacting a high price. He crossed himself and took a deep breath. He knew that he should not be afraid of death but he could not help but feel faint at the thought of his own. Clasping his hands together, the priest finally uttered. " *Da*, my son?"

"It has been ninety eight years, two hundred and eight days, and nineteen hours since my last confession," the stranger in the black suit continued on with the same rich, almost polite tone of voice. "Since then I have sinned too many times to mention, but with a minute of your time I will cover the most grievous of them. Do I have your permission to continue?"

He was so engrossed by the exotic stranger, Father Belsky did not even comprehend everything the man said. A smart but cautious man by nature, the priest had seen enough good and evil in his long career to know when he was in the presence of one or the other. Yet, he knew his duty and would not deny the gift of confession to any of the Lord's children. He ignored a fresh bead of sweat that appeared on his brow before he continued to speak. "Yes, yes of course my son. Continue, please."

"Very well," the strange man in the black suit stated before clearing his throat. "I've lied, cheated, gambled, tortured, been unfaithful to my spouse with all sorts of promiscuous women, and I have been blamed with the destruction of an entire family and nation. I feel the worst about that last one, I suppose. And oh yes, and I've committed murder. A number of times actually."

Taken aback by this unabashed list of behavior the good Father Belsky let several long, quiet moments pass between them before moving so much as a muscle in response. He had known of the existence of these men, these demons, for over twenty years now. The first occurrence of their intervention was during a church carnival in the early 1970's when a new church secretary, a gaunt man in his early fifties who wore glasses, disappeared with four of the local children, all wards of the state. When the angel arrived on the scene, his long beard, piercing blue eyes, and distinctive golden sword sensed the panic before the younger Father Belsky could explain the situation. The angel disappeared on foot, stayed gone for over four hours, and returned with three of the children walking behind him and one of them slumped over his shoulder asleep. All was well that day, and out of respect, Father Belsky never asked what became of the secretary. He remembered how grateful he was, how he begged the angelic stranger, known only as Turtledove, for a way to repay him for saving the children. So, it came to pass, that Father Belsky swore to protect the church from all invaders, both foreign and domestic; a promise that weighed heavily on his shoulders through the decades of cold war that he lived through. Father Belsky feared that with the destruction of one superpower would come the rise of multiple smaller, more vindictive, and less organized groups, each with their own leaders and agenda toward mankind's supposed universal prosperity. None of this mattered anymore, however, as there were no famous biblical stories of anyone ever escaping the lion's den. "You must seek forgiveness."

"This is part where I'm supposed to accept my penance and bask in the Lord's absolution, right Father?" came the almost amused sounding voice. "You see, I don't think that I can…"

"You must forgive yourself," Father Belsky interrupted in a nervous voice. He wondered if he could reach the alter to write a message to the angel in time but doubted greatly that he could manage to do so without giving away the system by which he communicated with heaven.

"Forgiveness," said the man in black, suddenly hissing a bit as he stressed each syllable.

"We all must have forgiveness in the end," Father Belsky said softly, almost to himself. The sweat on his forehead was now steadily falling in silent, drops onto his crimson and cream-colored ceremonial robes. Catching the white of the stranger's eyes for the first time through the mesh partisan the priest offered, "I absolve you, my son."

"What did you say, Father?" the man in black asked in voice that was almost a whisper.

"I absolve," Father Belsky said again in a louder, more confident tone of voice. A newfound sense of inner peace had stolen over him. "As a man of the Lord, I forgive your sins my sons."

"I cannot hear you, Father," the man in black said again, pressing his eyes closer into the mesh partisan.

"No matter what horrendous acts you have committed, you can still seek the Lord's forgiveness," spoke Father Belsky, his voice calm.

"Father, may we continue our confession face to face? I still cannot hear you."

The priest knew that he should not part the partisan, yet his hands, no longer shaking, began to move the mesh that separated them. He repeated his favorite Scripture verses in his head as he looked into the stranger's unnaturally bright eyes.

Without a second of hesitation the man in the black suit removed a large, severely jaded and curved blade from a holster attached to his suspenders on his back, lurched forward, and drove the knife, tip first, straight through the vulnerable neck of Father Belsky. It was over in an instant. Whereas barely minutes before the clergyman had been thinking, speaking, and sweating profusely he now amounted to nothing but a body with strings of sinew, tendon, and copious streams of blood that covered everything in its splash radius upon impact. With closed eyes the man in black breathed steadily, calmly, as his hand warmed with the holy blood of the empathic priest he knew to be an Eden spy. It was energy, it was life, it was.. satisfying.

The blood that fell from Father Belsky's neck collected in a small, oblong shaped pool near the wide open door of the confessional. Though the body was in a horizontal position, leaning up against the door's hinge, both the trickle, and flow of the dark red liquid seem to be taking on a mind of its own as it streamed south, as if being guided by an invisible brook. Within minutes a small pool of blood had formed in the middle of the church's long aisle. No sooner had the man in the black suit left the confessional booth than the earth cracked, split, and broke apart beneath the pool of holy blood to make way for the large object that jettisoned its way through the church floor. The object was a black stucco fountain, round, eight feet wide, eight feet high, layered, and covered in crudely drawn carvings. As the concrete rocks fell away, the spots of so much prayer and bene- diction, the freshly anointed sins of mankind reached out from Tartarus itself as a bright, deep purple candescent light sprayed out from the fountain, filling the entire cathedral in its ominous glow. Soon, the purple hues turned to black before breaking apart into a beautifully violent burst of the deepest orange. The man in black watched the spectacle while standing rigidly against a pillar. He noticed that the linen laid out to cover the old instruments old oak wood matched the dead priest's cloak almost exactly. The man in black laughed at that, distracting him slightly from the task at hand.

Within seconds two shadows appeared as silhouettes set against the purple light, small at first, then larger as they grew closer to the man in the black suit. It was like they were walk- ing down a long, well-lit hallway. He lowered his eyes as Edward Vilthe, Lord of Tartarus and Reaper of Souls. The other man he saw was Rudolph Hess. The murderer of Father Belsky waited until they were within earshot before falling to one knee in a sign of submissive respect to his master. It did not go unnoticed.

"Rasputin," Vilthe hissed, extending his hands upward a bit while simultaneously gliding closer to the man in black. "Well done my faithful one."

"Thank you, my lord," the man in black said. Though he was nervous, he was unsure if the slight shaking he felt in his legs, arms, and teeth were due to his nerves, or the cold, uneasy feeling his liege cast over every room he entered. Deciding that he did not really want to know the answer, Rasputin raised his head upward, making immediate eye contact with the dull, hazy eyes of the walking corpse that was Edward Vilthe. "Shall we..?"

The fading light of day was no friend to the dark trio, being as one of their party was completely masked by a long black robe, another was wearing the tattered remains of an SS uniform, and the third was wild haired and his suit was covered in blood. All in all it took but moments for a shocked public to take notice of their presence as they walked down the steep church steps and across the square towards the prize they sought.

They came. From fruit venders to butchers, to pedestrians on the street they came. Armed with an assortment of weapons, none more advanced than a meat cleaver, a small mob gathered on both sides of the street in a fraternity of revulsion for the grotesque strangers.

"Nazi Demon!" screamed a man in Russian as he took a swing at Hess with his broom handle. Although the German was able to easily duck the assault, it annoyed him nonetheless.

With sudden clap of his bony hands Vilthe brought the entire scene around the trio to a crawl of slow motion. Thanks his murder of Scott Wright, Vilthe still possessed some of Wright's abilities, including the slowing of time within his immediate vicinity. Although they could not see it, beneath the robe that had kept him hidden, Edward Vilthe cracked a smile.

Still feeling the adrenaline of the encounter with the priest, Rasputin tossed a dagger to Hess, who caught it flat palmed between his two, somewhat trembling hands. His look of disbelief only grew after the native German looked up from the newly acquired weapon to see his previously reluctant colleague with a goading grin that begged for mockery before offering a coy, "Do you think a Russian could still beat a German?"

Together the two hacked and slashed through the small mob, tearing open throats and disemboweling bellies, until all in their wake lay dead or dying. Hess paid special attention to the man with the broom, getting creative in ways Adolf Hitler only wished he could have conceived.

"Fools..." Vilthe hissed from beneath his shadowy cloak. With eerily translucent skin covering fragile bones created in a time forgotten by man, the immortal reaper of souls removed his hood that had rested there for over a century. A hairless, opaque shaded cranium sat like a crown over wisps of white eyebrows that in turn were overshadowed by eyes that were the very definition of the word black. His pupils were non-existent, which gave both his companions the impression that he was clearly not human. But it didn't matter, not in that moment. For Rasputin and Hess, two men whom had loathed one another until that day, only one memory would be shared regarding the moment Vilthe revealed his visage to the world - the hostile takeover of the powdery white skin disease that was creeping up around the evil creature's eyes, nose, and forehead before vanishing along his scalp. The pattern was not constantly symmetrical but instead appeared to be random with swirls and blots of chalky white skin advancing further upward more noticeably on Vilthe's right than his left. A pair of small, unmoving ears covered in liver marks rounded out the heavy breathing reaper of souls as he thought a vile thought, and sent the most negative mental energy ever conceived through the universal ether into his henchmen's direction.

Both of the hands holding the silver daggers were hit simultaneously with what felt like a large bee sting directly on the knuckle of their middle finger. Dropping his weapon before letting out a gasp of surprised pain, Rasputin keeled over a bit before looking up at his master pleadingly.

"You dishonor me, Rasputin," Vilthe hissed. Inside his mouth both men could see a strangely forked tongue that split into two at the tip. The effect would have been entrancing if not for the throbbing pain that lingered in the Russian madman's hand.

With another swipe of his hand the doors of the governmental building flew off of their hinges allowing Vilthe, Rasputin, and Rudolph Hess to walk inside to both a grand and foreboding entrance. Unsure of the noise, all seven of the guards on duty rushed toward the sounds of danger, not away from it. The decision, while valiant in its attempts to put duty first, even in the dying days of one's regime, would prove on par with that of a fish who takes the odd looking worm that happens to be randomly suspended two feet underwater in a lake. With less the effort than one would expel squinting Vilthe caught the eyes of three men in mid-run, levitated them nearly four feet off of the ground, and violently ejected their hearts from their chests before they fell to his feet. These three would prove to be the lucky ones.

The trio continued past the guard station with little interruption as Rasputin, who had done away with using weapons, calmly kissed the palms of both his thumbs before outmaneuvering two of the guards who ran at him, spinning around to throw the third off balance, and placed both thumbs on the center of the fourth guards neck. Armed with a standard issue Soviet rifle, the guards' eyes flashed a deep orange for a moment, like a computer booting up, before Rasputin released his grip and watched as the guard raised his rifle and shot his three companions to death. Then, without skipping a beat, the guard turned the rifle around, removed the sheath from the bayonet unit attached to the top, raised it to his chest above where his heart lie, and plunged it deep and true. The glow in the soldier's eyes did not leave until long after he had fallen to the ground.

An alarm sounded overhead prompting more guards, to pour into the hallway, the first two arriving almost instantaneously as if from nowhere. They ran toward the trio from Tartarus as their deceased comrades had done moments before. Vilthe caught the pair of guards that made the mistake of advancing on him in an invisible net of negative ions that enveloped them like molasses, completely stopping their momentum. With an smile that only appeared for the briefest of milliseconds, Vilthe repositioned their momentum, rearranging both of their fields of vision so that the two turned toward one another before ramming their foreheads with as much energy as they each could exert. The effect was painful, yet not paralyzing, which Vilthe knew. He had experimented in the past with other living dollies, other bits of human meat, and knew how much pain each could take before it cracked. Before it was either no longer useful, or just plain broken. Either way that's all that humans were really; little more than an evolutionary hiccups past the point of mosquitoes.

The labyrinth that was the Soviet governmental building housed a treasure of secret goods and government confidentiality. But the fate of dictators, and secret trail of government paid assassins on foreign soil were second to the calculated fixation Vilthe had set his sights on. The deeper the trio delved into the building the greener the uniforms to the guards, soldiers, and finally commandos who dared cross their path. One man's brains literally oozed out of his nose, ears, and eyes before Vilthe brushed him aside to die as another statistic in a massacre that would never be publicly known. Another man, a soldier, was fused together with the wall near where he stood in a particularly cruel twist by the reaper of souls. Ironically, Vilthe garnered the idea after Rasputin crudely pointed out that the particular soldier, the last alive from a group of eleven that came in with firearms shooting, was perhaps being cowardly and relying on the wall to shield him from their supernatural wrath. Using the ability he had stolen from a neurotic economist in the late 19th century, the Lord of Tartarus focused all of his negative energy, might, and connection with the Earth to accelerate the atoms inside the soldier's feet to blend with those atoms comprising the wall. When the effect traveled like a shock wave, liquidating the soldiers internal organs as it passed, the agony brought out a pitiful weeping sound from the blue, dead lips before they too became nothing but a congealed mass of organic mush.

For Hess, who had seen the faces of countless Soviet soldiers die while he was serving during the war, the needless slaughter of brave men chafed at him. The townspeople were one thing, but these were real men. He found himself hoping that the Soviets would simply give up on sending in reinforcements to stop their theft. But they kept coming; again and again the soldiers marched out toward the trio of extraordinarily villainous men. With their firearms held high and their chins tucked low they came, hurdling over their fallen comrades bodies as Vilthe again and again made short work of their feeble attempts at stopping them. A group of seven Soviet soldiers approached from their rear, catching Hess off guard. Though he was able to deflect the bullet aimed at him, it grazed his heel, knocking him down and leaving Vilthe completely exposed to the riot guard's fury. With a quickened haste they got into attack position, their boots squeaking against the tile floor as they approached.

Born in a cave, Vilthe had learned to rely on certain primal instinct. It was this desire; this need to protect himself, that killed any and all chance of intimacy he would ever feel with another living being. Like a shell he had built of his own accord it was inescapable. A prison. Yet for all of the loss of freedoms, trust, happiness, and contentment that go with being in your own personal prison there is one upside. No one else can get in. With this in mind Vilthe concentrated and suddenly, almost inexplicably, the tongue of each and every one of the Soviet attackers was ripped from their mouths with an invisible force equivalent to a giant's grip. Writhing over in pain, all seven allowed the trio from Tartarus to pass them down the corridor, their hands clutching their mouths in silent screams.

Hess limped along after the other two as they walked further into the compound. He knew what was likely coming; more fighting, more death, more bullets. Then again, and again, and again before they came to the room they had been looking for, the door to which was marked with large black numbers in bold print '112263'. Oddly, it was unlocked. Rasputin raised his own eyebrows at this before turning the knob and entering inside, coming face to face with an armed guard standing in front of a man in a white lab coat with classes who sat at a desk behind him. A large paining the size of an Oldsmobile sat situated on the wall behind them. The guard reached for his weapon, but was dead before his hand even had the opportunity to clasp the handle, all thanks to Hess' quick shot with his own Rugger pistol.

The lone Soviet survivor, a small, skinny, bald man wearing glasses and sweating profusely above his brow became rattled with fear as every part of his body besides his tightly clutched hands shook uncontrollably. His bladder released, causing the smell of urine to fill the small, cramped room.

"Humans are such a weak, disgusting species," Vilthe said crossing the threshold into room 112263 while simultaneously slowly turning his left hand over while focusing on the Soviet, causing the levitating scientist to do the same. "Did you know that they are made mostly of water? Strange really. The building block of life they call it. My question is, what happens when you take away the building blocks?"

Terrified by the candor being displayed by their long quiet, long admired from a distance liege Lord was nothing compared to the horrifyingly gruesome scene that played out before them. The spinning Soviet's skin went from pink to bright red within seconds before both eyes popped out from their sockets, bouncing off the sides of his head as he continued to spin counterclockwise. A small scream emitted from the man's lips as drop by drop every molecule of water leached itself from his body, beginning with his toes before creeping upward, creating a strange jerky like texture to his legs, groin, midsection, stomach, and finally, his head.

As if he had forgotten that his traveling companions too were human by nature, Vilthe gave a low, almost boyish chuckle before releasing the dehydrated corpse of the soviet scientist to fall to the ground next to the soldier tasked to keep him safe. Vilthe stared at them for a moment, his head tilted in an obvious sign of deep contemplation. Then, without bothering to look at Hess or Rasputin, he said, softly, "Find it."

Leaping into action both Rasputin, and the limping Hess ran to the back of the small room, grabbing for the painting that sat on the wall. After removing it the opening made way to reveal a false wall that contained no safe, no lock, nothing but a cache of weapons conceived by mankind in its darkest hours of oppression and domestic born evil. There, lying perfectly still within their cases, were two fully operational nuclear warheads. Mission accomplished.

"There..." Vilthe hissed, gliding toward the nearly six foot long beauty on the left. He touched it lightly; almost confirming it was real before barking another order at his two assistants. "Quickly."

Pulling a cart from the hallway, Hess wheeled it over to the warheads as obeyed his Vilthe turned his right hand over and focusing on the nuclear weapon and raising it nearly a foot off of it's already shaky holster. It rose steadily higher before gliding much in the same way Vilthe did toward the dolly before flipping over onto the flat part of its base and coming to a complete, restful stop on the dolly. A series of straps sprung around the bomb, nestling it in safely for transportation.

"Now the other," Vilthe said to Hess, motioning for his other henchman to join his mad pursuit.

Rasputin jumped at the beckoning of his master. After the pair of them did the same to the second bomb the trio wasted no time in exiting the room, traveling the corridors littered with corpses and the sounds of suffering, before popping back out the front door of the compound, crossing the deserted street, and back into the church.

When they approached the fountain, the two positioned themselves before Vilthe to make way for his glide after. Yet before they arrived at the last step to the fountain the withered, disfigured Vilthe held out a bony hand before Hess that stopped the German officer dead in his tracks.

"My lord?" Hess inquired.

"You will not be coming with us, Rudolph," Vilthe said before retracting his arm and using it to refasten his long black hood over his head. "You have unfinished business."

Hess thought about Vilthe's statement for a moment before realizing what he was insinuating. Alora, he was speaking of his sister's murder. "Sire, I.."

"You were struck at, Rudolph, see that you strike back accordingly," Vilthe said, turning to leave.

"I..." Hess offered before being thrown backward halfway across the church by a flick of Vilthe's wrist.

"You will not return to Tartarus until the girl is dead!" Vilthe said, his flat, matter of fact tone conveying the severity of Hess' situation, even if the man himself was in denial. "Come Rasputin."

The two left through the fountain before Hess, who waited nearly an hour to do the same. Then, without prompt, the fountain lowered itself back into the ground as if it were never there, leaving behind only the path of destruction caused by the inhabitants of the other end. The incident, though not publicized for the sake of keeping face, was a disaster from every perspective. For the already failing U.S.S.R. government the breach would ensure that the growing civil threat would result in a chaos resembling the French revolution. Not to mention the damage it would do to the newly conceived Russian government waiting in the wings to assume power. The ninety-two soldiers that lost their lives in defense of the arsenal stolen by Vilthe were called heroes who gave their lives to a country that no longer existed.

Chapter 20:
Lazarus Rising

Tortuga, Haiti - November 1802

Timing is everything.

Out of the sparse jungle that was early 19th century Haiti lay a clearing; one which saw a lone solider strolling through it toward the rocky hillside above. With a freshly shaven face of silk and a saber bobbing against his left knee the French solider named Charles LeClerc made his way toward a single tree that grew there, sitting in judgment, and looking high above the valley below. It was his favorite spot, as it provided not only the required shade to read his weekly correspondence, but also granted an excellent view of all of the camp's activities. Inquisitive by nature, results by fortitude: that was the maxim that earned this gentleman his high ranking of general in Napoleon Bonaparte's military. Well, that, and the marital familiarity that he enjoyed with the Emperor of France's sister. Charles was a pale skinned, grizzled looking fellow whose uniform of a high ranking French officer, dark blue tunic, faded, yet bleached white trousers, sturdy black leather boots, and a belt made of the same material, were always crisply pressed. As he walked, he found himself grappling with a growing sense of apprehension that settled haphazardly in the pit of his stomach. He touched his bayonet where it was dangling from its leather attachment to his belt, the presence of it bringing him a peace of mind that nothing else could offer.

At the age of thirty General Charles LeClerc was every bit the representation of a man of his age and circumstance. However it was not this distinction that made General LeClerc leader of the occupying French forces that held the island and more formidable than other men cut of the same cloth. It was a secret, one which other men could scarcely believe with their eyes, much less by the power of Charles' own lips. Few had ever witnessed him display his extraordinary ability, and with good cause. Long ago LeClerc swore to himself that it would only be during battle, or in life and death situations in which he would profit by displaying his... talents. These thoughts, which he almost despised of himself, Charles chose to ignore for the time being, focusing instead on the impending hours solitude ahead. With his father's looking glass strapped neatly to his belt by a small brown leather hook tied at the end, Charles was looking forward to nothing more than a leisurely afternoon, free from the burden of responsibility and duty toward France.

BOOM

The noise was thunderous, cascading like a wave of omnipotent fury throughout the entirety of LeClerc's world, causing him to fall down the rocky hillside he had begun to climb. Still some twenty yards from the top of the hill, and the tree where he thought to seek refuge, LeClerc settled for a large, misshapen bolder that had somehow found its own way four fifths of the journey upward toward the vantage point. Finding his bearings as quickly as he could, Charles LeClerc dropped to one knee before crouching cat-like, as low to the ground as possible.

BOOM

The bleak sky broke open to reveal a thin, golden colored slit that shimmered with crimson, lilac, and puce hues before ejecting multiple people into the clearing near the bottom of the hillside below. For two of the young men passing between the great rift that separated present day Eden from early 19th century Haiti, Rolland Wright and Stewart 'Dodger' Yick, the dangers would begin immediately. While their names were unknown to the French soldier, both became the targets of Charles LeClerc the moment their feet touched Haitian soil. Shortly thereafter Tiikeri, Marcus Turtledove, Kniff Youngblood, Jaime Gonzalez, Hannah, Gwendolyn Murrow, Tina, and Timothy Holmes, though LeClerc did know their names either. One by one they flew through the air, none of them falling with grace, not even Gwendolyn. For all but three the feeling of being ripped through time was a new experience, one which none of them enjoyed. Their point of entry, the slit in the sky above the hillside, detracted into itself to disappear within seconds of their arrival, further solidifying any suspicions of wrongdoing held by the otherwise unknown observer to the situation, LeClerc. He crouched even lower to the crowd and remained as quiet as humanly possible.

"Is everyone alright?" Turtledove asked, looking around tentatively before stopping Tina from exploring further by extending his hand to grasp her shoulder. Somewhere, quite nearby, someone was experiencing a great deal of unease and apprehension - two tell tale signs that someone had witnessed their arrival. Best case they are merely frightened, but worst case they are lying in wait to attack. "Stay close to me child."

"Turtledove is right, we need to move with caution," Rolland said, formulating a plan in his mind.

"Aye, extreme caution," Kniff agreed. " Which way, Mr. Turtledove?"

Folding his hands together, more than slightly unabashed by the group of young one's trust and confidence in his aged abilities Marcus Turtledove smiled broadly without showing a single tooth before stating unequivocally, "I am but a poor player upon this stage, my friends. Gone is my authority over you, replaced with not but reverence. Whomever your leader, I am theirs to command."

The cadets of the Class of the Tiger all blinked for a long moment before staring at one another with looks that ranged from mild confusion to outright skepticism. Regardless, one singular truth won out above all others and although they all knew it, Gwendolyn was the one to vocalize it. "So, Rolland is in charge then?"

Everyone but Rolland and Timothy murmured their agreement before their circle of cadets and Turtledove turned to face Rolland to hear their next course of action. Watching this interaction of power Charles LeClerc's mood went from agitated fear to one of aggressive disdain for these new strangers invading his territory. Based on first impressions alone he did not believe them to be native hostiles, or their rebel allies, though he hypothesized that if he was not aware of them, or their unusual means of arrival, then they must be at the very least sympathetic to that Toussaint L 'Overture's cause if not outright supportive. Even if only one of their party had the same dark complexion as the island rebels. Either way they seemed meek and easy to conquer based on looks alone. LeClerc again eyed Turtledove as the weakest of the herd based on advanced age. Perhaps striking fast and true toward one would rile the rest up enough to make a careless mistake and then.. No. Since they decided to put a mere boy in charge, then let their democratic body wither while the leader of their leader is severed from their pack.

"Kniff, Tim, Jaime, landing on this hilltop gives us a great vantage point to look out for potential unfriendlies. Let's create a perimeter around our position to double check," Rolland commanded, prompting the three young men to his left to all nod their heads before equipping themselves and moving about. They walked with an untrained precision that lent credence to a perception that their level of training left much to be desired.

The one the group called 'Rolland' then turned to the female next to him before giving a similar command LeClerc could not overhear. Off into the sky went Gwendolyn, much to the Frenchmen's astonishment. This left the black female, the old man, the girl he wanted near him, the leader, and the kid who had landed alongside of him when they landed.

"Mind if I head up to the top of that tree and take a look around?" Dodger asked, taking another quick peak in Hannah's direction before he completed his sentence. Noticing this, Rolland smiled at the possibility of things to come for his friend before nodding and turning to the others. From behind him Rolland heard, "Be back soon brother."

The gesture, though a little, inconsequential thing for one male to say to another landed square upon Rolland's pride giving him a second wind and boost of confidence. It was further by Tina, who looked up and smiled at him before giving him a kiss on the cheek and whispering into his ear, "I'm going to go with Turtledove to look around. I think, I think I might have heard something, someone's music maybe. Don't worry, I'll stay close. I love you."

Wanting to ask Turtledove but feeling rushed to make a decision, Rolland stared at Hannah, the only remaining cadet left without instructions. Smiling back at him and rolling her eyes she walked past him after Tina, insisting on going to help the duo look for the wild hair they both suspected. Touching his cheek gently Rolland noticed the huge smile that was nearly plastered there and tried to ignore the small voice in the back of his mind trying to spoil the moment with paranoia. Him, the orphan boy who lived in a car and had no home to bring a girl to in high school... was loved. Someone actually loved him. A girl! A fresh wave of wonder washed over Rolland as he turned to walk away toward the incline of the hillside and the large boulder while he reflected on his new fortune. With thoughts far away Rolland walked the short distance toward the large rock, ever closer to danger, ever closer to destiny. As it was Rolland could not see LeClerc, or his bayonet that lay clinched tightly in his right hand with the blade facing outward in the striking position.

Nearby, high atop a perch on a lonely branch roughly twelve feet off of the ground, attached to an ancient tree overlooking the rest of the hillside teleported Stewart 'Dodger' Yick. Landing with a startled balance on the branch the young cadet found an old fear of heights thought long forgotten creep its way back into his stomach. Steadying himself instead, Dodger swung both legs around until he was facing outward enough to see Tina kiss Rolland before walking away from him with a giggle. "That lucky son of a bitch."

Dodger then turned his attention to another group, this one consisting of Kniff, Timothy, and Jaime, join together with a returning Gwendolyn, who immediately fell into conversation with the others. As they joked with one another casually, Dodger watched them with a new sense of appreciation for their shared plight, absent-mindedly smiling as he did so. Gone were the feelings of division that tore them asunder a month previous; leaving behind nothing but unity, friendship, and a begrudging harmony based on mutual respect. It was hard to believe, but for the first time since he could remember Stewart felt accepted by a group of peers. So much so that he once again allowed his eyes to venture eastward toward the spot where Hannah was catching up to Tina and Turtledove. Tina. She was such a pretty girl. Dodger thought the world of all of them, well maybe except for Timothy, and was especially happy that Tina and Rolland had ended up together. Lumping them into the same category as peanut butter and jelly, Dodger scanned the clearing to the spot where Rolland and wondered over to.

Dodger saw movement from behind the large boulder first, followed immediately by Rolland's smiling face as he walked toward it, his expression one of a dazed man in love. As the shadows behind him lifted with the suns movement overhead something else became clearly visible in the vast distance between where Dodger stood and the trap Rolland was walking into. The reflection off of the Frenchmen's blade as he swung it upward into an attack stance was so bright it blinded Dodger for a split second, but a second was all he had before it was time to act. "Rolland behind you!"

Yet Rolland could not hear Dodger's warning. Closer and closer LeClerc crept around the boulder as Rolland passed, his back now facing the Frenchmen with saber poised to strike. With a silent rage LeClerc lunged toward Rolland with his bayonet hacking the air between them wildly. The first onslaught landed to the left of Rolland, who turned just in time to feel his earlobe being severed as 18th century French-made steel lopped it off before he even knew he was under attack. As the blood came, hot and sticky, Rolland's confusion mixed with the adrenaline of the moment.

"What?" Rolland asked as he witnessed his attacker gearing up for another lunge with the blade. Rolland whirled around, attempting to bring his hands together and slow time, yet he could not make it due to a mixture of sticky fingers and shock. But it did not matter as LeClerc's blade was already in motion, dead-set on taking Rolland's life for its mid-morning meal. In a moment that felt like an eternity Rolland watched, with baited breath, as life happened around him; all at once forcing him from center stage to relegated as a supporting character in the play of the cosmos. In the blink of an eye Dodger teleported between the two men with but a single thought in his mind - get to the knife first. Deciding to face the attacker Dodger gambled with both the timing, and the distance by which the Frenchmen's attack came.

A gamble the young Stewart Yick lost as the cold steel tip of LeClerc's bayonet met with the soft, inviting flesh square in the middle of the young man's chest. As the blade went in further Dodger's eyes widened in surprise as his hands groped in a vain attempt to stop the Frenchman's momentum. Instead LeClerc, fueled-on by a thirst for blood, twisted the blade counter-clock-wise inside Dodger's chest, simultaneously sinking it in deeper as it went.

"No!" Rolland screamed before kicking LeClerc fully in the small of his stomach. The Frenchman let go of the blade and fell backward onto the rocky hillside with the breathe knocked out of him. Dodger, no longer supported by the weight of another human being, fell instantly to his knees before toppling over onto his side; LeClerc's blade lodged more than half way into his chest.

"Help! Help!" Rolland screamed in a state of shock. He looked from LeClerc back to Dodger before hitting a knee and crawling to his friend's side. Dodger's face was pale to the point of becoming white if not for the streaks of crimson covering his chest, stomach, hands, and face. The blood was everywhere as Rolland cradled his friend in his arms, though the mess was the least of their worries. In the moments that followed Kniff, Timothy, and Jaime found them, all with the same expressions of disbelief donned on their faces as Rolland had a mere minute before. "I need help!"

"Arrggghhhh damn that hurts!" Dodger bellowed, his insides burning like fire. He looked down at himself for the first time, afraid of what he might see when he did. The bayonet that still stood at a nearly forty-five degree angle had become a part of him, one which he could feel moving around slightly inside with each small movement. Even breathing brought about a fresh wave of pain that hurt like a lightning strike. Somewhere, in the dark cavernous reaches of his still adolescent mind, Stewart Yick knew that he was in the deepest trouble he had ever encountered. "Take it out. Take it out... Take it out NOW!"

Dodger's screams did nothing to help the situation. Instead they had the effect of both alerting Turtledove's group to the incident, and re-invigorate the ailing LeClerc, who had managed to stay hidden from the new arrivals by keeping quiet and creeping back behind the large boulder from whence he came. Instant tears came to the eyes of both Tina and Hannah as they approached Rolland, who along with Hannah, held Dodger's shoulders as Turtledove gingerly pulled the bayonet from his student's chest. Once the blade was clear the wound overflowed with blood that Hannah was tasked with cleaning. It was in this confusion that LeClerc decided to once again to act. Regaining his courage, and with as much might as he could muster the Frenchman rose to his feet before lunging, again, at Rolland and Dodger, this time with a spare hunting knife he kept tied around his ankle.

Seeing this, both Jaime and Kniff leapt into action, disabling LeClerc with a practiced ease that came directly from their training sessions together. Kniff, a bit overzealous, got behind the man before intentionally bending LeClerc's arm backward until he heard the snapping sound of a broken bone. Smiling sadistically at this LeClerc snapped back, slamming his own head into Kniff's forehead twice until he let go, switched the knife to his non broken arm, and went after the Merman with all the strength he had left. Expecting this, Kniff waited until LeClerc had gained enough momentum before dropping to one knee, rolling sideways on the inclining hillside, and grabbing LeClerc's hand, reversing the General's momentum until the tip of the blade found its new home in the middle part of LeClerc's exposed neck. Choking sounds not dissimilar to the ones Dodger was making emanated out of LeClerc's mouth as he toddled backward, his non-broken arm searching for something solid to rest against. Unfortunately for LeClerc this action was underscored by Jaime, who sped past them into a crouching position to slam the General's head against the hard ground, drawing more blood from the open eyed, no longer breathing Frenchman. As he lay lifeless and sprawled out on a patch of dead grass, the cadets' collective attentions shifted back to Dodger.

Not knowing where the French soldier had come from, Jaime immediately barked orders to Timothy to take over for him while he did a perimeter sweep on foot, prompting the younger Holmes twin to snap out of his daze and jog over to where Rolland held Dodger. Panic filled his body, prompting a flight or fight sense he had faced but once before in his life. Instincts being what they are Timothy made his decision, turning on his heels, and ran in the opposite direction of his classmates toward the unknown safety he assumed lay at the bottom of the hillside. Yet after a few hundred feet of baited breathing Timothy ran into the one person he was hoping to avoid. The one person who could force him to turn back around.

"Timothy?" Tina asked apprehensively as she crooked her head at the sight of her twin brothers arms nearly covered in blood. Behind her both Hannah and Turtledove moved with an cautious curiosity that only intensified once they too saw the copious amount of blood and no visible wound that Timothy wore. Since her brother looked healthy, Tina assumed that it was not Timothy's blood, nor that of a potential victim. Her deductive reasoning lead Tina's thoughts to the worst possible scenarios, the dark part of her psyche filling in the gaps of the mental summersaults her worst fears were performing with relative ease. "Timothy, whose blood is that?!"

362

Unable to speak save for a croaking, half audible mumble Timothy instead lifted his left hand to point behind him in the direction from which he came. Without a second to waste all three broke out into a run, leaving Timothy Holmes standing alone on the open Haitian hillside. Unsure if he should feel like a failure, or a hero, he stood there, quietly, reflecting on the consequences of what had just transpired. The view along the north side of the hill gave full access to the large encampment that lay at the base, mostly consisting of row after row of structurally well-built tents and canopies. Beyond them were a great deal of horses and people that Timothy could not clearly. He took his time watching the movement of the little dots of people. They were like ants to Timothy, each with its own responsibility and duty to the whole.

On the ground nearby Dodger's pale white face cracked into a smile as he grew accustomed to the pain of the gaping wound in the middle of his chest. Until this point he had been afraid to touch the wound yet now something inside him gave him the proverbial green light to do so. With his left hand Stewart Yick felt the outer edges of the hole, the bits of mangled flesh reminding him of the angel hair pasta that his grandfather, Joseph, used to make for Sunday night dinners. It was a happy thought, one of many he had over the course of his short life. He shook his head ever-so-slightly as he reflected on the absurd humor that was the human condition. Birth, life, death, repeat; the eternal cycle of a limit release species, each trying to outwit and outmaneuver the generation before. Truly, it was a tale told by a fool. There was a peace in that.

"Hang in there buddy," Rolland said with a tone of conviction he had never felt before. He tried not to focus on the fact that his arms, legs, and clothes were mostly covered in his best friend's blood. "We're gonna get you cleaned up and out of here. You just hold on. Alright?"

Again Dodger smiled, his dry lips forcing themselves apart as his eyes found Rolland's against the warm, sunny sky overhead.

It was a nice day, and the breeze felt cool against Stewart's already cold cheeks. He was suddenly very thirsty as he felt more strength draining out of him. Knowing that he COULD fight simply wasn't enough anymore, not now, not after feeling such peace, such tranquility. As if he were playing an early model videogame with a life meter Dodger could read the writing on the wall as he used what little bit of energy he had to maintain his smile and say, "Rolland, you need to - you need to stop talking so much."

Despite himself Rolland smiled at this, slightly repositioning his friend in his arms as Dodger's face grew whiter.

"Dodger!" Tina screamed, running to his side. The wound was deep, jagged, and would require immediate medical attention in the best of circumstances. As it was, the wave of emotions washed over her in a flurry of shocked entanglements.

Due to his empathic abilities, Turtledove felt every bit of emotion resonating from the group of teenagers before him, both individually and as a group. Their collective energy was strong, nearly as strong as his own Knights of Time, yet he was not sure if they, or even he, was prepared to lose one of them this early on in their already illegal mission to the past. Fighting these thoughts Marcus pushed past the crying Hannah before lowering himself next to Rolland, squeezing Dodger's hand, and pulling it away to survey the damage done to his chest.

"The damage is too severe," Turtledove said silently, looking from Rolland to Tina, who had joined them on the ground. The older man shook his head sadly.

"Rolland," Dodger stated through now blood soaked lips and hard fought breathes. "You still there?"

"Yeah buddy, it's gonna be alright, you'll see," Rolland said, putting a hand on Dodger's face and directing it toward his own until their eyes met. The eyes that met Rolland's were glassy, unfocused, and barely lit with the same spark that had made Dodger such an excellent friend a mere minutes before. With the slightest of nods Dodger followed Rolland's lead for the last time.

"So pretty..." Dodger said, his eyes glazed as they fixed on Hannah, who joined Timothy and Kniff as they stood over the others, looking on at the tragedy as it unfolded. "I bet you like to dance. You look like the sorta girl who would like to dance. I should have asked you sooner.."

They all smiled despite themselves as the moments dragged while Dodger's breath became more and more labored.

'Rolland is going to make it, Rolland is going to make it,' Dodger thought to himself, over and over again in such a way that the phrase became soothing beyond comprehension. As the violent shivers took over his body, Stewart opened his eyes to see everyone he had grown to care about while at the academy was staring down at him with tears either streaming or being held back forcefully. This touched Dodger, so much so that he found the strength to lift his left hand slightly into the air. It grasped once, twice, and found Rolland's as he cradled his friend near the moment of expiration. A smile, such a simple thing, would become the lasting gift between them as they ended their living friendship on a high note.

'Rolland is going to make it...'

Rolland Alan Wright would forever remember that moment as the most inappropriate smile of his life; though, also one that he would never regret. For as soon as his lips parted, and teeth became visible - so did Dodger's. And with that final action, the spark of life within Stewart 'Dodger' Yick went out permanently, ending his time upon this Earth.

As it is with most things the ghosts of the past wait for no one. A mere twenty feet away the pale cheeks of the French officer known as General LeClerc were beginning to bloom with color, signaling the rejuvenation process to begin for the rest of his body. The wound in his neck, although serious enough to kill him once, had already begun to heal the moment the blade had been removed. His conscience clicked into being once the neural pathways had reversed their decaying process long enough, reminding him of the who, what, when, and where. Charles LeClerc's 'gift' had not only saved his life once again, but it had also given him the added gifts of both time, and the element of surprise on his enemy. As the feeling returned to his body, the French General sat up from his laying position where he had fallen dead, looked around, and immediately heard the sound of faint crying.

To LeClerc's astonishment the group of young people and the old man were still there, apparently mourning over the loss of the one he had killed. With a surge of glee blossoming within his chest LeClerc quickly went for his right boot, shaking it off from its position at his knee before it fell with a small *clunk* sound that did nothing to draw attention. Judging the group ill trained based on their inability to post either scouts, or a guard to monitor his body, Charles knew that he could pick off one or two more before they would even think to defend themselves against a creature like himself. It was the only chance he had, after all, considering what he was up against. Who he was up against. The freak-show was now in full force as the number of normal looking citizens with what he could only describe as biblically supernatural had gone from two to nearly a dozen. He could not allow that to happen... he would not.

All around Dodger's body the Class of the Tiger and Turtledove huddled in complete shock and astonishment. Tiikeri, her steps sure footed as ever, pranced into the space closest to where Dodger had fallen before sticking her little black and white head slightly into the air, her nose poking out the highest it could elevate before taking several sharp, deep breaths inward. Without looking the cub tensed its shoulders slightly before closing her eyes, and letting out a slight howling sound that bellowed unspoken cries of sorrow from the entire party. Rolland was especially moved by the cub's effort, even if it did last but eight seconds. Those moments, however brief, were all the world would afford Stewart Yick. For his is not a tale with a happy ending, but instead another scar on the soul of the maturing Father Time.

Had they been given more than thirty seconds to collect their thoughts, perhaps they would have decided to turn back toward Eden, back to the safety of further training and survival skills. But fate would have nothing of that.

"Rolland, sweetie," Tina said, her left hand resting gently on Rolland's free shoulder. She slowly eased it upward until it grazed his cheek comfortably before finally resting on his chin, tilting it upward until they were looking eye to eye. "You need to let go."

Nodding in agreement, Rolland allowed Kniff and Jaime to assist him to his feet as Turtledove stepped forward to help offer a supportive hand. "Your, your ear its-" Tina began, prompting Rolland to grasp at his left ear, and becoming shocked at what was, or was no longer, there.

Gwendolyn, returning for the first time since their arrival, landed with her usual practiced grace rivaling an Olympic gymnast before sprinting over to her group where she saw that someone had fallen. She pushed through Turtledove and Hannah just in time to be put to work in sliding Dodger's lifeless body off of Rolland's weight and onto the ground a few feet away. It was a sobering experience, one that took her away from the task at hand and the reason she had come back in such a hurry. As it was, the second Dodger's body was put down her attention focused back to the mission, spinning around and grabbing a still reeling Rolland by his wrist, forcing his attention onto her before stating, in no uncertain terms, "We're surrounded."

"What?" Rolland asked, his brain buzzing from the rush of adrenaline and grief. He looked at Gwendolyn for a long moment, his hand absentmindedly inching closer to the large knife attached to his belt. But no sooner had Gwendolyn opened her mouth to respond than a flash of orange colored light bolted into their presence. Jaime too had arrived from his scouting report.

"Rolland, Turtledove, we're surrounded by an army," Jaime said between gulps of air. None of them had ever heard him winded before yet there he was, nearly doubled over with his hands behind his head in an attempt to breathe easier and recover quicker.

"You should listen to them, Rolland," came the loud, confident voice in French accented English. As Charles LeClerc who stepped out from the place where Kniff and Turtledove had left his body, the cadets each took a defense stance ready to avenge their fallen classmates death a series of clicks followed by the rustling of movement of boots. Gwendolyn, impulsive as ever, even elevated herself up to eight feet to seem more intimidating.

Suddenly nearly three dozen French soldiers held the Class of the Tiger at gunpoint, their weapons pointed mainly at Jaime, Kniff, Turtledove, and oddly Tina. While the other soldiers shouted in French and gestured to the others, their commanding officer had his sights set on Rolland. Although they could not know it as they looked at one another, Rolland and LeClerc, both men were thinking the same thing. Both believed that while there was a good chance that Rolland could get away, at least half of his people, including most likely the two non-flying women, would die in the escape attempt. Guessing the non flying blonde female was precious to Rolland based on the interaction he had briefly heard earlier, LeClerc felt that he had his enemy in the palm of his hand. Choosing not to buy this bluff, Kniff continued to move across the clearing, only to be met with gunfire that landed a mere two feet from his location. Not knowing if the shooter missed, or was sending a warning the merman stopped his pursuit and surrendered. Looking beyond the guns Kniff could see the shooters hoisting them up into killing mode. Turtledove knew it too, as he could feel it in the essence of their respective bones. Their horses were tired from the climb, and did not intend to make the return journey empty handed. Behind the guns were men, French men, each ready and in position to take out as many members of Rolland's party as they possibly could before laying down their own lives for LeClerc. Weighing his options in a second Rolland knew that he was beat.

"Ok," Rolland said, tossing his father's knife to the ground in front of him. "Ok we surrender. You snuck up on us fair and square with your little party trick there."

Smiling, Charles LeClerc walked the short distance to Rolland. Returning the favor from earlier LeClerc lifted his size eleven military issue boot, cocked it back, and kicked Rolland as hard as he could directly in his stomach. Doubling over, Rolland fell to the ground before he was swarmed by a group of no less than six French guards who quickly tied his hands and shackled his legs together behind him. Likewise the same was done with the other males. The females, all three of them, had their hands tied in front of them and received no shackles about their ankles. While a somewhat cordial affair for all the others, the French soldiers who bound Rolland took many liberties in punching, kicking, and clawing at him. LeClerc included.

"Ahhhh that feels so much better!" LeClerc said with a practiced air of giddiness. He took a deep breath of the air before crouching low to meet Rolland at eye level as two of his guards raised the fallen leader up. With a bloody nose, busted bottom lip, and a swollen left eye Rolland was obviously still pissed off based on his facial expression, one which would never tell a lie so great as that of surrender.

"Since it seems that you want to be so difficult. I guess I will have to look to the women to get some answers." LeClerc said, looking down slightly at Rolland as he struggled for oxygen. "If they prove to be as difficult as you, I will fuck and torture all three of them."

The words brought fresh struggling and a new round of beating for Rolland Wright as the others stood by and watched. For Turtledove it was another painful experience, much like the one he had just gone through in losing his latest protégé. Likewise Tina hated every second, feeling much of the same empathy that she imagined Turtledove did for the man she loved. For Timothy Holmes, however, the occasion was long overdue but landed quite nicely as far as just desserts go. For Timothy nothing could have been finer, no matter what happened next.

"Divide them," LeClerc ordered before mounting a horse and rounding on himself. Two more officers on horseback soon pulled up beside him before they were given orders and the group dispersed. Then, just as suddenly as he had arrived, General Charles LeClerc galloped away on horseback followed by a dozen of his finest men.

"What are they doing?" Rolland asked through swollen lips, struggling against his bonds as the other cadets fell into two different categories on the left and right of him. Another guard stepped forward before likewise using the butt of his rifle to inflict a fresh round of assault to Rolland's torso.

"They want the men on the right, women over here," Tina proclaimed, prompting the rest of the travelers of light to quickly comply. Each of the three tiger women were lifted onto horse-back behind a French soldier; Gwendolyn first, then Hannah, and finally Tina. To their right, also sitting horseback with his hands both shackled, and tied behind his back was another man, though he was distinctly not French. Nor did he look European in any way, shape, or form. His chest, neck, and arms were covered in tattoos that looked tribal in nature, as did his long, braded black hair that set off his square jaw. Tina wondered to herself who he was and why he warranted double the restraints, but not enough to ask at his particular juncture.

"It will be ok," Tina said shakily, the mascara above her eyes smeared from crying. She met Turtledove's gaze before finding Timothy's, and Rolland's as well. A half hearted smile crossed her lips, but each man knew she didn't mean it. How could she, when directly behind her lay the body of one of their own?

As she was taken away at gunpoint, Hannah and Gwendolyn close behind her, Tina couldn't help but remember her time in Florida and her previous experience death. Being directly responsible for Alora's death was difficult enough to stomach, not to mention the headless corpse of Judah's friend Arbuthnot as it fell to the ground beside her. Now Dodger, a face she had gotten used to see every morning, joined their ranks as departed souls who left while in her immediate presence. Worse yet, she knew that this was probably only the beginning. A silent prayer in the mind of Tina Leigh Holmes was all that could do to ease her discomfort. A prayer of peace, safety, and rest for her fallen friend.

After the women were led away out of sight the remaining guards, all twelve of them, gathered the chained male cadets together before lining them up to be led away. It was at that time that Rolland noticed Turtledove speaking to the only French officer sitting upon a horse in hushed tones. The two them looked long and hard at one another before the officer proclaimed, "Gather their fallen. Place him upon the cart. Bring it forth."

Rolland was pleased at this statement, even if his mouth would not allow a smile to form as he watched Turtledove too be shacked, lined up with the rest of them, and marched toward somewhere LeClerc called 'The Bog'. Staggering the two parties in case of mutual attack, LeClerc rode ahead with the females, leaving behind a group of soldiers to lead Rolland, Kniff, Turtledove, Timothy, and Jaime back to the camp. Along with them, in the only cart left behind, was the body of Stewart 'Dodger' Yick. The path LeClerc took was the main road, little more than a dirt path meant to assist local farmers going up and down into the villages. But the one in which the men were taken was the older, more dangerous journey that would have been a death sentence for lesser men, hands tied behind their backs or not. After a while it became obvious to many of them that they were simply being marched along a path down to the bottom of the hillside. Thinking on this Kniff, the only non-pain ridden one amongst them in a mindset of leadership, began to formulate a plan of escape. Yet no sooner had he thought past the initial stages when their party was stopped by more unexpected visitors.

At the bottom of the hill, where the French soldier who had been barking orders a moment before stood nine dark skinned gentlemen, all armed with muskets, all but one of them aimed at the travelers chests. Their clothes were distinctly different from the Frenchmen, more tattered, old fashioned, and dirtier.

"Lay down your weapons!" The French private shouted at the small group of men, each of which began laughing at him and his fellows. Although the numbers were stacked against the rebels their cause was true, prompting each to train hard, practice harder, and smile in the face of death. With a practiced ease that could only come from preparedness the group of nine all drew their muskets and fired at the French soldiers, most of which fell dead or wounded immediately, including the commanding officer. The remaining three, none of which were hurt, all fled on foot back up the hillside, eliciting another fresh round of laughter from the nine rebels who then turned their attention on the captors that had been left behind.

Their leader, and only one among them still holstering his weapon, was a tall, broad shouldered gentleman with short, dark black hair adorning the top of his head in a widows peak pattern. A pair of spectacles rested upon the end of his nose as he eyed them curiously, looking from Jaime to Turtledove to Rolland in return.

"You are not French," the man said in an odd accent that sounded almost French itself. He appeared half scavenger, as he rummaged through the dead French soldier's pockets looking for goods, and half soldier with the training of a thief and the tactics of an outlaw.

"No, we are not," Rolland answered before spitting out a bit of blood onto the dirt between them. This odd act brought a smile to the stranger's face before he proclaimed that they would be returning with them.

Hoping that he could convince the leader to assist in retrieving the girls from their own captivity, Rolland's hopes of complete cooperation were soon dashed as his request to be set free from his bondage was denied. And so the Travelers of Light were led once again at gunpoint, this time with new captors, across the island toward an unknown leader who would decide their fate, and that of their fellows being marched away. Rolland could not help but feel like as a leader he had failed miserably.

The journey that followed took nearly two hours on foot, during which Rolland spent most of his time trying to process what had just transpired as well as worrying about the safety of his female classmates. It was clear that these people were serious, causing Rolland to fear that they were not above committing rape. It had been drilled into Rolland's head that neither a respectable Academy of Light graduate, nor a proper Knight of Time committed the act of murder lightly, only for the greater good. Still, the idea that something heinous might befall Tina made Rolland ready to equip himself to massacre the entire French fleet as a preventative measure. The rebels were camped in a geographically excellent position on a long stretch of land lodged between a Cliffside and a natural quarry, allowing for a great deal of protection. As they made their way through the camp it became obvious to Rolland that they had wandered into a slave revolt based on the presence of not just soldiers, but families as well. Men, women, and children were living side-by-side in a cause larger than themselves.

Upon entering a wide tent, Rolland noticed two things that piqued his curiosity. The first was a distinct smell of something that made his stomach rumble and his eyes perk up. A particular odor, it was one that he had grown both fond of and then sickened by after a year of living off of nothing but fast and cheap food following his father's disappearance. As the six soldiers marched him and Turtledove first into the darkest corner of the nearly twenty foot wide tent Rolland knew there was no mistaking it; somewhere within his immediate vicinity was fried chicken. What it was, when Rolland was finally marched by, was anything but chicken. The fried bit was crude, but looked serviceable. A thought he believed both pleasing, and completely out of place. The second thing that caught the teenager's attention was what looked like numerous black garments that littered the tents floor. At first he assumed they were bits of discarded cloth, but that was before Rolland noticed the extended arms, cut off sleeves, and hoods with distinctive eyeholes amassing beneath his feet. His senses over stimulated, Rolland did not notice the large, shadowy figure that lingered behind the large wooden table in the center of the room. That is, not until it moved.

"We captured the prisoners LeClerc had picked up," said the Haitian rebel who had guarded Rolland. "But C de Baca is... still with the French."

The distinct tone of terror that formed these words that sounded like English, yet seemed entirely foreign to Rolland's ears was reminiscent of but one other individual he had ever crossed paths with and the uncouth relationship that man, who coincidently also called himself a general, fostered with the indigenous population of that region. His resolved strangely affirmed by this familiar brand of injustice, Rolland's nerve returned in time to properly survey the room around him for the first time. Behind him and to the left he could hear Turtledove sniffling slightly, yet repetitively, as his bound hands preventing him from blowing his nose. Further behind them stood the pair of Kniff and Jaime, both of which were still experiencing an odd sense of onset shock at both witnessing Dodger's death, and the sudden resurrection of the man they had co-murdered in the wake of said event. Behind them still further, lingering off to the right of the group paced Timothy, who looked entirely bored of the entire scene playing out before him.

"I can scarcely believe it," a deep, somewhat familiar voice said in a shocked tone.

"C de Baca allowing himself to be captured like that, it's unthinkable," said the officer who brought them there.

A scrape of a chair followed by the deep, resonate thud of familiar footsteps came into focus as the figure turned, filling both Rolland Wright and Marcus Turtledove with an immediate sense of shocked dread. There, standing before them was Victor Aquasi III - but not as he was when they had last seen him.

Gone was the young man teetering on the edge of a bright future. He was now replaced by a man of broad chest, chiseled features, and a stern mouth and a demeanor that was reminiscent to Rolland of General Falocco in Eden. Even his once pearly white teeth were now a shade darker than before, matching the soul of a man who had been through hell in a decade without his friends.

"There was also a long bundle traveling with them. Inside was a young male, looks to be of the Orient," the Haitian guard said in a matter of fact tone that had no respect what-so-ever for the dead. Victor didn't so much as bat an eye at this news, only shifted his focus from the Haitian solider to Turtledove.

"One of yours?" Victor asked, allowing several more beats to pass before giving up on receiving an answer. Instead he quietly gave the order to have it stored somewhere discreet until the entire matter could be dealt with. He never once missed a beat, or seemed genuinely shocked to see them, nor was he grateful for their presence. It was almost as if he were ambivalent to them being there at all. Between the worry of what was happening to Tina and the shock of seeing Victor at what he guessed was ten years older Rolland understood all too late that the guard was speaking of Dodger's corpse. The timing of the question was undercut by the sudden onset of panic that gripped at Rolland's heart, reminding him of the look on Victor's face that fateful day he lost his Cadillac Deville outside the bookstore, the way Puck looked at him when he knew Rolland had just ended his life, and the face Dodger made immediately after he was stabbed in the chest. All of them shared one, undeniably common truth between them.

Timing is everything.

Chapter 21:
Thwack

Marshall Island - 1937

Growing up as a tomboy Amelia Earhart had taken her fair share of bumps and bruises. Still, none of them, not the time she broke her arm jumping off the roof of her father's house, nor when she broke her hip in her first plane crash, compared to the beating she took at the hands of Sephanie Kelly. With both hands tied behind her back, Amelia could do little about her situation but endure it. This lull led to the dropping of the guard that the hostage had held since she was abducted. Amelia never saw the chloroform laced rag as she turned the corner in her mind, its well directed aim courtesy of her would be abductor met its mark over her nose and mouth with little in the way of a struggle. The ease at her entrapment, mixed with her low body weight allowed Sephanie Kelly a lot of leeway in maneuvering the sleeping pilot back to her own encampment, one so deep into the brush of the island's natural foliage and fauna that she doubted anyone could, much less would track the pair.

Perish not, want not.

When Amelia awoke she found herself in a dark area of the woods surrounded on all sides by thick vegetation, trees, and the unmistakable smell of burning wood coming from the heated fire behind her. Despite her hands being tied behind her around a wooden stake of some kind, the American pilot had a good idea of the when, who and where of her situation. The sound of birds overhead drew her attention upward to reveal a mid-afternoon sky as blue as she had ever seen. The thought of flying through such a sky made her envious of the chattering animals and sad at the prospect being as impossible as it was enticing. A believer in fiction, based in large part on her own supernatural abilities, Amelia wished with all of her might that she could somehow float, or develop the ability to soar toward the opening in the otherwise tree line above. Instead, she was greeted, after several long minutes, by the somewhat familiar face of the girl Joan had confronted with back in the cabin filled with books; Sephanie.

In her hands Sephanie carried a clay pitcher of what Amelia guessed was water. Waiting for the receptacle to be brought close enough, Amelia prepped her legs for the perfect kick. The opportunity came when Sephanie crouched to lower the pitcher to the ground and it was Amelia's knee that did the honors of knocking the pitcher out of Sephanie's hands, where it shattered onto the dirt without touching Sephanie at all. Expecting some sort of reciprocation from this action, Amelia braced herself by closing her eyes and waiting for the blow to be struck. When none came after several seconds, she opened her eyes again to see Sephanie standing there, her arms folded like a disappointed parent standing over a child. She was so quick that Amelia never saw her arm drawback, feeling the punch as Sephanie clocked her squarely in the mouth.

"What kind of coward punches a person who can't fight back?" Amelia said as she spit the blood from her mouth.

"What did you just say?" Sephanie asked, crouching down further to become eye level with her coughing captive before catching Amelia's eyes, and cocking her head upward.

"I called you a coward, you chicken shit coward," Amelia said, spitting more blood onto the ground to her left. Although three of her teeth were loose she wasn't missing any, not yet anyway. Looking at her captor, weighing her options over again in her mind, Amelia Earhart did what she had always done - she took matters into her own hands. So, with no clear sign of rescue, she spoke with a clear confidence that would make her an American legend, "There's no way you couldn't take me if I wasn't tied up."

"Maybe," Sephanie said while turning her head slightly. "But we'll never know."

Walking around the clearing, Sephanie gathered the few materials she had brought while silently planning her next move. It wasn't enough to simply hide the girl from Otep and Vilthe, Sephanie had to formulate a plan to appease both her husband, as well as be able to explain to Joan so that she would forgive her. Or else... Sephanie didn't want to think about what else. Pushing these thoughts aside temporarily Sephanie bent over to pick up the shattered clay pit before something very strange happened.

At first Sephanie assumed that she had tripped, shaking her head as she pushed herself upward with both hands until she was in a kneeling position. Another sharp, stinging pain in her back, just below her shoulder blade told Sephanie just how wrong she had been. Without turning around to check for sure, Sephanie knew that somehow Amelia Earhart had gotten free of the ropes. Not only that, but she had one hand on the back of Sephanie's head while she faced the ground. With a sudden, quick jerking motion forward Sephanie's head hit the dirt hard enough to leave a bruise on her forehead. Straddling her abductor's back Amelia hesitated for the slightest moment before grabbing her again, this time with her hands around her neck. The feeling of hands squeezing seemed to bring Sephanie out of her stupor, allowing her to fight back, using her arms to claw at Amelia, using all of her strength to throw the woman from her back.

"What the hell are you?" Sephanie asked as she scrabbled to a crouching position before being struck by Amelia's foot. After sitting down hard, Sephanie could see little through her tangled hair that now covered the majority of her bruised face. The quickness of Amelia's movements suddenly dawned on her, "A fucking teleporter?"

Amelia did not reply except to kick the fallen Sephanie in her stomach hard enough to knock the wind out of her before taking several steps backward and raising her fists again. Although she did not exactly know what a teleporter was, per say, Amelia had an educated guess on the matter based on its root word. A teleporter she was not. She was angry at the inconvenience of her kidnapping, intolerant of the larger situation, and flat out pissed off by the constant interference of individuals who claimed no government affiliation what-so-ever. With all of this on her mind she (foolishly) allowed Sephanie Kelly to get back to her feet.

Raising her arms with a grace unparalleled by any individual at any time before or since her birth, Sephanie summoned the forces of the very fabric of nature itself. In channeling her cognitive energy into a single thought, in this case lightening, the embodiment of Earth herself was embed with the power of the very setting in which we all exist. Feeling the fear coming rising from Amelia as Sephanie closed her eyes to concentrate, the unseen clouds overhead formed in perfect unison with their time arrival in Sephanie's mind. Once they were in place, and an acceptable parting in the branches of the large trees could be scoped out by the inner, all-seeing eye Sephanie possessed, she unleashed the forces upon the helpless American pilot.

CRASH

The blinding light of the lightening striking nearly ten feet to Amelia's left startled her so badly it literally made her fall over before placing her head between her elbows. Nothing in her training could have prepared her for Sephanie's might. Nothing. Performing the tuck and role with little thought as to her destination, Amelia soon released the tight hold on her own head, her bleary vision giving her the bad news her mind feared might come to pass; she had fallen into Sephanie's trap. If there was any doubt in Amelia's mind about this, then the foot on her chest, with its annoying pressure, sure was telling a convincing lie.

"Damn it, just stay down!" Sephanie hollered, putting her full weight on the smaller Amelia but finding it difficult to keep it study for some reason.

With another well placed knee to Sephanie's midsection, Amelia was able to free herself as her captor doubled over in pain. Amelia paused to catch her breath, letting her guard down as Sephanie lay still in the dirt. She immediately went to the pile of goods Sephanie had gathered, sifting through them to see if any could be of use to her or Joan. So engrossed with her task she did not hear the rush of wind before it was too late. The last thing she remembered was seeing the long, dark brown club swinging from Sephanie's arm before the black wave of excruciating pain took her.

Thwack

Down went Amelia, torso first into a nearby pile of broken tree limbs that did nothing to soften her fall to the ground below.

"Finally," Sephanie said, dropping to her knees wearily, dropping the wooden club she had used to knock Amelia out with. It rolled away from her into a semi circle before coming to a stop, prompting her sigh before standing back up and eyeing the situation at hand. "Now what the hell am I going to do with you...?"

Joan was at her wits' end. She was feeling hopeless beyond measure, heartsick at what had happened with Sephanie and anxious that the orb would return again. She was also worried about Judah, and desperately needed to see him. Panic set into her chest, inviting it's best friends anxiety and irrational fear along for the ride. Where had Judah gone? Did Sephanie take him? If so, was he already dead?! The pain of everything burned inside of her like a cancerous ulcer. Also, Amelia had disappeared in the middle of the night and Joan was now currently searing for her, desperate for any sight of the young woman. Knowing her American history well enough to know that the great pilot vanished in/around the same place they were did little to ease Joan's worries. All this and more ran through her mind like a freight train as she wondered through the trees.

Suddenly, Joan caught a glint of sunlight reflecting from something across the wide clearing she had come across. As she moved cautiously closer, she realized the reflection was coming from a head of short blonde hair that she had spent many an hour running her hands through. She came to a stop as the person across from her also suddenly come to a halt as he spotted her. As he too realized who the person was he had spotted, the figure was running at full speed toward her with a reckless abandon reserved only for moments of such intense passion. The elation that coursed through Joan as she sprinted toward her husband, toward Judah Raines, was nearly tangible. The two met halfway, each throwing their arms around the other until they fell into the grass as their lips found the other's.

Joan clawed at Judah's shirt, ripping the garment slightly as she yanked it over his head. Surprised, Judah's breath caught in his throat as he rolled on top of Joan as she pressed her lips onto his. As their tongues found one another, caressing gently with the warmth of their bodies, the rest of their clothing managed to slip off with no regard to their surroundings, or the perceived danger that mattered so much a mere minute before. Not even the word betrayal existed in Joan's mind during this time, for it was time spent within true love's embrace.

" I've missed you.." said Joan between kisses. The tips of her fingers insisted on grazing Judah's back lightly, finding their way up and down his exposed flesh. Her favorite was the small of his back, right above his buttocks. There the muscles from his strong torso came together with the clashing of his bottom in a pleasing arch that sent shivers down Joan's own spine. Judah's hands found their way to the warm skin of her torso. Joan's shirt and bra were off and over her shoulders before she had a chance to think. She lay back so that her breasts were fully exposed, giving Judah easy access toward his favorite of her body parts.

"I missed you too, love," Judah said to his wife as he caressed the inside of her thighs slowly with the back of his hand. Her smooth ivory skin gave him goose bumps every time he looked at the area between her knees and waist, always tempting him with the road to paradise. As they held one another both knew how lucky they were to find each other at this time when both seemed so tough, yet so vulnerable.

What followed was the passions of two souls intermingled in a single, solitary purpose; to bring moments of happiness and pleasure to the other person. Afterward the two lay next to each other in the grass and in their joining, they found a small measure of bliss, their actions screaming joy into eternity.

"Love - that was the best sex I've ever had," Judah exclaimed, wrapping one arm around his wife's waist. "We should lose each other more often!

"Whoa there cowboy," Joan began, drawing her husband in for a kiss while reaching around for her ragged blouse. "We still have a honeymoon to experience."

"Yeah, about that," Judah said, as he too began rummaging for his clothes. "Don't we need to get the hell off of this island first?"

Joan wasn't ready to talk about what anything that had happened on this island so instead she changed the subject. After a brief back and forth rehashing their adventures while separated, which conspicuously omitted Sephanie's very presence, Judah told her of his time while away from his beloved. While she attempted to listen to her husband, she could not help but instead think of her new sequence of events, the one she had recited for Judah. The one where she greatly exaggerated Otep's role, including Noonan's death. Where Amelia was holding back on what she knew, that part was actually true, but Joan made it sound more like a spy thriller. She then let her mind linger to a dark thought that had she not been relaxed and in good company, never would have vocalized her feelings otherwise. "Can I ask you a question?"

"Shoot," Judah said, slipping his own underwear on and reaching for his pants.

"Remember when we first met and I told you about, you know, my abilities..?" Joan asked, her eyes cast downward to avoid his gaze.

Surprised by the sudden openness with a subject she didn't often discuss, Judah was eager to press the issue, but knew he had to tread lightly. "Vaguely.. what of it?"

"So you remember me telling you about my dreams.. and the voices.. and how I can speak to the dead...?" Joan said through muffled lips, still refusing to make eye contact with her husband.

"Yes," Judah said cautiously. "But you just brought up like three things, love. To which are you referring?"

"Well, the last one," Joan began, stopping to take a deep breath as her eyes welled up with tears, and her throat became dry. "Do you remember how much it scared me?"

"I do," Judah said to his wife, sitting back down next to her and placing one hand on her exposed knee. There was great comfort in that action, and Joan pressed on.

"If I talked to Fred Noonan," Joan began to say, before feeling her husband's hand under her chin, lifting it so it was parallel with his, their eyes meeting. "We could find the trigger and leave here sooner. Maybe as early as tonight."

Looking into Joan's eyes Judah saw it all. The hurt, the pain, even the betrayal that came with her previous life. Having been born into a regular, well adjusted upper middle class family on Earth, Judah never had to deal with the public rigors and pressure that went with being a high profile celebrity upon entering Eden like Joan did. It wasn't bad enough that the same group who claimed responsibility for the end to her time on Earth had made her into a saint, but to leave her with the eternal emotional scars that went with that life; well, it all just seemed very cruel and unusual to him. Still, he had to make an attempt at understanding the lemmings and their ways.

"Love, you should do whatever you are comfortable with. You also told me how draining it is for you to contact the dead, how weak it left you. Didn't you tell me that you haven't even attempted it since you've been in Eden?" Judah said, looking from one of his wife's beautiful blue eye to the other.

Nodding through her tears, Joan couldn't help but smile at her husband's obvious concern. Though she knew they came from very different worlds, and had they been born in the same century they would no doubt have been forced into war against one another, the two souls decided on a similar, yet less confrontational means of hostile diplomacy; **marriage**.

"I love you, Judah Jacob Raines," Joan said suddenly, a husky tone in her voice as, she reached for the button on his pants to loosen it again.

"Naughty girl!" Judah said, picking his wife up, holding her in a close hug as his hands grabbed her bottom. "Just for that I won't make you call me Doctor."

Nearby, on the shores of the what the indigenous dubbed Half Moon Bay, gathered nearly one hundred Imperialist Japanese warriors dressed in full military uniform. Standing at attention they all pledged allegiance to the man who stood at on the elevated boulder and looked down on them. With a nod of his head the entire force turned left once, their footwork perfectly synchronized as they moved, then again until they were all facing away from Otep and toward the ocean. For a brief moment Otep toyed with the idea of ordering them to walk into the ocean, an order he had already given more than one recruit. Born and bred within a feudal system these soldiers worshipped him just as they did their emperor, seeing both as more than mere mortal men. Riding the Imperialist recommendation to the point of divinity, Otep knew that whatever misgivings them might have would be squashed once he demonstrated him mastery over the dead.

"From the ashes of obscurity so shall you arise and make a lasting impact upon this Earth once again!" Otep screamed, lifting his arm slowly as his undead minions swayed, silently, in reverence to their creator, their giver of a second life. They were less than human, less than the excrement of livings things; as they possessed the ability to inflict harm upon those still walking around. Splintered fingers jammed with decades of caked on dirt, grime, and suffering broke free of the Earth into the fresh air of day, followed by hands, arms, and bits of torsos with the optional head on every other body. By controlling the remaining neural synapses surrounding their brainstems Otep could bend them toward his will with the simplest of collective thought.

Standing nearby the one hundred Japanese soldiers watched the crime against nature that was Otep's gift. A few men, soldiers stationed at the front of the lines, watched as their fallen comrades, some they even personally recognized, clawed their way back into the realm of the living, giving no thought as to the effect it had on the peace promised to the currently living once their number was called from the great beyond. Otep thought about this, and how ironic life was in the grand scheme of things. While he had a schedule to keep, Otep did not want to rush the process of creating his army, despite his current philosophy of quantity over quality.

With a word the one hundred Japanese Imperialist began their march across the island, back toward the site of the first of many victories for the Japanese Imperialist army. Each walked with a mixture of total fortitude and fear. For these were pilots of the highest order, and their eyes were set on taking the four dozen planes stationed on the other side of the island. It was their goal, their lot in this second life, their mission.

The mission, the one Otep could not forget. This march was the first step in their mission. It was the first step in starting the second world war in the Pacific nice and early. The first step toward manipulating the Time Stream towards Vilthe's ends. The first step toward getting what Otep really wanted; who Otep really wanted.

And it all began with killing Amelia Earhart.

After Judah and Joan finished making love a second time, they gathered themselves and made their way back to the barn where they had camped with Amelia and Noonan that first night. By the time they reached the barn, they were both so exhausted from emotional and physical fatigue; they succumbed to sleep as the midday sun blazed outside. After what seemed like hours, Judah awoke with a slightly sweaty brow and a sleeping wife collapsed on top of him. Judah had quite the time freeing himself from the equation, but free himself he did. Walking outside to urinate Judah Jacob Raines, the self proclaimed smartest man in all of Eden or Earth took no weapon despite knowing full well the danger that the island brought. After he located a tree that looked serviceable he unbuckled his trousers before removing himself and pissing on said tree. The relief in his bladder, mixed with the post orgasmic happiness from Joan only intensified the distractions stealing his focus as he closed his eyes. Regardless of the reasoning, when Judah did open his eyes again, he was no longer alone. Finishing his business with a few shakes of his member, Judah noticed something moving out of the corner of his right eye that was too large to be an animal, and too small to be an enemy.

Moving closer Judah saw what looked light brown skin belonging to a child, a boy who was hunched over in an attempt to hide in the brush from Judah. Smiling at the boy as he slowed his pace Judah too crouched downward to get a better view of the child.

"Well hullo there," Judah said to the native child who eyed him apprehensively. Though the boy was skinny he did not appear to be starved. He wore a simple green pair of makeshift shorts and no shirt. Though he was cautious he did not seem to be afraid as Judah approached, his eyes fixed on the stranger from Eden. "Aren't you sneaky little bloke?"

The boy grinned at Judah as he motioned him to come closer. Judah smiled back and began making his way to the boy, mentally wondering if the lad could help him find some food. So engrossed in his own thoughts was Judah that he failed to notice that the boy was no longer alone.

"Uh oh," Judah managed to say before the long, slender club of the dark skinned man with chapped lips hit him over the head.

Thwack

The strike was calculated, meant to disable without causing any long term damage. Heat from the sun, still clinging to life overhead fell upon Judah's shoulders and chest as he tried to look up against it, only to be greeted by an strange sound from the child who now appeared to have multiplied into four or five children. Judah looked at this with confusion for a moment before realizing that there were indeed multiple children dressed alike, albeit they seemed to be merely working in unison and not related. As the sun struck down on him Judah raised his hand to block the rays, providing shade, and the unfortunate knowledge that the large club was being lifted once again for the benefit of his noggin. The last thing Judah saw before losing consciousness was the giant shadow of the man standing above him.

"No.. don't," Judah pleaded brokenly. But his cries fell on deaf ears as the piece of lumber connected, once again, with Judah's skull.

Thwack

Chapter 22:
Something Reckless

Haiti - 1803

"Victor," Turtledove managed to say as his eyes locked onto the large, brooding, bulky man who stood before them flanked by at least five guards. He looked every bit the leader the men claimed him to be, and yet, he looked like their Victor. Except older. Much older. "Can it really be you?"

"Dismissed," Victor said in a tone much deeper than either of his fellow travelers of light remembered. The command prompted the guards to hesitantly step away from their posts. They each uttered softly, "Yes, Toussaint," as they filed out of the tent.

"Victor?" Rolland asked, cocking his left eyebrow. In a world of surreal this was the strangest thing to befall him yet. Or Victor, as it was, being that it was him who was suddenly ten years older than he was months ago.

"Aye," Victor said, nodding his head up and down while looking from Kniff to Jaime, to Timothy, to Turtledove, and finally to Rolland, who had yet to say anything but his friend's name. "You should not have come here. Not after all this time. The hour is late in our revolution, we are outnumbered, outgunned, and outmaneuvered. That being said, it is very good to see you."

"What happened to you?" Rolland asked. The ire of the large black man who stared daggers at him from behind him fancy desk made him uneasy, tense, and pissed off that no one was defending him like they would for each other.

"What happened to me?" Victor asked in an agitated voice. Slamming his right fist against his desk the full frustration from being unable to escape his plight for over a full decade bubbled to the surface of Victor Aquasi III's temper as small bits of splintered wood flew upward before falling back down to the desk from whence they came. A tear rested in the corner of Victor's right eye, glistening evilly in stark contrast to its creator's agenda of machismo and a strong front. "I've been here for almost twelve years!"

Seeing this, and feeling nothing but responsibility for his misfortune, Turtledove grieved for his fallen pupil. "Oh Victor. I came as quickly as I could."

"But not quickly enough," Victor retorted, dejected. He walked over to chest and removed a blue glass bottle, uncorked the top, and took a long swig of its contents.

"When I first got here, I landed with a broken leg," Victor said, smiling a bit as he spoke. The same pearly white teeth that both Turtledove and Rolland remembered from earlier experiences with the younger Victor showed through the years, offering something familiar. "Can you imagine me with a broken leg?"

The physics of the nearly three hundred pound Victor hobbling on one leg did seem a bit humorous to Rolland, even if he knew that the rest of his friend's story would not be so lighthearted. "So what happened?"

"Landed by the docks and some sailors thought I was a runaway slave so they captured me and brought me to the nearest plantation where the owner lied about my being a runaway so he could keep me. This plantation owner also got off on beating his slaves," Victor said, drinking more of the foul smelling liquid within the bottle. Took me months to get used to the food and drink here without getting sick. That's part of what made the recovery so difficult at first. My owner wanted to let me die or kill me himself, I was so sick and useless. I was almost relieved to die, cause I knew no one from Eden was going to come look for me."

Feeling his guilt squeeze in on him like a vise, Turtledove shifted uneasily, drawing Victor's eyes and a renewed focus to his tale.

"Problem was, whenever they tried to shoot me, I wouldn't die," Victor said, laughing loudly as he remembered being shot from every angle, only for the musket balls to flatten, and fall off of his body like they had never made impact at all.

Rolland remembered the pair of them being shot at in front of the bookstore, back when all of this had started for him. But he had never thought at the time that Victor was bullet proof. The very idea was... well...

"Didn't stop um' from trying though, for days and days. But word got out, and eventually C de Baca and the rebels came looking for the 'man who couldn't be killed'. They burst into the slave quarters late one night and the next thing I knew, I was waking up in the back of a wagon with my hands and feet tied. "

"Wait, they kidnapped you?" Rolland asked, the bluntness of his tone betraying his true thoughts. He had expected to hear that Victor had actually started the entire Haitian slave rebellion, not that he would have joined up against his will half way into it.

"Suppose so, yeah," Victor said, finally sitting down across from Rolland and Turtledove before taking notice of Kniff for the first time since their arrival. "Rode with them for a while as their prisoner, but it didn't take. Once they knew that I found fight with them, they trusted me with a blade. Days became weeks as I got to know them and they tried to know me. But I wouldn't let them know much. The only real talking I did was in battle."

Victor licked his lips before chewing on the bottom one in a nervous way that stretched the contours of his still youthful face. "You know, for the first year or so I would look to the sky during every clash with the French. Every battle! I felt like such a fool afterward when none of you would arrive. It was.. I was.. just so lonely... like it was that first day again. But my silence bred mystery, which created more distance between myself and the men. So, the cycle went on and on for another few years. Just me against the rest of the world. Just me."

The sinking feeling within Turtledove's stomach doubled on itself, calling out for an anchor or reprieve; yet none came to him as he stood, hands folded politely behind his back, and listened as Victor's tale grew darker, and more bloodstained.

"Remaining a Knight wasn't easy, but I can say with complete honesty that I've lived my oath, even in exile from Eden." Victor said with immense pride. "The other problem... took more convincing."

The tone of Victor's voice had changed after eyeing Kniff, although Rolland did not understand why until Turtledove spoke.

"He is trustworthy, Victor," Turtledove said while motioning toward Kniff's direction. "Kniff is the first Mer-person to ever attend the Academy of Light in an effort to improve relations between his people and ours."

The old Victor, the one who Rolland had happened upon unaware as both a captive in Andrew Jackson's camp, and a leader of a runaway slave group dressed in black, had always worn his emotions on his sleeve, out in the open. This Victor, however, betrayed absolutely no response, physical or verbal, to Turtledove's assurance that Kniff was on the up-and-up trust wise. Instead he let several moments pass before offering a curt nod and busying himself with signing a piece of parchment on the worn table in front of him before whistling, a cue for a guard to re-enter the tent. Without speaking the guard took the parchment from Victor and left the tent as silently as he had entered. "Never know who can be trusted these days."

"Yeah, that's all well and good Vic, but you're burying the lead. Why are people calling you Toussaint? And just how did you convince everyone to put you in charge?" Rolland asked, a feeling a bit like Judah in his bombardment of questioning concerning Victor's actions. He knew very little about Haitian history except for the bit he had learned in high school.

"On that first day, when C de Baca dumped me out of that wagon, I was frightened to say the least," Victor began. Looking from Marcus to Rolland the burden heavy eyes of Victor Aquasi III found solace in long forgotten traits of those he once held so dear. "Fear turned to shock as I was pulled to my feet, bad leg and all, by the man who was in charge. I soon learned that this leader of the slave rebellion a was a man named Toussaint L'ouverture, a former French citizen who defied Napoleon after he reversed his position on freeing the colonies slaves. C de Baca and his men gaped at Toussaint and me because the resemblance between us was striking, even I could see that."

"So you guys switched places? He became you, and you became Toussaint? Just couldn't keep out of trouble, right?" Rolland asked with only mild sincerity at desiring an answer. To his astonishment, however, Victor did not return the jovial mood. Instead he frowned, and showed more age in his face than Rolland guessed the ten or so year difference to be. "I guess not. So where is the real guy? Where is the real Toussaint?"

"Dead," Victor said, deciding not to mince words. "That same day we suffered a surprise attack from the French killing almost the entire party except for me and C de Baca. So, I did what I thought was the right thing, what I thought a Knight of Time would do, and I assumed Toussaint's role in history. After the firefight I searched Toussaint's body for his orders, fulfilled them, introducing myself as him, and continued to play my part. I've worked these past years to perform my duty."

The comment drew a snigger of laughter from Jaime, whose shackles made enough noise to remind Victor that his guests were still wearing signs of their encounter with LeClerc. With a quick whistle of his lips Victor summoned four Haitian guards who stepped forward through the tent to free the travelers from their confines, Timothy going last. The cool air felt good on Rolland's ankles and wrists, a freedom he hoped Tina was also enjoying. For Kniff the sensation that he was in the past, the real living past, and that anything could still happen at any time was an exhilarating experience he could only keep in due to the respect he felt necessary to show for Dodger's death. The guards disappeared as quickly as they had came, taking with them the shackles and along with them the last representation that any of the visiting Travelers of Light were anything but equal to the Haitian rebels or their families.

"So you assumed Toussaint's identity to protect the Time Stream," Turtledove asked, though he phrased it more in the form of an assumption, complete with broad grin that signified his approval for Victor's actions.

"Once a Knight of Time, always a Knight of Time," Victor said before a boy no older than twelve scurried into the tent before kneeling in front of Victor, a parchment of paper clutched in his left hand. With a bowed head the child revered Victor, or Toussaint as he was known to the boy, and his sense of respect was almost palpable. With a snap of his finger the boy rose, made eye contact with his leader, and produced the parchment, passing it to Victor as he grew ever closer. Standing up as he unraveled the paper Victor asked "Is this true?"

The boy nodded fervently before rising to his feet to reveal a tear soaked face and trembling hands.

"Apparently C de Baca has been captured by the French, but that much I knew already. But along with him were a group of females not of this island," Victor said, looking from the parchment over to Turtledove out of instinct. "I'm guessing they're with you?"

Rolland looked at Turtledove, unsure as to his next move. Never in his wildest dreams would he have guessed that the last few hours would have transpired, not even within the B.E.T.S.I. course itself. Still, whenever he let his mind drift it landed back to the inescapable fact that Dodger, his friend, was dead. Falling back on hold habits picked up from his time living out of his Cadillac, Rolland shut down that part of himself psychologically, choosing instead to revisit it once the immediate danger had passed.

"Tina," Rolland said while finding Victor's eyes. "Along with some others you've never met. Gwen and Hannah."

Recognizing the last name spoken, but not remembering where he had heard it before, Victor chose instead to ignore it. Instead he favored the direct approach, one in which he knew would get the job of retrieving the lost Edenites quicker than diplomacy ever would. "Then it is time we sent the French a message of our own."

With a renewed vigor Victor walked steadfast past the Travelers of Light toward his co-captains and guards, all of whom had assembled to hear their commanding officer address the rumors that his top general had been captured. Unsure as to what to do, Rolland and company lagged behind for a few moments as if remembering their roles in the living history unfolding before them. Since Victor had violated that rule, the only real rule involving manipulating the Time Stream, he could be held accountable for his actions. Still, the statute did not apply to those individuals thought lost within the Time Stream, meaning that as a person ruled so by Eden Superior Court Victor Aquasi III was not technically accountable for his actions.

Following Victor outside Rolland and Turtledove were greeted to the sight of hundreds of Haitian soldiers gathered around the tent they had just been inside, all waiting to hear from their leader on their next move. As Kniff and Jaime followed the crowd increased in size until a legitimate mob stood before a pacing, amped-up Victor. Each of the men, tired and physically depleted from the ravages of a long-standing guerilla war, looked toward their leader with a mix of hopeful apprehension..

"*Cinq le dique dur facon!,*" Victor bellowed to a roar of approval and applause amongst his men. Each either held up their right hand in a supportive gesture of unity, or the weapon they clutched within. Behind Victor half a dozen Haitian guards sprang into action, disappearing behind the assembled crowd like ants marching toward a common goal.

"What does that mean?" Rolland asked, hoping amongst himself, Turtledove, Kniff, and Jaime one of them would know. When all but Turtledove shook their heads to the negative the old man swallowed hard before tilting his head back toward the re-emerged Haitian guards.

Six French soldiers, who by the looks of their ragged clothing had been captives of the Haitians for many weeks, were chained up and marched out through the crowd until they stood, barefoot, before Victor and his Captains. One by one they were made to look into Victor's eyes as he walked past them, catching the sight of each man as he went along. The green, gray, and brown eyes of the damned souls stained the soul of the man known as Toussaint L'ouverture for only a moment before the memories of the countless dozens of lives of good, honest men killed at the brutal, unforgiving hands of the French oppressors. The years of wasted lies and friendship backfiring as colonists of St. Dominique, as the French called it, were granted their freedom, only to have it taken away just as haphazardly.

Then, quicker than a human eye could blink, Victor took to one knee and struck his fist like a match in a swinging pendulum motion, causing it to spark and ignite in flames. Within seconds the flame grew, creating a plethora of colors as it fed on the oxygen around it until it was more than a flame, as it was plainly obvious to everyone watching that this flame had become a literal extension of its bearer and served no other master. Indeed, the sight, which would otherwise draw shock and possibly even disgust, seemed instead to draw cheers and applause. From as far back as his voice might carry if shouted the applause for Victor's otherwise abnormal abilities involving his flint like skin was celebrated, verging on worship. But it did not end there.

He wasn't sure at first, yet the longer Rolland stared at it the more convinced he became. The flame itself, the fire comprising the active flame on Victor's arm was moving in a very specific, almost calculated pattern. It reminded him of the Time Stream, Ananke, in the way it moved with intention and purpose. Disturbed by this, he thought to give voice to the matter in case his eyes really did deceive him. "He can control the fire..."

None of his companions responded to this, save for the nodding of the heads that were too fixated on what the General of the Haitian army would do next. In that moment Rolland realized how far gone his friend really was, and knew that whatever came next, it would not be pretty.

The Haitian guards held their hostages steadfast as their leader rounded on their position, still eyeing them up. Then, seemingly at random, Victor pointed at a man with salt and pepper colored hair and green eyes who was brought close by two Haitian guards. The Frenchmen was held backward, his chest pointed upward as the two Haitian regulars giving him not an inch of freedom. The man struggled against the brute force of his captors to no avail as his destiny was sealed the moment he killed one of their fellow Haitian natives while his back was turned in an escape attempt. In their minds, his death would serve as both a warning to their enemies through word of mouth, and an uplifting morale booster for their cause of freedom. What came next was something Rolland had seen numerous times, though it had then been used as a party trick.

"Five the hard way! Five the hard way!" came a chorus of chants in broken English and French.

The Frenchmen's flesh singed at first, peeling away into a red, pulsating glow similar to a sunburn before spreading in an oval pattern while simultaneously continuing to relentlessly ravage the center with a white hot radiation burn. The flame was beautiful, including shades of the same white, blue, yellow, orange, and red that made it up over a decade before, yet it was refined somehow, sharp looking with an edgy undertone that looked deadly if pushed too hard.

"Victor this is madness!" Turtledove protested, drawing the ire of the seven Haitian guards stationed at the entrance of the tent behind them. This was not the genial Victor he had known; the man was a much different person. Gone was the boy, replaced by a man. A man who stared Turtledove directly in the eyes as he simultaneously wielded his flaming hand like the graceful weapon it was. Standing there, looking directly at the man Victor had become, Marcus Turtledove appealed to his better judgment and sense of self; two principals he had insisted be established within the character of every Knight of Time.

"Aye," Victor said, lowering his flaming hand. He let go of the middle-aged French prisoner, tossing him aside like an afterthought. Victor spit on the prisoner, who remained laying on his side as two guards hauled him upward toward his feet. "Put them all to work digging latrines."

The crowd, although disappointed, dare not speak a word to the contrary of their leader's decision. As the night wore on past the hour of nine o'clock the moon found a position at a most illuminated point, encouraging the digging of said latrines well into the wee hours of the morning. Many off duty guards would share a bottle of rum, still hoping that their supernatural leader will return to judge the work poorly and dole out retribution by flame. As it was, the sorely disappointed Haitians made do with their own forms of entertainment.

With a slow, unmotivated movement Tina brought her flat palm down hard against her exposed right calve muscle, leaving a small black dot of bug parts in the actions wake. It was the fifth time she had performed the action successfully since they began their stint in captivity. They were still surrounded by no less than two dozen or so French soldiers led by their General, Charles LeClerc. Their mission: re-enslave the populace of freedmen living on the island of St. Dominique, the country that would come to be known as Haiti. Although Tina did not realize this her time in Florida fighting alongside the Nabawoo people had given her a keen insight into the politics, stresses, and daily activities involved with mounting a major military campaign. There were certain signs, certain tells that LeClerc displayed; like a contentious need to crack his knuckles, neck, and limb joints. The soldiers too looked worse for wear, their tour of duty going into its fifteenth consecutive month.

'Why wouldn't they be wary?' Tina thought to herself as the large band of travelers crossed yet another stream with a low water crossing. The group had been marching for the better part of two hours along the tree line of the beach, careful to avoid going too far as to be detected by enemy or foe, before turning inland for roughly an hour. Their current location was a mystery past the obvious fact that it was far enough away from where they were taken that the possibility of finding the boys would be difficult at best. She wondered where Rolland had been taken to, and if he had escaped yet. She always suspected that he was never one who could be cooped up for long, even in Eden prison. No, Tina knew why Rolland stayed in the jail cell for as long as he did. Why he kept returning every evening for their midnight conversations. Her. This reverie was only interrupted by the arrival at their destination.

"Halt!" screamed a voice unseen to any of those a party to the caravan. All the French soldiers, especially the ones surrounding LeClerc, raised their weapons in response.

From all around them came French soldiers, making their way slowly from behind the bushes and trees. Armed to the teeth with both the numbers, and weaponry to cause a massacre beyond comprehension to any enemy that dare cross their path. The surprise caused all three of the females to jump in the saddle.

"That was... interesting," said the large man in double shackles who had been riding alongside them since their capture. He looked at Tina as he continued, "These dolts make quite a lot of mistakes, I'm afraid. Like not gagging you as it is obvious that you're the brains of your operation. Without you they're wandering in the dark. Gag you, remove you from the equation, and bide real time by which to form a plan for what to do with you. Whoever you all are."

"You understand English?" Tina asked the man, both surprised and a bit insulted at his estimation of her.

"Quite well," the man said, stepping away from a low hanging branch which swung backward to his Tina softly in the chest. "Or well enough to know that you are also the bossy one of the group, which usually indicates brains. The other blonde is the muscle, you can tell she is holding back something powerful, and the other one, well, she's also holding something back."

"Well if you're so smart, then how did you get captured?" Tina asked, a bit childishly. The man, although intimidating in stature, was coming off as arrogant enough to presume to know her based on assumptions alone and she didn't like that one bit.

"I said I spoke English, and that I was observant." the man said, taking another large step to avoid a bit of mud. "I did not say I wasn't careless."

Tina smiled sheepishly, more than a bit taken aback by the strangers eloquence and manner. Though he looked every bit the brute, there was a certain softness to his dexterity, making him personable in an indescribable way.

"What's your name, Mr. Observant?" Tina asked the man.

"C de Baca" the man said, smiling at Tina when she turned back around to face him. "It's nice to make your acquaintance."

"You as well, I'm Tina," Tina said instinctively. Something about the man, the oddity at which he carries himself mixed with the strange, almost pan-flute like music that surrounded him with every action made her definitely curious. She was about to speak again before being shushed by one of the French guards as he raised his weapon, prompting his comrades to do the same. Before them was a vast, flat land surrounded by naked branches belonging to trees that stood nearly twenty feet tall. An excellent position for cover, the soldiers looked both cautious, and a bit excited to cross into the threshold of the place, whatever it was. LeClerc held up one fist before inching slowly toward the closest line of trees and whistling twice. They all waited several moments before the whistling was repeated back in kind, and the end of a rifle protruded out from between two of the tree trunks.

"We're here."

As dusk grew in the French encampment the officers quartered themselves into their own dining tent, choosing to sup only with those in which they would back in regular society. The camp was large enough, hosting no less than four thousand French soldiers ready to lay down their lives for their glorious cause. Unfortunately for Tina that cause was neither the filling of her belly, or the freeing of her wrists from bondage. No sooner had their party arrived in the French camp than she began forming a plan of escape. Examining the assets at her disposal Tina deduced not only a plausible way by which to escape, but also the way by which would be the least dangerous for her and the others. The last thing they needed was another incident like Dodger's horrifying death. Shaking this unpleasant memory from her foremost thoughts she decided instead to focus on the newest member of their party. It did not take a genius to deduce that there was something uniquely special about C de Baca, the real question was what. If Victor had been sent to this place by Time Stream than perhaps it was for an extraction mission; perhaps even C de Baca's extraction mission.

Thinking on this, and much more, Tina gave Gwendolyn a slight nudge with her elbow, connecting with the blonde Nocturn's upper arm. This contact, if ever so slight, was completely optional for Gwendolyn, as the reflexes of the Nocturn species are three times faster than that of human beings. With plenty of time to move out of the way Gwen chose instead to allow her classmate to connect with her, skin on skin, before directing her attention toward Tina.

"What's your plan?" Gwendolyn asked, a spark of mischief in her beautiful Nocturn eyes; so *human*, yet not in the slightest.

"We need a distraction," Tina whispered, her own eyes meeting Gwendolyn's with purpose. "I'll take care of the rest."

Their conversation was cut short by the arrival of one Charles LeClerc, who entered the camp with boots stomping and a stride that whispered shades of the French Emperor himself. He was accompanied by a short, balding man wearing horn-rimmed spectacles who walked with a limp. The man's name was Captain Pierre Lavre, who was five years LeClerc's senior, despite his lower rank and eagerness to always be pleasing those whom he called 'Sir'. Looking over toward his recent female captives, the three of them, the small blonde, the mouthy one and the meek African girl. Charles knew he had some sort of leverage - he just wasn't sure what kind or who it could be used against. Still, two white women of breeding age didn't just fall from the sky every day. Especially these women, these, and troublesome women who found themselves his captives. Sensing trouble afoot from the three, Charles LeClerc passed his men before arriving at the largest tent within the encampment. Positioned outside were two young men who couldn't have been older than the age of thirteen. These two especially liked their jobs since they were in such close proximity to where Tina, Hannah, and Gwendolyn were tied up. Their teenage eyes looked past their duty toward another potential prize, one that disregarded consent in favor of early 19th century savagery on as personal of a scale as could be. In this the three Travelers of Light were united in their shared fear.

Annoyed with the choice of his personal guard, LeClerc chose to stick to the emotion he currently felt to be the strongest within him, a need for sleep, and he disregarded the boy soldiers and the female captives by going into his tent alone. After removing his boots, overcoat, and unfastening his pantaloons LeClerc began had just begun to feel the weight of the day fall off of him when he heard a faint clanging noise. Choosing to ignore it in favor of his hot-headed singular thoughts (,') As he felt his blood boil from within him, releasing a fresh wave of mitochondrial cells to regenerate his mortal coil, a part of him wished he hadn't been seen as a monster by any of the females outside of his tent. For no woman could love, or even pretend to love a monster. Killing their friend, a necessary act that he did not regret, was unfortunate in that now each one of them would be forced to look at Charles as the man who took away both their friend, and their dignity. No sooner had he taken one sock, his left sock, off than came the noise that stopped Charles in his tracks.

"Arrrrggghhhhh!" cried out a shrill voice of one of the prepubescent guards stationed outside LeClerc's tent.

Sitting bolt upright from his leaned position on his cot Charles LeClerc stared with wide eyes at the entrance to his tent. After groping madly at his nightstand for several minutes with his right hand LeClerc clasped the handle of a small dagger that he his sister had given his as a birthday gift. Armed with a lethal weapon the General crept toward the entrance of his tent with extreme trepidation at what he might find when he stepped outside.

Gone were his guards, the captive blonde and black women he had taken that afternoon, and the Haitian rebel with the long braided hair. A quick examination confirmed a distinct lack of foot prints or trail markings of any sort. It was almost as if each of them had disappeared. Then he saw her... the mouthy one. The woman he suspected belonged to that brat back at the hillside. The one he promised to hurt at the first sign of trouble. The young woman stood roughly ten feet away from LeClerc, her back straight as an arrow with both hands on her hips for added effect. He could see it then, the wanting deep within her. It wasn't a raging fire like the leader of the rebels, or a glacier of rock hard will that would cut through anything in its path to impose its will. Instead there was something else - something powerful, yet natural and free-flowing. Although she had cleared the immediate camp of his men, more soldiers, these men officers, began to file into the camp and into their situation, each watching with extreme curiosity. In total there were four, but in all honesty LeClerc was only vaguely counting them out of the corner of his eye as he couldn't force himself to take them off of his next chosen prey: Tina.

"Alright little one," Charles LeClerc said to the amusement of his fellow officers. They tittered and laughed at the young woman who stood steadfast with her hands on her hips. "You have released your friends yet you linger. Tell me sweet child, did you do it be alone with me? Hmm? Can it be that you desire to remain in my good graces? Or did you simply realize that you couldn't all escape, so you thought you would be noble and sacrifice yourself so that they could all leave? Either way, I'm afraid you have made a dreadful mistake my love, for as of this moment

I have found you, so you belong to me. And I have to warn you, I do not take very good care of my things."

Smiling sweetly Tina betrayed no sense of what was to come for the pompous Frenchmen. Instead she offered the same big-eyed grin that charmed Rolland and her father alike before quipping in no uncertain terms, "That's probably why you don't have nice things."

Meeting Tina's grin with his own before signaling for the officers behind him to attack her, LeClerc didn't even reach for his own weapon before the small skirmish was over in one swift action. The flash of blonde lightening that whizzed through the camp set the entire site on end, knocking over cups, plates, men in motion, and even the stray bit of food. But none of this was noticed, not even the missing loaf of bread from the baker's tray, due to the absence of the man barking orders but a minute prior. Charles LeClerc was gone.

Stumbling to their feet the French officers attempted to make sense of the situation, only to be met with greater confusion at the sight of their missing commanding officer. One of the men, LeClerc's second in command, Captain Piere Lavre, watched this with rapt attention. No longer spotting his commanding officer present, the Captain immediately raised the alarm by throwing his hands upward in a panicked motion. Nearby French soldiers, each within earshot, rushed to the Captains aid, only to in-turn witness another blonde streak of light that whizzed through the encampment, leaving behind nothing but the Captain's black officers cap.

Spotting this, many of the French regulars took to their arms, aiming them directly at Tina, who was now the only non-French individual left in the clearing to surround. At first there were five, and then three more young, very confused looking privates joined the others, making the number of rifles eight.

"Put those damn things down!" screamed the disembodied voice of General LeClerc to the eight French soldiers holding Tina. Looking around none could locate the officer until one of them, one of the privates who arrived late, turned his attention back to the attractive Tina, still sporting the same sweet smile as before. When she pointed upward, the private saw just what had become of both Captain Lavre, and General LeClerc. Sitting on two different thick branches, nearly thirty feet above the fire below them, each French officer sat helplessly as their captor, Gwendolyn, hovered silently between them and the trees that gave them support. Lavre, who was deathly afraid of heights, had both of his legs and arms wrapped around the branch for extra protection. LeClerc was irate at being tricked by women. "You have my attention. What is it that you desire?"

"We want an alliance," Tina offered in near perfect French, a language she had studied during her internship with the Knights of Time.

At this notion LeClerc smiled, an action that Tina could not see but Gwendolyn could. This dishonest toothy expression of amusement and repressed anger did nothing but solidify the already toxic impression of the Frenchman that the Nocturn had been forming since they arrived. She thought that perhaps, in the name of diplomacy, she could overlook his callous murder of her teammate as a casualty of war. Actions from humans like this; baser level beings with no forethought to the consequences of their actions disgusted her to the point of rage. She looked at the General with a blank stare of pity mixed with revolution before he returned her gaze, choosing instead to speak loudly and downward to Tina while keeping eye contact with Gwendolyn. "But my dear, you have my Captain and I at a disadvantage. You and your fellows could leave at any time. Why linger here for an easy recapture and a slow death?"

"I told you, we want an alliance," Tina reiterated. "You have been responsible for a lot of deaths, including my friend. This violence has to stop right now. Do you hear me? Now!"

"Bitch!" LeClerc screamed from his position, shaking the branch he rested on greatly. The entire top half of the tree shook, causing a cascade effect in shaking the tree, and subsequent branch where Captain Lavre held tight, to shake as well. A pitiful squeal came from Gwendolyn's right before the sound of night birds too fluttered about. Try as he might LeClerc could not, would not, wrap his mind around the idea of negotiating any type of surrender to a woman. "Bitch..."

"Call me names all you like, Mr. LeClerc," Tina shouted upward while separating her legs into a more formidable stance. In purposefully not addressing LeClerc by his title she knew it would rile his anger up more, forcing him into an even more uncomfortable position and realize how helpless he was. A gamble she was not sure would pay off. "But while you are up there I hold all the power."

"Fine, fine!" LeClerc screamed, his face turning a different shade of red than before. Confident in his ability to best the girl once he had shot the flying bitch in the face, Charles assumed that it was merely a matter of numbers - a game he would win once he was fighting with the French army back on his side.

"Bring him down," Tina ordered, prompting another squealing noise by Lavre before the trio glided gently, feet-first, back down to the campsite below. Gwendolyn shot upward again before returning with Hannah and C de Baca in a similar manner. LeClerc took the pause in action to dust off, collect his thoughts, and take stock of the situation around him. He knew that immediate action would result in much the same as before - with him up a tree without a rope. Still, his bullheaded nature forced him to attempt something foolish once again. Haphazardly brushing leaves off of his right shoulder; he gave the signal to the five nearby soldiers to capture the visitors.

The French guards were swift, grabbing both Hannah and the still unarmed C de Baca, who again offered no physical resistance. Tina could almost swear she saw the faintest of grins begin to spread across LeClerc's smug face before he was jolted back into reality by payback's harsh comeuppance. Taking flight again, Gwendolyn grabbed the back collar of LeClerc's shirt, lifting him off of the ground as she ascended. He squirmed for a moment before realizing his plight, offering no more resistance than one would a parachute. "Alright!"

"No," Tina said with a defiant air. She placed both hands on her hips while starring daggers into LeClerc's eyes. "We will honor our terms of amnesty if you allow us to leave here unharmed. Tell me, are you familiar with fire?"

A small chorus of nervous laughter rippled through the Frenchmen, some casting knowing looks at their comrades. LeClerc merely nodded his head.

"Then imagine fire, combustible, indestructible, unyielding fits of fire exploding all around you for miles and miles. THAT is the type of weapon we will unleash on your island. Your homeland. The very fucking queen of France herself."

"Napoloean was an Emperor," Gwendolyn muttered under her breath.

"Whatever. The point is - do not attempt to stop us, and do NOT follow us. In short, do NOT fuck with us! Is that understood?"

The reaction of the French was a mixed bag of cautious fear and unbridled rage at the women's audacity. LeClerc, who had very little experience with women in general, did not know when to stop pressing the issue, much to his soldier's dismay.

"A big threat. But why don't you want to be followed, little one?" LeClerc asked in a smarmy, underhanded tone of voice. "Because you know my numbers vastly outnumber yours and I'll eventually find you?"

"Again, no," Tina said, barely moving a muscle. "We'll honor our agreement because it's the right thing to do. Not that you would know anything about that."

"No," LeClerc answered, motioning toward the trail that led away from his camp and back inland. "I wouldn't."

"But you will offer us amnesty?" Tina asked with extreme apprehension, still somewhat surprised by the suddenly easing going nature of the terms of semi-surrender.

"Yes, that is what we are offering," Leclerc said, kicking a bit in a vain attempt to free himself from Gwendolyn's grip. "As long as you concede the rebel location."

"Now just wait a moment," Tina said in a sickingly sweet voice that was as direct as it was effective on men. "You will listen to me, *Monsieur* General LeClerc, or I will direct my colleague to drop you from a much higher distance. Ability to heal yourself or not, I cannot imagine anyone would bounce back from a splattering of over five hundred feet."

Tina's words resonated within Charles LeClerc's head along with all of the blood that rushed there from various parts of his body. Trapped, humiliated, and thirsty for an ounce of retribution over the bitch barking orders at him Charles decided to play her game, bide his time, and wait until the perfect moment to strike against her. Raising his left hand against the force of gravity LeClerc made the three finger salute that signified both his immediate surrender and honorable intention of following through with whatever agreements of peace Tina proposed. As Gwendolyn returned him to ground level he once again righted himself, straightened his back, and met Tina as an equal for the first time before bluntly stating, "I will agree to your terms."

The trek across the island took hours with little to no communication between the four companions, not for lack of interest, but due to extreme mental and physical exhaustion. This was especially true for the one member of the Class of the Tiger who had been doing the heavy lifting since their arrival, Gwendolyn. Not only was she the one to find their eventual location in the Haitian rebel camp, but she was also the one who was forced to lead them all there. This task proved more difficult than originally thought, as Tina's terrible sense of direction mixed with Hannah's constant stopping proved a frustration combination. Since arriving in this strange place Gwendolyn Murrow had experienced a sharp, yet increasing sense of anxiousness in pit of her stomach. Worse than any anticipation she experienced before the B.E.T.S.I trial was the current feeling that something was about to happen, remained unchanged, even during the sudden death of Dodger. It was with this in mind that she walked mindlessly through the gathering crowd of curious onlookers as she, Tina, and Hannah made their way into the group LeClerc had called the Haitian rebels. The area was crude, mostly comprised of small communal tents surrounding even smaller campfires. The men, as Gwendolyn observed, looked half starved though their eyes looked hungry for something other than food. Momentarily disturbed by the looks thrown their way, it did not take long to figure out that the glances were aimed at their guide, C de Baca. The man, by far the largest of stature amongst his fellow soldiers, commanded a certain level of respect, as all stood when their party came near and remained that way until they were out of site.

It was not difficult to surmise which tent belonged to the Haitian leader, as it was the biggest, cleanest, and situated in the middle of the entire camp for the best security. Gliding in behind the main fortification so as to not be seen by the guards on duty, Gwendolyn made her way around the cream colored tent until she came to a large hole at waist height in the cloth that was big enough for her to look inside comfortably. She heard voices, but saw nothing but the edges of a large wooden desk, so she moved on before finding a better, larger hole at nearly eye level. That is when Gwendolyn's life changed forever.

It was love at first sight. Rounding the corner Gwendolyn looked up to see Turtledove and Rolland standing next to a tall, broad shouldered, dark skinned man. He was handsome with a finely chiseled jaw line and eyes that spoke volumes of past experience and wisdom. Every thirty seconds or so a soldier who looked to be under his command would file in, whisper something into his ear, and scurry away just as quickly as he had arrived. The mental shift was evident as the handsome stranger attempted to right himself to conform with his present company, but try as he might he could not switch gears so fast. He was, whoever he was, a man torn apart from the inside. He was beautiful, mysterious, and utterly intoxicating to her sensibilities. In that moment Gwendolyn knew that this man, whoever he was, had stolen her heart without ever laying eyes upon her. She instantly adored the way he moved, the way he spoke. Then it hit her, as she remembered the purpose for their mission in the first place. Retrieve someone, someone very near and dear to Rolland, Turtledove, and Tina; but what was his name....Victor.

Gwendolyn Murrow, her beautiful Nocturn eyes glowing, looked on Victor with a deep and unequivocal sense of longing that was as powerful as it was immediate. It is often said that in natural instinct trumps everything else, even reason or sound judgment. Yet nature, just like the rest of the universe, had never met with the iron will that belonged to Gwendolyn, or the craftiness that came with belonging to a clan of Nocturns. She watched him for a few minutes more, taking in more of his silent persona as he interacted with the others. He seemed very sad, yet immeasurably happy at the same time, almost as if he had been forced to live two different lives that were now clashing together. Although Nocturns had no empathic abilities, Gwendolyn could sense Victor's soul crying out for comfort. Because of this, and due to the nature of their mission, she decided to wait on introducing herself. No, she didn't want to do something reckless upon making a first impression. Gwendolyn knew, almost instinctively, that the moment was not yet right to approach the man she immediately coveted, despite what her instincts told her to do.

"There you are!" came the voice of Tina Holmes, interrupting Gwendolyn's reverie. As she and Hannah made their way through the cramped line of tents that had set themselves up around General Toussaint's quarters toward her.

"Hey... you," Gwendolyn said with an awkward attempt at nonchalance, prompting the other two to look at her like she was crazy. No sooner had their suspicions arose than C de Baca, surrounded by a great deal of friends and well-wishers, followed them through the line of tents toward their party.

"Ladies," C de Baca said with a nod of his head toward all three.

"Is this the tent? Are the boys in there?" Tina asked, not waiting for an answer before following C de Baca inside. Thankfully, neither of them, nor Hannah, noticed that Gwendolyn did not follow them. Their reception was entirely too distracting.

"Tina!" Rolland shouted before crossing the threshold and nearly tackling his lady love. "Are you alright? How did you escape?"

"There is no time," Tina said, her eyes refusing to give an inch before expelling her news of impending invasion. "I'm certain that we were followed here by LeClerc's men. I'm not sure how many of them there are but-"

"But-" came the low, somewhat raspy voice of Victor Aquasi III as it hit the perked ears of Tina Holmes. Turning around slowly her baby blue eyes found his dark brown corneas before the instant shock of his different appearance hit her like a train. "It spells trouble no matter how many there are."

"Vic- tor?" Tina asked, her eyebrows raised to her hairline from the excitement of hearing her friend's voice. Tilting her head slightly in confusion she stared deeper into the soul of the man who stood before her, all grown up. "Oh Victor, how long have you been here?"

"Nearly a dozen years," Victor said, his eye right eye watering slightly at the sympathetic, although somewhat unexpected tone Tina immediately adopted. He had always appreciated that she was the kindest of her family, if not the gentlest person he had ever known. But to put her shock aside to think of his tribulations right off the bat was... something only a true friend would think to do. "But who's counting, ay? Bring it in here."

The two hugged, Victor wrapping his bear arms around Tina's midsection as they embraced as old friends made new again. Hannah walked into the tent behind them in time to witness this, filling her with happiness. She recognized Victor from the night when Scott Wright had died, and knew him to be an honorable man worth retrieving. Seeing him and Tina hug meant that not only had it all been worth it, but that they had one more ally on their side against the unpleasant General LeClerc. Though happy to see Victor alive, Tina's mind quickly shot back to the trepidation she felt the entire trip. "The French!"

"Yes, the French," Victor said before letting go of Tina. "They once gave the people of this island their freedom before Napoleon decided to take it away. This I cannot allow. Not in good conscience. Tell me, Tina Leigh, did you bring back anyone with you?"

"I did!" Tina said enthusiastically. "Hannah is right outside with one of your men, C de Baca."

The name caused Victor to turn his head slightly before smiling again. He had known all along that any clash with LeClerc could not be won without C de Baca, no matter how strong their conviction. The news that his top Lieutenant had been captured the day before had created something of a quandary for Victor, who had to decide if sacrificing one hundred of his soldiers to rescue one was a worthy enough end to justify the means. Fortunately, Tina and company solved this problem for him.

"Gwendolyn too... though I don't see her anywhere," Tina said looking around for her missing teammate. "Ugh, she's disappeared again. I swear she's around here somewhere. You'll meet her, I'm sure. Oh, Victor. It's just so good to see you!"

"You too," Victor said, flashing her pearly whites for her once again. He then nodded at Hannah, whom he barely recognized from their previous encounter before thinking on it again. "You're the girl from-"

But the sound of shouting signaled the presence of intruders within the camp; a signal that both Victor and his men knew quite well. Springing up from their various positions within the comfort of their tents, the men and women labeled as Haitian rebels quickly move to fortify what was near and dearest to them. The soldiers came all at once with no stagger to their attack. The French regulars, all on foot, none on horse, charged into the Haitian military camp with rifles and bayonets at the ready. Their fight, one which found them severely out-numbered and outmatched, was a futile one; a fact not lost on the one amongst them capable of thinking such higher level thoughts, Captain Lavre. Though a stout man he knew enough as a tactician to know that this was a precision strike, quick and clean; yet the orders he gave to his men completely lacked an exit strategy.

"French foot soldiers, all around us!" cried out a Haitian sol-ider who took an flaming arrow squarely to his chest immediately afterward.

The initial shock of the invasion caused nearly everyone to rush out of Victor's tent, though not all at once. Lingering behind a bit were both Rolland, and Victor, who took the time to re-attach his sword to his britches. Unfortunately this gave the invading French soldiers enough time to both locate, and begin their attack on the tent from the outside. Four of the Frenchmen took to one knee before readying their rifles toward the entrance to the tent. With a loud, thunderous voice that came from an authoritative place deep within, Lavre gave the order to fire.

Musket balls flew through the tent, narrowly avoiding Rolland's shoulder and thigh as they went. Two caught Victor in the chest and neck, though they like so many other projectiles flattened and fell once they made contact with his thick skin. Remembering that they needed time to re-load, both he and Victor looked at one another before running for the entrance to the tent and bum rushing the line of French soldiers half sitting on one of their knees. Extending his arms outward in a winged position Victor leapt on all four of the soldiers, immediately disarming them as they fell to his weight to the ground below.

Victor sprang up, his own sword at the ready. To his left came Lavre, his own sword drawn and aimed at Victor's weapon. They clashed twice before a new saber entered the fray, this one being held by another French soldier. Out of the corner of his eye Victor saw Rolland wrestling and fighting two more of the French, their weapons making zero impact as he attempted to clasp his hands together to gain the upper hand. *'The more things change...'* Victor thought, distracting him long enough for the missing French soldier to again raise his rifle, this time with the end of the barrel a mere three inches from Victor's exposed ear. The Haitian General heard two sounds, the first being the click of the rifle firing as both Captain Lavre and the other Frenchman, the one wielding a saber, launched a fresh round of attacks from both behind and in front of him. Being completely overwhelmed, Victor half expected for the bullet to penetrate his ear and take him down immediately. When he heard no shot, but instead more howling from behind him as he fought Lavre hand to hand, Victor assumed that it was Rolland pulling double duty in handling the soldiers.

The second sound, a buzzing noise accompanied by a light yellow, almost blonde colored blur that forced him backward off of his feet, left him confused and alone as he looked around for either the Captain or his saber holding charge. The remaining Frenchman too sat on the ground beside Victor, though he was severely favoring his hand as if it were in extreme pain. Reaching for the rifle, Victor picked it up, turned it over, and hit the man square in the forehead with the butt of the rifle, knocking him out instantly. Though he had no idea what the buzzing sound was that took the attacking French soldiers away, his rage over the fact that they had dared to enter into his peoples' land was tantamount to an excuse for all out war. He looked upward, only to see a night sky filled with stars and smoke from various parts of his camp where the invaders had set it ablaze. It both broke his heart, and emboldened him at the same time, bizarrely making him stronger in his convictions. A plan began to form in the dark reaches of Victor's mind, mixing bits of lessons learned from failed invasions and notes he had taken on past successful strategy against the imperialist occupiers. Things would be different this time, of that he was sure. This time Victor would use the weapon he had been afraid to unleash before.

This time Victor would unleash the beast.

Tina's feet had always had a mind of their own. When the fighting broke out in the Haitian camp Tina fled the tent right behind Turtledove and Hannah before ducking sharply to the right and making her way through the tree line to the medical tents. Deciding that there amongst the already sick and wounded was as good a place as any to make her stand Tina went about setting traps for the invading soldiers using shards of broken glass, pottery, and even a bit of fire in one or two spots. Suddenly she felt altogether useless at a time when those weakest around her needed her most.

"The French are awful," Tina said, looking past the fire positioned in front of the medical tents. Though her comments were directed toward the women acting as the nurses behind her, none but an unseen individual heard what it was she had to say. The man, unwashed for months and far from home, crept drunkenly toward her through the bramble bushes and thick tree line that surrounded the medical area. She would be the first women he had gotten his hand on in near five years, and he did not plan on being gentle with her. The closer he went, the more the air around him, the air between Tina and himself smelt like vanilla with a hint of honey. Overwhelmed by the pleasurable scents, the would-be rapist gave himself away before he could capitalize on his sense of surprise.

"Pretty thing," said the strange man in a gruff, uncaring voice from beyond the shadows. Tina heard his voice and the undertones of evil baritone balanced in perfect sync with the underhanded triangle and the devious trombone. His intentions were clear, regardless of what words he offered. Before she even turned around Tina knew she could not run but instead had to stay and fight, no matter how large the stranger was or how menacing he might appear. The nurses had fled, choosing to sacrifice Tina in exchange for their own safety. With a resolve unknown to her before recently Tina turned to face the shadowy figure as it edged in closer with the ticking seconds. From behind them a fresh round of screams were let out from across the field where Tina had come from originally. She did not allow herself to look in that, or any direction other than the one of the hand of fate waiting for her in the darkness.

Galloping noises from infantry officers led by Captain Lavre made their way into the camp due west, straight for the medical tents and Tina's position. There were ten in total, eight on horse and two marching on either side while holding long wooden torches with wicks dipped in whale fat. Passing the tree line as they entered the small patch of woods that separated them from their target location, Lavre rode hard to the left of his column before bending downward, further than other soldiers might have had to due to his short stature, and set ablaze to a small thicket of sticks nestled close to a grouping of trees. The ten then entered the woods ahead of the flames, it quickly nipping at their heels. The fire quickly spread upward, outward, and all around until it was chasing their party toward the rebel medical tents. A few of the lucky nurses, the ones not up to their elbows in infection or gangrene, witnessed this utter disrespect for the planet with abject horror.

Then, without warning, a sudden dizziness came over Tina as she was forced downward toward the hard ground. Her head was turned sideways as cold, sweaty fingers pressed against her right cheek while another pinned her chest. Her arms flailed wildly as they fell with little effect on her attackers chest. Thinking quickly her legs sprawled as much as they could given that his were forcing hers both downward, and simultaneously, apart. From behind her she could hear the French troops on horseback making their way out of the forest. Either they would kill her or he would, it was only a matter of time.

"Now *cheri*," the dirty stranger said in badly accented English through yellow teeth, "you don't need to be living for me to do what I need. Just go to sleep now like a good girl."

Tina could not breathe.

No sooner had her vision begun to blur than the heavy weight weighing her down disappeared entirely, leaving her gasping at the ocean of air available to her all at once. Terrifying, blood curdling sounds of anguish and horror filled her ears, spots from a lack of oxygen filled her eyes, and an undeniable sense of vulnerability filled Tina's thoughts as she slid and scooted out of the way of harm until she felt a long, hard, wooden barrier that she recognize to be one of the logs the Haitians used to sit on. Laying her back flat against it, she closed her eyes even tighter and tried to ignore the sounds of what she could only describe as a mix between a bear attack and a tiger mauling its prey. Then she coughed for what felt like a long time, what felt like minutes, before summoning the courage to brush away her matted hair from her eyes and look up at what had become of the situation. That's when Tina realized that several things had changed since her eyes were last opened.

The scene before her was full of carnage, that much was undeniable, though it was not the type she could have expected. Out of the French soldiers and the one French outsider that had stalked her in the shadows, Tina spotted the remains, or at least the partial remains of at least eight of them. The man who had attacked her, pinning her to the ground, lay closest to the fire, literally ripped in half from crotch to neck; his head nowhere to be seen. Miraculously, the forest was not on fire, but instead looked crisp and freshly wet with some sort of dew. But the most surprising thing of all, the one that Tina least suspected, was the one thrashing about nearly thirty feel above her head, still holding the ninth of the attacking French within it's massive, pointed claws. Whatever it was could fly, was fast, and strong enough to pick up and carry French soldiers before dropping them. It wasn't until the flying savior flew against the silhouette of the moonlight that Tina got her first look at the massive, nearly twenty foot wingspan of a creature that was distinctly not Gwendolyn Murrow. Indeed, the beast that had been defending Tina from the French assault seemed to be on her side, despite its grotesque appearance. This was never more evident than when it chose to land, letting go of its French prisoner when it was coming toward the group, still eight or nine feet from above. The soldier tucked, rolled, and got up to his feet before running in full sprint back toward the forest. The creature itself folded its massive wings around itself like a cloak before standing stock-still in the nighttime air. The sounds of its breathing were heavy, loud, and carried over to where Tina stood like an echo from the distant past.

As her vision cleared Tina raised her aching body into a sitting position; the sound of heavy, labored breathing still quite close-by. It did not take more than a few seconds to deduce the situation. There, standing at nearly eleven feet tall and at least five feet wide was a literal monster of a creature. While comparable to Puck in his Ballua state, this creature stood on two legs, had massive wings that nearly doubled his size, had gray skin from head to toe, wore a simple loincloth around his midsection, and had the most distinctive long, flowing black hair that was braided into multiple strands in random places. Tina looked closer at these, still too afraid to move more than her eyes. The creature turned, alerted by her presence, before it faced her full on to reveal its identity. "Oh my..."

The jagged, stone face of the large, gargoyle like-beast panted through each breath, causing his chest to rise and lower basked in the firelight. Large fangs, not unlike those of a fully grown tiger showed themselves as it howled as it threw its head back and raised its arms into the air. At the tips were claws, long, pointed, and frightening fingernails that yellowed and looked like small daggers at the end. No sooner had the creature roared, cocking it's head back and stomping its tail against the ground when another choked, shallow, and pitiful sound ebbed over Tina's ears. At first it sounded very far away, not demanding much of her attention; yet as the beast before her began to slow it's breathing it's back also hunched lower, lower, and lower to the ground until it's nearly eleven feet were a much more respectable six feet. Gone too was the gray skin, replaced by a darker hue recognizable as human. The fangs, wings, and tail too disappeared as the animal fell into a sitting, and crouched position on the ground before her. The only thing that remained true, that remained the same throughout the entire process was the hair. For although she had met him a mere couple of hours before the braided black hair would stick with Tina for a lifetime.

"C de Baca?" Tina asked the now fully composed after her attack.

With tear stained eyes the man who introduced himself as C de Baca, now completely naked save for the small cloth that covered his genitals, sobbed uncontrollably as his true nature was revealed to yet another potential ally. "I'm a monster."

Hannah was at a crossroads. Since arriving in Haiti the young woman had witnessed a death, been taken captive, and been released under the protection of a girl no less than seven years her junior. The final insult came with being summarily dismissed, she suspected due to her gender, before landing in a far flung part of the Haitian rebel camp where everyone looked at her as if she were made out of cheese. Hannah was a stranger, a traveler, and possibly a threat. After the battle had ended and things began coming to a state of normalcy for the Haitian encampment, male attention again turned to Hannah, making the young woman uncomfortable and wanting to find refuge elsewhere.

After making eye contact with the nearest guard Hannah was able to not only procure the correct directions, but also an armed guard that kept a respectable distance. Hannah was taken to one Mrs. Deanoux, a midwife and cook on the west side of the encampment. Together they walked to the kitchen area where Hannah requested permission to whip up a few batches of her grandmothers biscuits for the soldiers. Thinking the ideal splendid, Mrs. Deanoux fetched the supplies without a moment's hesitation.

"Many of us double our professions out of, how do you say, necessity," the midwife told Hannah, directing her to the smallest tent on the row. They entered to find that the place was much larger than it looked on the outside, almost twice as large. Two large fires that took up the majority of the tents space, one of which housed what appeared to be a wood-burning oven.

"I hope this will do, dear," the midwife said before excusing herself back to her previous task outside.

"It's perfect," Hannah said happily under her breath before setting off to work. For the next hour she sought out the eggs, flour, sugarcane, and began the ancient art of baking the stress and anxiety away. Once she had everything gathered and mixed together Hannah took the spot next to the large pot before sprawling her legs on either side of it, inserting a big wooden spoon handed to her by the midwife, who happened to buzz through at random intervals, grabbing this tool or that. When all the ingredients were in the pot Hannah stirred happily, and thought. Soon this mixture would be dough, it would be different, yet she would remain the same.

Hannah thought of Dodger and how he had chosen, with his dying words, to tell her how pretty she was. The ignorance she showed toward him, never once realizing his true feelings, his true self.. made her ashamed and saddened by what could never be between them. All the friendship, the chats, and the potential love, for who could not love such a charming young man, made her so sad that her stomach began to churn. Still, she kept mixing the dough.

Hannah switched gears, deciding to think about her other dilemma, the one she had purposefully been putting off discussing with Rolland. She knew that when approached with the idea he would have a passionate, if not extreme opinion on the matter, good or bad. It wasn't that she was afraid of his response, but knew that she could not in good conscience move forward without his blessing. It was a fascinating dilemma, one that tied neatly into the fact that she came along on this mission to rescue Victor, who was present at the event in question. She remembered that night fondly, and with great sadness. It was the night that Rolland's father had died protecting her - the night that she knew, for the first time, that she was not only equal to other folks, but that she, Hannah the house slave, could be considered special.

Tears formed in Hannah's eyes, the very tears she had hoped to conjure as the secret ingredient to her biscuits. She leaned over the large pot and let the tears drop into the dough, falling with no fanfare and becoming one with the mixture. She stirred some more, blending in a part of herself as she again thought of Dodger, of Scott Wright, and Dolley, whom reports and historic articles back in Eden had told her that even in this time, had passed away. All these people in her life, all gone in what felt like the blink of an eye... but what did it mean, and how could she honor them? More tears came and joined the dough as she stirred. Then more, and more until no salt was needed and the love that Hannah felt for the fallen, for the still standing, and for those who would never fight was felt in her creation. It was her love. It was her life. It was Hannah's protection.

Chapter 23:
Earhart M.I.A.

Lae Island - 1937

Deep within the confines of a dream Joan Raines found something she had been looking for in the waking realm. She awoke thinking on this as she reached her arm over to where she knew Judah to be laying in a thicket of hay from where they had made love. But Judah was not there. Startled to full awareness by this discovery Joan pushed herself upward in while yawning loudly and looking around the barn. With no sign of struggle and nothing strewn about Joan decided that her husband had probably stepped outside to relieve himself. No sooner had this thought crossed her mind than the distinct sound of wooden twigs breaking under human feet found its way to her ears.

Joan was to her feet and across the barn within seconds, running out the door and straight towards the sounds. She was caught up short by the sight of her husband's shirt lying in a heap on the ground. Snatching it up with her left hand Joan held it close to her chest as she looked around again, this time taking special notice of minor details. Pondering this, Joan slowly yet steadily moved the shirt to her nose, inhaling the scent of Judah and gaining comfort from the smell. Infused with a new sense of fortitude Joan crouched low to gain another perspective when she noticed a pair of dark skinned, very skinny feet that were standing facing toward her from the foliage of the forest.

"Hey!" Joan screamed before she could contain herself. Propelling her body forward through the hedge Joan saw for the briefest of moments who she was chasing; a small native child with no clothing save for a loincloth around his waist.

Trusting her instincts, Joan decided to follow the boy. She told herself that he would lead her to Judah and to think anything else would send her already frayed nerves into overdrive. Yet, she underestimated the boy's swiftness and she soon lost him as well as his trail. She had been wondering for nearly an hour when she came upon a familiar clearing. After thinking for a second, Joan realized she was where Fred Noonan had died. Where Sephanie Kelley - her best friend, had murdered him in cold blood.

When Joan came upon the pale body of Fred Noonan, he had already beginning to rot away around the corners of his mouth. The humidity of the island drew flies to the deceased co-pilot's nostrils. The large gash that ran across his throat was festering with a putrid infestation of maggots and dried blood. They had given his remains no dignity. This disrespect of a good man caused Joan's blood to boil. Setting the scene, Joan was confident that though she had not performed this particular ability in nearly two dozen years, she still had the ability to pull it off. With a great difficulty she was able to lay the body down so that the mouth muscles were able to move easier instead of against gravity. Crouching down low, so that she was eye level with the sitting Noonan, she leaned over to his ear before whispering.

"Where is the trigger?" Joan asked Noonan's corpse, though he had been dead for the better part of twenty-four hours. So much had happened during that time period that Joan felt she had forgotten more about the deceased American navigator before her than she had ever learned while he lived. With this thought in mind, Joan thought of her husband, Judah, and wondered if she would ever see him again. She wanted to drop everything, the pursuit of the trigger, the protection of Amelia, all of it, just to run to Judah. So lost in this illogical, worst case scenario fantasy that she nearly forgot her place. Feeling utterly foolish, and just as useless, Joan sat next to the navigator's corpse, pondering her own fate. What had began as a promised honeymoon had quickly turned into a full-blown extraction mission with much of the same chaos as the last one, the only positive addition being the impromptu barn sex with Judah. That WAS nice. Still, it hardly helped her current situation.

Joan thought of all the times she had performed this particular skillet as a part of her overall duty to Eden and the Knights of Time. Burbank California 1966. Memphis Tennessee 1977. New York City 2008. Each time more depressing than the last. Each man wishing for more life. Little worldly knowledge was gained at each interview with the departed, yet a clear picture of their death and the circumstances surrounding it always became clear once that conversation was over. More memories of the past again came to Joan's mind, though this time of her own volition and without the presence of a supernatural floating orb. She thought back to her time as a girl solider, and the day she was finally summoned before the king. It was a cold day for April, she remembered that much very clearly. When her caravan arrived at the castle their horses were taken before a group of men clad in armor escorted them through the castle to the great chamber.

Inside many people in various garbs lined the great processional hall, all-leading to the large, plush throne where a slim young man with a goatee sat proudly.

Seeing the great throne before her, something set off a warning alarm inside of Joan's mind that told her something was not quite right; a similar feeling she was feeling again as she looked at Noonan's body. To her left stood the women, many of which wore simple grey dresses to distinguish that they worked in laundry, or as housekeepers, or servants of some sort. On the right stood the men, whose outfits were of a larger variety, and no two the same. Half way down the aisle Joan got a good look at the king's eyes for the first time and something else, something she had not seen for a while. The orb was there, she remembered vividly, and it showed zero affection for the man who sat upon the throne. Yet for her, and oddly enough, for the pauper dressed in a crushed velvet suit who stood quite nearby, the orb seemed to become a flutter. Relying on this instinct, Joan continued to walk down the aisle, purposefully lingering a bit by the man who set the orb into a tizzy of loops, rolls, and bounces. Keen on watching his eyes out of the corner of her own, Joan swore that he too watched the orb, or at least looked in the orbs general direction on more than one occasion. It was in this that Joan finally understood what it was that providence was attempting to tell her. The monarch was attempting to fool her, this much she knew. Yet pointing him out was not enough in her mind to warrant his trust. No, it would require something more than that. Something divine.

As she approached the man who sat upon the throne Joan stood motionless after coming to a stop. All within the hall waited for Joan to kneel, yet when she did not no uproar transpired. Instead, the then young girl took another calculated risk, taking several carefully taken steps backward until she was again eye to eye and within speaking distance of the other orb attractor. With a single look into the man's eyes an chose the ones she knew would mean the most. Sitting there, her hair braided into a messy, unfiltered mess of a tangle, Joan repeated those words with tears in her eyes.

"You are on a righteous path," Joan whispered into the left ear of the corpse of the American navigator Fred Noonan.

The re-animated corpse lifted its head and opened its dead, hollow eyes before saying the last words she expected to hear. The same words that had once upon a time gained an army from a monarch dressed in a crushed velvet disguise. "You are on the righteous path; go with certainty and peace."

Smiling, Joan wiped away the tears that clung to her right eye before continuing on with her interrogation.

"Half...." Noonan said breathily.

"Half, half of what Noonan?" Joan asked.

"Amelia is half of the key to project... project...." Noonan said, his voice fading.

"Project? What Project?" Joan asked.

"She is the key..." Noonan whispered breathily, though he was not breathing at all. "Amelia. It must be her who uses the trigger."

"Why, why her?" Joan asked.

"Because of her abilities..." Noonan said before his head fell limp against the grass.

"What abilities?"

"The pilot," Noonan's corpse stated through blue, unmoving lips. The effect was creepy beyond words or description. Anyone unfortunate enough to be blessed with the curse of speaking with the dead knows what little good describing it is to those who cannot does.

"Amelia?" Joan asked, somewhat taken aback by the rather obvious answer. "Why wouldn't she have just told me that-"

"Kill you," Noonan's corpse said, prompting Joan to back away from the otherwise lifeless body.

"Excuse me?" Joan asked, adjusting her position as she crouched in closer to the corpse. In doing so she was totally unprepared for the eyelids that shot open like window blinds to reveal gray, veiled over eyeballs that looked somewhat sunken inward, rocking Joan to the core of her very soul.

"We knew you were coming..." said Noonan's corpse, his time on Earth coming to an end for the second time in as many days. "We were told to kill you."

Across the channel on a smaller island lived the tribe known as the Eke, a mostly peaceful people who had captured Judah, taking him hostage. The blonde traveler of light awoke to the sound of drums that he would ever miss-associate with going to war, when it reality it was closer to the sounding of a dinner bell. Considerably hungry himself, Judah tugged at his bonds lightly, finding them wrapped around the post in the middle of the dark enclosure. It wasn't for several moments until his eyes adjusted to the darkness of the room, but longer still before the figure sitting close by made even the slightest of movements to reveal himself.

"I have been watching you for days, sky traveler," said a low, husky voice in thickly accented English. All seemed to fade away as he spoke, including every thought inside Judah's head of escape, or even Joan's welfare. When the man moved out of the shadows Judah saw that he was older, pushing fifty years of age with a dark complexion.

Judah listened to this and despite his otherwise good intentions, could not help to stifle the snarky laugh that escaped his lips as he stared at the older man with mouth agape. "Listen Charlie, I hate to admit this even to myself but it was kids that did this to me, not one of what I'm guessing is many strapping warriors you'll unleash on me if I do somehow manage to escape. But guess what? I don't care! I've survived worse than this so go ahead mate."

"Who is this Charlie?" the old man asked with genuine confusion in his eyes.

"Right," Judah said, his hips wiggling a bit as he attempted to itch the mosquito bite on the middle of his lower back.

"Perhaps we start on wrong course of introduction," the dark skinned man said, rising to his feet and walking closer to Judah.

"I am Ono, Chieftain of the Eke tribe, father of Muitimbo," the old man said before bowing his head slightly. He then looked Judah dead in the eyes in a very serious way before saying "You are on my island. I have told you who I am, now please tell me who you are."

"Gladly," Judah said, giving a passive aggressive smile as he continued on with his spiel. "Doctor Judah Jacob Raines, PhD at your service. Creator of the Dream Phoenix, representative of Eden, and if we're just throwing out titles I've also won every science fair I entered from Kindergarten to college."

"Hello, Doctor Rain," The Eke Chief said, looking down upon the still restrained Judah. "Please forgive our distrust of those who are not of our kind. We see from your machinery that you are not only different from us, but also different from the other, more primitive men who have come here unwelcome. Is this because you are not of mankind?"

Impressed beyond words by the keen observational skills of the Eke chief, Judah could think of nothing else to say besides, "Yeah, guess you could say that. How's it you speak English by the way?"

"Very good then," the Eke Chief continued, lifting one hand and motioning for two of his guards to step forward and cut the robes that held Judah's hands together. "You must meet Muitimbo, as he too is like you. Come then, meet my people! Regale us with tales of your homeland."

At these words five very large Eke guards came into the tent, revealing a bright, blinding sunlight that forced Judah's hands over his eyes and away from the ropes that were soon free of his person. It was at this time that Judah realized that he had been inside of a tent of sorts the entire time, somewhat explaining the almost complete darkness. Then, without being aware before-hand, numerous hands grabbed at him until Judah was standing on his own two feet, a mere shoulder distance apart from the Eke Chieftain, who looked much older in the light of day. It was less than five seconds later, however, that the curiosity finally got the best of the crowd of Eke townsfolk outside the tent, most of which also came pouring inside like sunlight.

Feeling very put on the spot, but also fearing for his life, Judah thought for a moment about which homeland he would share with the Chief and his Eke people. He looked around at the sea of faces that stared back at him. He guessed eighty, maybe one hundred wide eyed and curious imaginations were fixated on him, wondering where he, the alien in their world, might have come from. He then remembered how Turtledove handled the same situation during their trip to Pensacola, Florida and the transparency he displayed with the Nabawoo people. In viewing the Eke, be it a latent prejudice toward the so-called 'uncivilized' Judah could not help but think of them much like the Nabawoo.

"It's a place called Eden," Judah said, not believing his own mouth as he spoke the words. The Eke Chief translated his words as Judah cracked his neck, knuckles, and fingers one by one. "It exists outside of this world in its own separate dimension. Kind of like a lost paradise where time as you know is represented by a stream. A Time Stream. "

The word 'stream' hit a nerve with the Eke people as in their language this was a grave insult on par with telling them to do something very vulgar with their own mother. After the laughter and commotion died down and order was once again restored the general feeling of cooperation hung in the air like a sign for Judah to take comfort in. This was further evidenced by the arrival of a nearly seven foot tall broad shouldered man whose septum was pierced with a thin, hollowed out wooden reed. His bulbous arms and frame made Judah look childish by comparison, despite being slightly larger than average himself, even in his middle age.

"This is my son, Muitimbo," the Eke Chieftain Ono said to Judah with great pride to his voice. At these words the large man bent downward and extended his right hand to Judah, who took it in turn to shake. Much to Judah's surprise the greeting was firm, but not uncomfortable, commanding yet not overly aggressive, and overall left him with a genuine impression of camaraderie.

"It is very nice to meet you," Judah said to Muitimbo as he shook the man's hand. He guessed his new friend to be in his early twenties at the latest, but no older.

"*Mbkhenry*," the giant Eke said between his somewhat mangled, though perfectly white teeth. He smiled ignorantly as he shook Judah's hand, revealing that he was at least somewhat familiar with Anglo customs.

"Do you speak any English?" Judah asked, his arm being shaken by the overly strong Eke.

"*Mbkhenry*," the Eke said again as he looked down on Judah and smiled while nodding repeatedly.

"*Mbkhenry*, huh?" Judah said, prompting Muitimbo to repeat himself again several times before nodding furiously. "Mind if I just call you Henry?"

Shaking his head at his son and Judah the Eke Chieftain stepped back from them both before walking over to greet the gathering of his people outside of his hut. In opening the flap he lifted the veil from both Judah's eyes, and that of the Eke community as the two sides saw one another full-on for the first time. "There is one more thing you should know, Doctor Rain."

Judah looked up from the happy crowd where he felt like an instant celebrity, looking at the old man casually. "What's that?"

"That would be the island where we found you," the Eke chieftain said, motioning to the distance with his hand. Judah didn't follow mentally but did jog the short distance through the crowd of Eke toward the beautiful, if not terrifying sight before him.

There, across a small divide of perhaps three miles of ocean, was the main island where he knew Joan and Amelia to be. "Oh shit."

"Welcome to the Eke," the chieftain said with a sly smile.

Amelia woke up to the feeling of cold water creeping uncomfortably down her throat, blocking her natural airways and making it nearly impossible to breathe properly. With a great inhaling of oxygen, and recognition of the situation upon consciousness, the curly haired pilot choked through multiple gasps as pockets of air filled her stomach.

"Where is the trigger?" Sephanie asked while pouring the boiling hot water from the pot over the fire into a cup on a nearby table.

Sephanie stopped completely before hesitating on her next action. Before her were numerous tools of the trade, various items to coerce even the staunchest of spies into revealing their inner secrets. Sure the Earhart girl was quiet now, but Sephanie was willing to bet that the dumb little pilot would be singing once she was down to only having six fingernails left. With this method of assault in mind Sephanie picked up a pair of slender, long, and silver plated items that resembled a pair of giant tweezers before turning back around to face her captive.

"Do you think I like doing this, Amelia?" Sephanie asked, pulling on the rope again, forcing the ends of the machine, and Amelia's shoulder from its socket, further apart. With a twinge of compassion for the pilot Sephanie stopped herself before turning away from her and taking a deep breath. She asked herself if this was the right thing to do, the moral thing, and moreover, did the ends justify the means? Pondering this, Sephanie turned around again to find Amelia gone.

As if she had phased through the very ropes themselves - they sat, still tied to the empty chair sitting beneath the large tree where Sephanie had left Amelia seconds before. Looking around for her for several minutes, Sephanie allowed herself to become riled up again, agitated, and distracted, never seeing the attack coming as the tables turned themselves quite beautifully. The kick was so hard, so decisive that it dislocated Sephanie's left arm instantly in addition to knocking her down and disorienting. This was part of Amelia's plan; the rock however, was just good timing, and Sephanie's hand landing on it expedited her escape nicely.

Amelia ran as fast as she could, her calve muscles burning with an intensity that reminded her of being a child again. Thinking about it for a few moments, Amelia could not recall a time since childhood when she had so greatly physically exerted herself in such a short amount of time. Between the odd bits of time travel, the physical battles (with both humans and zombie coconut crabs), and the long treks through the island Amelia was running on fumes as much as any plane she had ever flown. Thinking about the grand scheme of things, she came to the conclusion that perhaps it was time to retire from the life of espionage and piloting. She was still young enough after all, and could totally change careers to something more stable. Something safer. In the distance she saw what appeared to be a building, small, but sturdy and closed off behind a sturdy looking fence. It didn't look like much, but it was enough to catch her breath.

No sooner had these thoughts invaded her brain space then she ran headlong into what looked like a lone Japanese pilot relieving himself near a nearby bush, his back to her. Because he was leaning downward the soldiers helmet was weighted down over his eyes, giving Amelia a bit of the advantage as she decided to make a run for it. Once he finished the Imperialist soldier zipped up the fly on his standard issue pants before turning around, his helmet still dragging in front of his eyes. Thinking that perhaps if she did not move quickly Amelia would not draw attention to herself, and therefore, would not be caught before reaching the other side of the field, she took off running with a reckless abandon. This caused the breaking of grass beneath her, which finally prompted the soldier's attention.

Because the chinstrap chaffed his skin the helmet hung low over his eyes preventing him from seeing Amelia entirely, although he did see her bare feet and thought them to be both quite beautiful and imaginary. Because she was already in mid-run, Amelia did not see the comedic way in which the solider realized that not only was she indeed real, but also the fugitive that his commanding officers had ordered him to be on guard against. This dereliction of duty would not stand, especially around the Egyptian stranger who would rather have a dead soldier than a living one. Although Amelia did not understand the words that the soldier spoke, she knew enough by the way he pointed at her and screamed what sounded like obscenities that were quickly attracting other soldiers. The ant theory was in full effect.

"Run," Amelia said to herself through baited breathes as she went along. Her chest hurt, her lungs were on fire, and her legs felt like they were about to give out at any moment, yet she kept running as if her life depended on it.

And so it did.

Chapter 24:
The First Time

Before this night the most awkward moment Tina had ever experienced with her first encounter with showering after gym class at the academy. The very thought of leaving herself exposed and vulnerable to the world terrified her to the very core of her soul. Yet now, within the of the large stones that formed the enclosure where C de Baca had chosen to make camp, Tina had put herself out there despite this, only to be rewarded with re-experiencing the term 'awkward silence' on a whole new level. A mere seventeen feet away, the duration of the length of the distance between them, C de Baca sat with his knees pointed toward the sky and his arms crossed them, cradling his head in shame. Though he was no longer crying the shame had set-in deep enough to make eye contact between the two impossible; at least in C de Baca's eyes. Looking around for the first time since the revelation that C de Baca was living a double life Tina saw the destructive aftermath of the failed French sacking of the camp. Counting the four bodies that lay in various states of an oddly beautiful deathly tableau with their weapons nowhere within sight. What was visible was the tattered leather gauntlet that looked like it belonged on C de Baca's left hand. Reaching for it tentatively, careful not to disturb her companion's brooding, Tina retrieved the gauntlet, held it for a moment, turning it over in her hand several times as she inspected it, before deciding to give it back to its owner.

A mere seventeen feet away, the duration of the length of the distance between them, C de Baca sat with his knees pointed toward the sky and his arms crossed them, cradling his head in shame. Though he was no longer crying the shame had set-in deep enough to make eye contact between the two impossible; at least in C de Baca's eyes. Looking around for the first time since the revelation that C de Baca was living a double life Tina saw the destructive aftermath of the failed French sacking of the camp. Counting the four bodies that lay in various states of an oddly beautiful deathly tableau with their weapons nowhere within sight. What was visible was the tattered leather gauntlet that looked like it belonged on C de Baca's left hand. Reaching for it tentatively, careful not to disturb her companion's brooding, Tina retrieved the gauntlet, held it for a moment, turning it over in her hand several times as she inspected it, before deciding to give it back to its owner.

"Pretty sure this belongs to you." Tina spoke softly, offering the leather gauntlet back to C de Baca, which he took with a half-hearted half grin that spoke nothing of the monster within.

"Thank you," C de Baca offered, before returning his head to its resting position between his folded arms.

The exchange was small, but it gave Tina the confidence she needed to proceed. Guessing that C de Baca's transformation was based on anger, she hypothesized on how best to move forward. Deciding on the direct route, she dropped what little facade she held that the situation could be anywhere close to normal and spoke again, this time in a normal tone of voice. "So... what was that?"

Raising his head, slowly, the dark eyes of C de Baca found Tina's own before breathing deeply, yet calmly against the question. Then, without warning or further hesitation C de Baca let out a loud, deep belly laugh that shook the ground around him. After a few moments he noticed that Tina did not laugh in return, causing the deep lines in his face to harden into a somber façade once again.

Taken aback by this, Tina eyed him suspiciously before allowing her instincts to kick-in. Remembering her training from Doctor Duffy regarding channeling her body's natural energy into accelerated concentration Tina hit the proverbial 'off' switch in her mind, shutting down all sound but the one she felt - not with her ears - but with her soul. Softly, as if by orchestrated by a conductor at a private symphony for one, the sound of soft wind chimes playing an upbeat tune of joyous, yet still very peaceful celebration. It was not fast paced, nor catchy, yet the consistency of the melody was friendly, inviting, and emblematic of the one eternal thing that she had come to recognize at a young age: the truth. For most of Tina Holmes' life she had known the truth of when someone was lying to her based this ability of hers, and it had served her well. So too did she gamble that C de Baca, as crass and monstrous as he may appear, was not intending to hurt her. Having passed the first stage of her own lie detector test, Tina was eager to move on to stage two to verify the truth. For this, however, she would have to have the one thing C de Baca was not offering at the moment; eye contact. "Not used to people being direct with you?"

"In all of my years no one has ever come right out and asked me about my changing before," C de Baca said with another sudden grin. His jovial spirit was almost contagious as their eyes locked. "Truth is - I don't know exactly how it works. Or what my limitations are. Or even what causes me to start changing in the first place."

"Or what causes you to change back," Tina said in a way that made it sound like it wasn't quite a question but rather a statement. Taking immediate exception to this, C de Baca's inner music stopped on a sour note within Tina's inner ears.

"That I do know, Tina Holmes," C de Baca said as his spine straightened as he held his head higher than before. The firelight found his brown eyes as they offset themselves proudly while he began his tale. "I never really change all the way, you know. I've met others like me, other monsters that roam freely in the dark. I often find that we have little in common, yet a few things remain the same. Chief among them is this - a small part of me, my human conscience, the one I began my life with, never truly goes away while I am... not myself."

" So, you weren't born like this? You weren't born a.." Tina began before stopping herself. She didn't know what to call C de Baca exactly, as all the descriptive nouns she could think of would come across as either rude or insulting.

"A monster?" C de Baca asked, smiling wickedly before shaking his head. "No, no this is a curse."

"A curse?" Tina asked dumbfounded.

"I was so young when it happened, not much older than you are now," C de Baca began, his words falling hard, as if he had never recounted his story to anyone before, much less someone he genuinely trusted. For this Tina looked grateful, if not more than a bit apprehensive. Knowing full well the level of Tina's, or anyone's skepticism, C de Baca chose not the course of half truths and subject changes of his time on Earth, but a much more foreign idea; the unabridged truth.

"It began when I was a child, but that is not when I came to be on this island," C de Baca began, looking into the fire. The familiar cracks from burning wood were comforting, easing his way through the tale he knew he had to tell. "I was brought here by a Portuguese slave ship."

Doing some quick math in her head, appearing a million miles away in the process, Tina's face contorted for a moment before she said, "But the Portuguese haven't been involved in the slave trade for what.. almost one hundred years."

Turning his head to meet Tina's unexpected gaze, C de Baca's brown eyes found the blue ones looking quizzically back into his own. "I'm very old, Tina Holmes. My people were called Aztec by the people who conquered them. In the beginning I did not know a lot about my enemies, or life. But, at first I was also weak and helpless to stop my own subjugation."

The words were rich in conviction from their speaker, despite the fact that they were obviously biased. Admittedly, Tina did not want to believe the tale that C de Baca proceeded to tell, yet she had little choice in the matter, from both an emotional, and ethical standpoint. The more he spoke the more ridiculous, depressing, and disheartening the story became, Tina holding her tongue until the final word was uttered.

"When the Spanish arrived on our shores my people had two options; die or be enslaved," C de Baca said, his last words with a renewed sense of trepidation. "

Sensing a great deal of emotional strain on him, and fearing for a reprisal appearance of his alternate personality, Tina gave C de Baca another opportunity to change his mind by opening her mouth to speak, but he would have none of it. Silently he held up a hand, not in stern demand or control, but instead out of a genuine sense of mutual respect. This airing of his feeling, whatever they were, must have been cathartic for C de Baca somehow.

"This is not all, Tina Holmes," C de Baca said, his eyes filling with the tears of memories long past. The lines in his face betrayed no sense of his true age, or the true splendor of the soul that lay within C de Baca's breast. To the world he was, and always would be, flesh. Scarred, and unwanted in whatever form, beast or slave, he took in physical appearance. Yet here, with this woman, this near complete stranger, he made the conscious decision to speak the name he had long since cast aside. "I had a family. I had a wife who was with me. Her name was Yamira. I was put to work in the fields while Yamira became a house servant and as such, she lived in the house and we were only allowed to see each other one day a week."

The mere mention of the name said aloud brought not only a fresh wave of tears to the man's eyes, but also a weakening of his knees, which brought his already slumping shoulders down further, making his appear smaller somehow; less monster like in appearance. "For years I worked in the fields, toiling like an animal, all for the chance to see my wife, to see my beautiful Yamira at the end of each week."

"This arrangement was fine for a while until one day when my master was approached by the same man who had sold me to him while out at the market. This man, this officer as he called himself, instructed me to take him to the neighboring village and act as an interpreter. My master promised me an entire week off with Yamira. So, with him I went," C de Baca continued, his body stiff with the memories of a life, long since lived. "When we arrived we-"

The words were hard, caught in C de Baca's throat like an unwelcomed guest they stirred up emotions, memories, and worst of all, in his mind at least, actual feelings. Desiring, almost against his better nature, to share these thoughts with someone he decided on Tina Holmes upon their first meeting. She was a sweet girl, very smart, and had a tenacious spirit that emboldened him even in this dark hour. With that in mind he continued on with his tale, despite the feelings of incredible sorrow for all that he had once held dear and lost. "When we arrived to the village, Juniatai Avital, the conquerors did not want them to surrender. No. What they came for involved bloodshed, something that I could not allow."

C de Baca's hands shook as he crouched before staring long-ingly into the fire. There he found something that emboldened, if not strengthened him into continuing. "They started with the city leaders. Then all the men they could find, followed by the elderly. After that they forced the women to choose between their own lives, and their children's. You can guess what their decision was, even if the Spaniards lied by way of force. But you know what the truly shocking thing was, Tina Holmes? The horrific, mind numbingly simple fact that not once did I recall them asking a single question, or interrogate a single villager. Fore when they had finished, and when the conquerors thought the last one was dead, they piled the streets of its perceived riches of the dead and set the bodies ablaze. Later, a man in a long black cloak arrived. He carried with him a long, sharpened scythe. I have heard him called many names over the years, but, I believe I have heard Toussaint, er, your Victor, call him Vilthe."

A dual noise of repressed shock as well as an emotion fueled whimper let out from both parties before C de Baca turned to look Tina square in the eyes. She knew, in that moment, why he sat with her alone after saving her life. He needed to confess something, and she, Tina, was his choice of to whom he would be revealing his shame. "I fled from this man, Tina Holmes. My fear.. it overpowered everything."

Cries from an owl rung out in the night behind their camp, making C de Baca's story even more dramatic from Tina's seat on the ground where the dirty stranger had attacked her. She could feel sweat beading down her back a bit, making her skin clammy and uncomfortable against the humid night air. She could tell that C de Baca, however monstrous in appearance, was much gentler in spirit. The idea that looks could be deceiving was nothing new to her, though she often wondered how much she herself was missing out on simply by her initial opinion to pass on something, or not try it due to being slightly outside her comfort zone. So deep in thought was she that Tina gave a small jump when he spoke again, this time softer, slower, with a more melancholy timbre to his voice. Unlike before, which seemed like new territory for him, this part felt rehearsed somehow, as if he had recited it over and over again.

"When I returned to my own village there was little doubt that my neighbors had heard about Juniatai Avial's fate. After I had fled, those villagers still alive took to my example and left as well. They were captured, brought back, and made to witness the deaths of every person who remained. The Spaniards have no respect for human life. No more so then the French who invade this island now," C de Baca continued, purposefully avoiding Tina's stare once again. He could not take the weight of her tears on his heart, but he also could not stop his tale either. So, as he had done so many times before in his long life, C de Baca swallowed the saliva in his mouth and went on with his story.

"The captured broke free, killing many of the Spaniards before they themselves were slaughtered like dogs. All because of my example. All because of my cowardice. Yet worse, it was my ill luck to discover that one of the Spaniards killed at Juniaitai Avial was also the brother of my master, Aldo," C de Baca said with deep regret in his voice. It did not take a priest to see how guilty he felt about the situation as his breathing became heavier with each sentence.

"I pleaded with Aldo, I told him that I didn't know about his brother's death, and I told him about the man in the black cloak with the long scythe. But he didn't believe me. Instead he beat me, called me a swine, and cursed me for all eternity. That I could take, but what I could not abide was the harm he promised to inflict on Yamira. So I took her far, as far as our feet would carry us the next day. But that night I went to sleep and awoke to find my love with her hands bound behind her back and clothes removed for Aldo's pleasure. He required..." C de Baca stuttered, remembering the horror that led him to Tina. "Aldo required a blood sacrifice, which he took from my wife. He cut her chest, Tina Holmes, so I took a sacrifice of his blood from the same place. I bit into his neck like a mad dog, Tina Holmes, I ripped into his flesh with all the frustration and penance I could. In that moment I was more animal than man, I was, I was.."

C de Baca trailed off as he turned, still further away from Tina and the firelight. Though she still slightly feared him, Tina instinctively followed his movements so that she could hear him clearly as he continued. "Yamira was not gravely hurt, nor did Aldo did not die right away. Instead, he cursed me, this time accompanied by great lights and otherworldly colors from the sky. Aldo attempted many incantations as he grabbed my hands, holding me into his viselike grip as he slipped his mortal coil. He died while turning me into the monster before you, Tina Holmes. It was his blood magic, I know now. Yet for all of his tricks, I felt no different after I took his life. Not at first."

"David," Tina said with a barely audible voice, "There is no such thing as magic."

Ignoring her, C de Baca went on with his tale.

"Yamira and I returned to our lives, hiding Aldo's body and acting if as normal. When the Spaniards came around again, they did much the same as they had done before at Juniatai Avial, lining people up and grouping them based on gender and age. I alone realized what was happening, and I decided that grief or no, I would not allow events to unfold twice the same," C de Baca finished proudly.

"I attempted to peacefully stop the Spaniards, but when that proved folly I lost my temper. It was strange the first time, almost dream like in its ballet of elements of a hazy blur. The only constant were the screams, I remember that much at least. I know because that is when they first started," C de Baca continued, hesitant in fear of being judged too harshly for the actions of his youth. "It was then that I first turned in to the monster that you saw. While I cannot deny it is a part of me, I can apologize for offending you with its presence. Yamira saw this monster, and saw me turn into it. Worse, she feared that she was responsible for my plight following Aldo's actions. Years past, many of our enemies fell, yet she and I.. we could not get back to what you might call 'normal'. It was simply too late. Regretfully, the guilt consumed her into taking her own life upon a knife's edge."

"So you've lost... everything..." Tina stated flabbergasted, realizing only too late the rudeness in her tone of voice.

"Yes, everything but these," C de Baca said while simultaneously raising his hands to reveal the golden cuffs interwoven into his brown leather gauntlets surrounding his wrists. They were horrifically beautiful in their simple, yet elegant design of servitude, and yet at the same time they represented the complexity of his inner warrior. "I have discovered over the centuries that these gauntlets, chains surrounding my wrists and all, are what harbor the curse Aldo placed upon me. For when I transform they remain, unseen, yet appear once I revert back to my original self. They alone keep me from joining Yamira in the afterlife. They alone keep me from the peace I seek."

With these words a fresh tear fell from Tina's left eye before cascading down her cheek and landing on her shirt with a dull sound against the still crackling fire.

"But it isn't all bad, I have traveled. All of that happened in America, so I came here to St. Dominique to be free. I have lived long, lived large, and I have learned some things," C de Baca stated, his voice upbeat and prouder than Tina could have reasonably expected given his sad tale. When she looked over at him, fully expecting to see a broken, disheveled shell of man who had lost all control over his life, instead saw a hard jawed Lieutenant of the Haitian rebel army.

"What?" Tina asked, her pale, tear-stained cheeks betraying deeper feelings of regret. This drew a smile from C de Baca, further confusing the youngest Holmes child. 'What words of wisdom on inspiration could someone who has witnessed so much death possibly offer to give comfort in a time like this?'

"The hope that tomorrow might be better..."

Elsewhere, the bright illuminating glow from a piece of technology, a cell phone, completely misplaced in time, filled the night with zoomed-in images of a young woman quite familiar to the viewer. Timothy Holmes watched the video he had taken the night his sister had gone to visit Rolland in Eden's jail with eyes glazed over in lustful ambiguity. It was a quiet spot that Timothy had found for himself, quite a bit away from the main part of the Haitian camp near what appeared to be an old grouping of trees that were cut down but never moved. One of the trees had become the long, yet solid log that he rested his back upon, giving him both the leverage to sit comfortably and the necessary height to be hidden from anyone who might be curious as to his doings. The screen flashed again, this time with a slow motion series of still images that slowed Tina turning around slowly, somewhat facing the camera so that a bit of her cleavage was evident from full-on. Becoming aroused at this sight, Timothy did what all teenage boys do when faced with such temptation, and proceeded to unzip his jeans. As he went along in a repetitive motion of self gratification the privacy he so desired was granted to him in order to spend time lusting after the one bit of real gratification that he could never have.

Within the confines of General Toussaint's, also known as Victor Aquasi III, tent sat a large table set up in a council like environment. The position of the chairs suggested debate, and the shape of the table said equal footing for the participants. With such green cadets as the likes Turtledove brought with him, save Rolland and Tina, Victor was little surprised by the brash attitude displayed by the Mer who called himself Kniff as he pressed again and again for an attack by sea instead of land.

"The topic at hand is strength by land," said Turtledove after pouring himself a cup of tea from the kettle that sat over the fire in the middle of the tent. He circled around before heading back over to the desk and the despondent council that formed. They gathered, in various forms of standing, with Victor taking the position of power behind his desk, Rolland pacing a bit, and Kniff upright, attempting to make his case. "We need not focus so much on the sea!"

"We waste our resources in folly," Kniff proclaimed in an exasperated tone before closing his eyes in frustration. It had been long, too long, since the cool crisp feeling of hydrogen molecules danced with oxygen molecules upon his skin. The refreshing hydration of the open ocean called for him, even in this time period, when its voice was distinctly different than the oceans of Eden. "Our might is great upon the sea. Toussaint, I know that you have ships, I've seen them. Four at least, if not five. Why not use them to draw the French out into the open water? They would be sitting ducks!"

"No," Rolland said, shaking his head. "I see where you are coming from logistically but there are too many variables here to risk a sea battle. First and foremost being LeClerc himself."

"Yes," Turtledove interjected, attempting to cut the tension. "His death must be witnessed in order to be catalogued as complete."

The others, all of which disagreed with this sticking point, knew that the burden of past battle experience weighed heaviest upon the shoulders of Turtledove, therefore questioning his wisdom would prove just as folly as Kniff's plan of attack.

"Just his death, then?" Kniff asked with zero sense of the graveness of such a topic. "Not all of the French? I mean, I am not familiar with this time and culture. Are these French likely to flee if their leader is captured? Or will they appoint another in his stead?"

"I want them dead for what they've done to my peop-" Victor said, stopping himself mid sentence, his speech betraying his inner thoughts.

"Your people," Rolland said slowly looking Victor straight in the eyes. He recognized them well. They were the same that just a few months prior looked up at him briefly after the bookstore fire that started his journey of the otherworldly. Still, he had considered Victor a friend, a confidant, a member of his inner circle. The fully grown man who stood there, now, stooped over a large map of the island with sullen eyes. Who was this man? "You were going to say you want him dead for what he did to your people, right?"

The gravity of the insinuation made them all uneasy, including the eavesdropping Haitian guard stationed just outside the tent. Belonging to a group, be it a family unit, military squad, or even a partnership can be filled with pitfalls and tribulations, even for the most skilled or personable individual. But even the heart, filled with vessels and arties of feelings of all-to human dreams and desires will expire if not nourished enough. In the early days of being in Haiti, all those years ago, Victor's heart was not nourished. Indeed, it took self-sustainment through multiple campaigns, multiple nights of crying himself to sleep, and numerous self-reminders that Haiti was his home, not Eden, before he could even begin to get over the trauma that brought him to the 19th century version of hell on Earth.

Yet how could he make them, any of them, understand his tribulations when they had been parted for a mere few months by their estimation. They did not understand. They could not understand. So, instead Victor attempted to change the subject. "I believe that LeClerc is uniquely evil in both his extra abilities, and his lack of respect for human life. History tells us the French will be back, and so be it. The purpose is keep with the timeline by removing LeClerc now, not in maintaining the free republic these people deserve."

"But you just called the Haitians your people," Kniff quipped before his brain could tell his tongue to stop speaking. "You're speaking of the Republic that *YOUR* people deserve. Right?"

"It is none of your concern, Merman," Victor said, laying the rolled up map upon his desk as he looked outward onto his camp. Through the tent flaps he saw soldiers hurrying by carrying large knapsacks and supplies for what would be the Haitians final stand against their would-be enslavers and knew that his cause was just.

"There are too many voices and not enough ears listening," Turtledove wisely stated, drawing a series of agreeing nods from the others. "Rolland, you were chosen to lead this company from Eden. That being the case, I think that we should leave the two leaders alone for a bit of time to decide our next course of action."

As Kniff and Turtledove left the tent a knowing glance passed between the two that spoke volumes of their shared past and potential future. Indeed, the wise whiskered face of Marcus L. Turtledove conveyed much to his two students, neither of which were the same men whom he had known mere months before. Their voyages were complicated beyond measure, yet he still attempted to do just that as he sized each up softly before exiting the tent.

"So," Victor said, sitting behind his desk once again before righting his chair and placing his hands on his desk. The position was one he had taken many times with many soldiers over the years, lending him an air of both authority, and respect. Rolland did not subscribe.

"Dude," said Rolland, forever cementing 20th century slang into the 19th century vernacular. "You're really going to try to strong-arm me?"

"Ugh," began Victor, genuinely surprised at what Rolland had turned the conversation in to with his first verbal volley. "I'm not sure that I-"

"Let me stop you right there, General," Rolland stated in his thickest voice of a sarcastic Colonel Sanders impression that he could muster before dropping it entirely with his next words. "You aren't the picnic I expected either.

"You should not have come," Victor said with a cold voice that chilled Rolland's heart.

"Yeah, I know that now," Rolland responded before standing quickly, his wooden chair falling over behind him. At the sound, the two Haitian guards outside the tent gripped their weapons tighter in preparation to defend their General. As the seconds ticked by both Rolland and Victor watched each other before eyeing the guards.

"It isn't them you should be worried about," Victor said, motioning toward the guards outside. "It is me who should concern you. Me who could take you out if I wished it to be so."

"Oh, could you now?" Rolland asked, raising one eyebrow. "Well if that's how you feel about it then I am super sorry that I came here. Sorry that I dragged everybody else here thinking I was going to be helping you out."

"Then why are you still here, huh?" Victor asked, placing both of his hands on his hips like a small child. "Why do you stay? Why do you fight?"

"I don't fight because I support what you believe in, Victor," Rolland said, looking his friend dead in the eye as he delivered his honest, if not blunt, assessment of their situation. "I'll fight because once upon a time I used to believe in you."

Silence filled the tent as the two leaders stared at one another with a wide eyed curiosity. It was clear that much had changed between them, not only as a duo but as individuals as well. Victor had grown ten years in age, true, but he had also gained many fighting abilities in battle, many leadership skills, and had overcome numerous failures in order to learn and persevere for himself and his adopted Haitian populace. All the while Rolland too had done his fair share of growing, although at a much slower pace. Each knew the absurdity of their situation, as each knew that within the other could do much more damage to their cause than taking out two 19th century human guards. So, instead of going to war, or fighting amongst brothers, the two did as they had done more than once and would continue to do for the rest of their days as friends; they let go of their grudges.

"I'm sorry," Rolland offered, knowing how deep his words cut.

Victor smiled, his pearly teeth gleaming off the firelight as he bent his head a bit in bashful camaraderie. "I would like to apologize as well. It has been hard here, yes, but it does not excuse my shameful manners toward you, my friend."

The two shook hands, hugged for a moment and then sat to discuss plans in more intricate detail. Roughly thirty minutes into their talk over Haiti's geographic features, Rolland brought up a point that led to the brief calling of a skinny ammunitions expert with a mustache before he too was dispatched as Victor took notations. Then, when the two could scheme no more, Victor came up with a plan of attack that both agreed would best utilize their strengths, both Haitian and Edenite alike.

"You want to share this with the others?" Victor asked.

"Yes," Rolland said quickly with a suddenly nervous look. "But there is just one thing more. About earlier."

But it was too late as the others had already walked past the guards and were filing back into the tent. Not knowing if they would survive the forthcoming battle, or the perils that lie before then, neither young man knew if they would ever continue their conversation again. But with a single nod of the head from each, both knew that whatever the case their friendship would remain study.

"Would you all mind coming back in now?" Rolland asked with a polite smile, beckoning the remainder of them back into the tent. This time Jaime and a few other Haitians that Rolland did not know followed suit and filled in the empty gaps around the table. Finally the mustached man walked in as well, carrying a large barrel that looked larger than himself.

"We lay a trap at dawn. We'll go south to the tip of the peninsula," Victor ordered, looking from the ammunitions expert to Turtledove, and finally to the trio of Rolland, Turtledove, and Kniff.

"I will tell Tina and Gwendolyn," Rolland confirmed, simultaneously taking a mental note to perform the task.

"Some of us are going to go sit by the fire and listen to the soldiers tell their stories," Turtledove said to his former pupil with a hopeful smile. The inner guilt he felt for what had become of Victor was second only to the pride that swelled within him for the man he had grown to be. There was a strength there, even if it was quickly being overtaken by the longing for something more. Something unseen. A gilded beam of something lit within the fire inside him, forcing a smile despite himself. The moment was close at hand.

"Thank you for the offer, but I would like to be alone right now," Victor retorted automatically.

Gwendolyn, knowing she had but one chance at a first impression, walked slowly into the tent, peeling back the canvas flap, bending low as she entered and stood before Victor for the first time. At first he did not hear her, but instead smelt something wonderful, something like cinnamon mixed with vanilla that instantly made his heart warm. Looking up not expecting to see anything but perhaps the backside of one of his guards outside, Victor saw Gwendolyn, immediately doing a double take to ensure that she was real.

"Hello," Gwendolyn said with a small smile that showed her teeth a bit. Her tilted head gave her eyes, so round and pure in their bright majesty, an extra hue of color that cast a spell on him, drawing him in immediately. Her skin was pale, yet creamy and looked smooth to the touch. Whoever she is, whatever she was, to Victor she felt like a cool drink of water in a desert of woe. The worries and stress he had been carrying for years melted away into a completely new sensation; one of openness, trust, and a clear fulfillment of his dreams. He breathed, for that was all he could think to do so caught off his guard.

"My name is Gwendolyn Murrow," the young Nocturn woman said, extending her left hand out as she had seen the human custom in films. Victor took it without a second of apprehension, their skin contact sending a small, yet very noticeable static electric charge through the two of them as they touched, both exclaiming. "Ow!"

Looking down at her with a broad smile Victor saw the culmination of multiple hopes, secret desires, and personal fantasies of happiness regarding a family springing to fruition from the seed of a simple touch. The two stood there, hands held, in silence for a long minute as their eyes looked into that of their newfound attraction. It was odd, yet familiar. Strange, yet comforting. Within his mind's eye he knew that the worst words, the first real words he said to her would define him in her eyes. Then and there he made the choice of who he was, and who he would be moving forward.

"Victor," he said with a soft smile that warmed her heart even further. For it was love at first sight, or at least as close as one comes to it in the 'real' world.

Leaving the tent in a bit of a huff due to lingering feelings of guilt surrounding the situation, Rolland assumed that nothing short of torturing LeClerc within an inch of his life would put him in a better mood. That theory was quickly tested as he heard the small, yet familiar voice of Hannah calling his name as he began to march back off into the woods to find Tina. Turning around Rolland approached Hannah for their first one on one conversation since coming to Haiti, an overdue occurrence given their shared loss of a teammate.

"I've been meaning to speak with you about something," Hannah began, biting her lip in an old, bad habit that she fell back on when she was nervous. "Something I've been waiting to get you alone to talk about."

"Oh?" Rolland asked, coming to a stop to give her his full, undivided attention. He had absolutely no clue what it was she wanted to talk to him about, but by the tone of her voice it wasn't anything good. "What's up Hannah?"

"Ok, I do not know how to say this without it sounding odd, so I am just going to say it and hope that you do not judge me too harshly. I, Hannah, do not have a last name. I have noticed that a lot of people have a last name. What I mean is that everyone but me has one," Hannah spoke in a steady, but wary tone of voice. "So, I was thinking about people I admire whose names I might take on as my own. I have Madison. I have..."

"You're looking for a last name?" Rolland interrupted her, not seeing his relevance to any of what Hannah was talking about. "I don't understand why you need to discuss this with me. I think Madison is a fine last name."

"But Madison is not the name that I have chosen, Rolland Wright. The name I have chosen is, well," Hannah stuttered, looking downward and losing what was left of her confidence. "It is your own."

"My own?" Rolland asked, confused.

Taking his hand within her own Hannah felt the lines of Rolland's skin as they ran from one side to the other, forming what some might call a lifeline. Tracing it with her index finger Hannah pressed down firmly before finding Rolland's eyes with her own and asked the question she had held within her heart for days. "I would like to be known, from this day onward, as Hannah Madison Wright."

Rolland's eyes widened for a moment as he felt his mouth hang open at the sound of this request. Flabbergasted, he could think of nothing to say in the immediate moment. He was not insulted, or offended, or any negative emotion what-so-ever. Instead he was more confused. Mainly, confused as to why Hannah troubled herself so long in broaching the subject with him in the first place. Then, as that thought knocked around in his subconscious, a darker, more menacing thought crept up to take the proverbial throne of neurotic power; why? Why did Hannah, a girl he barely knew and who had spent approximately five minutes with his father desire to take his name? Was this a play at his heart? He had never felt any sexual tension between himself and Hannah, even while she held his hand.

"I cannot pretend to understand your reasoning, and honestly I would prefer if you do not give it. Not now, anyway. But if this is what your heart so desires, then I will totally give you my blessing, Hannah Madison Wright," Rolland said proudly with a large, brotherly smile toward his newest, self-adopted sibling.

The two embraced in a long, happy hug that sealed the deal between them before Hannah went back off to the kitchen area to finish the final preparations for her tear-laden biscuits. She felt slight guilt for not telling Rolland what she was up to, but cared not anymore for she had the support and loyalty that came with being called Hannah Wright.

An hour went by before C de Baca decided to call it a night and go to sleep. Excusing himself like a true gentleman he kissed Tina's left hand before going to his tent. She watched him leave the fireside, eyeing his back and looking for any indication that giant, sprawling wings could pop out to transform him any second. Based on his demeanor, the thought seemed preposterous to her, an idea that kept her attention rapt as she too, instinctively, walked through men's camp toward the divide that kept it from her own camp. As the lights fell to darkness the further away she got from the fire the more her own regrets in life bubbled to the surface of her mind.

A rustling came from the bushes to Tina's left; a noisy, busy bit of movement that left little doubt that whoever it was made an attempt to be sneaky. She held her breath for a split second before letting it go, still filled with the wonderful feeling of luck and accomplishment that her talk with C de Baca gave her. Then, with as much pomp as he had ever respected, Rolland Wright popped out from the brush, bits of leaves falling upon his broad shoulders as his head and toothy smile found Tina in the darkness.

"Hey," Rolland said, happy to both be seeing her, and to be seeing her alone.

"Hey yourself," Tina said with a nervous smile. She could not contain herself. With emotions stemming from C de Baca's tale and the pheromones experienced by the element of danger they constantly lived under the spirit of passion overtook her, and by default, took Rolland as well. Tina wanted to forget about the attack in the woods, the death of her friend, and the menacing eyes of her attacker... eyes that she did not want to remember. No. No, Tina wanted to replace them in her memory, and sooner the better.

"What are you-?" Rolland asked before being cut off by a gentle, yet firm finger pressed against his lips. Removing it, Tina's hand slid downward until it reached his belt buckle, zipper, and finally with slight, yet determined tug, dropped his pants from around his waist.

"Shhhhh," Tina said, the glow of the firelight reflecting off of her baby blue eyes. She removed her shirt, then her bra with a practiced ease that drew Rolland in closer. "No talking.. just let your body speak to mine. The two kissed, groped, and held one another tight as they took of article after article of clothing beneath the pale Haitian moonlight. As the moment took them, each held their breath as two became one, both that this place known as Haiti, this land of death, love, and life was special to them somehow. That this moment, their bodies intertwined, would live on in their memories forever after in a sea of time and shadow.

The Haitian night time was one of sounds that shook Timothy Holmes to the core of his soul. With a list of fears that ran no less than fifty nouns deep, any number of which could jump out at him without notice, Timothy walked a bit aimlessly before arriving close to where he thought his destination to be. In search of food, he wished to find the same kitchen area he knew Hannah was headed to, hoping to pester her into making him something. Hearing noises from what sounded like young people he moved quicker through the brush until he came upon a series of bushes that stood before a clearing where he saw two people. Two people, one man and one woman, who were having sex. A feeling of elevation, one that shot up within him so quickly that it would have been exquisite if not for the next feeling. One that hit him so hard that the long-held fantasy of seeing his twin sister's bare backside in the flesh was forever ruined.

Before he knew what to do he was already running, awkwardly, in the opposite direction from the clearing where Tina and Rolland were being intimate. His Tina. His one. His only. A dead oak tree fallen over would do as shelter while he gathered his thoughts. There Timothy stayed, his brain playing mental gymnastics, as he tried again and again to convince himself that Tina wasn't doing what he knew she was doing. That she wasn't giving herself... to him. The uneasy feeling that bit away at the inside of his stomach aside Timothy knew that eventually he would have to leave the dark safety of the hiding place he had found beneath the dead oak tree.

The first time that Rolland or Tina had consummated the act of love with another person was everything either had ever wanted it to be. Tina was sore, satisfied, and happy with her new-found intimacy with Rolland, despite the less than perfect circumstances surrounding it.

A strange rustling in the trees nearby shocked both travelers upright, their clothes falling to their sides to reveal their shared nudity to the elements of nature. Thinking quickly, and deciding that she did not want her dead body to be found naked, Tina grabbed her panties and shirt with her left toes before flinging them upward and catching them with her right hand. From behind her Tina thought she heard something that sounded like a small animal running toward them, but thought nothing of it as she got dressed and looked over at her loving boyfriend.

Watching her, Rolland forgot the potential danger of whatever it was coming from the dark forest in lieu of the naked, soon to be fully dressed teenage girl that stood before him..

It was that state of mind that Timothy Holmes, running away from the shame of masturbating for the fourth time that evening to the various pictures of his sister on his cell phone, found the pair of lovers as Rolland pulled on the pants that Tina tossed him.

"Oh, hey Timothy," Tina said awkwardly as she hurried to put her shirt back on. "What are you, um, doing here?"

"I, uh," Timothy uttered between bated breaths as he stuffed his hands into his jeans pockets. He both wanted to be next to Tina, and at the same time, nowhere near her or her stupid boyfriend. "I just wanted to see if you were safe is all. We going soon? I want to go soon."

Tina looked at her twin brother with a mix of trepidation and humiliation. She knew that he knew what she had been doing with Rolland mere minutes beforehand, and dreaded him relaying that information to their parents. Thaddeus especially would blow his top at the idea of his little girl having relations with the outlaw Rolland Wright. Thinking about her outlaw boyfriend gave her a chill through her spine that brought a smile to her lips despite what her brain wanted. Trying to cover for this, she locked her lips before shaking her head a bit and stating, "Yes, I think so. Meet me back at the fire in ten minutes? The one in front of Victor's tent."

Timothy looked at his sister with a doe eyed expression that betrayed his inner thoughts, if only for a moment, to Rolland who watched with an crooked eye. The hair on the back of Rolland's neck stood on end with a strange suspicion that he did not know how to place. He did, however, form a question within himself that demanded an immediate answer, lest he continue down a path that he did not fully understand.

"Hey, can I ask you a question? Even if it's a little weird," Rolland asked Tina as Timothy disappeared into the main part of the woods toward the Haitian camp. "Or personal."

"Wait, we just had sex and you feel weird asking me about a personal question?" Tina asked, putting her jacket back on over her shoulders. Her smile was soft, so soft that Rolland was again aroused by her femininity. The look she gave him was a mix between skepticism and mild curiosity.

"It's about how you hear people's... inner music or whatever," Rolland said as his face went white. "Did you not hear Timothy coming, or... what's up with that?"

"I can see why you would ask that," Tina said, her voice muffled a bit as she hung her head.

"I don't know. Rather, I don't really know. I figure that because we're twins that he and I might share the same music and I've just learned to ignore my own, you know? Like I'm so used to it that I tune myself out and therefore, I tune him out as well," Tina sputtered all at once before falling into Rolland's arms.

With a kiss he reassured her that no more words were needed on the matter. Nor would there be, for better - or worse.

Chapter 25: What Now?

Lae (Eke) Island - 1937

For all the knowledge possessed by the self-proclaimed smartest man alive Doctor Rain (as the Eke people had been calling him for the past several hours) had many ideas on how to assist his wife find her way to him, or vice versa; but they all ended with the same result - failure. Despite this pessimism Judah soldiered on by way of not only forming a plan, but also taking another page out of his young friend Victor's playbook in recruiting a local army to wield. Though this strengthen his resolve, the uneasy feeling that he would never see Joan again crept into his heart like a deadly poison. To be clear it was not the transportation, or even the timing that was an issue. What Judah was really having trouble with were the unknown variables like Vilthe's minions that were inevitably lurking about, and anyone else sent to derail their mission. Then Judah thought of what he felt should have been obvious all along. Their mission.

Looking over at the Eke men stacking wood for smoke piles Judah spotted Muitimbo, with his seven foot tall stature and overly broad frame hauling twice the wood of the other men. Thinking the Eke man to be quite strong, an advantageous trait in battle, Judah stood up to get a better look at the potential recruit; a fateful decision. In studying him for a moment, Judah noticed something odd about the young man, something that he had never noticed before. Despite the large muscles that he bolstered proudly for all to see, none of the wood was actually touching any part of his dark skin. This development was too much for Judah, who could not stop himself from getting a closer look as Muitimbo, who led the pack in wood stacking, being the first to go back to the pile delivered by the convoy of Eke brethren appearing from out of the sparse woods. Judah craned his neck in a continued act of voyeurism, feeling his age as he moved. Yet sure enough, there walking along with what appeared to be a small skip in his step was Muitimbo, a large bundle of wood hovering slightly above his hands, despite being nearly three feet wide and four feet tall in its own right. Being the tactful sort (when he remembered) Judah waited until Muitimbo put the pile down before rushing down the hill toward him.

Muitimbo saw Judah coming, stopped what he was doing, and waited politely as the stranger approached. Incidentally, all of the items within his general vicinity that were moving independently moments before, also stopped their motion, many lowering themselves to a resting position with a practiced ease that only comes over time.

"Good day," Judah said, immediately thinking to himself how weird and inadvertently Australian he sounded. Then with a second thought he remembered geographically where he was in the world and believed the gesture might slip past as normal.

"Bmhenry," Muitimbo said, nodding his head up and down as he only made brief eye contact with Judah. The phrase, whatever it meant, was the only one the overly muscled small giant could, or would say. Unsure if he was a simple minded fellow or not, Judah decided to call the bluff anyway, certain in what he saw that prompted him to approach.

"How long have you been able to levitate, err, lift things with your mind?" Judah asked. First impressions were tedious enough, much less when a language gap stood in the way. Yet, for some reason that he could not put his finger on - there seemed to be little to no confusion in the young native man's eyes. On the contrary, a vague sense of understanding wafted over them as a betraying look made both feel nervous.

"Bmhenry," Muitimbo stated yet again, breaking his resolute gaze on the white stranger.

"You understand me, don't you?" Judah asked, knowing that they had zero time to mince words. "Every fucking word I say."

"A little," Muitimbo finally allowed with a shy, boyish air to his response. "But I not so good with, eh, how you say, lake of con-ver-sat-ion. Or fook- king. I know not that word."

Feeling very much the successful poker player Judah beamed with a great feeling of accomplishment at rooting out this farce. Deciding to take it one step further he further bet he could get more information out of Muitimbo by asking direct questions; as long as he did it in a happy tone of voice. What Judah could not figure out, or if it was even strictly necessary, is if this was an opportunity for recruitment for this young man, or if it was one problem too many.

"That thing you were just doing, making the sticks move," Judah said in a cool, calm tone that purposefully did not display any hint of judgment. "I know a lot of people who can do that sort of thing."

"People who come from the sky?" asked, his English skills going well beyond the single word of 'Henry'.

"Why, yes!" Judah said happily, offering an unyielding sword of optimism toward the potential new recruit. "How long have you been able to do that for?"

Muitimbo thought on this for a moment, scratching behind his ears and chin before coming up with a satisfactory answer. "Since I became a man."

Judah smiled at this attempt at modesty. Then, as the two had very little else to say to one another, Muitimbo excused himself to go back to working on the moving of large sticks with the other Eke. Watching this while reflecting on the intricate workings of the world, how these supernatural abilities did not discriminate in who, or what kind of person would be born with them, or how they were used. All of this and more he had learned since he himself became a man like Muitimbo.

"There is a beautiful balance in nature," Judah said aloud as he held Muitimbo and his people in bewilderment. For all of the pain he had experienced since arriving there, both literally and figuratively, he was still thankful for the experienced. Judah loved his job. Not knowing who else might be listening to this, he was taken aback when a response came in the form of the lad's father.

"Agreed," said the Eke Chieftain as he made his way slowly down the hillside to where Judah stood watching the workers build larger piles for even more smoke signals to get Joan's attention. The plan was to summon the two women using the smoke and perhaps a plane or two for the Eke to use later. This deal sat well with both parties involved, but Judah wished to sweeten it a bit more. "Within each of us."

"I'll cut right to the chase, Mr. Eke. Your Honor," Judah said before swallowing and taking a deep breath. The spiel was well rehearsed, despite the fact that he had never heard it himself. "Your boy, your son is special like me, isn't he?"

Snapping his head toward Judah faster than he would have thought possible the elder Eke eyed the traveler with a fresh sense of skepticism that renounced all but that of paternal love for a child. This was the moment that travelers of light prepared for, the one in which those ordinary citizens who were in the know as to the supernatural realities of the non-fiction world would turn their ire on the Knight of Time. But instead of vocally berating Judah with the troubles of his people, or the evils of the modern world, the Eke Chieftain simply gave a curt, if not short answer. "I believe he has exceptional cognitive acuity, yes."

Impressed by the large vocabulary the Chieftain harbored, Judah suddenly felt a great respect for the stranger, deciding to shoot straight with the man for the sake of progress.

"Sir," Judah asked directly, cutting out any semblance of bullshit. "Do you know what it is I am asking you?"

"You are asking if you can take my son with you when you leave," the Eke Chieftain said in so uncertain terms.

"Papa?" came Muitimbo's voice as he eyed his father curiously. He had apparently overheard the conversation between his father and the stranger, and decided to sneak away from his work to join. The discussion of his future was a topic Muitimbo held great interest in, even if it was ultimately his father who decided. It wasn't that he had a desire to leave the only home he had ever known, but more of a certainty that whatever his fate, it lied far away from Eke Island.

"He will go with you," the Chieftain said before turning to face his son. "His destiny is truly beyond these waters. I have known this for a long time."

"No su en, Papa?" Muitimbo asked his father with a hurt look in his dark brown eyes. The young man was intimidating due to his stature, but was also kind in a way that reminded Judah of Victor's good nature. Both were much closer to children than men in their outlook on how life would play itself out. Naive was their opinion, and shortsighted their goals. "What about our people?"

"You will be missed," the Eke Chieftain said, placing is right hand on his sons chest in the closest sign of paternal love he could given their size difference. Despite this, the tears welling within the eyes of the elder Eke spoke volumes to the words left unspoken between father and son. Mentor and protégé. "But you will go."

It was not but an hour later when their party finally got under way. After making their tearful goodbyes the Eke Chieftain departed from his son and warriors by electing to stay behind with a defending force. Though they lacked formal military training, including the use of modern positions such as advanced scouts, they were still a very organized, and effective force. A practical people, the Eke also pledged to send an emergency party out just in case Judah perished in battle and Joan's whereabouts became unknown. Amused by the idea that Joan was helpless enough to need assistance should Judah die, the traveler of light decided instead to dismiss the good gesture as just that.

"Light them up!" Judah exclaimed as he gathered the last remaining bits of necessities before heading across the island to where the landing strip was. With any luck his wife would understand the meaning of his messages and report to the spot of them at once. From there the Eke people would cover fire as the four of them made their way back to Eden, recruiting two new travelers for the price of one. This luck continued, as Judah even found an old arrowhead matted in dirt when he went to tie his shoe a few minutes later. With this newly positive outlook seeping into his brain Judah felt the heat from the fires popping up around him as he walked through the piles of wood, each now crackling loudly with the signs of new flames.

Yet without further incident Judah led the band of warriors out from their camp on the far side of Eke Island and into the mainland of hostility that he knew awaited them. The journey across was smooth, much smoother than Judah would have expected given the larger size of their party. However, the strength in numbers advantage did little to quell the lingering feelings of self-doubt that plagued Judah's psyche. Even with the strength quota (Muitimbo) without the numbers. The addition of Muitimbo was of little comfort as Judah could only guess that any trust between them was goal oriented and not personal; a trait that while respectable, was not a relationship that you wanted to forge before going into battle. Lost in this train of thought as they rounded a mossy bend in the dirt road that was covered in vegetation and fallen trees, neither man saw the overly modern encampment before walking straight into it. It was then that the next obstacle in Judah's path back to Joan presented itself in the way of an ancient Egyptian relic named Otep.

From Judah's perspective it appeared as if Otep had re-created his favorite parts of 21st century living nearly one hundred years in the past. This included what looked like a full sized recreational vehicle (RV), camping equipment, picnic tables, multiple propane powered grills, and even a sound system complete with speakers that would not be released to the public until early 2015. From a Knight of Time's point-of-view, Otep had broken every protocol and procedure in the book related to time appropriate technology and advances. He had no time to dwell on this, however, as the zombified Imperialist Japanese troops took their own positions, each defending against one of the Eke soldiers with both their rifles, and jaws equipped for attack, the less-than experienced fighters among them began to sweat and slightly break formation.

"No," Muitimbo said, softly, yet in a commanding tone under his breath. While the momentary reassurance did settle the nerves of a few of the 'greener' Eke, the command also had the unintended consequence of amusing Otep, drawing out a wicket, toothless smile across his chiseled face. The greasy haired, dark-skinned man stood with a rigid posture and still wore the same black cloak he donned when torturing Judah. The re-introduction did little except reignite within Judah a sense of unfinished business, despite being taken by nearly complete surprise.

"Traveler," said the cold, unforgiving tone of the master of the dead, Otep, as he sauntered into the clearing between where the Eke stood in uncomfortably close proximity to nearly a dozen dead-eyed, Imperialist Japanese. They were gathered with rifles armed at the tribesman though they did not, or rather, could not stare at them for want of eyeballs in their hollowed out skulls. Due to this translucent skin many of their blue, blood-clotted veins were either prominent, or highly visible to the naked eye.

"So, it's you then! You're the daft bloke who's been telling these lemming what to do then, eh?" Judah asked Otep, arming himself with the arrowhead as his thumb gently pushed the flat end higher into his palm, causing the sharp end to poke out behind his fingers, creating the perfect hidden weapon.

"Please" Otep said, moving to a nearby counter bar that played host to a large pitcher of clear liquid. After pouring himself a portion into a small, clay cup Otep turned to Judah to offer it without looking. The cup sat there, clutched in the old Egyptian's putrefied hand as he poured himself another amount into a second cup. "We are still gentlemen, after all. Let us discuss this."

"Why do you sons of bitches always wanna talk, eh?" Judah asked, throwing both of his arms up in the air before crossing them in a gesture of throwing away garbage, or wiping his hands from a situation.

"Whatever do you mean?" Otep asked, sipping from the small clay cup in his hand while taking a seat on a nearby plush couch. The furniture was black, the same black as Otep's eyes, and much more luxirious than anything any member of the Eke had ever laid eyes upon before.

"This always happens to me. The big bad never just fights, they always HAVE to talk, share their feelings, tell me their freaking life story..." said Judah, his voice betraying the bits of frustration his words could not.

"I see" Otep offered, shifting his position on the black, leather couch opposite an identical loveseat, across from an empty glass coffee table that reached Judah's shin. The master of the undead removed one of his lethal hands from his cup and gestured, somewhat modestly, for Judah to sit down across from him. "And how does that make you feel?"

"Encourage-able," Judah stated, matter-of-factly, his fingers but few inches from his weapon. The Eke, including Muitimbo, all stood frozen to the spot, not knowing how to proceed except to look to Judah for guidance. Sensing this, Judah knew that when in a precarious situation, especially one where defeat is likely, walking in with your head held high made all the difference in the world. In that vein

Judah smiled, removed the crudely made sword given to him from the Eke that morning, and held it high before shouting loudly.

"Bring it, bitch!"

Meanwhile, across the distance between the two islands walked a despondent Joan Raines, whose quest to find the answer to a riddle from a dead man yielded mixed results. One the one hand Joan held the trigger to Project Dreamcoat, which she still did not know or understand the importance of such a ridiculously named top secret mission. On the other, it came at the cost of knowing that all people, even new, blonde people who inexplicably travel through time with you, are just as big of snakes as the ones you already knew. It wasn't the fact that Amelia was an American spy, she had figured that much out days ago. What really bothered Joan was that Amelia lied to her, just like Sephanie did, to protect a secret that Joan otherwise wouldn't have cared about. This pattern of repetition struck Joan like a stake through the heart, for how was she to look Amelia into the eyes again knowing what she knew? After learning the dead man's secret, much of what Joan assumed about her new friend was only a half-truth; making it barely better than an outright lie. Or was Joan the one who was being jaded? This toxic thought process was disrupted as Amelia got close enough to be heard coherently.

"Joannie!" Amelia screamed, immediately throwing Joan off of her game with the level of familiarity she had come to expect. The American pilot came running at full pace out of a thicket of shrubs that ran parallel with the furthest part of the island.

"Where did you go off to?" Joan asked half-heartedly as Amelia came to a brief stop while trying to catch her own breathe. Through choked intakes of oxygen she tried to tell Joan something but for the life of her it could not come out properly. Then the sparkling green eyes of the pilot caught a glimpse of what Joan held in her possession.

"Is that it? The device. Is that the trigger?" Amelia asked Joan, pointing at the remote control in her friend's hand.

"Yep," Joan said with a false sense of confidence to her voice. It wasn't the way in which she spoke the word, but the tone of voice behind it.

Amelia couldn't be sure, but she suspected something less than honest, or at the very least, hidden, regarding the trigger's journey into Joan's possession. Then, almost as if she had made it happen with her mind, Amelia watched as the sleek metal device slid from Joan's experienced hand, through the air, and onto the mud covered ground below.

"Merde," Joan cursed under her breath, before bending down to grab the silver metal trigger, but noticed something else instead. A white piece of something curved, smooth, and oddly beautiful to her. Scooping both up in her left hand, Joan squinted her eyes a bit to get a finer look at its detail while presenting the new item to her comrade for a closer inspection. "Is this part of a propeller?"

"Yeah, I think so," Amelia said without giving it much thought. She had seen hundreds of them in her career, thousands if you counted the broken shards from her own propellers. "But they're very handy. You never know when you might need one."

"Right," Joan said before rolling her eyes and pocketing the trigger. She highly doubted the importance of trash in the grand scheme of her life and was about to voice this train of thought out loud when the two were interrupted by the stinging sound of sudden bullets whizzing by their ears.

PFHEW - PFHEW

Suddenly there was a man flanked by four tall, slender elemenos wearing plum colored sweater vests. Joan knew the squat,
balding man as Ivan, but the world called him Terrible, a title
bestowed upon him by Vilthe upon recognizing kinship in savagery. There were no words spoken, only the click of the rifles as
the elemenos opened fire upon the women. The pair scrambled,
running in opposite zigzagging patterns that allowed only the
most experienced of gunmen to get a good sight on them for
a clear shot. Joan noticed this as she looked over her shoulder,
fully expecting to see Amelia behind her. Instead, the sight Joan
did see gave her an immediate hollow feeling in the bit of her
stomach. Behind Ivan and his small band of elemenos stood the
advancing small army of Imperialist Japanese soldiers who had
been following Amelia.

"Merde, shit, fuck," Joan swore under her breath as she doubled
her pace, passing Amelia on the right before making a hard left turn
into the protection of the tree line. She knew that maneuvers like
this sent a message, one which she controlled, as a finer time for
leadership she would be hard-pressed to find. "This way!"

"Where... are... we... going?" Amelia shouted to Joan as she
dodged a tree limb as tall as she stood. Even though Amelia understood why Joan didn't want to stop their momentum, she couldn't
help but believe that going at such a breakneck pace was sure to get
them both killed due to error. Especially when the margins were so
small. At first she thought this was just her pilot's logic, but as the
minutes dragged on and her healthy 'glow' of sweat turned to a full
on drenching of her shirt, the American made up her mind to infer
as to their destination between baited breaths. "What's..?"

"Your plane," Joan screamed, pushing another sycamore limb
forward, hearing the ricochet as it righted itself in front of Amelia,
who chose to duck beneath it instead. The rocks beneath her feet

made the already uncomfortable position outright miserable, yet Joan could not waver. Would not waver. Not when she felt so close. In truth she feared another reprisal of the damned white orb interrupting her mission, though she couldn't admit this to anyone; especially herself. So, the two pushed on, through the same thicket of woods that Joan had gone through a few times, past Sephanie's camp from that fateful first evening, and back, back to the landing strip where she had met Amelia. "Figure it's our best shot."

"Good idea," Amelia offered, not knowing what else to say as she leaped over a large rock that resembled a cross between a football and a footlocker. Joan's peak physical condition allowed her to keep up with Joan, if only barely. The rigorous work-out had a finite destination, that she knew. The trick would be keeping her shit together long enough to make it to the landing strip. Hoping she wouldn't panic, Amelia pressed her courage to its sticking place and moved onward.

In the distance the sound of cautionary gunfire gave way to stray shouts in a foreign tongue. Amelia instinctively reached for her gun, only to feel Joan's hand there stopping her draw.

"Wait," Joan whispered without moving her lips. The ventriloquist act was wise given that seconds later the gunfire doubled, prompting the American pilot to grab Joan's hand instead before bolting in the opposite direction of the noise. Sprinting, the two majestic women hurdled their way through the unforgiving, unkempt, wild marshland that was Lae Island in the early 20th century before finally finding a clearing that lead to the coast. Once clear it took the pair less than five minutes of climbing up a large oak tree to get a better view of where they were going. The landing strip was roughly a mile and a half away from them, a distance easy to cover on foot.

With no haste the pair of women made their way back down the oak tree before heading due South to where their chariot awaited. The short journey was hallmarked by its inescapable silence as the two traveling companions spoke not one syllable to one another the entire time. This was done neither for love, nor hate, as the two were simply focused on that task at hand so much that they forgot their pleasantries. As they walked each thought of their immediate futures. For Amelia the question of how Fred Noonan was murdered would need to be addressed first. Then, she supposed, she would go with Joan wherever she went. If these people, these travelers of light as they called themselves, were telling the truth, then she had a chance at a whole new life. One where she could start over and not be known as just some American flying woman. She could be... whatever the hell she wanted to be! The smile brought a smile to the young American's face that did not go unnoticed by her French counterpart.

Joan could not decide between Los Angeles, California or Venice, Italy for her honeymoon with Judah. On the one hand, the beaches of California offered a certain ambiance of wild seclusion with nature. But on the other hand, Venice did have a rich history, maybe even with some relation to her time in the 15th century. Both had excellent shopping, food, and activities enough that even Judah would find something to enjoy. She knew that he liked one sport in particular, though she could not tell which one it was. There was a ball involved, she knew that. Joan laughed to herself as the two approached the far side of the landing strip with a sense of optimistic caution that bordered on cocky given the circumstances. A sudden cough caused Joan to crouch over and away to be polite. It was then that Joan saw them, the little flecks of black dots that multiplied like crazy the closer they got.

"Merde," Joan said, quickening her pace as she speed walked back to where Amelia stood before passing her completely and heading for the plane with a renewed vigor to her step. With a final thought she grabbed Amelia's hand, pulling her along just in time to spare the pilot the scene that slowly gained on them as the seconds turned into minutes, and the specs turned into reanimated corpses of men. As the two women made their way across the landing strip toward Amelia's plane without incident, other than the constant barrage of gunfire nearby. Observing the scene around her, Joan saw no sign of the imminent danger that her 'other' senses told her was lurking nearby.

For Amelia, the fiberglass, oval shaped hatch that protected the two pilot seats from the elements of nature, had always been like a second home. Yet now, under these conditions, she found no solace in taking the controls as she slipped into the pilot's chair. Flipping the appropriate switches via her route memory, Amelia knew approximately how long it would take for the engines to spring to life, saying a silent prayer under her breath that they might fly away unnoticed.

Like a spray of fresh rain the hailstorm of lead bullets fired all around the plane holding the two women came down with no apology. Quickly, Joan too clamored into the plane before righting herself, and returning fire using the Gatling gun attached to the plane's backside. Her shots were wide and off target due to her unfamiliarity with the early 20th century technology. Still, Joan's defensive moves were beneficial in allowing Amelia time to work on getting the plane started. No sooner had Joan began to worry that something may be wrong with Amelia, or the plane, then another distraction reared it's ugly head - the Gatling gun was out of ammunition. Thinking quickly, Joan removed her sidearm, the gun that Judah had left behind in the barn the evening before, took aim, and began shooting at the nearest targets to them. One by one they fell as Joan attempted to study her breathing and gain a sense of control on her actions. War is hell, even for the most experienced veterans.

What typically took seconds under normal circumstances became a tedious, if not downright stressful task under the hail of gunfire and promise of bodily harm. With the correct switches turned on, and the corresponding systems checked, the plane was ready for liftoff, or would have been, if not for the near empty gasoline tank that stared angrily back at Amelia before her own reflection shown off of the glass.

"What's the hold up?" Joan asked, her blonde ponytail bobbing against the middle of her back gracefully as she loaded another clip into her pistol before opening fire again, nailing two re-animated Imperial Japanese soldiers. They fell to the ground nearly twenty feet from the ladies plane, a breach in the mental perimeter that Joan had established before they were sky bound. Using her left foot Joan nudged her co-pilot, perhaps a bit harder than she meant to in order to prompt the curly haired woman into action. The force, it seemed, knocked Amelia out of whatever stupor she had been-in, as seconds later they were underway.

Amelia thought of bringing up the gasoline issue to her companion, but the longer she stared at the plane's dashboard, the longer she remembered the ordeal that Joan had already gone through in their short time together. Doing some quick math in her head, Amelia made the judgment call that the pair could reach the next island as long as they did not deviate from the prescribed route. Smiling wickedly to herself, Amelia gave a short "Nothing" to Joan before they were in business. With a methodical roar of its engines the small plane began to move forward before gaining momentum, and finally taking off into the air where it soared high above the Pacific waters for several long, interrupted moments.

THIS was Amelia's element, this was her world - high up in the air along with the clouds and smells of the Earth as they wafted toward the heavens above. For the briefest of moments, all was well. Then, simultaneously, they both smelt the smoke followed by the sounds of fresh gunfire behind them. The Imperial Japanese were still in pursuit. Out of ammunition, fuel, and options Amelia knew what it was she would need to do in order to get both of them out alive; the problem was that would involve revealing herself, her TRUE self, to Joan.

"Is that..?" Joan asked, turning to Amelia before looking out the window to see the flames of the oil fire holding on for dear life as the speed of the wind attempted to quench them. Thinking quickly, Joan popped opened the hatch of the plane, creating an escape route that quickly backfired, as two Imperialist Japanese planes appeared to be in route from the same landing pad they had left from minutes before. "Merde!"

A volley of shots fired from one of the Japanese two planes knocked the aircraft sideways, sending Amelia tumbling from the controls. Acting quickly, Joan shut the hatch door open again, this time much wider, before grabbing the plane's controls herself, righting the plane best she could given her total lack of experience as a pilot.

After checking that she wasn't injured, Amelia made the quick decision that she had over-estimated her skills during combat, accepting that this plane was doomed to crash, even if the two of them were night. Temporarily ignoring Joan as she reached over Amelia to guide the plane's controls, the American pilot reached for two large packs out of sight on the side compartment of the hatch space. What she retrieved there were two standard issue United States military parachute packs. Amelia picked up the first parachute pack, checking its chord for proper placement. But upon picking up the second pack she discovered that the actual shoot itself was completely missing. Without thinking, she turned around and shoved the functional parachute into Joan's lap before grabbing the controls from her new friend and telling her to go ahead. As Joan slid the straps over her shoulders, shifting her weight to go with the still zigzagging plane as it sped away from the two Japanese planes, she couldn't help but notice the horrible, yet subtle whistling noise that filled the inside cabin as the gunfire whizzed by their aircraft. An ominous sign.

The final straw came when Joan, who had trusted Amelia's piloting skills up until that point, peered over her colleagues

shoulder only to be greeted to the sight of the gasoline pedom-
eter firmly placed over the large, white letter E.

"Are we out of fuel?" Joan shouted over the sound of gunfire
and plane engines. No sooner had she stated the question than the
jarring feeling of the rear propeller being shot out interrupted her,
throwing their plane completely off balance. Falling onto her bottom in the seat, Joan did not hesitate to hit the large OPEN button
that launched the hatch door completely off of its hinges, out into
the open sky, and brought it down flat on top of one of the two
remaining Imperialist Japanese planes. "We need to go, now!"

"You do," Amelia said, stone-faced with the utmost sincerity
to her voice.

"WE do," Joan corrected her, deciding not to mince words.
"I'm not leaving you behind. I'm not leaving you to die like, like
Fred died. Sephanie and I.. we're already too much alike."

"What?" Amelia asked Joan, the sound of wind drowning
out almost all other noises. All save Amelia's voice, which rang
out righteous, and true. "Why would you say such a thing? You're
nothing like her."

"I am," Joan admitted without missing a beat, almost as if
she were expecting the question. In truth she wasn't, though it
would hardly matter in a few heartbeat's time. Casting her eyes
downward in shame, Joan admitted what she had been holding
back from Amelia for days.

"Just like her I hid something from you.. I didn't tell you that I
watched as Sephanie murdered your co-pilot. I watched her.. and
did nothing to stop it."

The color in Amelia's face, normally a vivacious shade of
glow that gave strength to those around her, fled in an instant.

It's removal heralded the final straw in her decision to evacuate the plane, though Joan knew nothing of it. In fact, the last thing that Joan felt was the hard push from her right side as Amelia body checked her over the side of the plane, causing her to free fall from the dying plane.

Catching her wits as quickly as she could, Joan felt the fall for a mere seconds before collecting herself enough to pull the rip cord on her parachute, releasing the tent, and surrounding her in its massive, poorly packed tufts of cloth. Joan opened her eyes with a sharp pain in her temples and a creak in her neck. The wind from the deceleration of free falling, albeit slower than she would without the parachute, still snapped at her skin like strong frostbite. A loud BOOM noise followed by immense heat told her that once again she was alone in her mission and without Amelia.

"Damn it all!" Joan cried out as the plane exploded. The heat from the blast forced her eyes away. Closing them for several long seconds as gravity brought her downward, back toward her inevitable destination of the new island, Joan couldn't help but feel an immense sense of failure, followed secondly by discomfort as several small bits of shrapnel hit her skin, leaving small searing bits of pain. When she looked back there was nothing in the sky but smoke, followed by the faint light of fire off in the water, glistening, and mocking her feeble attempt at completing her mission.

What was left to do? What COULD she do? Amelia was dead, the mission was a failure, and Judah was nowhere to be found.

"What now?"

Chapter 26:
Had to Be

Haiti - 1803

Black was the sky the morning the Haitian rebels set out to meet the French army in full battle. Their company split by purpose, each gathering their weapons, ammunition, and other supplies for the reckless plan Victor and Rolland had imagined. It was a gamble, yes, but one they both hoped would pay off. Yet for all of their bluster, all of their fiery patriotism and desire to be free of French oppression barely any Haitian stirred from their rough beds before the fourth hour of the day. No. The first awake that morning, if she ever truly slept at all, was Hannah, who laid out a stolen battered French navel flag over four barrels where she placed her homemade biscuits. As the morning sun arose the men began stirring, she encouraged them to each take a biscuit take as they exited the camp for the battlefield. She was tired, but the long hours without making over one hundred biscuits seemed even more than worth it when she saw the grateful smiles of the men.

"Thanks Miss," a soldier offered politely as he took a biscuit from Hannah's tray. A knowing smile graced her lips as the young woman passed out more and more of the biscuits to the good soldiers defending the freedom of St. Dominique, what Rolland had told her would one day be known as the nation of Haiti.

"You, girl!" C de Baca called out to Hannah, who stopped dead in her tracks before turning around slowly. "Do you know how to handle a gun?"

"N-no, no sir." said Hannah shakily, swallowing a bit of saliva to clear her suddenly bone dry throat.

"How about a sword?" C de Baca asked in a cool tone of voice, all the while removing a sword from the scabbard on his left hip.

"No sir." Hannah responded, now curious as to what he wanted of her.

"Well then, I suppose you will have to figure it out if the French make it through our lines," C de Baca said, wrapping her hand around his own sword before removing his own fingers, one by one, until Hannah was holding it independently.

"But don't you need...?" Hannah asked him before being cut off.

"I'll find another," C de Baca said with a rueful smile as he reached for a biscuit from her the top of her barrels. He bit into it with gusto before winking at her and riding onward.

"Move it along soldiers!" C de Baca cried out, one of the last to leave the camp. His assigned companion for the march was Marcus Turtledove, a man that he had yet to communicate much with since his arrival. Yet looking at Turtledove now, as the older man made his way through the crowd of soldiers with the aid of a long, plain looking walking stick that was slightly taller than himself, C de Baca finally saw a glimmer of the wisdom that Toussaint spoke so highly of on so many occasions.

Shoulder to shoulder the two men marched, each coming from a distinctly different worlds. For C de Baca the prospect of his long life coming to an end was not one that came accompanied by fear, but rather a sense of long awaited relief. He longed to see Yamira again, even if it wasn't in a physical way, he knew that eternal slumber would bring their souls together once again.

For Turtledove the mental barriers were beginning to degrade beyond reasonable repair. The despair of war had always weighed heavily upon his empathic shoulders, yet the sudden death of young Stewart Yick, or Dodger, as Rolland and the other young ones had known him, struck deep within the old man's heart unlike many other deaths he had experienced beforehand. It wasn't the loss of life so much as the direct responsibility he felt for even placing the young man in that position in the first place. He knew that someone would have to pay for this, and he also knew that as the only real sanctioned traveler of light authorized to use the Dream Phoenix to gain access to the Time Stream that he would be held most culpable for Stewart's death. This train of thought continued to thinking of the moment he most dreaded; telling Councilman Yick, Stewart's only remaining family member, that his grandson had died.

They walked along like two normal men despite their unspoken troubles. But unlike normal men these two were followed by nearly two thousand Haitian rebel soldiers, each armed with a combination of crudely made swords, rifles, shovels, gardening equipment, and other makeshift weaponry they had found to defend their newly won freedom. One thought; a life spent outside the cruel bondage of slavery. The French would take try that away from them, so, they would fight Napoleon Bonaparte's puppet soldiers to send a bold message back across the Atlantic. Every ninth and tenth soldier carried upside-down barrels of gunpowder with a round, two inch in diameter hole carved out in bottom to create a controlled pour of the fine substance into a trail behind them. This phenomenon caused the other soldiers in the columns behind these men to give them a wide birth, creating a ripple effect and making new rows before the process started over as the columns made their way through the twisting landscape of what would someday be called Haiti.

"Have you thought about what happens if this does not work?" Turtledove asked, his wise old eyes looking sideways toward the soldiers on either side of him. The one on the left was still munching on what remained of his Hannah biscuit, while the one on the right seemed to have a bum left knee. The slight hobble to his step was misleading, Turtledove knew, as he had seen the man use the rifle swung over his shoulder and knew the deadly accuracy that guarded his and C de Baca's path into enemy territory.

"I've tried not to," C de Baca said, his vision focusing on the rendezvous spot a hundred yards away. Sticking his nose in the air he smelt the unmistakable whiff of unwashed bodies mixed with alcohol and rough spun wool that he knew to be French soldiers on the march.

"Is that how you deal with all of your problems, C de Baca?" Turtledove asked, cutting right to the point of his line of questioning. This was greeted with a split second of what looked to Turtledove like a complete look of unadulterated honesty from C de Baca before silence fell between them and their eyes never made contact again.

When they arrived at the rendezvous point their party stopped and surveyed their surroundings, finding themselves surrounded by the ocean on three sides and only one way back, the one in which they had came. Many piles of wood, accompanied by small trees that measured no less than nine feet high spotted the cliff-side sparsely.

"Dismount!" C de Baca ordered, prompting the few men with horses to jump off. Chipping away with their axes and hammers, the two thousands Haitian soldiers that followed the two men out onto the peninsula set up what appeared to be a makeshift village complete with tents, fire pits, and multiple hammocks made out of hemp. Their instructions were to build as many as possible before French scouts sent word that their commanders, who were sure to be watching their actions, attempted to pin them into a corner between them and the ocean. This they knew and hoped to use to their advantage, but the plan needed something more. A distraction.

Back toward their camp, at the head of the second wave of Haitian forces Victor sat upon a horse, going over the mental checklist that he had prepared the evening before as he trotted along. It seemed like no less than every thirty seconds another scout would approach with a report on French movement. Based on the estimates of General LeClerc's army Victor thought that they had about an hour to lay the trap for the French to fall into.

"Fear is but a four letter word, not a state of mind," Victor shouted in a perfectly balanced voice that conveyed as much hope as it did terror. Their numbers were large, their armor impenetrable, and their mission clear; take back the island or die trying. No longer were they serving the crown of their fathers and forefathers, but instead fighting for the right to own a country, and yes, a very class of people, slaves, for themselves. In this there was no denying, the dream of every single Frenchman was to climb the latter of peasantry through social status and the symbolism thereof. Slaves were a clear representation of that, and one they would not be giving up easily. Yet how could he put these ideas into words? How could so much expression of liberty, freedom, and a hope for a better tomorrow be conveyed?

"Let's kill those sons of bitches."

The proud French force of five thousand strong stood ready to weed out the rebel scum before setting sail on the next morning's tide. They marched outward, both LeClerc and his Captain Lavre positively giddy with the prospect of ending this rebel farce once and for all. It stood to astonishment when, besieged by his own hubris, General Charles LeClerc saw with his own two eyes the single man standing in front of many, weaponless. Instantly he knew the man, but did not fear him, for he knew the scent of death was strong upon him and saw it as a sign of divine intervention. In his human form C de Baca did not scare LeClerc, only the randomness of his moods and quickness of his transformation could strike undue fear into LeClerc's heart. But C de Baca was not meant to inspire fear, no. Instead he was designed to be the bait for the Haitian trap, but LeClerc would have none of it. Sensing this, and knowing that the numbers were his advantage, and it was numbers by which he would use to inflict the most damage.

"Attack!" LeClerc shouted, raising his sword his in a wavering way that went mostly unnoticed by his mean. Behind him the first wave rushed out on foot, their swords aloft as they stormed the enemies' front line, each ready for single combat. While this unorthodox fighting technique had taken some getting used to, especially given the primitive, ungentlemanly use of bows with arrows, yet the resources were scarce in St. Dominique, all except the wood from the trees that grew naturally in the colony. And so it was that the second line of LeClerc's forces was comprised entirely of a line of archers, no less than four hundred deep, each practiced with many years at their craft readied their own weapons before pointing them toward the heavens in anticipation. With a word from their General they let loose their trigger fingers, launching a thick line of arrows onto the rebels rear side. Gracefully they flew upward before coming down, down to the Earth from which they came to once again land, every one, among the dirt and soil until it resembled a small version of the mighty tree that it once was apart.

Perplexed at this, but not entirely dismayed, General LeClerc looked past the failed barrage to his first line of soldiers that were now making first contact. Not surprisingly, many of them had chosen to gang up on C de Baca, as he was the first rebel they encountered, isolated from the others, and appeared easy pickings. Using their swords as skewers. Each took a turn attempting to end C de Baca by simple stabbing, all failing to do so when their time came. What they did do, however, is sufficiently piss him off enough to unleash the beast within his soul.

Changing forms before his eyes, C de Baca cried out in intense agony as the transformation into the creature within him began. Rolland could hardly believe what he watched as memories of Puck flooded his mind. Claws, fangs, and a tale sprouted from the Aztec warrior's body as expanded to the point of enormity before filling out with broad muscle and landing with a practiced grace that only comes from experience. It took the soldiers approximately two seconds after his transformation was complete for them to decide to advance their attack once again. Unfortunately for them, it took C de Baca but one second.

The tail swung into the nearest French soldiers, striking each in the chest and knocking them off their feet, could not be stopped despite all of the musket balls fired at it. Looking up at the beast, the remaining eight or so soldiers that remained circled around C de Baca gawked with reactions that ranged from sheer curiosity, to fear, and to genuine hate for a creature so unlike human beings. The fear emanating from the French was so evident that Turtledove, who fought the few stragglers of the first French wave as they entered rebel territory, could feel it tangibly as the soldiers circled the Aztec. With a loud roar the monster shed his human mind for an instant, and relying on instinct alone, flung his arms at the Frenchmen, catching three of them with his razor sharp claws in the chest, thigh, and neck. Two of the soldiers chose to flee back toward their camp, deciding this was the time to leave. C de Baca not only went after them, but killed them both by stomping them to death like bugs beneath his feet.

The two remaining Frenchmen knew that their time was numbered, and as such decided to take a gamble. One was able to finally remove his sword from its scabbard, chose to arm with the hope of getting picked up with the beast's claws, he thought to ram the spear through his jaw, sealing it shut. The other soldier had a more practical idea. As C de Baca turned around he peered over his shoulder to see the cause of the remaining commotion. There he saw the sword holding Frenchman, and without a seconds further hesitation, C de Baca turned around with clenched fist in an upper cut punch, sending the soldier flying no less than fifty feet in the air. But he was not done yet, as with a kick of his heel the other soldier, the one who thought he might scale the beast somehow, too went flying backward into his own line of people, taking out four approaching soldiers as he fell into their company. Although none of them died, they did not do any more fighting that day. With another loud roar C de Baca let the French army know what would befall them soon enough.

"Enough!" LeClerc pronounced loud enough for his men to hear. "Lavre, you will lead the next advance. If all else fails I want you to take a group of men and infiltrate their lines until you get their leader, Toussaint. Do you hear me? Toussaint must die."

Captain Lavre looked up at his General with an uneasy feeling. Unable to speak he simply nodded before scurrying off to fulfill his orders. Left alone once again LeClerc gave the order to launch the second wave of his attack. Another hundred or so French soldiers, each of them armed, stormed straight for the Haitian rebel line. LeClerc watched in horrified dismay as half-starved slaves cut down his men like they were stick soldiers. Like lambs to the slaughter their fellow soldiers, all standing behind their commanding officers, but with weapons drawn and ready for the command to advance, looked on with great trepidation as some of their best swordsmen were made into afterthoughts by well places Haitian swords and strategically placed blows. More than one thought of dropping their weapons entirely, and making a run for it.

Unsheathing his sword the General LeClerc threw his left leg over his horse, free fell to the ground below, caught himself, and began spiriting across the distance between his army and the rebels. With his sword held high he met one, a tall bulky man who moved slowly. LeClerc then appeared to zig left, but instead zagged to the right before kicking the man squarely in the buttocks until he fell over. The game, it seemed to LeClerc, was that the enemy had somehow developed an impenetrable protection, perhaps via magic or some other form of sorcery. He then performed very similar fighting techniques on to two other seemingly random Haitian rebels before gaining a clear path to the clearing where he saw C de Baca fighting two of his French officers.

"Stop wasting your time with these weaklings and fight me monster," LeClerc asked C de Baca loudly, drawing Turtledove's attention away from using his walking stick to disarm another four or five French soldiers whose aim was elementary at best. After fending off the last attacker with a sharp slam to the head, the leader of the Knights of Time rushed back to his horse. He managed to gallop the distance between himself and C de Baca and once he arrived he saw something extraordinary. C de Baca, monster or not, did not engage LeClerc, but instead spread his majestic wings and flew up into the air away from the fight. The grace of the creature was majestic and terrifying, even to the most skeptical observer. With his long claws, fangs, and tail the beast resembled the closest thing anyone present had seen to a storybook dragon brought to life.

From afar Turtledove could sense the doubt emitting from the hostile French army. Through the smoke and confusion of the battle he found LeClerc's eyes, pale and terrifying in their lack of empathy. Marcus tried with all of his might to reach out, to touch the inner intent of the soul resting within Charles LeClerc, closing his eyes for added concentration. This perceived violation of Charles' mind brought the anger to the forefront of his mind. Without thinking the brash French officer walked to the nearest solider and wrenched the man's pistol from his hands. Trembling with rage LeClerc fired as accurately as he knew how toward the old man and his too-knowing eyes.

The bullet flew into the air with evil intent that was quickly extinguished by the presence of sudden whizzing blur into the fray. The blur spun once, twice, then slowed long enough to reveal legs, a torso, and a blonde head that grinned before crashing head first into the dirt behind French territory. LeClerc turned and ran through his men, pushing and shoving until he was face to face with Gwendolyn Murrow. The blonde Nocturn was with her left hand clenched, her head perfectly crooked to look them all in the eye. She suddenly opened her hand and tossed the bullet to LeClerc with a wink before propelling herself back upward into the sky. Taking off without a word escaping her lips, Gwendolyn bent her legs, concentrating upward while folding her free hand to her chest. In moving upward, further away from the ground below, she left behind all sense of what it meant to be amongst the human populace, entering into a world of her own; a world above the clouds. She heard small popping noises as the men below attempted to fire their primitive guns at her up in the sky. The foolish Frenchmen either did not, or could not know that the same balls they shot would travel upward only so far before hurtling down toward them with a similar velocity to that in which they left. Gwendolyn looked down to see a few of the small standing dots on the ground turn into fallen over dots, elongated to give the impression that they had fallen asleep.

Then, the memory of the likewise fallen Dodger entered Gwendolyn's mind, and the deceased soldiers below no longer slept a peaceful sleep. They were, for better or worse, all at rest.

"I want them all dead. Every single one of them dead, do you hear me?!" General LeClerc screamed at the surrounding men.. He knew that he held the numbers advantage, and that if he acted quickly he could force the bulk of the Haitian rebels off of the steep cliff and into the ocean they had foolishly blockaded themselves upon. Finding a new horse, LeClerc climbed upon its saddle before righting himself and galloping to the front line and until he found the man he was looking for.

"Lavre, I've changed my mind. You are to stay behind while I lead the next wave, understood?"

"But General, I..." Captain Lavre said with confusion before resigning himself. "Yes, General, I understand"

The next wave of French soldiers came at the Haitian rebels, this time in a greater number and with their General in the lead. The melee increased as this time both French and Haitians fell under the might of the passions of war. The rebels continued to hold their own, far surpassing their French counterparts in both sheer determination. Even LeClerc himself, who was quickly de-horsed by a rather skinny, hungry looking young rebel who stabbed the animal in the side in an ungentlemanly manner. LeClerc grappled with the young man after losing his footing falling off the horse. Yet while the young rebel had the initial advantage, the end of his fight came when the young buck who challenged him didn't move quite fast enough, leaving his neck exposed. Charles smiled as the obligatory squirt of fresh blood sprayed onto his face, forearms, and chest as his victim fell to the ground. His victory, though cherished for him, was short lived, as screams from French officers fell on his ears from both his left, and right.

Death reigned down upon the French in the form of flaming arrows as Victor led a freshly inspired group of rebels into their rear and through the French lines. Broken by their lack of discipline, many of the French soldiers broke rank and fled even further away from their position, back into the trap Rolland, Tina, Hannah, and the remaining fifteen hundred Haitian forces rebels were waiting to add their support to the cause. Splitting with his men halfway through the fray, Victor broke off in search of the man he now came face to face with as the battle reached its next phase. Victor dismounted his horse, drew his sword, and pointed it at LeClerc before opening his mouth to speak. But the words never came. Instead all hell broke loose in the form of a giant monster, bursting onto the scene and casting both Victor and LeClerc sideways with its massive frame that sometimes went by the name C de Baca. Caring not for who he inflicted his carnage on, C de Baca thrashed his giant claws forward, swiping at as many of the fleeing Frenchmen as possible before they made their way back to the safety of their lines.

Shots were fired, each bouncing off the thick skin of the beast, whose eyes glowed red with a passionate rage. Scrambling to his feet Charles LeClerc felt his mind very much reeling from the sudden loss of both his coordination, and his senses. What he did know, however, was that the rock embedded in his side was sharp, pointed, and went in almost four inches. Pawing at it with his non dominant hand he was able to remove the largest chunk, but could feel smaller pieces still lodged inside. This discomfort momentarily alleviated he was able to get back to his feet and meander toward his army as C de Baca turned his attention to the rebel front line and distracting them from LeClerc's departure. Once at the large, off-white war tent that his men had constructed in case of the elements, there LeClerc was greeted by no less than nine other soldiers, each offering to assist or serve him in some way as they led him through the lines to his personal tent. There he was sat as a doctor bustled in past the soldiers, all still speaking at the same time and taking no notice of LeClerc's dazed state, or the doctor attempting to do his job.

"Be quiet," LeClerc ordered. His heavy breathing made his orders difficult to discern, even if he did not also brandish a gaping wound that looked fatal to all who saw him. Sweat poured heavily from his brow. Then the thought struck him, where was Lavre?! A roaring noise from outside suddenly broke LeClerc's concentration. Shaking madly the Frenchman jumped up from his seat, hobbled to the tent's entrance flap and lifted it. He managed to make it outside the tent, and gazed across the divide into the enemies camp as the magic of the transformation took shape before his eyes. LeClerc watched as the once large monster, clearly visible from so far away due to his massive size and girth, shrunk to little more than the size of a normal man before disappearing into the crowd of soldiers that readied themselves for the next excursion. He was one of them, just another rebel. Just another mortal. Just another life to take. "Belay that order. Ready the men for another wave, and find Captain Lavre. Stop this damned doctor from following me everywhere, and-"

"You're surrounded, General Asshole," Rolland Wright said, flanked by both Tina and Hannah as the trio walked confidently into what was left of the French line. Many weapons drew on them at once, including guns, arrows, and swords that all seemed to guarantee that none would leave their alive, no matter what the outcome of the battle might be. "I could kill you and these men this very second, but I won't. Not if you do something for me." The young man took a deep breath before saying, "You're going to stop your advance right now."

"I do not take orders from children," retorted General LeClerc in heavy French-accented English through gritted, yellowing teeth. "I serve for the glorious cause of my country, I always have. Faithfully. I won't stop that service because you asked me nicely."

Rolland shook his head, disappointed but not surprised that things were going this way. Victor had insisted that LeClerc would never listen to reason and he appeared correct. The only other recourse was intimidation. From a crudely sown leather bag strapped across her chest, Tina pulled out a glass bottle stuffed with a yellowish looking cloth and gingerly handed it to Rolland. From his back pocket, Rolland produced a smaller item; a unique item that no person present besides Tina had ever seen before. A disposable lighter. Flicking the device on Rolland instantly created a flame, and held it close to the cloth sticking out of the bottle. As the flame touched the cloth, Rolland said defiantly, "Oh Charles, I never said please."

Tossing the bottle, Rolland, Tina, and Hannah ran in the opposite direction for a few split seconds before the detonation took place. The explosion sounded, sending bits of flaming logs from the fire in front of it in all directions. Knowing what to expect, it took the trio of travelers but a moment or two to gather their wits enough to retreat back across the hostile territory into the rear. With the ensuing confusion and chaos, the trio were able to stay covered by the tree-line as they made their way to Victor and Turtledove.

LeClerc, whose body had still yet to heal fully from the jagged rock, felt the pieces embedded themselves now deeper due to the explosion. Looking at his left hand he saw but two fingers remaining, a middle and an index, before the small nubs began to once again grow into full blown fingers. The small flesh colored bulbs opened like flowers in the spring as LeClerc watched himself heal like clockwork. Sucking in all of the wetness from his mouth Charles spit sideways, releasing a large glob of blood and snot that got caught between his lips as he smiled. 'The ships,' he thought to himself as he felt his body slowly righting itself. 'All we have to do is lead them towards the ships.'

Before he had died Stewart Yick imparted a bit of wisdom he had learned from his grandfather to his classmate, Kniff Youngblood, around a campfire one evening. When in a bad situation, one where you're feeling hopeless beyond measure, distract yourself by humming. This will not only make you feel better, but also give those around you the false sense of calm. When pressed further, Dodger would admit that he would believe anyone who was humming before killing others that they're going into battle with a crazy person, and will attract most of the initial enemy fire. Despite the fact that he was crouched down in a crab position, sandwiched between Jaime, and a very dirty young man who called himself Tolva, who wore a very thin mustache over his naturally dark lips. Looking from one to the other Kniff knew, deep inside himself, that Dodger had been right. With no further thought he began a low, resonate hum from the bottom of his stomach.

Jaime knew it was Kniff, but for some reason could not bring himself to ask his teammate why he was doing so. Instead Jaime chose to begin humming as well, his baritone voice joining Kniff's deep alto in a blend of agreeable resolve. As both fought on, their weapons clashing against those of various French soldiers, some who fell, some who were merely disarmed, a strange thing happened to the Haitian forces around them. Falling in step with their foreign, seemingly sudden appearing saviors, the company of men within a six foot radius too began to hum. At first it was but seven who headed the call, their voices carrying over the sounds of a French retreat to a song that few recognized, an old Mer nursery rhyme Kniff's mother had sung to him as a young child. Their voices began to die down as they neared the water. Kniff looked at Jaime and nodded to his friend. It was time.

Outside on the ridge, the recovered LeClerc led a band of soldiers upward toward the edge of the peninsula, spotting the rebels as they ran out to engage. They each carried large axes which they swung, one at LeClerc, and one at the private behind him. Though the private fell, LeClerc was able to disarm the guard, dislocate his swinging arm, and move onward toward the rebel line. Charles looked over his shoulder to see a slew of Frenchmen doing the same, keeping close on his heels with both their pace, and passion for bloodshed.

It was with that image in mind that he met with the literal looming shadow of the French ships he had been expecting weeks before as they made their way, one on each side of the peninsula, toward the area where his troops were rallying toward. Each ship was equipped with no less than eight side cannons a piece, all aimed at the location where rebel troops were now pushing French soldiers, ensuring that the shooting gallery would have plenty of targets. LeClerc's sword arm went limp as he realized what was happening. Then, without another warning, the other shoe dropped hard in the form of screams from behind him on the ridge. Cannon fire spread throughout the opening between the lines, knocking down numerous groupings of Frenchmen, and forcing the survivors to scramble away in unexpected horror.

Standing at the front of one of the ships was Kniff, arms at his side, a smug, self satisfied expression etched onto his handsome face. More explosions filled the air as the two ships rained down cannon fire on the French regulars fleeing for their lives. Miraculously, not a fragment of debris, stray cannon, nor single shot of enemy fire so much as grazed any of the Haitian soldiers as they drove their invaders further back from the peninsula in which they assumed was the Haitian forces death march. LeClerc himself ran backward, engaging as many rebels as he could along the way, yet did no lasting damage to any of the men he encountered.

A strange phenomenon was taking place, one that was not going unnoticed by soldiers on either side of the conflict. For whenever a Frenchmen would attempt to strike, or kill any of the rebels some unseen force of luck or quick timing would prevent them from being so much as scratched. Sure, there were Haitian casualties, but they were few and far between, almost as if they represented a statistical necessity instead of realistic numbers of men lost in war. The last wave of French soldiers, which LeClerc discovered only consisted of a third of his forces before the rest turned to coward, nearly all were slain or wounded.

Maddened beyond reason, Charles LeClerc swung his axe wildly, hoping to connect with anyone, friend or foe, who crossed his path. While he managed to knock over a very green French private who had already wet himself and was fleeing the scene, he did no other damage to anyone, or anything but his own pride. 'What the hell is going on?!' he thought to himself.

Victor watched his enemy's frustration and felt a surprising surge of pity for the man. Was it LeClerc's fault that he fought for a cause that was doomed to failure? Should he, Victor Aquasi

III, break from tradition and attempt to change the time stream by calling a truce with LeClerc, rather than advancing until they were both dead? Inhaling sharply the big man yelled at the top of his voice, "Cease fire for parlay!"

His voice brought the fighting to a halt and both sides warily moved away from each other. All except LeClerc, who was the last to leave the battlefield and retreat to the French side of the conflict. Unlike their General the French were tired and confused at their inability to hurt the Haitians and confused as to why the ships fired upon them. Even Charles LeClerc suspended himself in his blood lust to listen to what the man he knew as the rebel Toussaint L 'Overture had to say.

"Noble sons of France, we have you surrounded. Throw down your weapons and we will return your ships and allow sail back to your homeland. We have not harmed any of the crew, only those who actively resisted takeover. Go now and no harm will come to you. Stay and you will die before the day is at an end," Victor said in near perfect French as his loud, resolute tone of voice that carried over the distance to ring upon the ear of every French soldier left in the battle. Victor made a point not to look LeClerc in the eyes as he spoke, though it did not make a difference.

"It is you, *Monsieur* Toussaint, who will die," LeClerc shouted back at the rebel, though his voice carried none of the oratory drama that Victor's did. By this point LeClerc was one of only a handful of the French invaders left that still held both the necessary amount of sway from keeping the men from a revolt, and the tenacious spirit for more battle that left the rest of the war-weary soldiers. There was still no sign of Captain Lavre, nor were their battleships coming to their rescue. To many the choice seemed clear - surrender, or follow LeClerc to their certain deaths. Perhaps sensing this, LeClerc moved through the ranks as fast as he could, taking a quick inventory of his resources and muttering under his breath. It was time that he needed, time and more men to distract the bulk of the rebels so he could sneak past them and kill Toussaint himself.

"I will give you one last chance," Victor said again, his tone calm.

Knowing that he was defeated, or at least that his current cause was lost, the battered French General began formulating a plan of escape for himself under the guise of faking his own death. Yet each way he thought of the act it felt unseemly and cowardly. Charles looked at the rebels, revulsion covering his thoughts. Then he cast his gaze upon Rolland, Tina, and the rest of the new arrivals that he knew to be supernatural abominations. Loathing beyond measure filled the French officer as he thought of all the horrible things he would like to do to each of them. Facing Rolland he suddenly shouted, "How dare you come here? How dare you insert yourself into a situation that you have no right to infringe upon!"

"No, *Monsieur* LeClerc," said a timid, yet strong female voice from behind Rolland Wright. She walked into the space between the two sides, while looking confidently at General LeClerc and his army of guns drawn on her. Her demeanor was that of someone who had done this sort of thing before, even if that was a lie. "It is you who misunderstands the situation. Have you not noticed how little you have hurt these people today? These soldiers, all of them - are under my protection."

"Your protection eh?," LeClerc sneered derisively as he examined Hannah for a long moment before laughing, encouraging those behind him to do the same. It was true, his forces had been what felt like a step behind the rebels all morning, himself included. But to go so far as for the meekest among them to boast responsibility for such an act? Charles thought this preposterous. He had wondered if she was also a supernatural like the others, but had come to realize she was probably their servant or even an escaped slave from the island. For how could she, a simple young girl, be the cause of so much bad fortune? A fresh chorus of laughs accompanied this line of questioning, though it did not seem to faze Hannah in her role as self-appointed representative. "Understand this, all of you, I will not surrender. We will not stop until every last one of us is dead, and I do mean every, last, one."

The cold words found their mark, finally making Hannah wince before she took one giant step backward, followed by several more before turning and sprinting to safety. Embarrassed, Hannah could not understand what brought on her bit of boldness. Regardless, both Victor and Rolland were thankful that she did. Eyeing one another they seemed to exchange the same bleak thought as Tina and Gwendolyn comforted the now shaking Hannah; regardless of what happened to any of them, LeClerc had to die in order for the conflict to end. Period.

"It's time," Rolland said with the utmost certainty, prompting their final sequence of events to be set into motion.

"Light them up!" Victor screamed as loud as he could, prompting the group of skinny rebels holding wooden clubs to scatter like ants in all different directions into the no-man's-land between the two groups. The large General bent low, swung his left arm in a now familiar pendulum motion, and with a masterful friction force set his entire hand, forearm, and eventually entire appendage aflame.

As each of the young rebels ran past Victor they held out the dark tips of their clubs, igniting them in blue and gossamer flames that held true to their purpose as they bobbed along with the children's momentum. When they reached the end of the rebel territory each fanned out into an evenly spaced line until they met with what looked like pre-marked lines on the ground. These 'lines' were comprised entirely of the gun powder that ran from where the Haitian teens stood, through the French lines, clear through to the other side, where more rebels waited to catch any stragglers. Without further trepidation each of the men lowered their flames, igniting the lines of gunpowder, before running at full speed back to the Haitian lines.

"Forward!" LeClerc screamed at his soldiers as the explosions all around them began. As many of them as possible ran toward the Haitian line and the resulting clash was as loud as it was frightening. Victor's warriors met the French foot soldiers head on, steel on steel, forming the sort of allegiances that transcend everything, including the grave. From C de Baca, to the lowest of the low enlisted former slave long past their prime, every one aimed to hold on to the newly claimed rights of freedom, choice, and self governance; none of which they planned on giving up, especially without a fight. All around men were crying out in pain and agony. In fits of homicidal rage to his immediate left Victor, or as he was known on this battlefield, General Toussaint, watched as his long time second in command, Lt. C de Baca, led a band of Haitians into a line of armed, yet reloading French soldiers, massacring them with an almost immaculate proficiency.

Charles LeClerc suddenly found himself facing the man who had been the beast. He drew his sword with a gallant movement that would put even the most courtly knight to shame. Yet the way in which he met C de Baca's sword was less about courtliness, and more about inflicting pain on another man. Though LeClerc was smaller than the still human C de Baca, his quickness gave him the advantage when it came to small, albeit annoying attacks, such as stomping on his enemies foot when he drew close enough to lay his hands upon the Frenchmen.

"Come now, monster," LeClerc said in a goading tone of voice. "It will only hurt for a second. I'm jealous, really. You get to leave his wretched place before I do."

The feeling of regurgitation overpowered C de Baca, causing him to raise his brows, open his mouth, and belch a loud, reverberating burp that also brought with it a quarter sized pink bubble. Astonished by this, both he and LeClerc looked at the small bubble as its smooth, thin layer of pink coating that gave it the spherical shape doubled over on itself again and again, making it bigger each time. This continued until the bubble was the size of a beach ball, still gliding gracefully as it made its way toward LeClerc. The general watched it come toward him, feeling apprehensive. He tried to run but it was too late as the bubble landed against him harder than he expected popping instantly and spraying a mist of a noxious pink pudding-like substance all over LeClerc's thigh, foot, chest, and arm. A beat went by before the real effect set-in, the one that began with the steaming burn that ate through the uniform LeClerc wore before finding the tender flesh underneath.

General LeClerc screamed in agony as nearly his entire right side of his body was rotting away before the eyes of both armies, many of which had stopped fighting to watch this horrifying display. Suddenly nearly every member of the Haitian forces began to violently hiccup. This not only prompted their French counterparts to retreat but shocked many of them enough into dropping their weapons.

Apprehensive due to the still screaming LeClerc, who clung to his side as he lay in the fetal position by a worried looking C de Baca's feet, the rebels nearly all closed their eyes when the bubbles circled around to run back into their originators. But this time, instead of creating a spray of toxic puss that incapacitated their fellows, the bubbles encircled each one, creating a cocoon of protection and safety from any outside element, including enemy weaponry. From a place unseen by nearly all who the wave affected, a pinkish hue of hope washed over the battlefield like a tidal wave of invisible water, incapacitating every person who consumed one of Hannah's fireside biscuits. The treats themselves were not so important as what was in them; the pain, the fear, the regret for not being able to foresee the danger surrounding Dodger's death - Hannah didn't want that to happen again. She wouldn't let that happen again.

Rolland watched this in amazement at what one person could do with their abilities. He knew that Hannah wanted to use his last name and felt vindicated in his decision to give it to her. Nearby he reached for Tina's hand, not sure if she too abstained from one of Hannah's biscuits, which he knew was the source for the hovering pink bubbles, but found nothing there but Timothy, whose bubble was three times as thick as everyone else's'.

"Hey," came Victor's voice through the fog of pink and increasingly intense smell of sulfur. By this point more of the noxious bubbles had appeared, all emitting from C de Baca, whose insides apparently disagreed with whatever Hannah used in her recipe. These toxic bubbles frightened the few hundred remaining French troops to their core, convincing them all to retreat backward and take their chances with the rebels in the rear to make their escape. Few did. The timing of Hannah's 'attack' could not have been worse timed it seemed, as though it dealt the 'deciding blow' to the morale of the remaining French forces, it also only hardened the remaining passionate Frenchmen who saw their only options to be win, or die where they stood. Many hacked away at the bubbles with their weapons, often meeting with mixed results. If not for the secondary forces of rebels who had not eaten any of Hannah's biscuits the bubble protected to non-bubble protected rebels would be even more skewed. Victor watched this, taking it all in before a sudden realization hit him hard. Turning to Rolland once again he exclaimed, "You're not in a bubble. Didn't you eat a biscuit?"

"Nope, no time. Looks like you didn't either," Rolland observed, looking Victor up and down. The dual realization that neither was protected in the same way that the others were, making them vulnerable both terrified them, and comforted them at the same time, knowing that despite the changes between them since the last time, they were once again fighting side by side as brothers in arms. Yet brothers aside, the teenage libido knows what it wants. "Have you seen Tina?"

"No man, sorry," Victor said, before their attention was drawn to the figure slowly rising out of the mud before them. Standing there, holding a dagger in his left hand, with his flesh half rebuilt around a terrible burn that exposed his internal organs, General LeClerc again rose to defend his honor as the last Frenchmen to take the field. Victor looked to Rolland who began to speak, but was cut off by the sound of steel as Victor removed his own saber from his hip. "Go find Tina. I've got this."

Without another word Rolland ran off into trees alone, but Victor didn't have time to think about that. The stage was set for his greatest, final showdown with the man who had haunted his dreams for the past fifteen months. Looking to his right, Victor could clearly see the curved line of unlit gunpowder as it hugged the outside perimeter of the peninsula, the same was true on the left. The lines, which had been prepared for his unique skill set, were laid out with a mere two foot distance between their two ends, one of which Victor was stepping on.

"Whoops," Victor said to himself before side stepping to his right and dropping to one knee. Raising his head slightly he looked for General LeClerc, finding him in mid attempted battle with three Haitian soldiers who were floating away in their bubbles above him, before their eyes met. In a moment of transfixed hatred Charles LeClerc dropped the dagger he held, looked around briefly, smiled, and righted himself brandishing a proper sword that no doubt belonged to a deceased French officer. Victor lit the lines of gunpowder and watched as they blew at the feet of his enemy, causing them to burn through the shoes, LeClerc to lose him composure, and balance. But Victor knew that it ultimately amounted to nothing more than delaying the inevitable. Lost in this thought, and frankly unsure as to how to proceed in killing the un-killable man, Victor did not anticipate how quickly LeClerc recovered from his attack, coughing politely to get the rebel leader's attention. Victor jumped up, his right fist immediately catching a flame as he took a fighting posture.

"Let me guess," LeClerc said in his cockiest tone of voice as he stared directly into Victor's soul. "You can control fire?"

The catchphrase that had followed Victor for so many years had slipped his mind in the last few due to the pressures and responsibilities that came with mounting a resistance against a world power. Still, the reminder of his boyhood cockiness was a mental advantage, one in which he would gladly accept. Yet, something was amiss with the phrase now that he heard it coming out of someone else's mouth, even if it was being applied to him. "No," Victor said softly before resuming his fighting stance.

"I am the fire."

They never included him in their secrets. Timothy Holmes watched them from the inside of his bubble, though he could not hear what they were saying. Outside both Rolland and Victor spoke frantically before Rolland ran into the woods and Victor went to fight the mad Frenchman. He hated how they would always have little secrets, all of his teammates, but would never include him in on any of them. This thought, though important he felt it was, soon gave way to a much more panicked and worrisome trouble as he thought about what Rolland could be running toward. Looking around furiously and not seeing her anywhere Timothy removed his cell phone from his pocket and put it into his palm with the edge facing outward before scraping it against the bubble. Again and again he repeated the scrapping motion until a large POP sound gave way at the same time as the ground beneath him.

It wasn't the two foot fall that Timothy hated, more the fact that there was no one there to reassure him that he should be getting up and moving along. His whole life either his mother, or his sister had been around to hold his hand. Now he knew it was his turn to go find Tina. Timothy stood up and began running toward the tree line before disappearing into the wood. Once inside he found it dark and quiet, much quieter than he remembered it being the night before. He wished that he knew how to track, how to tell direction, hell anything would be helpful in a moment like this.

"Help!" came a loud female voice that Timothy recognized as belonging to his sister. As fast as his thick legs would take him Timothy made his way through the trees toward the sound of the single scream, confident that he could do whatever needed to be done. He ran for several long minutes, straining to see as the sun began to sink. Suddenly smelling smoke and catching a glimpse of a fire, Timothy darted through the trees toward the fire, not looking before he leapt directly onto the scene of the attempted assault on his sister by Captain Lavre.

"Wha-?" Lavre asked as Timothy looked down at the man who was laying on top of Tina's back with his hand over her mouth. A few feet away the man's knife, nearly five inches long and serrated with a sharp tip, laid in its holster. Timothy snatched it up before Lavre could, but his gloating left him blind to the sneak attack the Captain launched immediately after. Wrestling Timothy to the ground. The two fought with all the tenacity of two declawed cats, the summation of their efforts being that the knife was pushed a good two feet further away from both of them than when they started.

It was in this state, both men on the ground, arms wrapped around one another in a defensive manner, which Rolland Wright wandered in on the two as they wrestled next to the unconscious Tina. Not particularly caring about either of them he stepped over them with quick footedness, Rolland cradled his girlfriend within his arms for a moment before checking her pulse and breathing. From what little he knew about first aid he felt like everything was normal, she must have passed out from the result of something her brother did, no doubt. Still, Timothy was a member of his team, and Rolland was loyal to his team.

Walking the short distance between them Rolland grabbed Captain Lavre by the scruff of his neck before taking the bottom of his uniform jacket with the other and tossing him completely off of Timothy. The small man doubled over in pain and began cowering. As if on cue large crocodile tears, the kind that only came from years of practice filled the Captain's eyes as he plead for mercy before Rolland. "Please, Sir. Spare my life."

Rolland shook his head in amazement, and looked at the man with astonished equal amounts of both pity and disdain. Removing his father's knife from its hilt before turning around to place the sharpened point at Lavre's jugular the teenager had nothing but contempt in his heart. Too long, too hard, and too much fighting had since they came to Haiti, despite his best efforts. Too much had gone wrong, completely wrong, and no matter what the outcome none of them would ever be the same. Especially Victor.

"Rolland...." came Tina's meager voice from the ground. Her left eye opened ajar as she saw her boyfriend holding her attacker at knifepoint. "Don't. He... is... asshole..."

With a growing sense of what it meant to grow up and learn values such as compassion, faith in happenstance, and trust in others, Rolland relaxed his grip on his father's dagger and let his arm fall to his side. "Just get the hell out of here already."

With that the portly Captain Lavre hastily stood up before taking off into the forest, leaving Rolland and Timothy alone with the unconscious Tina. Rolland went over to her, scooped her up in his arms, and walked over to Timothy before proceeding to hand her over to him. With an odd look on his face, Timothy took his sister in his arms.

"Take her back to Victor's tent in the main camp," Rolland instructed Timothy. "Stay to the trees and take the long way out of sight. When this is over we'll come and get you both."

As Timothy nodded hesitantly, Rolland wondered whether this was a wise choice, but decided that yes, this was the right thing to do. He was needed back in the battle and Victor's side. He knew that Timothy, whatever his other faults may be, would take care of his sister.

"Get her out of here, alright?" Rolland told Timothy. He then kissed Tina's head and squeezed her hand before letting it and her go into her twin's care. He started jogging back towards the battle but the thought of leaving Tina unsettled with Timothy though he couldn't quite understand why.

For some reason, and he would never be able to explain this to himself much less anyone else, the voice of Anake reverberated through his mind as clear as day. The words *tell no one of this* repeated twice, forcing Rolland to stop what he was doing and turn back. He ran at a full sprint back to the clearing where he had left the twins, feeling a sense of relief at seeing Timothy still there. That relief quickly faded as Rolland Wright noticed that Tina was now on the ground. He then encountered the most improbable thing he had yet to experience since coming to Eden. If he had not seen it with his own two eyes Rolland would not have believed it, but see it he did. As horrified disgust coiled in his belly, Rolland witnessed the ever-so-gentle slide of fingers make their way into Tina's pants, and into her underpants. A lightning bolt of electricity went off in Rolland's head at this sight.

"Hey!" Rolland screamed, prompting Timothy to look up at him automatically, his fingers still in Tina's panties. "What the fuck do you think you're doing?"

At this Timothy finally removed his fingers, placing his hand back on Tina's hip before his cheeks turned a bright shade of scarlet as he looked at the ground. "Well, I, uh...."

But Rolland never let him finish.

It took Rolland three steps to reach Timothy, punching the Holmes heir squarely in the orbital bone below his right eye, causing him to drop flat on his back as he took the pain. Rolland not only moved Tina quickly out of the way but stood ready to also take any retribution coming his way for inflicting the blow. When none came after a few moments, Rolland felt satisfied enough to let Timothy, who sat up knees crying for mercy, alone for the time being.

What felt like a heartbeat later C de Baca, through the mist of gathering sulfur, found them in their awkward tableau. Choosing to address Rolland over Timothy he briefly asked what he could do before accepting the task of taking Tina somewhere safe. Carrying her as easily as one would a pound of sugar, C de Baca set off into the night. Glaring at him one last time Rolland Wright shook his head at Timothy, wondering how in the hell he would explain this to Tina once she awoke. Dreading that conversation, Rolland glared at the perverted Holmes brother one more time before turning back to the dark woods, and disappearing into them.

Sitting there, feeling more alone than he had in quite a long while, Timothy found himself counting down the seconds before he would stand up. He wasn't sure where that beast was taking his sister, but he knew that he would be there when she woke up. He also knew that he could take the credit for her save, and most of all he, Timothy, would be the one would could brag to their parents that he took care of his sister in the field. His mother was going to be so proud of him.

Rolland ran for a while before he found them. The noises of the battle were offset by the ocean waves smacking against the rocks below the peninsula below. No sooner did he hear and make out a voice that he recognized to be Victor's than he heard a loud explosion that forced Rolland to take cover by diving onto the ground beneath him. Long gone was the time for thinking - thought was a luxury for others, people no in the middle of a battlefield. Once the smoke cleared, he attempted to open his eyes to deduce the situation, though he found it very difficult to do so at first.

"Damn," Rolland said aloud to no one while bringing his still strong right arm forward. Laying it flat underneath him like a carjack, Rolland pushed himself upward until he was resting on his knees, closing his eyes as he went. Head pounding, eyes watering, and nose running from the sulfuric smell of Hannah's giant pink bubbles, he could still think of little else but Dodger, and the difference his friend would have made on the battle. Stuffing down the thoughts of Timothy's perversions and the Pandora's box that problem would later bring, he chose to focus on yesterday's issues instead. The pain, the regret, and the inner sense of responsibility like a dagger through his heart, Rolland once again did what he swore to himself he wouldn't do, letting the pity into the small gaps left on his emotional plate.

Forcing his eyes open again, against his bodies urges to keep them closed, Rolland surveyed the scene around him with a new resolve. To his left were fallen bodies of Frenchmen, most with plainly visible open wounds in the form of claw marks across their chests and backs where C de Baca had skewered them with his gargantuan wings; a gruesome end punctuated by the bodies scattered and intermingled limbs. To his right, Rolland saw nothing save more smoke that irritated his eyes all over again, drawing fresh tears forward to join his familiar friend, grief.

Once upon a time Rolland would have put his mother's face to that emotion above all else. Then, in chronological order, perhaps his Cadillac would be next, followed by his great grandmother, Princess Blaisey, and most recently Victor, and Dodger. Grief was a bitch, and had sadly become Rolland's most consistent friend over the years, cropping up again and again. Yet this time, unlike the others, the emotion was somehow different.

"Fucking, just die already!" came a loud, angry voice from the smoke behind Rolland. Rising to his feet unsteadily he turned around to see that what he needed most was not a reprieve from the grief that held his heart like a parasite, but time. Time, the one thing that he could control, manipulate, and bend to his will. Time - the great divider of all things, and the one thing he needed in order to sort out the mess that he had helped to create. Speeding his pace into a full out jog, Rolland hung his head low, cast his eyes upward, and followed the sound of grunting until he found them, roughly fifty yards away; one victor, one vanquished in an ironic pose of battlefield dramatics. There, standing above a fallen Victor was the Frenchman LeClerc with both hands wrapped around what looked like the hilt of the same sword Rolland recognized as the weapon that took Dodger's life. Bringing it high into the air above him, Charles wasted zero time in lowering the glistening blade downward as fast as he could toward Victor's exposed and vulnerable throat.

"No!" Rolland heard himself cry out, though he would later suspect that it might have just been a strong thought within his own head. For at that moment a small, yet curiously strong flash of black and white fur streaked across his line of sight, obscuring the action just long enough for Rolland to run the short distance that separated them. A mashing of teeth on skin, resulting in a smearing of bloody arms found LeClerc wrestling with the newest, and most opportune member of the class of the tiger, Tiikeri. With as much ferocity as the cub could muster she tore and gnawed at the foul smelling Frenchmen, creating a distraction long enough for Rolland to act.

"Can you move?" Rolland asked Victor, who nodded slightly before his eyes opened. Although only semi-conscious due to the altercation with LeClerc, Victor could stand well enough if supported, at least at first. Yet when he lifted one hand toward LeClerc to propel himself forward, his feet gave out and Victor fell down onto the Haitian soil he had spent nearly a decade defending. Flustered, Rolland realized that his question had been answered just as another flash of white and black fur whizzed by as Tiikeri lost her fight against the much larger LeClerc. Landing a few feet away the tiger cub stood, rounded on herself, and walked behind Rolland's legs before beginning to growl once again at their shared enemy. The moment had come to decide; stand and fight, or retreat with Victor and their collective dignity. Though Rolland suspected he knew where Tiikeri's vote would lie, the literal weight of Victor upon his shoulders had an effect on his conscience.

"Fine," LeClerc said with baited breath as he turned and his left hand lifted a pistol in Rolland's direction. The Frenchmen's once white uniform was painted red from the deep cuts and hanging flesh Tiikeri had taken from the officer's arms, separating the skin from bone. Despite this LeClerc wore the same smug smile that greeted Rolland immediately after murdering Dodger in cold blood. It was then that a profound change happened within Rolland Wright that he would not fully understand for many years. It was then that something primal, dangerous, and unspeakable clawed its way to the surface of his psyche before taking control of Rolland.

Behind them came light footsteps that Rolland knew belonged to C de Baca in his human form. Together they stood and stared at LeClerc's pistol; all three forming their own plan of attack. For C de Baca the choice seemed clear - use the number to their advantage. There were three of them after all, including Tiikeri and a half conscious Victor,. Despite the odds of one, if not two of them failing in the attempt at least he knew it might also rile him up enough to transform, possibly even long enough to rip the General in half length wise and scatter his body about various parts of the island. No sooner was C de Baca making plans for exact locations to stash LeClerc's liver than all were broken from their reverie by a calm, calculated voice.

"Take Victor," Rolland said to C de Baca, drawing LeClerc's eyes to his own. C de Baca hesitated for a moment, but soon Rolland felt the weight of Victor being taken off of his shoulder. A gust of the sulfuric seaside air mixed with salted wind carried over the peninsula where they stood. Rolland knew the repercussions of his words, even before he had said them. He also knew what they meant, and what had to happen next. Knew that C de Baca's quarrel with LeClerc stretched back longer than his own and by doing what he had to do next would rob his new ally from any form of revenge. Still, Rolland could not bring himself to care, or feel any emotion past the all-encompassing feeling of righteousness that filled every bit of his soul. "Take Victor and go. Now!"

"Like hell I will," C de Baca said, his much larger frame able to both support Victor's massive weight on one shoulder and steady himself for a fight with LeClerc with his free hand. Yet when he shuffled his feet, C de Baca accidently kicked Victor's leg a bit, noticing for the first time the deep cut that his leader, and friend, had sustained. Memories of their years fighting together, talking to one another, and scheming to survive onslaught after onslaught came to light as Victor again opened his glassy eyes to see his most loyal lieutenant there with him. With what remaining strength he had left, Victor raised his less battered arm to C de Baca's, and rested his hand on top of it, hoping to draw from their friendship the same strength he felt was keeping the other going. Feeling this, and remembering all those had lost before, including his own son, C de Baca ignored the tears in his eyes. He nodded at Rolland as he turned away to disappear into the smoky darkness with Victor with Tiikeri following them closely at their heels.

Rolland, with a late model 18th century pistol aimed at his chest, had never felt more confident in his decision. With a slow, meticulous pace he took a small step to his left before turning his torso to move closer and in LeClerc's direction. This action, not surprisingly, resulted in LeClerc mimicking Rolland, before moving away from him until the two were literally walking in a circle around one another in a reverse game of cat and mouth.

"You've seen that I can heal," LeClerc said, attempting to regain the upper hand. He felt a strange sense of foreboding now that he was alone with the young man, still not knowing fully who or what he was. "You know you cannot beat me."

"I don't have to beat you," Rolland said, walking straight toward LeClerc until the barrel of the pistol in the Frenchmen's hand was resting on the teenager's chest. With a now practiced ease Rolland was able to slide one hand behind him to grab the hilt of Scott's dagger. "I just have to outlive you long enough to separate your head from your body."

"You won't," LeClerc said with a bloody gummed grin. The crimson mask of battle was everywhere, painting a picture of the man's values as he wavered upon his knees, his catlike qualities still ever-present as he rose to his feet. Scott Wright's knife still held close to the Frenchmen's chest. "You can't."

The words, meant to coerce an action, instead inexplicably created a crystal clear image of Andrew Jackson saying something similar at the end of a bow and arrow within Rolland's mind eye - and any chance of mercy became an afterthought. Sensing his opponent's momentary distraction, LeClerc made a quick movement to his left, hoping to avert Scott's blade.

BANG

A sudden pang of immense pain hit LeClerc squarely in the chest, stealing him of both breathe and balance before he fell forward into a sitting position on both knees. As the smoke cleared the French officer saw that the shot rang out from a concealed pistol Rolland must have been keeping hidden in the waistband behind his back. The shot was not meant as a fatality, both knew, but as a precursor of the thing to come. The thing Rolland knew he had to do in order to end all of this.

With the sunken eyes of a condemned man LeClerc looked up at Rolland in full surrender. Gone was the confident air of upper class sophistication he held on that fateful day when the Class of the Tiger arrived in Haiti. Shaking his head slightly, LeClerc pulled nervously at his tunic, hoping to see the extent of the wound and judge if it would heal within the short period of time he had before Rolland continued his assault. As it was, Charles LeClerc, General of the French occupying forces on the island of Haiti, never saw the tip of Scott's blade as it plunged deep into the middle of his throat, twisted, and stayed there, half propped up by Rolland's hand holding the dying man's hair until the life within his Earthly vessel expired and he was no more. With surprising ease Rolland cut the muscle and sinew until his knife was clean through. Fighting back both tears, and the urge to

vomit, Rolland stood and held LeClerc's lifeless head by the hair
as the crackling of fires, dying men's moans, and other sounds of
a fresh battlefield filled the air around them.

With less enthusiasm than he had for any task in his entire
life Rolland half tossed, half dropped LeClerc's head onto the
blood stained battlefield before watching it roll slowly down the
incline. When it reached the bottom it almost leapt off into the
dark abyss below. A faint, yet distinctive splash told Rolland that
the ordeal, no matter how tiresome and trying, was finally over.
LeClerc's reign of terror was done. The wrenching feeling in his
stomach made him throw up, and as his body lurched forward
he lost control of himself for a moment, letting the tears come,
though silent in their arrival. His side had won, but at what cost?
Dodger was still dead. Victor was still ten years older than he
was supposed to be, and not any better off for it. Add to it,
the lows that Rolland had sunk to in the last few minutes, the
summation of which made Rolland feel as unlike himself as he
ever had before. Yet in these thoughts, himself almost despis-
ing, Rolland Wright remembered his first day of basic individual
training with Captain Nareau. He remembered the centaur and
the long-winded speech on the responsibilities of taking a life...
another life. LeClerc joined a short, exclusive list that had but one
other member; Puck.

"It had to be done," Rolland said aloud to himself as he gazed
out into the ocean and wondered, one last time, if LeClerc's head
would spend eternity attempting, in vain, to regenerate. There
is a difference between knowing right from wrong and actively
encouraging one over the other. But within his heart of hearts,
deep down in a vault of secrets he would never share with anyone
else, Rolland hoped that yes, part of LeClerc was alive enough to
spend eternity attempting to reconnect with something he had
lost. Something special to him that would never be found.

Chapter 27:
What Defines Us

Tina awoke shortly after being unceremoniously dropped against a tall tree in a grassy clearing by her twin brother Timothy. The spot was secluded yet close enough to the coast to where Timothy could hear the waves of the ocean splashing against the rocks. Still rattled from his confrontation with Rolland, and genuinely wishing that his fellow cadet would perish in the confrontation with the French, Timothy cared little for following Rolland's instructions very well. His shirt was stained now with day of sweat, as were his boxer shorts. He wanted nothing but to go home and take a long hot shower. Timothy closed his eyes, content.

Stirring, Tina groggily asked for several things in her confused state. The responses she received from Timothy were short, curt, and she did not know what she had done to deserve his ire. Following a copious amount of rubbing her eyes she sat up, surveyed her surroundings, and after seeing only herself and her brother began to prepare a verbal line of questioning for Timothy that would never come to fruition. For no sooner had

Tina stood upon her wobbly legs than she too heard the noise coming from the nearby tree line that her twin was already staring at. Images of beasts both great and small flashed through Tina's mind, ending in C de Baca's transformed state bursting through the trees to... do what, exactly? Someone had cried out very near to the spot where she stood, just before the sharp pain the back of her head that made everything a blur, and she went to sleep. No. Not sleep. She had been attacked, and worse, from behind in a cowardly flee of retreat. Worrying for a moment that LeClerc might be getting away she dismissed the notion as absurd, especially with her friends standing in the way. No. Tina reminded herself that she was not remembering the facts. The last thing she remembered was a voice ordering her brother to carry her away while...

"I sense a great deal of confusion," Turtledove stated as he suddenly glided into the clearing with a half smile. Immediately thankful that these two were alive, the old man thought of how tough and full of potential the two Holmes children were, even Timothy. His skin tingled with the familiar sense of angst that came after a battle and loss of life. Unsure which one of the Holmes children was releasing it, due to both their close physical proximity, and their shared genetics as twins, he decided to assume it was both. Though Turtledove was relieved to see two of his students alive, the leader of the Knights of Time saw no one else, and merely did his best to not only don a happy face and attitude, but also project it to the others as well. "Are you both well?"

It was this more than anything that bothered Tina, for she could sense the lie somehow, as if Turtledove's subtle forms of manipulation were beginning to wane on her as time went on. They both nodded enthusiastically, though Tina could tell Timothy was faking it as well, and for the first time, found herself siding with her parents' views on Marcus L. Turtledove. This realization changed him in Tina's mind, making Marcus Turtledove less revered and more human. But it was almost disrespectful, the way believed her to be stupid and susceptible to his simple tricks. No sooner had Tina begun to delve into this then the strange sound of birds flocking away from their location signaled the preamble to the arrival of another one of their teammates.

Rocketing into the clearing came Jaime, whose trail of destruction through the field leading to their location was nearly as bad as the one Timothy had left in dragging his sister there. To the untrained, fleeing French eye a grouping of broken branches and smashed leaves would appear inconsequential; but if LeClerc had succeeded on the beach, then his skill set would make quick use of Jaime's trail to find the others. Happy to see the others Jaime exchanged pleasantries before looking to Turtledove for an update on the others. This action became a bit repetitive as Hannah, Kniff, and Gwendolyn made their way likewise into the clearing for safety.

Tiikeri, still spry, took the low point as Gwendolyn went high to secure the perimeter as they waited for any sign of those who had stayed on the peninsula the longest. When none came they returned to their friends and the hollow thought that if Rolland were or Victor were dead, then their sacrifice in coming to Haiti, that Dodger's sacrifice would be in vain. It was time now to figure out what they would do if Rolland, their only way in and out of Eden, might not be coming back. Despite their unanimous silence, the thought bubbled beneath the surface of every one of their minds. The only question was, which one of them would bring up their predicament first.

"Damn it, Rolland Wright," Tina whispered to while gazing at the morning haze burning away into the afternoon sun. "Where are you?"

The mentality of a person who has just committed the act of murder is one of a dual spirit. On one hand the individual might feel vindicated in some way, as if their action was done for the greater good, or justified by some cosmic scale. This sense of self-adulation is counterpointed by the crippling, almost psyche crushing guilt of knowing that you are only able to take your next breath because you decided another man wouldn't be able to. This toxic combination of cat and mouse somersaulted through Rolland's head as he made his way away from the body littered piles of death and destruction on the Haitian peninsula. Yet the stark sight of a distinct lack of Haitian rebel bodies actually made Rolland smirk a bit, and ponder Hannah's effectiveness as a member of his team.

Rolland walked along, adrift in his own thoughts, until the smoke from the beach behind him was no longer haunting his eyes, only his nostrils. The path inland was littered with weapons, and blood. There was a loose plan in his mind to begin walking toward the designated rendezvous point where he could find Tina and the others; but somehow he did not feel as though he could join them quite yet. Without realizing it, he had wandered near the seaside dock where Kniff had commandeered nearly all of the French ships fit for sail upon the sea. One ship, a smaller vessel, more comparable to a schooner than a full-sized ship, had been left behind. Watching it, Rolland saw that its decks gave life to a multitude of hustle and bustle from multiple French soldiers, their dumb looking white uniforms still crisp from the inaction of battle. Flashes of LeClerc's blood-stained uniform shot through his mind life a bolt of lightning, quick and unforgiving, before disappearing without a trace left of its majesty upon the proverbial heaves of Rolland's mind. Wearing the shame he felt on his sleeve, Rolland thought of the best way to approach the situation, his quota for bloodshed spent on the days previous task. But it hurt to think.

Taking several steps backward until he was a safe distance away Rolland watched the unguarded dock with great interest for several long minutes. Captain Lavre was the commanding officer, directing all of the action with his stout sense of authority. The portly officer barked orders to the seven or so Frenchmen as they scurried to do his bidding. Shaking his head Rolland turned around and walked for what felt like a good half of an hour in silence, save for the sound of his feet moving against the ground. In reality it was but five minutes. It was not until Rolland came to a particularly odd looking hedge, one in which was bent inward toward the top, like someone very tall was holding it to shield themselves from sight. Eyeing it suspiciously, Rolland approached with less caution than he should have given the circumstances. He offered a cautious, "Hello?"

"Rolland!" said a deep but quiet voice that came from behind the patch of tall grass and overgrown trees. Rolland immediately recognized that it belonged to C de Baca, who was holding the unconscious Victor up as best as he could. With his other hand the giant of a man let go of the top of the hedge, which was indeed being held to hide their location from passing French soldiers. Rolland rushed over to them before scooping up Victor's free side onto his own shoulder, immediately feeling the massive weight of his unconscious friend. With a quick look to C de Baca for confirmation Rolland nodded his head back in the direction he had come, back to the rendezvous point, and with a nod the two set off, slowly, but surely, through the island's many fields of four-foot tall grass. Making their way toward the port-side docks where Captain Lavre made his escape, Rolland and C de Baca crouched low while ducking, and running as fast as they could with Victor's unconscious, nearly seven foot tall body dragging between them. Every couple of feet Victor would stir a bit, and once Rolland even thought he saw his friend open his eyes slightly, only to close them and begin his loud, yet oddly comforting, snoring routine.

Victor's snoring, a noise which is not found in any form of nature, immediately alerted all eight of the remaining French troops to their presence. At first they were cautious, fearing the appearance of C de Baca in his beastly form. Yet when no sight of wings or claws appeared on the horizon, and each Frenchmen remembered that they were armed, the mental switch of aggression flipped before they collectively made their pursuit. A fever of French shouts and footsteps from heavy boots came running along the wooden dock, rifles drawn, as they made their way toward the company of rebels hidden in the tall grass. Running as fast as they could to the left the three found shelter behind a large overturned wooden wagon beside a boulder. The space, although technically big enough for the three of them, was anything but comfortable given Victor's enormous, unconscious girth. Spotting a discarded French pistol inside the wagon, C de Baca grabbed it with his free hand, and without saying a word to Rolland, returned fire on the advancing French officers.

"What are you doing? We can't fight them all!" Rolland shouted while simultaneously attempting to untangle his arms from Victor. If he could just slow time a bit, then perhaps he could defuse the situation.

Tilting his head slightly, as if Rolland had suddenly become an odd-looking bug, C de Baca spoke in a definitive tone. "Don't we have to try?"

Rolland thought for a moment, taking in C de Baca's words. Their mission was to retrieve Victor, which he had done, and that was contingent upon stopping the French invasion of Haiti, which was down to less than a dozen soldiers and a portly, cowardly officer. Guessing these invaders to be rather uncoordinated under Lavre's leadership, Rolland did not believe that they posed much of a threat, despite their gunfire and superior numbers. Never once had he stepped outside himself, never once had Rolland stopped to think that perhaps his mission was different from C de Baca's mission, or even Victor's mission for that matter. "Let's just move elsewhere, alright? We have to get Victor out of here!"

Still eyeing Rolland curiously, C de Baca reluctantly dropped the pistol before recommitting himself to supporting Victor's weight, and moving onward with Rolland, past the point where the French planned to meet. Crouching low to avoid detection, they moved swiftly yet were seen by only one rogue French soldier who broke from formation to pursue them. Without missing a beat C de Baca dropped his side of Victor, took four mighty steps, and close-lined the soldier by extending his arm straight outward seconds before the soldiers' chin was to meet with it. Due to the way the Frenchmen's head bounced off the ground, his neck had probably been snapped, killing him instantly. The move was so clean, so efficient that it reminded Rolland of the wrestler Paul Levesque in the ring; graceful, yet deadly. A fresh wave of awe coursed through him as he watched the man, not the monster, turn back around to face his allies.

Re-joining Rolland, C de Baca helped him westward a few hundred yards until they came to a hill where they would be forced to climb in order to pass. With a nod of his head upward Rolland caught C de Baca's eye before looking toward the hill and silently asking if they should proceed. Looking past him, C de Baca slowly shook his head 'no' before tilting it upward a bit to signal a silent 'look' request. There, outflanking their company of rebels, six French officers rode in on horseback from above, over the hill, coming down on their location fast. Panicked, Rolland looked around furiously for a way out but found only one. A madcap, Hail Mary, bum rush of the inner perimeter of the French line to force their way clean through to the ocean. It was crazy, and a bit suicidal, but it was possible. Otherwise...

They were trapped.

Then it hit Rolland like a ton of bricks - the logic of the situation. So transfixed had he been in focusing on the variables surrounding rescuing Victor, the battle on the beach, and even Timothy violating Tina that he had nearly forgotten the ONE thing that he had known all along; the history of Haitian independence. Going over the events he remembered in his mind the endgame formed a picture that sounded uncomfortably familiar. There was a great battle where the French were defeated, but only at the cost of the Haitian leaders life. "But that would mean..."

Rolland's words, stated out loud without intention, were the first spoken from himself to C de Baca since he had requested that they NOT fight the French. Their context was perplexing, adding to the growing discontent within C de Baca. "Speak plainly, Rolland Wright. We do not have much time."

"You're right, I'm sorry," Rolland said, his manners moving faster than his brain. "We are from another time, remember?"

"Yes, you and the general said as much during the meeting," C de Baca said, remembering the multitude of questions he held that than none of their party would answer. "What does that have to do with our current situation?"

"This has already happened," stated Rolland, looking up at the French officers on horseback again as they sat in idol judgment. Even in defeat they seemed pompous and arrogant. He had little doubt that the remaining French would attempt a measure of retribution on them if caught, but he had no intention of giving them the satisfaction. "I already know how this ends. We've known all along, even though I guess no one wanted to admit it. Victor, Toussaint, or whatever, he gets taken on that ship by Captain Lavre and he, well, he dies on the way to France to stand trial."

The news did not faze C de Baca the way Rolland had anticipated, as the Aztec warrior of old betrayed not a muscle in his response. "That is unacceptable."

"I don't want to kill anyone else," the words escaped Rolland's lips, landing squarely upon C de Baca like they were meant to be there all along.

"Neither do I," C de Baca retorted with the utmost sincerity. It was clear that whatever actions they took, it would be them doing it, not the beast. Never again would the beast decide.

"Right," Rolland answered, the anxiety building in his stomach as the seconds ticked by. He knew that even if he could slow time down around them, leaving them time enough to escape, it still would not give them the time needed to move Victor uninhibited. "I do have a terrible plan, if that helps matters."

"What is it?" C de Baca asked, re-positioning Victor in case he needed to change forms. Even thinking upon the change, both physical, and mental, gave C de Baca the tense, uneasy feeling of shame and impending regret. "Quickly!"

"Well," Rolland began, looking past C de Baca for a moment before drawing in a large breath and continuing on. "I slow-down time, go get that large wheelbarrow we ran by back there, all while not getting shot. Then you and I would throw Victor into it, bum rush through the weak point in the French defenses, still while not getting shot, and keep running until we hit the beach. From there we basically haul ass to the rendezvous point."

Nodding his head slowly C de Baca watched as the first two of the six French officers on horseback began to make their way down the steep hill toward them. The Aztec warrior again played with his leather gauntlet, untethering and tethering the leather string that tied it into place. Rolland watched this, and for a moment, thought of what Dodger would make of such a quirky habit being displayed by such a hard ass. Because of the severity of the situation, or in spite of it, Rolland felt oddly uncomfortable, almost as if his skin was crawling. It was then when the sobering realization hit him.

"This won't work!" Rolland exclaimed, grabbing C de Baca's shoulder without thinking. Though he quickly realized his error when the man beast's eyes began to glow red, the impetuous leader of his class never loosened his resolve, only his grasp. "We can't escape!"

"And why not?" C de Baca asked, a bit of smoke escaping from his left nostril.

"Because that's not the way that it works." Rolland said, his squatting position turning into a full on sit with both legs stretched out in front of his like a large letter V. "History cannot be changed. Whatever originally happened has to happen again."

"Or else what?" C de Baca asked, he too finally calming down from the post battle adrenaline high.

"Or else the Time Stream will self correct," Rolland said, meeting C de Baca dead in the eyes to convey complete honesty. "Toussaint has to die on that ship or history as we know it can be changed forever, and I do not know what that will mean."

Sitting down next to Rolland, leaving Victor's weight entirely for Rolland to take on himself, C de Baca donned a posture reminiscent of the masterpiece known as 'The Thinker'. He stared off into the sea of carnage that surrounded them before stating, " I will take his place."

"What?" Rolland asked, sweat forming upon his brow as the third and forth Frenchmen on horseback followed their fellows. All of them had golden sabers fastened to their belts that bobbed off the sides of their horses and glistened in the sunlight.

"Can I trust you with my final request?" C de Baca asked suddenly, still refusing to look at Rolland. " I have a living son, Rolland Wright. He is much like me in that he too is an outcast. I bedded his mother shortly before she was sold up North into your United States."

"Why are you telling me this?" Rolland asked as the fifth and sixth horsemen followed the line of the others. As the first horse found its way toward the bottom of the hill, its rider drew his saber before raising it high and crying out in his native tongue.

"Because I want you to take him, take the man you call Victor, the man that I called General for so long. Take him and keep him well. I am spent, Rolland Wright. I am old and feel it in my bones. What I am not, however, is a bad parent. Not to my last remaining child. He lives in the land of New Jersey, and I hope against hope that someday you will find him. Promise me this, Rolland Wright, promise me that you will find him."

"I-" Rolland began, completely taken aback by the change of subject. "I don't know. I mean I-"

"You are the one, the only one who can do this. Only you can save my son," C de Baca stated. "For this I will grant both you and our mutual friend here, your lives."

"Ok," Rolland said without thinking, almost as if his mouth had decided for him. Flabbergasted, Rolland watched as C de Baca stood, ran over to the wheelbarrow near the boulder, flipped it over, wheeled it back to them, and helped him place Victor inside. Then, without another word, he took one half of the wooden poles that pushed the device and pushed, refusing Rolland's help what so ever. He thought of what it was C de Baca was offering to do, and on the conditions he himself had to agree to. Could he abide by this? Looking at the man he had come to know as both trustworthy and dependable, Rolland could not bear the thought of another death on his conscious. "You can't do this."

"Go," C de Baca said under his breath. His voice was low, his eyes cast downward, and his hands balled up in determined fists of acceptance. "Go now."

"Fuck that," Rolland retorted. " I won't leave you."

Without saying another word C de Baca stretched out his left hand, grasping Rolland by the back of his denim jeans, lifted him up nearly a foot off of the ground, and tossed him as easily as an adult would a doll before screaming, "Now!"

After his unexpected flight, and subsequent landing amongst a pile of ash that he assumed used to be a large tent, Rolland was feeling anything but cooperative. Unluckily for him, C de Baca was quick in his response time as well, seemingly gliding past the distance between them and standing upright, his back as rigid as the day is long, when Rolland finally made it to his own feet.

"You will take your people, take the one you call Victor, and leave, now!" C de Baca ordered Rolland, before turning around to job the short distance back to the dock. Bullets from French rifles fired at C de Baca as he went along, though none found their mark. Arriving at the gate outside of the ship he was greeted at gunpoint by the last remaining five officers under Lavre's command, all of who instantly both recognized, and feared the man they had all come to associate with a quick and painful death.

"Lavre!" C de Baca screamed after the French Captain and last surviving officer he knew of left on the island. "I, Toussaint L 'Overture, surrender!"

Not moments later nearly two beady little brown eyes attached to a stout body came peeking out of the ship's hull, onto the deck, down the ramp, and up to C de Baca. His initial thought being that Lavre's pace was as slow as his wit, C de Baca saw numerous opportunities to lose his cool and kill them all. Swallowing his pride for the sake of his friend and commanding officer, he chose instead the path of least resistance. Fiddling with the fringe of his leather gauntlet, he accidentally pulled when he should have pushed, and the string came spilling out, loosening the garment greatly.

"You?" Lt. Lavre asked, eyeing C de Baca up and down like one would a prized animal, checking for something he had not previously seen. "You are not L 'Overture! Have your forgotten your tenure with our army? You're just some rebel wretch, I was there when you were captured!"

Breathing in deeply, his lungs filling with the sickly sweet mixture of early morning air and freshly spilt blood, C de Baca choose his fate one final time. "I kept my identity a secret in the hopes that as a ordinary prisoner I could glean information to take back to my army when I escaped from your camp. The man on the battlefield today was a decoy, a good friend who took my name to protect me and protect our cause, which I know now is lost."

His eyes wary Lt. Lavre stared at C de Baca for a long moment. Even if this man were not the real Toussaint, no one would have to know the truth and he, Lavre, would be hailed a hero. He thought for another minute before ordering his men to seize the rebel.

Rolland watched from afar as the French soldiers came at C de Baca all at once, nearly throwing themselves on top of him until his hands and legs were clasped in chains. They were rough, so rough in fact that the left leather gauntlet, the treasured possession that was both a blessing, and a curse, slipped off of its long time owner's arm and fell onto the wooden deck below.

Suddenly, C de Baca let out a booming laugh that continued as he was carried further away from his enchanted coverings and further away from life as he knew it. With death all but a foregone conclusion, the old warrior thought back on the centuries he had spent upon the Earth, and wept silently for everything he had not done. A Frenchman picked up the gauntlet and examined it for a moment before tossing it into the water. Rolland would never forget the laugh of the condemned man who had sacrificed himself for Victor and himself. It was a deep laugh, resonant, and full of an unadulterated wisdom that boasted gleefully that this; this life and everything in it was nothing but one big elaborate joke on the user.

"Fear not," Gwendolyn said to Tina, despite the panic bordering on electricity charging through her body. While Tina could not feel this biological display stemming from her teammate, she did sense that something was amiss. Days later, once Tina saw both Victor and Gwendolyn holding hands for the first time, she would recall this moment when the two women locked eyes in the Haiti as the moment their friendship truly began. "I believe them to be alive, Tina Holmes. Both he and Victor."

"I hope you're right," Tina said before releasing a sudden cry of relief as she spied her boyfriend trudging up the trail toward them straining with the effort of pushing Victor's unconscious body in the wheelbarrow. Leading the charge she greeted Rolland with a large, open armed hug that he only slightly returned.

"Thanks darlin'," Rolland said half heartedly, his mind still reeling from the guilt of taking yet another life in the heat of battle.

"What did you do?" Kniff asked, shouldering his rifle and motioning to Victor.

"Something reckless," Rolland said. Though plagued with guilt he knew that showing it at that juncture would only spell doom for their nearly complete mission. "Is everyone accounted for?"

"Everyone but you, Victor and C de Baca," replied Tina, her eyebrows rising in anxious fear. "Where is he? We thought he was with you."

Looking into Tina's eyes Rolland knew there was no way he could either lie, or do a sufficient enough job of telling her what he believed to be the truth. In the end he ended up merely shaking his head at her and hoping that she would accept that as enough. She placed a hand on his shoulder before they went their separate ways; she to tend to Victor and he to discuss the next step with Turtledove. Rolland told Turtledove everything, detail by painful detail. Despite his ache at what he knew Rolland must be feeling, Marcus Turtledove set about the task of righting his group and returning them all to Eden. His frustrations themselves, manifested themselves in the rope binding Dodger's body.

Doing as he was told, and doing it quickly, Rolland gathered every other traveler he could find before booking it toward the spot where they had initially arrived. All save one traveler, the fallen companion, that Turtledove himself went to fetch. Walking back with the body of Stewart Yick, tucked neatly in sheets of linen and rope, tied around the body's arms, head, and ankles to keep them in place while rigor mortis set in. The leader of the Knights of Time passed by Rolland, the stench of death and decay stronger than the teenager was prepared for, before Turtledove proceeded to place the bundle on the ground reverently near their exit point. The scene gave Rolland a lurching feeling, not dissimilar to a dry heave, as the entirety of the past few days stuck him in relation to the implications for the future. Deciding at once not to think about this, or anything else which might lead him back to an Eden jail cell, Rolland focused instead on the first step; getting them all back. While his previous attempt at returning to Eden took some help from Turtledove, this one felt easier, more natural somehow. With complete focus Rolland closed his eyes, cleared his mind, and thought of nothing but his objective, clear, and true.

BANG

Springing to life like a spark came a clear ripple of time as it fluctuated around itself in a counter-clockwise motion before the crowd of travelers. A widening gap in the middle, filled with white and purple light shown through clearly, beckoning onlookers inside as it became large enough to accommodate each while standing. Rolland could feel it, feel its power as it coursed through his veins. But he wouldn't admit that to himself. Not for many battles to come. Attributing it instead to the adrenaline to his time in Haiti, Rolland worked up the nerve to actually open his eyes following the opening of the passage. Deciding to do just as he had in Florida, Rolland surveyed the scene, and retaining early 19th century Haiti to his memory one last time. The water hitting the shore in the distance looked black with debris from the battle and the air smelled of a mixture of blood, gunpowder, fish, and death.

Death. Rolland knew that once they arrived in Eden he would be the one who would take Dodger's body back into Eden Town Proper. He knew that he, perhaps along with Turtledove, would be the one to inform Councilman Joseph Yick that his only living relative, his grandson, was now at peace with the rest of their family. So deep in thought was Rolland that he barely noticed when Tina joined him, taking him silently by the hand.

The pain in Rolland's chest was so severe that it bordered on the memory of being shot with an arrow on the beaches of Pensacola. All at once panic filled his mind, heart, shoulders and knees as the thought of not only traveling through the portal he had just made, but also once again taking responsibility for the safety of his classmates, Turtledove, Victor, and Tina. Tina, whose sweet innocence left no thought in her mind as to her brother's true intentions toward her. Tina, who had come to trust and believe in him so much. He squeezed her hand tightly and led her to the portal.

"Geronimo..." Rolland shouted, leaping forward into the Time Stream, one hand extended outward for navigation, the other clasped tightly to Tina's hand, creating a chain that held the other eight people in their party, along with Dodger's wrapped body, and the tiger cub, Tiikeri.

Upon entering the time stream, the first thing Rolland noticed was that his light-headedness went away immediately. As if someone had removed a blindfold from his eyes, Rolland now clearly saw the beautifully ornate tunnel of transforming colors as they meshed into one another. Gossamer and scarlet hues cascading into memories of colors long forgotten to mortal eyes showed the way back, back to Eden, back to wherever it was Rolland wanted to go. As if he was sitting back in the driver's seat of his Cadillac El Dorado once again; Rolland knew that he was in complete control of their destination. Smiling, the revelation came with a high that was quickly followed by a low of the oddest variety.

It was then that Rolland saw something strange, something he was, and never would be, sure if it was real or imagined. There, amongst the sea of beautiful colors and tapestry of elegance was the outline of what appeared to be two men standing back to back as they zigged and zagged in an unnerving pattern that left the tunnel opposite the one Rolland was traveling. Thinking to call out to them Rolland was extended his right hand in a 'stop' motion, but his words never left his tongue. Furrowing his brow, Rolland simultaneously struggled to create noise of any sort, and attempt to comprehend the streaking bits of white and black that flashed past the two men, almost as if it was hunting them. Then - the pain came.

A searing, white-hot burning behind his eyes gave Rolland immediate reason to pause. He cried out, but again no sound came. Instead a voice that was distinctly not his own filled his ears with foreboding words that spelled his doom.

'You did not heed my warning, Rolland Wright,' said a voice from beyond the void that was the Time Stream. Knowing immediately that it was Anake, the Time Stream itself, Rolland at first choose purposefully to ignore it, searing pain be damned. With the weight of responsibility of handing out life or death to those he surrounded himself with was bad enough without the gloating of a supernatural, metaphysical, entity.

'I will not warn you again...'

Chapter 28:
Join or Die

The call came later than expected. Although Councilman Anthony Varejao was unclear as to exactly how Rolland Wright was able to manipulate the Time Stream, he knew the boy was powerful, possibly the most powerful being to ever set foot in Eden. There had been no sign of Wright or the others anywhere outside of the academy for days, but Varejao had placed a scout outside of the Academy and the Halls of Time to alert him immediately when the little bastard left. The unpredictability of Rolland and his abilities were the last in a series of variables that the Councilman had sifted through to set the deck exactly as he wanted it for his ultimate plans. The boy had managed to worm his way out of the Florida incident and Eden Prison where Varejao had hoped he would rot. He grew giddy at the thought of catching Rolland in another act of manipulating the Time Stream but first he must deal with the task at hand. He pushed thoughts of Wright aside as he faced what was to come tonight. This night was the one he had been both dreading and looking forward to for months.

After locking the door of the office, Anthony Varejao walked the short distance to the middle of the three large bookshelves that stood behind his desk. Kicking his chair to the side, he scanned the shelves until he found the tome he sought easily within the alphabetized shelf. As he gently pulled out *A Connecticut Yankee in King Arthur's Court* by Mark Twain a soft clicking sound was heard. The action caused the entire bookcase to move outward, revealing a trapdoor that allowed the entire shelf to be supported by its left hinges. Turning around, the councilman opened the bottom left drawer in his oak desk and retrieved a long black flashlight that he immediately clicked on via the button atop its smooth shaft. He then turned, breathed deeply, and made his way into the catacombs of the Eden courthouse.

As Anthony Varejao entered the dark passageway and began descending down the steps, he felt a deep sense of apprehension, even though he had used this passageway dozens of times throughout his tenure on the Council of Light. A German born architect had designed the tunnel following the passage of Eden's Sapien Act, before passing on the knowledge to none but those who served more than one term on the council itself. The man was concerned about a potential Elemeno uprising following the legislation and built the tunnel with a quick escape in mind. Although he appreciated the man's ingenuity, Anthony yearned for fresh air, increasing his pace down the stairway as the minutes lingered on his mind. Finally, the passage gave way to a steel door, which he opened with great effort.

"That was easier when I was younger," Councilman Varejao said aloud to himself as he stepped out into the fresh Eden air.

The tunnel had taken him from his office, through the city, and out near the main entrance to Eden Town Proper. To his left Anthony could see the sentry, Michael, on duty for the evening. This was Anthony's favorite time of day, a thought that brought a smile to his face as he took out his cellular phone and proceeded to text an unsaved phone number.

'GO'

Setting out on foot the Councilman walked the path with the apprehension he had felt all night and hoped that finding the car would alleviate his nervousness. The vehicle, hidden behind a thicket of fallen logs and tall grass, was an older model Rip-Rora that Anthony suspected hadn't been used in decades. Yet the message had him it would work and had told Anthony where to find the keys. After brushing aside a few leaves and insects he unlocked the driver's side door and sat down behind the wheel. Upon retrieving the keys under the driver's side seat, he began surveying the inside of the vehicle. The gasoline gauge read exactly one quarter of a tank full, the perfect amount for Anthony's plans. Putting the keys in the ignition, the Rip-Rora roared to life, lifting off the ground smoothly and the engine purring softly. Eying the compass on the dashboard, Varejao saw that it pointed south. Turning the steering wheel to the right slightly until the small "S" turned into a "W," Varejao stepped on the gas with mild enthusiasm.

The councilman sped along onward for nearly four miles, passing through the back entrance to Eden Town Proper into the wide open fields that held the Blackard Family Orchard and the Academy of Light. Multiple villages speckled the green valleys and lush landscapes he flew over, giving the impression that they were very close, even if they were in actuality quite far away. The Eden hillside beyond the Academy of Light was vast in its grassy valleys and hills before hitting the dense oak trees that comprised the Solomon Forest. This dense, lush vegetation went on as far as anyone, human or Elemeno, could know, just like the Time Stream itself. The sheer vastness made him wonder if he should keep going, yet onward he went, along places few had been for many years, if ever. Rangers and the occasional adventure types would make the this trek every now and then, but few had reason to seek this far off the beaten path on the outskirts of the Time Stream, or the odd, crudely constructed bridge that reached across it like an arch.

As Varejao brought the Rip-Rora to a halt, he was immediately met with a cacophony of sounds seemingly coming from the Time Stream itself. Nearby a rustling from what Anthony assumed to be a deer fleeing gave way into the night as it mixed with the other sounds of disturbed nature, angry and alive. It sounded like thunder bellowing, prompting Varejao to get out of the vehicle. The sky around the area became cloudy overhead, blotting out the night stars that had shown the way to the otherwise peaceful area.

Without warning, an immensely powerful beam of light from inside the Time Stream burst forth toward Varejao, propelled by intense upward momentum and delivering with it a giant cylindrically shaped object that stood nearly seven feet tall. It shot upward before landing somewhat gently on the archway above the Time Stream, retracted upon itself, and revealed two men; Rudolph Hess and the assassin Nero. Both men were ragged, their clothes torn and faces drawn in a defensive posture. Each sported at least one long set of claw marks on their person. They looked around for a moment before spying Varejao, who breathed a sigh of relief as he approached the men with a cautious optimism. When he was close enough, he noticed that neither of the men looked apprehensive, but instead rather appeared mystified by their surroundings to the point of carelessness.

"How is this possible?" Hess asked in his heavy German accent, utterly confused at finding himself in the one place he never dreamed he would be allowed entrance; Eden.

"You will find, Mr. Hess, that a great many things are possible when you know the right people," Varejao said, a smug resolve washing over his overly stretched facade.

"And you are?" Hess asked, his left hand sliding gingerly toward the sidearm he had lodged in the small of his back. The weapon was of cold comfort.

"The right people," stated Varejao coyly, "Allow me to introduce myself gentlemen; Councilman Anthony Varejao."

The revelation of the name in the clandestine meeting gave way to a rustling in the nearby woods, causing both sides to wonder if their mutual destruction was momentarily at hand. It would have been foolish to think that anyone would venture so far out into the Eden wilderness, but then again, it would be a foolish bet that these two would ever normally cross paths. After a long moment the two men returned the odd sense of hospitality they were being shown, albeit devoid of any compassion what-so-ever.

"Rudolph Hess," the Nazi responded before looking to Nero, who grunted, turned around, and unceremoniously dived head first off of the archway into the Time Stream. At this Varejao let out a small, but noticeable gasp that amused Hess enough to comment. "Do not worry about him. This is how he acts naturally. The snake is a solitary animal, you see."

"Indeed," Varejao agreed, suddenly wary. Perhaps this wasn't a good idea.

"I must admit to being impressed by your..." Hess began, his voice dripping with derision. "Confidence. You obviously seem to know who we are, even expected us to be here. My question is, how?"

Anthony Varejao felt the heat rising in both of his cheeks and a fresh band of sweat forming on his forehead. Betrayed by his nerves the councilman knew that he had better speak fast if he hoped to accomplish anything of merit during this meeting, or even establish the chance for another. With a raspy throat and shaky hand he began to speak. "I-"

"What I also suspect is that you share a relationship with a certain…. individual shall we say, the same individual that my associate and myself are working for," Hess said, continuing as if Varejao had not even spoken.

"You suspect many things, so it would seem," Varejao stated, regaining his confidence. The reaction was delayed, yes, but he felt comfortable enough with it for his cheeks to return to their normal shade. "I work only for myself."

Hess smiled thinly at this proclamation as he proceeded to light a cigarette while eyeing the Councilman Varejao down like a jackal would a helpless doe. Hungry.

"Vhat is it you what?"

"Rest assured, Mr. Hess," Varejao said briskly. "That what I want is something that you yourself also want. To put it bluntly, I mean to overthrow the Council of Light, disband the governing bodies of Eden, and segregate a large majority of the planet's regions into quadrants with Governors who oversee Vilthe's rule of law in exchange for riches beyond measure."

"And where would I fit into your new vision for Eden?" Hess asked sharply, cutting right to the bone of their main issue. Despite the bit of spittle that came jettisoning out of the German's mouth at this accusatory line, Varejao remained still, almost stoic in his physical response. "Would I presume correctly that you would offer me, what did you call it, *das* Governorship? In exchange for all of my assistance for putting you into power?"

"No," Varejao said without moving. For the first time in their meeting Hess noticed the age lines that marked the Edenite's face. "Though you would be free to command the Governors as you wish. Thus would be your prerogative as my second in command. This is what I am offering you, *Herr* Hess."

This prompted a lingering laugh from Hess that carried loudly through the trees to the ears of another person. Lying in a The originator of the noise that garnered the attention of Hess, Nero, and Varejao kept as low and silent as he possibly could, knowing it could mean his death if he was discovered. Well within earshot of the clandestine meeting camped the intrepid reporter Brad Burkhart, who despite being on a holiday from his regular duties, found himself lying in a large dirt hole, playing dead. Normally Brad found leisure in the seclusion of the woods, especially the remote spots. He had taken women he was seeing out there, even brought a tent along so that they could visit his favorite spots overnight, but none of them appreciated the seclusion and one-ness with nature that Brad found there.

To Brad, nature was like a childhood pet. A wild, ever-changing animal that was never quite the same in reality as it was within one[s mind. Dangerous to the stranger, useful to the master - the alpha of their pack. They knew the rules. He had always followed the rules, always left a note detailing where he was going so that he could do everything to avoid unnecessary danger. But tonight he had found the danger he had evaded as it happened upon a small clearing through the vegetation that gave him a clear view of just who it was meeting way out in the woods. What Brad saw astonished him.

There, standing in the middle of the forest was a real live Nazi speaking in what appeared to be friendly conversation with one of the most prominent political figures in all of Eden. Reaching for the cell phone in his right front pocket Brad opened up the video recorder application before hitting the round, red,

RECORD button and aiming the camera at the pair. The story would be huge if he could get it back to the station. In the meantime, all he had to do was not get caught.

"You speak of a utopia based upon what? One man's idea of what that should be. You have no sense of communal good, or superior race. I've heard nothing of the betterment of your lands under your reigns, what makes me think that your image of the future is any better than Vilthe's? Or the Council of Light? Tell me, do you plan to totally betray your master, or only piss him off a little bit?" Hess asked, his resolve steelier than it had been since arriving.

"I dream of a future made in my image," Varejao said, pacing back and forth as his mind wandered to a yet unseen version of paradise.

"So my choice is that I join you, overthrow the Council of Light, and be the third most powerful man in the universe, or, what exactly? Die?" Hess asked, half genuinely curious, half disdainful at the prospect of meeting his end by such an unimpressive looking warrior.

"Yes, two options; either you join or you die," Varejao said smoothly, now firmly in control again.

"You will find, Councilman Varejao, that zhere are always more than two options in life," said Hess. "Almost all of them involve agendas from men like you."

"Men like me?" Varejao asked before being cut off.

"Narcissists," Hess said with a hiss that resembled his master's so perfectly that had Anthony Varejao's eyes been closed, he would have sworn it to be Vilthe himself.

"Call me what you will, but the fact remains that I plan to do what I plan to do for the greater good of our kind. The time for decisions is at hand wouldn't you agree? It is time to pick a side. Either way you, me, both of us will eventually be guilty of betrayl," Varejao offered.

"It is not betrayal!" Hess seethed before catching his own anger and bringing it back into check. The momentary dropping of his guard gave Varejao what he believed to be a peak beneath the armor of the former Nazi. But what he did not know, that Hess would never forget, was the old slogan that once you became a Nazi, you were a Nazi for life.

"Let us be honest. You're but a soft bureaucrat. Your kind isn't exactly known for being so domineering. The fuehrer one time even-" Hess said, but was cut off by a sudden lack of oxygen in both of his lungs. Both of his hands flew to his throat as Rudolph Hess felt the back of his throat close tightly upon itself, making future breathing impossible.

"One thing you'll find out about me, Mr. Hess, is that I am much more than just a bureaucrat," Varejao said, holding one hand out before snapping his fingers, seemingly returning the oxygen to Hess by way of the former Nazi's airways. "Now, will you really hear me out or not?"

With a stinging in his chest, and a thumping in his head, Rudolph Hess felt something that he had not felt in over a month; anger. Not since Alora's death had his mind wandered from anything but pity and self-loathing.

"Go on..."

"My sources tell me that you and your master took something recently that did not belong to you, is that correct?" Varejao asked, beginning to pace parallel to where Hess stood rooted to the spot on the wooden bridge.

"Yes," Hess uttered underneath his breath, the steady stream of building fury within him intensifying with each second he stood in the man's presence.

"A nuclear bomb, correct?" Varejao pressed.

When Hess did not respond, Varejao continued. "How does he plan to use it?"

"To celebrate his birthday." Hess offered with no remorse to his voice. He was growing tired of this game and wanted to leave.

"Fine," Varejao said, stopping his pace and looking Hess dead in the eye. "But when he does use it, make sure that he does it when a door to Eden is open."

"What?" Hess asked, genuinely surprised by this request.

"The doors to Eden, you know, the ones scattered across the planet Earth," Varejao said to Hess, piquing the man's curiosity. "If a doorway is open at the time of detonation, then Eden too will be affected by the blast if in proximity. If the doorway is closed, then it will not."

"And you want Eden destroyed? I thought you wanted to rule it for yourself." Hess asked Varejao suspiciously, his left eyebrow rising higher on his pale, skinny face.

"In order to build a paradise worth living in, we must first cleanse the garden of a few weeds." Varejao said in his oily voice.

Hess took a step backward on the bridge before turning away from the councilman. This time Varejao did not advance but waited silently as he watched the German stare into the Time Stream. Rudolph Hess thought on those words for several moments, battling back the bombarding memories that ravaged his violent mind. All the while the former Nazi's heart kept reminding his mind of the promise made to his sister, who he missed desperately. There on his left arm were the burns that would not heal. The burns inflicted by the same flames created by Judah Raines and Tina Holmes that had taken Alora's, his dear sweet sister, life.

"I shall consider it, *Herr* Varejao," Hess said softly, stepping back up onto the ramp above the gate to the Time Stream. "Strongly consider it."

Hidden amongst the brush, Brad Burkhart watched as the two concluded their business, hitting the END button on the recording option on his phone. Almost instinctively, he then proceeded to send the video file directly to his partner and fellow anchor, Jennifer Morrison. If anyone would know what to do with such a juicy tidbit of political dirt it would be her. The file took a few long moments to download to the message, and then twice as long to send. But send it did, with a timestamp to confirm the delivery. A silent smile of relief crossed Brad's lips as his attention was brought back to reality.

"I don't think you know what you're-" Varejao began but stopped speaking immediately after seeing the rising form of the assassin Nero as he emerged from the Time Stream, this time standing on a cylindrical podium type object. He landed behind the diminutive Nazi, offering him a quick exit without saying a word.

"Goodbye, councilman," Hess said, as he stepped upon the podium. The object they stood upon swirled counter clockwise into a myriad of color and sound once again before hovering over the lapping waters of the Time Stream. A slight pause, and then the podium dipped under the water, taking the two men with it. Before they were fully submerged Rudolph Hess called out, "You shall have my answer soon."

Brad observed this exchange in awed silence. After the Nazi and the Roman looking man disappeared, he watched as Varejao cursed to himself and then began walking away toward the broken down Rip-Rora that was parked nearby. Believing himself to be in the clear Brad took his phone and began to dial Jennifer's number to see if she had opened the video yet.

"Come on, Jen, pick up your phone," Brad Burkhart said to himself softly but impatiently while mentally preparing the tirade of words he planned to unleash on his co-anchor. This story was big, even as far as corruption stories go. Deciding this was too good to share over the phone anyway, Brad hit the end button before turning to leave. He had crept along a few feet, pocketing his phone as he went, before he heard the most terrifying thing that would ever befall his ears.

"Human," came a low, growl from the darkness of the trees. The tail made itself known before the rest of the beast, larger even for his breed than 98% of those who would ever live. The figure, a tall Elemeno with bright green fur covering his entire body save his eyes and nose, stepped forward out from the darkness of shadow into the sporadic moonlight in order to face his prey. He was wearing combat gear including what appeared to be a bulletproof vest. For a moment, Brad wanted to laugh aloud at the sight but he never got the chance.

Wasting no time the giant Elemeno pounced on Brad, launching himself nearly ten feet into the night sky before it landed on top of the now fleeing news anchor's back. Digging his claws into Brad's shoulders, the elemeno tore at the human flesh, then began using his fangs to rip at the back of Brad's neck until the tangy taste of blood drenched his lips. In a vain attempt to defend himself Brad batted at the beast with his hand to no avail, causing only a slight disruption in the attack. Brad knew that he had to do something. Deciding to go completely limp the reporter mimicked a tactic he had learned regarding bear attacks as a boy. It seemed to work as the giant Elemeno did let go of Brad, dropping him for a long moment but watching him warily. Believing himself to be smarter than the Elemeno,

Brad waited several long beats before slowly rolling onto his side, ignoring the pain in his gaping neck wound. Using his forearms to propel himself forward, Brad crawled away from his attacker, getting what he guessed to be at least fifty yards, and thinking that he was doing quite well for himself. Brad was quickly taught the folly of his assumptions, however, as his panicked crawling was halted when the Elemeno grabbed him roughly by the forearm without stopping its own forward momentum as it flew toward him.

Brad heard his arm snap before he cried out in pain, twisted free, the beast released him, and he fell the three feet to the ground with an unforgiving thud. Although Brad knew instinctively that his arm wouldn't work, Brad knew that his legs would carry him as far as they could, so he crawled out from under the beast, kicking him in the face as he went. He had a second to hear the see the hulking figure double over from the kick before he made a mad dash away from the trees.

Brad knew that he was fucked, but couldn't logically admit it to himself just yet. In his mad desperation for the next place to turn his uneasy legs, which found themselves instinctly pointing toward Eden. It was only then that Brad thought of the one lifeline he knew he still had within his power to call-upon. Literally.

The cell phone.

Fumbling with his pocket Brad removed the cell with a shaking right hand before turning it over and popping the battery out with more ease than he anticipated. He turned and threw the small object as far as he could before anticipating a noise to let him know that it had landed somewhere in the darkness. A noise did come, but from behind Brad, not in front of him. The loud stomping of the Elemeno gave no time for pause as it began to chase the reporter, falling onto its hind legs for added speed in its pursuit. Brad ran as fast as he could, thinking quickly about zigzagging patterns to slow the Elemeno's momentum, but all he managed was a weakly maneuvered turn around a rather large tree that gave him little choice but to turn. His end came when Brad forgot that his arm was broken, and, after realizing that he could not run any more, turned around to defend himself with the useless appendage.

The Elemeno was on him in a flash, knocking him hard to the ground and the breath from his lungs. Gasping for air, the familiar feelings of claws digging themselves into his skin made itself known in no less than eight different spots in Brad's torso. Reaching around him for something, anything, to help him escape Brad found a small, adult fist sized rock that he palmed with his right hand before bringing it down hard on the closest part of his attacker, the tip of his tail.

The giant Elemeno roared as he whirled around to catch Brad who was again to his feet in mid-run. Unfortunately the combination of catlike grip and fleeing fragility do not combine together well, and accidents happen. Thus was the case in the moments proceeding as the Elemeno reached out with both paws, latched onto both sides of Brad's head, and held on as he kept running; instantly breaking his neck.

Brad's body fell to the ground as soon as it was released, the life fleeing from its vessel as fast as it could under the circumstances. In a matter of seconds Brad Burkhart had gone from a living, breathing, human to nothing more than the monster's plaything. The thought brought a smile to the blood stained lips of the giant Elemeno, whose ears perked backward when he heard the rustling coming from the bushes in front of him. Taking a defensive posture, the Elemeno waited for the intruder to make itself known. Then, from out of same spot Brad had been spying earlier came the very subject himself, emerged Anthony Varejao, now face to face with the Elemeno. The two stared at one another for a long moment, each surprised but not afraid.

"What's this? What have you done?" came the voice of Councilman Varejao as he made his way to where the Elemeno stood over the body of Brad Burkhart. "What have you done, Eugene?"

The Elemeno cocked his catlike head to one side quickly, giving the immediate impression that he resented this line of questioning. This was further evidenced by the way both of his ears pointed backward in an automatic response the any accusation, a nervous tick he had picked up when he and his brother were taken away from their parents as children, sent to the human schools, and re-educated as something Eugene knew deep down that he was not. Checking his emotions while simultaneously retracing all twenty two of his claws back inward, Eugene opened his mouth before stating, "He saw you, followed you out here somehow. I didn't want him as prey, I swear it. I had no choice!"

Councilman Varejao looked at the corpse once again, kicking it with his heel a bit until it rolled onto its back, giving them a clear view of Brad Burkhart's face and bruising around his broken neck.

"He's a newscaster," Varejao said before sighing deeply and raising his eyebrows. He shook his head once, twice before scrunching up the sides of his mouth and stating briskly "This will draw attention. We have no choice but to dispose of the body."

"You mean that you want *me* to dispose of the body," the giant Elemeno said, looking down at the councilman with barely concealed contempt.

Varejao looked at the Elemeno for a moment and wondered why he did not fear the beast. For all intents and purposes he should be afraid of the large monster; he was over two feet taller and had a good two hundred pounds on the council member. Yet Anthony held no feelings of fear, nor concern, nor any variation in between for the beast he kept in his employee. "Yes, Eugene, you're right. YOU will dispose of the mess you've made."

The large Elemeno named Eugene snarled once, twice, and then turned around to scoop up the body of Brad Burkhart for disposal. What he would do with it Anthony Varejao did not want to know. What he did notice, however, as he looked away from the pair as they disappeared into the moonlight, was the broken cellular telephone that sat idly on a large rock nearby. The screen was cracked and battery missing, but it was a troublesome sign nonetheless.

Elsewhere, in the apartment of the news anchor Jennifer Morrison sat the undisturbed cell phone containing the last message that her friend and co-anchor Brad Burkhart would ever send; and with it the only concrete evidence that something was terribly wrong in Eden. When she awoke, somewhere between the packing of her emergency suitcase, and the fleeing of her apartment, Jennifer took what belongings that she could think of in the moment. The video proved many things, but foremost, that Brad, if he was still alive, was in more danger than she could assist him with. Most likely he was dead, and more likely, Jennifer was next.

Chapter 29:
Kiss Me

Lae (Eke) Island

"Bring it, bitch! Bring it bitch! Bring it bitch!"

The shrill, staggered cries of the Eke warriors filled the sticky Pacific air as they drew a smile from the foreign British scientist's lips. Judah threw his head back and laughed in a dominating sign of intimidation that struck Otep's mental armor like a battering ram. What began as a jest had quickly transformed into an unintentional battle cry for the small, but fierce band of Eke warriors. Otep was not amused, causing Judah to then shift his focus to the tall Egyptian. Anticipating that his next planned move was out of the question, Judah could think of little else except for his building annoyance at the situation, and overwhelming desire to find Joan before returning to Eden. It was amidst these thoughts that Judah found himself watching Otep's reanimated Imperialist soldiers renew their firing positions, guns at the ready, as Otep opened his mouth to give the order to fire when Judah took action.

"Henry!" Judah screamed, prompting Muitimbo to take notice and launch into a defensive action. It was like poetry in motion. With a singular, yet definitive thought that was strong enough to cascade through the group of corpses like a tidal wave, he force of Muitimbo's abilities made itself known for the first time in battle. Though, it was not released on the undead themselves, but instead, their weapons. Aimed at dislodging the rifles the cascade of mental energy beamed outward with a bluish hue not dissimilar to the reflection of the Time Stream in the early morning hours. Muitimbo's shot rang outward before catching each firearm like a vacuum and lifting them twelve feet into the air. In the span of ten seconds Otep's army of the undead was rendered all but impotent.

"Neat," Judah said under his breath.

Otep seethed with rage at the sight of the Eke warrior's powers as he motioned for his small army to attack the natives with their full unarmed might. Spotting this Judah did something similar, triggering the tribal war calls from the loudest warriors who immediately propelled themselves forward into the fray. The fighting was ugly, with men literally attempting to tear one another apart. In most cases the undead corpses would gang up in groups of two or three against one Eke. With death being in the air the Eke unleashed their own brand of savagery, hacking at limbs and heads even after their foes were already slain.

The cold ocean water hit Joan's legs past the ankle when the tide came in. Despite landing cleanly in the poorly made American parachute tangled and bunched beneath her feet beneath the water, almost drowning before she was able to disentangle herself from it. Angry about losing Amelia in such a fashion, the only solace she could find was that soon she would find the trigger, kill her former best friend, retrieve her husband, and go home. After a brief swim Joan found the tireless trudge up from the water onto the sandy shoreline extremely tiring. Then, amidst an ocean of self-pity she was heaping upon herself mentally, Joan spotted the metal glinting in the distance. The wreckage of Amelia's plane was scattered all over the sandy beach. She sighed, wondering how she would ever find the trigger amongst all the metal.

The wreckage from the plane, and the scattered body parts from dismembered Imperial Japanese soldiers scattered about were enough to make the Commander of the Knights of Time wince. Though she had been on hundreds of battlefields in her life there was something extremely unsettling about this one. It was almost as if it were not yet the climax, despite the fact that the Imperial Japanese had been defeated, and Nero had been sent back through the Time Stream via the Dream Phoenix. She was so tired that she sat down hard on the wet sand. She tried to breathe, to gather her thoughts and calm herself of her uneasy feelings. After many moments of her breath mixing with deafening silence from the now empty battlefield before her, she stood up gingerly and slowly made her way across the scattered remains of the day.

On the island on Joan's island sat the barn where she and Judah had made love the day before. It was much too far to swim and even if she did have the energy for it, the darkness of night was beginning to fill the sky. To her right lay the wreckage of Amelia's plane, debris sticking out and odds and ends everywhere she looked. Again pondering how she could ever find the trigger, Joan was so distracted that she completely missed the sound of Sephanie's arrival behind her. This rare lapse in senses threw both women, as neither was used a Joan who was not constantly on alert.

"It is time," said Sephanie as she approached her former best friend. There was no home for her in Eden or Tartarus without the trigger, or the cover that Joan threatened to blow. This spite toward a woman she had only recently described as like a sister to her left Sephanie with a bitter taste in her mouth.

"Damn straight," Joan retorted before launching herself forward, her shoulder connecting with Sephanie's forehead. The hit was hard and further punctuated by the sudden jolt of pain in her back Sephanie felt as she landed on the sand. Not wasting any time Joan grabbed for Sephanie's neck, getting one hand around it before Sephanie countered with a finger to Joan's nostril, pulling it backward. This was accompanied by a bent knee kick to Joan's left hip, which finally forced her rolling off to the side. Sephanie then got to her knees and turned around, hoping Joan wouldn't be standing there ready for her. She was wrong.

With a smile bordering on sadistic Joan Raines, or Joan of Arc as she had been called at the height of her glory, readied herself for more physical combat. Right hook after left the saint showed her traitorous best friend what happened to those who double crossed her. In Joan's mind it did not matter if Sephanie was the victim of what modern psychologists would call Stockholm syndrome, or that she had been taken as a child and perhaps did not know any better than the life she grew into. No. It was past the point of caring, or asking why. For Joan the need for vengeance overshadowed everything else. Onward she pressed, this time with nothing but malice in her heart.

"Give me the trigger!" Joan hollered, gambling that Sephanie may have found it amongst the plane wreckage before she had the opportunity.

"No!" Sephanie shouted back, gripping her friend's wrist like her life depended on it. Any thoughts to a quick escape with the trigger were dashed, as Sephanie subtly touched her back pocket where the metallic trigger still sat comfortably. Uninterrupted.

It was at this juncture in the story when another player, one all too familiar to Joan, made their appearance. Without any introduction the white orb that had haunted Joan for days appeared just over the horizon, making itself known from the corner of her eye. She thought of utilizing it, somehow ditching Sephanie in the past, but then remembered that strategy, however brief she may have held it, did not work for Amelia. Deciding all too quickly that she would deal with Sephanie first and the orb second, Joan pressed onward, again with her offensive attack. It was then that Sephanie too noticed the orb for the first time.

Digging her fingernails deep into her best friend's bare flesh, Sephanie held on as tight as she could. Something inside of her beckoned her to accept the role as villain, move on from Joan, toward the ride she knew would we waiting for her, and the trigger. Still, something inside of her was forcing Sephanie to hold on to what she knew, what was comfortable; for her that was with Joan and the life she had made for herself in Eden.

The orb suddenly whirled into their collective line of vision, hopping buoyantly through the air as it went clockwise twice around a tall tree. It went low, swinging close by the place where Joan and Sephanie wrestled, coming so near that it nearly engulfed Sephanie's head. Both women stopped their harassment of each other and watched the orb as it floated serenely to a spot between two boulders. Before the orb even reached its destination, Joan knew what it was telling her. She vaulted into the air and broke out into a run towards the orb with Sephanie following closely behind her.

"What the hell?" Sephanie inquired as the orb whirled upward about around them in a sporadic, almost agitated pattern. "What is that thing?"

Joan was shocked that Sephanie, in addition to herself and Amelia, could see the orb. Given any other circumstances they might have dropped whatever it was that they were doing in order to investigate. The two women thought on this for a full minute of subdued silence before the next threat made itself known. Suddenly the ground shook, just as it had in the barn with the 'Beware the Sheep' sign, giving Joan an uneasy feeling in the pit of her stomach. She thought of acting first, but the coming battle met them head on, giving them the only option of re-acting to whatever it was coming their way. The wait was short, however, as soon the two women came face-to-face with their would-be attackers.

The dead, decaying faces were sinister in their intent for the women, not caring one iota where Sephanie's true allegiances lay. The sheer numbers alone told Joan that neither would survive the clash, even with the assistance of extra-human abilities. There were simply too many to...

"Bring it, bitch! Bring it, bitch!" came the faint, but still very audible battle cry for just over the horizon-line. The Eke warriors had breached the line of Otep's undead men, and were making their way towards the undead Imperialist's who were aimed at Mrs. Raines. Sephanie smiled, not knowing what, or who, had taught these men such a crass phrase, but thankful that they did. It was funny. Perhaps the only funny part of their current situation. As the chanting grew louder the numbers of the undead also multiplied, until the sound of a single gunshot signaled the official begin to the battle. Looking at one another with a longing look of trepidation, both Sephanie and Joan went to work on their closest ghastly attackers with all of the gusto they could reasonably use.

Some minutes went by as Joan fought, hand-to-hand, against multiple foes. All around them stood half naked men in tribal paint fought a coalition of undead soldiers in Imperialist garb. Then, through the midst of an especially tenacious scene of carnage she found her husband Judah leading a group of especially large tribesmen against the main bulk of the undead forces. She watched as his blonde hair, somewhat crazy in the heat of battle, whipped around his head as he maneuvered his way through cutting down one, two, three lifeless monsters that Otep had brought to life. Joan again smiled, knowing full well that no matter the outcome of the day, she could be alright as long as Judah was there to comfort her afterward. Though he didn't see her, or rather couldn't see her as he was surrounded by a contingent of much larger men, and much smaller re-animated Imperialists, his very presence brought her comfort. She watched as the caravan of both armies moved through, and back near the area where they had come from. It was chaos, but, the sort of chaos that Joan knew her husband found opportunity.

Snapping out of her stupor, simultaneously realizing that Judah was inadvertently providing the cover she needed, Joan turned her attention back to Sephanie only to find her gone. Luckily their intimate relationship as best friends gave Joan the advantage in this situation, or so she thought. This doubt was further reinforced when she looked at the spot the orb had led them to and saw that the trigger was gone. The pursuit did not go far before Joan caught up with Sephanie in a large clearing. Sephanie looked across at Joan with mild panic before vaulting herself into the air and scrambling up the nearest tree..

But that was the least of Joan's worries as she focused on the reflective glow bouncing off the setting sun onto the object in Sephanie's right hand. The trigger to Project Dreamcoat was now the prize both women openly fought for, not their friendship.

For Judah, the battle was not going as well as planned. With the dead constantly being re-animated the Eke were beginning to tire and succumb to their foes. To make matters worse Otep suddenly cast some sort of strange incantation upon the entire battlefield that quite literally knocked the wind out of Judah's lungs, sending him and all the living around him flat on their backs. The remaining corpses immediately took at advantage of the situation. The sounds of fresh screams filled the air, prompting many of the Eke to panic and try to prematurely get up, only to fall back down.

Laying flat on his back and struggling to breathe, Judah felt nothing of the hero on high he had pretended to be so often while walking around Eden. As the breath painfully returned to his lungs he struggled to roll back to his feet, making small bits of progress as the moments trickled by. No sooner had he finally managed to get upright before Otep sent another wave of power knocking him and the others down again. Suddenly, a pair of decomposing limbs reached for his face and began clawing at him savagely. Rolling to his left in order to avert the two groping hands he found himself firmly grasped within the determined palm of another, much dirtier arm with a long sleeve plaid shirt extending all the way to its cuff. He very soon could no longer breath began to feel as if he would pass out.

"On my command they are going to pull as hard as they can until your limbs pop off," Otep spoke while looking down at Judah. The wind caught his black hair a bit as he bent and his unblinking resolve chilled the Knight of Time to his soul, even if his outward demeanor betrayed no sense of his terror. Instead Judah, in his typical fashion, called his enemies bluff with a simple nod of his head.

No sooner had the corpses begun to pull than the first of their heads popped off before shooting into the sky like rockets. This process repeated for the near skeleton remains clutching his right leg, then the left. Struggling against the confused corpses Judah was not only able to break free, but also take a shot at

Otep, who was now staring at Muitimbo, the cause of the head popping, in shock. Striking the Egyptian man with a blow to the knee cap, Judah clamored to his feet before feeling the sting of Otep's retribution in the form of yet another skeletal hand jettisoning up from the ground below before clasping itself around his ankle. Trying to release himself from it Judah kicked furiously, only to uproot the skull and torso of the creature as its blank, nearly flattened face rose from the mound. The capture was short lived however, as a well placed kick by a third party sent the head skidding across the field. Only then did the skeletal hand let go of Judah's ankle.

"Lost head," Muitimbo said through his white set of teeth as the pair made their way through the field away from their attackers. Looking back briefly, the son of the Eke Chieftain did see five or six of his fellow tribesmen run in the opposite direction, helping to scatter Otep's group a bit. He was able to afford this split of attention due to the long strides of his powerfully agile legs that nearly formed one step for every two of Judah's. He looked back again, spotting another two Eke warriors standing their ground to fight. In his heart and mind he wished them luck before redistributing his attention back to Judah, their retreat, and what to do next.

"Over there!" Judah screamed, spotting an old chicken coup the size of a small barn. While it offered little in the way of shelter, it could serve well enough as a fortification of sorts until the other Eke were able to circle back around to help them. Once concealed by the foliage, the pair finally caught their breath. Scattered dots of bodies, parts, and weapons checkered the green field of grass that had not until that day known warfare of any sort. Deciding it safe enough the two rushed inside only to see how run-down the old structure really was. The odd, familiar noise of whispers of the unseen told them both to turn around and see the enemy coming toward them through the holes in the wooden walls.

"Damn it all," Judah cursed as the creeping figure of Otep gliding in their direction. There wasn't much there to work with, but that never stopped Judah before. Taking quick stock he found the items that he needed to fashion an effective killing device, hoping that he wouldn't end up as the beneficiary.

"Muitimbo," Judah then said, garnering the Eke warrior's full attention as he came to a halt after sprinting up beside the blonde traveler. This was the first time Judah had ever called him by his own name, which meant that all jovialness had been dropped in lieu of warfare. "You ever play baseball? Or throw rocks?"

"Yes..." Muitimbo offered in thick English, crooking one eyebrow upward. "Throw rocks but baseball...."

Yet before Muitimbo could speak any further Judah had began picking up any large jagged rocks he could find. He placed one in Muitimbo's hand before enacting a mock throw toward Otep who had now appeared to be floating above a tree. Nodding in understanding Muitimbo launched rock in a blur towards the Egyptian, hitting him squarely in the forehead and interrupting his wordless incantation.

The mad Egyptian cried out in pain yet managed to stay in the air. The second time Muitimbo's arm let a rock fly Otep was not so lucky and he came crashing to the ground, bleeding from a deep cut on his forehead.

"Oh, no magic words now eh?" Judah asked as he yanked the man up to his feet. The Egyptian simply smiled before latching his hands on to the outside of Judah's arms. Within seconds Judah could feel that something was very wrong. His arms felt hot, as though an entire mound of fire ants had bitten him. As he bellowed in pain and tried to fight back Muitimbo charged at Otep only to be hit hard in the side of the head. Watching Muitimbo crumple to the ground, Judah was more than surprised when Otep gave him what he recognized as a 'spear' or the ramming of his shoulder into Judah's stomach after a running start. Smiling to himself as he went flying alongside Otep, Judah seized the opportunity to ensure that both the hook, and the chain were in their proper positions for what he had in mind next. Their landing hurt, as did the respective repetition of getting back to his feet. But once there, even if he had to wait for Otep, whose blood was seeping out of the wound from his belly where the hook had lodged itself, Judah found comfort in knowing he could always rely on his wits. Behind him Muitimbo also stirred, both he and Otep in a race to get to their feet while Judah enjoyed an adrenaline high that kept him one step ahead.

"Think again twinkle toes," Judah said before pulling on the metal chain as hard as he could, releasing the mechanism that triggered the makeshift pulley system, activating the upward movement of the tree limb, which he watched rise slowly behind the sauntering Otep. Catching the villain square in stomach Judah noticed how the hook had not gone in very deep. "Damn it all. Here Henry, when I give the word you pull as hard as you call. Got that? Pull!"

An enthusiastic nod assured Judah that his new companion comprehended his instruction, allowing him the time to spring the distance between them and the spot where Otep stood. The hook was stabbed within his stomach, and was not possible to dislodge with one hand. No sooner was he about to muster his strength for an attempt with both hands when Judah came sprinting up to Otep before landing a running dropkick into his stomach, pushing the hook in all the way to the hilt. A loud groan fell over the area as Judah screamed something incomprehensible behind him.

Taking this as his cue to act, Muitimbo pulled with all of his might on the chain, forcing it to jerk upward, taking the vulnerable Otep with it. Acting like a zipper the hook forced its way upward through Otep's body, ripping it in half while splaying his innards out all over the barn. After counting one and two inside his own head, Judah crouched low as the spray of rotten intestines sprayed about the small barn, covering everything. Covering his head with his arms Muitimbo shielded himself from much of this downpour, but not all. Alas, his christening as a traveler of light was that not only by fire, but something far, far more disgusting.

Jumping from the tree like a flying squirrel, Sephanie landed on top of Joan elbow first and dug in hard into Joan's chest. Joan instantly retaliated and the scratching and squeezing of necks quickly turned into the pulling of hair and biting of exposed flesh. The tide turned however when Sephanie somehow managed to get upright and wrapped her legs around Joan's and began squeezing with all of her might. So focused was Sephanie that she did not feel the metallic trigger slide out from her pants pocket, and onto the Earth below.

"Seph-" Joan chocked, her bloodshot eyes and purple face pleading for mercy as the legs continued to squeeze tighter. The cold dispassion that Sephanie displayed in that moment left zero doubt in Joan's mind that her former best friend was ready to end her life. She thought of her husband and feared that Sephanie might go after him next. In not knowing of Sephanie's betrayal, Judah was left vulnerable and exposed. Yet the only reason that he did not know was because Joan hadn't told him yet. Before this fights, a small part of her wouldn't, nay, couldn't admit it to herself. With her last seconds of consciousness Joan thought of how guilty she felt for signing Judah's death warrant when suddenly the pressure of Sephanie's hands were released, and the pressure around Joan's neck was inexplicably gone.

"Bullseye!" came the female voice from beyond Joan's line-of-vision. The youthful tone from a baited breath elicited nothing but swears from Sephanie, who fell over from taking a piece of plane debris to the side of her head.

As oxygen flooded into Joan's lungs the fuzzy shapes that comprised the world around her took to becoming recognizable again. Two people were fighting very near to where she sat on her hands and knees. One was Sephanie. But who was the other? It would be several minutes of this confused state before Joan's brain would communicate with her logically again and she would recognize Amelia as the one who had come to her aid.

Amelia Earhart was not holding back any of the Special Forces training she had received via the United States military. In being the first female to fly across the Atlantic, and Pacific Oceans she was also the first female to successfully complete many of the U.S. militaries' most stringent guidelines and techniques for battle, even if those records have been lost to time. This conflict was not won via superior ability, or skill set, but by chance of time. By carefully concealing a rock in her left hand, Amelia was able to not only block Sephanie's next attack, but also, smoothly, bring her hand up right to the young girl's temple and connected with it, causing Sephanie to double-over in pain where she once stood. Though not unconscious, Sephanie looked dazed to the point of deliriousness. Joan saw this, all of this play out as she stumbled to her feet, yet was still wary.

"Careful," Joan said, trying and failing to get to her feet. "She tried that one on me before giving me the slip."

"Noted," Amelia retorted, her eyes still on the still Sephanie. She was looking for something.. but could not see it with her naked eye.

"Hey, aren't you dead?" Joan asked with a slight smile. "I didn't think that you could teleport."

Amelia laughed as she helped Joan stay on her feet, despite some wobbly knees. "You mean the plane? I've crashed lots of planes. That was no big deal."

"But.."

Yet Joan had no time to ask more questions as she watched in open-mouthed horror the sight that was creating itself directly behind where Amelia stood. On the far side of the clearing was a newly created portal, a rip in the fabric of time and space represented by a vortex of colors that led to the Time Stream. This one looked nearly identical to the one that she and Judah had arrived through days before. Not knowing of any active time travelers, save for the cadet Rolland Wright, Joan knew it must be a rogue vortex created by Vilthe or one of his agents. But how? None of them possessed such abilities.

"How...?" Joan asked, genuinely confused at what it was that she was seeing.

"What is that?" Amelia asked, her mouth open in wonder.

Joan knew that explaining it to her would take longer than the time they had, so instead she dropped the matter entirely. Joan took one last look at the Sephanie moaning on the ground before deciding it wasn't worth her time.

"We should go, now," Joan said, grabbing Amelia's arm and pulling her a few steps in the opposite direction from the time vortex before meeting with resistance.

"No," Amelia said before catching her own words. "I mean, just, not yet. Ok? I have something that I need to do. Something that I need to get."

Smiling at Amelia Joan removed the shiny metal trigger from her pocket before waving it at her newfound friend to see. "The trigger for Project Dreamcoat, right?"

Flabbergasted, Joan took two giant steps back before looking at Amelia with a renewed sense of intimidation. "Uh, yeah. How did you know?"

The attack came from out of nowhere, hitting Joan's right knee, knocking the trigger out of Amelia's hands, and into the air as Sephanie Kelly snatched it. Holding the prize aloft she ran as fast as she could away from the pair toward the nearly appeared time vortex. Wasting no time Amelia sprinted after her, catching her only via the small stone wall, which Joan could have sworn she saw Amelia literally disappear into as she ran. Seconds later Amelia, bent over, pulled the trigger out from Sephanie before holding it up for Joan to see. Jogging over to them, Joan watched as Sephanie mounted another offensive, a typical move from someone who does not know when they have been defeated.

"Back for more bitch?" spat Amelia as she lunged for Sephanie. Countering this, Sephanie kicked Amelia in the stomach before shifting gears to work on Amelia's chest. The two women rolled, arms inter-tangled in a fierce battle for superiority, making their way down the grassy incline toward the sea.

Still shaky from Sephanie's choking, Joan staggered to her feet after them. Something about Amelia's reappearance did not seem normal, although knew that the Amelia had possessed some sort of supernatural ability, particularly one that the early 21st century United States government would be willing to exploit. Suddenly, everything seemed to click instead Joan's brain. The only way Amelia could have survived a plane crash like that was if she was able to get out of the plane in time. The only way she could have possibly done that without a scratch was if she could teleport. Now, the ramblings of Noonan's corpse made sense - Amelia was the key. She was *THE* key to the entire operation - any operation! When Joan finally caught up to the pair, they were still locked in a heated battle.

Prying the trigger from Sephanie's hand with all of her might, Amelia clawed and scratched while Joan suddenly entered the fray and pulled the metal object free, eliciting a scream from Sephanie who punched Amelia hard in the face, breaking her nose. Then, seeing how weak Joan was, and how precarious her hold on the trigger was in proximity to the time vortex, Sephanie took one last gamble in a running dash toward both goals at once.

"No," Joan cried out before gathering her strength and kicking Sephanie in the stomach, knocking her backward into the solid white light, and away from the situation for good. With a look of shock and flailing limbs Sephanie made eye contact with her best friend one more time before disappearing.

Breathing heavily Joan looked at the white void of light for a long moment, half expecting Sephanie to somehow crawl back out and resume the fighting. When nothing happened, and the sound of shouts in the distance caught her ears, Joan turned to see who it was that made the noise. There, walking toward her was her husband accompanied by a very tall, very broad shouldered looking islander who wore no shirt. Judah smiled broadly at the sight of his wife and began jogging towards her as fast as he reasonably could.

Joan watched as he came closer to her, a smile plastered on her face that matched his own. A wave of joy crashed inside of her, filling Joan with a newfound happiness that was reflected on her husband's face for the briefest of moments. But then Judah's expression turned from one of joy to that of disbelief and abject horror.

The first person to notice the figure emerging from the white light was Amelia, whose eyes grew large as saucers as Joan met them in confusion and surprise. Judah was too far away for any physical confrontation, and although he screamed his wife's name, it was already too late.

Joan didn't feel the knife as it made its way to the front of her neck, or the sharp pull as the assassin Nero grabbed her hair, forcing her head backward for a clean slice. What Joan did feel, was the fear in the eyes of those she had grown to know and love, as her flesh was torn open, making it near impossible to breath before she was suddenly let go. Down, down, downward toward the cold, hard Earth. Yet no sooner had she fallen than she was again within her attackers grasp, this time with the knife looming over her heart. Instinctively, Joan reached into her pockets for anything that could aid her escape. There, nestled in the deep confines of her pocket was the broken piece of propeller that Amelia had handed her on the other island. Clasping it within her hand and summoning all the strength that she had left, Joan jammed the metal directly into the eye socket of her attacker.

Instantly Joan felt her hair being let go, sending her forward and eliciting a greater pain in her throat. Every breath she took brought a fresh round of flames to her lungs. It wasn't easy to stand, but somehow Joan did, before taking three uneasy steps toward her sprinting husband, and falling to the ground onto her side. The trigger to Project Dreamcoat likewise fell out of her hand, joining Joan on the hard Earth where they all, friend and foe alike, stood.

Amelia immediately launched into a defensive posture, attacking the assailant with as much intensity as she had exerted with Otep, and Sephanie. She phased out with every attack he launched, stealthy in her precision of punches afterward. She could see how impressed he was with the amount of control she wielded over her ability, but said nothing despite several non-verbal cues by way of odd faces. He managed to catch her though and his quick kick to the head knocked the pilot to her knees. Though wounded due to Joan's quick thinking, Nero knew that he need only escape back to the Time Stream in order to heal. Silently, Nero pledged revenge on the individuals who mourned for the women whom he had just attacked as he moved into the portal.

It wasn't until the assassin was gone, and the time vortex closed, that Amelia's thoughts once again returned to Joan. She stood about ten feet away, watching her friend's life expire as the moments ticked away into an eternity of nightmares and regrets. Although it had been the man who had attacked Joan, all Amelia could think of was Sephanie, and her blood ran cold with unadulterated fury at the repeated betrayal. She swore revenge, but something more as well. Looking at Joan, lying in the arms of the man she loved, Amelia swore to herself that she would honor her friend by fulfilling the promises she made. No sooner had Amelia given thought as to what exactly this would mean when she heard the sputtering of blood in Joan's cough that snapped her back to the present reality of the situation.

"Don't worry love," Judah said in a steady, comforting voice as he held his wife's head up in an attempt to slow the bleeding. "We'll get you back home and patched up right away. You'll see. "

"Ju, Jud-" Joan tried to say through gasping, shallow breaths. Her left hand found Judah's in the increasing darkness surrounding her. It was unfair, so unfair that she would meet her end this way. But then again, it was better than the literal flames she had been saved from long ago. As a teenager she had been rescued by a stranger who brought her deliverance, a new hope and new life of adventure just beyond the realm of believability. That man had become her husband, whom loved her so he would do anything she asked. But Joan wanted for only one thing.

"What is it love?" Judah asked, fighting back the tears gathering behind his eyes. The lines in his face told the story that his own words could not. Countless words left unsaid, a multitude of careless fights about petty things, and a lifetime of love lost between them hung upon this moment; their last moment together.

"Kiss me," Joan asked through choked breaths. Blood escaped her drenched lungs before trickling out her mouth and down her neck before landing in a pool on the ground below. She was colder now, colder than she had ever felt before. And Judah was warm. So warm. Her hand found his as she relinquished the strength to raise her own head again, resting it within the crook of her husband's arms. Above them, unseen to anyone but the fading Joan, the white orb that traveled with her through so much of her life came gently downward until it laid upon her chest, and disappeared within her departing soul.

Despite the knowledge that it would be the last time he did so, Dr. Judah Jacob Raines lowered his weary head down onto his dying wife and gave her one final embrace as she slipped away.

One final kiss to mark the end of the greatest love Dr. Judah Jacob Raines would ever know.

One final kiss to say goodbye to a Saint.

Chapter 30:
In My Life

Eden: Before Sunrise

As the morning sun filled the sky the hillside outside of the Halls of Time life was already bustling with activity. Nearly two hundred volunteers from all over Eden had arrived the evening before to assist in the preparations. They came from as far east as the McFadden village, the last outpost of Eden before the Elemeno lands. All came to pay their respects to the fallen knight and hero, the patron saint of the planet Earth and Eden, Joan Raines of Orleans.

Inside the Halls of Time all of the occupants stirred within their respective quarters. For some, like Victor and Rolland, their loss was a sad reminder of other fallen ones who had crossed their paths, exiting the world too soon. Visions of Dodger, C de Baca, and others danced in their respective heads, forging a bond between them that neither could speak of. Others, like Tina and Turtledove, wept openly for their fallen friends; especially Turtledove, who had been in a tormented daze since he had been told of Joan's untimely passing.

Then, there was Judah. Judah the brave. Judah the genius. Judah - the man whom everyone held such high expectations. After using the portable Dream Phoenix to get them back to Eden, Amelia and Muitimbo had followed him back to the Halls of Time, where they had hardly left his side. At least at first. His new entourage aside, the grief that enveloped Judah was so powerful that it consumed every second of his thoughts, sending him into a steady decline of depression that kept getting worse.

Joan's body had been lying in state within the main entrance of the Halls of Time for last two days. The first day had been the private memorial for her fellow knights and close friends while the second day had been open to the public, many of whom had brought gifts or tokens to place around her casket. The occasion brought out both the best, numerous classes of Edenites ranging from affluent business holders to impoverished Elemenos, and the worst - including two separate visits by Councilman Varejao and a very public altercation between Councilman Holmes and his daughter. These incidents were small, however, compared to the real crisis going on upstairs within the guest quarters of the Halls of Time.

In the dormitory wing, inside the last room on the right, Dr. Judah Jacob Raines was laying upon a twin sized mattress. Curled into the fetal position, with caked snot and tears clinging to his face due to over twenty-four hours of uninterrupted grieving and seclusion. None knew how to comfort Judah for none could understand the pain from missing his other half. Therefore most of his fellow Knights, including the ever present Amelia and Muitimbo, shared his grief in silence.

Unable to sleep for want of his thoughts Rolland decided to dress and head to the cemetery early before the bulk of the main crowd arrived. As he moved through the building the sound of sobbing could be heard from down the hallway. Outside the main door he found Geoffrey standing on the massive front porch, silent save for the exhaling of his lungs from the drag of a cigarette. The only good thing that had occurred in the last few days was the release of Geoffrey from Eden Prison, where he had been languishing since Victor had fallen through the Time Stream. With a half hearted wave the newly released shape shifter watched Rolland leave the grounds and disappear over the horizon towards the cemetery where so many of their fallen comrades lay at rest and where Joan would soon join them in eternal slumber.

No sooner had the Halls of Time disappeared behind him than the limestone and marble headstones of the cemetery came into view. Still being early morning only a few people were walking through the iron gates. One of which Rolland saw had a hose that he was using to water the flowers outside the illustrious gates. Assuming this to be the groundskeeper, or perhaps even undertaker, Rolland gave him a cordial wave as he passed into the sacred ground and towards the folding chairs that marked the site of the service.

Yet before Rolland could reach the chairs he saw a solitary figure to his left. There, next to a fresh grave stood an older man with glasses and thin black hair. He was dressed in an impeccable suit and his hands were clasped tightly behind his back. He was silent, yet reflective as he stared at the same grave where Rolland had buried another friend the day before. The grave of Stewart 'Dodger' Yick.

"Councilman Yick," Rolland said softly, remembering that he was one of five votes that acquitted him at his trial that seemed like a lifetime again now. Despite the older man's wrinkles and air of wisdom, Rolland saw so much of Dodger within his grandfather that his heart ached. Rolland felt both compelled, and foolhardy offering him the customary greeting, "Good morning."

"Morning," Councilman Yick said in a courteous tone. The mourning of his only surviving family member had been especially hard on Joseph, given all that he had lost already. When they had buried his grandson he sat in stony silence, his face giving no indication to the aching in his heart and in his bones.

"Are you here for Joan's service? "Rolland asked awkwardly, unsure as to what he should say.

"Yes, and to visit my grandson" Councilman Yick said shortly, though still very politely. He was now wringing his hands, his stiff façade breaking for the first time. Rolland did not respond, but bowed his head respectfully.

"Stewart was…" Councilman Yick began to say, his eyes drifting off toward the morning sunrise. The age lines were more visible in the natural light than they were under the fluorescents of the council chambers. Warm tears formed against the eyes of the distinguished man, his stoic nature gave way to his raw emotion.

The injustice of it was maddening to Rolland, and his hand went up to the missing lobe of his ear. This habit was one he had picked up since the day of Dodger's death, and one he had yet to decide if he wanted to get rid of or not, as the physical reminder of his friend's sacrifice was one he carried. Still, the loss hurt Rolland deeply. How could he even begin to describe the soul crushing guilt that had consumed his mind like a thick blanket of fog ever since Dodger's last breath? The remorse, though worse than the guilt, had changed him in ways that he was only beginning to understand. But then he remembered something he had heard long ago from his mother, Taylor Wright.

'Friendship holds no expectations, only gratitude for the time spent together.'

The thought of his mother cracked Rolland's own façade and he swallowed hard before forcing himself to look at Councilman Yick.

"He was a good man," Rolland offered in a strained yet strong voice.

"Was he?" Councilman Yick asked in a rush. "Tell me about him. Please. I only knew the boy, but- "

With an surge of pleasure, the first he had felt in many days, Rolland knelt down at Dodger's grave and proceeded to relay the story of their friendship, Nero's attack during the B.E.T.S.I. trial, being roommates, and above all else how Stewart had been the best friend that he had ever had.

"Let me tell you about the man."

With the turning of the tenth hour, the day brought a flood of those into the cemetery to pay their respects. Lines and lines of chairs, amounting to roughly four hundred sitting positions were filled with mourners. In the front row sat Turtledove, surrounded by those who had stood by him in the darkest hours of the past few weeks. Victor and Gwendolyn too sat close by, along with a stone-faced Geoffrey.

As the time to begin neared so did Judah, who despite being dressed in a very crisp looking dark blue suit with an ironed white dress shirt underneath looked wretched. The blonde hair that had been his signature was unkempt and dirty. His bloodshot eyes seemed not to register all of the people around him. Never one for large groups, Judah could only grimace at the turnout for the woman that he, and so many others, had loved. Hoping for a savior from this attention Judah's silent wishes were answered in the form of Turtledove, who opened the funeral proceedings by walking to the podium and beginning to speak.

"Today we mourn the loss of one of Eden's greatest citizens, one of its greatest friends, Joan Raines," Marcus Turtledove said, tears already beginning to form in his eyes. The potential he saw in Joan was always so vast, so grand in its scope that he could scarcely fathom until now that none of it would ever transpire. No children would ever spring from her and Judah's loins, nor the fruits of her labors enjoyed in positions of leadership. Fighting back his emotions Turtledove looked at Judah, who sat bent over a bit but with his head held high and full attention on Marcus.

"Joan was the best student that I ever had the privilege to teach," Turtledove said to the crowd, the lines surrounding his mouth twitching madly as he attempted to keep his emotions in check. "So imaginative, and so eager to learn. But what I never understood about the girl was where all of her energy came from."

As the eulogy continued, the two most junior members sat at the end of the fourth row, listening intently. For Rolland, who was acting as both a fainting couch and tissue dispenser for Tina, the entire ordeal was as intense as it was surreal. Memories of Joan greeting him upon his entrance to Eden rushed back to the forefront of his mind, again and again. The possibility of dying because of that stupid plant monster, a sprocket, a mere hour after arriving in Eden would have made him look like an idiot worthy of receiving a Darwin award. She, like Dodger, and his parents would be burned forever into his heart. So preoccupied with his own thoughts was Rolland that he did not notice Turtledove sit down and another person take his place at the podium.

"Joan was a trend setter, with the main trend being that women could be equal to men in the field. In that, Joan was the most influential woman in all of Eden," Doctor Fluker said with a vehement attitude on the matter. Her passion toward her fellow Edenite was inspiring to all that heard it, stirring up the feelings of pride in just who Joan was to not only Eden, but the history of Earth as well.

A few more individuals, such as Jesse James, Councilman Oskam, and even Michael the Eden town sentry came to pay their respects, each passing by Joan's casket after they spoke. Apparently Michael had been one of Joan's students at the Academy of Light, with her having a heavy influence on what career path he took in life. The more people spoke the more memories were evoked, and more dots were connected as far as relationships go to people within Rolland's mind.

Extending her hand, Tina found Rolland's free one and clasped onto it tightly. The feeling was wonderful, filled with hope and meaning, and both felt comfort from their togetherness. Though their fallen friends, both Dodger and Joan, were in all of their thoughts, the future looked was still hopeful.

Judah's heart literally hurt from the pain of what he had lost. The only outlet, however, was through the song he found himself repeating over and over in his head. Again he looked at the casket that held what was left of his eternal love, his soul mate, and best friend. Then, as he suddenly found himself standing at the podium, waiting for the words to come, the words by which he could best make his wife proud of him in her final hour upon life's stage, none would reveal themselves, save these.

There are places I'll remember all my life,
Though some have changed...

Feelings of heartache ripped at Judah's chest. He wouldn't give in to the feelings of grief, he couldn't; it wasn't what Joan would have wanted. Instead he pressed onward.

Some forever not for better
Some have gone
And some remain...

The lyrics rang true of his life, his fallen friends, such as Scott & Taylor Wright, and his wife, Joan. They were all gone now, all but him. Like Turtledove, Judah was the last of the old guard of his class, the last remaining Knight from a bygone era. The pressure within his head built, crying out for an outlet to express themselves. The tears where there, yet Judah would not let them come. He wanted Joan to be proud, even now. Even after she was gone.

Though these places have their moments
With lovers and friends, I still can recall.

Again, Judah fought the tears.

Some are dead and some are living
In my life, I love you more.

The sea of faces faded away as Judah left the podium and went straight to the headstone. He traced his wife's name and the fleur de lis that were etched into the white stone. Beside her, at rest, lay the earthly remains of Taylor Wright, with her husband, and Rolland's father, Scott Wright on the other side. The trio of headstones stood, not as monument to the lives lost in action, but as a testament to the accomplishments, friendship, and esteem each held one another in during their time amongst the living. Judah saw this, understood this, but cared not. For him the stones were just stones, holding no symbolic meaning except as markers. He took a deep breath and suddenly found himself singing aloud again.

But of all these friends and lovers
There is no one, compares with you

Memories of Joan's face glistening in the sun found their way into Judah's mind as he fought back the tears of the bereaved. Memories of his courtship with Joan flooded Judah's mind accompanied by a physical pain that grasped at his heart with a fierce, unforgiving pull toward her grave.

And these memories lose their meaning
When I think of love.. As something new

It couldn't be over between them, it just couldn't. He still owed her a bloody honeymoon! Judah wanted to be with Joan, dead or alive. Still, he knew that even now, much like their lives together, it wasn't about what he wanted. So, with all the strength that he could muster in the moment, Judah continued on with the song.

Though I know I'll never lose affection
For People and Things
That Came before

Sorrow. Sweet sorry would be Judah's nightly companion now, the warmer of his bed.

I know I'll often stop and think about them..
In my life...

The words caught once, but came when called. Judah had to finish, he had to.

I've loved you more.

The tears came freely as Judah tried in vain to finish the song without falling apart. What fell from his mouth was little more than a whisper for the benefit of himself, and perhaps the first row of people who could hear him. They were all Knights, or future Knights of Time. They were all that was left of his family.

In my life...
I've loved you more.

Silence filled the air as no one dared move, speak, or even whisper about the sight before them. In this moment another mourner appeared on the scene, one who also bore the tear-stained cheeks of someone who missed Joan. Sephanie Kelly walked catlike around the corner of the cemetery unnoticed by everyone in attendance save one man, Anthony Varejao. From her vantage point she heard the tail end of Joan's favorite Beatles song and guessed that it was Judah singing.

"Thank you for coming. You can all kindly fuck off now," said Judah with a ghost of his old smile before striding through the aisle and towards the gates. He disappeared into the mid-morning sunshine, a man freed of any tangible emotional connections to the living. A man without a cause. A man without hope.

The rest of the bereaved sat in muddled silence, each waiting for another person to stand before them to end the ceremony. Moments passed, and none came. Silence engulfed every soul, forcing everyone, including the youngest gathered, to look within themselves for closure to the senseless loss that was Joan Raines' death. Once the awkwardness had worn off and the spectators began to trickle out all but the close friends and family stayed to shake hands and seek solace in being together. Lt. James and Sgt. Tillman, both fellow faculty members of the academy along with Joan, also lingered for a while.

Rolland and Tina finally met Amelia Earhart and Muitimbo, who in turn also got a chance to meet Kniff and Timothy Holmes. These connecting of worlds left Rolland mentally reeling. So far he had seen Turtledove, Tina, Victor, Judah, and Geoffrey, yet Rolland had been looking around for Sephanie, surprised and concerned that he had not seen her since his return. A twinge of guilt struck him as he caught Tina's eye once again, causing a faint smile to form despite his best efforts to remain solemn. Shelving thoughts of Sephanie in favor of happier ones, he squeezed the hand that had found his minutes before and looked into the baby blue eyes of his first love. It was a good moment, a happy moment. One they would each treasure.

The path to the cemetery exit saw a steady stream of people leaving for the first ten minutes or so, leaving Sephanie ample time to lie in wait until an opening presented itself. Once it did she continued her catlike behavior in stepping out unnoticed from the gate, looking over her shoulder as she went. As she turned back around she found herself surrounded.

Standing there were a small coalition of council and community members including Doctor Duffy, Doctor Yick, Councilwoman Oskam, Doctor Fluker, Councilman Varejao, Councilman Holmes, and Marcus Turtledove all looking stone faced.

"Sephanie, if you please.." Turtledove said insistently while holding out his hand.

Reaching between her breasts, Sephanie retrieved the metal trigger for Project Dreamcoat that had cost Joan her life, centering it within her palm before handing it over to Turtledove with a morose look. The stern looks upon all of their faces melted at once, turning into bright smiles of approval. Almost giddy with anticipation, Councilman Varejao quickly snatched the remote from Turtledove immediately, producing a large, silver briefcase from behind him, and opening it to reveal a very plain looking compartment.

"Well done, Ms. Kelly," Councilman Varejao said, his hands folded behind his back in a smug tone of voice. "But your duties are not done yet, so, best be off to continue on with them."

Confused by this, Sephanie looked from Varejao to Turtledove, then to Fluker, and back to Turtledove again, desperate for some sort of answer. Wasn't it enough that she was not only a double agent, but a triple agent for these people as well? Did they not appreciate that she, and only she, was in a unique position to bring Vilthe down. Holding her thoughts and tongue Sephanie took a deep breath before approaching the conversation from a more diplomatic perspective.

"My next mission.." Sephanie asked, somewhat apprehensively. "Is there any way that you could-"

"Sorry, Ms. Kelly," Councilman Varejao said, interrupting Sephanie before she could make her request. "But you are needed right where you are. Kindly return to Vilthe at your earliest convenience."

"But-" Sephanie began, looking desperately from Varejao to Turtledove, even to Doctor Duffy, whom she had never even spoken to before. If she had not been watching closely she might not have seen Turtledove shake his head at her.

"Yes councilman," Sephanie said, dejected, and full of regret for her actions. She turned and left their group before doubling back around, waiting until they were all distracted with Varejao's suitcase, and snuck back in toward the casket. Come hell or high water, she had some things to tell Joan before she was laid to rest.

And yet, Sephanie was not the only bystander observing the clandestine scene. For although Amelia Earhart knew nothing of the politics, deceit, or lives lost in order for the meeting she eavesdropped on to take place, she knew enough about espionage to know when a plot was being hatched. As she stood, clad in a tasteful black dress that she had herself borrowed from Joan's own closet, a plot of her own took form within her own imagination. A plot that involved revenge, deceit, and trickery. Amelia knew that she was being sent to some academy where she would learn how to use her powers toward the communal good; but all that she could think about was the slow burn of revenge, and the merry way her teenage blood would look covering the sword that Joan had dug up outside the church. Once Joan had passed, the sword fell to her, Amelia, who could think of no better use for it than to exact revenge on the young woman who took Fred Noonan's life. The one responsible for Joan's sudden murder. The one responsible for Judah's pain.

"Let her forget," Amelia said as Sephanie marched away from the scene with a stern, yet vulnerable cadence to her walk, fighting back the tears behind her eyes. "I won't forget."

With fat, nubby fingers Councilman Varejao took the prized suitcase, flipped it around, and presented it to the group before clicking the two locks on either side of its rectangular front into the 'open' position. He then inserted the metallic trigger before turning it in counter-clockwise motion, causing it to spring ajar. The trigger Varejao had installed in the open slot was now illuminated with a green light that ran the entire duration of the inside of the case, including a switch in the middle that was currently in the *off* position.

"This is Project Dreamcoat," Varejao began, looking each of them in the eye. "Or as some of you may know it, the inter-dimensional gateway cooperation project."

A few curious glances exchanged by council members Yick and Oskam gave Varejao pause to worry. Perhaps they suspected his credibility.

"Now before anyone gets any ideas we are NOT talking aliens here. Quite the contrary. We are talking about something much, much more dangerous. Copies of ourselves. Now the multi-universe theory dictates that for every decision we make a new universe is sprouted from that moment onward with its own history, consequences. You get the picture?" Varejao asked bluntly. "Well then, I'm here to tell you the worst fucking news you will ever hear in the history of your life. So brace yourselves, because here it comes."

The preamble did little to quell the nerves of the already worried councilmen and women. Even Marcus Turtledove, already knowing the coming announcement and lamenting on it for weeks, dreaded hearing it out loud for a second time. Yet still, there he was serving as Protector of Eden until the bitter end.

"There did exist hundreds, maybe even thousands or millions of these multi-verses at one point. But then Vilthe, for some unknown reason, decided to go on a massive genocidal rampage right through each and every damn one of them. We received proof of this via another dimension's version of Marcus Turtledove before he went dark last month. He provided us with intelligence on what Vilthe was doing, how he had succeeded before, and how we could work together in order to stop him once and for all. But that was then, and now we estimate there aren't many of these multi-universes left, including our own."

"How many do you estimate are left?" Doctor Duffy asked, her throat dry from the magnitude of the terror coming to their doorstep.

"Two or three," Turtledove responded, joining the conversation for the first time.

"But now with this trigger, we're able to open a portal, er, gateway between our universes to amass a larger defense. Just think of the potential. Twice as many troops at the academy, twice as many combatants against Vilthe," Varejao said with a mindless giddiness that Turtledove felt an obligation to put a stop to.

"Twice the taxation on our already small resources," Turtledove spoke, obviously against Varejao's proposal.

"Never the less," Varejao offered, turning his attention back toward the group at large. "We have gathered here today to take a vote on if this machine shall be turned on. Vote 'yay' if in the opinion of yes, 'nay' if no. All the yays?"

When all but Turtledove voted in the affirmative he capitulated and watched as Varejao flipped the switch into the ON position. At first nothing happened, prompting a burst of whispers from Fluker and Duffy. Yick was disgusted, and felt that he needed to excuse himself. Then, without warning a large tremor shook the ground beneath them, filling each with panic for the briefest of moments. Lasting only three seconds the shaking caused more fear than actual damage, yet left each member of the clandestine group felt a surge of guilt and responsibility in the action. With a vague promise between them, except Turtledove, who again abstained from the vote, each swore to keep their actions a secret.

"I officially declare Project Dreamcoat a go. This meeting and any attached to it, never happened," Varejao said before shutting the silver suitcase and scurrying off.

Sephanie watched this, eyed Turtledove, who again nodded at her, and made her way into the small crowd that was still milling about in front of Joan's casket. Knowing that both Judah and Amelia would be there, and not knowing what to say to either of them, nor wanting to make a scene, Sephanie resigned herself to this being the closest she would ever be to Joan again. Barely able to make-out the outline of her face, Sephanie said a small prayer for her friend's forgiveness in an impossible situation. She then turned her attention to the right of the casket to see the row of cadets sitting there, including Rolland... and Tina Holmes. Holding hands.

There the two sat, surrounded by friends including a Nocturn and a Mer-person. Again she looked at Rolland and Tina holding hands. It bothered her a great deal, just like Joan had said it would way back in Pensacola. Another fresh wave of pain hit Sephanie's heart, bringing the tears quicker this time than before. Looking around at the scene before her, Sephanie could not help but feel a sense of empty hopelessness. A strange thought considering the amount of positive memories of Joan being shared so openly, the genuine affection coming from the Class of the Tiger's group, and the interagency cooperation that allowed to her steal the remote trigger for the Council of Light.

Still, the fact that her best friend was dead, very much due to the actions she had committed, weighed so heavily upon Sephanie's consciousness that she did not know how she could possibly move beyond them. Her mind turned to vices of the flesh, and looked around for Rolland, finding him still hand in hand with Tina and tucking a piece of hair behind her ear. She felt a pang again but hardened her hear in resolve. He was lost to her. Just as Joan's advice on the matter was also lost.

The list of names to comfort her came and went like a database of the deceased; Taylor, Scott, Joan... all of them, her entire support network save Turtledove, dead and gone. Sephanie missed them more than words could say. She hated the feelings of isolation forced upon her by playing every side for all it was worth. She hated that no one loved her. She hated feeling alone.

Thus is the price for loyalties that waver.

The End

Epilogue:
Earth 8008

Present

Historian's Note:

This is not our universe.

As Major General Anthony Varejao stated immediately following Joan Raines' funeral, there are were thousands of multi-verses that somewhat resembled our own. That is, before Vilthe got to them. Now only two exist; ours (Earth Prime), and Earth 8008. In this universe there never was a United States of America, no Knights of Time, no nuclear technology. The tapestry of Earth 8008 is comprised of key differences, both large and small, that vary from our own world in surprising ways. Yet what they lack in centralized authority they make up for in scientific innovation - being the first universe to successfully open Project Dreamcoat.

Time: Present

Location: Central Tejas Desert

The scorching noon sun that sat high above their head was ominous, its purple hue filling the grassless valley with a foreboding sense of doom. It was almost as if the heavens themselves were weeping due to the sins of mankind. For despite the woes of mankind this land known as Tejas had never been settled. The sprawling metropolitans of Dallas, Houston, and Austin were never established, leaving nothing but the vast stretches of sparse grasslands and cacti that served as a last bastion of solitude for those few survivors who numbered in the hundreds, not thousands.

For the teenager Rolland Wright the setting sun was more than an omen of the battle to come, it was a promise. A promise to his dead mother Taylor, a promise to all of the deceased friends that he had lost in the past few years, in both Eden and on Earth. And most of all, a promise to the man responsible for destroying Eden, the province of California, severing his left hand from his arm, and murdering half of Earth's civilization; Edward Vilthe.

Still struggling with the mental anguish from phantom limb syndrome in the year since it had happened, as if it were an itch that he could not scratch the desire to revenge the lost portion of himself gnawed at him with every breath that he took. Without realizing it his teeth began to grind against one another as he wished with all of his might that he might face Vilthe in single combat upon the battlefield, that his utter destruction would be as excruciating as as it would be final. A whistle sounded from somewhere far off, yet close enough to catch his attention and break him from his concentrated self-pity.

The sound belonged to an officer marching in front of a long line of troops. Rolland watched as the soldiers mobilized on the horizon, all of them armed with weapons he could only dream of possessing. Each held a sleek silver paneled rifle slung over their right shoulder as they marched along toward what would be their final hour. Rolland's reverie was interrupted by a sudden snapping of a broken tree limb from the clearing behind their camp. It was always noises that made him jump, or to break his concentration. Rolland pondered this as he turned around to investigate the cause of the noise; not at all shocked by what he saw once he faced the culprit.

"Just me, son," Scott Wright said, stepping over the trap he had set the evening before around their immediate encampment as he made his way toward Rolland.

"The soldiers," Rolland began, shrinking slightly as the words spilled out from chapped lips, his reward for surviving so long in such an unforgiving world. "I think they'll be distracted long enough for us to activate the device."

Scott smiled, as he often did when he recognized a bit of her in his son. When his wife Taylor was murdered by Vilthe nearly two years prior Scott knew he had two choices regarding Rolland - hide him further, or share his secret pride with the world. Not a day had passed since he had gone public had Scott regretted his decision. At first many in Eden society shunned the boy, calling him a bastard and swearing him to be the downfall of the entire planet. Yet the news of Rolland's secret parentage quickly faded once the other new arrival to Eden made bigger headlines.

He went by the name Marcus L., claimed that he was the leader of the Commanders of Time, and was the last survivor of his own universe, Earth 009. At first Scott and the Rangers of Time were hesitant to accept his tale as the truth, despite him being a literal doppelganger of their Marcus L. Turtledove, except that he had one eye missing. The inter-dimensional traveler claimed that he had arrived from a parallel universe, a claim that many balked at until he produced evidential proof in the form of the two words that changed it all.

Nuclear weaponry.

The previously unheard-of technology rocked the core of Eden's defensive capabilities from any prospective outside threat; or it would have, if it didn't take nearly six months to complete the assembly of the bombs that were to accompany the enriched uranium the one-eyed Marcus L. brought with him to Earth 8008. The beginning of the build was successful, with the team even ahead of schedule by week nine. Then the Incident occurred, and the project, along with every government sponsored activity, and any semblance of life died in Eden. Likewise, the revelation that there existed parallel universes was not surprising to many citizens of Eden; what was surprising, however, was the idea that most of the near infinite universes had already been destroyed by Vilthe's megalomania and obsession of killing humans.

Still, Scott did not regret his decision to bring Rolland into the life that he had once shielded him from as a Ranger of Time. The simple fact was that Rolland was not only a quick learner, but naturally talented as well. It was shame he couldn't be trained by the best, by his mentor, Bradford Nareau. The man who had taught him how to control his own time traveling abilities had been brutally murdered by the beast known as Ballua during the Battle for the Academy. The Rangers lost the battle, and Scott was forced to watch as Ballua and Vilthe's invading armies brought down the Academy of Light, and the Blackard Family Orchard. Even the humans who sought refuge in lesser known locations were killed. Among the nearly three thousand dead were Rolland's classmates, and fellow Junior Rangers, the Holmes twins Timothy and Thaddeus Jr., the Nocturn woman who could fly, and all of Eden's government officials, civil servants, and bureaucratic groupies.

Allowing his mind to wander back to that fateful day, Scott thought back on his own actions, and the lives he lost along the way. More images of Eden's destruction filled his memory, scattering pain onto every inch of his psyche. The literal vaporizing of the Council of Light by Vilthe's forces was the hardest to stomach. In the evenings, whenever Scott found a free moment to let his mind wander he would always ask himself if the nuclear weaponry would have helped to prevent the Incident that led to Eden's destruction, or merely delayed it until it was too late.

Scott, along with his ragtag crew of remaining Rangers, were the only travelers of light left alive to tell the tale and finish what his forbearers had started. In a fashion befitting the late Marcus Turtledove, Scott took command, relocating the remaining travelers of light to present day Earth and organizing numerous missions against the Vilthe. But their efforts to preserve Earth, much like their efforts to keep Eden free and righteous, fell to the wrath of the reaper of souls.

Russia was the first to forfeit their lands, handing them over to Vilthe's henchman Nero in exchange for safety under the new world regime. Unfortunately, Nero did not keep his word, almost immediately ordering his own lieutenant, Otep, to engage the masses in chemical warfare. Seven million were lost in the first week alone. Along with these act of horrendous annihilation came the tactics Vilthe dubbed Operation Extinction. Despite Nero's public deception of the Russian people, other nations jumped at the chance to strike a peace with Vilthe. China, Japan, and Germany all willingly disbanded their governments and armed forces in the name of peace. To reward their complacency Vilthe poisoned their drinking water, culling the population of each country by one third before a common thread could be determined. Another estimated 80,000 lives were lost. The reaper of souls ate well.

When it was established that peace would not be reached despite mankind's best attempts to do so, The Sovereign States, a mostly isolationist superpower, entered the fray. But by that point it was too late. Once the war came down to the federal capitol city of Lafayette, the site of one of Vilthe's only early failures, Operation Extinction went into effect. If he had not seen it with his own two eyes, Scott would have never believed what he knew to be true. The initial, and only, report released by the Sovereign States Bureau of Statistics approximated the casualties in the hundreds of millions following Vilthe's first 30 following Eden's destruction. Shortly after the release, much of Lafayette was destroyed in a fire started by the beast Ballua. The first tactic implored by Vilthe during the operation was utilizing his necromancer Otep to raise the recently departed souls. All over the world the living dead walked amongst their living peers, luring them into traps, enticing them with final goodbyes, and then consuming their flesh with a vivacious spirit reserved for those whose mind and souls have passed beyond the mortal realm. One of Scott's fellow Rangers, a shape-shifter by the name of Geoffrey fell victim to such a luring. Poor Geoffrey.

But even Geoffrey's death was not an isolated event. Many more millions of souls perished in the second round of Vilthe's attacks, all aimed at targeting local water supplies throughout the so-called 'civilized' human world. One by one cities went dark across the once illuminated night sky of Earth. When the most sacred of resources became scarce, distrust in remaining public officials quickly led to rioting, revolution, and appeasement from the human populace in a vain attempt to beg Vilthe to cease his assault on their species. Offering him what was left of North America, including all of the territories formerly held by the now defunct governments, and a portion of their future food supply, Vilthe begrudgingly agreed not to attack any more humans on one condition; that every remaining homosapian relocate to Australia and never return to the mainland again.

It was in this dark hour that the Rangers of Time revealed themselves to the world at large, finally breaking the veil of secrecy that the founders of Eden insisted upon. First hailed as heroes, then as demons, finally what was left of the general public was forced to recognize them as their greatest weapon in defeating Vilthe during the Battle of Thousand Oaks, in which the mysterious Marcus L. and Marcus Turtledove both lost their lives. From then onward it was a slow, but gradual slide into oblivion. Although the world governments had done the heavy lifting against the nearly immortal reaper, the Rangers had made significant advances since the last of the remaining great world powers, Great Britain, was eradicated via a massive tsunami that wiped the great island off the face of the Earth. The estimated sixty million dead all attributed to Vilthe's bride, the gothic, vindictive young Queen of Tartarus, Sephanie.

It had all started with Sephanie, the young, beautiful Queen of the Underworld, and her introduction to the mix as a power player. Groomed from a young age to be Vilthe's equal, the mortal, female version of Death Incarnate propped the so-called 'Destroyer of Eden' up to a status higher than icon, or even that of ruler. The power couple, Vilthe and Sephanie, had coordinated their ceremony with the announcement that segregation amongst species would be the wave of the future, before proclaiming themselves monarchs of a new world order where select travelers of light and elemenos ruled over a lower class of human beings. Their wedding, a surreal event to behold, came on the heels of a mysterious spree of deaths in Eden, concluding with Taylor Wright. Shortly after the double agent Sephanie fled Eden, taking with her what she believed to be the only weapon the travelers of light possessed against the reaper of souls. Presenting it to her love as a wedding gift, Sephanie handed over the decoy briefcase that had cost Taylor her life. It was crimson red with golden edges that shimmered under any light. The silver clasps that held its contents secure were bookended around a small lock with an unusually odd keyhole the likes of which none who laid eyes upon it had, or would ever see again. Written across both its front, and back in large black letters were the words:

'PROJECT DREAMCOAT'

Questions had been surrounding the strange parcel for months after it came to Eden. The contents of the briefcase were as complex as they were complicated. So much so that both Turtledove, and the Marcus L. insisted that two decoys be made and the case be traded amongst a small group of trusted individuals. Unfortunately for both Taylor, and Sephanie, the case Scott Wright's wife held on that fateful day was indeed a decoy after all. The real case had been fully converted into a device capable of something extraordinary. That is, it could be extraordinary if they could ever get it to work properly.

"You alright, Pop?" Rolland asked his father while waving his remaining hand back and forth.

"Uh, yeah," Scott offered, rolling his eyes a bit and smiling paternally. "Just a bit nervous is all. You were saying something about the device? Is it good to go?"

"Yeah, I think so, actually," Rolland said cheerfully before talking two quick steps closer to his father before jogging past him completely to the long stretch of barren wasteland that lay between their makeshift rig and where they stood. "Let me show you!"

Mere moments later Scott gave out the call to gather, attracting the attention of all the remaining Rangers of Time to take the proverbial knee. One by one they found their way, Kniff, Jeremy, Vic, and Julie Michelle. Except his son, who much like teenagers everywhere, in every time period throughout recorded history, ignored his father's call and continued to work. Scott could not help but laugh at Rolland's enthusiasm, even in the face of mortal danger.

"Julie, would you mind?" Scott asked the girl who had finally settled upon a seat atop the metal rig that housed one of the nuclear devices that they planned to detonate should Vilthe overpower them. The petite, half Chinese girl rolled her eyes before batting them twice and hopped off of her perch, onto the dirt ground below.

Crossing over to where her boyfriend stood, furiously pressing buttons on keyboards - seemingly at random to Julie's eyes, the baser teenage instincts kicked in as she leaned in close behind Rolland, raised her mouth to his left ear, and whispered something inaudible to the rest of them. This simple action prompted the teenage Wright to move with incredible haste away from the terminal in which he had been devoting his undivided attention, down the small flight of metal safety stairs, and over to the line of other Rangers. With a knowing grin Julie followed the object of her affection with the confidence that can only come from an intimate relationship.

"I don't want to know," Scott proclaimed, closing his eyes. This bit of humility brought a welcome smile to the joyless faces of the remaining Rangers, all of which embraced the moment like it was one of their last of the kind.

The levity was broken by the unmistakable sounds of warfare as the soldiers from the allied coalition of mankind met with Vilthe's forces beyond eyesight; but not beyond earshot.

"Focus," Scott said, commanding the attention of his five underlings. "Mission status report; we are a go on the equipment. Kniff and Vic have successfully set up the nuclear technology and thanks to Rolland there, we can safely ensure that the blast radius will effectively kill Vilthe, and all of his underlings should it come to that."

The silent nodding of heads from all five of the Rangers spoke silent volumes to the lengths each would go to see the job finished, Vilthe obliterated from the face of the Earth. Each had sacrificed something, and someone, in order to be standing there that day.

"This spot has been chosen as the epicenter of what has come to be known as Project Dreamcoat. It is our duty to execute this operation and send two representatives through the portal in order to converse with what appears to be the only other remaining universe left this side of oblivion," Scott said, the logic falling from his words as he spoke them. Once upon a time he grew up, not as a child does, but as an adolescent becoming a man, in a magical place that resembled a planet out of time called Eden. But that dream was lost now - replaced by yet another desolate wasteland, just like the one he stood upon.

"But why here? Why Tejas of all places?" Julie asked as her chapped lips cracked beneath the southern sun.

Scott's paternal sense of patience only stretched so far, a sight that was apparently evident to Julie alone.

"To be honest with you I'm not entirely sure. Turtledove, the other Turtledove, the one with one eye, told us that something happens in a place called 'Dallas' in the early 1960's. Something to do with a world leader," Scott said through gritted teeth. The small group of Rangers of Time watched their haggard leader explain their task with collective baited breath. The plan is - if we can get the world's attention to warn them that Vilthe is coming, then maybe we can get the Rangers of Time from those universes to help as well."

"Universes?" Rolland inquired, knowing full well that they were one of two universes left in a multi-verse that once housed billions, if not trillions of alternate realities.

"What can I say," Scott retorted, the sounds of far-off automatic gunfire sending a shiver down his spine before he could get the rest of his sentence out. "I'm optimistic."

Nods of approval for the plan, even if it was a long shot went through the rangers like the wave at a sporting event. A large

BOOM sound, followed by a bright flash of orange light gained all of their attention. In the far off distance over the horizon Rolland could hear heavy gunfire along with the shouts of dying men and women. Though he could not see them due to their position over the hill, he knew that the thousands of survivors who marched on Vilthe's forces were not meant to win the fight, but merely to bide time for he and his father to complete their mission; to activate Project Dreamcoat.

"Kniff, you'll be taking point," Scott said, nodding to Kniff before turning to his son. "Rolland, you know what to do."

"Alright ladies, let's get in position," Kniff spouted off, making his way over to the metal scaffolding that propped up the would-be gateway to a parallel dimension. Gripping both sides of the latter, Kniff climbed effortlessly upward before grabbing a rifle with his left hand despite the absence of both a ring and middle finger. The war had been hard on the last surviving Merman, making this mission more than personal; it was necessary for the continued survival of his species.

Following close behind Kniff was Scott Wright, who more than anything wanted to ensure his son's safety through this ordeal. He thought about this as he ignored more sounds of warfare coming from somewhere too close for comfort. With a practiced hand and expert finesse, Scott Wright affixed a blue, rubber encased wire around the steel gateway's main conduit, joining it and the suitcase together, forming a locking seal that melded together instantaneously.

Nearby, the younger Wright made himself useful by doing his duty in the last minute preparations and preparing to actually go through the gateway. He had no idea about what he might find when he got to the other side, but suspected that it could be something truly wild. Maybe in another universe he would be super muscular, or extremely good at Bliss Ball, or maybe even just... still have a second hand. The thought depressed Rolland to no end, causing his missing appendage to itch once again.

"You ready big guy?" Vic asked Rolland as they both watched the horizon for the coming onslaught.

"Yeah," said Rolland, wishing to change the subject at any cost. "You know, I'm thinking about becoming a fireman."

"A fireman, huh?" Vic asked, smiling his toothy smile for the first time in weeks. His teenage face stained with the minor burns and pockmarks of battle. The set-up of the nuclear weapons that morning had already taken a toll on his muscles, making them sore. "I could see that."

"Thought you might like it," Rolland answered while simultaneously clasping his stump to his body to hold his rifle. "Probably be a big need for them when this is all over."

"Whenever that may be," Vic said, talking before his mind could tell him not to speak. He looked at Rolland quickly with a fear in his eyes, recalling the last time the 'wrath of Rolland' had reared its ugly head in his direction. It wasn't that Victor could blame his friend for finding faith in an unwavering sense of optimism after losing his hand, or that he took personal offense whenever any of those around him weren't likewise optimistic regarding their predicament.

"What's a three syllable phrase for dictator?" Rolland asked with a stone face.

"I don't, I don't know," Vic retorted quickly, his nervousness apparent. He loved how whimsical Rolland had become since losing his hand, but suspected it was merely a ruse to mask his anger. That was so like Rolland Alec Wright. Remembering how solemn his friend had been in the past, Vic lived with the lie, feeding into it for fear that there would be no tomorrow. Coping was a learned skill in a post-Eden life on Earth 8008, one Vic had yet to learn. So instead, Vic kept his mouth shut and prepared to laugh politely at Rolland's joke.

Rolland hated making jokes, hated the light-hearted feelings that people had during times of war. But more than that, what Rolland really hated was the way that his friends kept looking at him after the accident. He hated that bit of pity in their eyes. So, many moons ago, he had decided to lie. Lie to himself, lie to others, hell, lie to the world at large. With this thought in mind Rolland continued on with his joke. His eyes caught the line of modified nuclear warheads that ran the two sides of their camp, surrounding them in a death-trap of their own making. There were thirty in all. It was a dark world, a cruel world, but Rolland wasn't. Rolland wanted to be different. Smiling slightly to put his friend at ease, Rolland tilted his head a degree before revealing the answer. "A penis potato."

From close by Jeremy chuckled slightly at the two knuckle-heads that comprised the best prospect planet Earth had at survival in the next generation. Ridiculous word-play aside, they were both formidable in their own right. Despite a missing hand, Jeremy had seen Rolland save hundreds of civilians. His valor was beyond measure, even if he was differently-abled. Vic though.. Vic was a strange one. Beneath the surface Vic seemed to be growing darker, meaner, more vindictive during battle. The irony was that Jeremy was half proud of Vic's newfound sense of vengeance - since they were on the same side of the war. Otherwise...

Suddenly a loud hum filled the air around them, gaining the attention of all six Rangers of Time within its vicinity. They all stood frozen as the hum grew louder with each passing moment before upon itself into a crescendo of discontent. For Rolland, the hum grew higher pitched and focused in on the worst parts of his mind's eye. Burrowing deep into his psyche, confusing his thoughts, and causing him to lose focus. He needed that focus, need it, if he were to use any of his time traveling abilities.

So too were Scott, Vic, Julie, and Kniff losing their own physical balance and control of the situation, rendering none of them capable of seeing the onslaught of arrows that poured from the very horizon they had been watching so intently. Only Jeremy alone could see the rain of terror hurdling toward them at breakneck speed.

"Fuck nugget," Jeremy said under his breath, before launching into action. Running to the console where he knew the camp's defenses to be, Jeremy quickly pulled up the menu on the monitor before selecting the SHIELDS option. The result was a large, half bubble-like shield that propelled itself forward from the ground, catching the arrows midair, rendering them inert and ineffective. Breathing a sigh of relief at this act of quick thinking, Jeremy let his guard down enough to stop watching his physical back as nearly a dozen armed elemenos snuck into the Rangers camp from the rear. Each furry green monster was armed with small armor machine guns, each firing .38 caliber rounds directly at the Rangers, and their line of nuclear warheads. Being inside of the protective bubble their ammunition was very effective as it kept the other Rangers in a shocked state of frozen, momentary panic. Jeremy cursed himself again, knowing that he had given the elemenos that luxury. Pressing another button on the console next to him resulted in the ignition of a magnetic charge that yanked each of the firearms from the elemenos paws, again giving the young Ranger of Time a temporary win.

Ironically, it was the lone elemeno who carried a bow, and arrows, who managed to get the lucky shot. For Jeremy the oversight proved to be costly, as he was the first, and subsequently the only, Ranger of Time hit by Vilthe's first wave, taking an arrow to the left shoulder, knocking him off of the scaffolding, and into the sand below. The other rangers saw this, and, returning to their wits, began running toward their respective battle stations. All except the kindhearted Julie Michelle.

"Jeremy!" Julie exclaimed, teleporting away from her post before reappearing one hundred yards to the North where her friend lay. Quickly turning him over onto his back so she check his pulse, she barely missed a fresh spray of bullets that rained down on their position, courteous of Vilthe's second wave, who had managed to breach the defenses somehow.

It was actually Julie's distraction that allowed the elemeno archer to complete the first wave's main objective - turn off the Ranger's shields. Taking a bullet to the head for his troubles (courteously of a fully pissed off Kniff) the elemeno died without receiving a bit of the praise he so highly craved. Hunched over the control panel on the second story of the scaffolding the elemenos body acted as a shield for the next elemeno who double-checked the work of the first before turning to leave, only to likewise be rewarded with a bullet between his eyes via Kniff. Creating a small radius of protection that stretched from the scaffolding platform to the entrance of their camp, the marksman was able to pick off seven more invading elemenos with ease. Kniff, it seemed, was on a roll.

Yet one against many rarely results in a positive outcome for the minority. Soon enough Vilthe's forces responded in kind. More bullets from return fire landed indiscriminately amongst the Rangers encampment as their enemy made their appearance known for the first time in mass, barreling toward the scaffolding with destruction on their minds. Leading the charge was Hess, accompanied by his wicked tempered sister, Alora. Behind them trailed an entire heard of elemenos, each wearing protective body armor and armed with semi-automatic machine guns.

"Kill them all!" screamed Alora, holding her makeshift sword high above her head. Gone was her electric green whip that had once been used to bend many a Ranger to her will, replaced with an item stolen from the private study of the Queen of France herself. Following this command a large wave of two hundred elemenos in turn raised their furry paws above their hairy, extended ears and marched in unison toward the Rangers position. In a shocking display of uncharacteristic carnage, more bullets rained down on to the Rangers of Time as advanced fire gave way to the ominous sounds of something large, and very angry that approached from the south.

Ballua, the beast formerly known as Puck - that is, until after the interaction with Rolland in Paris. The mission was one that the Rangers, even before Eden's destruction, rarely ever discussed, as it brought great shame on both Wright men, it being Rolland's first mission. Yet after that incident, and Rolland's stupid, dangerous actions, the mental facilities of the ginger haired man were on par with a small child. Due to this, the once joking spirit of a changeling had morphed into the beast and had never changed back. Stuck in the form of a ruthless, bloodthirsty monster with a penchant for destruction, and two massive tusks; the brain damaged soul inside wept, and wished for the sweet release of death from his bondage. But his master would never allow that, so, instead Ballua pressed on with all of his might to kill, destroy, and finally meet a warrior worth ending his reign of terror.

Storming into the camp of the Rangers of Time Ballua made short work of the land mines set-up there by Scott as traps. Pawing at them in a scooping motion with its gigantic front claws, Ballua sent them each flying toward the gathering elemenos. Multiple POPPING noises followed, accompanied by many screams of agony and finally silence. Both Rolland and Scott saw this, each picking up a nearby weapon, a pair of plasma rifles left by Kniff, before beaming down a layer of protective fire to ensure that Ballua did not go after their weapons expert Mer-Man. The result was nothing more than a severely pissed off beast who knew precisely where to look for his next kill; the Wright men.

"Hey, ugly," came a lone voice from the sand by Ballua's feet. There, standing amongst the bloodstained backdrop and scaly, cracked skin of the beast who used to be a man was the already battle-worn Jeremy. He held something long and metal over his non-injured shoulder. The item was dark green and weighed him down heavily."Fuck you!"

The rocket launcher fired only once, but its force was felt for the rest of the battle. The explosion sent Jeremy flying backward and upward into the air, away from the platform that housed the briefcase for Project Dreamcoat. For his part, Ballua acted much the way any beast would who sees small prey suddenly fly backward through the air. Swatting at Jeremy like a cat would a fly, mere milliseconds passed before the payload of the rocket made contact with the monster's midsection.

"I have to go check on him," Vic proclaimed, hopping out from his hiding place across from where the two Wright men stood. Climbing down the scaffolding and jogging over toward the direction where he spotted Jeremy being sent, the broad shoul-dered teenager saw little risk to doing this before the elemeno regulars advanced close enough to make a difference. Spotting both the Project Dreamcoat briefcase, and a frantic Julie Michelle punching in coordinates onto a keypad beside a large window-like entryway, Vic formed a mental strategy. First, he would find Jeremy, then he would take him directly to the gateway, drop him off, and rendezvous with the Wrights. Yet no sooner had these thoughts formed than the long, green, electric whip that haunted so many of his dreams re-introduced itself to the war, this time with HIM as its intended prey. Without any hesitation Alora unsheathed and held the stolen French sword aloft, blade pointed at Vic's face.

"Little shit," Alora said with a smirk. With a forceful pull the teen went from confident to submissive, literally cowering at her feet, in a second.

"Vic!" Rolland screamed, seeing this transpire from across the distance. Deciding to act before thinking, once again, he lunged forward off of the scaffolding to protect his fallen friend. If not for the cover fire provided by Kniff, Rolland would have been taken out by any one of the elemeno soldiers who had found their way into the poorly defended encampment. After taking a few practiced steps, breathing steadily as he went while making the instant decision to do so, Rolland took aim at Alora's mid-section from behind her - and fired. Down Alora went, the fatal shot releasing her of her wits as she fell. Vic gasped for air as the whip loosened around his neck. Rolland's brain began to work again when he looked down and saw the panic stricken gaze of terror Vic emitted as he looked past Rolland to something on the horizon.

"We've got to move," Vic said through a raw throat as he scrambled to his feet.

Together they moved, past more armed elemenos, each of which belonged to various undisciplined units that went from soldiering to pillaging, and back again; often getting lost along the way. The two teens were halfway back to the spot where the vortex was primed when the feelings began to make themselves known. Rolland could tell that something was wrong, Taylor's genetic gifts had told him that much. Vic's head start provided him the time enough to get to the scaffolding, but Rolland was not so lucky.

The ground around him shook as the beast made its presence known to the battle once again, clawing and scrapping its way onto planet Earth. Ballua, or what was left of the monster, was back. Nearly the entire right side of its torso and face were missing due to the rocket launcher. A burnt out eye socket stared at Rolland as it's duplicate pierced him with a deadly glare. Its skull was plainly visible to the naked eye.

Moving quickly toward the workstation to his right, Rolland whirled around in time to grab the edge of the computer as the ground beneath it lifted in one solid piece with him on top. The mound of flesh, dirt, and electronics was flung aside before freefalling for seven or eight feet and crashing to the earth. With his eyes closed as tight as he could make them Rolland tucked, rolled, and landed among what he could feel to be a large patch of hot sand, or dirt, as a bit was kicked up with his landing and fell into his mouth. A dirty tongue aside, the only other pain from the ordeal was stemming from his bad arm. Part of him was glad that he was missing the hand, for he knew without a doubt that the bones in the arm where broken, and that without breaking them he would not have survived the crash.

So distracted by this was Rolland, that he never saw Rasputin arrive, survey the scene, and plan the most effective way to bring his own particular brand of chaos to the mix. Whistling to the beast, Rasputin gave a masculine, yet distinctive wave toward Ballua, drawing its attention while Rolland was still dazed.

"Quickly, give me your hand!" Rasputin told Rolland, offering to assist him out of the wreckage. Rolland took it in turn, stretching as far as he could in a vain attempt at freedom. As he rose to his feet, Rolland began to cough, then panic when he saw just who his supposed savior was.

"What...?" Rolland began to ask before he felt the icy breath of Ballua on the back of his neck. With a quick motion forward Rasputin plunged a knife into Rolland's stomach. Something grabbed his legs from behind, as the next thing Rolland knew he fell forward into the dirt, the knife going in further and twisting a bit. Still holding Rolland's hand from before, Rasputin then flipped Rolland over, allowing the teenager to see his attackers full-on for the first time.

Ripping at Rolland's stomach with its strong paw, three of Ballua's eight inch wide claws found their way into the tender parts, drawing blood and a look of bewilderment from the teenager. Perhaps it was the shock of seeing his own intestines that convinced Rolland he had made a fatal mistake in trusting Rasputin, regardless, he let go of the man's hand, allowing himself to slip back into the pile of wreckage and land with a sharp, painful thud.

As his face turned white from blood loss and the world around him grew dark, Rolland heard the screams of his father coming from somewhere close-off, and felt a sudden breeze from something large moving quite near his head. The object was Ballua's claw, coming back to finish Rolland off as it came down, hard, on the teenagers midsection. By this time Rolland had lost all feeling in the majority of his body, making the painful impact of the three hundred pound smash against his body almost numb. Almost. The literal catch came when Ballua raised his paw upward, netting Rolland's intestines on the end of its claw. This resulted in the teenager being carried upward, not unlike how a cat plays with a string. Bringing the object close to its remaining eye, the beast eyed what it had caught before tossing Rolland expertly up into the air, opening its oddly shaped mouth, each row of razor sharp teeth primed, and catching him between its jaws. It crunched once, twice, and then swallowed, taking what was left of Rolland Wright off of the battlefield.

"No!" Scott screamed, rushing across the scaffolding in Ballua's direction. But before he could take another step a fresh spray of bullets reigned down from above him, catching the two elemenos attempting to sneak behind him toward the machinery where the Project Dreamcoat generator was roaring loudly. Kniff was doing his job. So distracted by his grief was Scott, that he missed the wisps of black smoke that bellowed into the camp landing nearby before swirling in a counter-clockwise formation until the atoms formed the outline of a short, thin man wearing a dark cloak. Although he stood nearly twenty feet away and below them, and his face was hidden due to its grotesque nature, all that saw him knew who he was. Edward Vilthe.

With a flick of his wrist the reaper of souls flipped the unsuspecting Scott Wright over the second story of the scaffolding, turned him around, and off of his feet until he lay on the flat of his back on the sand. His arms pinned beneath him, the middle-aged time traveler looked at the man who had taken everything from him as he approached with more hatred than trepidation. The loathing emitting from the heart of Scott Wright that day was enough to tear the sun from the sky. With a touch of his hand Vilthe could, and would end the life of Scott Wright. He leaned in to do so, brining his bewitched finger down onto Scott's temple.

A purple mist filled the small space between them, temporarily filled with a petite Asian girl with fresh tears in her eyes.

"I have to go back!" Scott hollered, thinking of using his time travelling abilities to save his son. "We have to get Rolland back!"

Julie knew this would happen, knew that the day would come when either Scott or Rolland fell in battle, and the other would immediately jump to this conclusion. Any other day, any other time and she would agree with Scott. But at this juncture, at this time, when Vilthe's literal destruction was so close.. they could not afford it. Not even for Rolland. Not even for the love of her life. Instead, Julie simply shook her head before she grabbed Scott's wrist, and the two of them vanished, replaced by another cloud of purple smoke. A few moments later the pair re-appeared, this time back atop the scaffolding where Victor had joined Kniff in returning fire on the invading elemeno foot soldiers.

"Can we do this now?" Vic asked, prompting Scott to break himself from the grief-induced stupor he had imposed long enough to drag himself to the control panel. There on the screen was the button he needed, followed by the password he put in R0!!andWrighT, before pressing execute. The moment he had been waiting months for came and went with no nervous apprehension, or joyous occasion. It just went. Just like Rolland. When nothing happened, the looks among the three functioning rangers spoke volumes of what would need to happen next. Plan B. One nod from Kniff to Vic was all it took to set the teenager along. "I'm on it."

With a great gust of wind from the skies above the entire desert was washed in a blanket of ultraviolet light, briefly blinding everyone for a moment before the phenomenon subsided. When it did, all of the fires had been extinguished, along with every electronic device being turned off, and every weapon jamming. This cosmic ceasefire, as distracting as it was, paled in comparison to the actual development post blackout.

"Scott," Julie said to her colleague, but the time traveler was not listening. Too preoccupied with Rolland's death to care about anything else, including the safety of his own teammates, Scott Wright completely ignored the pearly, swirling vortex that filled the doorway beside the monitor where the scaffolding was the sturdiest. The act he had been working toward for months had finally come to pass, yet Scott did not care in the slightest. To him all was lost now with Rolland's death. All was in vain.

But there it was - a literal vortex to another dimension.

Suddenly the game had changed and everything had become very real, including a means for escape for the surviving Rangers. Spotting Victor running from one station to the next, reactivating the generators and nuclear devices attached to each of them, Kniff took out yet another round of ammunition and affixed it into his semi-automatic machine gun. He had never held a taste for human weapons before this war, and he hoped to return to that opinion following its conclusion. Ironic that he above all the rest became the groups weapons officer. Humans. For the time being, however, the weapon he held would come in handy, as both Alora and Rasputin had made their way onto the first level of the scaffolding. After laying down a few warning shows in their direction Kniff scanned his general vicinity for any other hostiles. When he expanded his perimeter outwardly, he spotted Vilthe, standing there staring at the vortex. Beyond that he saw elemenos, sand, and... another Ranger?!

"Well I'll be damned," Kniff said to himself, smiling. There, wading through sand in shoes that were a size too small for his feet was Jeremy, half of the arrow from before still lodged in his shoulder. Kniff watched as he flagged down someone who appeared at his side a moment later. Julie had gone to get him. All was going according to pl-

A sharp pain from behind his eyes interrupted Kniff's thoughts. Then he noticed the blood coming from his nose. No. Not his nose.. then.. he simply fell asleep.

The rock that Vilthe telekinetically lifted from the desert sand did not know it would be the instrument of Kniff's murder before it entered his temporal lobe. Yet as it lodged itself there, causing his eyes to cross in a last moment of utter confusion and fear, the Mer Man found solace in knowing that he would be joining his people soon.

The nerves in Kniff's hand clutched at the trigger of the semi-automatic machine gun in his fingers, firing it repeatedly as his body fell onto the scaffolding face first. The spray of bullets were aimed directly at Vilthe's line of lieutenants, one of which, Rasputin, caught two in the leg and chest. This last ditch distraction allowed Vic to sneak around the super group of evildoers on his way to yet another device.

High atop the scaffolding, where's Kniff's body lay, a poof of purple smoke appeared before depositing both a still crying Julie and Jeremy beside it. A horrific scream followed by the stifled sobbing was in order as Jeremy simultaneously attempted to both control Julie from alerting Vilthe to their position, and find anyone else left alive. Preferably Scott Wright. Unfortunately for them, Scott was still alive, but not at his station.

The pair watched as Scott, brazen as ever, marched toward Vilthe to meet the ghoul in open combat. Seeing the time traveler coming, Vilthe gave a billowy gesture to his lieutenants by stretching his arms backward, causing them to disperse a bit before he took a step toward the man intent on doing him bodily harm. With his head held high Scott Wright walked straight at the reaper of souls - a bold move. One that was greeted not by reward, but by a single, bright red spark of a beam that shot out of Vilthe's palm like a laser beam, went through Scott's sternum, and killed him instantly.

Harsh sobs from the terrified teenage girl sitting next to him brought Jeremy back to the grim reality that the two of them faced. Taking the chance to survey the battlefield one final time from their vantage point, high atop the scaffolding, Jeremy saw no sign of Rolland. Vic, on the other hand was quite visible, as he fought off an elemeno soldier before taking its weapon, killing two more, and altering the nuclear device they were guarding. After a few seconds the tension within Jeremy's stomach told him not to linger, and he turned his attention back to Julie. He never did find out if Victor was successful in setting off those devices.

"We need to help him," Julie said between sobs. "We need to find Rolland, and Vic."

"No, we have to leave now," Jeremy said, his left hand already pushing the small of Julie's back, moving her along in a crawl toward the vortex. They arrived within seconds, and before she could argue again, he was propelling her forward into the strange, jettisoning vortex. "Someone has to survive, why not us?"

But before Julie could answer, she was already half way across the royal blue platform, and face to face with the white, swirly vortex. Eyeing it with the greatest trepidation, and courage that her youthful experiences could muster within the moment, she closed her eyes and leapt head first into the great unknown.

"You can run," Vilthe howled over the loud buzzing sound of the now armed nuclear device closest to him. They seemed to grow louder the more Victor activated, almost as if they were working in unison somehow. Vilthe feared not the weaponry of mankind, and as such, took little notice of its various noises. "But you will die!"

"Not today, asshole," Jeremy stated bluntly before standing upright and turning around to jump headfirst into the vortex behind Julie. Bullets followed them, but none found their mark as both Rangers of Time escaped Earth 8008 and the tyranny of Vilthe's empire.

And then there was one. Earth 8008's last defender against Vilthe's oppression, a boy who would never get the chance to exist on Earth Prime due to circumstances beyond his control; the teenager, Vic.

With all of the devices armed Vic made his way up the metal scaffolding that led to the swirling vortex with a renewed energy to his actions. Spying the formation of individuals at the entry point, Vic assumed that his teammates, all save the Wrights, had made their way there and were awaiting his arrival. With enemies closing in all around him the number of options for escape was down to one, the vortex.

The rude awakening Vic received when he lifted his head to see Vilthe, Rasputin, and Alora waiting for him at the briefcase was enough to take his breath away. Since the other two had gone through the vortex they had moved toward it and were also making plans to follow. It was then that Vic both saw Kniff's corpse, and was shocked to find that he had been detected by the extrasensory perceptions of the Lord of Tartarus.

"You have been abandoned," Vilthe hissed, the hood of his cloak slipping slightly to the side, revealing the fleshy pink skin and bone below.

Instinctively the teenager panicked, hurtling himself sideways behind the cover of the nearest computer station. The hot metal of the scaffolding on his skin reminded him that despite Kniff's corpse, and Vilthe's presence, this was no dream. No, this was a waking nightmare, one that had but one ending; his own death.

Then Vic saw the button; the button that he had longed to find. Without thinking he propelled himself toward it, throwing almost his entire nearly three hundred pound frame behind the palm of his hand. He was up and to his feet before he let go of the trigger, turning to face those whom he had once been taught to fear and hate. The alarms overhead and all around the perimeter of the camp activated, causing blinking red beams to emit a warning pulse, scaring numerous stray elemenos who pillaging the camp.

Vic flashed his toothy grin at Vilthe before jumping headlong into the swirling vortex, the tips of his feet missing a fresh spray of bullets by millimeters. The opening whirled for a moment or two before appearing to grow tired, and slowed to a near stop before disappearing entirely.

Vilthe stood, face to face, with the closed vortex that he had pinned all of his hopes on. Out of the corner of his eye ticked a silent timer with red, block like numbers

0:02

"No..." Vilthe began to say before the counter hit zero, triggering the chain of nuclear weapons. The first one went off, instantly vaporizing everything within a city block, including the remains of the intrepid Rangers who had fallen, Kniff, Scott, and Rolland Wright. Yet their deaths did not come without the assurance that Vilthe, the Vilthe of 8008, the man who had destroyed their Eden and their way of life on Earth was destroyed for good.

Then the next device exploded. Followed by another, and another, and another, until nothing remained of Earth 8008 but stardust.

Earth 001 aka Earth Prime (Our Earth) - 1586

The British Colony of Roanoke

All three of the travelers from an extinct Earth broke through into our own universe with zero fanfare beyond the curious animals that overheard the opening and closing of the vortex. The swirling entryway opened fifty feet out to sea from the beach before depositing Julie Michelle into the icy depths of the Atlantic.

Kicking with all of her might Julie Michelle fought against the never-ending tide to survive, even in the cold Atlantic waters. As she spotted land, the hope for a continued life filled her lungs almost as much as the water. Almost. Shear will and determination, thinking of Rolland's final moments, Julie fought her way to the sandy beach before her before lying out in the hot, mid-morning sunshine.

Yet making it to shore was the least of her worries, as no sooner had she begun to relax when the opening of another portal in the sky, nearly a mile away, prompted her to once again take action. Friend, or foe, Julie's life was about to change, forever.

Jeremy, who had never experienced exceptionally good luck in matters of battle and conquest, continued his streak upon arrival onto Earth 001.

But that is another story for another time.

For the unconscious Vic the sweet taste of victory against Earth 8008 Vilthe would soon be replaced with the bittersweet realization that he was no longer in his own universe. This universe, Earth Prime, stands very different than his; a rude awakening that awaited the sleeping teenager as he stirred on the mossy wetland of a Roanoke swamp.

Yet for the moment, safely away, in the last remaining universe not lost to Vilthe - our universe, three souls displaced from time and space landed safely.

Project Dreamcoat was a success.